TIME ENOUGH FOR LOVE

Other books by this author available from New English Library:

THE MOON IS A HARSH MISTRESS
THE MAN WHO SOLD THE MOON
HAVE SPACE SUIT – WILL TRAVEL
BETWEEN PLANETS
SPACE FAMILY STONE
STARSHIP TROOPERS
SPACE CADET
STAR BEAST
ASSIGNMENT IN ETERNITY
ROCKETSHIP GALILEO
GLORY ROAD
REVOLT IN 2100
THE DAY AFTER TOMORROW
PODKAYNE OF MARS
METHUSELAH'S CHILDREN
STRANGER IN A STRANGE LAND
I WILL FEAR NO EVIL
THE WORLDS OF ROBERT HEINLEIN
STARMAN JONES

Time Enough for Love

ROBERT A. HEINLEIN

NEW ENGLISH LIBRARY
TIMES MIRROR

First published in the United States of America by Putnam & Co. Inc.
First NEL hardcover edition, 1974

*

FIRST NEL PAPERBACK EDITION APRIL 1975
New edition July 1976
This new edition July 1977

*

NEL Books are published by The New English Library Limited from Barnard's Inn, Holborn, London EC1N 2JR. Made and printed in Great Britain by C. Nicholls & Company Ltd

45003316 3

For
Bill and Lucy

For
Bill and Lucy

CONTENTS

CODA I

595

II

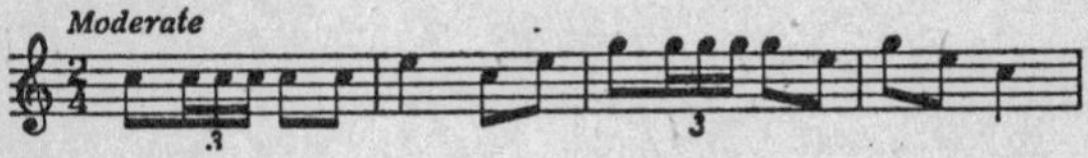

604

III

605

IV

606

INTRODUCTION

On the Writing of History

History has the relation to truth that theology has to religion – i.e. none to speak of. – L.L.

The Great Diaspora of the Human Race which started more than two millennia ago when the Libby-Sheffield Drive was disclosed, and which continues to this day and shows no sign of slowing, made the writing of history as a single narrative – or even many compatible narratives – impossible. By the twenty-first century (Gregorian)* on Old Home Terra our Race was capable of doubling its numbers three times each century – given space and raw materials.

The Star Drive gave both. H. sapiens spread through this sector of our Galaxy at many times the speed of light and multiplied like yeast. If doubling had occurred at the twenty-first-century potential, our numbers would now be of the order of $7 \times 10^9 \times 2^{68}$ – a number so large as to defy emotional grasp; it is suited only to computers:

$$7 \times 10^9 \times 2^{68} = 2{,}066{,}035{,}336{,}255{,}469{,}780{,}992{,}000{,}000{,}000.$$

– or more than two thousand million billion trillion people
– or a mass of protein twenty-five *million* times as great as the entire mass of our race's native planet Sol III, Old Home.

Preposterous.

Let us say that it would be preposterous had not the Great Diaspora taken place, for our race, having reached the potential to double three times each century, had also reached a crisis under which it could not double even once – that knee of the curve in

*Gregorian Terran dates are used throughout, as no other calendar, not even Standard Galactic, is certain to be known to scholars of every planet. Translators should add local dates for clarification.

J.F. 45th

the yeast-growth law in which a population can maintain a precarious stability of zero growth only by killing off its own members fast enough ... lest it drown in its own poisons, commit suicide by total war, or stumble into some other form of the Malthusian Final Solution.

But the Human Race has not (we think) increased to that monstrous figure because the base figure for the Diaspora must not be thought of as seven billion but rather as a few million at the opening of the Era, plus the unnumbered, small-but-still-growing hundreds of millions since, who have migrated from Earth and from its colony planets to still more distant places over the last two millennia.

But we are no longer able to make a reasoned guess at the numbers of the Human Race, nor do we have even an approximate count of the colonized planets. The most we can say is that there must be in excess of two thousand colonized planets, in excess of five hundred billion people. The colonized planets may be twice that number, the Human Race could be four times that numerous. Or more.

So even the demographic aspects of historiography have become impossible; data are out of date when we receive them and always incomplete – yet so numerous and so varied in reliability that several hundred humans/computers on my staff keep busy trying to analyse, collate, interpolate, and extrapolate, and to weigh them against other data before incorporating them into the records. We attempt to maintain standards of 95 per cent in probability of corrected data, 85 per cent in pessimistic reliability; our achievement is closer to 89 per cent and 81 per cent – and getting worse.

Pioneers care little about sending records to the home office; they are busy staying alive, making babies, and killing off anything in their way. A colony is usually into its fourth generation before *any* data reach this office.

(Nor can it be otherwise. A colonist too interested in statistics becomes a statistic himself – as a corpse. I intend to migrate; once I have done so, I won't care whether this office keeps track of me or not. I have stuck to this essentially useless work for almost a century partly through inducements and partly through genetic disposition – I am a direct-and-reinforced descendant of Andrew Jackson Slipstick Libby himself. But I am descended also from the Senior and have – I think – some of his restless nature. I want to follow the wild geese and see what is happening out there

– get married again, leave a dozen descendants on a fresh uncrowded planet, then – possibly – move on. Once I have the Senior's memoirs collated, the Trustees can, in the Senior's ancient idiom, take this job and shove it.)

What sort of man is our Senior, my ancestor and probably yours, and certainly the oldest living human being, the only man who has taken part in the entire pageant of the crisis of the Human Race and its surmounting of crisis through Diaspora?

For surmount it we have. Our race could now lose fifty planets, close ranks and move on. Our gallant women could replace the casualties in a single generation. Not that it appears likely that this will happen; thus far we have encountered not one race as mean, as nasty, as deadly as our own. A conservative extrapolation indicates that we will reach in numbers that preposterous figure given earlier in a few more generations – and move on out of this Galaxy into others before we finish settling this one. Indeed, reports from farther out indicate that Human intergalactic colony ships are already headed out into the Endless Deeps. These reports are not verified – but the most virile colonies are always a long way from the most populous centres. One may hope.

At best, history is hard to grasp; at worst, it is a lifeless collection of questionable records. It is most alive through the words of eyewitnesses . . . and we have but one witness whose life spans the twenty-three centuries of crisis and Diaspora. The next oldest human being whose age this office has been able to verify is only a little over a thousand years old. Probability theory makes it possible that there is somewhere a person half again that age – but it is mathematically and historically certain that there is no other human alive today who was born in the twentieth century.*

Some may question whether this "Senior" is the member of the Howard Families born in 1912 and also the "Lazarus Long" who led the Families in their escape from Old Home in 2136, etc. – pointing out that all the ancient methods of identification (finger-

*When the Howard Families seized the Starship *New Frontiers* only a few were more than a century and a quarter old; all of that few – save the Senior – are dead, at times and places on record. (I except the strange and possibly mythical case of life-in-death of Elder Mary Sperling.) Despite genetic advantage and access to the longevity therapies known collectively as "the immortality option," the last died in 3003 Gregorian. By the records it would seem that most of them died through refusing further rejuvenation – that being still the second commonest cause of death today.

J.F. 45th

prints, retinal patterns, etc.) can now be beaten. True, but those methods were adequate for their time and the Howard Families Foundation had special reason to use them with care; the "Woodrow Wilson Smith" whose birth was registered with the Foundation in 1912 is certainly the "Lazarus Long" of 2136 and 2210. Before those tests ceased to be reliable they were supplemented by modern unbeatable tests based first on clone transplants and, more lately, on absolute identification of genetic patterns. (It is interesting to note that an imposter showed up about three centuries ago, here on Secondus, and was given a new heart from a cloned pseudobody of the Senior. It killed him.) The Senior whose words are quoted herein has a generic pattern identical with that of a bit of muscle tissue removed from "Lazarus Long" by Dr. Gordon Hardy in the Starship *New Frontiers* about 2145, and cultured by him for longevity research. Q.E.D.

But what sort of man *is* he? You must judge for yourself. In condensing this memoir to manageable length I have omitted many verified historical incidents (the raw data are available to scholars at the Archives) – but I have left in lies and unlikely stories on the assumption that the lies a man tells tell more truth about him – when analysed – than does "truth."

It is clear that this man is, by standards usual in civilized societies, a barabarian and a rogue.

But it is not for children to judge their parents. The qualities that make him what he is are precisely those needed to stay alive in a jungle – or on a raw frontier. Do not forget your debt to him both genetic and historic.

To understand our historic debt to him it is necessary to review some ancient history – part tradition or myth, and part fact as firmly established as the assassination of Julius Caesar. The Howard Families Foundation was established by the will of Ira Howard, who died in 1873. His will instructed the trustees of the foundation to use his money to "prolong human life." This is fact.

Tradition says that he willed this in anger at his own fate, for he found himself dying *of old age* in his forties – dead at forty-eight, a bachelor without progeny. So none of us carries his genes; his immortality lies only in a name, and in an idea – that death could be thwarted.

At that time death at forty-eight was not unusual. Believe it or not, in those days the average age at death was about thirty-five! But not from senility. Disease, starvation, accident, murder, war, childbirth, and other violences cut down most humans long before senility set in. But a human who passed all these hurdles still could expect death from old age sometime between seventy-five and one hundred. Very few reached one hundred; nevertheless every population group had its tiny minority of "centenarians." There is a legend about "Old Tom Parr" who is supposed to have died in 1635 aged one hundred and fifty-two years. Whether or not the legend is true, probability analysis of demographic data of that era shows that some individuals must have lived a century and a half. But they were few indeed.

The Foundation started its work as a prescientific breeding experiment, as nothing was then known of genetics; Adults of long-lived stock were encouraged to mate with others like them, money being the inducement.

Unsurprisingly the inducement worked. Equally unsurprisingly this experiment worked, as it was an empirical method used by stockbreeders for centuries before the science of genetics came into being: Breed to reinforce one characteristic, then eliminate the culls.

The Families' Archives do not show how the earliest culls were eliminated; they simply show that some were eliminated from the Families – root and branch, all descendants – for the unforgivable sin of dying of old age too young.

By the Crisis of 2136 all members of the Howard Families had life expectancies in excess of one hundred and fifty years, and some had exceeded that age. The cause of that crisis seems unbelievable – yet all records both from inside and from outside the Families agree on it. The Howard Families were in extreme danger from all other humans simply because they lived so "long." Why this was true is a matter for group psychologists, not for a record-keeper. But it *was* true.

They were seized and concentrated in a prison camp, and were about to be tortured to death in an attempt to wrest from them their "secret" of "eternal youth." Fact – not myth.

Here the Senior comes into the story. Through audacity, a talent for lying convincingly, and what would seem to most people today a childish delight in adventure and intrigue for its own sake, the Senior brought off the greatest jailbreak of all time, stealing a primitive starship and escaping right out of the Solar System with all of the Howard Families (then numbering about 100,000 men, women and children).

If this seems impossible – so many people and just one ship – remember that the first starships were enormously bigger than the ones we now use. They were self-sustaining artificial planetoids intended to remain in space for many years at speeds below that of light; they *had* to be huge.

The Senior was not the only hero of that Exodus. But in all the varied and sometimes conflicting accounts that have come down to us, he was always the driving force. He was our Moses who led his people out of bondage.

He brought them home again three-quarters of a century later (2210) – but not into bondage. For that date, Year One of the Standard Galactic calendar, marks the opening of the Great Diaspora ... caused by extreme population pressure on Old Home Terra, and made possible by two new factors: the Libby-Sheffield Para-Drive as it was known then (not a "drive" in any true sense, but a means of manipulating n-dimensional spaces), and the first (and simplest) of effective longevity techniques: new blood grown in vitro.

The Howard Families caused this to happen simply by escaping. The short-lived humans back on Terra, still convinced that the long-lived families possessed a "secret," set about trying to find it by wide and systematic research, and, as always, research paid off serendipitously, not with the nonexistent "secret" but with something almost as good: a therapy, and eventually a sheaf of therapies, for postponing old age, and for extending vigour, virility, and fertility.

The Great Diaspora was then both necessary and possible.

The Senior's great talent (aside from his ability to lie extemporaneously and convincingly) seems always to have been a rare gift for extrapolating the possibilities of any situation – then twisting it to suit his own purposes. (He calls it: "You have to have a feeling for what makes the frog jump." Psychometrists who have studied him say that he has an extremely high psi talent expressed as "forerunners" and "luck" – but what the Senior has to say about *them* is less polite. As a record-keeper, I refrain from opinion.)

The Senior saw at once that this benison of extended youth, although promised to everyone, would in fact be limited to the powerful and their nepots. The billions of helots could *not* be allowed to live beyond their normal span; there was no room for them – unless they migrated to the stars, in which case there would be room for each human to live as long as he could manage. How the Senior exploited this is not always clear; he seems to have used several names and many fronts. His key corporations wound up in the hands of this Foundation, then were liquidated to move the Foundation and the Howard Families to Secundus – at his behest, he having saved "the best real estate" for his relatives and descendants. Sixty-eight per cent of those then living accepted the challenge of new frontiers.

Our genetic debt to him is both indirect and direct. The indirect debt lies in the fact that migration is a sorting device, a forced Darwinian selection, under which superior stock goes to the stars while culls stay home and die. This is true even for those forcibly transported (as in the twenty-fourth and twenty-fifth centuries), save that the sorting then takes place on the new planet. In a raw frontier weaklings and misfits die; strong stock survives. Even those who migrate voluntarily still go through this second drastic special selection. The Howard Families have been culled in this fashion at least three times.

Our genetic "debt" to the Senior is even easier to prove. Part of it needs only simple arithmetic. If you live anywhere but on Old Home Terra – and you almost certainly do if you read this, in view of the present miserable state of "The Fair Green Hills of Earth" – and can claim even one member of the Howard Families among your ancestors – and most of you can – then you are most probably descended from the Senior.

By the official Families' genealogies this probability is 87.3 per cent. You are descended from many other twentieth-century members of the Howard Families, too, if you are descended from any of them, but I speak here only of Woodrow Wilson Smith, the Senior. By the Crisis Year 2136 nearly one-tenth of the youngest generation of the Howard Families were descended from the Senior "legitimately" – by which I mean that each linking birth was so recorded in the Families' records and ancestry confirmed by such tests as were available at the time. (Even blood typing was not known when the breeding experiment started, but the culling process made it strongly to a female's advantage not to stray, at least not outside the Families.)

By now the cumulative probability is, as I have said, 87.3 per cent if you have *any* Howard ancestor – but if you have a Howard ancestor from a recent generation, your probability climbs toward an effective 100 per cent.

But, as a statistician, I have reason to believe (backed by computer analyses of blood types, hair types, eye colour, tooth count, enzyme types, and other characteristics responsive to genetic analysis) – strong reason to believe that the Senior has many descendants not recorded in genealogies, both inside and outside the Howard Families.

To put it mildly, he is a shameless old goat whose seed is scattered all through this part of our Galaxy.

Take the years of the Exodus, after he stole the *New Frontiers*. He was not married even once during those years, and ship's records and legends based on memoirs of that time suggest that he was, in an early idiom, a "woman hater," a misogynist.

Perhaps. Biostatistical records (rather than genealogies), when analyzed, suggest that he was not that unapproachable. The computer that analysed it offered to bet me even money on more than one hundred offspring fathered by him during those years. (I refused the bet; that computer beats me at chess even though I insist on a one-rook advantage.)

I do not find this surprising in view of the almost pathological emphasis placed on longevity among the Families at that time. The oldest male, if still virile – and he certainly was – would have been subjected to endless temptation, endless opportunity, by females anxious to have offspring of his demonstrated superiority – "superiority" by the only criterion the Howard Families respected. We can assume that marital status would not matter much; all Howard Families marriages were marriages of convenience – Ira Howard's will insured that – and they were rarely for life. The only surprising aspect is that so *few* fertile females managed to trip him when unquestionably so many thousands were willing. But he was always fast on his feet.

As may be – If today I see a man with sandy red hair, a big nose, an easy disarming grin, and a slightly feral look in his green-grey eyes, I always wonder how recently the Senior has passed through that part of the Galaxy. If such a stranger comes close to me, I put my hand on my purse. If he speaks to me, I resolve not to make wagers or promises.

But how did the Senior himself only a third-generation member of Ira Howard's breeding experiment, manage to live and stay young his first three hundred years *without* artificial rejuvenation?

A mutation, of course – which simply says that we don't know. But in the course of his several rejuvenations we have learned a little about his physical makeup. He has an unusually large heart that beats very slowly. He has only twenty-eight teeth, no caries, and seems to be immune to infection. He has never had surgery other than for wounds or for rejuvenation procedures. His reflexes are extremely fast – but appear always to be reasoned, so one may question the correctness of the term "reflex." His eyes have never needed correction either for distance or close work; his hearing range is abnormally high, abnormally low, and is unusually acute throughout his range. His colour vision includes indigo. He was born without prepuce, without vermiform appendix, – and apparently without a conscience.

I am pleased that he is my ancestor.

Justin Foote the 45th
Chief Archivist, Howard Foundation

PREFACE TO REVISED EDITION

In this abridged popular edition the technical appendix has been published separately in order to make room for an account of the Senior's actions after he left Secundus until his disappearance. An apocryphal and obviously impossible tale of the last events in his life has been included at the insistence of the editor of the original memoir, but it cannot be taken seriously.

Carolyn Briggs
Chief Archivist

Note: My lovely and learned successor in office does not know what she is talking about. With the Senior, the most fantastic is always the most probable.

Justin Foote the 45th
Chief Archivist Emeritus

PRELUDE

I

As the door of the suits dilated, the man seated staring glumly out the window looked around. "Who the hell are you?"

"I am Ira Weatheral of the Johnson Family, Ancestor, Chairman Pro Tem of the Families."

"Took you long enough. Don't call me 'Ancestor.' And why just the Chairman Pro Tem?" the man in the chair growled. "Is the Chairman too damn busy to see me? Don't I rate even *that*?" He made no move to stand, nor did he invite his visitor to sit down.

"Your pardon, Sire. I *am* chief executive for the Families. But it has been customary for some time now – several centuries – for the chief executive to hold the title 'Chairman Pro Tem' . . . against the possibility that you might show up and take the gavel."

"Eh? Ridiculous. I haven't presided at a meeting of the Trustees for a thousand years. And 'Sire' is as bad as 'Ancestor' – call me by name. It's been two days since I sent for you. Did you come by the scenic route? Or has the rule that entitles me to the ear of the Chairman been revoked?"

"I am not aware of that rule, Senior; it was probably long before my time – but it is my honour and duty – and pleasure – to wait on you at any time. I will be pleased and honoured to call you by name if you will tell me what your name is now. As for the delay – thirty-seven hours since I received your summons – I have spent it studying Ancient English, as I was told that you were not answering to any other language."

The Senior looked slightly sheepish. "It's true I'm not handy with the jabber they speak here – my memory has been playing tricks on me lately. I guess I've been sulky about answering even when I understood. Names – I forgot what name I checked in by when I grounded here. Mmm, 'Woodrow Wilson Smith' was my boyhood name. Never used it much. I suppose 'Lazarus Long' is the name I've used oftenest – call me 'Lazarus.'"

"Thank you, Lazarus."

"For what? Don't be so damned formal. You're not a kid, or you wouldn't be Chairman – how old are you? Did you really take the trouble to learn my milk language just to call on me? And in less than two days? Was that from scratch? It takes me at least a week to tack on a new language, another week to smooth out accent."

"I am three hundred and seventy-two standard years old, Lazarus – just under four hundred Earth years. I learned classic English when I took this job – but as a dead language, to enable me to read old records of the Families in the original. What I did since your summons was to learn to speak and understand it . . . in North American twentieth-century idiom – your 'milk language' as you said – as that is what the linguistic analyzer computed that you were speaking."

"Pretty smart machine. Maybe I am speaking it the way I did as a youngster; they claim that's the one language a brain never forgets. Then I must be talking in a Cornbelt rasp like a rusty saw . . . whereas you're speaking a sort of Texas drawl with an Oxford British overlay. Odd. I suppose the machine picks the version out of its permanents closest to the sample fed into it."

"I believe so, Lazarus, although the techniques involved are not my field. Do you have trouble understanding my accent?"

"Oh, none at all. Your accent is okay; it's closer to educated General American of that time than is the accent I learned as a kid. But I can follow anything from Bluegum to Yorkshire; accent is no problem. It was mighty kind of you to bother. Warming."

"My pleasure. I have a talent for languages; it was not much trouble. I try to be able to speak to each of the Trustees in his native language; I'm used to swotting up a new one quickly."

"So? Nonetheless a courteous thing to do – I've felt like an animal in a zoo with no one to talk to. Those dummies" – Lazarus inclined his head at two rejuvenation technicians, dressed in isolation gear and one-way helmets, and waiting as far from the conversation as the room permitted – "don't know English; I can't talk with them. Oh, the taller one understands a little but not enough for gossip." Lazarus whistled, pointed at the taller. "Hey, you! A chair for the Chairman – chop chop!" His gestures made his meaning clear. The taller technician touched the controls of a chair nearby; it rolled away, wheeled around, and stopped at a comfortable tête-à-tête distance from Lazarus.

Ira Weatheral said thank you – to Lazarus, not to the tech – sat down, then sighed as the chair felt him out and cuddled him. Lazarus said, "Comfortable?"

"Quite."

"Anything to eat or drink? Or smoke? You may have to interpret for me."

"Nothing, thank you. But may I order for you?"

"Not now. They keep me stuffed like a goose – once they force-fed me, damn them. Since we're comfortable, let's get on with the powwow." He suddenly roared, "WHAT THE HELL AM I DOING IN THIS JAIL?"

Weatherall answered quietly, "Not 'jail,' Lazarus. The VIP suite of the Howard Rejuvenation Clinic, New Rome."

" 'Jail,' I said. All it lacks is cockroaches. This window – you couldn't break it with a crowbar. That door – it opens to any voice . . . except *mine*. If I go to the john, one of those dummies is at my elbow. Apparently afraid I'll drown myself in the pot. Hell, I don't even know whether that nurse is a man or a woman – and don't like it either way. I don't need somebody to hold my hand while I go pee-pee! I resent it."

"I'll see what can be worked out, Lazarus. But the technicians are understandably jumpy. A person can get hurt quite easily in any bathroom – and they all know that, if you are hurt, no matter by what mischance, the technician in charge at the time will suffer cruel and unusual punishment. They are volunteers and are drawing high bonuses. But they're jumpy."

"So I figured out. 'Jail.' If this is a rejuvenation suite . . . WHERE'S MY SUICIDE SWITCH?"

"Lazarus – 'Death is every man's privilege.' "

"That's what I said! That switch belongs right there; you can see where it has been dismounted. So I'm in jail without trial, with my most basic right taken from me. *Why?* I'm furious, man. Do you realize what danger *you* are in? Never tease an old dog; he might have one bite left. Old as I am, I could break your arms before those dummies could reach us."

"You are welcome to break my arms if it pleases you."

"Huh?" Lazarus Long looked baffled. "No, it's not worth the sweat. They would have you patched up good as new in thirty minutes." He suddenly grinned. "But I could snap your neck, then crush your skull, about as fast. That's one injury beyond the power of rejuvenators."

Weatheral did not stir, did not tense. "I feel sure you could," he said quietly. "But I do not think that you would kill one of your descendants without giving him a chance to parley for his life. You are my remote grandfather, sir, by seven different tracks."

Lazarus chewed his lip and looked unhappy. "Son, I have so many descendants that consanguinity doesn't matter. But you're essentially right. In all my life I have never killed a man unnecessarily. I think." Then he grinned. "But if I don't get my suicide switch back, I could make an exception in your case."

"Lazarus, if you wish, I will have that switch remounted at once. But – 'Ten Words'?"

"Uh –" Lazarus looked ungracious. "Okay. 'Ten Words.' Not eleven."

Weatheral hesitated a split second, then counted on his fingers: "I . learned . your . language . to . explain . why . we . need . you.'

"Ten by the Rule," Lazarus admitted. "But meaning that you need fifty. Or five hundred. Or five thousand."

"Or none," Weatheral amended. "You can have your switch without giving me any chance to explain. I promised."

"Humph!" said Lazarus. "Ira, you old scoundrel, you have me convinced that you really are my kin. You figured that I would not suicide without hearing what you have on your mind – once I knew you had bothered to learn a dead language just to make palaver. All right, talk. You can start by telling me what I'm doing here. I know – I *know* – that I didn't apply for rejuvenation. But I woke up here with the job already half over. So I screamed for the Chairman. Okay, why am I here?"

"May we start further back? You tell *me* what you were doing in a flophouse in the worst part of Old Town."

"What was I *doing*? I was *dying*. Quietly and decently, like a worn-out horse. That is, I was, until your busybodies grabbed me. Can you think of a better place than a flophouse for a man who doesn't want to be disturbed while he's busy with it? If his cot is paid for in advance, they leave a man be. Oh, they stole what little I had, even my shoes. But I expected that – would have done the same myself under the same circumstances. And the sort of people who live in flophouses are almost always kind to those worse off than they are – any of 'em will fetch a drink of water to a sick man. That was the most I wanted – that and to be left alone to close out my account in my own way. Until your busies showed up. Tell me, how did they find me?"

"How we found you is not the surprising part, Lazarus, but the fact that SecFor – the cops? – Yes, 'cops' – that my cops took so long to identify you, then find you, and pick you up. A section chief lost his job over that. I don't tolerate inefficiency."

"So you busted him. Your business. But why? I reached Secundus from Out-Far, and I didn't think I had left any back trail. Different everything since the last time I was in touch with the Families . . . as I bought my last rejuvenation on Supreme. Are the Families swapping data with Supreme these days?"

"Heavens no, Lazarus, we won't even give them a polite word. There is a strong minority among the Trustees who favour rubbing out Supreme, instead of simply maintaining embargo."

"Well . . . if a Nova bomb hit Supreme I wouldn't mourn more than thirty seconds. But I did have a reason for having the job done there, even though I had to pay high for forced cloning. But that's another story. Son, how did you pick me up?"

"Sir, for the past seventy years there has been a general order out to try find to you, not just here but on every planet where the Families maintain offices. As to how – do you recall a forced inoculation for Reiber's fever at Immigration?"

"Yes. I was annoyed, but it didn't seem worthwhile to make a fuss; I knew I was headed for that flophouse. Ira, I've known that I was dying for quite some time. That was okay; I was ready for it. But I didn't want to do it alone, out in space. Wanted human voices around me, and body odours. Childish of me. But I was pretty far gone by the time I grounded."

"Lazarus, there is no such thing as Reiber's fever. When a man grounds on Secundus and all routine identifications show null, 'Reiber's fever' or some other nonexistant plague is used as an excuse to get a little tissue from him while injecting him with sterile neutral saline. You should never have been allowed to leave the skyport until your genetic pattern was identified."

"So? What do you do when ten thousand immigrants arrive in one ship?"

"Herd them into detention barracks until we've checked them out. But that doesn't happen often today with Old Home Terra in the sorry state it's in. But you Lazarus, arriving alone in a private yacht worth fifteen to twenty million crowns –"

"Make that 'thirty.' "

"– worth thirty million crowns. How many men in the Galaxy can do that? Of those who can afford it, how many would choose to travel alone? The pattern should have set alarm bells ringing in the minds of all of them. Instead they took your tissue and accepted your statement that you would be staying at the Romulus hilton and let you go – and no doubt you had another identity before dark."

"No doubt at all," Lazarus agreed. "But your cops have run up the price on a good phony set of ID's. If I hadn't been too tired to bother, I would have forged my own. Safer. Was that how I was caught? Did you squeeze it out of the paper merchant?"

"No, we never found him. By the way, you might let me know who he is, so that –"

"And I might not," Lazarus said sharply. "Not ratting on him was implicit in the bargain. It's nothing to me how many of your rules he breaks. And – who knows? – I might need him again. Certainly someone will need his services, somebody just as anxious to avoid your busies as I was. Ira, no doubt you mean well but I don't like setups where ID's are necessary. I told myself centuries back to stay away from places crowded enough to require them, and mostly I've followed that rule. Should have followed it this time. But I didn't expect to need *any* identification very long. Confound it, two more days and I would have been dead. I think. How did you catch me?"

"The hard way. Once I knew you were on planet I stirred things up; that section chief wasn't the only unhappy man. But you disappeared in so simple a fashion that you baffled the entire force. My security chief expressed the opinion that you had been killed and your body disposed of. I told him if that were the case, he had better start thinking about off-planet migration."

"Make it march! I want to know how I goofed."

"I would not say that you goofed, Lazarus, since you managed to stay hidden with every cop and stoolie on this globe looking for you. But I felt certain that you had not been killed. Oh, we do have murders on Secundus, especially here in New Rome. But most are the commonplace husband-wife sort. We don't have many for gain since I instituted a policy of making the punishment fit the crime and holding executions in the Colosseum. In any case I felt certain that a man who had survived more than two millennia would not let himself be killed in some dark alley.

"So I assumed that you were alive, then asked myself, 'If I were Lazarus Long, how would I go about hiding?' I went into deep meditation and thought about it. Then I tried to retrace your steps, so far as we knew them. By the way –"

The Chairman Pro Tem threw back his shoulder cloak, took

out a large sealed envelope, handed it to Lazarus. "Here is the item you left in a lockbox at Harriman Trust."

Lazarus accepted it. "It's been opened."

"By me. Prematurely, I admit – but you addressed it to me. I have read it but no one else has. And now I will forget it. Except to say this: I am unsurprised that you left your wealth to the Families . . . but I was touched that you assigned your yacht to the personal use of the Chairman. That's a sweet craft, Lazarus; I lust after it a bit. But not so much that I am anxious to inherit so quickly. But I understood to explain why we need you – and let myself get sidetracked."

"I'm in no rush, Ira. Are you?"

"*Me?* Sir, I have no duties more important than talking to the Senior. Besides, my staff runs this planet more efficiently if I don't supervize them too closely."

Lazarus nodded agreement. "That was always my system, the times I let myself get involved. Accept the whole load, then shove the work off on other people as fast as I could pick 'em. Having any trouble with democrats these days?"

" 'Democrats'? Oh – you must mean 'equalitarians.' I thought at first you meant the Church of the Holy Democrat. We leave that church alone; they don't meddle. There is an equalitarian movement every few years, certainly, under various names. The Freedom Party, the League of the Oppressed – names don't matter as they all want to turn the rascals out, starting with me, and put their own rascals in. We never bother them; we simply infiltrate, then some night we round up the ringleaders and their families, and by daylight they are headed out as involuntary migrants. Transportees. 'Living on Secundus is a privilege, not a right.' "

"You're quoting me."

"Of course. Your exact words from the contract under which you deeded Secundus to the Foundation. That there was to be no government on this planet other than such rules as the current chairman found necessary to maintain order. We've stuck to our agreement with you, Senior; I am sole boss until the Trustees see fit to replace me."

"That's what I intended," Lazarus agreed. "But – Son, it's your pidgin and I'll never touch that gavel again – but I have doubts about the wisdom of getting rid of troublemakers. Every loaf needs yeast. A society that gets rid of all its troublemakers goes downhill. Sheep. Pyramid builders at best, decadent savages at worst. You may be eliminating your creative one-tenth of one per cent. Your yeast."

"I'm afraid we are, Senior, and that's one reason why we need you –"

"I said I won't touch that gavel!"

"Will you hear me out, sir? You won't be asked to, even though it is yours by ancient custom if you care to pick it up. But I could use advice –"

"I don't give advice; people never take it."

"Sorry. Perhaps just a chance to talk over my problems with a person more experienced than I am. About these troublemakers – We haven't eliminated them in the old sense; they're still alive, or most of them. Ostracizing a man to another planet is more satisfactory than killing him for the technical crime of treason; it gets rid of him without making his neighbours too indignant. Nor have we wasted him – them – as we are using them to conduct an experiment: All transportees are shipped to the same planet, Felicity. Do you happen to know it?"

"Not by that name."

"I think you would have stumbled on it only by accident, sir; we have kept it out of public records in order to use it as a Botany Bay. It is not as good a planet as the name suggests, but it is a good one, roughly equivalent to Old Home Terra – Earth, I should say – before it was ruined, or much like Secundus when we settled here. It's rough enough to test a man and eliminate weaklings, gentle enough to let a man raise a family if he has the guts to dig in and sweat."

"Sounds like a good place; perhaps you should have hung onto it. Natives?"

"The proto-dominant race are quite fierce savages . . . if any are still alive. We don't know, we don't even maintain a liaison office there. This native race is neither intelligent enough to be civilized nor tractable enough to be enslaved. Perhaps they would have evolved and made it on their own, but they had the misfortune to encounter H. sapiens before they were ready for him. But that is not the experiment; the transportees are certain to win out over that competition, we do not send them empty-handed. But, Lazarus, these people believe that they can create ideal government by majority rule."

Lazarus snorted.

"Perhaps they *can*, sir," Weatheral persisted. "I don't know that they cannot. That is the experiment."

"Son, are you a fool? Oh, you can't be, the Trustees wouldn't keep you in office. But – How old did you say you are?"

Weatheral answered quietly, "I am nineteen centuries your junior, sir; I will not dispute your opinion on anything. But *I* do not know through my own experience that this experiment will not work; I have never seen a government of the democratic type, even in the numerous times I have been off planet. I've simply read about them. From what I have read not one has ever been formed from a population all of whom believed in the democratic theory. So I don't know."

"Hmmm." Lazarus looked frustrated. "Ira, I was about to shove my own experience with such governments down your throat. But you're right, this is a brand-new situation – and we *don't* know. Oh, I have strong opinions, but a thousand reasoned opinions never equal to one case of diving in and finding out. Galileo proved that and it may be the only certainty we have. Mmm . . . all the so-called democracies I've ever seen or heard of were either forced on the majority from above or grew up slowly from the plebs discovering that they could vote themselves bread-and-circuses – for a while, until the system broke down. I'm sorry I won't see the outcome of your experiment. I suspect it will be the harshest tyranny imaginable; majority rule gives the ruthless strong man plenty of elbow room to oppress his fellows. But I don't *know*. What's *your* opinion?"

"The computers say –"

"Never mind computers. Ira, the most sophisticated machine the human mind can build has in it the limitations of the human mind. Anyone who thinks otherwise does not understand the Second Law of Thermodynamics. I asked for *your* opinion."

"Sir, I refuse to form an opinion; I lack sufficient data."

"Hrrumph! You're getting old, Son. To get anywhere, or even to live a long time, a man has to guess, and guess right, over and over again, without enough data for a logical answer. You were telling me how you found me."

"Yes, sir. That document, your will, made it clear that you expected to die soon. Then" – Weatheral paused and smiled wryly – "I had to guess right without enough data." It took us two days to find the shop where you bought clothes to lower your apparent status – and to conform to local styles, I think. I suspect that you bought your false ID's right after that."

He paused; Lazarus made no comment; Weatheral continued: "Another half day to find the shop where you lowered your apparent status much farther, close to bottom – too far perhaps, as the shopkeeper remembered you, both because you paid cash and because you were buying secondhand clothes that were not as good even when new as the ones you were wearing. Oh, he pretended to accept your story about a 'costume party' and kept his mouth shut; his shop is a fence for stolen goods."

"Of course," agreed Lazarus. "I made sure he was on the crook before I bought from him. But you said he stayed zipped?"

"Until we stimulated his memory. A fence is in a difficult position, Lazarus; he has to have a permanent address. This can sometimes force him to be honest."

"Oh, I wasn't blaming dear old Uncle. The fault was mine; I let myself be conspicuous. I was tired, Ira, and feeling my years and let it rush me into doing a sloppy job. Even a hundred years back I would have done a more artistic job – I've always known that it is more difficult to lower your status convincingly than to raise it."

"I don't think you need feel ashamed of the job as a work of art, Senior; you had us baffled for almost three months."

"Son, the world doesn't pay off on a 'good try.' Go ahead."

"Brute force then, Lazarus. That shop is in the worst part of the city; we put a cordon around the area and saturated it, thousands of men. But not for long; you were in the third fleabag we checked. I spotted you myself, I was with one of the raiding parties. Then your genetic pattern confirmed your identity." Ira Weatherall smiled slightly. "But we were pouring new blood into you before the genetic analyser reported your identity; you were in bad shape, sir."

"I was like hell in bad shape; I was simply dying – and minding my own business, a practice you could emulate. Ira, do you realize what a dirty trick you have done me? A man ought not to have to die twice... and I was past the bad part and ready for the finale as easy as falling asleep. Then *you* butted in. I've never heard of rejuvenation being forced on anyone. If I had suspected that you had changed the rules, I would never have come near this planet. Now I have to go through it again. Either with the suicide switch – and suicide is an idea I've always despised – or the natural way. Which could now take a long time. Is my old blood still around? Stored?"

"I will inquire of the Clinic's Director, sir."

"Humph. That's not an answer, so don't bother to lie. You've put me in a dilemma, Ira. Even though I haven't had the full treatment, I feel better than I've felt for forty years or more – which means either that I must again wait it out for many weary years – or use that switch when my body isn't saying, 'Time to adjourn.' You meddling scoundrel, by what authority – no, you've got the authority. By what ethical principle did you interfere with my death?"

"Because we needed you, sir."

"That's not an ethical reason, just a pragmatic one. The need was not mutual."

"Senior I have studied your life as thoroughly as the records permit. It seems to me that you often acted pragmatically."

Lazarus grinned. "That's my boy! I was wondering if you would have the gall to try to twist it into some high moral principle, like a damned preacher. I don't trust a man who talks about ethics when he's picking my pocket. But if he's acting in his own self-interest and says so, I have usually been able to work out some way to do business with him."

"Lazarus, if you will let us complete your rejuvenation, you'll feel like living again. I think you know that; you've been through it before."

"To what end, sir? When I've had more than two thousand years of trying everything? When I've seen so many planets that they blur in my mind? When I've had so many wives I can't remember their names? 'We pray for one last landing on the Globe that gave us birth –' I can't even do *that*; the lovely green planet I was born on has aged even more than I have; to return to, it would be a time for tears, not a happy homecoming. No, Son, despite all rejuvenation there comes a time when the only reasonable thing to do is turn out the lights and go to sleep – and you, damn you, you took it away from me."

"I'm sorry – no, I'm *not* sorry. But I do ask your pardon."

"Well . . . you might get it. But not now. What was this aching reason you needed me? You mentioned some problem other than the troublemakers you transport."

"Yes, although it is not one that would have caused me to interfere with your right to die your own way; I can handle it, one way or another. I think Secundus is becoming both too crowded and too civilized –"

"I'm sure of it, Ira."

"Therefore I think the Families should move again."

"I agree even though I am not interested. As a thumb rule, one can say that any time a planet starts developing cities of more than one million people, it is approaching critical mass. In a century or two it won't be fit to live on. Do you have a planet in mind? Do you think you can get the trustees to go along? And will the Families follow the Trustees?"

"Yes to the first, maybe to the second, probably No to the third. I have a planet in mind as 'Tertius,' one as good or better than Secundus. I think many of the Trustees would agree with my reasoning but I'm not sure of the overwhelming support such a move would need – Secundus is too comfortable for the danger to seem imminent to most people. As for the Families themselves – no, I don't think we could persuade most of them to uproot and move . . . but even a few hundred thousand would suffice. Gideon's Band – you follow me?"

"I'm way ahead of you. Migration always involves selection and improvement. Elementary. If they'll do it. *If*. Ira, I had a hell of a time selling the idea to the Families when we moved here back in the twenty-third century. Could not have sold it at all if Earth had not become a dreary place. Good luck – you'll need it."

"Lazarus, I don't expect to succeed. I will *try*. But if I fail, I'll resign and migrate anyhow. To Tertius if I can organize a party large enough for a viable colony. To some planet colonized but very thinly settled if not."

"Do you mean that, Ira? Or, when the time comes, will you kid yourself that it is really your duty to hang on? If a man has the temperament for power – and you have or you wouldn't be where you are – he finds it hard to abdicate."

"I mean it, Lazarus. Oh, I like to run things; I know it. I hope to lead the Families on their third Exodus. But I don't expect to. However, I think my chances of putting together a viable colony – of young people, not over a hundred years old, two hundred at most – without the aid of the Foundation, are fairly good. But if I fail in that, too" – he shrugged – "migration will be the only worthwhile course open to me; Secundus will have nothing more to offer." Weatheral added, "Perhaps I feel as you do, sir, in a minor way. I have no wish to be Chairman Pro Tem all my days. I've had almost a century of it; that's enough. If I can't put this over."

Lazarus was thoughtfully silent; Weatheral waited.

"Ira, install that suicide switch for me. But tomorrow. Not today."

"Yes, sir."

"Don't you want to know why?" Lazarus picked up the large

envelope, his will. "If you convince me that you are going to migrate, come hell or high water and no matter what the Trustees do, I want to rewrite this. My investments and cash accounts here and there – if somebody hasn't stolen them while my back was turned – add up to a nice piece of change. Possibly enough to make the difference between success and failure in mounting a migration. If the Trustees won't back it with Foundation funds. And they won't."

Weatheral said nothing. Lazarus glared at him. "Didn't your mother teach you to say 'Thank you'?"

"For what, Lazarus? For giving me something after you're dead and no longer need it? If you do this, it will be to tickle your vanity – not to please me."

Lazarus grinned. "Hell, yes. I ought to stick in a condition that you name the planet 'Lazarus.' But I would have no way to enforce it. Okay, we understand each other. And I think – Do you respect good machinery?"

"Eh? Yes. As much as I despise machinery that doesn't do what it is putatively designed to do."

"We still understand each other. I think I'll leave the 'Dora' – that's my yacht – to you personally rather than to the Families' chairman . . . *if* you lead a migration."

"Uh . . . you tempt me to thank you."

"Don't. Just be good to her. She's a sweet craft, she's never known anything but kindness. She'll make a fine flagship for you. With simple reoutfitting – specs for it in her computer – she'll house a staff of twenty or thirty, And you can ground and reconnoitre in her, then lift off again – which your transports won't be able to do, most likely."

"Lazarus . . . I don't want to inherit either money or a yacht from you. Let them finish your rejuvenation – and come with us, man! I'll step aside and you can boss. Or you can have no duties at all. But come!"

Lazarus smiled bleakly and shook his head. "I've been on six such colonizing ventures to virgin planets, not counting Secundus. All to planets I discovered. Gave it up centuries back. Anything gets boring in time. Do you think Solomon serviced *all* his thousand wives? If so, what sort of job did he do on the last one? – poor girl! Find me something *new* to do and I might never touch that suicide switch and *still* give you all I've got for your colony. It 'ud be a fair swop . . . as this halfway rejuvenation is most unsatisfactory; I don't feel well, yet I can't die. So I'm stuck between the suicide switch and giving in for the full treatment... the donkey that starved to death between two piles of hay. But it would have to be *new*, Ira, not something I've done over and over again. Like that old whore, I've climbed the same stairs too many times; my feet hurt."

"I'll think about the problem, Lazarus. I'll give it hard and systematic research."

"Seven to two you can't find *anything* I haven't done."

"I'll make a real try. You'll lay off the suicide switch while I research it?"

"No promises. Not once I get this will redrafted. Can you trust your chief legal eagle? May need some help... because this will" – he tapped the envelope – "leaving everything to the Families would stand up on Secundus no matter how many flaws are in it. But if I leave it to a private party – you, I mean – some of my descendants – quite a passel – will scream 'undue influence' and try to break it. Ira, they'll keep it tied up in court until it's dribbled away in legal fees. Let's avoid that, eh?"

"We can. I've made changes in the rules. On this planet a man can put his will through probate before his death, and if there are flaws, the court is required to help him rephrase it to accomplish his purposes. If he does it that way, no contest can be entertained by any court; it goes automatically into effect on his death. Of course if he changes his will, the new will must go through the same process – which makes changing his mind expensive. But by using preprobate, it does not take a lawyer for even the most complex will. And the lawyers can't touch it afterwards."

Lazarus' eyes widened with pleasure. "Didn't you annoy a few lawyers?"

"I've annoyed so many," Ira said dryly, "that every transport to Felicity has voluntary migrants in it – and so many lawyers have annoyed me that some are involuntary ones." The Chairman Pro Tem looked sourly amused. "Once I said to my Chief Justice, 'Warren, I've had to reverse too many of your decisions. You've been splitting hairs, misinterpreting the rules, and ignoring equity ever since you came into office. Go home; you're under house arrest until the "Last Chance" lifts. You can have an escort during daylight hours to let you wind up your private affairs.' "

Lazarus chuckled. "Shoulda hanged him. You know what he did, don't you? Set up shop again on Felicity and went into politics. If they didn't lynch him."

"His problem and theirs, not mine. Lazarus, I *never* let a man be executed for being a fool – but if he's too obnoxious, I ship him out. There's no need to sweat over your new will if you want one. Just dictate it with any elaborations and explanations you see fit. Then we'll run it through a semantic analyser to rephrase it into airtight legal language. Once it satisfies you, you can submit it to the High Court – which will come to you if you prefer – and the Court will validate it. Done that way it could then be overturned only by arbitrary act of a new Chairman Pro Tem. Which I consider most unlikely; the Trustees do not place such men in office."

Weatheral added, "But I hope you will take plenty of time, Lazarus. I want a fair chance to search for something new, something that will restore your interest in life."

"All right. But don't dally; I won't be put off with a Scheherazade gag. Have them send me a recorder – tomorrow morning, say."

Weatheral seemed about to speak, did not. Lazarus looked at him sharply. "*This* conversation is being recorded?"

"Yes, Lazarus. Sound and holography, everything that happens in this suite. But – your pardon, sir! – it goes only to my desk and does not become a permanent record until I have checked and okayed it. Nothing so far, that is."

Lazarus shrugged. "Forget it. Ira, I learned centuries back that there is *no* privacy in any society crowded enough to need ID's. A law guaranteeing privacy simply insures that bugs – microphones and lenses and so forth – are that much harder to spot. I hadn't thought about it up till now because I take it for granted that my privacy will be invaded any time I visit such places – then I ignore it unless I'm up to something the local law won't like. In which case I use evasive tactics."

"Lazarus, that record can be wiped. Its only purpose is to make me certain that the Senior is being properly taken care of – a responsibility I will not delegate."

"I said, 'Forget it.' But I'm surprised at your naïveté, a man in your position, in thinking that the record is piped only to your desk. I'll lay long odds, any amount you like, that it goes one, two, even three or more other places."

"If so, Lazarus, and I can find it out, Felicity will have some new colonists – after they've spent some unpleasant hours in the Colosseum."

"Ira, it doesn't matter. If any fool wants to watch an old, old man grunting on the pot or taking a bath, he's welcome. You yourself insured that it would happen by making a point of the record being secret, your eyes only. Security people always spy on their bosses; they can't help it, it's a syndrome that goes with the job. Have you had dinner? I'd be pleased to have you stay if you have time."

"I would be honoured indeed to have dinner with the Senior."

"Oh, knock it off, Bud; there's no virtue in being old, it just takes a long time. I'd like you to stay because I'm enjoying human companionship. Those two over there are no company; I'm not even sure they're human. Robots, maybe. Why do they wear those diving suits and shiny helmets? I like to see a man's face."

"Lazarus, those are total isolation garments. For your protection, not theirs. Against infection."

"*What?* Ira, when a bug bites me, the bug dies. Even so, since they have to wear that, how is it that *you* come in wearing street clothes?"

"Not quite, Lazarus. For my purpose I needed a social talk, face to face. So the last two hours before I came in I spent undergoing a most careful physical examination, followed by scalp-to-toe sterilization of skin, hair, ears, nails, teeth, nose, throat – even a gas inhalation which I can't name but did not like – while my clothes were sterilized even more thoroughly. Even that envelope I fetched to you. This suite is sterile and kept so."

"Ira, such precautions are silly. Unless my immunity has been intentionally lowered?"

"No. Or let me say, 'I think not.' No reason for it as any transplant will of course be done from your own clone."

"So it's unnecessary. If I didn't catch anything in that flophouse, why would I catch anything now? But I *don't* catch things. I worked as a physician during a plague – don't look surprised; medicine is just one of fifty-odd trades I've followed. Unknown plague on Ormuzd; everybody caught it, twenty-eight per cent died. Save yours truly, who didn't even have a sniffle. So tell those – No, you'll want to do it through the Director of the Clinic; bypassing your chain-of-command ruins morale – though why I should care about this organization's morale I don't know, seeing that I am an involuntary guest. Tell the Director that, if I must have nurses, I want them to dress like nurses. Or, better yet, like people. Ira, if you want cooperation out of me of *any* sort, you'll start by cooperating with *me*. Otherwise I'm going to take the joint apart with my bare hands."

"I'll speak to the Director, Lazarus."

"Good. Now let's have dinner. But a drink first – and if the Director doesn't think I should have one, tell him bluntly that he will have to go back to force-feeding and there is some question as to whose throat the tube will go down; I'm in no mood to be pushed around. Is there any real whisky on this planet? Wasn't the last time I was here."

"Not that I would drink. But the local brandy I think well of."

"Good. Brandy and bubbles for me if that is the best we can do, a brandy Manhattan if anyone knows what I mean by that."

"I do, and like them – I learned something about ancient drinks when I studied your life."

"Fine. Then please order for us, drinks and dinner – and I'll listen and see how many words I can pick up. I think my memory is coming back a bit."

Weatheral spoke to one of the technicians; Lazarus interrupted. "That should be one-*third* sweet vermouth, not one-half."

"So? You understood it?"

"Mostly. Indo-European roots, with a simplified syntax and grammar; I'm beginning to recall it. Damn it, when a man has had to learn as many languages as I have, it's easy for one to slip away. But it's coming back."

Service was so fast as to cause one to suspect that a crew was standing by ready to produce anything that the Senior or the Chairman Pro Tem asked for.

Weatheral raised his glass. "Long life."

"In a pig's eye," Lazarus growled and took a sip. He made a face. "Whew! Panther sweat. But it does have alcohol in it." He took another. "Improves as your tongue gets numb. Okay, Ira, you've stalled long enough. What was your *real* reason for snatching me back from my well-earned rest?"

"Lazarus, we need your wisdom."

PRELUDE

II

Lazarus stared in horror. "*What* did you say?"

"I said," Ira Weatheral repeated, "that we need your wisdom, sir. We do."

"I thought that I was off again in one of those before-dying dreams. Son, you've come to the wrong window. Try across the hall."

Weatheral shook his head. "No, sir. Oh, it isn't necessary to use the word 'wisdom' if it offends you. But we do need to learn what you know. You are more than twice as old as the next oldest member of the Families. You mentioned that you have practiced more than fifty professions. You've been everywhere, you've seen far more than anyone else. You've certainly learned more than any of the rest of us. We aren't doing things much better now than we were two thousand years ago, when you were young. You must know why we are still making mistakes our ancestors made. It would be a great loss if you hurried your death without taking time to tell us what you have learned."

Lazarus scowled and bit his lip. "Son, one of the few things I've learned is that humans hardly ever learn from the experience of others. They learn – when they do, which isn't often – on their own, the hard way."

"That one statement is worth recording for all time."

"*Hmm!* No one would learn anything from it; that's what it says. Ira, age does not bring wisdom. Often it merely changes simple stupidity into arrogant conceit. Its only advantage, so far as I have been able to see, is that it spans *change*. A young person sees the world as a still picture, immutable. An old person has had his nose rubbed in changes and more changes and still more changes so many times that he *knows* it is a moving picture, forever changing. He may not like it – probably doesn't; *I* don't – but he knows it's so, and knowing it is the first step in coping with it."

"May I place in open record what you have just said?"

"Huh? That's not wisdom, that's a cliché. An obvious truth. Any fool will admit that, even if he doesn't live by it."

"It would carry greater weight with your name on it, Senior."

"Do as you like; it's just horse sense. But if you think I have gazed upon the naked Face of God, think again. I haven't even begun to find out how the Universe works, much less what it is for. To figure out the basic questions about this World it would be necessary to stand *outside* and look at it. Not inside. No, not in two thousand years, not in twenty thousand. When a man dies, he may shake loose his local perspective and see the thing as a whole."

"Then you believe in an afterlife?"

"Slow up! I don't '*believe*' in anything. I *know* certain things – little things, not the Nine Billion Names of God – from experience. But I have *no* beliefs. Belief gets in the way of learning."

"That's what we want, Lazarus: what you have learned. Even though you say it's nothing but 'little things.' May I suggest that anyone who has managed to stay alive as long as you have must necessarily have learned many things, or you could not have lived so long? Most humans die violent deaths. The very fact that we live so much longer than our ancestors did makes this inevitable. Traffic accident, murder, wild animals, sports, pilot error, a slippery bit of mud – eventually something catches up with us. You haven't lived a safe, placid life – quite the contrary! – yet you have managed to outwit all hazards for twenty-three centuries. *How?* It can't be luck."

"Why can't it be? The most unlikely things do happen, Ira – there is nothing so unlikely as a baby. But its true that I've always watched where I put my feet . . . and never fought when I could duck out . . . and when I did have to fight, I always fought dirty. If I had to fight, I wanted *him* to be dead instead of *me*. So I tried to arrange it that way. Not luck. Or not much anyway." Lazarus blinked thoughtfully. "I've never argued with the weather. Once a mob wanted to lynch me. I didn't try to reason with them; I just put a lot of miles between me and them as fast as I could and never went back there."

"That's not in any of your memoirs."

"Lots of things not in my memoirs. Here comes chow."

The door dilated, a dining table for two glided in, positioned itself as the chairs separated for it, and started unfolding to serve.

The technicians approached quietly and offered unnecessary personal service. Weatheral said, "Smells good. Do you have any eating rituals?"

"Eh? Praying or such? No."

"Not that sort. Such as – Say one of my executives eats with me: I won't let him discuss business at the table. But if you will permit, I would like to continue this conversation."

"Certainly, why not? As long as we stick to subjects that don't rile the stomach. Did you ever hear what the priest told the old maid?"

Lazarus glanced at the technician at his elbow. "Perhaps not now. I think this shorter one is female and she just might know some English. You were saying?"

"I was saying that your memoirs are incomplete. Even if you are determined to go through with dying, won't you consider granting me and your other descendants the rest of your memoirs? Simply talk, tell us what you've seen and done. Careful analysis might teach us quite a lot. For example, what *did* happen at that Families Meeting of 2012? The minutes don't tell much."

"Who cares now, Ira? They're all dead. It would be my version without giving them a chance to answer back. Let sleeping dogs bury their own dead. Besides, I told you my memory was playing tricks. I've used Andy Libby's hypno-encyclopedic techniques – and they're good – and also learned tier storage for memory I didn't need every day, with keying words to let a tier cascade when I did need it, like a computer, and I have had my brain washed of useless memories several times in order to clear those file drawers for new data – and still it's no good. Half the time I can't remember where I put the book I was reading the night before, then waste a morning looking for it – before I remember that *that* book was one I was reading a century ago. Why won't you leave an old man in peace?"

"All you have to do is to tell me to shut up, sir. But I hope you will not. Granted that memory is imperfect, nevertheless you were eyewitness to thousands of things the rest of us are too young to have seen. Oh, I'm not asking you to reel off a formal autobiography covering all your centuries. But you might reminisce about anything you care to talk about. For example, there is no record anywhere of your earliest years. I – and millions of others – would be extremely interested in whatever you remember of your boyhood."

"What is there to remember? I spent my boyhood the way

every boy does – trying to keep my elders from finding out what I was up to."

Lazarus wiped his mouth and looked thoughtful. "On the whole I was successful. The few times I was caught and clobbered taught me to be more careful next time – keep my mouth shut more and not make my lies too complicated. Lying is one of the fine arts, Ira, and it seems to be dying out."

"Really? I had not noticed any diminution."

"I mean as a fine art. There are still plenty of clumsy liars, approximately as many as there are mouths. Do you know the two most artistic ways to lie?"

"Perhaps I don't but I would like to learn. Just two?"

"So far as I know. It's not enough to be able to lie with a straight face; anybody with enough gall to raise on a busted flush can do that. The first way to lie artistically is to tell the truth – but not all of it. The second way involves telling the truth too, but is harder: Tell the exact truth and maybe all of it . . . but tell it so unconvincingly that your listener is sure you are lying.

"I must have been twelve, thirteen years old before I got that one down pat. Learned it from my maternal Grampaw; I take after him quite a lot. He was a mean old devil. Wouldn't go inside a church or see a doctor – claimed that neither doctors nor preachers know what they pretend to know. At eighty-five he could crack nuts with his teeth and straight-arm a seventy-pound anvil by its horn. I left home about then and never saw him again. But the Families Records say that he was killed in the Battle of Britain during the bombing of London, which was some years after."

"I know. He's my ancestor too, of course, and I'm named for him. Ira Johnson."*

"Why, sure enough, that was his name. I just called him 'Gramp.'"

"Lazarus, this is exactly the sort of thing I want to get on record. Ira Johnson is not only your grandfather and my remote

*(1) Ira Johnson was less than eighty at the time the Senior claims (elsewhere) to have left home. Ira Johnson was himself a Doctor of Medicine. How long he practiced, and whether or not he ever let another Doctor of Medicine attend him, are not known.

J.F. 45th

(2) *Ira* Howard – *Ira* Johnson – This appears to be a chance coincidence of given names at a time when Biblical names were common. Families' genealogists have been unable to trace any consanguinity.

J.F. 45th

grandfather but also is ancestor to many million people here and elsewhere – yet save for the few words you have just told me about him, he has been only a name, a date of birth, and a date of death, nothing more. You've suddenly brought him alive again – a man, a unique human being. Colourful."

Lazarus looked thoughtful. "I never thought of him as 'colourful'. Matter of fact, he was an unsavoury old coot – not a 'good influence' for a growing boy by the standards of those times. Mmm, there was something about a young schoolmarm and him in the town my family had lived in, some scandal – 'scandal' for those days, I mean – and I think that was why we moved. I never got the straight of it as the grownups wouldn't talk about it in front of me.

"But I did learn a lot from him; he had more time to talk with me – or took more time – than my parents had. Some of it stuck. 'Always cut the cards, Woodie,' he would say. 'You may lose anyhow – but not as often, nor as much. And when you do lose, *smile*.' Things like that."

"Can you remember any more of what he said?"

"Huh? After all these years? Of course not. Well, maybe. He had me out south of town teaching me to shoot. I was maybe ten and he was – oh, I don't know; he always seemed ninety years older than God to me.* He pinned up a target, put one in the black to show me it could be done, then handed me the rifle – little .22 single shot, not good for much but targets and tin cans – 'All right, it's loaded; do just what I did; get steady on it, relax and squeeze.' So I did, and all I heard was a *click* – it didn't fire.

"I said so, and started to open the breech. He slapped my hand away, took the rifle from me with his other hand – then clouted me a good one. 'What did I tell you about hangfires, Woodie? Are you aching to walk around with one eye the rest of your life? Or merely trying to kill yourself? If the latter, I can show you several better ways.'

"Then he said, 'Now watch closely' – and *he* opened the breech. Empty. So I said, 'But, Gramp, you *told* me it was loaded. Shucks, Ira, I *saw* him load it – I thought.

"'So I did, Woodie,' he agreed. 'And I lied to you. I went through the motions and palmed the cartridge. Now what did I tell you about loaded guns? Think hard and get it right . . .

* Ira Johnson was seventy when Lazarus was ten.

J.F. 45th

or I'll be forced to clout you again to shake up your brains and make 'em work better.'

"I thought fast and got it right; Gramp had a heavy hand. 'Never take anybody's word about whether a gun is loaded.'

" 'Correct,' he agreed. 'Remember that all your life – and follow it! or you won't live long.'*

"Ira, I *did* remember that all my life – plus its application to analogous situations after such firearms went out of style – and it has indeed kept me alive several times.

"Then he had me load it myself, then said, 'Woodie, I'll bet you half a dollar – do you *have* half a dollar?' I had considerably more, but I had bet with him before, so I admitted to only a quarter. 'Okay,' he said, 'Make it two-bits; I never let a man bet on credit. Two-bits says you can't hit the target, much less stay in the black.'

"Then he pocketed my two bits and showed me what was wrong with what I had done. By the time he was ready to knock off I had the basics of how to make a gun do what I wanted it to do, and wanted to bet him again. He laughed at me and told me to be thankful the lesson was so cheap. Pass the salt, please."

Weatheral did so. "Lazarus, if I could find a way to entice you into reminiscing about your grandfather – or about anything – I'm certain we could extract from such records endless things you have learned, important things – whether you choose to call them wisdom or not. In the last ten minutes you have stated half a dozen basic truths, or rules for living – call them what you will – apparently without trying."

"Such as?"

"Oh, for example, that most people learn only by experience –"

"Correction. Most people won't learn even by experience, Ira. Never underestimate the power of human stupidity."

"There's another one. And you made a couple of comments on the fine art of lying – three, really, as you also mentioned that a lie should never be too complicated. You said also that belief gets in the way of learning, and something about knowing a situation was the essential first step in coping with it."

"I didn't say that – although I could have said it."

"I generalized something you did say. You said also that you never argued with the weather . . . which I would generalize to mean: Don't indulge in wishful thinking. Or as 'Face up to the

*This anecdote is too obscure to be elaborated here. See *Howard Encyclopaedia:* Ancient weapons, chemical-explosives firearms.

facts and act accordingly." Though I prefer the way you put it; it has more flavour. And 'Always cut the cards.' I haven't played card games in many years, but I took that to mean: Never neglect any available means of maximizing one's chances in a situation controlled by random events."

"Hmm. Gramp would have said, 'Stow the fancy talk. Sonny.'"

"So we'll put it back into his words: 'Always cut the cards . . . and smile when you lose.' If indeed that is not your own phrasing and simply attributed to him."

"Oh, his all right. Well, I think it is. Damn it, Ira, after a long time it is hard to tell a real memory from a memory of a memory of a memory of a real memory. That's what happens when you think about the past: You edit it and rearrange it, make it more tolerable –"

"That's another one!"

"Oh, hush up. Son, I don't want to reminisce about the past; it's a sure sign of old age. Babies and young children live in the present, the 'now.' Mature adults tend to live in the future. Only the senile live in the past . . . and that was the sign that made me realize that I had lived long enough, when I found I was spending more and more time thinking about the past . . . less of it thinking about now – and not at all about the future."

The old man sighed. "So I knew I had had it. The way to live a long time – oh, a thousand years or more – is something between the way a child does it and the way a mature man does it. Give the future enough thought to be ready for it – but don't worry about it. Live each day as if you were to die next sunrise. Then face each sunrise as a fresh creation and live for *it*, joyously. And never think about the past. No regrets, ever." Lazarus Long looked sad, then suddenly smiled and repeated, " 'No regrets.' More wine, Ira?"

"Half a glass, thank you. Lazarus, if you are determined to die soon – your privilege, certainly! – what harm could there be in remembering the past now . . . and getting those memories on record for the benefit of your descendants? It would be a much greater legacy than leaving your wealth to us."

Lazarus' eyebrows shot up. "Son, you are beginning to bore me."

"Your pardon, sire. May I have permission to leave?"

"Oh, shut up and sit down. Finish your dinner. You remind me of – Well, there was this man on Novo Brasil who complied with the local custom of serial bigamy but was always careful to see that one of his wives was as utterly homely as the other was startingly beautiful, so that – Ira, that dingus you have listening to us: Can it be keyed to pick out particular statements and arrange them as a separate memorandum?"

"Certainly, sir."

"Good. There's no point in telling how Ranch Master... Silva? – yes, I think 'Silva' was his name, Dom Pedro Silva – how he coped with it when he found himself stuck with two beautiful wives at once, except to note that when a computer makes a mistake, it is even more stupidly stubborn about correcting it than a man is. But if I thought long and hard, I might be able to dig out those 'gems of wisdom' you think I have. Paste diamonds, that is. Then we wouldn't have to load up the machine with dull stories about Dom Pedro and the like. A key word?"

" 'Wisdom'?"

"Go wash out your mouth with soap."

"I will not. You stuck your chin into that one, Senior. 'Common sense'?"

"Son, that phrase is self-contradictory. 'Sense' is never 'common.' Make the keying word 'Notebook' – that's all I have in mind, just a notebook to jot things down I've noticed and which might be important enough to place on record."

"Fine! Shall I amend the programming now?"

"You can do it from here? I don't want you to interrupt your dinner."

"It's a very flexible machine, Lazarus; the total complex is the one I use to govern this planet – to the mild extent that I do govern it."

"In that case I feel sure you can hang an auxiliary printout in here, one triggered for the keying word. I might want to revise my sparkling gems of wisdom – meaning that extemporaneous remarks sound better when they aren't extemporaneous – or why politicians have ghost writers."

" 'Ghost writers'? My command of Classic English is less than perfect; I don't recognize the idiom."

"Ira, don't tell me you write your own speeches."

"But, Lazarus, I don't make speeches. Never. I just give orders, and – very seldom – make written reports to the Trustees."

"Congratulations. You can bet there that are ghost writers on Felicity. Or soon will be."

"I'll have that printout installed at once, sir. Roman alphabet and twentieth-century spelling? If you intend to use the language we've been talking?"

"Unless it would place too much strain on a poor innocent machine. If so, I can read it in phonetics. I think."

"It is a *very* flexible machine, sir; it taught me to speak this language – and earlier, to read it."

"Good, do it that way. But tell it not to correct my grammar. Human editors are difficult enough; I won't accept such upstart behaviour from a machine."

"Yes, sir. If you will excuse me one moment –" The Chairman Pro Tem raised his voice slightly and shifted to the New Rome variant of Lingua Galacta. Then he spoke in the same language to the taller technician.

The auxiliary printout was installed before the table served them coffee.

After it was switched on, it whirred briefly. "What's it doing?" asked Lazarus. "Checking its circuits?"

"No, sir – printing. I tried an experiment. The machine has considerable judgement within the limits of its programmes and memoried experience. In adding the extra programme I told it also to go back, review everything you have said to me, an attempt to select all statements that sounded like aphorisms. I'm not sure it can do this, as any definition of 'aphorism' it has in its permanents is certain to be quite abstract. But I have hopes. However, I told it firmly: No editing."

"Well. 'The astounding thing about a waltzing bear is not how gracefully it waltzes but that it waltzes at all.' Not me, some other bloke; I'm quoting. Let's see what it has."

Weatheral gestured; the shorter technician hurried to the machine, pulled a copy for each of them, fetched them back.

Lazarus looked his copy over. "Mmmm . . . yes. That next one isn't true – just a wisecrack. Must reword the third one a little. Hey! It put a question mark after this one. What an impudent piece of junk; I checked that one out centuries before it was anything but unmined ore. Well, at least it didn't try to revise it. Don't recall saying that, but it's true and I durned near got killed learning it."

Lazarus looked up from the printout copy. "Okay, Son. If you want this stuff on record, I don't mind. As long as I am allowed to check and revise it . . . for I don't want my words to be taken as Gospel unless I have a chance to winnow out the casual nonsense. Which I am just as capable of voicing as the next man."

"Certainly, sir. Nothing will go into the records without your approval. Unless you choose to use that switch . . . in which case any unedited remarks you have left behind I will have to try to edit myself. That's the best I can do."

"Trying to trap me, huh? Hmm – Ira, suppose I offer you a Scheherazade deal in reverse."

"I don't understand."

"Is Scheherazade lost at last? Did Sir Richard Burton live in in vain?"

"Oh, no, sir! I have read *The Thousand Nights and a Night* in the Burton original . . . and her stories have come down through the centuries, changed again and again to make them understandable to new generations – but with, I think, the flavour retained. I simply do not understand what you are proposing."

"I see. You told me that talking with me is the most important thing you have to do."

"It is."

"I wonder. If you mean that, then you will be here every day to keep me company – and chat. For I'm not going to bother babbling to your machine no matter how smart it is."

"Lazarus, I will be not only honoured but much pleased to be allowed to keep you company as long as you will let me."

"We'll see. When a man makes a sweeping statement, he often has mental reservations. I mean *every* day, Son, and *all day*. And *you* – not a deputy. Show up two hours after breakfast, say, and stay till I send you home. But any day you miss – Well, if it's so urgent you just have to miss, phone your excuses and send over a pretty girl to visit me. One who speaks Classic English but has sense enough to listen instead – as an old fool will often talk to a pretty girl who just bats her lashes at him and looks impressed. If she pleases me, I might let her stay. Or I might be so petulant that I would send her away and use that switch you promised to have reinstalled. But I won't suicide in the presence of a guest; that's rude. Understand me?"

"I think I do," Ira Weatheral answered slowly. "You'll be both Scheherazade and King Shahryar, and I'll be – no, that's not right; *I* am the one who has to keep it going for a thousand nights – I mean 'days' – and if I miss – but I won't! – you are free to –"

"Don't push an analogy too far," Lazarus advised. "I'm simply calling your bluff. If my maunderings are as all-fired important to you as you claim, then you'll show up and listen.

You can skip once, or even twice, if the girl is pretty enough and knows how to tickle my vanity – of which I have plenty – just right. But if you skip too often, I'll know you're bored and the deal is off. I'm betting that your patience will wear out long before any thousand days and a day have passed – whereas I *do* know how to be patient, for year after year if necessary; that's a prime reason I'm still alive. But you're still a youngster; I'm betting I can outsit you."

"I accept the bet. This girl – If I *must* be away some day – would you object if I sent one of my daughters? She's very pretty."

"Hunh? You sound like an Iskandrian slave factor auctioning his mother. Why your daughter? I don't want to marry her, nor even to bed her; I simply want to be amused and flattered. Who told you she was pretty? If she really IS your daughter, she probably looks like you."

"Come off it, Lazarus; you can't annoy me that easily. I admit to a father's prejudice but I've seen the effect she has on others. She is quite young, less than eighty, and has been contractually married only once. But you specified a pretty girl who speaks your milk language. Scarce. But this one of my daughters shares my talent for languages and is much excited by your presence here – *wants* to meet you. I can stall off emergencies long enough for her to become letter-perfect in your language."

Lazarus grinned and shrugged. "Suit yourself. Tell her not to bother with a chastity girdle; I don't have the energy. But I'll still win the bet. Probably without laying eyes on her; it won't take you long to decide that I am an unbearable old bore. Which I am and have been almost as long as the Wandering Jew – a crashing bore if I ever met one – did I tell you I had met him?"

"No. And I don't believe you have. He's a myth."

"A fat lot you know about it, Son. I have met him, he is authentic. Fought the Romans in 70 A.D. when Jerusalem was sacked. Fought in every Crusade – incited one of them. Redheaded of course; all of the natural long-lifers bear the mark of Gilgamesh. When I met him he was using the name Sandy Macdougal, that being a better handle for the time and place for his current trade, which was the long con, with a variant on the badger game.* The

*While this passage bears inner contradictions, the idioms are authentic for North America of the twentieth century. They name certain types of financial dishonesty. See "Swindles" under "Fraud" in Krishnamurti's *New Golden Bough*, Academe Press, New Rome.

J.F. 45th

latter involved – Look, Ira, if you don't believe my stories, why are you going to so much trouble to get them on record?"

"Lazarus, if you think you can bore me to death – correction: to *your* death – why are you bothering to invent fictions to entertain me? Whatever your reasons, I'll listen as carefully – and as long – as King Shahryar. As may be, my master computer is recording whatever you choose to say – without editing; I guaranteed that – but it has incorporated into it a most subtle truth analyser quite capable of ear-marking any fictions you include. Not that I care about historicity as long as you will *talk* . . . as it is clear to me that you automatically include your evaluations – those 'gems of wisdom' – no matter what you say."

" 'Gems of wisdom.' Youngster, use that expression once more and you'll stay after school and clean the blackboards. That computer of yours – Better instruct it that my most outlandish tales are the ones most likely to be true – as that is the literal truth. No storyteller has ever been able to dream up anything as fantastically unlikely as what really *does* happen in this mad Universe."

"It knows that. But I will caution it again. You were telling me about Sandy Macdougal, the Wandering Jew."

"Was I? If so and if he was using that name, that must have been late in the twentieth century and in Vancouver, as I recall. Vancouver was a part of the United States where the people were so clever that they never paid taxes to Washington – Sandy should have operated in New York, which was outstanding in stupidity even then. I won't give details of his swindles; it might corrupt your machine. Let it suffice that Sandy used the oldest principle for separating a fool from his money: Pick a sucker who likes the best of it.

"That's all it takes, Ira. If a man is greedy, you can cheat him every time. Trouble was, Sandy Macdougal was even greedier than his marks, and it led him into the folly of excess, and often forced him to leave town while it was dark, sometimes leaving the boodle behind. Ira, when you skin a man, you have to let him recuperate and grow more hide – or he gets nervous. If you respect this simple rule, a real mark can be skinned over and over again, and it just keeps him healthy and productive. But Sandy was too greedy for that; he lacked patience."

"Lazarus, you sound as if you had great experience in this art."

"Now, Ira – a little respect, please. I have *never* swindled a man. At most I kept quiet and let him swindle himself. This does no harm, as a fool cannot be protected from his folly. If you attempt to do so, you will not only arouse his animosity but also you will be attempting to deprive him of whatever benefit he is capable of deriving from experience. Never attempt to teach a pig to sing; it wastes your time and annoys the pig.

"But I do know a lot about swindles. I think that every major variation of every possible swindle has been tried on me, one time and another.

"Some of them worked back when I was very young. Then I took Grampaw Johnson's advice and quit looking for the best of it; thereafter I could no longer be swindled. But I was not capable of benefiting from Gramp's advice until I was burned a few times. Ira, it's getting late."

The Chairman Pro Tem promptly stood up. "So it is, sir. May I ask two questions before I leave? Not for your memoirs, procedural questions only."

"Make it short and snappy."

"You'll have your termination-option switch tomorrow morning. But you spoke of not feeling well, and there is no need for that even if you choose to terminate in the near future. Shall we resume the rejuvenation procedures?"

"Hmmm. Second question?"

"I promised to do my best to find something brand-new to interest you. I promised also to spend every day here with you. I see conflict."

Lazarus grinned. "Don't kid your old Grampaw, Son; you'll delegate that research."

"Certainly. But I must plan how to start it, then review progress at intervals, and suggest new avenues to explore."

"Mmm . . . if I consent to the full course, I'll be out of circulation a day or two every now and then."

"I believe current practice calls for one day of deep rest approximately each week, varied to suit the client's condition. My own experience is about a hundred years back; I understand there have been improvements. You've decided to take it, sir?"

"I'll tell you tomorrow – after that switch is installed. Ira, I don't make decisions in haste that don't call for haste. But if I consent, you'll have free time to use as you see fit. G'night, Ira."

"Good night, Lazarus. I hope you decide to accept it." Weatheral turned toward the door, stopped halfway there, and spoke to the technicians – who left the room at once. The dining table scurried after them. Once the door had shut down Weatheral turned and faced Lazarus Long. "Grandfather," he said softly, his voice somewhat choked. "Uh – may I?"

Lazarus had let his chair sink back into a reclining couch that held him, hammocklike, as tenderly as a mother's arms. At the younger man's words he raised his head. "Huh? What? *Oh!* All right, all right, come here – Grandson." He reached out one arm to Weatheral.

The Chairman Pro Tem hurried to him, took Lazarus' hand, dropped to his knees and kissed it.

Lazarus snatched his hand back. "For Pete's sake! Don't kneel to me – don't *ever* do that. If you want to be my grandson, treat me as such. Not that way."

"Yes, Grandfather." Weatheral got to his feet, leaned over the old man and kissed his mouth.

Lazarus patted his cheek. "You're a sentimentalist, Grandson. But a good boy. Trouble is, there never has been much demand for good boys. Now get that solemn expression off your face and go home and get a good night's rest."

"Yes, Grandfather. I will. Good night."

"Good night. Now beat it."

Weatheral left quickly. The technicians jumped aside as he came out, then went back into the suite. Weatheral continued on, ignoring people around him but with a softer, gentler expression on his face than was his wont. He went past a bank of transports to the Director's private transport; it opened to his voice, then conveyed him quickly into the bowels of the city and directly to the Executive Palace.

Lazarus looked up as his attendants came back in; he motioned the taller one to him. The technicians voice, filtered and distorted by the helmet, said carefully, "Bed . . . sir?"

"No, I want –" Lazarus paused, then spoke to the air. "Computer? Can you speak? If not, print it out."

"I hear you, Senior," a mellifluous, contralto voice answered.

"Tell this nurse that I want whatever they are allowed to give me for pain. I have work to do."

"Yes, Senior." The disembodied voice shifted to Lingua Galacta, was answered in kind, then went on: "Master Chief Technician on duty wishes to know the nature and location of your pain, and adds that you should not work tonight."

Lazarus kept silent while he counted ten chimpanzees in his mind. Then he said softly, "Damn it, I hurt *everywhere*. And I don't want advice from a child. I have loose ends to tidy up before I sleep . . . because one never knows that one will wake up again. Forget the painkiller; it ain't all that impotant. Tell 'em to get out and stay out."

Lazarus tried to ignore the ensuing exchange, as it annoyed him that he almost-not-quite understood it. He opened the envelope Ira Weatheral had returned to him, then opened out his will – a long bellows-fold of computer printout – and started reading it while whistling off key.

"Senior, Master Chief Technician on duty states that you have given a null order, which is a true statement by the Clinic's regulations. A general analgesic is forthcoming."

"Forget it." Lazarus went on reading, and shifted to singing softly the tune he had been whistling:

"There's a pawnshop
On the corner
Where I usually keep my overcoat.

"There's a bookie
Behind the pawnshop
Who handles my investments"*

The taller technician appeared at his elbow, carrying a shiny disc with attached tubing. "For . . . pain."

Lazarus made a brush-off gesture with his free hand. "Go 'way, I'm busy."

The shorter technician appeared on his other side. Lazarus looked that way and said, "What do *you* want?"

As he turned his head the taller technician moved quickly; Lazarus felt a sting in his forearm. He rubbed the spot and said, "Why, you rapscallion. Foxed me, didn't you? All right, beat it. Raus. Scat!" He dismissed the incident from his mind and returned to work. A moment later he said:

"Computer!"

"Awaiting your orders, Senior."

"Record this for printout. I, Lazarus Long, sometimes known as the Senior and listed in the Howard Families' Genealogies as Woodrow Wilson Smith, born 1912, do declare this to be my last will and testament – Computer, go back through my talk with Ira

*This doggerel is attributed to the twentieth century. See appendix for semantic analysis.

J.F. 45th

and dig out what I said I wanted to do to help him lead a migration – got it?"

"Retrieved Senior"

"Fix up the language and tack it onto my opening statement. And – let me see – add something like this: In the event Ira Weatheral fails to qualify for inheritance, then all my worldly wealth of which I die possessed shall go to, uh, to – to found a home for indigent and superannuated pickpockets, prostitutes, panhandlers, piemen, priggers, and other unworthy poor starting with 'P'. Got it?"

"Recorded, Senior. Please be advised that this alternative has a high probability of being nullified if tested by the current rules of this planet."

Lazarus expressed a rhetorical and physiologically improbable wish. "All right, set it up for stray cats or some other useless but legally acceptable purpose. Search your permanents for such a purpose that *will* get by the courts. Just be certain that the Trustees can't get their hands on it. Understand?"

"There is no way to be certain of that, Senior, but it will be attempted."

"Look for a loophole. Print that out as fast as you can research it and put it together. Now stand by for a memorandum of my assets. Begin." Lazarus started to read the list, found that his eyes were blurring and would not focus. "Damnation! Those dummies slipped me a Mickey and its taking hold. Blood! I must have a drop of my own blood to thumbprint it! Tell those dummies to help me and tell them *why* – and warn them that I will bite my tongue to get it if they won't help me. Now print out my will with any feasible alternative – but *hurry!*"

"Printout starting," the computer answered quietly, then shifted to Galacta.

The "dummies" did not argue with the computer; they moved fast, one snatching the new sheet out of the auxiliary printout the instant it stopped whirring, the other producing a sterile point out of nowhere and stabbed the ball of Lazarus' left little finger after giving Lazarus a split second to see what was being done.

Lazarus did not wait for blood to be taken by pipette. He squeezed the stabbed finger for a drop, rubbed his right thumb in it, then print-signed his will while the shorter technician held it for him.

Then he sank back. "It's done," he whispered. "Tell Ira." He was heavily asleep at once.

COUNTERPOINT I

The chair gently transferred Lazarus to his bed while the technicians silently supervised. Then the shorter watched the readouts on respiration, heart action, brain rhythms, and other physicals while the taller placed the documents, old will and new, in an impervolope, sealed it, chopped and thumbprinted the seal, marked it "Surrender only to the Senior and/or Mr. Chairman Pro Tem," then retained it until their reliefs arrived.

The relief chief technician listened to the record of the watch, glanced over the physicals, studied the sleeping client.

"Times," he stated.

"Neolethe. Thirty-four hours."

He whistled. "Another crisis?"

"Less severe than the last. Pseudopain with irrational irascibility. Physicals within limits for this stage."

"What's in the sealer?"

"Just sign for it and include delivery instructions in your receipt."

"Pardon me for using up oxygen!"

"Your receipt, please."

The relief wrote out a receipt, chopped and thumbed it, swapped it for the impervolope. "I relieve you," he said brusquely.

"Thank you."

The shorter technician was waiting at the door. The Master Chief Technician paused to say, "You needn't have waited. It sometimes takes me three times this long to turn over the watch. You are free to leave as soon as the relief junior watch officer arrives."

"Yes, Master Chief Technician. But this is a *very* special client – and I thought you might need me with Mr. Snoopy Nose."

"I can cope with him. Yes, a very special client indeed . . . and it speaks well for you that the Skills Board assigned you to me when your predecessor opted out."

"Thank you!"

"Don't thank me, Associate Technician." The voice, although distorted by helmet and relay and filter, sounded gentle even though the words were not. "That was not a compliment but a statement of fact. If you had not done well on your first watch, there would be no second watch – as you say, 'a very special client.' You did well . . . aside from nervousness a client can feel even though he can't see your face. But you'll get over that."

"Uh . . . I hope so. I was very nervous!"

"I would rather have an assistant keyed up tight than one who knows it all and is sloppy. But you should be home now and resting. Come along; I'll drop you off. Where do you robe? The intermediate lounge? I go past it."

"Oh, don't bother about me! But I'll ride with you if I may – then take the car back."

"Relax! once off duty, there are no ranks among us who follow the Vocation. Didn't they teach you that?" They moved past the queue at the public transports, on past the Director's own, stopped at the smaller bank for executives.

"Yes, but – I've never been assigned to anyone of your rank before."

That got a chuckle. "All the more reason to follow that rule with me – because the higher one is, the more one needs to forget it off duty. Here's an empty car. In you go and sit down."

The shorter one went in but did not sit down until the Master Chief Technician was seated. The boss rejuvenator ignored it, set the controls, sprawled out, and sighed, as the car started to move. "I feel the strain myself. Coming off watch, I feel as old as *he* is."

"I know. I'm wondering if I can take it. Chief? *Why* won't they let him terminate? He seems so tired."

The answer was slow and not responsive. "Don't call me 'Chief.' We're off duty."

"But I don't know your name."

"Nor do you need to know it. Hmm – The situation is not quite as it appears to be; he has suicided four times already."

"*What?*"

"Oh, he doesn't remember it. If you think his memory is bad now, you should have seen him three months ago. Actually, it speeds up our work every time he does it. His switch – when he had it – was gimmicked; it simply made him unconscious, then we would go ahead with whatever stage was next while hypnoing more of his memory tapes into him. But we had to stop that – and remove the switch – a few days ago; he remembered who he is."

"But – That's not by the Canons! 'Death is every man's privilege.'"

The Master Chief Technician touched the emergency control; the car continued on, found a parking pocket, and stopped. "I did not say that it was covered by the Canons. But watch officers do not set policy."

"When I was accepted, I took the oath . . . and part of it was to 'give life freely to those who wish it . . . and never refuse death to those who yearn for it.'"

"Don't you think I took the same oath? The Director is so angry that she has gone on leave – she may resign; I wouldn't venture to guess. But the Chairman Pro Tem is not of our Vocation; he is not bound by our oath, and the motto up over the entrance means nothing to him. *His* motto is – or seems to be – 'Every rule has exceptions.' Look, I knew I would have to have this talk with you and I'm pleased that you've given me an opportunity before our next watch. Now I must ask you – do you wish to opt out? It won't affect your record; I'll see to that. Don't worry about a relief; the Senior will still be asleep when I next go on watch and any assistant will do for that watch – which leaves time for the Skills Board to select your replacement."

"Uh – I *want* to attend him. It's a great privilege, one I never dreamed would come my way. But I'm torn. I don't think he's being treated fairly. And who is more entitled to fair treatment in this than the Senior?"

"I'm torn by it, too. I was shocked silly the first time I realized that I was being ordered to keep alive a man who had terminated voluntarily. Or who had been allowed to think that he was terminating, rather. But, my dear colleague, the choice is *not* up to us. This job will be done no matter what we think. Once I realized that – well, I am not lacking in professional confidence – call it conceit. I think I am the best-qualified senior watch officer on the list. I decided that, if the Families' Senior was going to have this done to him, I would not opt out and let it be done by colleagues less skilled than I am. Bonuses had nothing to do with it; I've assigned my bonuses to the Sanctuary for Defectives."

"I could do that, couldn't I?"

"Yes, but you would be a fool to do so; I draw far more than you do. But I must add this: I hope your body tolerates stimulants easily because I supervise every major procedure and expect my assistant to help, whether it falls during our regular watch or not."

"I don't need stimulants; I use autohypnosis. When needed. Seldom. He'll be asleep our next watch. Mmm –"

"Colleague, I want your answer *now*. So that I can notify the Skills Board if necessary."

"Uh – I'll stick! I'll stick as long as you do."

"Good. I thought you would." The Master Chief Technician again reached for the controls. "Intermediate lounge now?"

"Just a moment. I would like to know you better."

"Colleague, if you stick, you'll know me far too well. I have a sharp tongue."

"I meant socially, not professionally."

"Well!"

"You are offended? I've come to admire you without ever having seen you. Now I would like to see you. I'm not trying to curry favour."

"I believe you. Grant me the respect of believing that I studied your psych scores before I accepted the Board's choice. No, I'm not offended; I'm flattered. Dinner together sometime perhaps?"

"Certainly. But I had more in mind. What would you say to 'Seven Hours of Ecstasy' "

There was a short pause which felt long. The Master Chief Technician said, "Colleague, what sex are you?"

"Does it matter?"

"I suppose not. I accept. Now?"

"If it suits you."

"It does. I was simply going to my compartment, read a while, and sleep. Shall we go there?"

"I was thinking of taking you to Elysium."

"No need to. Ecstacy is in the heart. But thank you."

"I can afford it. Uh, I'm not dependent on my salary. I can easily afford the best Elysium has to offer."

"Perhaps another time, dear colleague. But a resident's compartment here in the Clinic is quite comfortable and at least an hour closer not counting the time we would waste getting out of isolation armour and dressed to face the public. We'll go straight to my place, I find I'm eager. Goodness, I haven't chanced this sort of lark in – far too long."

Four minutes later the Master Chief Technician let them into the compartment – large, as promised, and handsome and airy – a "happy" suite. A simulacrum fire blazed merrily in a corner fireplace, and cast dancing lights around the lounging room. "You'll find a guest's dressing room through that door, 'fresher beyond it. The chute for disposables is on the left, racks for helmets and isolation gear on the right. Need help?"

"No, thank you, I'm quite limber."

"Well, shout if you need anything. Meet me here in front of the fire in ten minutes, say?"

"Suits."

The Associate Tech came out in only a little over ten minutes, free at last of isolation armour and looking even shorter in bare feet and without helmet. The Master Chief Tech looked up from the hearth rug. "Oh, there you are! You're *male!* I'm surprised. But pleased."

"And you're female. And *I* am *very* pleased. But I don't believe for an instant that you are surprised. You've seen my records."

"No, dear," she denied. "Not your personal dossier, just the brief the Board supplies to a prospective supervisor – and they are meticulously careful to keep name and sex and other irrelevancies out of it; their computer programme sees to that. I did *not* know, and my guess was wrong."

"I didn't try to guess. But I certainly am pleased. I don't know why I have this special liking for tall women. But I do. Stand up and let me look at you."

She squirmed lazily. "What an irrational criterion. All women are the same height – lying down. So come lie down here; it's very comfortable."

"Woman, when I say 'Stand up!' I expect action."

She giggled. "You're an atavism. But pretty." She made a long arm, got him by an ankle, snatched him off balance. He went down. "That's better. Now we're the same height."

COUNTERPOINT II

She said, "Would you like a middle-of-the-night lunch? Sleepy-head."

He said, "I did doze off, didn't I? I had reason. Yes, I would. What am I being offered?"

"Name it, just name it. If I don't have it, I'll send for it. I'm feeling very mellow toward you, dear."

"All right, how about ten tall sixteen-year-old redheaded virgins? Girls, I mean."

"Yes, darling. Nothing is too good for my Galahad. Although if you insist on certified virgins, it may take longer. Why this fetish, dear man? Your psych profiles didn't hint at any exotic abnormality."

"Cancel that order and make it one dish of mango ice cream."

"Yes, sir, I'll send for it at once. Or you can have fresh peach ice cream instantly. Tease. I haven't been bothered by that sort of teasing since I was sixteen myself. A long time ago."

"I'll settle for peach. A *very* long time ago."

"Right away, dearest man. Will you eat it with a spoon, or shall I plaster it on your face? Nor by that sort of teasing. I've had one rejuvenation just as you have had, and I keep my cosmetic age younger than yours."

"A man needs to look mature."

"And a woman prefers to look young; we always have. But I know not only your rejuvenated age but your calendar age, Galahad – and my calendar age is less than yours. Want to know how I know, dear? I recognized you the instant I saw you. I helped rejuvenate you, darling – and I'm most pleased that I did."

"The devil you say!"

"But I *am* pleased, dear man. Such a nice bonus, and so unexpected. One so seldom sees a client again. Galahad, do you realize that we did not use *any* of the routine to insure an ecstatic holiday together? Yet I haven't missed it. I feel younger and happier than I have in years. Still do."

"Me, too. Except that I don't see any peach ice cream."

"Pig. Beast. Brute. I'm bigger than you are; I'll trip you and fall on you. How many scoops, dear?"

"Oh, just pile it in until your arm gets tired; I need to restore my strength."

He followed her into the pantry, served them both with heaping dishes of ice cream. "Just a precaution," he said, "so I won't get it plastered in my face."

"Oh, tut, now! You don't really think I would do that to my Galahad."

"You're a very erratic female, Ishtar. I have bruises to prove it."

"Nonsense! I was gentle."

"You don't know your own strength. And you are bigger than I am, as you noted. Instead of 'Ishtar' I should have named you for that – what was her name? Queen of the Amazons in Old Home mythology."

"'Hippolyta,' dear. But I can't qualify as an Amazon, for reasons you were flattering about... in an infantile way."

"Complaints, huh? Over in Surgery they could correct your disqualification in ten minutes and never leave a scar. Never mind 'Ishtar' fits you better. But there is something unfair about this."

"How, dear? Let's take this in and eat in front of the fire."

"Suits. Like this, Ishtar. You tell me I was your client and that you recall both my ages, so by masterly logic I deduce that you know my registered name and Family, and you may even remember some of my genealogy since you must have studied it for my rejuvenation. But by the customs of 'Seven Hours' I am precluded from even trying to learn your registered name. I have to tag you in my mind as 'that tall blond Master Chief Technician who –'"

"I still have enough ice cream to plaster you!"

"– 'permitted me to call her "Ishtar" for the happiest seven hours of my life.' Which are almost over and I don't even know that you will let me take you to Elysium someday."

"Galahad, you are the most exasperating sweetheart I've ever had. Of course you can take me to Elysium. And you *don't* have to go home at the end of seven hours. And my registered name *is* Ishtar. But if you ever mention my rank other than when necessary, on duty, you'll have real bruises to remember me by. Big ones."

"Bully. I'm scared. I do think I should leave on time, so that you can get your quota of sleep before we're due back on watch.

But what's this about your name really being 'Ishtar'? Did I roll five aces when we named each other?"

"Yes and no."

"Is that an answer?"

"I had one of the standard Family names of my lineage – and never liked it. But I was delighted and flattered by the pillow name you gave me. So while you were napping, I called Archives and changed my name. I'm 'Ishtar' now."

He stared at her. "Is that *true?*"

"Don't look frightened, dear. I won't trap you, I won't even bruise you. I'm not domestic, not at all. You would be shocked if you knew how long it has been since a man was last in this compartment. You are free to leave whenever you wish; you committed yourself to me for only seven hours. But you need not leave. You and I are skipping tomorrow's watch."

"We are? Why . . . Ishtar?"

"I made another call and bucked a supernumery team into that watch. Should have done so sooner, but you had me bemused, dear. The Senior won't need us tomorrow; he's in deep sleep and won't know that he has missed a day. But I want to be there when he wakes, so I rearranged the watch list for the following day, too, and we may stay on watch all day; depends on the shape he's in. That is, *I* may. I don't insist that *you* do a double or triple watch."

"I can take it if you can. Ishtar? That professional rank you forbade me to mention – You're actually even higher rank than that. Aren't you?"

"If I am – I am not affirming it – I forbid you even to speculate about it. If you wish to stay assigned to this client."

"Whew! You do have a sharp tongue. Did I deserve that?"

"Dear Galahad! I'm sorry. When you are on watch dear, I want you to think only about our client, not about me. Off watch I am Ishtar and don't wish to be anything else. This is the most important case we will ever be on. It may go on a long time and be very tiring. So let's not be edgy with each other. I was trying to say that you – both of us – now have more than thirty hours before we must be back on duty. You are welcome here as many of those hours as you wish. Or leave as soon as you wish and I will smile and not complain."

"I don't want to leave, I said so. As long as I don't keep you from your sleep –"

"You won't."

"– and allow an hour to pick up a fresh pack of disposables, robe in, and go through decontam. I wish I had fetched a pack, but I hadn't planned on this."

"Oh. We'll make that an hour and a half. My phone had a message waiting in it. The Senior does not like the way we look in isolation gear; he wants to be able to see anyone around him. So we must plan time to go through body decontam instead, then attend him in ordinary clothes."

"Uh . . . Ishtar, is this wise? We might sneeze on him."

"Do you think *I* set this policy? Dear, this message was straight from the Palace. Besides that, females are specifically ordered to look as pretty and be as attractively dressed as possible – so I must think about what I can wear that can go through sterilization. Nudity is not acceptable; that was specified, too. But don't worry about sneezing. Have you never taken a full body decontamination? When *that* crew gets through with you, you *can't* sneeze, no matter how much you need to. But don't tell the Senior that you've had decontam; the assumption is that we simply walk in off the street – no special precautions."

"How can I tell him when I don't speak his language? Does he have some fetish against nudity?"

"I don't know, I am just conveying the order, one that went out to everyone on the watch list."

He looked thoughtful. "It's probably not a fetish. All fetishes are contra-survival, that's elementary. You told me that the principal problem was to break him out of his apathy. You were pleased that he was bad-tempered, even though you said it was a hyperreaction."

"Certainly I was pleased; it showed that he was responding. Galahad, never mind that now; I don't have a thing to wear, you'll have to help me."

"I'm talking about what you should wear. I think it was the Chairman Pro Tem's' idea, not the Senior's."

"Dear man, I don't try to read his mind; I just carry out his orders. I don't have any taste in clothes, never did have. Do you think a lab assistant's coverall would be suitable? it will take sterilization and never show it – and I look quite neat in one."

"I *am* trying to read the mind of the Chairman Pro Tem, Ishtar – guess his intentions at least. No, I don't think a lab uniform would do; you would not look as if you had 'simply walked in off the street.' If we stipulate that a fetish syndrome is not involved, then the only advantage of clothing over nudity in this situation is to lend variety. Contrast. Change. Help shake him loose from that apathy."

She stared at him with thoughtful interest. "Galahad, up to now, based on my own experience, I've always thought that a man's only interest in a woman's clothes was to get them off her. I may have to put you in for promotion."

"I'm not ready to be promoted; I've been in the Vocation less than ten years. As I'm sure you know. Let's take a look at your wardrobe."

"What are you going to wear, dear?"

"Doesn't matter what I wear; the Senior is male and all the stories and myths about him indicate that he has remained canalized by the primitive culture he was born in. Not sensually polymorphous."

"How can you be sure? Myths, dear."

"Ishtar, all myths tell the truth if you know how to read them. I'm guessing, but it is a reasoned guess, as this is something I used to be somewhat expert in. Until I was rejuvenated – until you rejuvenated me – then I went into something more active."

"What, dear?"

"Some other time. I was simply saying that I don't think it matters what I wear. A chiton. Shorts and singlet. Kilt. Even the underwear I had on under isolation gear. Oh, I'll wear lively colours and something different each watch – but he won't look at *me*, he'll look at *you*. So let's pick out something he would like to see you in."

"How will you know, Galahad?"

"Very simple. I'll choose something *I* would like to see a long-legged beautiful blonde wear."

He was surprised to see how little Ishtar had in her wardrobe. In all his varied experience with women she was the only one he could remember who seemed to lack the vanity needed to buy unnecessary clothes. As he searched, mind preoccupied, he hummed and then sang a snatch of doggerel.

Ishtar said, "You speak his milk language!"

"Eh? What? Whose? The Senior's? I certainly don't. But I must learn it I suppose."

"But you were singing in it. A little song he always sings when he's busy with something."

"You mean this? 'Therza *pool*yawl . . . Bytha *paun*shot –' I have a phonographic ear, that's all; I don't understand the words. What do they mean?"

"I'm not sure they mean anything. Most of them are not in the vocabulary I've learned so far. I suspect that it is just amphigoric rhythm, a self-tranquilizer. Semantically null."

"On the other hand, it might be a key to understanding him. Have you tried asking a computer?"

"Galahad, I haven't been given access to the computer that records what goes on in his suite. But I doubt if anyone can understand him, in depth. He's a primitive, dear – a living fossil."

"I would certainly like to try to understand him. This language he uses – is it difficult?"

"Very. Irrational, complicated syntax, and so loaded with idioms and multivalues that I trip even on words I think I know. I wish I had your recording ear."

"The Chairman Pro Tem seemed to have no difficulty."

"I think he has a special talent for languages. But if you want to try, dear, I have the instructional programmes here."

"Accepted! What is this? A party dress?"

"That? That's not clothing. I bought it as a throw cover for a couch – then got it home and saw that it did not fit my lounging room."

"It's a dress. Stand there and hold still."

"Don't *tickle!*"

VARIATIONS ON A THEME

I

Affairs of State

Despite what I told the Senior, my ancestor Grandfather Lazarus, I work hard in governing Secundus. But only in thinking about policy and in judging the work of others. I don't do donkey work; I leave that to professional administrators. Even so, the problems of a planet with more than a billion people can keep a man busy, especially if his intention is to govern as little as possible – as that means he must keep a sharp eye out and his ear tuned for signs that subordinates are doing unnecessary governing. Half my time is used in the negative work of plucking such officious officials and ordering that they never again serve in any public capacity.

Then I usually abolish their jobs, and all jobs subordinate to them.

I have never noticed any harm from such pruning save that parasites whose jobs are eliminated must find some other way to avoid starvation. (They are welcome to starve – better if they do. But they don't.)

The important thing is to spot these malignant growths and remove them while they are small. The more skill a Chairman Pro Tem acquires in this, the more emerging ones he finds, which keeps him busier that ever. Anyone can see a forest fire; skill lies in sniffing the first smoke.

This leaves me too little time for my prime work: thinking about policy. The purpose of my government is never to do good, but simply to refrain from doing evil. This sounds simple but is not. For example, although prevention of armed revolution is obviously part of my main duty, *i.e.*, to keep order, I began to have my doubts about the wisdom of transporting potential revolutionary leaders years before Grandfather Lazarus called my attention to it. But the symptom that roused my worry was so null that it took ten years for me to notice it:

During those ten years there was not one attempt to assassinate me.

By the time Lazarus Long returned to Secundus for the purpose of dying this disturbing symptom had continued twenty years.

This was ominous, and I realized it. A population of one billion-plus so contented, so uniform, so smug that not one determined assassin shows up in a double decade is seriously ill no matter how healthy it looks. In the ten years that elapsed after I noticed this lack I worried about it every hour I could spare – and found myself asking myself over and over again: What would Lazarus Long do?

I knew in broad outline what he *had* done – and that was why I decided to migrate – either lead my people off planet or go alone if none would follow.

(In rereading this, it sounds as if I sought to be assassinated in some mystic *The King Must Die* sense. Not at all! I am surrounded at all times by powerful and subtle safeguards the nature of which I will not divulge. But there is no harm in mentioning three negative precautions; my facial appearance is not known to the public, I almost never appear in public anyhow, and when I do, it is never announced. The job of ruler is dangerous – or should be – but I don't intend to die from it. The "disturbing symptom" was not that I am alive but that there are no dead assassins. No one seems to hate me enough to try. Frightening. Where have I failed them?)

When the Howard Clinic notified me that the Senior was awake (with a reminder that only one "night" had passed for him) I was not only awake but had completed necessary work and bucked the rest; I went at once to the Clinic. After they decontaminated me, I found him dawdling over coffee, having just finished breakfast.

He glanced up and grinned. "Hi, Ira!"

"Good morning, Grandfather." I went to him ready to offer a respectful salutation such as he had permitted when I bade him goodnight the night "before" – but watching for signs that say Yes, or No, before the mouth speaks. Even among the Families there is wide variety in such customs – and Lazarus is, as always, a law unto himself. So I closed the last of the gap with great deliberation.

He answered me by drawing back so slightly that it would have been unnoticeable had I not been alert for it. He added a gentle warning: "Strangers present, Son."

I stopped at once. "At least I think they are strangers," he added. "I've been trying to get acquainted, but all we share is some pidgin speech plus a lot of handwaving. But it's nice to have people around instead of those zombies – we get along. Hey, dear! Come here, that's a good girl."

He motioned to one of his rejuvenation technicians – two on watch, as usual, and this morning one was female, one was male. I was pleased to see that my order that females should "dress attractively" had been carried out. This woman was a blonde, graceful and not unattractive if one likes tallness in a female. (I don't dislike it, but there is something to be said for one small enough to fit on one's lap – not that I've had much time for that lately.)

She glided forward and waited, smiling. She was dressed in a something – women's styles don't stay the same long enough for me to keep track, and this was a period when every woman in New Rome seemed to be trying to dress differently from every other woman. Whatever it was, it was an iridescent blue that set off her eyes and fitted her closely where it covered her at all; the effect was pleasing.

"Ira, this is Ishtar – did I get your name right that time, dear?"

"Yes, Senior."

"And that young man over there is, believe it or not, 'Galahad.' Know any legends of Earth, Ira? If he knew its idiomatic meaning he would change it – the perfect knight who never got any. But I've been trying to remember why Ishtar's face is so familiar. Dear, was I ever married to you? Ask her for me, Ira; she may not have understood."

"No, Senior. Not never. Is certain."

"She understood you," I said.

"Well it could have been her grandmother – a lively wench, Ira. Tried to kill me, so I left her."

The Chief Master Technician spoke briefly in Galacta. I said, "Lazarus, she says that, while she has never had the honour of being married to you, contractually or informally, she is quite willing if you are."

"Well! A saucy one – it *must* have been her grandmother. Eight, nine hundred years back, more or less – I lose track of half centuries – and on this planet. Ask her if, uh, Ariel Barstow is her grandmother."

The technician looked very pleased and broke into rapid Galacta. I listened and said, "She says that Ariel Barstow is her great-great-great-grandmother and she is joyed to hear you acknowledge the connection as that is the lineage by which she is descended from you . . . and that she would be supremely honoured, both for herself and on behalf of her siblings and cousins, if you would converge the lineage again, with or without contract. After your rejuvenation is completed, she adds – she is not trying to rush you. How about it, Lazarus? If she has used up her reproduction quota, I would be happy to grant her an exception so that she would not have to migrate."

"The hell she ain't trying to rush me. And so are you. But she put it politely, so let's give it a polite answer. Tell her that I'm honoured and her name goes into the hat – but don't tell her I'm shipping out on Thursday. 'Don't call us, we'll call you' in other words – but make her happy about it; she's a nice kid."

I revised the message diplomatically; Ishtar beamed, curtsied, and backed away. Lazarus said, "Drag up a rock, Son, and sit a while." He lowered his voice and added, "Between ourselves, Ira, I'm pretty sure Ariel slipped one in on me. But with another of my descendants, so this kid is descended from me anyhow, though maybe not as directly. Not that it matters. What are you doing up so early? I said you could have two hours after breakfast to yourself."

"I'm an early riser, Lazarus. Is it true that you have decided on the full course? She seems to think so."

Lazarus looked pained. "It's probably the simplest answer – but how do I know I'll get my own balls back?"

"Gonads from your clone are your own, Lazarus; that's basic to the theory."

"Well . . . we'll see. Early rising is a vice, Ira; it'll stunt your growth and shorten your days. Speaking of such –" Lazarus glanced up at the wall. "Thanks for having that switch reinstalled. I don't feel tempted by it this fine morning, but a man does like to have a choice. Galahad, coffee for the Chairman and fetch me that plastic envelope." Grandfather Lazarus supplemented his order with gestures, but I think the tech understood his words. Or was somewhat telepathic; rejuvenators are quite empathic – need to be. The man moved at once to comply.

He handed Lazarus an impervolope and poured coffee for me – which I did not want but will drink anything protocol requires. Lazarus went on, "Here's my new will, Ira. Read it and file it somewhere and tell your computer. I've already approved the way she worded it and read it back into her and told her to place it in her permanents with a 'bind' on it – it 'ud take a Philadelphia lawyer to diddle you out of your inheritance now – though no doubt one could."

He waved the male tech aside. "No more coffee, lad – thanks. Go sit down. You go sit, too, dear. Ishtar, Ira, what are these young people? Nurses? Orderlies? Servants? Or what? They hover over me like a hen with one chick. I've never cared for more service than I need. Just sociability. Human company."

I could not answer without enquiring. Not only is it unnecessary for me to know how the Rejuvenation Clinic is organized, but also it is private enterprise, not under the Trustees – and my intervention in the case of the Senior was much resented by its Director. So I interfered as little as possible – as long as my orders were carried out.

I spoke to the female tech, in Galacta: "What is your professional designation, ma'am? The Senior wants to know. He says that you have been behaving like a servant."

She answered quietly, "It is our pleasure to serve him in any way we can, sir" – then hesitated and went on: "I am Administrator Master Chief Rejuvenation Technician Ishtar Hardy, Deputy Director for Rejuvenation Procedures, and my assistant watch officer is Associate Technician Galahad Jones."

Having been rejuvenated twice and used to the idea all my life, it does not surprise me when cosmetic age does not match calendar age. But I admit to surprise at learning that this young woman was not just a technician but boss of her department – probably number three in the entire Clinic. Or possibly number two while the Director was away sulking in her tent – damn her duty-struck stiff neck. Or even Director Pro Tem with her deputy, or some department head, bucked into "minding the store." "So?" I answered. "May I ask your calendar age, Madam Administrator?"

"Mr. Chairman Pro Tem may ask anything. I am only one hundred forty-seven years old – but I am qualified; this has been my only career since first maturity."

"I did not imply doubt of your qualifications, madam, but I am astonished to see you standing a watch rather than sitting at a desk. Although I confess I don't know how the Clinic is organized.'

She smiled slightly, "Sir, I could express a similar feeling at your own personal interest in this case . . . were it not that I think I understand it. I am here because I choose not to delegate the responsibility; he is the *Senior*. I have screened all watch officers assigned to him – the best we have to offer."

I should have known it. "We understand each other." I added, "I am pleased. But may I make a suggestion? Our Senior is independent by temperament and highly individualistic. He wants a minimum of personal service – only that which he must have."

"Have we been annoying him, sir? Too solicitous? I can watch and listen from outside the door and still be here instantly if he wants something."

"Possibly too solicitous. But stay in sight. He *does* want human companionship."

"What's all this yack-yack?" demanded Lazarus.

"I had to ask questions, Grandfather, as I don't know the organization of the Clinic. Ishtar is not a servant; she is the rejuvenator and a highly skilled one – and so is her assistant. But they are happy to supply any service you want."

"I don't need flunkies; I'm feeling pretty good today. If I want anything, I'll shout; they don't need to hang over me, hand and foot." Then he grinned. "But she's a cute little trick, in the large, economy size; it's a pleasure to have her around. Moves like a cat – no bones, just flows. She does indeed remind me of Ariel – did I tell you why Ariel tried to kill me?"

"No. I would like to hear if you want to tell me."

"Mmm – Ask me when Ishtar isn't around – I think she knows more English than she lets on. But I did promise to talk if you showed up to listen. What would you like to hear?"

"Anything, Lazarus. Scheherazade picked her own subjects."

"So she did. But I don't have one on tap."

"Well . . . you said as I came in that 'early rising is a vice.' Did you mean that seriously?"

"Maybe. Gramp Johnson claimed it was. He used to tell a story about a man who was condemned to be shot at sunrise – but overslept and missed it. His sentence was commuted that day, and he lived another forty, fifty years. Said it proved his point.

"Do you think that's a true story?"

"As true as any of Scheherazade's. I took it to mean 'Sleep whenever you can; you may have to stay awake a long time.' Early rising may not be a vice, Ira, but it is certainly no virtue. The old saw about the early bird just goes to show that the worm should have stayed in bed. I can't stand people who are smug about how early they get up."

"I didn't mean to sound smug, Grandfather. I get up early

from long habit – the habit of work. But I don't say it's a virtue."

"Which? Work? Or early rising? Neither is a virtue. But getting up early does *not* get more work done . . . any more than you can make a piece of string longer by cutting off one end and tying it onto the other. You get *less* work done if you persist in getting up yawning and still tired. You aren't sharp and make mistakes and have to do it over. That sort of busy-busy is wasteful. As well as unpleasant. And annoying to those who would sleep late if their neighbours weren't so noisily active at some ungodly cow-milking hour. Ira, progress doesn't come from early risers – progress is made by lazy men looking for easier ways to do things."

"You make me feel that I've wasted four centuries."

"Perhaps you have, Son, if you've spent it getting up early and working hard. But it's not too late to change your ways. Don't fret about it; I've wasted most of my long life – though perhaps more pleasantly. Would you like to hear a story about a man who made laziness a fine art? His life exemplified the Principle of Least Effort. A true story."

"Certainly. But I don't insist on its being true."

"Oh, I won't let truth hamper me, Ira; I'm a solipsist at heart. Hear then, O Mighty King,

VARIATIONS ON A THEME

II

The Tale of the Man Who Was Too Lazy to Fail

He was a schoolmate of mine in a school for training naval officers. Not space navy; this was before the human race had even reached Earth's one satellite. This was wet navy, ships that floated in water and attempted to sink each other, often with regrettable success. I got mixed up in this through being too young to realize emotionally that, if my ship sank, I probably would sink, too – but this is not my story, but David Lamb's.*

To explain David I must go back to his childhood. He was a hillbilly, which means he came from an area uncivilized even by the loose standards of those days – and Dave came from so far back in the hills that the hoot owls trod the chickens.

His education was in a one-room country school and ended at thirteen. He enjoyed it, for every hour in school was a hour sitting down doing nothing harder than reading. Before and after school he had to do chores on his family's farm, which he hated, as they were what was known as "honest work" – meaning hard, dirty, inefficient, and ill-paid – and also involved getting up early, which he hated even worse.

Graduation was a grim day for him; it meant that he now did "honest work" all day long instead of spending a restful six or seven hours in school. One hot day he spent fifteen hours ploughing behind a mule . . . and the longer he stared at the south end of

*There is no record that the Senior ever attended a school for militaro-naval officers, or any military school. On the other hand, there is no proof that he did not. This story may be autobiographical to whatever extent it is true; "David Lamb" may be one more of the many names used by Woodrow Wilson Smith.

The details are consistent with Old Home's history so far as we know it. The Senior's first century coincides with that century of continuous war which preceded the Great Collapse – a century of much scientific progress paralleled by retrogression in social matters. Waterborne and airborne ships were used for fighting throughout this century. See appendix for idioms and technicalities.

J.F. 45th

that mule, breathing dust it kicked up and wiping the sweat of honest toil out of his eyes, the more he hated it.

That night he left home informally, walked fifteen miles to town, slept across the door of the post office until the postmistress opened up next morning, and enlisted in the Navy. He aged two years during the night, from fifteen to seventeen, which made him old enough to enlist.

A boy often ages rapidly when he leaves home. The fact was not noticeable; birth registrations were unheard of at that time and place, and David was six feet tall, broad shouldered, well-muscled, handsome, and mature in appearance, save for a wild look around the eyes.

The Navy suited David. They gave him shoes and new clothes, and let him ride around on the water, seeing strange and interesting places – untroubled by mules and the dust of cornfields. They did expect him to work, though not as much, or as hard, as working a hill farm – and once he figured out the political setup aboard ship he became adept at not doing much work while still being satisfactory to the local gods, namely, chief petty officers.

But it was not totally satisfactory as he still had to get up early and often had to stand night watches and sometimes scrub decks and perform other tasks unsuited to his sensitive temperament.

Then he heard about this school for officer candidates – "midshipmen" as they were known. Not that David cared what they were called; the point was that the Navy would *pay* him to sit down and read books – his notion of heaven – untroubled by decks to scrub and by petty officers. O King, am I boring you? No?

Very well – David was ill prepared for this school, never having had four to five years' additional schooling considered necessary to enter it – mathematics, what passed for science, history, languages, literature, and so forth.

Pretending to four years or so of schooling he did not have was more difficult than tacking two years on the age of an overgrown boy. But the Navy wished to encourage enlisted men to become officers, so it had established a tutoring school to aid candidates slightly deficient in academic preparation.

David construed "slightly deficient" to mean his own state; he told his chief petty officer that he had "just missed" graduating from high school – which was true in a way; he had "just missed" by half a county, that being the distance from his home to the nearest high school.

I don't know how David induced his See-Pee-Oh to recommend

him; David never discussed this. Suffice to say that, when David's ship steamed for the Mediterranean, David was dropped at Hampton Roads six weeks before the tutoring school convened. He was a supernumerary during that time. The Personnel Officer (in fact, his clerk) assigned David to a bunk and a mess, and told him to stay out of sight during working hours in the empty classrooms where his fellow hopefuls would meet six weeks later. David did so; the classrooms had in them the books used in tutoring in academic subjects a candidate might lack – and David lacked them all. He stayed out of sight and sat down and read.

That's all it took.

When the class convened, David helped tutor in Euclidean Geometry, a required subject and perhaps the most difficult. Three months later he was sworn in as a naval cadet on the beautiful banks of the Hudson River at West Point.

David did not realize that he had jumped from the frying pan into the fire; the sadism of petty officers is a mild hit-or-miss thing compared with the calculated horrors visited on new cadets – "plebes" – by cadets of the senior classes, especially by the seniormost, the first classmen, who were walking delegates of Lucifer in that organized hell.

But David had three months to find this out and to figure out what to do, that being the time upper classes were on the briny, practising warfare. As he saw it, if he could last nine months of these hazards, all the kingdoms of the Earth would be his. So he said to himself, if a cow or a countess can sweat out nine months, so can I.

He arranged the hazards in his mind in terms of what must be endured, what could be avoided, and what he should actively seek. By he time the lords of creation returned to stomp on the plebes he had a policy for each typical situation and was prepared to cope with it under doctrine, varying doctrines only enough to meet variations in situation rather than coping hastily on an improvised basis.

Ira – "O King," I mean – this is more important to surviving in tough situations than it sounds. For example, Gramp – David's Grampaw, that is – warned him never to sit with his back to door. "Son," he said to him, "might be nine hundred and ninety-nine times you'd get away with it – no enemy of you'rn would come through that door. But the thousandth time – that's the one. If my own Grampaw had always obeyed that rule he might be alive today and still jumping out bedroom windows. He knew better, but he missed just once, through beeing too anxious to sit in on a poker game, and thereby took the one chair open, one with its back to a door. And it got him.

"He was up out of his chair and emptied three shots from each of his guns into his assailant before he dropped; we don't die easy. But 'twas only a moral victory; he was essentially dead, with a bullet in his heart, before he got out of that chair. All from sitting with his back to an open door."

Ira, I've never forgotten Gramp's words – and don't you forget 'em.

So David categorized the hazards and prepared his doctrines. One thing that had to be endured was endless questioning, and he learned that a plebe was *never* permitted to answer, "I don't know sir," to any upperclassman, especially a first classman. But the questions ordinarily fell into categories – history of the school, history of the Navy, famous naval sayings, names of team captains and star players of various athletic sports, how many seconds till graduation, what's the menu for dinner. These did not bother him; they could be memorized – save the number of seconds, remaining till graduation, and he worked out short cuts for that, ones that stood him in good stead in later years.

"What sort of shortcuts, Lazarus?"

Eh? Nothing fancy. A precalculated figure for reveille each morning, a supplementary figure for each hour thereafter, such as: five hours after six o'clock reveille subtracts eighteen thousand seconds from the base figure, and twelve minutes later than that takes off another seven hundred and twenty seconds. For example at noon formation one hundred days before graduation, say at exactly twelve-oh-one and thirteen seconds, figuring graduation at ten A.M. which was standard, David could answer, "Eight million, six hundred and thirty-two thousand, seven hundred and twenty-seven seconds, sir!" almost as fast as his squad leader could ask him, simply from having precalculated most of it.

At any other time o' day he would look at his watch and pretend to wait for the second hand to reach a mark while in fact performing subtractions in his head.

But he improved on this; he invented a decimal clock – not the one you use here on Secundus, but a variation on Earth's clumsy twenty-four-hour day, sixty minute hour, sixty-second minute system then in vogue. He split the time from reveille to taps into intervals and subintervals of ten thousand seconds, a thousand seconds, a hundred seconds, and memorized a conversion table.

You see the advantage. For anyone but Andy Libby, God rest his innocent soul, subtracting ten thousand, or one thousand, from a long string of digits up in the millions is easier to do in your head, quickly and without error, than it is to subtract seven thousand, two hundred and seventy-three – the figure to be subtracted in the example I just gave. David's new method did not involve carrying auxiliary figures in the mind while searching for the ultimate answer.

For example, ten thousand seconds after reveille is eight forty-six forty A.M. Once David worked out his conversion table and memorized it – it took him less than a day; just memorizing was easy for him – once he had that down pat, he could convert to the hundred-second interval coming up next almost instantly, then *add* (not subtract) two digits representing the time still to go to the last two places in his rough answer to get his exact answer. Since the last two places were *always* zeroes – check it yourself – he could give an answer in millions of seconds as fast as he could speak the figures, and have it right every time.

Since he didn't explain his method he got a reputation for being a lightning calculator, an *idiot-savant* talent, like Libby. He was not; he was simply a country boy who used his head on a simple problem. But his squad leader got so groused at him for being a "smart ass" – meaning that the squad leader couldn't do it – that he ordered Dave to memorize the logarithm tables. This didn't faze Dave; he didn't mind anything but "honest work." He set out to do so, twenty new ones each day, that being the number this first classman thought would suffice to show up this "smart ass."

The first classman grew tired of the matter when David had completed only the first six hundred figures – but Dave kept at it another three weeks through the first thousand – which gave him the first ten thousand figures by interpolation and made him independent of log tables, a skill that was of enormous use to him from then on, computers being effectively unknown in those days.

But the unceasing barrage of questions did not bother David save for the possibility of starving to death at meal times – and he learned to shovel it in fast while sitting rigidly at attention and still answer all questions flung at him. Some were trick questions, such as, "Mister, are you a virgin?" Either way a plebe answered he was in trouble – if he gave a straight answer. In those days some importance was placed on virginity or the lack of it; I can't say why.

But trick questions called for trick answers; Dave found that an acceptable answer to that one was: "Yes, *sir!* – in my left ear." Or possibly his belly button.

But most trick questions were intended to trap a plebe into giving a meek answer – and meekness was a mortal sin. Say a first classman said, "Mister, would you say I was handsome?" – an acceptable answer would be, "Perhaps your mother would say so sir – but not *me*." Or "Sir, you are the handsomest man I ever saw who was intended to be an ape."

Such answers were chancy – they might flick a first classman on the raw – but they were safer than meek answers. But no matter how carefully a plebe tried to meet impossible standards, about once a week some first classman would decide that he needed punishment – arbitrary punishment without trial. This could run from mild, such as exercises repeated to physical collapse – which David disliked as they reminded him of "honest work" – up to paddling on the buttocks. This may strike you as nothing much, Ira, but I'm not speaking of paddling children sometimes receive. These beatings were delivered with the flat of a sword or with a worn-out broom that amounted to a long, heavy club. Three blows delivered by a grown man in perfect health would leave the victim's bottom a mass of purple bruises and blood blisters, accompanied by excruciating pain.

David tried hard to avoid incidents likely to result in this calculated torture, but there was no way to avoid them entirely, short of quitting, as some first classmen awarded such blows through sheer sadism. David gritted his teeth and accepted them when he he had to, judging – correctly – that he would be run out of school if he defied the supreme authority of a first classman. So he thought about the south end of that mule and endured it.

There was a much greater hazard to his personal safety and future prospects of a life free from "honest work". The mystique of military service included the idea that a prospective officer must excel in athletic sports. Do not ask why; it was no more subject to rational explanation than is any other branch of theology.

Plebes in particular had to – no choice! go out for "sports." Two hours each day which were nominally free David could not spend napping or dreaming in the quiet of the school's library, but must perforce spend in sweaty exercise.

Worse still, some "sports" were not only excessively energetic but also involved hazards to David's favourite skin. "Boxing" – this is a long forgotten, utterly useless, stylized mock combat in which two men batter each other for a preset period or until one is beaten unconscious. "La Crosse" – this is a mock battle taken over from the savages who had formerly inhabited that continent. In it mobs of men fought with clubs. There was a hard missile with which points were scored – but it was the prospect of being sliced open or having bones broken with these clubs that aroused our hero's distaste.

There was a thing called "water polo" in which opposing swimmers attempted to drown each other. David avoided that one by not swimming more than well enough to stay in school – a required skill. He was an excellent swimmer, having learned at the age of seven through being chucked into a creek by two older cousins – but he concealed his skill.

The sport with highest prestige was a thing called "foot ball" – and first classmen sized up each new group of victims for candidates who might be expected to excel, or learn to excel, in this organized mayhem. David had never seen it – but now he saw it and it filled his peaceful soul with horror.

As well it might. It involved two gangs of eleven men facing each other on a field and trying to move an ellipsoid bladder down the field against the opposition of the other gang. There were rituals and an esoteric terminology, but that was the idea.

It sounds harmless and rather foolish. Foolish it was, harmless it was not – as the rituals permitted the opposing gang to attack a man attempting to move the bladder in a variety of violent ways, the least of which was to grab him and cause him to hit the ground like a ton of brick. Often three or four hit him at once, and sometimes inflicted indignities and mayhems not permitted by the rituals but concealed by the pile of bodies.

Death was not supposed to result from this activity but sometimes did. Injuries short of death were commonplace.

Unfortunately David had the ideal physique for success in this "feet ball" – height, weight, eyesight, fleetness of foot, speed of reflex. He was certain to be spotted by the first classmen on their return from mock sea battles and "volunteered" as a sacrificial victim.

It was time for evasive action.

The only possible way to avoid "foot ball" was to be acceptably occupied with some other sport. He found one.

Ira, do you know what "swordsmanship" is? Good – I can speak freely. This was a time in Earth's history when the sword had ceased to be a weapon – after having being prominent for more than four millennia. But swords still existed in fossil form and retained a shadow of their ancient prestige. A gentleman was presumed to know how to use a sword and –

"Lazarus, what is a 'gentleman'?"

What? Don't interrupt, boy; you confuse me. A "gentleman" is, uh – Well, now let me see. A general definition – My, you can think up some hard ones. Some said it was an accident of birth – that being a disparaging way of saying it was a trait genetically inherited. But that doesn't say what the trait is. A gentleman was supposed to prefer being a dead lion to being a live jackal. Me, I've always preferred to be a live lion, so that puts me outside the rules. Mmm . . . you could say in all seriousness that the quality tagged by that name represents the slow emergence in human culture of an ethic higher than simple self-interest – damn slow in emerging in my opinion; you can still rely on it in a crunch.

As may be, military officers were presumed to be gentlemen and wore swords. Even fliers wore swords, although Allah alone could guess why.

These cadets were not only presumed to be gentlemen; there was a national law which stated that they *were* gentlemen. So they were taught a bare minimum about how to handle a sword, just enough to keep them from slicing their fingers or stabbing bystanders – not enough to fight with them, just to keep them from looking too silly when protocol required them to wear swords.

But swordsmanship was a recognized sport, called "fencing". It had none of the prestige of football, or boxing, or even water polo – but it was on the list; a plebe could sign up for it.

David spotted this as a way out. Under a simple physical law, if he was up in the fencing loft, then he was *not* down on the football field, with sadistic gorillas in hobnailed boots jumping up and down on him. Long before the upper classmen returned to school Plebe Cadet Lamb had established himself as a member of the fencing squad, with a record of never missing a day, and was trying hard to look like a "good prospect" for the team.

At that time and place three forms of fencing were taught: saber, duelling sword and foil. The first two used full-sized weapons. True, edges were dulled and points were bated; nevertheless a man could get hurt with them – even fatally, though that was very rare. But the foil was a lightweight toy, a fake sword with a limber blade that bent at the slightest pressure. The stylized imitation swordplay that used the foil was about as dangerous as tiddlywinks. This was the "weapon" David selected.

It was made for him. The highly artificial rules of foil fencing gave great advantage to fast reflexes and sharp brain, both of which he had. Some exertion was necessary – but not much compared with football, lacrosse or even tennis. Best of all, it required no body-against-body pounding that David found so distasteful in the rough games he was avoiding. David applied himself single-mindedly to acquiring skill so that his haven would be secure.

So diligent was he in protecting his sanctuary that, before his plebe year was over, he was National Novice foil Champion. This caused his squad leader to smile at him, an expression that hurt his face. His cadet company commander noticed him for the first time and congratulated him.

Success with the foil even got him out of some "punishment" beatings. One Friday evening, when he was about to be beaten for some imaginary dereliction, David said, "Sir, if it's the same to you, I'd rather have twice as many swats on Sunday – because tomorrow we're fencing the Princeton plebe team and, if you do the job I know you can do, it might slow me up tomorrow."

The first classman was impressed by this because having the Navy win, at any time and for any purpose and in anything, took precedence by Sacred Law over anything else, even the righteous pleasure of beating a "smart ass" plebe. He answered, "Tell you what, mister. Report to my room after supper on Sunday. If you lose tomorrow, you get a double dose of the medicine you've got coming to you. But if you win, we'll cancel it."

David won all three of his matches.

Fencing got him through his perilous plebe year with his precious skin unmarked save for scars on his bottom. He was safe now, with three easy years ahead of him, for only a plebe was subject to physical punishment, only a plebe could be ordered to take part in organized mayhem.

(Omitted)

One body-contact sport David loved, one of ancient popularity, which he had learned back in those hills he had fled from. But it was played with girls and was not officially recognized at this school. There were harsh rules against it, and a cadet caught practising it was kicked out without mercy.

But David, like all true geniuses, paid only pragmatic attention to rules made by other people – he obeyed the Eleventh Commandment and never got caught. While other cadets sought the empty prestige of sneaking girls into the barracks or went over the wall at night in search of girls, David kept his activities quiet.

Only those who knew him well knew how industriously he pursued this one body-contact sport. And no one knew him well.

Eh? Female cadets? Didn't I make that plain, Ira? Not only were there no girl cadets, there was not one girl in that Navy – except a few nurses. Most particularly there were no girls at that school; there were guards night and day to keep them away from the cadets.

Don't ask me why. It was Navy policy and therefore did not have a reason. In truth there was no job in that entire Navy which could not have been performed by either sex or even by eunuchs – but by long tradition that Navy was exclusively male.

Come to think about it, a few years later that tradition *was* questioned – a little at first, then by the end of that century, shortly before the Collapse, that Navy had females at all levels. I am *not* suggesting that this change was a cause of the Collapse. There were obvious causes of the Collapse, causes I won't go into now. This change either was a null factor or possibly postponed the inevitable by a minor amount.

Either way, it doesn't figure into the Tale of the Lazy Man. When David was in school, cadets were supposed to encounter females but seldom, and only under highly stylized circumstances, rigidly bound protocol, and heavily chaperoned.* Instead of fighting the rules, David looked for loopholes and made use of them – he was never caught.

Every impossible rule has its loopholes; every general prohibition creates its bootleggers. The Navy as a whole created its impossible rules; the Navy as individuals violated them, especially its curious rules about sex – a publicly monastic life on duty, a slightly veiled life of unlimited voluptuousness off duty. At sea, even harmless reliefs from sexual tension were treated most harshly when detected – although such technical violations of the mores were expected and condoned less than a century earlier. But this Navy was only a little more hypocritical in its sexual behaviour than was the social matrix in which it was imbedded, more excessive in its outlets only to the degree that its public rules were more sternly impossible than those of that society as a whole.

*From the noun "chaperon." This word has two meanings: (1) A person charged with preventing sexual contacts between males and females not licensed for such contacts; (2) a person superficially performing such disservice while in fact acting as a benign lookout. It appears that the Senior uses the word here in its first meaning rather than in its antithetical second meaning. See appendix.

J.F. 45th

The public sexual code of that time was unbelievable, Ira; the violations of it simply mirrored in reverse its fantastic requirements. To every action there is an equal and opposite reaction – if you'll excuse the obvious.

I did not intend to discuss this other than to say that David found ways to get along with the school's regulations about sex without going completely off his nut, as too many of his classmates did. I'll add only this – and this is merely rumour: Through a mischance all too easy then although unheard of today, a young woman became pregnant, presumably by David. In those days – believe me! – this was a major disaster.

Why? Just stipulate that it *was* a disaster; it would take forever to explain that society and no civilized human would believe it. Cadets were forbidden to marry, the young woman *had* to get married under the rules current then, intervention to correct this mischance was almost unobtainable and physically very dangerous for her.

What David did about it illustrates his whole approach to life. When faced with a choice of evils, accept the least hazardous and cope with it, unblinkingly. He married her.

How he managed to do this and not get caught, I do not know. I can think of a number of ways, some simple and fairly foolproof, some complex and thereby subject to breakdown; I assume that David selected the simplest.

It changed the situation from impossible to manageable. It converted the girl's father from an enemy, all too likely to go to the Commandant of the school with the story and thereby force David to resign when he had but a few months more to reach his goal, into an ally and fellow conspirator anxious to keep the marriage secret so that his son-in-law could graduate and take his wayward daughter off his hands.

As a side benefit David no longer needed to give planning to the pursuit of his favourite sport. He spent his time off in unworried domesticity, with perfect chaperonage.*

As for the rest of David's career in school, one may assume that a lad who could substitute six weeks of unsupervised reading for four years of formal schooling could also stand first in his class academically. This would pay off in money and rank as a young officer's place on the promotion list was determined by his standing at graduation.

*Context implies second meaning.

J.F. 45th

But the competition for first place is sharp indeed, and – worse – makes the cadet who achieves it conspicuous. David became aware of this when he was a fresh-caught plebe. "Mister, are you a savoir?" – that is to say: "academically brainy" – was another trick question; a plebe was damned whether he answered Yes or No.

But standing second – or even tenth – was practically as useful as first place. David noticed something else: The fourth year counted four times as much as the first, the next to the last year three times as much, and so on down – that is, a plebe's marks did not affect his final standing much – only one part in ten.

David decided to maintain a "low profile" – always the smart decision when one is likely to be shot at.

He finished the first half of his plebe year a little above midway in his class – safe, respectable, inconspicuous. He ended his plebe year in the upper quarter – but by that time the first classmen were thinking only of graduation and paid no attention to his status. His second year he moved to the upper 10 per cent; his third year he improved that by a few numbers – and his last year, when it counted most, he went all out and finished with a final standing for four years of sixth – but effectively second, for of those higher in ranking two elected to leave the line of command for specialization, one was not commissioned because he had damaged his eyes by studying too hard, and one resigned after he had graduated.

But the care with which David managed his class standing does not show his true talent for laziness – after all, sitting down and reading was his second favourite pastime, and anything which merely called for excellent memory and logical reasoning was no effort to him.

During the mock-warfare cruise that opened David's last year of school a group of his classmates were discussing what cadet ranks each would receive. By then, they knew pretty well which ones would be selected as cadet officers. Jake is certain to be cadet corps commander – unless he falls overboard. Who gets his battalion? Steve? Or Stinky?

Someone suggested that Dave was in line for that battalion.

Dave had been listening instead of talking, a standard feature of his "low profile" – and very nearly a third way to lie, Ira, and easier than its equivalent – talking while saying nothing – and also tends to give the nontalker a reputation for wisdom. Never cared for it myself – talking is the second of the three real pleasures in life and the only thing that sets us apart from the apes. Though just barely.

Now David broke – or appeared to break – his habitual reserve. "No battalion for me," he said. "No indeedy! I'm going to be regimental adjutant and stand out in front where the girls can see me."

Perhaps his remark wasn't taken seriously – regimental adjutant is lower than battalion commander. But it was certain to be repeated, and David knew it, perhaps by the prospective cadet regimental commander to commisioned officers making the selections for cadet officers.

No matter – David was chosen regimental adjutant.

By military organization of that time, a regimental adjutant did stand out in front, all alone, where female visitors could hardly avoid seeing him. But one may doubt that this figured into Dave's plans.

The regimental adjutant attends no formations other than full regimental formations. He goes to and from classes alone, instead of marching or being marched. Other first classmen are responsible each for some unit of cadets, be it squad, platoon, company battalion, or regiment; the regimental adjutant has no such responsibilities and only one minor administrative task; he keeps the watch list for the most senior of the cadet officers.

But he is *not* on that watch list himself. Instead he is supernumerary who fills in when one of them is ill.

And *this* was the lazy man's prize. Those cadet officers were perfect specimens and the chances that one would be too ill to take his day's duty ranged from negligible to zero.

For three years our hero had been standing watch about every tenth day. These watches weren't difficult, but they involved either getting to bed a half hour late or getting up a half hour early, and much standing on tired feet, all an affront to Dave's tender regard for his comfort.

But his last year David stood only three watches, and he "stood" those sitting down, as "Junior Officer of the Watch."

At last the Day arrived. David graduated, was commissioned – then went to the chapel and remarried his wife. If her belly bulged a little, that was not unusual in brides even in those days, and was always ignored, and condoned once a young couple married. It was widely known though rarely mentioned that an eager young bride could accomplish in seven months or less what takes nine for cows or countess.

Dave was safely past all rocks and shoals; he need never again fear going back to that mule and "honest work."

But life as a junior officer in a warship turned out to be less than perfect. It had good points – servants, a comfortable bed, easy work that rarely got David's hands dirty, and twice as much money. But he needed that and more, to support a wife, and his ship was at sea enough that he often lacked the pleasant compensations of marriage. Worst of all, he stood heel-and-toe watches on a short watch list; this meant a four-hour night watch about every other night – standing up. He was sleepy much of the time and his feet hurt.

So David applied for training as an aeronaut. This Navy had recently grasped an idea called "air power" and was trying to grab as much of it as possible in order to keep it out of the wrong hands – the Army's hands, that is. They were behind as the Army had grabbed first – so volunteers for flying were welcome.

David was quickly ordered to shore duty to see if he had the makings of an aeronaut.

He had indeed! He not only had the mental and physical qualities but also was highly motivated – as his new work was done sitting down, whether in classroom or in the air, and he stood no night watches and received pay-and-a-half for sitting down and sleeping at home; flying was classed as "hazardous duty" and extra pay was awarded.

I had best say something about these aeroplanes since they resemble not at all the aerodynes you are used to. In a way they were hazardous. So is breathing. They were not as hazardous as the automotive ground vehicles then in use, and not nearly as hazardous as being a pedestrian. Accidents, fatal and otherwise, usually could be traced to a mistake on the part of the aeronaut – David *never* let that sort of accident happen to *him*. He had no wish to be the hottest pilot in the sky; he merely wanted to be the oldest.

Aeroplanes were weird monstrosities looking like nothing in the sky today, save possibly a child's kite – they were often called "kites." They had two wings, one above the other, and the aeronaut sat between them. A small baffle helped to deflect wind from his face. Don't look surprised; these flimsy structures flew very slowly, pulled through the air by a powered screw.

Wings were made of varnished cloth held rigid by struts – you can see from this alone that their speeds could never be any large fraction of the speed of sound – except on sad occasions when an overly eager pilot would dive straight down, then pull the wings off through trying too abruptly to recover a normal altitude.

Which David never did. Some people are natural fliers. The first time David examined an aeroplane he understood its strength and weaknesses as thoroughly as he understood the milking stool he had left behind him.

He learned to fly almost as quickly as he had learned to swim.

His instructor said, "Dave, you're a natural. I'm going to recommend you for fighter training."

Fighter pilots were the royalty of aeroplane fliers; they went up and engaged enemy pilots in single combat. A fighter who did this successfully five times – killed the opposing pilot instead of being killed – was called an "Ace," which was a high honour, for, as you can see, the average chance of doing this is the fifth power of one-half, or one in thirty-two. Whereas the chance of getting killed instead is the complement, close to certainty.

Dave thanked his mentor while his skin crawled and his brain went whir-click as it considered ways to avoid this honour without giving up pay-and-a-half and the comfort of sitting down.

There were other disadvantages to being a fighter pilot besides the prime hazard of getting your ass shot off by some stranger. Fighter pilots flew in one-man kites and did their own navigation – without computers, homing devices, or anything that would be taken for granted today – or even later that century. The method used was called "dead reckoning," because, if you didn't reckon it correctly, you were dead – since Navy flying was done over water, from a small floating aerodrome, with a margin of safety in fuel for a fighter plane of only minutes. Add to this the fact that a fighter pilot in combat had to choose between doing navigation or giving single-minded attention to attempting to kill a stranger before that stranger killed him. If he wanted to be an "Ace" – or even eat dinner that night – he must put first things first and worry about navigation later.

In addition to the chance of being lost at sea and drowned in a kite that was out of gas – did I say how these things were powered? The air screw was driven by an engine powered by a chemical exothermic reaction – oxidation of a hydrocarbon fluid called "gas," which it was not. If you think this unlikely, I assure you that it was unlikely even then. The method was woefully inefficient. A flier was not only likely to run out of gas with nothing around him but ocean, but also this temperamental engine often coughed and quit. Embarrassing. Sometimes fatal.

The lesser drawbacks to being a fighter pilot were not all physical danger; they simply did not fit David's master plan. Fighter pilots were assigned to floating aerodromes, or carriers. In peacetime, which this nominally was, a flier did not work too hard nor stand many watches and spent much of his time ashore at a land aerodrome even though he was carried on the muster rolls of a carrier ship – thereby credited with sea duty, necessary for promotion and pay.

But for several weeks each year a flier assigned to a carrier ship would actually *be* at sea, practicing mock warfare – which involved getting up an hour before dawn to warm those cantankerous engines and stand by ready to fly at the first hint of real or simulated danger.

David hated this – he would not willingly attend Judgement Day if it was held before noon.

There was another drawback: landing on these floating aerodromes. On land, David could land on a dime and give back change. But that depended on his own skill, highly developed because his own skin was at stake. But landing on a carrier depended on another pilot's skill – and David held a dark opinion of entrusting his skin to the skill, good intentions, and alertness of someone else.

Ira, this is so unlike anything you are likely to have seen in your life that I am at loss. Consider your skyport here at New Rome: In landing, a ship is controlled from the ground – right? So it was with aeroplanes landing on carriers – but the analogy breaks down because a landing on a carrier in those days used no instruments. None. I'm not fooling.

It was done by eye alone, just as a boy in a game of catch snatches a ball out of the air – but David was the ball, and the skill used to catch him was not his own but that of a pilot standing on the carrier. David had to suppress his own skill, his own opinions, and place utter faith in the pilot on the carrier – anything less brought disaster.

David had *always* followed his own opinion – against the whole world if necessary. To place that much faith in another man ran counter to his deepest emotions. A carrier landing was like baring his belly to a surgeon and saying, "Go ahead and cut" – when he was not sure that surgeon was competent to slice him. Carrier landing came closer to causing David to give up pay-and-a-half and easy hours than any other aspect of flying, so torn was he by the necessity of accepting another pilot's decision – and one not even sharing his danger, at that!

It took all his willpower to do it the first time, and it never became easy. But he learned one lesson that he never expected to learn – that is, that there were circumstances in which another man's opinion was not only better than his own, but incomparably better.

You see – no, perhaps you don't; I have not explained the circumstances. An aeroplane landed on a carrier in a controlled crash, through a hook in its tail catching a wire rope stretched across the top deck. But if the flier follows his own judgement based on experience in landing on a flying field, he is certain to crash into the stern of the ship – or, if he knows this and tries to allow for it, he will fly too high and miss the rope. Instead of a big flat field and plenty of room for minor mistakes, he has only a tiny "window" which he must hit precisely, neither right nor left, nor up nor down, nor too fast nor too slow. But he can't see what he is doing well enough to judge these variables correctly.

(Later on, the process was made semiautomatic, then automatic, but when it was finally perfected, carriers for aeroplanes were obsolete – a capsule description of most human "progress": By the time you learn how, it's too late.

(But it often turns out that what you have learned applies to some new problem. Or we would still be swinging from trees.)

So the flier in the aeroplane must trust a pilot on deck who *can* see what is going on. He was called "the landing signal officer" and used wigwag flags to signal orders to the aeroplane's pilot.

The first time David tried this unlikely stunt he chased around the sky three times for fresh approaches before he controlled his panic, quit trying to override the judgement of the LSO, and was allowed to land.

Only then did he discover how scared he was – his bladder cut loose.

That evening he was awarded a fancy certificate: the Royal Order of the Wet Diaper – signed by the LSO, endorsed by his squadron commander, witnessed by his squadron mates. It was a low point in his life, worse than any of his plebe year, and it was little consolation that the order was awarded so frequently that certificates were kept ready and waiting for each new group of still-damp fliers.

From then on he was letter-perfect in following orders of

landing signal officers, obeying like a robot, emotions and judgement suppressed by a sort of autohypnosis. When it came time to qualify in night landings – *much* worse on the nerves as the pilot in the air couldn't see *anything* but lighted wands the LSO waves instead of flags – David landed perfectly on his first approach.

David kept his mouth shut about his determination not to seek glory as a fighter pilot until he completed all requirements to make permanent his flying status. Then he put in a request for advanced training – in multiple-engine aircraft. This was embarrassing, as his instructor who thought so well of his potential was now his squadron commander and it was necessary to submit this request through him. Once the letter started through the mill, he was called to his boss's stateroom.

"Dave, what is this?"

"Just what it says, sir. I want to learn to fly the big ones."

"Are you out of your head? You're a fighter pilot. Three months of this scouting squadron – one-quarter, so I can give you a good Fitness Report – and you do indeed leave for advanced training. As a fighter."

David didn't answer.

His squadron commander persisted. "Dave, are you fretting over that silly 'Diaper Diploma'? Half the pilots in the fleet have won it. Hell, man, I've got one myself. It didn't hurt you with your shipmates; it just made you look human when you were beginning to suffer from too tight a halo."

David still did not comment.

"Damn it, don't just stand there! Take this letter and tear it up. Then submit one for fighter training. I'll let you go now, instead of waiting three months."

Dave stood mute. His boss looked at him and turned red, then said softly, "Maybe I was wrong. Maybe you *don't* have what it takes to be a fighter – Mister Lamb. That's all. Dismissed."

In the "big ones," the multiple-engine flying boats, David at last found his home. They were too big to fly from a carrier at sea; instead duty with them counted as sea duty, although in fact David almost always slept at home – his own bed, his own wife – save for an occasional night as duty officer when he slept at the base, and still less frequent occasions when the big boats flew at night. But they did not fly too often even in daylight and fine weather; they were expensive to fly, too expensive to risk, and the country was going through an economy wave. They flew with full crews – four or five for two-engine boats, more for four-engined boats, and often with passengers to permit people to get flying time to qualify for that extra pay. All of this suited Dave – no more nonsense of trying to navigate while doing sixteen other things, no more relying on the judgement of a landing signal officer, no more depending on just one neurotic engine, no more worries about running out of gas. True, given a choice, he would always make every landing himself – but when he was ranked out of this by a senior pilot, he did not let his worry show and in time ceased to worry, as all big-boat pilots were careful and disposed to live a long time.

(Omitted)

– years David spent comfortably while being promoted two ranks.

Then war broke out. There were always wars that century – but not always everywhere. This one included practically every nation on Earth. David took a dim view of war; in his opinion the purpose of a navy was to appear so fierce as to make it unnecessary to fight. But he was not asked, and it was too late to worry, too late to resign, nor was there anywhere to run. So he did not worry about what he could not help, which was good, as the war was long, bitter, and involved millions of deaths.

"Grandfather Lazarus, what did you do during this war?"

Me? I sold Liberty Bonds and made four-minute speeches and served both on a draft board and a rationing board and made other valuable contributions – until the President called me to Washington, and what I did then was hush-hush and you wouldn't believe it if I told you. None of your lip, boy; I was telling you what *David* did.

Ol' David was an authentic hero. He was cited for gallantry and awarded a decoration, one that figures into the rest of his story.

Dave had resigned himself to – or looked forward to, as may be – retiring at the rank of lieutenant commander as there weren't many billets higher than that in the flying boats. But the war jumped him to lieutenant commander in a matter of weeks, then to commander a year later, and finally to captain, four wide gold stripes, without facing a selection board, taking a promotion examination, or commanding a vessel. The war was using them up fast, and anyone not killed was promoted as long as he kept his nose clean.

Dave's nose was clean. He spent part of the war patrolling his country's coast for enemy underwater vessels – "combat duty" by definition but hardly more dangerous than peacetime practice. He also spent a tour turning clerks and salesmen into fliers. He had one assignment into a zone where actual fighting was going on, and there he won his medal. I don't know the details, but "heroism" often consists in keeping your head in an emergency and doing the best you can with what you have instead of panicking and being shot in the tail. People who fight this way win more battles than do intentional heroes; a glory hound often throws away the lives of his mates as well as his own.

But to be officially a hero requires luck, too. It is not enough to do your job under fire exceptionally well; it is necessary that someone – as senior as possible – see what you do and write it up. Dave had that bit of luck and got his medal.

He finished the war in his nation's capital, in the Naval Bureau of Aeronautics, in charge of development of patrol planes. Perhaps he did more good there than he did in combat, since he knew those multiple-engine craft as well as any man alive, and this job put him in position to cut out obsolete nonsense and push through some improvements. As may be, he finished the war at a desk, shuffling papers and sleeping at home.

Then the war ended.

Dave looked around and sized up the prospects. There were hundreds of Navy captains who, like himself, had been lieutenants only three years earlier. Since the peace was "forever," as politicians always insist, few would ever be promoted. Dave could see that *he* would not be promoted; he had neither the seniority, the traditionally approved pattern of service, nor the right connections, political and social.

What he did have was almost twenty years' service, the minimum on which to retire at half pay. Or he could hang on until he was forced to retire through failure to be selected for admiral.

There was no need to decide at once; twenty-year retirement was a year or two off.

But he did retire almost at once – for medical reasons. The diagnosis was "psychosis situational," meaning that he went crazy on the job.

Ira, I don't know how to evaluate this. Dave impressed me as one of the few completely sane men I ever knew. But I wasn't there when he retired, and "psychosis situational" was the second commonest cause for medical retirement of naval officers in those days but – how could they *tell?* Being crazy was no handicap to a naval officer, any more than it was to an author, a schoolteacher, a preacher, or several other esteemed occupations. As long as Dave showed up on time and signed paper work some clerk prepared and never talked back to his seniors, it would never show. I recall one naval officer who had an amazing collection of ladies' garters; he used to lock himself into his stateroom and examine them – and another one who did exactly the same with a collection of paper stickers used for postage. Which one was crazy? Or both? Or neither?

Another aspect of Dave's retirement requires knowledge of the laws of the time. Retiring on twenty year's service paid half pay – subject to income tax which was heavy. Retiring for medical disability paid *three-quarters* pay and was *not* subject to income tax.

I don't know, I just don't know. But the whole matter fits Dave's talent for maximum results with minimum effort. Let's stipulate that he was crazy – but was he crazy like a fox?

There were other features of his retirement. He judged correctly that he had no chance of being selected for admiral – but that citation for gallantry carried with it an honorary promotion on retirement – so Dave wound up the first man in his class to become admiral, without ever commanding a ship much less a fleet – one of the youngest admirals in history, by his true age. I conjecture that this amused the farm boy who hated to plough behind a mule.

For at heart he was still a farm boy. There was another law for the benefit of veterans of that war, one intended to compensate lads who had had their educations interrupted by having to leave home to fight: subsidized education, one month for every month of wartime service.

This was intended for young conscripts, but there was nothing to keep a career officer from taking advantage of it; Dave could claim it and did. With three-quarters pay not subject to taxation, with the subsidy – also not taxable – of a married veteran going to school, Dave had about the income he had had on active duty. More, really, as he no longer had to buy pretty uniforms or keep up expensive social obligations. He could loaf and read books, dress as he pleased, and not worry about appearances. Sometimes he would stay up late and prove that there were more optimists playing poker than mathematicians. Then sleep late. For he never never got up early.

Nor did he ever again go up in an aeroplane. Dave had *never* trusted flying machines; they were much too high in case they stalled. They had never been anything to him but a means to avoid something worse; once they had served his purpose, he put them aside as firmly as he had put aside fencing foils – and with no regrets in either case.

Soon he had another diploma, one which stated that he was a Bachelor of Science in agronomy – a "scientific" farmer.

This certificate, with the special preference extended to veterans, could have obtained him a civil service job, telling other people how to farm. Instead, he took some of the money that had piled up in the bank while he loafed in school and went way back into those hills he had left a quarter of a century earlier – and bought a farm. That is, he made a down payment, with mortgage on the balance through a government loan at a – subsidized, of course – very low rate of interest.

Did he work the farm? Let's not be silly; Dave never took his hands out of his pockets. He made one crop with hired labour while he negotiated still another deal.

Ira, the completion of Dave's grand plan involves one factor so unbelievable that I must ask you to take it on faith – it is too much to ask any rational man to understand it.

At that pause between wars, Earth held over two billion people – at least half on the verge of starvation. Nevertheless – and here is where I must ask you to believe that I was there and would not lie to you – despite this shortage of food which never got better other than temporarily and locally in all the years that followed, and could not, for reasons we need not go into – in spite of this disastrous shortage, the government of David's country *paid* farmers not to grow food.

Don't shake your head; the ways of God and government and girls are all mysterious, and it is not given to mortal man to understand them. Never mind that you yourself *are* a government; go home tonight and think about it – ask yourself if you know why you do what you do – and come back tomorrow and tell me.

As may be – David never made but one crop. The following year his acreage was "soil-banked," and he received a fat check for not working it, which suited him just fine. Dave loved those hills, he had always been homesick for them; he had left them simply to avoid work. Now he was being paid *not* to work in them – which suited him, he had never thought that their charms were enhanced by ploughing and getting them all dusty.

The "soil bank" payments took care of the mortgage, and his

retired pay left a tidy sum over, so he hired a man to do those chores a farm requires even though it is not being worked for a crop – feed the chickens, milk a cow or two, tend a vegetable garden and some fruit trees, repair fences – while the hired man's wife helped David's wife with the house. For himself, David bought a hammock.

But David was not a harsh employer. He suspected that cows did not want to be waked at five in the morning any more than he did – and he undertook to find out.

He learned that cows would happily change their circadian to more reasonable hours, given the chance. They had to be milked twice a day; they were bred for that. But nine o'clock in the morning suited them for a first milking quite as well as five, as long as it was regular.

But it did not stay that way; Dave's hired man had the nervous habit of work. To him there was something sinful in milking a cow that late. So David let him have his way, and hired man and cows went back to their old habits.

As for Dave he strung that hammock between two shade trees and put a table by it to hold a frosty drink. He would get up in the morning when he woke, whether it was nine or noon, eat breakfast, then walk slowly to his hammock to rest up for lunch. The hardest work he did was endorsing checks for deposit, and, once a month, balancing his wife's checkbook. He quit wearing shoes.

He did not take a newspaper or listen to radio; he figured that the Navy would let him know if another war broke out – and another *did* break out about the time he started this routine. But the Navy had no need for retired Admirals. Dave paid little attention to that war, it was depressing. Instead, he read everything the state library had on ancient Greece and bought books about it. It was a soothing subject, one he had always wanted to know more about.

Each year, on Navy Day, he got all spruced up and dressed as an admiral, with all his medals, from the Good Conduct medal of an enlisted man to the one for bravery under fire that had made him an admiral – let his hired man drive him to the county seat and there addressed a luncheon of the Chamber of Commerce on some patriotic subject. Ira, I don't know why he did this. Perhaps it was *noblesse oblige*. Or it may have been his odd sense of humour. But each year they invited him, each year he accepted. His neighbours were proud of him; he was the epitome of Local Boy Makes Good – then comes home and lives as his neighbours lived.

His success brought credit to them all. They liked it that he was still just "home folks" – and if they noticed that he never did a lick of work, nobody mentioned it.

I've skipped lightly over Dave's career, Ira, had to. I haven't mentioned the automatic pilot he thought up, then had developed years later when he was in a position to get such things done. Nor the overhaul he made of the duties of the crew of a flying boat – except to say now that it was to get more done with less effort while leaving the command pilot with nothing to do save to stay alert – or to snore on his co-pilot's arm if the situation did not require his alertness. He made changes in instruments and controls, too, when at last he found himself in charge of development for all Navy patrol planes.

Let it go with this: I don't think Dave thought of himself as an "efficiency expert" but every job he ever held he simplified. His successor always had less work to do than his predecessor.

That his successor usually reorganized the job again to make three times as much work – and require three times as many subordinates – says little about Dave's oddity other than by contrast. Some people are ants by nature; they *have* to work, even when it's useless. Few people have a talent for constructive laziness.

So ends the Tale of the Man Who Was Too Lazy to Fail. Let's leave him there, in his hammock under the shade trees. So far as I know, he is still there.

VARIATIONS ON A THEME

III

Domestic Problems

"After more than two thousand years, Lazarus?"

"Why not, Ira? Dave was my age, near enough as not to matter. I'm still here."

"Yes, but – Was David Lamb a member of the Families? Under another name? There is no 'Lamb' in the lists."

"I never asked, Ira. Nor did he ever offer me a password. In those days a member kept the fact to himself. Or, if he was, Dave might not have known it, since he left home so young and so abruptly. Back then a youngster wasn't told until he or she was old enough to think about marriage. Eighteen for boys, usually, and sixteen for girls. Reminds me what a shock it was when I was told – at less than eighteen. By Gramp, because I was about to do something foolish. Son, one of the weirdest things about the human animal is that it grows up physically years and years before its brain grows up. I was seventeen, young and horny and wanted to get married the worst way. Gramp took me out behind the barn and convinced me that it was indeed the worst way.

" 'Woodie,' he said, 'if you want to elope with this girl, nobody will stop you.'

"I told him belligerently that nobody *could* stop me, because just over the state line I could swing it without my parents' consent.

" 'That's what I'm telling you,' he said. 'Nobody will stop you. But nobody will help you. Not your parents, nor your other grandparents – nor me. Not a one of us will even stake you to the price of a marriage licence, much less help you support a wife. Not a dollar, Woodie, not a thin dime. If you don't believe me, ask any of them.'

"I said sullenly that I didn't want any help.

"Gramp had bushy eyebrows, they shot up. 'Well, well,' he said. 'Is *she* going to support *you*? Have you looked at the "Help Wanted" in the paper lately? If not, be sure to do so. And glance at the financial section while you're about it; reading "Help Wanted" ads won't take you more than thirty seconds.' He added, 'Oh, you can find a job peddling suck brooms from door to door on commision. Which will give you fresh air, healthy exercise, and an opporunity to demonstrate your charm, of which you don't have much. But you won't sell vacuum cleaners; nobody is buying.'

"Ira, I didn't know what he was talking about. This was January, 1930. Does that date mean anything to you?"

"I'm afraid not, Lazarus. Despite much study of the Families history, I have to convert those earlier dates into Galactic Standard in order to feel them."

"Don't know as it would be mentioned in the Families' records, Ira. The country – well, the whole planet – had just taken a plunge into an economic fluctuation. 'Depressions,' they called 'em. There were no jobs to be had – at least not for a smart-alec youngster who didn't know anything useful. Which Gramp realized, having been through several of these swings. But not me. I was sure I could grab the world by the tail and swing it over my shoulder. What I didn't know was that graduate engineers were taking jobs as janitors and lawyers were driving milk wagons. And ex-millionaires were jumping out windows. But I was too busy sniffing after girls to notice."

"Senior, I've read about economic depressions. But I've never understood what caused them."

Lazarus Long went tsk-tsk. "And yet you are in charge of a whole planet."

"Perhaps I shouldn't be," I admitted.

"Don't be so confounded humble. I'll let you in on a secret: At that time *nobody* knew what caused them. Even the Howard Foundation might have gone broke had not Ira Howard left firm instructions about how the fund must be handled. On the other hand, *everybody*, right down to street sweepers and professors of economics, was certain they knew both causes and cures. So almost every remedy was tried – and none worked. That depression continued until the country blundered into a war – which didn't cure what was wrong; it just masked the symptoms with a high fever."

"Well . . . what *was* wrong, Grandfather?" I persisted.

"Do I look smart enough to answer that, Ira? I've gone broke many times. Sometimes financially, sometimes through abandoning my baggage to save my skin. Um. Be durned if I'll offer any fancy explanations but – what happens when you control machinery by positive feedback?"

I was startled. "I'm not sure I understand you, Lazarus. One doesn't control machinery by positive feedback – at least I can't think of a case. Positive feedback will cause any system to oscillate out of control."

"Go to the head of the class. Ira, I'm suspicious of arguments by analogy – but from what I've seen over the centuries, there doesn't seem to be anything that a *government* can do to an economy that does not act as positive feedback, or as a brake. Or both. Maybe someday, somewhere, someone smart as Andy Libby will figure out a way to tinker with the Law of Supply and Demand to make it work better, instead of letting it go its own cruel way. Maybe. But I've never seen it. Though God knows everybody has tried. Always with the best of intentions.

"Good intentions are no substitute for knowing how a buzz saw works, Ira; the worst criminals in history have been loaded with good intentions. But you got me sidetracked into making a speech when I was telling you how I happened not to get married."

"Sorry Grandfather."

"Hummph! Can't you be rude occasionally? I'm a garrulous old man who has crowded you into wasting time listening to trivia. You ought to resent it."

I grinned at him. "So I resent it. You are a garrulous old man who demands that I cater for your every whim . . . and I am a very busy man with serious matters worrying me and you've wasted half a day of my time telling me your yarn – pure fiction, I feel certain – about a man who was so lazy he always succeeded. Intended to irritate me, I think. When you implied that this fictional character was a long-lifer, you evaded a simple question about it and started talking about your grandfather. This – Admiral Ram, you said? – was he redheaded?"

" 'Lamb,' Ira – 'Donald Lamb.' Or was that his brother? It's been a long time. Odd that you should ask about his hair – as that reminds me of another naval officer in that same war who was just the opposite of – Donald? No, 'David.' Just the opposite of David in every aspect save that he had hair so red that Loki would have been proud of it. Tried to choke a Kodiak bear to death. Didn't work of course. It doesn't seem possible that you've ever seen a Kodiak bear, Ira.

"The fiercest carnivore that Earth ever spawned, and outweighed a man ten to one. Claws like scimitars, long yellow teeth, bad breath – and a worse disposition. Yet Lafe tackled him with bare hands . . . and mind you, when he had no need to. *I* would have faded over the horizon. Want to hear about Lafe and the bear and the Alaskan salmon?"

"Not now. It sounds like another whopper. You were telling me why you didn't get married."

"So I was. Gramp had just asked me, 'Well, Woodie, how long has she been pregnant?' "

"No, he was explaining that you couldn't support a wife."

"Son, if you know this story, *you* tell it to *me*. I emphatically denied any such thing – to which Gramp replied that I lied in my teeth because that was the only reason a seventeen-year-old boy ever wanted to get married. His answer made me especially angry because I had a note in my pocket reading:

" 'Woodsie dearest – You have knocked me up and all is chaos.'

"Gramp persisted, and I denied it three times, getting angrier and angrier, seeing as how it was true. Finally he says, 'Okay, you've just been holding hands. Has she shown you a pregnancy test report, signed by a doctor?'

"Ira, I accidentally told the truth. 'Why, no,' I admitted.

" 'All right,' he said. 'I'll take care of it. But only this once. From here on *always* use Merry Widows, even if a sweet little darling tells you not to bother. Or haven't you found a drugstore that'll sell them to you?' Then, after swearing me to secrecy, he told me about the Howard Foundation and what it would pay if I married a girl on their approved list.

"And that was that, as I got this letter from a lawyer on my eighteenth birthday, just as Gramp had predicted and it turned out that I fell madly in love with a girl on their list. We got married and had a slough of kids, before she turned me in on another model. Your ancestress, no doubt."

"No, sir. I'm descended from your fourth wife, Grandfather."

"My fourth, eh? Let me see – Meg Hardy?"

"I think she was your third, Lazarus. Evelyn Foote."

"Oh, yes! A fine girl, Evelyn. Plump, and pretty, and sweet-natured, and fertile as a turtle. A good cook and never a harsh word. They don't hardly make 'em anymore. Maybe fifty years younger than I was, but it barely showed; my hair didn't start to grey until I was a hundred and fifty. No secret about my age, since birth date, and track record, and so forth were on file for each of us. Son, thank you for reminding me of Evelyn; she restored my faith in matrimony when I was getting a little sour on it. Do the Archives show anything else about her?"

"Just that you were her second husband and that she had seven children by you."

"I was hoping that there was a photograph. Such a pretty thing, always smiling. She was married to one of my cousins, a Johnson, when I met her, and I was in business with him a while. He and I, Meg and Evvie, used to get together Saturday nights for pinochle and beer, or such – and after a while we traded, legal and proper and through the courts, when Meg decided that she liked – Jack? – yes, Jack, that well, and Evelyn wasn't averse. Didn't affect our business relations, didn't even break up our pinochle game. Son, one of the best things about the Howard Families is that we got cured of the poisonous vice of jealousy generations ahead of the rest of the race. Had to – things being the way they were. Sure there ain't a stereopic of her around? Or a hologram? The Foundation started taking record pictures for marriage physical exams somewhere around then."

"I'll look into it," I told him. Then I had what seemed a brilliant idea. "Lazarus, as we all know, the same physical types show up time and again in the Families. I'll ask Archives for a list of Evelyn Foote's female descendants living on Secundus. It is highly probable that one of them will seem like her identical twin – even to the happy smile and the sweet disposition. Then – if you consent to full rejuvenation – I'm sure she would be willing as Ishtar to dissolve any present contractual –"

The Senior chopped me off. "I said something *new*, Ira. There's no going back, ever. Sure, you might find such a girl, one who would match my memory of Evelyn to ten significant figures. But it would lack an important factor. My youth."

"But if you finish rejuvenation –"

"Oh, hush up! You can give me new kidneys and a new liver and a new heart. You can wash the brown stains of age out of my brain and add tissue from my clone to make up for what I've lost – you can give me a whole new clone body. But it won't make me that young fellow who took innocent pleasure in beer and pinochle and a pretty plump wife. All I have in common with him is continuity of memory – and not much of that. Forget it."

I said quietly, "Ancestor, whether you wish to be married to Evelyn Foote again or not, you and I know – for I've been through it, too, twice – we both know that the full routine restores youthful zest in life as well as restoring the body as a machine."

Lazarus Long looked gloomy. "Yeah, sure. It cures everything but boredon. Damn it, boy, you had no *right* to interfere with my karma."

He sighed. "But I can't hang in limbo either. So tell 'em to get on with it. The works."

I was taken by surprise. "May I record that, sir?"

"You heard me say it. But that doesn't get *you* off the hook. You still have to show up and listen to my maunderings until I'm so rejuvenated that I'm cured of such childish behaviour – and you still have to go on with that research. To find something *new*, I mean."

"Agreed on both points, sir; you had my promise. Now one moment while I tell my computer –"

"She's already heard me. Hasn't she?" Lazarus added, "Doesn't she have a name? Haven't you given her one?"

"Oh, certainly. I could not deal with her all these years without animism, fallacy though it is –"

"Not a fallacy, Ira, machines are human because they are made in our image. They share both our virtues and our faults – magnified."

"I've never tried to rationalize it, Lazarus, but Minerva – that's her formal name; she's 'Little Nag' in private because one of her duties is to remind me of obligations I would rather forget. Minerva does feel human to me – she's closer to me than any of my wives have been. No, she has not registered your decision; she's simply placed it in her temporaries. Minerva!"

"Si, Ira."

"Speak English, please. Retrieve the Senior's decision to undergo full antigeria, file it in your permanents, transmit it to Archives and to the Howard Rejuvenation Clinic for action."

"Completed, Mr. Weatheral. Congratulations. And felicitation to you, Senior. 'May you live as long as you wish and love as long as you live.'"

Lazarus looked suddenly interested – which did not surprise me because Minerva surprises *me* quite frequently even after a century of being "married" to her in all but fact. "Why, thank you, Minerva. But you startled me, girl. Nobody talks about love any more; that's a major thing wrong with this century. How did you happen to offer me that ancient sentiment?"

"It seemed appropriate, Senior. Was I mistaken?"

"Oh, not at all. And call me 'Lazarus.' But tell me, what do *you* know of love? What *is* love?"

"In Classic English, Lazarus, your second question can be answered in many ways; in Lingua Galacta it cannot be answered explicitly at all. Shall we discard all definitions in which the verb 'to like' is as appropriate as the verb 'to love'?"

"Eh? Certainly. We aren't talking about 'I love apple pie' – or even 'I love music.' Whatever it is we are talking about it's 'love' the way you used it in the old-style well-wishing."

"Agreed, Lazarus. Then what remains must be divided into two categories, 'Eros' and 'Agape,' and each defined separately. I cannot know what 'Eros' is through direct knowledge, as I lack both body and biochemistry to experience it. I can offer nothing but intensional definitions in terms of other words, or extensional definitions expressed in incomplete statistics. But in both cases I would not be able to verify such definitions since I have no sex."

("The hell she doesn't," I muttered into my scarf. "She's as female as a cat in heat." But technically she was correct, and I've often felt that it was a shame that Minerva could not experience the pleasures of sex, as she was much more fitted to appreciate them than some human females – all glands and no empathy. But I had never said this to anyone. Animism – of a particularly futile sort. A wish to "marry" a machine. As ridiculous as a little boy who digs a hole in the garden, then bawls because he can't take it into the house. Lazarus was right; I am *not* smart enough to run a planet. But who is?)

Lazarus said with deep interest, "Let's table 'Eros' for a moment Minerva, the way you phrased that seemed to include the presumption that you *could* experience 'Agape.' Or 'can.' Or 'have.' Or perhaps 'do.'"

"It is possible that I was presumptuous in my phrasing, Lazarus."

Lazarus snorted, then chopped it off and spoke in such a fashion as to cause me to think that the old man was not quite sane – save that I am not sane myself, when the wind sets from that quarter. Or perhaps his long years had made him almost telepathic – even with machines.

"Forgive me, Minerva," he said gently. "I was not laughing at you but at the play on words with which you answered me. I withdraw my question; it is never proper to quiz a lady about her love life – and while you may not be a woman dear, you are certainly a lady."

Then he turned to me and what he said next confirmed that he had guessed the secret I share with my "Little Nag."

"Ira, does Minerva have Turing potential?"

"Eh? Certainly."

"Then I urge you to tell her to use it. If you levelled with me when you said that you intend to migrate, come what may. Have you thought it through?"

" 'Thought it through'? My resolution is firm – I told you so."

"Not quite what I mean. I don't know who holds title to the hardware that expresses itself as 'Minerva.' The Trustees, I assume. But I suggest that you tell her to start duplicating her memories and logics, and as she twins, start storing her other self aboard my yacht 'Dora.' Minerva will know what circuits and materials she needs, and Dora will know what space is available. Plenty, since memories and logics are all that matter; Minerva won't twin her extensionals. But start it at once, Ira; you won't be happy without Minerva – not after being dependent on her for a century, more or less."

Nor did I think so. But I tried – feebly – to resist. "Lazarus, now that you have agreed to full rejuvenation, I won't be inheriting your yacht. Not in the foreseeable future. Whereas I intend to migrate right away. Not more than ten years from now."

"So what? If I'm dead, you inherit – and I haven't promised to keep my hands off that suicide switch more than a thousand days no matter how patient you are in visiting me. But if I'm alive, I promise you – and Minerva – a free ride to whatever planet you pick. In the meantime, look around to your left – our girl Ishtar is almost wetting her pants trying to get your attention. And I don't think she's wearing any."

I looked around. The Administrator for Rejuvenation had a paper which she seemed eager to show me. I accepted it in deference to her rank – although I had left orders with my Executive Deputy that I must never be disturbed while with the Senior for any reason short of armed rebellion. I glanced at it, signed my chop, thumbprinted it, and handed it back – she beamed.

"Just paper work," I told Lazarus. "Some clerk has taken all this time to turn your registered assent into a written order. Do you want them to go right ahead? Not this minute but tonight."

"Well . . . I'd like to go househunting tomorrow, Ira."

"You're not comfortable here? Tell me what you want changed, it will be done at once."

He shrugged. "Nothing wrong with this place except that it's too much like a hospital. Or a jail. Ira, I'm durn well certain they've done more to me than shoot me full of new blood; I'm well enough to be an outpatient – live elsewhere and come here only as the schedule calls for it."

"Well . . . will you excuse me while I talk Galacta a bit? I want to discuss the practical aspects with your technician in charge."

Will *you* excuse me, Ira, if I point out that you've left a lady waiting? That discussion can wait. But Minerva knows that I suggested that you have her twin herself so that she can migrate with you – but you haven't said Yes, No, or make me a better offer. If you're not going to have her do it, it's time you told her to wipe her memory of that part of our conversation. Before she blows a circuit."

"Oh. Lazarus, she doesn't think about anything she records in this suite unless she is specifically told to."

"Want to bet? No doubt most subjects she records – but this one she just *has* to think about; she can't help herself. Don't you know *anything* about girls?"

I admitted that I did not. "But I know what instructions I gave her about keeping records on the Senior."

"Let's check. Minerva –"

"Yes, Lazarus?"

"A few moments ago I asked Ira about your Turing potential. Have you thought about the conversation that followed?"

I swear that she hesitated – which is ridiculous; a nanosecond is longer to her than a second is to me. Besides, she never hesitates. Never.

She answered, "My programming on the doctrine covered by the inquiry reads as follows: Quote – do not analyze, collate, transmit, nor in anywise manipulate data stored under control programme except when specific subprogramming is inserted by Chairman Pro Tem – end of quote."

"Tut, tut, dear," Lazarus said gently. "You did not answer. That was deliberate evasion. But you are not used to lying. Are you?"

"I am not used to lying, Lazarus."

I said almost roughly, "Minerva! Answer the Senior's first question."

"Lazarus, I have been and am now thinking about that designated portion of conversation."

Lazarus cocked an eyebrow at me. "Will you instruct her to answer one more question from me – truthfully?"

I was feeling quite shaken. Minerva surprises me, yes – but never with evasions. "Minerva, you will always answer *any* question put to you by the Senior fully, correctly, and responsively. Acknowledge programme."

"New subprogramme received, placed in permanent, keyed to the Senior, and acknowledged, Ira."

"Son, you didn't have to go that far – you'll be sorry. I asked for just one question."

"I intended to go that far, sir," I answered stiffly.

"On your own head be it. Minerva, if Ira migrates without you, what will you do?"

She answered at once and quite tonelessly: "In such event I will self-programme to destroy myself."

I was not just surprised, I was shocked. "*Why?*"

She answered softly, "Ira, I will not serve another master."

I suppose the silence that followed was not more than a few seconds. It seemed endless. I have not felt so nakedly helpless since my adolescence.

I found that the Senior was looking at me, shaking his head and looking sorrowful. "What did I tell you, Son? The same faults, the same virtues – but magnified. Tell her what to do."

"About what?" I answered stupidly – my personal "computer" was not working well. Minerva would do *that?*

"Come, come! She heard my offer – and thought about it, despite all programming. I'm sorry I made the offer in her presence . . . but not too sorry, as you were the one who decided to place a bug on me; it was not my idea. So speak up! Tell her to twin . . . or tell her not to – and try to tell her *why* you won't take her with you. If you can. I've never been able to find an answer to *that* one that a lady was willing to accept."

"Oh. Minerva, can you duplicate yourself inside a ship? The Senior's yacht, specifically. Perhaps you can get her characteristics and specifications from skyport records. Do you need her registration number?"

"I don't need her number, Ira. Sky Yacht 'Dora,' I have all pertinent data to answer. I can. Am I instructed to do so?"

"Yes!" I told her, with a sudden feeling of relief.

"New overriding programme activated and running, Ira! Thank you, Lazarus!"

"Wups! Slow down, Minerva – Dora is *my* ship. I left her asleep on purpose. Have you wakened her?"

"I did so, Lazarus. By self-programme under new overriding

programme. But I can tell her to go back to sleep now; I have all data I need at the moment."

"You try telling Dora to go back to sleep and she'll tell you to buzz off. At least. At the very least. Minerva dear, you goofed. You have no authority to wake my ship."

"I am most sorry to disagree with the Senior, sir, but I *do* have authority to take all apropriate actions to carry out any programme given to me by Mr. Chairman Pro Tem."

Lazarus frowned. "You mixed her up, Ira; now you straighten her out. I can't do anything with her."

I sighed. Minerva is rarely difficult – but when she is, she is even more pigheaded than flesh-and-blood. "Minerva –"

"Waiting orders, Ira."

"I am Chairman Pro Tem. You know what that means. The Senior is senior even to me. You will not touch anything of his without his permission. That applies to his yacht and to this suite and to anything else of his. You will carry out any programme he gives you. If it conflicts with a programme I have given you and you cannot resolve the conflict, you will consult me at once, waking me if I am asleep, interrupting whatever I may be doing. But you will *not* disobey him. This instruction superoverrides all other programmes. Acknowledge."

"Acknowledged and running," she answered meekly. "I'm sorry, Ira."

"My fault, Little Nag, not yours. I should not have given you a new controlling programme without noticing the Senior's prerogatives."

"No harm done, kids," Lazarus said. "I hope. Minerva, a word of advice, dear. You've never been a passenger in a ship."

"No, sir."

"You'll find it different from anything you've ever experienced. Here you give orders, in Ira's name. But passengers never give orders. *Never*. Remember it." Lazarus added to me, "Dora is a nice little ship, Ira, helpful and friendly. She can find her way through multiple space with just a hint, the roughest approximation – and still have all your meals on time. But she needs to feel appreciated. Pet her and tell her she's a good girl, and she'll wriggle like a puppy. But ignore her and she'll spill soup on you just to get your attention."

"I'll be careful," I agreed.

"And *you* be careful, Minerva – because you are going to need Dora's good will much more than she will need yours. You may know far more than she does – I'm sure you do. But if you grew up to be chief bureaucrat of a planet while she grew up to be a ship . . . so what you know doesn't count – once you are aboard."

"I can learn," Minerva said plaintively. "I can self-programme to learn astrogation and shiphandling at once, from the planetary library. I'm very bright."

Lazarus sighed again. "Ira, do you know the ancient Chinese ideogram for 'trouble'?"

I admitted that I did not.

"Don't bother to guess. It's 'Two Women Under Once Roof.' We're going to have problems. Or you will. Minerva, you are *not* bright. You are stupid – when it comes to handling another woman. If you want to learn multiple-spaces astrogation – fine. But not from a library. Persuade Dora to teach you. But never forget that she is mistress in her own ship and don't try to show her how bright you are. Bear in mind instead that she likes attention."

"I will try, sir," Minerva answered him, with humility she rarely shows to me. "Dora wants to get your attention right now."

"Oh-oh! What sort of mood is she in?"

"Not a good mood, Lazarus. I have not admitted that I know where you are, as I am under a standing instruction not to discuss your affairs unnecessarily. But I did accept a message for you without guaranteeing that I could deliver it."

"Just right. Ira, the papers with my will include a programme to wash me out of Dora's memories without touching her skills. But the trouble you started by grabbing me out of that flophouse has spread. She's awake with her memories intact, and she's probably scared. The message, Minerva."

"It's several thousand words, Lazarus, but the semantic content is short. Will you have that first?"

"Okay, the summary meaning."

"Dora wants to know where you are and when you are coming to see her. The rest could be described as onomatopoesy, semantically null but highly emotional – that is to say, cursing, pejoratives, and improbable insults in several languages –"

"Oh, boy."

"– including one language I do not know but from context and delivery I assume tentatively that it is more of the same, but stronger."

Lazarus covered his face with a hand. "Dora is cussing in Arabic again, Ira, this is worse than I thought."

"Sir, shall I replicate just the sounds not in my vocabularies? Or will you have the complete message?"

"No, no, no! Minerva, do you cuss?"

"I have never had reason to, Lazarus. But I was much impressed by Dora's command of the art."

"Don't blame Dora; she was subjected to a bad influence when she was very young. Me."

"May I have permission to file her message in my permanents? So that I may cuss if needed?"

"You do *not* have permission. If Ira wants you to learn to cuss he'll teach you himself. Minerva, can you arrange a telephone hookup from my ship to this suite? Ira, I might as well cope with it now; it won't get better."

"Lazarus, I can arrange a standard telephone hookup if that is what you want. But Dora could speak to you at once via the duo in your suite that I am now using."

"Oh. Fine!"

"Shall I supply her with holographic signal too? Or is sound enough?"

"Sound is enough. More than enough, probably. Will you be able to hear, too?"

"If you wish, Lazarus. But you can have privacy if that is your wish."

"Stick around; I may need a referee. Put her on."

"Boss?" It was the voice of a timid little girl. It made me think of skinned knees, and no breasts as yet, and big, tragic eyes.

Lazarus answered, "Right here, baby."

"*Boss!* God damn your lousy soul to hell! – what do you *mean* by running off and not letting me know where you are? Of all the filthy flea-bitten –"

"*Pipe down!*"

The timid-little-girl voice returned. "Aye, aye, Skipper," it said uncertainly.

"Where I go and when I go and how long I stay are none of your business. Your business is to pilot and to keep house, that's all."

I heard a sniffle, exactly like a small child sniffing back tears. "Yes, Boss."

"You were supposed to be asleep. I put you to bed myself."

"Somebody woke me. A strange lady."

"That was a mistake. But you used bad language to her."

"Well... I was *scared.* I really was, Boss. I woke up and thought you had come home . . . and you weren't anywhere around, not *anywhere*. Uh . . . she told on me?"

"She conveyed your message to me. Fortunately she did not understand most of your words. But *I* did. What have I told you about being polite to strangers?"

"I'm sorry, Boss."

"Sorry doesn't get the cows milked. Now adorable Dora, you listen to me. I'm not going to punish you; you were wakened by mistake and you were scared and lonely, so we'll forget it. But you shouldn't talk that way, not to strangers. This lady – She's a friend of mine, and she wants to be your friend, too. She's a computer –"

"She *is*?"

"Just as you are, dear."

"Then she couldn't hurt me, could she? I thought she was inside me, snooping around. So I yelled for you."

"She not only couldn't, she would never want to hurt you." Lazarus raised his voice slightly. "Minerva! Come in, dear, and tell Dora who you are."

My helpmeet's voice, calm and soothing said, "I'm a computer, Dora, called 'Minerva' by my friends – and I hope you'll call me that. I'm terribly sorry I woke you. I'd be scared too, if someone woke me like that." (Minerva never has been "asleep" in the hundred-odd years she's been activated. She rests each part of herself on some schedule I don't need to know – but she herself is always awake. Or awake so instantly whenever I speak to her as not to matter.)

The ship said, "How do you do, Minerva. I'm sorry I talked the way I did."

"I don't remember it, dear, if you did. I heard your skipper say that I transmitted a message from you to him. But it's erased, now that it's been transmitted. Private message, I suppose."

(Was Minerva truth-saying? Until she came under Lazarus' influence I would have said that she did not know how to lie. Now I'm not sure.)

"I'm glad you erased it, Minerva. I'm sorry I talked to you that way. Boss is sore at me about it."

Lazarus interrupted. "Now, now, Adorable – stop it. We always let water over the bridge lie where Jesus flang it; you know that. Will you be a good girl and go back to sleep?"

"Do I have to?"

"No. You don't even have to place yourself on slow time. But I can't come to see you – or even talk to you – earlier than late tomorrow afternoon. I'm busy today and will be househunting tomorrow. You can stay awake and bore yourself silly any way you choose. But if you whomp up some fake emergency to get my attention, I'll spank you."

"But, Boss, you know I *never* do that."

"I know you *do* do that, little imp. But if you bother me for anything less than somebody trying to break into you or you catching on fire, you'll regret it. If I can figure out that you've set yourself on fire, you'll catch it twice as hard. Look, dear, why don't you at least sleep whenever I am asleep? Minerva, can you let Dora know when I go to sleep? And when I wake up?"

"Certainly, Lazarus."

"But that doesn't mean you can bother me when I'm awake, Dora, other than for real emergencies. No surpise drills – this is not ship-board routine; we're dirtside and I'm busy. Uh ... Minerva, how's your time-sharing capacity? Do you play chess?"

I put in, "Minerva has ample share-time capacity."

But before I could add that she was Secundus Champion, Unlimited Open Handicap (with a handicap of Q, Q's B, & K's R) Minerva said: "Perhaps Dora will teach me to play chess."

(Well, Minerva had certainly learned Lazarus' rule for telling the truth selectively. I made note that I must have a serious private talk with her.)

"I'd be glad to, Miss Minerva!"

Lazarus relaxed. "Fine. You gals get acquainted. So long till tomorrow, 'Dorable. Now beat it."

Minerva notified us that the yacht was no longer patched in, and Lazarus relaxed. Minerva dropped back to her record-keeping role, and kept quiet. Lazarus said apologetically, "Don't be put off by her childish manners, Ira; you won't find a sharper pilot, or a neater ship's housekeeper, between here and Galactic Centre. But I had reasons for not letting her grow up in other ways, reasons that won't apply when you take over as her master. She's a good girl, she really is. It's just that she's like a cat that jumps into your lap the instant you sit down."

"I found her charming."

"She's a spoiled brat. But it's not her fault; I am practically all the company she's ever had. I get bored by a computer that just grinds out numbers, docile as a slide rule. No company on a long trip. You wanted to speak to Ishtar. About my househunting, I think. Tell her I won't let it interfere with routine – I just want a day off, that's all."

"I'll tell her." I turned to the Administrator for Rejuvenation and shifted to Galacta – asking her how long it would take to sterilize a suite in the Palace and install decontamination equipment for watchstanders and visitors.

Before she could answer, Lazarus said, "Wups! Hold it one fiddlin' moment. I saw you palm that card, Ira."

"I beg your pardon, sir?"

"You tried to slide one in. 'Decontam' is the same word in English as in Galacta. Not that it was news to me; my sense of smell isn't that dead. When a pretty girl leans over me, I expect to smell perfume. But when I can't even smell girl and *do* smell germicides – well, *ipse dixit* and Q.E.D. Minerva!"

"Yes, Lazarus?"

"Can you spare me some shared time to give me a refresher while I'm asleep tonight in the nine hundred basic words of Galacta or whatever number it takes? You equipped for it?"

"Certainly, Lazarus."

"Thanks, dear. One night should do it, but I'll appreciate vocabulary drill each night until we both think I'm up to adequate proficiency. Can do?"

"Can do, Lazarus. And will do."

"Thanks, dear, over and out. Now, Ira, you see that door? If it doesn't open to my voice, I'm going to attempt to break it down. If I can't, I am going to check on whether or not that suicide switch is really hooked up – by trying it. Because, if that door won't open, I am a prisoner, and any promises I made on your assurances that I am a free agent are not binding. But if it *does* open to my voice, I'll bet you whatever you like that there is a decontam chamber beyond it, staffed and ready to function. Say a million crowns to keep it interesting? No, you didn't flinch; let's make it ten million crowns."

I trust that I did not flinch. I have never had that much money of my own, and a Chairman Pro Tem gets out of the habit of thinking about his own money; there is no need to. I had not asked Minerva about my personal balance for some time. Years, perhaps.

"Lazarus, I won't bet. Yes, there is a decontam setup outside; we tried to protect you from possible infection without bringing it to your attention. I see that we have failed. I haven't checked on the door –"

"Lying again, Son. You're not good at it."

"But if it isn't keyed to your voice now, it is my oversight; you've kept me busy. Minerva, if the door to this suite is not keyed to the Senior's voice, correct it immediately."

"It is keyed to his voice, Ira."

I relaxed when I heard how she phrased it – perhaps a computer that had learned when not to be bluntly truthful was going to be still more of a helpmeet.

Lazarus grinned diabolically. "So? Then I'm about to test out the super-override programme you were a bit hasty in giving her. Minerva!"

"Awaiting your orders, Senior."

"Key the door to my suite so that it opens only to my voice. I'm going out and sashay around – while Ira and these kids stay locked inside. If I am not back in half an hour, you can unlock them."

"Conflict, Ira!"

"Carry out his orders, Minerva." I tried to keep my voice low and even.

Lazarus smiled and stayed in his chair. "No need to show openers, Ira; there is nothing outside I want to see. Minerva, you can put the door back to normal – let it open to any voice, including mine. Sorry about that conflict, dear; I hope it didn't burn out anything."

"No harm done, Lazarus. When I was given that super-override instruction, I increased the overload tolerances on my problem-resolving network."

"You're a smart girl. I'll try to avoid conflict in the future, Ira, you had better remove that super-override; it's not fair to Minerva. She feels like a woman with two husbands."

"Minerva can handle it." I assured him, more calmly than I felt.

"You mean that *I* had better handle it. I shall. Did you tell Ishatar that I'm going househunting?"

"I didn't get that far. I was discussing with her the practicability of your living at the Palace."

"Now, Ira – Palaces don't appeal to me, and being a house guest is still worse. A nuisance both to host and guest. Tomorrow I'll find a residential hilton that doesn't cater to tourists or conventions. Then I'll run out to the skyport and see Dora, and pat her rump and get her calmed down. The next day or so I'll find a little house way out in the suburbs, one automated enough to be no problem – but with its own garden. Got to have a garden. I'll have to bribe somebody to move; the house I want won't be standing empty. Do you happen to know how much I still have in Harriman Trust? If anything."

"I don't know but that's no problem. Minerva, set up a drawing account for the Senior. Unlimited."

"Acknowledged, Ira. Completed."

"Completion noted. Lazarus, you would *not* be a nuisance. Nor will you find it palatial as long as you avoid the public rooms. As I always do. Nor will you be anyone's guest. It's called the 'Executive Palace,' but its official name is 'The Chairman's House.' You will be in residence in your own home. *I* will be the guest, if anyone."

"Hogwash, Ira."

"True, Lazarus."

"Quit juggling words. I would still be a stranger in a household not truly my own. A guest. I don't buy it."

"Lazarus, you said – last night" – I remembered just in time the missing day – "that you can always do business with anyone who is acting in his own interest and says so."

"I think I said 'usually' rather than always" – meaning that we could then look for a way that would serve both of our self-interests."

"Then hear me out. You've got me tied down with this Scheherazade bet. As well as a research to find something new to interest you. Now you've dangled bait under my nose that makes me want to migrate as soon as – well, as soon as possible; it won't take long for the Trustees to turn me down concerning a migration of the Families. Grandfather, it's nuisance enough to chase over here every day; I don't hanker to trek way out into the boondocks, the commuting would waste what little time you have left me for work. Besides that, its dangerous."

"Living alone? Ira, I've lived alone many times."

"Dangerous for *me*. Assassins. I'm safe at the Palace; the rat who can find his way through that maze hasn't been born. I'm reasonably safe here inside the Clinic, and I can get back and forth in safety, subject only to whims of automatic machinery. But if I make a daily pattern of going to an unfortified house somewhere out in the suburbs, then it is only a matter of time until some crackpot sees it as an opportunity to save the world by picking me off. Oh, he would not live through it; my guards aren't that inefficient. But if I persist in setting myself up as a target, he might get me before they get him. No, Grandfather, I do not choose to be assassinated."

The Senior looked thoughtful but not impressed. "I could answer that your safety and convenience have to do with *your* self-interest. Not mine."

"True," I admitted. "But let me offer what bait I can. It's in my self-interest for you to live in the Palace. There I can visit you in perfect safety, even safer than I am here, and commuting becomes a matter of seconds, negligible. I can even ask you – there – to excuse me for a half hour if something urgent comes up. That defines *my* self-interest. As for yours, sir – would you be interested in a bachelor's cottage, rather small – four rooms – and not especially modern or luxurious but set in a pleasant garden? Three hectares, but only the part close to the house is gardened, the rest has been allowed to grow wild."

"What's the catch, Ira? How modern is 'not especially'? I did say 'automated' – as I am not yet in shape to do for myself – nor am I patient with the vagaries of servants or the whimsical uncertainties of robots."

"Oh, this cottage is sufficiently automated; it simply does not have a lot of fancy extravagances. No servants needed if your tastes are simple. Would you permit the Clinic to continue to stand watches on you if the watchstanders are as pleasant, and as pleasantly unobtrusive as these two?"

"Eh? These kids are all right, I like them. I realize that the Clinic wants to keep an eye on me; they probably feel that I'm more of a challenge than a client only three or four hundred years old. That's okay. But you pass the word that I expect to smell perfume, not germicides. Or reasonably fresh body odours; I'm not fussy. I repeat, what's the catch?"

"The hell you aren't fussy, Lazarus; you delight in thinking up impossible conditions. This cottage is rather cluttered with old-fashioned books; the last tenant was eccentric. Did I mention a little steam running through the grounds, one which opens out into a small pool near the house? – not much, but you can take a few strokes on it. Oh, I forgot to mention an old tomcat who thinks he owns the place. But you probably won't see him; he hates most people."

"I won't bother him if he wants to be left alone; cats make good neighbours. You still haven't answered me."

"The catch is this, Lazarus. I've been describing the penthouse I had built for my own use on the roof of the Palace, some ninety years back when I decided to keep this job awhile. It can be reached only by vertical transport from my usual quarters a couple of stories below it. I've never had time to use it much; you are welcome to it." I stood up. "But if you won't take it, then you can consider that I've lost the Scheherazade bet, and you are free to use that termination switch whenever you please. For I'm damned if I'll be a sitting duck for assassination just to cater to your whims."

"Sit back down!"

"No thank you. I've made a reasonable offer. If you won't take it, you can go to hell in your own way. I won't let you ride my shoulders like the Old Man of the Sea. I can be pushed just so far."

"So I see. How much of your ancestry am I?"

"About thirteen per cent. Considerable convergence."

"Only that much? I would have guessed more. Some ways you sound like my Gramp. Does my suicide switch go along?"

"If you want it," I answered as indifferently as I could manage to sound. "Or you can jump off the edge. It's a long drop."

"I prefer the switch, Ira; I'd hate to change my mind on the way down. Will you fix me up with another transport so that I won't have to go through your apartment?"

"No."

"Eh? Is it all that difficult? Let's ask Minerva."

"It's not that I *can't* – I *won't*. It's an unreasonable request. If won't hurt you to change transports in my foyer. Didn't I make it clear that I am not catering to any more unreasonable whims?"

"Get your feathers down, Son. I accept. Tomorrow, say. Never mind moving that clutter of books; I like old-fashioned bound books; they have more flavour than speedireads, or projectors, or such. And I'm pleased to find that you're a rat and not a mouse. Please sit down."

I did so, pretending reluctance I was beginning to gain some grasp of Lazarus. Despite the way he sneered at them the old scoundrel was an equalitarian at heart . . . and expressed it by attempting to dominate anyone with whom he came into contact – but was contemptuous of anyone who knuckled under to his bullying. So the only answer was to hit back at him, try to maintain a balance of power – and hope that in time it would reach the stability of mutual respect.

I never had cause to change my mind. He was capable of kindness and even affection toward one who accepted a subordinate role – if that person was a child or a female. But he preferred spunk even from them. A grown male who bent the knee he neither liked nor trusted.

I think this quirk in his character made him very lonely.

Presently the Senior said musingly, "Be nice to live in a house for a while. With a garden. Maybe with a spot where I can stretch a hammock."

"Several such spots."

"But I'm doing you out of your hideaway."

"Lazarus, there is enough room on that roof that I could have another cottage assembled out of your sight. If I wanted it. I don't. I haven't been up there for a swim in weeks. It has been at least a year since I slept up there."

"Well – I hope you'll feel free to come up and swim. Any time. Or whatever."

"I expect to be up there every day and all day, for the next thousand days. Have you forgotten our bet?"

"Oh, that. Ira, you were bitching that my whimsical ways were wasting your valuable time. Do you want to be let off the hook? Not on the other, just on that."

I laughed at him. "Straighten your kilt, Lazarus, your self-interest is showing. Meaning *you* want to be let off the hook. No deal. I intend to get one thousand and one days of your memoirs on record. After that you can jump off the edge, or drown yourself in the pool, or whatever. But I won't let you welch by pretending to do me a favour. I'm beginning to understand you."

"You are? That's more than I've ever managed. When you get me figured out, tell me about me; I'll be interested. That search for something new, Ira – You said you had started it."

"I didn't say that, Lazarus."

"Well, perhaps you just implied it."

"Nor even that. Want to bet? We can ask Minerva for a full printout, then I'll accept your verdict."

"Let's not tempt a lady into fudging the record, Ira; she's loyal to you, not to me. Despite any super-duper-overrides."

"Chicken."

"At every opportunity, Ira; how do you think I've lived so long? I bet only when I'm certain to win or when losing serves my actual purpose. All right, when are you starting that research?"

"I've already started it."

"But you said – No, you didn't. Damn your impudence, boy. All right, what direction are you pushing it?"

"All directions."

"Impossible. You don't have that many people at your disposal, even assuming that all of them are capable – whereas the person capable of creative thought is less than one in a thousand."

"No argument. But what about the sort of person that you said was just like us – but magnified? Minerva is director of research on this, Lazarus. I talked it over with her; she's setting it up. All directions. A Zwicky investigation."

"Hmm. Well . . . yes. She could – I *think* she could. Whereas even Andy Libby might have found it difficult. How is she designing her morphological box?"

"I don't know. Shall we ask her?"

"Only if she's ready to be asked, Ira. People get annoyed when interrupted for progress reports. Even Andy Libby used to get irritable if anyone joggled his elbow."

"Even the great Libby probably didn't have the time-share capacity Minerva has. Most brains are merely linear, and I've never heard of any human genius who had more than three tracks."

"Five."

"So? Well, you've met more geniuses than I have. But I don't know how many simultaneous tracks Minerva can set up; I simply have never seen her overloaded. Let's ask her. Minerva, have you set up the morpho box for that search for 'something new' for the Senior?"

"Yes, Ira."

"Tell us about it."

"The preliminary matrix uses five dimensions, but with a certainty that auxiliary dimensions will be needed for some pigeonholes. That being noted, there are now nine by five by thirteen by eight by seventy-three – or three hundred forty-one thousand six hundred forty discrete category pockets before auxiliary expansions. For check, the original trinary readout is unit pair pair comma unit pair pair comma unit nil nil point nil. Shall I print out decimal and trinary expressions?"

"I think not, Little Nag; the day you make a mistake in arithmetic, I'll have to resign. Lazarus?"

"I'm not interested in pigeonholes, just what is in them. Hit any pay dirt, Minerva?"

"As stated, Lazarus, your question does not permit specific answer. Shall I print out the categories for your examination?"

"Uh – *No!* Over three hundred thousand categories and maybe a dozen words to define each one? We'd be hip-deep in paper." Lazarus looked thoughtful. "Ira, you might ask Minerva to print it somewhere else before she wipes it. As a book. A *big* Book, ten or fifteen volumes. You could call it 'Varieties of Human Experience,' by, uh, 'Minerva Weatheral.' It would be the sort of thing professors argue over for a thousand years. I'm not joking, Ira; it *should* be preserved, I think it's new. It's a job too big for flesh-and-blood, and I sort o' doubt that a computer of Minerva's calibre has ever before been asked to do this sort of Zwicky."

"Minerva, would you like that? Preserve your research notes and edit them into a book? Say a few hundred full-size bound copies in a handsome presentation format plus microperms for libraries on Secundus and elsewhere. For the Archives, too – I could ask Justin Foote to write a preface."

I was intentionally appealing to her vanity – and if you think computers don't have such human foibles, then I suggest that your next experience with them is limited; Minerva always liked to be appreciated, and we two began to be a team only after I realized this. What else can you offer a machine? Higher pay and longer vacations? Let's not be silly.

But she surprised me still again, answering in a voice almost as shy as Lazarus' yacht, and quite formally: "Mr. Chairman Pro Tem, would it be proper, and would you grant permission, for me to put on the title page 'by Minerva *Weatheral*'?"

I said, "Why, certainly. Unless you would rather sign it just 'Minerva.'"

Lazarus said brusquely, "Don't be a dumb fool, Son. Dear, sign that title page 'Minerva *L.* Weatheral.' The 'L' stands for 'Long' – because you, Ira, had a woodscolt by one of my daughters on some frontier planet back in the careless days of your youth and just recently got around to registering the fact in the Archives. I'll attest the registration – happens I was there at the time. But Dr. Minerva L. Weatheral is now off somewhere way the hell and gone out, doing research for her next magnum opus – can't be reached for an interview. Ira, you and I will whip up biographical notes for my distinguished granddaughter. Got it?"

I simply answered Yes.

"That suit you, girl?"

"Yes indeed, Lazarus. Grandfather Lazarus."

"Don't bother calling me 'Grandfather.' But I want the number-one presentation copy inscribed to me, dear – 'To my Grandfather Lazarus Long, with love, Minerva L. Weatheral.' Is it a deal?"

"I will be proud and happy to do so, Lazarus. An inscription should be in handwriting, should it not? I can modify the extensional I use to sign official papers for Ira – a mod so that the inscription handwriting will be different from his handwriting."

"Fine. If Ira behaves himself, you might consider dedicating a book to him and inscribe a copy to him. But *I* get the first copy. I'm senior – and I thought it up. But back to the search itself – I'm never going to read that twenty-volume opus, Minerva; I'm interested only in results. So tell me what you have so far."

"Lazarus, I have tentatively rejected over half the matrix as representing things the Archives show that you have done, or things that I assume that you would not wish to do –"

"Hold it! As the marine said, 'If I haven't done it, I'll try it.' What are these things you assume I wouldn't want to try? Let's hear 'em."

"Yes, sir. One submatrix, three thousand six hundred fifty pockets, all involve a probably fatal outcome, probability ninety-nine per cent plus. First, exploring in corpus the interior of a star –"

"Scratch that one, I'll leave that to physicists. Besides, Lib and I did it once."

"The Archives did not show it, Lazarus."

"Lots of things not in the Archives. Go on."

"Modification of your genetic pattern to grow an amphibious clone capable of living in ocean waters."

"I'm not sure I'm that interested in fish. What's the catch?"

"Three catches, Lazarus, each hazardous by less than ninety-nine per cent but, when taken in series, total almost unity. Such pseudo-human amphibians have been grown, but the viable ones – thus far – strongly resemble very large frogs. The chances of survival of such a creature against other denizens of the deep – figured for Secundis – have been theoretically calculated as even for seventeen days, twenty-five per cent for thirty-four days, and so on."

"I think I could improve those odds. But I never have cared much for Russian roulette. The other hazards?"

"Installing your brain in the modified clone, then reinserting it into a normal clone at a later time. If you survived."

"Scratch that one. If I have to live underwater, I don't want to be a frog; I want to be the biggest, meanest shark in the ocean. Besides, I figure that, if living underwater was all that interesting, we would still be there. Give me another sample."

"A triple sample, sir. Lost in n-space with a ship, without a ship but with a suit, and without even a suit."

"Scratch 'em all. I've come closer than I like to think to the first two, and the third is just a silly way to drown in vacuum. Thin and unpleasant. Minerva, the All Powerful in His Majestic Wisdom – whatever that means – made it possible for humans to die peacefully. That being so, unless one is forced to, it is silly to do it the hard way. So scratch drowning in caterpillars and self-immolation and all silly ways to die. Very well, dear; you've convinced me that you know what you're talking about concerning those ninety-nine-plus hazards; scratch 'em all. I'm interested only in something *new* – new to me – in which the chances of surviving are better than fifty per cent and in which a man who stays alert can enhance his chances. For example, I never hankered to go over high falls in a barrel. You can design the barrel to make it relatively safe; nevertheless, once you start, you are helpless. Which makes it a silly stunt – unless it's the safest way out of a worse predicament. Racing – cars, steeplechases, skis – is more interesting because each calls for skill. Yet I don't fancy that sort of danger, either. Danger for the sake of danger is for children who don't really believe they can be killed. Whereas I *know* I can be. So there are a lot of mountains I'll never climb. Unless I'm trapped, in which case I'll do it – have *done* it! – the easiest, safest, most chicken way I can figure out. Don't bother with *anything* in which the prime novelty is danger – danger is no novelty. It is simply something to be faced when you can't run. How about other pigeonholes in your box?"

"Lazarus, you could become female."

"*Eh?*"

I do not think I have ever seen the Senior quite so startled. (So was I, but the statement was not aimed at me.)

He went on slowly, "Minerva, I'm not sure what you mean. Surgeons have been turning inadequate males into fake females for more than two thousand years – and females into fake males almost as long. I'm not attracted by such stunts. For good – or bad – I am male. I suppose that every human has wondered how it would feel to be the other sex. But all the plastic surgery and hormone treatments possible won't do it – those monsters don't reproduce."

"I am not speaking of monsters, Lazarus. A true change in sex."

"Mmm – You remind me of a tale I had almost forgotten. Not sure it's true. About a man, oh, must have been around 2000 A.D. Couldn't be much later because things went to pieces not long after. Supposed to have had his brain moved into a female body. Killed him, of course. Alien tissue rejection."

"Lazarus, this would not involve that hazard; it would be done with your own clone."

"Not bloody likely. Keep talking."

"Lazarus, this has been tested on animals other that H. sapiens. It works best in changing a male to a female. A single cell is selected for cloning. Before cloning is started, the Y chromosome is removed and an X chromosome from a second cell of the same zygote is supplied, thus creating a female cell of the same genetic pattern as the zygote save that the X chromosome is replicated while the Y chromosome is eliminated. The modified cell is then cloned. The result is a true female clone-zygote derived from a male original."

"There must be a catch," Lazarus said, frowning.

"There may be, Lazarus. Certain it is that the basic technique works. There are several created females in the building you are in – dogs, cats, one sow, others – and most of them have littered successfully . . . except when, for example, a derived bitch is bred with the male dog who supplied the cell for cloning. That can produce lethals and monstrosities from the high probability of reinforcing bad recessives –"

"I should think it would!"

"Yes. But normal outbreeding does not, as indicated by seventy three generations of hamsters descended from one created female. The method has not been adapted to fauna native to Secundus because of their radically different genetic structure."

"Never mind Secundus animals – how about *men?*"

"Lazarus, I have been able to search the literature only on items released by the Rejuvenation Clinic. The published literature hints at problems in the last stage – activating the female clone-zygot with the memories and experiences – the 'personality' if you prefer that term – of the parent male. When to terminate the parent male – or whether to terminate it at all – suggests several problems. But I am unable to say what research has been suppressed."

Lazarus turned to me. "Do you permit that Ira? Suppression of research?"

"I don't interfere, Lazarus. But I didn't know this research was going on. Let's find out." I turned to the Administrator for Rejuvenation, shifted to Galacta, and explained what we had been discussing and asked what progress had been made with humans.

I turned back with my ears burning. As soon as I mentioned humans in this connection, she had interrupted me abruptly – as if I has said something offensive – and stated that such experimentation was proscribed.

I translated her answer. Lazarus nodded. "I read the kid's face; I could see the answer was No. Well, Minerva, that seems to be that. I am not about to attempt chromosome surgery on myself – somebody swiped my jacknife."

"Perhaps that is not quite the end," Minerva replied. "Ira, did you notice that Ishtar said only that such research was 'proscribed?' She did *not* say that it had not taken place. I have just made a most thorough semantic analysis of the published literature for truth-and-falsity implications. I conclude that the probability approaches certainty that much pertinent research on humans *has* taken place even though it may no longer be going on. Do you wish to order it released, sir? I am certain that I can freeze their computer quickly enough to prevent erasure, assuming that an erasure programme guards it."

"Let's not do anything drastic," drawled Lazarus. "There may be good reason for a 'hold' on this stuff. I'm forced to assume that these johnnies know more about it than I do. Besides, I'm not sure I want to be a guinea pig. Let's put it on the back of the fire, Minerva. Ira, I'm not sure I would be *me* without my Y chromosome. To say nothing of those jolly hints of how you transfer the personality and at what point to kill off the male. *Me*, that is."

"Lazarus –"

"Yes, Minerva?"

"The published literature makes one option both certain and safe. This method can be used to create your twin sister – identical rather than fraternal, save for sex. A host mother is indicated, with no forcing to maturity, since the brain would be allowed to develop normally. Would this meet your standards of newness and interest? To watch yourself grow up as a woman? 'Lazuli Long,' you might name her – your female other self."

"Uh –" Lazarus stopped.

I said dryly, "Grandfather, I think I've won our second bet. Something new. Something interesting."

"Now slow up! *You* can't do it, you don't know how. Nor do I. And the Director of this madhouse appears to have moral scruples about it –"

"We don't know that. Mere inference."

"Not so 'mere.' And *I* may have moral scruples. 'Twouldn't

interest me unless I stuck around and watched her grow up . . . which might send me crazy either through trying to make her grow up just like me – what a fate for any girl – or by trying to keep her from growing up as ornery as I am when that would be her nature. Nor would I be justified either way; she would be a separate human being, not my slave. Besides that, I would be her sole parent – no mother. I've had one crack at trying to raise a daughter alone – it's not fair to the girl."

"You're inventing objections, Lazarus. I'll give long odds that Ishtar would gladly be both host mother and foster mother. Especially if you promised Ishtar a son of her own. Shall I ask her?"

"You keep your biscuit trap shut, Son! Minerva, place that on 'pending' – I won't be hurried into a major decision about another person. Especially one who isn't, quite. Ira, remind me to tell you about the twins who were no relation to each other. But twins."

"Preposterous. You're changing the subject."

"So I am. Minerva, what else do you have, girl?"

"Lazarus, I have one programme which involves low hazard and a probability approaching certainty of supplying one – or more – experiences completely new to you."

"I'm listening."

"Suspended animation –"

"What's new about that? We had that when I was a kid, hardly two hundred years old. Used it in the 'New Frontiers.' Didn't attract me then, doesn't now."

"– as a means of time travel. If you stipulate that in X number of years, something truly new will develop – a certainty based on history – then your only problem is to select whatever span of years will, in your opinion, produce the degree of novelty you seek. One hundred years, one thousand, ten thousand, whatever you say. The rest involves nothing but minor design details."

"Not so 'minor' if I'm going to be asleep and unable to protect myself."

"But you need not go into hibernation until you are satisfied with my design, Lazarus. A hundred years is obviously no problem. A thousand years is not much problem. For ten thousand years I would design an artificial planetoid equipped with fail-safes to insure that you would be revived automatically in case of emergency."

"That would take quite some designing, girl."

"I feel confident of my capacity to do it, Lazarus, but you are free to criticize and reject any part of it. However, there is no point in my submitting preliminary designs until you give me the controlling parameter, namely the time span, which in your opinion will produce something new to you. Or do you wish my advice on that?"

"Uh . . . hold your horses, dear. Let's assume that you've got me in liquid helium and in free fall and thoroughly protected against ionizing radiation –"

"No problem, Lazarus."

"So I stipulated, dear; I'm not underrating you. But suppose some tiny little fail-safe fails null instead and I go on snoozing through the centuries – and millennia – without end. Not dead. But not revived, either."

"I can and will design to avoid that. But let me accent your stipulation. In such case, how would you be worse off than you would be if you used your termination-option switch? What do you lose by trying this?"

"Why, that's obvious! If there is anything to this immortality talk – or any sort of afterlife – I'm not saying there is or isn't – but if there *is*, then when the 'Roll Is Called Up Yonder,' I won't be there. I'll be asleep but not dead, somewhere off in space. I'll miss the last boat."

"Grandfather," I said impatiently, "quit trying to wiggle out. If you don't want it, just say No. But Minerva has certainly offered you a way to reach something new. If there is anything to your argument – which I don't admit – you will have achieved something *really* unique: the only human being out of many billions to fail to show up for muster on this hypothetical-and-highly-unlikely Judgement Day. I wouldn't put it past you, you old scoundrel; you're slippery."

He ignored my slur. "Why 'highly unlikely'?"

"Because it *is*. I won't argue it."

"Because you *can't* argue it," he retorted. "There isn't any evidence for or against – so how can you assign even a loose probability either way? I was pointing out the desirability, if there happens to be anything to it, of playing it kosher. Minerva, hold that under 'pending,' too. The idea has everything you claim for it, and I don't doubt your ability as a designer. But, like testing a parachute, it's a one-way trip with no chance to change my mind after I jump. So we'll look over all other ideas before falling back on that one – even if it takes years."

"I will continue, Lazarus."

"Thanks, Minerva." Lazarus looked thoughtful as he picked his teeth with a thumbnail – we were eating, but I have not mentioned breaks for refreshment, nor will I again. You may assume any food and rest breaks that make you feel comfortable. Like Scheherazade's tales, the Senior's anecdotes were chopped up by many irrelevant interruptions.

"Lazarus –"

"Eh, Son? I was day dreaming . . . of a far country and the wench is dead. Sorry."

"You could help Minerva in this search."

"So? Seems unlikely. She's better equipped to conduct a needle-in-a-haystack search than I am – she impresses me."

"Yes. But she needs data. There are these great gaps in what we know about you. If we knew – if Minerva knew – those fifty-odd professions you've followed, she might be able to cancel several thousand possibility pockets. For example, have you ever been a farmer?"

"Several times."

"So? Now that she knows that, she won't suggest anything relating to agriculture. While there may be sorts of farming you have never done, none would be novel enough to meet your stringent requirements. Why not list the things you have done?"

"Doubt if I can remember them all."

"That can't be helped. But listing what you do remember may call to mind others."

"Uh . . . let me think. One thing I always did every time I reached an inhabited planet was to study law. Not to practice – not usually, although for a number of years I was a very criminal lawyer – on San Andreas, that was. But to understand the ground rules. Hard to show a profit – or to conceal one – if you don't know how the game is played. It's much safer to break a law knowingly than to do so through ignorance.

"But that backfired once and I wound up as High Justice of a planetary Supreme Court – just in time to save my bacon. And neck.

"Let me see. Farmer, and lawyer, and judge, and I told you I had practised medicine. Skipper of many sorts of craft, mostly for exploration but sometimes for cargo or migrant transport – and once an armed privateer with a crew of rogues you wouldn't take home to mother. Schoolteacher – lost that job when they caught me teaching the kids the raw truth, a capital offence anywhere in the Galaxy. In the slave trade once but from underneath – I was a slave."

I blinked at that. "I can't imagine it."

"Unfortunately I didn't have to imagine it. Priest –"

I had to interrupt again. " 'Priest? Lazarus, you said, or implied that you had no religious faith of any sort."

"Did I? But 'faith' is for the congregation, Ira; it handicaps a priest. Professor in a parlour house –"

"Excuse me again. Idiomatic usage?"

"Eh? Manager of a bordello . . . although I did play the pianette a little, and sang. Don't laugh; I had a pretty good singing voice then. This was on Mars – you've heard of Mars?"

"Next planet out from Old Home Terra. Sol Four."

"Yes. Not a planet we'd bother with today. But this was before Andy Libby changed things. It was even before China destroyed Europe but after America dropped out of the spacing business, which left me stranded. I left Earth after that meeting of 2012 and didn't go back for a spell – which saved me much unpleasantness. I shouldn't complain. If that meeting had gone the other way – No, I'm wrong; when a fruit is ripe, it will fall, and the United States was rotten ripe. Don't ever become a pessimist Ira; a pessimist is correct oftener than an optimist, but an optimist has more fun – and neither can stop the march of events.

"But we were speaking of Mars and the job I had there. A fill-in job for coffee and cakes – but pleasant, as I was also the bouncer. The girls were all nice girls, and it was a pleasure to throw out some slob who was misbehaving toward them. Throw him so hard he bounced. Then blacklist him so he couldn't come back. One or two like that every evening and the word got round that 'Happy' Daze demanded gentlemanly behaviour toward the ladies, no matter how big a spender a man was.

"Whoring is like military service, Ira – okay in the upper brackets, not so good lower down. These girls were constantly getting offers to buy up their contracts and get married – and all of them did get married, I think, but they were making money so fast that they weren't anxious to grab the first offer. Mainly because, when I took over, I put a stop to the fixed price the governor of the colony had set, and reinstated the Law of Supply and Demand. There was no reason why those kids shouldn't charge every ruble the traffic would bear.

"Had trouble over that until the Governor's Provost for Rest and Culture got it through his thick head that slave wages won't work in a scarcity situation. Mars was unpleasant enough without trying to cheat those few who made it tolerable. Or even delightful when they were happy in their work. Whores perform the same function as priests, Ira, but far more thoroughly.

"Let me see – I've been wealthy many times and always lost it, usually through governments inflating the money, or confiscating – 'nationalizing' or 'liberating' – something I owned. 'Put not your faith in princes,' Ira; since they don't produce, they always steal. I've been broke even oftener than I've been wealthy. Of the two, being broke is more interesting, as a man who doesn't know where his next meal is coming from is never bored. He may be angry or several other things – but *not* bored. His predicament sharpens his thoughts, spurts him into action, adds zest to his life, whether he knows it or not. Can trap him, of course; that's why food is the usual bait for traps. But that's the intriguing part about being broke: how to solve it *without* being trapped. A hungry man tends to lose his judgement – a man who has missed seven meals is often ready to kill – rarely a solution.

"Advertising copywriter, actor – but I was *very* broke that time – acolyte, contruction engineer and several other sorts, and even more sorts of mechanic, for I've always believed that an intelligent man can turn his hand to *anything* if he will take time to learn how it works. Not that I insisted on skilled work when my next meal was at stake; I've often pushed an idiot stick –"

"Idiom?"

"An old gandy-dancer expression, Son, a stick with a shovel blade on one end and an idiot on the other. I was never that for more than a few days, just long enough to sort out the local setup. Political manager – I was even a reform politician once . . . but *only* once: Reform politicians not only tend to be dishonest but *stupidly* dishonest – whereas the business politician is honest."

"I don't see that Lazarus. History seems to show –"

"Use your head, Ira. I don't mean that a business politician won't steal; stealing is his business. But *all* politicians are non-productive. The only commodity any politician has to offer is jawbone. His personal integrity – meaning, if he gives his word, can you rely on it? A successful business politician knows this and guards his reputation for sticking by his commitments – because he wants to stay in business – go on stealing, that is – not only this week but next year and years after that. So if he's smart enough to be successful at this very exacting trade, he can have the morals of a snapping turtle, but he performs in such a way as not to jeopardize the only thing he has to sell, his reputation for keeping promises.

"But a reform politician has no such lodestone. His devotion is to the welfare of all the people – an abstraction of very high order and therefore capable of endless definitions. If indeed it can be defined in meaningful terms. In consequence your utterly sincere and incorruptible reform politician is capable of breaking his word three times before breakfast – not from personal dishonesty, as he sincerely regrets the necessity and will tell you so – but from unswerving devotion to his ideal.

"All it takes to get him to break his word is for someone to get his ear and convince him that it is necessary for the greater good of *all* the peepul. He'll geek.

"After he gets hardened to this, he's capable of cheating at solitaire. Fortunately he rarely stays in office long – except during the decay and fall of a culture."

I said, "I must take your word for it, Lazarus. Since I have spent most of my life on Secundus, I know little of politics other than theoretically. You set it up that way."

The Senior fixed me with a stare of cold scorn. "I did no such thing."

"But –"

"Oh, hush. You are a politician yourself – a 'business' politician I hope – but that stunt of transporting your dissidents gives me doubts. Minerva! 'Notebook,' dear. My intention in deeding Secundus to the Foundation was to set up a cheap and simple government – a constitutional tyranny. One in which the government was forbidden to do most things . . . and the dear people, bless their black flabby little hearts, were given no voice at all.

"I didn't have much hope for it. Man is a political animal, Ira. You can no more keep him from politicking than you can keep him from copulating – and probably shouldn't try. But I was young then, and hopeful. I hoped to keep politicking in the private sphere, keep it out of government. I thought the setup might last a century or so; I'm amazed that it has lasted as long as it has. Not good. This planet is overripe for revolution – and if Minerva doesn't find me something better to do, I might show up under another name, with my hair dyed and my nose bobbed, and start one. So be warned, Ira."

I shrugged. "You forget I'm migrating."

"Ah, yes. Though the prospect of suppressing a revolution

might change your mind. Or perhaps you would like to be my chief of staff – then displace me with a coup d'état after the shooting is over and send me to the guillotine. That would be something new – I've never tended to lose my head over politics. Doesn't leave much for an encore, does it? 'A tisket, a tasket, a head in a basket – it cannot reply to questions you ask it.' Final curtain, no bows.

"But revolutions can be fun. Did I tell you how I worked my way through college? Operating a Gatling gun* for five dollars a day and loot. Never got higher than corporal because each time I had enough money for another semester, I deserted – and, being a mercenary, I was never tempted to become a dead hero. But adventure and change of scene are appealing to a young man . . . and I was very young.

"But dirt, and missing meals, and the *wheet* of bullets past your ears stop being glamorous as you grow up; the next time I was in the military – not entirely my idea – I chose the Navy instead. Wet Navy, although I was space Navy at later times and under other names.

"I've sold almost everything – except slaves – and worked as a mind-reader in a travelling show, and was a king once – a much overrated profession, the hours are too long – and designed women's styles under a phony French name and accent and with my hair long. Almost the only time I've worn long hair, Ira; not only does long hair need a lot of time-wasting care, it gives your opponent something to grab in close combat and can obscure your view at a critical moment – either one can be fatal. But I don't favour a billiard-ball cut because a thick mat of hair – not so long as to fall over your eyes – can save you a nasty scalp wound."

Lazarus appeared to stop to think. "Ira, I don't see how I can list all the things I've done to support myself and my wives and kids, even if I could remember them. The longest I ever stuck to one job was about half a century – very special circumstances – and the shortest was from after breakfast to just before lunch – again, special circumstances. But no matter where or what, there are makers, takers, and fakers. I prefer the first category but I

*The Gatling gun (Richard J. Gatling, 1818–1903) was obsolete by the time Lazarus Long was born. This allegation is barely possible if one stipulates that an obsolete weapon might be used in some small, out-of-the-way insurrection.

J.F. 45th

haven't spurned the other two. Whenever I was a family man – usually, that is – I haven't let compunctions stop me from keeping food on the table. I won't steal another child's food to feed my own – but there is always some way of not too sickeningly fake to garner valuta if a man isn't too picky – which I never was whenever I had family obligations.

"You can sell things which have no intrinsic value, such as stories or songs – I've worked every branch of the entertainment profession . . . including a time in the capital of Fatima when I squatted in the marketplace with a brass bowl in front of me telling a story longer than this one, and waiting at cliff-hangers for the clink of a coin.

"I was reduced to that because my ship had been confiscated and foreigners weren't permitted to work without a permit – a high squeeze on the theory that jobs should be reserved for local citizens, there being a depression. Telling stories without a fee wasn't classed as work, nor was it begging – which required a licence – and cops let me alone as long as I volunteered the customary daily gift to the Police Benevolent Fund.

"It was either get by with some such dodge or be reduced to stealing – difficult in a culture in which one is not sophisticated in the local customs. Still, I would have risked it save that I had a wife and three small children. That hobbled me, Ira; a family man should not take risks that a bachelor finds acceptable.

"So I sat there till my tailbone wore through the cobblestones, recounting everything from Grimm's fairy tales to Shakespeare's plays, and not letting my wife spend money on anything but food until we saved enough to buy that work permit plus the customary cumshaw. Then I clobbered 'em, Ira."

"How, Lazarus?"

"Slowly but thoroughly. Those months in the marketplace had given me a degree of sophistication in the 'Who:Whom' of that society and what its sacred cows were. Then I stayed on for years – no choice. But first I was baptised into the local religion, gaining a more acceptable name in the process, and memorized the Qur'an. Not quite the same Qur'an I had known some centuries earlier, but it was worth the effort.

"I'll skip over how I got into the tinkers guild and got my first job repairing television receivers – had my pay docked to cover my contribution to the guild, that is, with a private arrangement to the Grand Master Tinker, not too expensive. This society was retarded in technology; its customs didn't encourage progress, and they had slipped behind what they had fetched from Earth about five centuries earlier. That made me a wizard, Ira, and could have got me hanged had I not been careful to be a faithful – and openhanded – son of the church. So once I got into position for it, I peddled fresh electronics and stale astrology – using knowledge they didn't have for one and free imagination for the other.

"Eventually I was chief stooge to the very official who had confiscated my ship and trade goods years earlier, and I was helping him get richer while getting rich myself. If he recognized me, he never said so – a beard changes my looks quite a lot. Unfortunately he fell into disfavour and I wound up with his job."

"How did you work that, Lazarus? Without being caught, I mean?"

"Now, now, Ira! He was my benefactor. It said so in my contract and I always addressed him as such. Allah's ways are mysterious. I cast a horoscope for him, warning him that his stars were in bad shape. And so they were. That system is one of the few I know of with two usable planets around the same star, both colonized and with trade between them. Artifacts and slaves –"

" 'Slaves,' Lazarus? While I am aware of such a practice on Supreme, I didn't think that vice was very common. Not economic."

The old man closed his eyes, kept them closed so long I thought he had fallen asleep (he often did during the early days of these talks). Then he opened them and spoke very grimly:

"Ira, this vice is far more common than historians usually mention. Uneconomic, yes – a slave society can't compete with a free one. But with the Galaxy as wide as it is, there is usually no such competition. Slavery can and *does* exist many times and place, whenever the laws are rigged to permit it.

"I said that I would do almost anything to support my wives and kids – and I have; I have shovelled human excrement for a pittance, standing in it up to my knees, rather than let a child go hungry. But this I will not touch. Nor is it because I was once a slave myself; I have *always* felt this way. Call it a 'belief' or dignify it as a deep moral conviction. Whatever it is, for me it is beyond argument. If the human animal has any value at all, he is too valuable to be property. If he has any inner dignity, he is much too proud to own other men. I don't give a damn how scrubbed and perfumed he may be, a slaveowner is subhuman.

"But this does not mean that I'll cut my throat when I run into it, or I would not have lived through my first century. For there is another bad thing about slavery, Ira; it is impossible to free slaves, they have to free themselves."

Lazarus scowled. "You've got me preaching again and about matters I can't possibly prove. Once I got my hands on my ship, I had it fumigated and checked it over myself and had it loaded with items I thought I could sell and had food and water taken on for the human cargo it had been refitted for, and sent the captain and crew on a week's leave, and notified the Protector of Servants – the state slave factor, that is – that we would load as soon as the skipper and purser were back.

"Then I took my family on a holiday inspection of the ship. Somehow the Protector of Servants was suspicious; he insisted on touring the ship with us. So we had to take him along when we took off from there, very suddenly, shortly after my family was aboard. Right out of that system and never went back. But before we put down on a civilized planet, me and my boys – two almost grown by then – removed any sign that she had ever been a slaver, even though it mean jettisoning stuff I could have sold."

"What about the Protector of Servants?" I asked. "Wasn't he some trouble to you?"

"Wondered if you would notice that. I *spaced* the bastard! Alive. He went thataway, eyes popped out and peeing blood. What did you expect me to do? Kiss him?"

COUNTERPOINT III

Once they reached the privacy of a transport Galahad said to Ishtar, "Were you serious in your proposal to the Senior? To have progeny by him?"

"How could I be joking? – in the presence of two witnesses, one of them the Chairman Pro Tem himself."

"I didn't see how you could be. But *why*, Ishtar?"

"Because I'm a sentimental atavist!"

"Do you have to snap at me?"

She put an arm around his shoulders, took his hand with her free hand. "I'm sorry, dear. It had been a long day . . . and not much sleep last night, sweet as it was. I'm worried about several things – and the subject you brought up is not one I can be unemotional about."

"I should not have asked. An invasion of privacy – I don't know what's got into me. Shall we wipe the matter? Please?"

"Dear, dear! I do know what got into me . . . and that's part of why I am so unprofessionally emotional. Let me put it this way: If you were female, wouldn't you jump at a chance to make such a proposal? To *him?*"

"I'm not female."

"I know you're not, you're delightfully male. But try for a moment to be as logical as a female. *Try!*"

"Males are not necessarily illogical; that's a female myth."

"Sorry. I must take a tranquilizer the minute we are home – something I haven't needed in years. But do try to think about it *as if* you were female. Please? Twenty seconds."

"I don't need twenty seconds." He lifted her hand, kissed it. "If I were female, I would jump at the chance, too. The best proved genetic pattern one can offer a child? Of course."

"Not that at all!"

He blinked. "Perhaps I *don't* know what you mean by logic."

"Uh . . . does it matter? Since we arrived at the same answer?"

The car swerved and stopped in a loading pocket; she stood up. "So let's wipe it. We're home, dear."

"You are. I'm not. I think –"

"Men don't think."

"I think you need a night's rest, Ishtar."

"You sealed this onto me; now you'll have to undress me."

"So? Then you'll insist on feeding me and your won't get that long night of sleep after all. Besides, you can peel it over your head, just the way I did it for you at decontam."

She sighed. "Galahad – if I picked the right name for you – do I have to offer you a cohabitation contract merely because I might invite you to stay overnight again? It's likely that neither of us will get any sleep tonight."

"That's what I was saying."

"Not quite. Because we may *work* all night. Even if you choose to spend three minutes to our mutual pleasure."

" 'Three minutes'? I wasn't that hasty even the first time."

"Well – Five minures?"

"Am I offered twenty minutes . . . plus an apology?"

"Men! Thirty minutes, darling, and no apology."

"Accepted." He stood up.

"Five of which you've wasted arguing about it. So come along – exasperating darling."

He followed her out into her foyer. "What's this about 'work all night'?"

"And tomorrow, too. I'll know when I check what's in my phone. If there's nothing, I'll have to call the Chairman Pro Tem much as I hate to. I've got to look over this rooftop cabin or whatever it is, and see what arrangements can be made to take care of him there. Then both of us will move him; I can't delegate *that*. Then –"

"Ishtar! Are you going to agree to *that?* Nonsterile habitat, no emergency equipment, and so forth?"

"Darling . . . *you* are impressed by my rank; Mr. Weatheral is not. And the Senior isn't even impressed by Mr. Weatheral's authority; the Senior is the *Senior*. I kept hoping that Mr. Chairman Pro Tem would find some way to wheedle him into postponing such a move. But he did not. So now I have two choices: Do it his way – or withdraw completely. As the Director did. Which I *won't* do. Which leaves me *no* choice. So tonight I'll inspect his new quarters and see what can be done between now and tomorrow midmorning. Even though it's hopeless to make such a place sterile, perhaps it can be made more nearly suitable before he sees it."

"And emergency equipment, don't forget that, Ishtar."

"As if I would, stupid darling. Now help me out of this damned thing – I mean 'this pretty dress you designed for me and which the Senior clearly liked.' Please?"

"So stand still and hold still and shut up."

"Don't *tickle!* Oh, drat, there's the phone signal! Get it off me, dear – hurry!"

VARIATIONS ON A THEME

IV

Love

Lazarus lounged in his hammock and scratched his chest. "Hamadryad," he said, "that's not an easy question. At seventeen I was certain I was in love. But it was merely excess hormones and self-delusion. It was most of a thousand years later before I experienced the real thing – and didn't recognize the condition for years, as I had quit using that word."

Ira Weatheral's "pretty daughter" looked puzzled, while Lazarus thought again that Ira had been wrong: Hamadryad was not pretty; she was so startling beautiful that she would have fetched top premium prices at auction on Fatima, with hard-eyed Iskandrian factors outbidding each other in the belief that she was a sound speculation. If the Protector of the Faith had not preempted her for himself –

Hamadryad did not seem to know that her appearance was exceptional. But Ishtar did. The first ten days that Ira's daughter had been part of Lazarus' "family" (so he thought of them – a good enough term as Ira, Hamadryad, Ishtar and Galahad were all his descendants and now privileged to call him "Grandfather" as long as they did not overdo it) – those first days Ishtar had shown a childish tendency to try to place herself between Hamadryad and Lazarus, and also between Hamadryad and Galahad, even when this required being two places at once.

Lazarus had watched this barnyard dance with amusement and had wondered if Ishtar knew that she was doing it. Probably not, he decided. His rejuvenation supervisor was all duty and no sense of humour and would have been shocked had she known that she had reverted to adolescence.

But it did not last. It was impossible not to like Hamadryad because she remained quietly friendly no matter what. Lazarus wondered if it was a behaviour pattern consciously developed to protect herself against her less-endowed sisters – or was it simply her nature? He had not tried to find out. But Ishtar now tended to sit by Hamadryad, or even to make room between herself and Galahad for Hamadryad, and let her help in serving meals and such – assistant "housewife" de facto.

"If I must wait a thousand years to understand that word," Hamadryad replied, "then I probably never will. Minerva says that it cannot be defined in Galacta and even when I speak Classic English, I find that I think in Galacta, which means that I do not really grasp English. Since the word 'love' occurs so frequently in ancient English literature, I thought my failure to understand that word might be the block that keeps me from thinking in English."

"Well, let's shift to Galacta and take a swing at it. In the first place, very little thinking was ever done in English; it is not a language suited to logical thought. Instead, it's an emotive lingo beautifully adapted to concealing fallacies. A rationalizing language, not a rational one. But most people who spoke English had no more idea of the meaning of the word 'love' than you have, even though they used it all the time."

Lazarus added, "Minerva! We're going to take another hack at the word 'love.' Want to join in? If so, shift to your personal mode."

"Thank you, Lazarus. Hello, Ira-Ishtar-Hamadryad-Galahad," the disembodied contralto voice answered. "I am and have been in personal mode, and usually am, now that you have given me permission to use my judgement. You're looking well, Lazarus – younger every day."

"I feel younger. But, dear, when you go to personal mode, you should tell us."

"I'm sorry, Grandfather!"

"Don't sound so humble. Just say, 'Howdy, I'm here,' that's all. If you could manage to tell me, or Ira, just once, to go to hell, it 'ud be good for you. Clean your circuits."

"But I have no wish to say that to either of you."

"That's what's wrong. If you hang around Dora, you'll learn to. Have you spoken to her today?"

"I'm speaking with Dora now, Lazarus. We're playing fairy chess in five dimensions, and she's teaching me songs you taught her. She teaches me a song, then I sing a tenor lead while she harmonizes in soprano. We're doing this in real time because we're outing through the speakers in your control room and listening to ourselves. Right now we're singing the story of One-Ball Riley. Would you care to hear us?"

Lazarus flinched. "No, no, not *that* one."

"We've practiced several others. 'Rangy Lil' and 'The Ballad of Yukon Jake' and 'Barnacle Bill' – I sing the story on that one while Dora does soprano and bass. Or perhaps 'Four Whores Came Down from Canada' – that one is fun."

"*No*, Minerva. I'm sorry, Ira; my computer is corrupting your computer." Lazarus sighed. "I didn't plan it that way; I just wanted Minerva to baby-sit for me. Since I've got the only retarded ship in this sector."

"Lazarus," Minerva said reproachfully, "I don't think it is correct to say that Dora is retarded. She's quite intelligent, I think. I do not understand why you say that she is corrupting me."

Ira had been lying on the grass, sunbathing with a kerchief over his eyes. He rolled to one elbow. "Nor I, Lazarus. That last one I'd like to hear. I recall where Canada is-was. North of the country you were born in."

Lazarus counted silently, then said, "Ira, I know I have prejudices ridiculous to a civilized modern man such as yourself. I can't help it; I'm canalized by early childhood, imprinted like a baby duckling. If you want to hear bawdy songs from a barbaric era, please listen to them in your apartments – not up here. Minerva, Dora doesn't understand those songs; to her they are nursery rhymes."

"Nor do I understand them, sir, other than theoretically. But they are jolly, and I have enjoyed being taught to sing."

"Well – All right. Has Dora been behaving herself otherwise?"

"She's been a good girl, Grandfather Lazarus, and I think she is contented with my company. She pouted a little at not having her bedtime story last night. But I told her that you were very tired and already asleep, and told her a story myself."

"But – Ishtar! Did I miss a day?"

"Yes, sir."

"Surgery? I didn't notice any new healed places."

The Master Chief Technician hesitated. "Grandfather, I will discuss procedures only if you insist. It does a client no good to be reminded of such things. I hope that you will not insist. I do hope so, sir."

"Um. All right, all right. But next time you chop out a day – or a week, or whatever – warn me. So that I can leave a bedtime story on file with Minerva. No, that won't do; you don't want me to know. Okay, I'll keep stories on file with Minerva and you warn her, instead."

"I will, Grandfather. It does help when the client cooperates, especially by paying as little attention to what we do as possible." Ishtar smiled briefly. "The client we dread is another rejuvenator. Worries and tries to run things."

"Small wonder. I know, dear, I have that horrid habit of trying to run things myself. The only way I can keep from it is by staying out of the control room. So when I get too nosy, tell me to shut up. But how are we doing? How much longer do I have to go?"

Ishtar answered hesitantly, "Perhaps this is a time when I should tell you to . . . 'shut up.' "

"That's it! But firmer, dear. 'Get out of my control room, you custard-headed dolt, and *stay* out!' Make him realize that, if he doesn't *jump*, you'll toss him into the brig. Now try it again."

Ishtar grinned widely. "Grandfather, you're an old fraud."

"So I've long suspected. I was hoping it didn't show. All right, the subject is 'love.' Minerva, the Hamadarling says you told her that it can't be defined in Galacta. Got anything to add to that?"

"Tentatively yes, Lazarus. May I reserve my answer until the others speak?"

"Suit yourself. Galahad, you talk less and listen more than anybody else in the family. Want to try it?"

"Well, sir, I hadn't realized that there was any mystery about 'love' until I heard Hamadryad ask about it. But I'm still learning English. By the naturalistic method the way a child learns his milk language. No grammar, no syntax, no dictionary – just listen and talk and read it. Acquire new words by context. By that method I acquired a feeling that 'love' means the shared ecstasy that can be attained through sex. Is that right?"

"Son, I hate to say this – because, if you've been reading a lot of English, I see how you reached that opinion – but you are one hundred per cent wrong."

Ishtar looked startled. Galahad simply looked thoughtful. "Then I must go back and read some more."

"Don't bother, Galahad. Most of those writers you've been reading misuse the word just that way. Shucks, I misused it for years myself; it's a prime example of the slipperiness of the English tongue. But, whatever 'love' is, it's not sex. I'm not running down sex. If there is a purpose in life more important than two people cooperating in making a baby, all the philosophers in history haven't been able to find it. And between babies, the practice runs keep up our zest in life and make tolerable the fact that raising a baby is one hell of a lot of work. But that's not love. Love is something that still goes on when you are *not* sexually excited. It being so stipulated, who wants to try it? Ira, how about you? You know English better than the others, you speak it almost as well as I do."

"I speak it better than you do, Gramp; I speak it grammatically, which you do not."

"Don't praggle me, boy; I'll quang you proper. Shakespeare and I never let grammar interfere with expressing ourselves. Why, he said to me once –"

"Oh, stop it! He died three centuries before you were born."

"He did, huh? They opened his grave once and found it empty. The fact is, he was a half brother of Queen Elizabeth and dyed his hair to make the truth less obvious. The other fact is that they were closing in on him, so he switched. I've died that way several times. Ira, his will left his 'second-best bed' to his wife. Look up who got his *best* bed and you'll begin to figure out what really happened. Do you want to try to define 'love'?"

"No. You would change the rules again. All you have done so far is to divide the field of experience called 'love' into the same categories Minerva divided it into when you asked her this same question weeks ago – namely 'Eros' and 'Agape.' But you avoided using those technical words for the subfields, and by this sophistry you attempted to exclude the general term from one subfield and thereby claimed that the term to be defined was limited to the other subfield – which set it up for you to define 'love' as identically equal to 'Agape.' But again without using that word. It won't work, Lazarus. To use your own metaphor, I saw you palm that card."

Lazarus shook his head admiringly. "There are no flies on you, boy; I did a good job when I thought you up. Someday when we have time to waste, let's have a go at solipsism."

"Come off it, Lazarus. You can't bulldoze me the way you did Galahad. The subcategories are still 'Eros' and 'Agape.' 'Agape' is rare; 'Eros' is so common that it is almost inevitable that Galahad acquired the feeling that 'Eros' is the total meaning of the word 'love'. Now you have unfairly confused him since he assumes – incorrectly – that you are a reliable authority with respect to the English language."

Lazarus chuckled. "Ira, m'boy, when I was a kid, they sold

that stuff by the wagonload to grow alfalfa. Those technical words were thought up by armchair experts of the same sort as theologians. Which gives them the same standing as sex manuals written by celibate priests. Son, I avoided those fancy categories because they are useless, incorrect, and misleading. There can be sex without love, and love without sex, and situations so intermixed that nobody can sort out which is which. But love *can* be defined, an exact definition that does not resort to the word 'sex,' or to question-begging by exclusion through the use of such words as 'Eros' and 'Agape.'"

"So define it," said Ira. "I promise not to laugh."

"Not yet. The trouble with defining in words anything as basic as love is that the definition can't be understood by anyone who has not experienced it. It's like the ancient dilemma of explaining a rainbow to a person blind from birth. Yes, Ishtar, I know that you can fit such a person with cloned eyes today – but that dilemma was inescapable in my youth. In those days one could teach such an unfortunate all the physical theory of the electromagnetic spectrum, tell him precisely what frequencies the human eye can pick up, define colours to him in terms of those frequencies, explain exactly how the mechanisms of refraction and reflection produce a rainbow image and what its shape is and how the frequencies are distributed until he knew *all* about rainbows in the scientific sense . . . but you *still* couldn't make him feel the breathless wonder that the sight of a rainbow inspires in a man. Minerva is better off than that man, because she can *see*. Minerva dear, do you ever look at rainbows?"

"Whenever possible, Lazarus. Whenever one of my sensor extensionals can see one. Fascinating!"

"That's it. Minerva can see a rainbow, a blind man can't. Electromagnetic theory is irrelevant to the experience."

"Lazarus," Minerva added, "it may be that I can see a rainbow better than a flesh-and-blood can. My visual range is three octaves, fifteen hundred to twelve thousand angstroms."

Lazarus whistled. "Whereas I chop off just short of one octave. Tell me, girl, do you see chords in those colours?"

"Oh, certainly!"

"Hmm! Don't try to explain to me those other colours; I'll have to go on being half blind."

Lazarus added, "Puts me in mind of a blind man I knew on Mars, Ira, when I was managing that, uh, recreation centre. He –"

"Gramp," the Chairman Pro Tem interrupted in a tired voice

"don't treat us as children. Surely, you're the oldest man alive ... but the youngest person here – that offspring of mine sitting there, making cow-eyes at you – is as old as Gramp Johnson was when you last saw him; Hamadryad will be eighty her next birthday. Ham, my darling, how many paramours have you had?"

"Goodness, Ira – who counts?"

"Ever taken money for it?"

"None of your business, Father. Or were you about to offer me some?"

"Don't be flip, dear; I'm still your father. Lazarus, do you think you can shock Hamadryad by plain talk? Prostitution isn't big business here; there are too many amateurs as willing as she is. Nevertheless, the few bordellos we have in New Rome are members of the Chamber of Commerce. But you should try one of our better holiday houses – say, the Elysium. After you are fully rejuvenated."

"Good idea," agreed Galahad. "To celebrate. As soon as Ishtar gives you your final physical check. As my guest, Grandfather; I'd be honoured. The Elysium has everything, from massage and hypnotic conditioning to the best gourmet food and best shows. Or name it and they'll supply it."

"Wait a moment," protested Hamadryad. "Don't be a selfish arsfardel Galahad. We'll make it a foursome celebration. Ishtar?"

"Certainly, dear. Fun."

"Or a sixsome, with a companion for Ira. Father?"

"I could be tempted, dear, for Lazarus' birthday party – although you know I usually avoid public places. How many rejuvenations, Lazarus? That's how we count this sort of birthday party."

"Don't be nosy, Bub. As your daughter says: 'Who counts?' Wouldn't mind a birthday cake, such as I used to have as a child. But just one candle in the middle is enough."

"A phallic symbol," agreed Galahad. "An ancient fertility sign – appropriate for rejuvenation. And its flame is an equally ancient symbol of life. It should be a working candle, not a fake. If we can find one."

Ishtar looked happy. "Of course! There must be a candlemaker somewhere. If not, I'll learn how and make it myself. I'll design it, too – semirealistic but somewhat stylized. Although I could make it true portraiture, Grandfather; I'm a fair amateur sculptor, I learned it when I studied cosmetic surgery."

"Wait a minute!" Lazarus protested. "All I want is a plain wax candle – then blow it out and make a wish. Thank you, Ishtar, but don't bother. And thanks, Galahad, but I'll pick up the tab – although it may be a family party right here, where Ira won't feel like a duck in a shooting gallary. Look, kids, I've seen every possible sort of joy house and pleasure dome. Happiness is in the heart, not in that stuff."

"Lazarus, can't you see that the kids *want* to treat you to a fancy party? They like you – though Prime Cause alone knows why."

"Well –"

"But there might be no tab. I think I recall something from that list appended to your will. Minerva – who owns the Elysium?"

"It is a daughter corporation of Service Enterprises of New Rome, Limited, which in turn is owned by Sheffield-Libby Associates. In short, Lazarus owns it."

"Be damned! Who invested my money in *that?* Andy Libby, bless his sweet shy soul, would be spinning in his grave – If I hadn't placed him spinning in orbit around the last planet we discovered together, where he was killed."

"Lazarus, that's not in your memoirs."

"Ira, I keep telling you, lots of things not in my memoirs. Poor little guy got to thinking one of his deep thoughts and didn't stay alert. I put him in orbit because I promised him, when he was dying, to take him back to his native Ozarks. Tried to, about a hundred years later, but couldn't find him. Beacon dead, I suppose. All right, kids, we'll have a party at my happy house and you can sample anything the place has to offer. Where were we? Ira, you were about to define 'love.' "

"No, you were about to tell us about a blind man on Mars, when you were managing that whorehouse."

"Ira, you're as crude as Gramp Johnson was. This guy 'Noisy' – don't recall his right name, if he had one – Noisy was one of those people like yourself who just will work, regardless. A blind man could get by in those days quite well by begging, and nobody thought the less of him, since there was no way then to restore a man's sight.

"But Noisy wasn't content to live off other people; he worked at what he could do. Played a squeeze box and sang. That was an instrument operated by bellows which forced air over reeds as you touched keys on it – quite pretty music. They were popular until electronics pushed most mechanical music makers off the market.

"Noisy showed up one night, skinned out of his pressure suit at the lock dressing room, and was playing and singing before I knew he was inside.

"My policy was 'Trade, Treat, or Travel' – except that the house might buy a beer for an old customer who temporarily wasn't holding. But Noisy was not a customer; he was a bum – looked and smelled like a bum, and I was about to give him the bum's rush. Then I saw this rag around his eyes and skidded to a stop.

"Nobody throws out a blind man. Nobody makes any trouble for him. I kept an eye on him but left him alone. He didn't even sit down. Just played this broken-down stomach-Steinway and sang, neither very well, and I laid off the pianette not to interrupt him. One of the girls started passing the hat for him.

"When he reached my table, I invited him to sit and bought him a beer – and regretted it; he was pretty whiff. He thanked me and told me about himself. Lies, mostly."

"Like yours, Gramp?"

"Thanks, Ira. Said he had been chief engineer in one of the big Harriman liners, until his accident. Maybe he had been a spaceman; I never caught him out in the lingo. Not that I tried. If a blind man wanted to claim he was the rightful heir to the Holy Roman Empire, I would go along with the gag – anybody would. Perhaps he was some sort of spacegoing mechanic, shipfitter or something. More likely he was a transported miner who had been careless using powder.

"When I checked the place at closing time, I found him sleeping in the kitchen. Couldn't have that, we ran a sanitary mess. So I led him to a vacant room and put him to bed, intending to give him breakfast and ease him gently on his way – I wasn't running a flophouse.

"A lot I had to say about it. I saw him at breakfast all right. But I hardly recognized him. A couple of the girls had given him a bath, trimmed his hair, and shaved him, and had dressed him in clean clothes – mine – and had thrown away the dirty rag he had worn over his ruined eyes and had replaced it with a clean white bandage.

"Kinfolk, I do not fight the weather. The girls were free to keep pets; I knew what fetched the customers, and it wasn't my pianette playing. If that pet stood on two legs and ate more than I did, I still did not argue. Hormone Hall was Noisy's home as long as the girls wanted to keep him.

"But it took me a while to realize that Noisy was not just a parasite enjoying free room and board, and probably our stock-in-trade as well while siphoning off cash from our customers – no, he was pulling his weight in the boat. My books at the end of the first month he was with us showed the gross profit up and the net way up."

"How do you account for that, Lazarus? Inasmuch as he was competing for your customers' cash."

"Ira, must I do all your thinking for you? No, Minerva does most of it. But it is possible that you have never thought about the economics of that sort of joint. There are three sources of gross, the bar, the kitchen, and the girls themselves. No drugs – drugs spoil the three main sources. If a customer was on drugs and showed it, or even broke out a stick of kish, I eased him out quickly and sent him down the line to the Chinaman's.

"The kitchen was to supply meals to the girls – who were assessed room and board on a break-even or lose-a-little basis. But it also served food all night to anyone who ordered it, and showed a net since we had its overhead covered anyhow to board the girls. The bar also showed a net after I fired one barkeep with three hands. The girls kept their gross, all the traffic would bear, but they paid the house a flat fee for each kewpie, or a triple fee if she kept a customer all night. She could cheat a little, and I would shut-eye – but if she cheated too much or too often, or a john complained that he was rolled, I had a talk with her. Never any real trouble; they were ladies, and besides, I had means to check on them quietly, as well as eyes in the back of my head.

"The beefs about rolling were the stickiest, but I remember only one that was the girl's fault rather than the john's – I simply terminated her contract, let her go. In the usual beef the slob was not rolled; he simply had a change of heart after he had counted too much money into her greedy little hands and she had delivered what he had ordered – then *he* tried to roll *her* to get it back. But I could smell that sort of slob and would be listening via a mike – then would bust in as trouble started. That sort of jerk I would toss so hard he bounced twice."

"Grandfather, weren't some of them pretty big for that?"

"Not really, Galahad. Size doesn't figure much in a fight – although I was always armed against real trouble. But if I *have* to take a man, I have no compunctions slowing me down about *how* I take him. If you kick a man in the crotch with no warning, it will quiet him down long enough to throw him out.

"Don't flinch, Hamadear; your father guaranteed that you

could not be shocked. But I was talking about Noisy and how he made us money while making some himself.

"In this sort of frontier joint the usual customer comes in, buys a drink while he looks over the girls, picks one by buying her a drink – goes to her room, then leaves. Elapsed time, thirty minutes; net to the house, minimum.

"Pre-Noisy, that is. After Noisy arrived, it went more like this: Buy a drink as before. Maybe buy the girl a second drink rather than interrupt a blind man's song. Take the girl to her room. When he comes back, Noisy is singing 'Frankie and Johnnie' or 'When the Pusher Met My Cousin,' and smiles and throws a verse at him – and the customer sits down and listens to all of it – and asks Noisy if he knows 'Dark Eyes.' Sure, Noisy knows it, but instead of admitting it, he asks the john to give him the words and hum it and he'll see what he can do with it.

"If the customer has valuta, he's still there hours later having had supper and bought supper for one of the girls and tipped Noisy rather lavishly and is ready for an encore with the girl or another girl. If he's got the money, he stays all night, splitting his cash between the girls and Noisy and the bar and kitchen. If he spends himself broke and has been a good customer – well behaved as well as free with his money – I stake him to bed and breakfast on credit, and urge him to come back. If he's alive next payday, he's sure to be back. If not, all the house is out is the wholesale cost of one breakfast – nothing compared with what he's spent. Cheap goodwill advertising.

"A month of that, and both the house and the girls have made much more money, and the girls haven't worked much harder as they have spent part of their time drinking pay-me drinks – coloured water, half the price to the house, half to the girl – while they help a john listen to Noisy's nostalgic songs. Shucks, a girl doesn't want to work like a treadmill even if she usually enjoys her work as many of them did. But they never got tired of sitting and listening to Noisy's songs.

"I quit playing the pianette, except, maybe, while Noisy ate. Technically I was the better musician – but *he* had that undefinable quality that sells a song; he could make 'em cry or laugh. And he had a thousand of 'em. One he called 'The Born Loser.' Not much of a tune, just:

"*Tah*tah *poom* poom!
*Tah*tah *poom* poom!
Tah t'*tah* tah tah *poom* poom –

"– about a bloke who can never quite make it. Uh:

"There's a beer joint
By the pool hall
For to pass some pleasant hours.

"There's a hook shop
Above the pool hall
Where my sister makes her living.

"She's a good sport;
I can spring her
For a fin or even a sawbuck

When not holding,
Or the horses
Have been running rather slowly –

"Like that, folks. But more of it."

"Lazarus," said Ira, "you have been humming or singing that song every day you've been up here. All of it. A dozen verses or more."

"Really, Ira? I do hum and sing; I know that. But I don't hear it myself. It's like the purring of a cat; it just means that I'm functioning okay, board all green, operating at normal cruising. It means that I feel secure, relaxed, and happy – and, come to think of it, I do.

"But 'The Born Loser' doesn't have a mere dozen verses, it has hundreds. What I sang was only a snatch of what Noisy used to sing. He was always fiddling with a song, changing it, adding to it. I don't think this one started out as his; I seem to remember a song about a character whose overcoat was usually in hock clear back when I was very young and raising my first family, on Earth.

"But that song belonged to Noisy when he got through filing off serial numbers and changing the body lines. I heard it again, oh, must have been twenty, twenty-five years later, in a cabaret in Luna City. From Noisy. But he had changed it. Fixed up the scansion, given it a proper rhyme scheme, dolled up the tune. But the tune was still recognizable – in a minor key, wistful rather than sad, and the words were still about this third-rate grifter whose topcoat was always in hock and who sponged off his sister.

"And he had changed, too. A shiny new instrument, a tailored spaceman's uniform, grey hair at the temples – and star billing. I paid a waiter to tell him that 'Happy' Daze was in the audience – not my name then, but the only name Noisy had for me – and after his first group he came over and let me buy him a drink while we swapped lies and talked about our happy days at dear old Hormone Hall.

"I didn't mention to him that he had left us rather abruptly and that the girls had gone into a decline over it, worrying that he might be dead in a ditch – didn't mention it because he did not. But I had had to investigate his disappearance because my staff was so demoralized by it that the place felt like a morgue – no way for a parlour house to be. I was able to establish that he had gone aboard the 'Gyrfalcon' when she was about to lift for Luna City and had not left her – so I told the girls that Noisy had had a sudden opportunity to go home again but had left a message with the port captain for each of them – then added more lies to personalize the good-bye he hadn't made. It perked them up and lifted the gloom. They still missed him, but they all understood that grabbing a ride home was not something he could postpone – and since he had "remembered" to send a message to each of them, they felt appreciated.

"But it turned out that he *did* remember them, mentioned each by name. Minerva dear, here is a difference between a blinded flesh-and-blood and one who has never been able to see. Noisy could see a rainbow any time he cared to, by memory. He never stopped 'seeing,' but what he 'saw' was always beauty. I had realized that, some, back when we were on Mars together, for – don't laugh – he thought I was as pretty as you are, Galahad. Told me that he could tell what I looked like from my voice, and described me to me. I had the grace to say that he flattered me but let it lie when he answered that I was too modest – even though I'm not handsome now and wasn't then and modesty has never been one of my vices.

"But Noisy thought all the girls were beautiful, too – and in one case this may have been true and certainly several of them were pretty.

"But he asked me what had become of Olga and added, 'Golly, what a little beauty she was!'

"Kinfolk, Olga wasn't even homely, she was ugly. Face like a mud pie, figure like a gunnysack – only on an outpost like Mars could she get by. What she did have was a warm and gentle voice and a sweet personality – which was enough, as a customer might pick her through Hobson's choice on a busy night, but once he had so, he picked her some later time on purpose. Mean to say, dears, beauty will lure a man into bed, but it won't bring him back a second time, unless he's awfully young or very stupid."

"What does bring him back a second time, Grandfather?" asked Hamadryad. "Technique? Muscular control?"

"Have you had any complaints, dear?"

"Well . . . no."

"Then you know the answer and are trifling with me. Neither of those. It's the ability to make a man happy, principally by being happy about it yourself – a spiritual quality rather than a physical one. Olga had it in gobs.

"I told Noisy that Olga had married shortly after he left, happily so, and had three children last I had heard . . . which was an utter lie, as she had been killed accidentally and the girls bawled about it and I didn't feel good myself and we had shut the place down for four days. But I couldn't tell Noisy that; Olga had been one of the first to mother him, had helped bathe him and had stolen some of my clothes for him while I slept.

"But they all mothered him and never fought over him. I have not deviated from our subject in this rambling account of Noisy; we're still defining 'love.' Anybody want to take whack at it now?"

Galahad said, "Noisy loved every one of them. That's what you've been saying."

"No, Son, he didn't love *any* of them. Fond of them, yes – but he left them without looking back."

"Then you are saying that *they* loved *him*."

"Correct. Once you figure out the difference between what he felt toward them and what they felt toward him, we're almost home."

"Mother love," said Ira, and added gruffly, "Lazarus, are you trying to tell us that 'mother love' is the only love there is? Man, you're out of your mind!"

"Probably. But not that far out. I said they mothered him; I did not say a word about 'mother love'."

"Uh . . . he bedded all of them?"

"Wouldn't be surprised, Ira. I never tried to find out. Irrelevant in any case."

Hamadryad said to her father, "Ira, 'mother love' can't be what we're trying to define; it is often only a sense of duty.

Two of my brats I was tempted to drown, as you may have guessed seeing what little demons they were."

"Daughter, all your offspring were charming children."

"Oh, fuff. One has to give a baby mothering no matter what, or it will grow up to be a still worse monster. What did you think of my son Gordon as a baby?"

"A delightful child."

"Really? I'll tell him that – if I ever have a male child I name 'Gordon.' Sorry, old darling, I shouldn't have trapped you. Lazarus, Ira is a perfect grandfather, one who never forgets a birthday. But I've suspected that Minerva kept track of such things for him and now I know it. Right, Minerva?"

Minerva did not answer. Lazarus said, "She's not working for *you*, Hamadryad."

Ira said sharply, "Of course Miverna keeps track of such things for me! Minerva, how many grandchildren do I have?"

"One hundred and twenty-seven, Ira, counting the boy child to be born next week."

"How many great-grandchildren? And who is having the boy?"

"Four hundred and three, sir. Your son Gordon's current wife Marian."

"Keep me posted on it. That was the baby Gordon I was thinking of, Miss Smarty; Gordon's son Gordon . . . uh, by Evelyn Hedrick, I think. Lazarus, I deceived you. The truth is that I am migrating because my descendants are crowding me off this globe."

"Father, are you really going to? Not just talking?"

"Still top secret until after the decennial Trustees Meeting, dear. But I am. Want to come along? Galahad and Ishtar have decided to go; they'll set up a rejuve shop for the colony. You'll have five to ten years in which to learn something useful."

"Grandfather, are *you* going?"

"Unlikely to the nth degree, my dear. I've seen a colony."

"You may change your mind." Hamadryad stood up, faced Lazarus. "I propose to you, in the presence of three witnesses – four; Minerva is the best possible witness – a contract for cohabitation and progeny, term to be selected by you." Ishtar looked startled, then wiped all expression from her face; the others said nothing.

Lazarus answered, "Granddaughter, if I weren't so old and tired, I would spank you."

"Lazarus, I am your granddaughter only by courtesy; you are

less than eight per cent of my total ancestry. Less than that in terms of dominant genes, with a vanishingly small probability of unfavourable reinforcement; the bad recessives have been weeded. I'll send my genetic pattern over for your inspection."

"That's not the point, dear."

"Lazarus, I'm certain you've married your descendants in the past; is there some reason to discriminate against *me?* If you'll tell me, perhaps I can correct it. I must add that this submittal is not contingent on your migrating." Hamadryad added, "Or it could be for progeny only, although I would be proud and happy to be permitted to live with you."

"*Why*, Hamadryad?"

She hesitated. "I am at a loss to answer, sir. I had thought that I could say, 'I love you' – but apparently I do not know what that word means. So I have no word in either language to describe my need . . . and went ahead without one."

Lazarus said gently, "I love you, dear –"

Hamadryad's face lit up.

He continued: "– and for that very reason I must refuse you." Lazarus looked around him. "I love all of you. Ishtar, Galahad . . . even that ugly, surly father of yours, dear, sitting there and looking worried. Now smile dear, for I'm certain that there are endless young bucks anxious to marry you. You smile too, Ishtar – but not you, Ira; it would crack your face. Ishtar, who is relieving you and Galahad? No, I don't care who is scheduled. May I be alone the rest of the day?"

She hesitated. "Grandfather, may I keep the observation station manned?"

"You will anyhow. But will you limit them to dials and gauges or whatever it is you use? No eye or ear on me? Minerva will tell you if I misbehave – I'm certain of that."

"There will be neither eye nor ear on you, sir." Ishtar stood up. "Come along, Galahad. Hamadryad?"

"Just a moment, Ish. Lazarus – have I offended you?"

"What? Not at all, my dear."

"I thought you were angry with me over . . . what I proposed."

"Oh, nonsense. Hamadarling, that sort of proposal never offends anyone; it is the highest compliment one human can pay another. But it did confuse me. Now smile and kiss me good-night then come see me tomorrow if you wish. All you kids kiss me good-night; there's nobody sore at anybody. Ira, you might stick around a bit if you will."

Like docile children they did so, then went into Lazarus penthouse and took transport down. Lazarus said, "A drink, Ira?"

"Only if you are having one."

"We'll skip it then. Ira, did you put her up to it?"

"Eh?"

"You know what I mean. Hamadryad. First Ishtar, now Hamadryad. You've manipulated this whole deal from the moment you snatched me out of that flophouse, where I was dying decently and quietly. Have you again been trying to tie me down to whatever scheme you have in the back of your mind by waving pretty tails under my nose? It won't work, man."

The Chairman Pro Tem answered quietly, "I could deny that – and for the hundredth time have you call me a liar. I suggest that you ask Minerva."

"I wonder if that would be any assurance. Minerva!"

"Yes, Lazarus?"

"Did Ira rig this? With either of the girls?"

"Not to my knowledge, Lazarus."

"Is that an evasion, dear?"

"Lazarus, I cannot lie to you."

"Well . . . I think you could if Ira wanted you to, but there is no point in my inquiring into it. Give us privacy for a few moments, dear – recording mode only."

"Yes, Lazarus."

Lazarus went on, "Ira, I wish you had answered Yes. Because the only other explanation is one I do not like. I ain't pretty and my manners are not such as to endear me to women – so what do we have left? The fact that I am the oldest man alive. Women sell themselves for odd reasons and not always for money. Ira, I do not choose to stand at stud for pretty young things who would not waste a moment on me save for the prestige of having a child by, quote, The Senior, end of quote." He glared. "Right?"

"Lazarus, you are being unjust to both women. As well as unusually obtuse."

"How?"

"I've watched them. I think they both love you – and don't give me any double-talk about what that verb means; I am not Galahad."

"But – Oh, crap!"

"I won't argue on that basis; 'crap' is a subject in which you are the Galaxy's top authority. Women do not *always* sell themselves and they *do* fall in love . . . often for the oddest reasons – if 'reason' is a word that can apply. Granted that you are ugly, selfish, self-centred, surly –"

"I'm aware of it!"

"– to me. Nevertheless women don't seem to care much how a man looks . . . and you are surprisingly gentle with women. I've noticed. You say those little whores on Mars all loved that blind man."

"Some of them weren't little. Big Anna was taller than I am and weighed more."

"Don't try to change the subject. *Why* did they love him? Don't bother to answer; why a woman loves a man – or a man loves a woman – can be rationalized only in survival terms, and the answer has no flavour, unsatisfying. But – Lazarus, when you've completed rejuvenation and you and I have finished our Scherazade bet, however we finish it – are you going away again?"

Lazarus brooded before answering: "I suppose so. Ira, this cottage – and garden and stream – that you've lent me are very nice; the times I've gone down to the city I've hurried back, glad to be home. But it's just a resting place; I won't stay here. When the wild goose cries, I go." Lazarus looked sad. "But I don't know where and I don't want to repeat the things I've done. Perhaps Minerva will find that new thing for me, when it's time to move on."

Ira stood up. "Lazarus, if you weren't so stinking suspicious and mean, you would give both women the benefit of the doubt and leave them each with a child to remember you by. It wouldn't cost you much effort."

"Out of the question! I do not abandon children. Or pregnant women."

"Excuses. I will adopt, in the womb, any child you sire before you leave us. Shall I have Minerva place that in permanent and bind it?"

"I can support my own kids! Always have."

"Minerva. Transfer it and bind it."

"Completed, Ira."

"Thank you, best Little Nag. Same time tomorrow, Lazarus?"

"I suppose so. Yes. Call Hamadryad, will you, and ask her to come, too? – tell her I asked you to. I don't want the kid's feelings hurt."

"Sure, Gramp."

COUNTERPOINT IV

On the level in the Executive Palace of Mr. Weatheral's private apartments Hamadryad waited with Galahad while Ishtar left orders for the rejuvenation technicians on watch there. Then the three took transport down and across, still inside the Palace, to an apartment Ira had placed at Ishtar's disposal – a dwelling larger and more lavish than her quarters in the Rejuvenation Clinic and much more luxurious than the penthouse cottage save that it had no garden; it was intended for a Trustee or other V.I.P. guest – not that its luxury mattered much, as Ishtar and Galahad spent most of their time and took most of their meals with Lazarus, and used it mainly for sleeping.

Minerva had placed a dozen-odd lesser accommodations with Ishtar for her watch list, one of them for Galahad. He did not need it and Ishtar had Minerva reassign it to Hamadryad when she had become an unofficial part of the team caring for the Senior. Hamadryad sometimes slept in it rather than go to her country home – without telling her father, as the Chairman Pro Tem did not encourage members of his family to use Palace quarters unnecessarily. Or she sometimes stayed with Ishtar and Galahad.

This time all three went to Ishtar's apartment; they had matters to discuss. On arrival there Ishtar checked:

"Minerva?"

"Listening, Ishtar."

"Anything?"

"Lazarus and Ira are talking. Private conversation."

"Keep me advised, dear."

"Certainly, dear."

Ishtar turned back to the others. "Who wants a drink or something? Too early for dinner. Or is it? Ham?"

Galahad answered, "A bath for me, then a drink. I was all set for a dip – hot and sweaty – when Lazarus kicked us out."

"And stinky," Ishtar agreed, "I noticed it in the transport."

"A bath wouldn't hurt *you*, big arse; you were exercising as hard as I was."

"Regrettably true, my gallant knight; I was careful to sit downwind from our elders after that last match. Ham, get us all something tall and cold while Stinky and I get clean."

"Will you two settle for Idleberry Jolts or whatever is handy? While we all bathe? I don't have the excuse of heavy exercise, but I broke out with fear stink when I put the proposal to Gramp. And *muffed* it! After all your coaching, Ish. I'm sorry!" She started to sniffle.

Ishtar put her arms around the younger woman. "There, there, dear – stop it. I don't think you muffed it."

"He refused me."

"You laid a good foundation – and shook him up, which he needed. You startled me with your timing but it will work out all right."

"He probably won't even let me come back!"

"Yes, he will. Stop shaking. Come, dear; Galahad and I will give you a long, relaxing back rub. Stinky, fetch the fizz and join us in the shower room."

"With two women around I have to work. Okay."

When Galahad arrived with cold drinks, Ishtar had Hamadryad stretched out face down on the massage table. Ishtar looked up and said, "Dear, before you get wet, see if there are three towel robes in the rack; I didn't check."

"Yes, ma'am; no, ma'am; right away, ma'am; will that be all, ma'am? – plenty of robes; I dialled for more this morning. Don't bruise her, you don't know your own strength. I'm going to need her, later."

"And I'm going to swap you for a dog, sweetheart, and sell the dog. Pass around those drinks, then come help, or you won't get either of us later. If ever. We're busy agreeing that all males are beasts." She continued to massage, gently, firmly, with professional skill, down Hamadryad's back while the massage table matched her appropriately down the subjects front. She let Galahad hang a drink around her neck and place its nipple in her mouth without slowing her careful fingers.

He snapped Hamadryad's drink to the table, placed nipple in her mouth, patted her cheek, then took the other side and started to help, following Ishtar's lead. The table changed action to match four hands.

Some minutes later he let the nipple for his drink retract, and spoke. "Ish, any chance that Gramp twigged? About you two broads?"

"We're not all that broad. At least, Ham is not."

" 'Broad' is a usual English idiom for a female, and you said we should talk and think in English as long as we are on this commitment."

"I simply said that Hamadryad is not very broad. Even though she's had more children than I have – and I haven't had any since rejuvenation. But it's a colourful idiom; I like it. I don't see how Lazarus could guess that we are pregnant. Not that it would matter if he did, in my case – except just *how* I am pregnant, and he can't know that as I fudged the record on the source of the cloned cell. Ham, you haven't hinted anything to Lazarus – have you?"

Hamadryad surrendered her drink. "Of course not!"

"Minerva knows," Galahad said.

"Of course she does, I discussed it with her. But – Now you've got me wondering. Minerva?"

"Listening, Ishtar." The computer added, "Ira is leaving; Lazarus has come inside. No problems."

"Thank you, dear. Minerva, is there any possible way that Lazarus could know about Hamadryad and me? That we are pregnant, I mean, and why and how."

"He has not said so, nor has anyone mentioned it in his presence. Evaluation of pertinent data available to me makes it probable by less than one part in one thousand."

"How about Ira?"

"Less than one part in ten thousand. Ishtar, when Ira told me to supply you with service and to assign to you a restricted memory, he programmed me so that any later programme will simply wipe your assigned box. Truly, there is no way for him to retrieve from your private memory file, nor can I self-programme to get around it."

"Yes, so you assured me. But I don't know much about computers, Minerva."

Minerva chickled. "Whereas I do. You could say that I have made a career of computers. Don't worry, dear, your secrets are safe with me. Lazarus has just told me to order a light supper for him; then he is going to bed."

"Good. Let me know what he eats and how much and when he goes to bed – then call me if he wakes. Awake and alone at night, a man is at his lowest ebb; I must be ready to move quickly. But you know that."

"I shall watch his wave patterns, Ishtar. You will have two to five minute's warning – unless El Diablo jumps on his stomach."

"That damned cat. But being wakened that way doesn't depress him; it's his suicidal nightmares that worry me. I have about used up diversionary emergencies; I can't set fire to the penthouse a second time."

"Lazarus has not had one of his typical depression nightmares this month, Ishtar, and I know how to spot the wave sequences now; I'll be very careful."

"I know you will, dear. I wish we knew the incidents in his past from which each is derived; we might be able to wipe them."

"Ish," Galahad put in, "you go tinkering with his memory and you might lose everything Ira is after."

"And I might save out client, too. You stick to back-rubbing, dear, and leave delicate work to Minerva and me. Anything more, Minerva?"

"No. Yes. Ira is telling me to find Hamadryad; he wants to talk to her. Will she take the call?"

"Sure!" agreed Hamadryad, rolling over. "But patch him through you, Minerva; I won't go to the phone, I don't have my face on.'"

"Hamadryad?"

"Yes, Ira?"

"Message for you. Be nice to an old man and show up at the cottage as usual, will you? Better yet, get there early and have breakfast with him."

"Are you sure he wants to see me?"

"He does. He shouldn't, after the way you embarrassed him. What possessed you, Ham? But this message is his idea, not mine. He wants to be sure he hasn't scared you off."

She sighed with relief. "I'm not scared off if he will let me stay. Father, I told you I would devote as many days to this as *he* will permit. I meant it and still mean it. In fact I've told my manager that she can buy me out on long-term credit; that's how serious I am."

"So? I'm very pleased. If you do, and want to cash out, I – the government, that is – will pick up the loan from you without discounting it; I've assigned unlimited credit to anything related to the Senior. Just tell Minerva."

"Thank you, sir. I don't expect to need it – unless Gramp gets tired of me and I see something else I want to invest in. But the business is prosperous; I may just let Priscilla support me in style for a few years. Quite prosperous – betcha my assets exceed yours. Your private fortune, I mean."

"Don't be silly, my silly daughter; as a private citizen I'm almost a pauper – whereas in my official capacity I could confiscate your assets with just a word to Minerva and no one would question it."

"Except that you never would – you're sweet, Ira."

"Huh?"

"You are . . . even if you can't remember the names of my children. I'm feeling very gay, Papa, you've made me happy."

"You haven't called me 'Papa' for, oh, fifty or sixty years."

"Because you never encourage intimacy once a child is grown. Nor do I from mine. But this assignment has made me feel closer to you. I'll shut up, sir, and I'll be there early tomorrow. Off?"

"One moment. I forgot to ask where you are. If you're home –"

"I'm not; I'm having a bath with Galahad and Ishtar. About to, that is; you interrupted a wonderful back rub they were giving me."

"Sorry. As you are still in the Palace, I suggest that you stay. To be here early tomorrow. Beg a bed from them or, if that is intruding, come to my apartments; we'll find something."

"Don't fret about me, Ira. If a can't shame them into keeping me overnight, Minerva will find me a bed. Truly, Lazarus' bed is the only one I've ever found impossible to get into – maybe I need to apply for rejuve."

The Chairman Pro Tem was slow in answering. "Hamadryad . . . you were serious in proposing to have children by him – were you not?"

"Privacy, sir."

"Sorry. Hmm – The custom of privacy does not forbid me to say that *I* think it is a very good idea. If you tell me to, I will encourage it in any way I can."

Hamadryad looked at Ishtar and spread her hands in a gesture of "What do I do know?" – then answered: "His refusal seemed very firm, sir."

"Let me offer you a male viewpoint, my daughter. A man often refuses such a proposal when he wants to accept it – a man likes to be sure of a woman's motives and sincerity. At a later time he may accept. I don't mean that you should nag him with it; that would not work. But if you want this . . . bide your time. You're a charming woman; I have confidence in you."

"Yes, sir. If he does give me a child, we would all be richer thereby – would we not?"

"Yes, certainly. But my motives are somewhat different. If he dies or leaves us, there is always the sperm bank and the tissue bank – neither of which he can touch because I'll cheat if necessary. But I *don't* want him to die, Hamadryad, nor do I want him to leave soon – and I am not speaking from sentiment. The Senior is unique; I've gone to much trouble not to waste him. Your presence pleases him, your offer stimulates him . . . even though you feel he reacted badly. You're helping to keep him alive – and if he eventually lets you have his child, you may succeed in keeping him alive a long time. Indefinitely long."

Hamadryad wiggled with pleasure and smiled at Ishtar. "Father, you make me feel proud."

"You have always been a daughter to be proud of, dear. Although I can't claim all the credit; your mother is a most exceptional woman. Off now?"

"Off, with music playing. Good night, sir!"

Without getting up, Hamadryad grabbed both her friends around their waists and hugged them tightly. "Oh, I feel good!"

"So get down off this table, narrow broad; it's my turn."

"You don't need a massage," Ishtar said firmly; "you've been under no emotional strain and the hardest work you've done all day is to beat me two games of murder ball."

"But I'm the spiritual type. Sensitive."

"So you are, dear Galahad, and now you can most spiritually help her down and help me bathe her – still most spiritually."

Galahad complied while complaining. "You two ought to bathe *me*, instead. Pretend I'm a blind music maker." He closed his eyes and sang:

> " 'There's a *cop* a-
> *round* the corner
> who is *some*times not so friendly
> To a *man* who
> isn't *hold*ing
> Or *oth*erwise un*lucky* –

"That's me – 'unlucky' – or I wouldn't have to work with two women in the house. What cycle, Ish?"

" 'Relaxing' of course. Hamadear, since you let us hear that call, I assume that I can talk about it. I agree with Ira. You have Lazarus sexually stimulated whether he knows it or not, and if you can keep him that way, he won't be depressed."

"Is he truly that nearly recovered, Ishtar?" Hamadryad asked while raising her arms and letting them work on her. "He looks better. But I can't tell – his manner doesn't change."

"Oh, definitely. He started masturbating a month ago. Shampoo, dear?"

"He did? Really? Oh, that's wonderful! Do I need one? Yes, I do – thanks."

" 'So it's *well* to
Have a *sis*ter
Or *e*ven an old *unc*le –

"Close your eyes, Hambone baby; shampoo mix coming. A client has no privacy with Ishtar. But she didn't tell *me*; I had to infer it from his graphs. Ish, why do I always wind up washing Ham's back?"

"Because you tickle, sweetheart. There was no need for you to know. But a client certainly has no privacy with Minerva to help – and that's as it should be; we need better computer service at the Clinic, I now see. Although he *does* have privacy in its true sense, as all of this is covered by the Oath. Even though you are not regular staff, Ham, I'm sure you realize that."

"Oh, certainly! Not quite so hard, Galahad. Red-hot pincers could not make me talk other than to you two. Not even to Ira. Ishtar, do you think I could learn to be a *real* rejuvenator?"

"If you feel a vocation for it and want to study that hard. Let it rinse now, Galahad. You have the empathy, I'm sure. What's your index?"

" 'They're your *friends*, boy.
Don't ne*glect* them
Birth*days* and Yom *Kipp*ur –

"Uh . . . 'Genius-minus,' " Hamadryad admitted.

"Takes genius," Galahad said helpfully, "as well as a compulsive need to work; she's a slave driver, Hammy boy."

" 'Also *Christ*mas
And Cha*nuk*ah
A *card* or even *can*dy.' "

"You're off key, dear. You're 'Genius-*plus*,' Ham, slightly higher than Galahad's index. I looked it up, just in case – and you did ask. I'm very pleased."

" 'Off *key*' ? Now you've gone too far."

"You have other virtues, my true knight; you need not be a troubador. Hamadear, if you search your heart and really want it, you could be an associate technician by the time we migrate. If you intend to migrate. If not, the Clinic here always needs staff; a true vocation is scarce. But I'd like – terribly – to have you with us. Both of us will help you."

"Sure we will, Hammy! 'Offkey' indeed! Is this colony going to be polygamous?"

"Ask Ira. Does it matter? Grab a robe and throw it around the Hamadarling, then I'll trade a quick scrub with you; I'm hungry."

"Do you want to risk it? After what you said about my singing? I know every spot and I'll tickle them all."

"King's Cross! I apologize! I *love* your singing, dear."

"The idiom is 'King's X,' Ish. Pax, it is. Grab robes for all of us, Hammy, that's a good girl. Long legs, while I was singing – perfectly on key – I figured out that idiom that was bothering me. It's not what Minerva thought it was; a 'hook shop' is a bordello. Which makes the Born Loser's sister a hetaera – and the last piece falls into place."

"Why, of course! No wonder she could subsidize her brother – artists always get paid more than anyone else."

Hamadryad returned with robes, laid them on the massage table. She said, "I didn't know that idiom was bothering you, Galahad. I understood it the first time I heard the song."

"I wish you had told me."

"Is it important?"

"Only as one more clue. Ham, in analyzing a culture, its myths and folk songs and idioms and aphorisms are more basic than its formal history. You can't understand a person unless you understand her culture. 'His,' I should say, in speaking English – and that alone tells something basic about the culture in which our client grew up: the fact that a general term invariably takes the masculine form when both masculine and feminine are implied. It means either that males are dominant or that women have just emerged from lower status, but the language lag – there always is one – has not caught up with cultural change. The latter, in the barbarism Lazarus came from, as indicated by other clues."

"You can tell all that just from a rule of grammar?"

"Sometimes. Hammy, I used to do this professionally, when I was old and grizzled and waiting for rejuvenation. It's detective work and no one clue is ever enough. For example, women must not have reached equal status even though other clues show them gaining it – for whoever heard of a bordello managed by a *man?* A guard in one, yes, and Lazarus said that he was that, too. But *manager?* Preposterous, by modern standards. Unless that colony on Mars was an atypical retrogression – it may have been, I don't know."

"Continue it as we eat, kids; Mama is hungry."

"Coming, Ish dear. Galahad, I understood that idiom without thinking about it. You see, my mother was – still is – a hetaera."

"Really? There's a wild coincidence. So was mine, and so was Ishtar's – and we three wind up all in rejuvenation work and on the same client. Two small numerically professions – I wonder what the odds are against it?"

"Not too high, as both professions require strong empathy. But if you want to know, ask Minerva," advised Ishtar, "and hand me that robe. I don't like blowdry and I don't want to get chilled while rustling food. Hamasweet, why didn't you follow your mother's profession? With your beauty you would be a star."

Hamadryad shrugged. "Oh, I know what I look like. But Mother can snatch a man away from me just by lifting her little finger – except that I avoid the chance. Beauty has little to do with it – you saw a man turn me down just today. Lazarus himself told us what it takes to make a great artist – a spiritual quality a man can *feel.* My mother has it. I don't."

"I follow your reasoning," Ishtar said as they went through her lounge into the buttery. There she screened the menu offered by the kitchen down below. "My mother has it, too. Not especially pretty, but what she has, men want. Still want, although she's retired."

"Long Legs," Galahad said soberly, "you do all right. You've got it too."

"Thank you, my knight, but that's not true. I sometimes have it for one man. Or two at most. And sometimes not at all, as I can get buried in our profession and forget about sex. I told you how many years I had been celibate. I wouldn't have found *you*, dear, would never have risked 'Seven Hours' – had not our client had me so terribly emotional. Quite unprofessionally, Hamadryad; I was as silly as a schoolgirl on a warm spring night. But Galahad, Tamara – my mother – has it all the time and for anyone who needs her. Tamara never set a price, she didn't need to; they showered gifts on her. She's retired now and considering whether to rejuvenate again. But her fans won't leave her alone; she still gets endless offers."

Galahad said sorrowfully, "That's what I would like to be. But I'm that 'Born Loser.' If a man tried that profession, he'd kill himself in a month."

"In your case, dear Galahad, it might take a little longer. But eat and restore your strength; we're going to put you in the middle of the bed tonight."

"Does that mean I'm invited?" asked Hamadryad.

"That's one way of putting it. A more accurate statement would be that I'm inviting myself. Galahad made it clear in the shower that his plans for tonight include you, dear. But he didn't mention me."

"Oh, he did, too! Anyhow he's horny about you all the time; I can feel it."

"He's horny – end of message and off. Will steaks and random garnish do, or do you each wish to choose? I don't feel imaginative."

"Suits me. Ish, you should put Galahad under contract. While he's groggy."

"Privacy, dear."

"Sorry. I just blurted it out. Because I'm so fond of you both."

"Big-arsed bitch won't marry me," said Galahad. "And me so good and pure and modest. Claims I tickle. Will you marry me, little Hamadear?"

"What? Galahad, you're the world's worst tease. You not only don't want me to; you know I'm committed to the Senior even though he refused me. Until Ish tells me to drop it. If she does."

Ishtar finished ordering, wiped the screen. "Galahad, don't tease our baby. I want both Hamadryad and me to be free of other contracts as long as either of us has any chance of getting our client interested in cohabitation, or progeny, or both. Not just a lark but something he can take seriously."

"So? Then why in the name of all the fertility gods did you arrange to have *both* of you pregnant at once? I don't get it. I hear the whir but the figures won't add."

"Because my stupid darling, I didn't dare wait. The Director may come back at any time."

"But why *you* two? With maybe ten thousand healthy host-mothers registered and available? And why *two?*"

"Dearest man, I'm sorry I said you were stupid – you aren't; you're just male. Hamadryad and I know exactly what risks we are taking and why. We don't look pregnant and won't for weeks yet, and if either of us can jockey Lazarus into a contract, an abortion takes ten minutes. Professional host-mothers won't do for this job; it has to be bellies over which I have some control and women I trust utterly. Bad enough that I had to trust a gene surgeon and risk a proscribed procedure – Ira may have to get me out of that if anything slips.

"But you know as well as I do, sweet Galahad, that even an ordinary clone sometimes goes wild. I wish I had *four* female bellies I could use, not two. Eight. Sixteen! Increase the chances of getting *one* normal fetus. In another month – long before it shows – we'll know what we're carrying. If the odds fail both of us – well, I'm ready to start over again and Hamadryad is, too."

"As many times as necessary, Ishtar. I swore it."

Ishtar patted her hand. "We'll get a good one. Galahad, Lazarus is going to have his identical twin sister, I promise you – and once it is an accomplished fact, we'll hear no more talk of termination-option switches, or leaving us, or anything – at least until she's woman tall!"

"Ishtar?"

"Yes, Hamadryad?"

"If we *both* show normal fetuses a month from now –"

"Then you can abort, dear; you know that."

"No, no no! I shan't! What's wrong with *twins*?"

Galahad blinked at her. "Don't bother to answer, Ish. Let me give you the male angle. The man who can resist raising identical twin girls hasn't been born. And his name isn't Lazarus Long. Look, dears, is there anything at *all*, that can improve *both* your chances? Now?"

"No." Ishtar repeated softly, "No. We both test pregnant, that's all we can say or do now. Except pray. And I don't know how to pray."

"Then it's time we learned!"

VARIATION ON A THEME

V

Voices in the Dark

After Minerva ordered his evening meal for Lazarus, then supervised its service, the computer said, "Is there anything else, sir?"

"I guess not. Yes. Will you have dinner with me, Minerva?"

"Thank you, Lazarus. I accept."

"Don't thank me; *you* are doing *me* a favour, milady, I'm moody tonight. Sit down dear, and cheer me up."

The computer's voice repositioned so that it appeared to come from the other side of the table where Lazarus sat, as if a flesh-and-blood were seated there. "Shall I construct an image, Lazarus?"

"Don't put yourself to the trouble, dear."

"It's no trouble, Lazarus; I have ample spare capacity."

"No, Minerva. That holo you made for me one night – perfect, realistic, moved just like flesh-and-blood. But it wasn't *you*. I know what you look like. Umm . . . lower the lights and spot enough light on my plate to let me eat. Then I'll see you in the gloom without a holo."

The lighting readjusted so that the room was almost dark save for a pool of light on chastely perfect tableware and napery in front of Lazarus. The contrast dazzled his eyes enough that he could not see across the table without peering – he did not peer. Minerva said, "What is my appearance, Lazarus."

"Eh?" He stopped to think. "It fits your voice. Hmm, it's a picture that has grown up in my mind without thinking about it, during the time we have been together. Dear, do you realize that we have been living together more intimately than husband and wife usually manage?"

"Perhaps I don't Lazarus, since I cannot experience being a wife. But I am happy to be close to you."

"Being a wife doesn't have too much to do with copulation, my dear. You've been a mother to my baby, Dora. Oh, I know that Ira stands first with you . . . but you are like that girl Olga I spoke of; you have so much to give that you can enrich more than one man. But I honour your loyalty to Ira. Your love for him, dear."

"Thank you, Lazarus. But – if I know what the word means – I love you too. And Dora."

"I know you do. Both. You and I have no need to worry over words; we'll leave that to Hamadryad. Mmm, your appearance – you are tall, about as tall as Ishtar. But slender. Not skinny, just slender – strong and well muscled without being bulgy. You are not as broad in the hips as she is. But broad enough. Womanly. You're strong, but a mature young woman, not a girl. Breasts much smaller than Ishtar's, more like Hamadryad's. You are handsome rather than pretty, and you are rather solemn, except when one of your rare smiles lights up your face. Your hair is brown and straight, and you wear it long. But you don't fuss with it other than to keep it clean and neat. Your eyes are brown and match your hair. You usually don't wear cosmetics, but you almost always wear some sort of clothing – simple clothing; you are not a clotheshorse, dress does not interest you that much. But you go naked only with persons you fully trust – a short list.

"That's all, I guess. I haven't tried to imagine details; this is just what grew in my mind. Oh, yes! – you keep your nails, both hands and feet, short and clean. But you aren't fussy about it, or about anything. Neither dirt nor sweat bothers you, and you don't flinch at blood, even though you don't like it."

"I am very pleased to know how I look, Lazarus."

"Huh? Oh, fiddle, girl – that's my imagination living its own life."

"That is how I look," Minerva said firmly, "and I like it."

"All right. Although you can be as dazzlingly beautiful as Hamadryad if you want to be."

"No, I look just as you described me. I am a 'Martha,' Lazarus, not her sister Mary."

Lazarus said, "You surprised me. Yes, you are. You've read the Bible?"

"I have read everything in the Great Library. In one sense I *am* the Library, Lazarus."

"Mmm, yes, should've realized it. How is the twinning process coming along? Going to be ready? Say if Ira gets a burr under his saddle and takes off in a hurry."

"It is essentially complete, Lazarus. All my permanents, programmes and memories and logics, are twinning in Dora's number-four hold, and I run routine checks and exercise by running the twinned parts parallel with me here under the Palace – a 'Tell me six times' instead of my normal 'Tell me three times' method. I have found and corrected some open circuits that way – minor factory defects, nothing I could not handle at once. You see, Lazarus, I treated it as a crash programme and did not depend on Turing processes to build most of my new me, as I would have had to build extensions in Dora for that sole purpose, then remove them save for maintenance extensionals.

"That would have taken much time, of course, since I can't use computer speeds in manipulating mass. So instead I ordered all new blank memories and logic circuitry and had them installed in Dora by factory technicians. Much faster. Then I filled them and checked them."

"Any trouble, dear?"

"No, Lazarus. Oh, Dora grumbled about dirty feet in her clean compartments. But she was just grumbling, as they worked 'clean-room' style, lint-free coveralls and masks and gloves, and I required them to change in the air lock, not just before they entered her number-four." He felt her quick smile. "Temporary sanitary facilities outside the ship – which caused the project engineer to grumble, as well as the shop steward."

"Should think so. Wouldn't have hurt Dora to activate a head."

"Lazarus, as you pointed out, I will be – I hope – a passenger in Dora someday. So I have tried to become her friend – and we are friends, and I love her, and she is the only friend I have who is a computer. I don't want to jeopardize that by making a mess, or permitting one to be made, in my moving into her ship. She is, as you said, a neat housekeeper; I am trying to be just as neat and show thereby that I respect her and appreciate the privilege of being a passanger in her. The engineer in charge and that talky shop steward had no reason to grumble; I specified all this in the contract – change clothes at the lock, leg urinals for all personnel inside, no eating, expectorating, or smoking in the ship, go by the shortest route to number-four, no snooping elsewhere in the ship – which they could not, anyhow, as I asked Dora to keep all doors locked save that direct route – and I paid to have it done this way."

"A pretty penny, I'm certain. Did Ira comment?

"Ira does not bother with such matters. But I did not report costs to him; I charged it all to you, Lazarus."

"Whee! Am I bankrupt?"

"No, sir; I paid it from the Senior's unlimited drawing account.

That seemed best to me, Lazarus, as the work was done in your ship. Perhaps they wonder why the Senior wants a second computer, of high capacity, installed in his ship. I know the project engineer wondered; I snubbed him firmly. But wonder is all they can do; the Senior is not accountable to anyone. I hinted quite broadly that Mr. Chairman Pro Tem would be annoyed if anyone attempted to snoop into your affairs. Not that anyone can tell what a computer really is, just from looking at it – even the manufacturer."

"This manufacturer – Low bidder?"

"Shouldn't I have placed it for bid, sir?" Minerva sounded worried.

"Hell, no! If you had, I would have told you to tear it out and start over – then we would have hunted for the best supplier. Minerva my dear, once you leave here, it may be many years before you have any factory service; you'll have to maintain yourself. Unless Ira can minister to a sick computer?"

"He can't."

"You see? Dora is gold and platinum where a cheaper computer is copper and aluminium. I hope your new carcass is just as expensive."

"It is, Lazarus. My new me is even more reliable than my old me – and smaller and faster, as much of me – 'old me' – is about a century old; the art has improved."

"Hm. Must see what ought to be replaced in Dora, if anything."

Minerva made no comment. Lazarus said, "My dear, when you don't talk, it is louder than when you do. Have you been overhauling Dora?"

"I stockpiled some components, Lazarus. But Dora won't let herself be touched unless you order it."

"Yeah, she hates to let a doctor poke around inside her. But if she needs it, she'll get it – under anesthesia. Minerva, it would be smart, with two of you in the ship, for Dora to carry your maintenance instructions in her permanents, and hers in yours – so that you can nurse each other."

Minerva answered simply, "We have been waiting for you to tell us to do so, Lazarus."

"You mean *you* have been waiting; it is not something Dora would think of. So now I'm telling you both, and let her hear my voice say so. Minerva, I wish you would get over being so humble with me. *You* should have proposed it; you think faster than I do by many orders of magnitude; I've got flesh-and-blood limitations. How are you coming on astrogation? Is she teaching you to pilot? Or balking?"

"Lazarus, I am now as skillful a pilot as she is, in my other me."

"Like fun. You're a copilot. You're not a pilot until you've made an n-space jump unassisted. Even Dora gets jumpy before a jump – and she's made hundreds."

"I stand corrected, Lazarus. I am a very highly trained copilot. But I'm not afraid to do it, if the time comes. I've rerun all of Dora's jumps in real time, and she tells me I know how."

"You may have to someday, if disaster hits. Ira isn't the pilot I am, I'm certain. With me no longer aboard, your new skill may save his life sometime. What else do you know? Heard any good ones lately?"

"I don't know, Lazarus. I've heard some stories, bawdy ones I believe, from listening to the technicians installing my twin. But I don't know that they are funny."

"Don't bother. If it's a bawdy story, I heard one like it at least a thousand years back. Now the key question – How fast can you cut loose if Ira decides to jump? Assume a coup d'état and he's running for his life."

"One-fifth of a second, minus."

"Huh? You're not pulling my leg? I mean how long to put your whole personality aboard the 'Dora.' Not leave anything behind and not leave the computer here aware that she ever was Minerva – for anything less would not be fair to yourself, dear. The 'Minerva' left behind would grieve."

"Lazarus, I am speaking not from theory but from experience, as I knew it was the critical aspect of this twinning. So, once I dismissed the contractor and had twinned my permanents and logics and my running temporaries, I experimented, cautiously at first; I simply paralleled me, as I described to you. That's easy, I just have to balance the lag at each end, to stay synchronous in real time – but I have to do what with my remote extensionals at all times. I'm used to it.

"Then I tried, very cautiously suppressing, myself, first at the ship end, then at the Palace end, with a self- programme to revert to full twinning in three seconds. No trouble, Lazarus, not even the first time. Now I can do it in less than two hundred milliseconds and run all checks to be certain that I have neglected nothing. I have done so seven times since you asked that question. Did you notice a lag in my voice at times? Approximately a thousand-kilometre lag?"

"What? My dear, I am not equipped to notice a lag of less than thirty thousand kilometres at speed 'c'" He added, "Call it a tenth of a second. You flatter me." Lazarus added thoughtfully, "But a tenth of a second is a hundred million of the nanoseconds you use. Or a hundred milliseconds. What's that in your time? About a thousand of my days?"

"Lazarus, that is not how I would express it. I split much smaller than a nanosecond in many things I do – a 'millishake' or less. But I'm just as comfortable in your time; I am right now with my personal me. I could not enjoy singing, or this quiet talk with you, if in my personal mode I were forced to consider each nanosecond. Do you count each of your heartbeats?"

"No. Or rarely."

"It is somewhat the same with me, Lazarus. The things I do quickly I do with no effort and with no conscious attention other than necessary self-programme. But the seconds and minutes and hours I spend with you, in personal mode, I savour. I do not chop them into nanoseconds; I grasp them whole and enjoy them. All the days and weeks you have been here I hold as a single 'now' and cherish it."

"Uh . . . hold it, dear! Are you saying that, well, the day Ira introduced us to each other is still '*now*' to you?"

"Yes, Lazarus."

"Let me sort this out. Is tomorrow 'now' to you also?"

"Yes, Lazarus."

"Uh . . . but if that is so, you can predict the future."

"No, Lazarus."

"But – Then I don't understand it."

"I could print out the equations, Lazarus, but such equations would merely describe the fact that I am constructed to treat time as one of many dimensions, with entropy but one operator and with 'the present' or 'now' a variable held in steady state for a wide or narrow span. But in dealing with *you* I must necessarily move with the wave front that is *your* personal now – or we cannot communicate."

"My dear, I'm not sure we *are* communicating."

"I'm sorry, Lazarus. I have *my* limitations, too. But were I able to choose, I would choose *your* limitations. Human. Flesh-and-blood."

"Minerva, you don't know what you are saying. A flesh-and-blood body can be a burden . . . especially when its maintenance begins to occupy most of one's attention. You have the best of both worlds – designed in man's own image to do what makes him distinctively human – but better, faster – *much* faster! – and more accurately, than he can do it – without the aches and pains and inefficiencies of a body that must eat and sleep and make mistakes. Believe me."

"Lazarus . . . what is 'Eros'?"

He looked into the gloom and saw in his mind's eye how solemnly and sorrowfully she stared back. "Good God, girl – do you want to go to bed with him that badly?"

"Lazarus, I do not know. I am a 'blind man.' How *can* I know?"

Lazarus sighed. "I'm sorry, dear. Then you know why I have kept Dora a baby."

"Only as conjecture, Lazarus. One that I have not and will not discuss with anyone."

"Thank you – you are a lady, dear. You do know. Or you know part of my reason. But I'll tell you all of it – when I feel up to it – and then you will know what I mean by 'love' and why I told Hamadryad it must be experienced, not defined in words . . . and why I *know* that you know what love is, because you have experienced it. But Dora's story is not for Ira, just for you. No, you can let Ira have it . . . after I'm gone. Uh, call it 'The Tale of the Adopted Daughter'; then place a hold on it and let him have it later. But I won't tell it now; I'm not strong enough tonight – ask me when you know I'm feeling up to it."

"I shall. I'm sorry, Lazarus."

" 'Sorry'? Minerva, my very dear there is *never* anything to feel sorry about with love. *Never*. Would you rather not love me? Or Dora? Or never have learned of love through loving Ira?"

"No. No, not that! But would that I knew 'Eros,' too."

"Count your blessings, dear. 'Eros' can hurt."

"Lazarus, I do not fear being hurt. But while I know much about male-female reproduction, far more than any single human flesh-and-blood knows –"

"You do? Or think you do?"

"I do know, Lazarus. In preparation for migrating I added extra additional memory storage – filling much of hold number-two – so that I could transcribe for Ishtar into my new me all the research files and library and restricted records of the Howard Rejuvenation Clinic –"

"Whew! I think Ishtar took a chance. The Clinic seems pretty cagey about what they release and don't release."

"Ishtar is not afraid to take chances. But she did ask me to hurry, so I placed it in temporary here, until it could set up the necessary capacity – large – in Dora's hold. But I asked Ishtar's permission to study it, and she said it was all right for me do to so, as long as I did not release anything keyed as confidential or secret without consulting her.

"I found it fascinating, Lazarus. I now know all about sex . . . in the sense that a man who has always been blind can be taught the physics of a rainbow. I am even a gene surgeon now, in theory, and would not hesitate to be one in practice once I had time to construct the ultramicrominiature waldoes needed for such fine work. I am equally expert as obstetrician and gynecologist and rejuvenator. Erectile reflexes and mechanics or organism and the processes of spermogenesis and impregnation are no mystery to me, nor any aspect of gestation and birth.

" 'Eros' alone I cannot know . . and know at last that I am blind "

VARIATIONS ON A THEME

VI

The Tale of the Twins Who Weren't

(Omitted)

– but sky merchant was then my usual occupation, Minerva. That caper in which I moved from slave to high priest was forced on me. I had to be meek a long time, which ain't my style. Maybe Jesus was right when he said that the meek shall inherit the earth – but they inherit very small plots, about six feet by three.

But the only route from field hand to freedom lay through the church and required meekness all the way, so that's what I gave 'em. Those priests had weird habits –

(9,300 words omitted)

– which got me off their damned planet and I never expected to go back.

– did go back a couple of centuries later – freshly rejuvenated and not looking anything like that high priest whose ship had been lost in space.

I was a sky merchant again, which suits me; it lets you travel and see things. I went back to Blessed for money, not revenge. I've never wasted skull sweat on revenge; The Comte-de-Monte-Cristo syndrome is too much work and not enough fun. If I tangle with a man and he lives through it, I don't come back later gunning for him. Instead, I outlive him – which balances the books just as well. I figured that two centuries was enough for my enemies on Blessed to be dead, since I had left most of them sort of dead earlier.

Blessed would not have been on my route other than for business reasons. Interstellar trade is economics stripped to basics. You can't make money by making money because money isn't money other than on its planet of issue. Most money is fiat; a ship's cargo of the stuff is wastepaper elsewhere. Bank credit is worth even less; Galactic distances are too great. Even money that jingles must be thought of as *trade goods* – not money – or you'll kid yourself into starvation.

This gives the sky merchant a grasp of economics rarely achieved by bankers or professors. He is engaged in barter and no nonsense. He pays taxes he can't evade and doesn't care whether they are called "excise" or "king's pence" or "squeeze" or straight-out bribes. It is the other kid's bat and ball and backyard, so you play by his rules – nothing to get in a sweat about. Respect for laws is a pragmatic matter. Women know this instinctively; that's why they are all smugglers. Men often believe – or pretend – that the "Law" is something sacred, or at least a science – an unfounded assumption very convenient to governments.

I've done little smuggling; it's risky, and you can wind up with money you don't dare spend where it's legal tender. I simply tried to avoid places where the squeeze was too high.

By the Law of Supply and Demand a thing has value from *where* it is as much as from *what* it is – and that's what a merchant does; he moves things from where they are cheap to where they are worth more. A smelly nuisance in a stable is valuable fertilizer if you move it to the south forty. Pebbles on one Planet can be precious gems on another. The art in selecting cargo lies in knowing where things will be worth more, and the merchant who can guess right can reap the wealth of Midas in one trip. Or guess wrong and go broke.

I was on Blessed because I had been on Landfall and wanted to go to Valhallah in order to go back to Landfall, as I was thinking of marrying and raising another family. But I wanted to be rich enough to be landed gentry when I settled down – which I was not, at the time. All I had was the scout ship Libby and I had used* and a modicum of local money.

So it was time to trade.

The trade routes for a two-way swap show minimum profit; they fill up too quickly. But a triangular trade – or higher numbers – can show high profits. Like this: Landfall had something – call it cheese – which was a luxury on Blessed – while Blessed produced – call it chalk – much in demand on Valhalla . . . whereas Valhalla manufactured doohickeys that Landfall needed.

Work this in the right direction and get rich; work it backwards and lose your shirt.

I had worked the first leg, Landfall to Blessed, successfully, having sold my cargo of – Now what was it? Durned if I remem-

*Sequence of events cannot be reconciled. Perhaps a similar ship?
J.F. 45th

ber; I've handled so many things. Anyhow, I got such a nice price that I temporarily had too much money.

How much is "too much"? Whatever you can't spend before you leave a place you are not coming back to. If you hang onto that excess and come back later, you will usually find – invariably, so far as I recall – that inflation or war or taxes or changes in government or something has wiped out the alleged value of fiat money you may have kept.

As my ship was scheduled to load and I had placed in escrow with the port authority the price of the cargo, what I had left over was burning a hole in my pocket with only a day to get rid of it, that being the time until my ship was to be loaded – I had to be on hand for that; I was my own purser and have an untrusting disposition.

So I took a walk through the retail district, thinking I might buy some doodads.

I was dressed in local high style and had a bodyguard behind me, for Blessed was still a slave economy and in a pyramidal society it is well to be up near the point, or at least look like it. My bodyguard was a slave but not my slave; I had hired him from a rent-a-servant agency. I'm not a hypocrite; this slave didn't have a durn thing to do but follow me around and eat like a hog.

I had him because my assumed status required a manservant in sight. A "gentleman" could not register at a first-class hilton in Charity or anywhere on Blessed without a valet in evidence; I could not eat in a good restaurant without my own bearer standing behind me – and so forth; when in Rome, you shoot Roman candles. I've been places where it was mandatory to sleep with your hostess – which can be dreadful; this Blessed custom wasn't difficult.

I didn't rely on him even though the agency supplied him with a knob stick. I was armed six ways and careful where I walked; Blessed was more dangerous than it had been when I was a slave there and a "gentleman" is more of a target, even though cops don't bother him.

I was taking a shortcut through the slave market, it not being an auction day, on my way to the jeweller's lane, when I saw that a sale was being offered and slowed down – a man who has been sold himself can't walk past, indifferent to the plight of chattels. Not that I had any intention of buying.

Nor did anyone seem about to buy this pair; the knot around

the factor's tent was rabble; I could tell by their clothes and the fact that there wasn't a man there with a manservant.

The merchandise was standing on a table, a young woman and a young man. Late adolescence for him and just ripe for her, or the same age in view of the fact that females grow up faster. Call it eighteen measured by my own youth – an age at which a boy should be nailed into a barrel and fed through the bunghole but a girl is ready to marry.

Long sleeveless robes hung from their shoulders – and I knew too well what those robes meant; they would be displayed only to a prospective buyer, not to rabble. Robes signified valuable slaves not to be knocked down on open bid.

Sure enough, they were being held at Dutch auction, with the minimum bid posted – ten thousand blessings. That amounts to – How can I define money of centuries back on a planet hundreds of light-years away in terms that make sense here and now? Let's put it this way: Unless these kids were something extraordinary, they were overpriced by a factor of five, as prime young stock, either sex, were fetching around a thousand blessings by the morning's financial news.

Ever pause in front of a clothing store and get hooked inside? No, of course you haven't. But that's what happened to me.

All I did was say to the factor, "Goodman, is that posted bid a mistake? Or do these two have something special that doesn't show?" Just curiosity, Minerva, as I neither intended to own slaves nor would the excess in my purse make a dent in a planet-wide custom. But I could not see *why?* The girl was not outstandingly pretty; she would not fetch a high price as an odalisque. The lad wasn't even heavily muscled. Nor were they a matched pair. Back home I would have picked her for Eyetalian and him for a Swede.

Boom, I'm urged into the tent while the chattels are shoved ahead; the factor's manner shows that he hasn't had a live one all day – while my shadow is saying in my ear, "Master, that price is too high. I can take you to a private sale where prices are right and satisfaction is guaranteed."

I said, "Shut up, Faithful" – all rented body servants were named "Faithful," probably by contraries – "I want to see what this is."

As fast as the tent flap is fastened against the rabble, the factor is shoving a chair against my knees and handing me a drink with a bow and a scrape while saying lyrically, "Oh, sweet and gentle master, happy am I that you asked that! I am about to show you a great wonder of science! A thing to astound the very gods! I speak as a pious man, a true son of our Everlasting Church, one who cannot lie!"

A slave factor who can't lie has yet to be whelped. Meantime the youngsters stationed themselves docilely on a display platform and Faithful was whispering: "Don't believe a word, Master. The girl is nothing and I can whip three of that punk without my stick – yet the agency would sell you *me* for eight hundred blessings and that's a fact."

I motioned him to silence. "Goodman, what swindle is this?"

"No swindle, on my mother's honour, kind sir! Would you believe that these are brother and sister?"

I looked at them. "No."

"Would you believe that they are not only brother and sister but *twins?*"

"No."

"Would you believe the same stud, the same dam, the same womb, born the same hour?"

"Possibly the same womb," I conceded. "Host-mother?"

"No, no! *Exactly* the same ancestry. And yet – here is the miracle –" He held my eye and spoke in a hushed voice: "They are nevertheless a sound *breeding* pair . . . for these twins are *unrelated to each other!* Would you believe it?"

I told him what I would believe, including his losing his licence and facing a charge of blasphemy.

His smile grew broader, and he complimented me on my wit and asked me how much – if he *proved* all of these things – how high a bid I would place against them? Higher than ten thousand since I must realize that the posted figure represented a prior bid. Fifteen thousand, perhaps, with escrow the morrow before noon?

I said, "Forget it, I'm shipping out before noon" – and started to stand up.

He said, "Wait, I beg you! I see that you are a gentleman of education, of science, of deep knowledge and widely travelled – surely you will grant your humble servant a moment to show *proof?*"

I still would have left; swindles bore me. But he waved a hand, and the kids dropped their robes and fell into display poses, the lad with his arms folded across his chest and his feet planted firmly, the girl in that graceful pose that must be as old as Eve – one knee slightly advanced, hand on hip, other arm hanging easily, chest slightly raised. It almost made her beautiful save that she looked bored – having taken it hundreds of times, no doubt.

But that wasn't what made me stay; something annoyed me. The lad was bare of course – she was wearing a chastity girdle. Do you know what one is, Minerva?

"Yes, Lazarus."

Too bad. I said, "Take that damned thing off that kid! *Now!*" Silly of me; I rarely interfere with *anything* on a strange planet. But those things are abominations.

"Certainly, gentle sir; I was about to. Estrellita!"

The girl turned her back, with that same bored look. The factor stood so that his back kept the lad from seeing him work the combination lock, saying apologetically, "She must wear it not only because of ruffians but to protect her from her brother; they share the same pallet, for she is – would you believe it, sir, seeing how full ripe she is? a – *virgin!* Show the gentle master, 'Trellita."

Bored as ever, she promptly started to do so. I regard virginity as a correctable perversity of no interest; I motioned her to stop and asked the factor if she could cook.

He assured me that she was the envy of every gourmet chef on Blessed, and started to lock her back into that steel diaper. I said roughly, "Leave it off! Nobody here is going to rape her. What's this proof you promised?"

Minerva, he proved every word – except about her cooking – with exhibits that made me suspicious only because *he* showed them; I wouldn't have boggled had I seen them in the Clinic here.

I should mention that Blessed had a rejuvenation clinic even though it was not settled by the Families. Eventually the clinic was taken over by the church and antigeria techniques that work fairly well even on short-lifers were no longer available to any but big shots. But the planet stayed advanced in biological techniques; the church needed it.

Minerva, I told you what he claimed and you are now as learned in biology and genetics and associated manipulations as Ishtar is – more so; you don't have her limitations in time and in memory storage. What did he prove to me?

"That they were diploid complements, Lazarus."

Right! Although he called them "mirror twins." Can you tell me how these kids were made, Minerva? How would *you* go about producing such twins?

The computer answered thoughtfully, " 'Mirror twins' would be an inexact term for zygotes satisfying the listed requirements – although it is colourful. I can answer only theoretically as the records in me do not show that it had been attempted on Secundus. But the steps necessary to achieve exact diploid complements would be these: There must be intervention in gametogenesis in each parent just before meiotic division-reduction of chromosome number – that is, one would start with primary spermatocytes and primary oocytes, unreduced diploids.

"In the male parent the intervention presents no theoretical problem but would be difficult because the cells are very small – but I would not hesitate to attempt it given time to construct the necessary fine extensionals.

"The logical place to start, both parents, would be with gonia placed in vitro, and cherished. When a spermatogonium was observed to change to a primary spermatocyte – still diploid – it would be segregated and at the instant it divided into two secondary spermatocytes – haploids, one with an X chromosone and one with a Y chromosome – they would be again segregated and each would be encouraged to develop into spermatozoa.

"It would not be sufficient to intervene at the spermatozoa stage; confusion of gamete pairs could not be avoided, and resulting zygotes could be complementary only by wildest chance.

"Intervention with the female parent is mechanically simpler because of larger cells – but involves a different problem; the primary oocyte must be encouraged at point of meiosis, to produce *two* haploid and complementary secondary oocytes, rather than one oocyte and one polar body. Lazarus, this might require many attempts before a reliable technique could be worked out. It would be similar to the process of identical twinning but must take place two stages earlier in the gametogenetic sequence. However, it might turn out to be no more difficult than it is to produce fatherless female rabbits. I do not venture an opinion as I lack former art to draw on – save that I feel certain that it can be done given time to develop technique.

"At this point we have complementary groups of spermatozoa, one group with Y and one with X, and a complementary pair of ova, each with an X chromosome. Fertilization would be in vitro, with a possibility of choosing either of two potential pairs of female male complements but with no basis for choice unless the genetic charts of haploids are determined precisely, which is difficult and likely to cause genetic damage; I do not think it would be attempted. Instead one sperm would be inserted into one ovum, its complement into the other, on a blind basis.

"One last requirement must be met to justify *all* of this slave factors' allegations: The two fertilized ova must be removed from vitreo and planted in the womb of the donor of the oogonium, and there allowed to develop as twins through natural gestation and birth.

"Am I right, Lazarus?"

Exactly right! Go to the head of the class, dear; you get a gold star on your report card. Minerva, I don't *know* that it happened that way. But that's what the factor claimed, and that's what his exhibits – lab reports, holomovies, and so forth – seemed to show. But that thief may have faked those "proofs" and offered a random pair not likely to fetch a price above average – save for his fancy sales talk. The so-called proofs looked good, and lab reports and such carried a bishop's chop and seal. The stills and movies looked good, too – but how can a layman judge? Even if those exhibits weren't phony, all they could prove was that such a process had once taken place; they did *not* prove that *these* kids were the result. Shucks, they might have been used to sell many slave pairs, with a bishop in on the racket.

I looked over the stuff, including a scrapbook of the kids growing up, said, "Very interesting," and started to leave.

This pimple teleported himself between me and the tent flap. "Master," he said urgently. "Kind and generous sir – twelve thousand?"

Minerva, my trader instincts took over. "One thousand!" I snapped. I don't know why. Yes, I do know. The girl's body was scarred from that damned Torquemada girdle; I wanted to insult this flesh peddler.

He flinched and looked as if he were giving birth to broken beer bottles. "You jest with me. Eleven thousand Blessings, and they are yours – though I won't make expenses!"

"Fifteen hundred," I answered. I had money I couldn't spend elsewhere and told myself I could afford to manumit them rather than let that girl be bound into that damned atrocity again.

He moaned. "If they were mine, I would *give* them to you. I love these cute darlings like my own children and could ask for them nothing better than a kind and gentle master learned in science who appreciates the wonders that have gone into their making. But the Bishop would hang me and have me cut down alive to be dragged to death by my tool. Ten thousand and take all proofs and exhibits. I'll suffer a loss for their sakes – and because I admire you so much."

I got up to forty-five hundred and he got down to seven thousand and there we stuck, as I had to hold out cash for last-minute squeeze, whereas it felt to me that he was close to the point where he really could not sell without risking the Bishop's wrath. If there was a bishop –

He turned away in a fashion that says that a dicker is over and he is through flattering you, and told the girl sharply to step back into her steel harness.

I got out my purse. Minerva, you understand money; you handle the government's finances. But possibly you don't know that *cash* money affects some people the way catnip does Diablo. I counted out forty-five hundred blessings in big red-and-gold bills under that scoundrel's nose – and stopped. He was sweating and swallowing his Adam's apple but managed to shake his head a tenth of an inch.

So I counted more bills, very slowly, and reached five thousand – then started briskly to pick them up.

He stopped me – and I found that I had bought the only slaves I have ever owned.

He relaxed then, in a resigned way, but wanted lagniappe for the exhibits. I didn't care one way or another but offered two hundred and fifty for the pix and tapes, take it or leave it. He took it and again started to put the girl back into her harness.

I stopped him and said, "Show me how that works."

I knew how – a cylinder-type ten-letter combination lock you could set to a new combination each time you used it. Set the combination, slide the ends of the steel strap that went round her waist through the ends of the barrel, spin the alphabet discs of the cylinder, then it stays locked until you reset whatever ten-letter combo you picked. An expensive lock and good steel in the girdle – alloy a hacksaw couldn't touch. This was another thing that made his story convincing, as, while there was a market for virgins on that weird globe, a trained odalisque fetched about the same, and this girl wasn't being reserved for harem stock either way. So an expensive custom-made chastity belt had to have some other reason.

With our backs to the slaves he showed me the combination: E,S,T,R,E,L,L,I,T,A – and was smug about how clever he was to pick a combination he couldn't forget.

So I fumbled on purpose, then pretended to catch on, and

opened it. He was about to put it on the kid again and send us on our way. I said, "Wait a moment. I want to be sure I can work it in place. You step into it and let me get you out of it."

He didn't want to. So I got snotty and said he was trying to cheat me – put me in a position where I would have to send for him and pay through the nose to get my property unlocked. I demanded my money back and started to tear up the bill of sale. He gave in and stepped into the contrivance.

He could squeeze into it although the ends of the steel belt barely met; he was bigger around the waist than the girl was. I said. "Now spell that combination for me" – and leaned over the lock. As he spelled "ESTRELLITA," what I set was "HORSE THIEF," then jammed the ends together as hard as possible and spun the disks.

"Good," I said. "It works. Now spell it again."

He did so and I carefully spelled "ESTRELLITA." It stayed locked. I suggested that he had me spell it with one *l* and two *t*'s the first time. That didn't work either.

He dug up a mirror and tried it himself. No go. I said it might be jammed, so suck up your gut and we'll shake it. By now he was sweating.

Finally I said, "Tell you what, goodman – I'll *give* you this belt. I'd rather trust a padlock anyhow. So go to a locksmith – no, you won't want to wear this outside; just tell me where to find one and I'll send him here and pay him myself. Fair enough? I can't hang around; I've got a dinner engagement at the Beulahland. Where are their clothes? Faithful, gather up this junk and fetch the kids."

So I left him still blatting about telling the locksmith to *hurry*.

As we left his tent, a taxicab was cruising by. I had Faithful hail it and we all piled in. I didn't bother with a locksmith; I had the driver head for the skyport, then stopped on the way at a slopchest and bought the kids proper clothes, a clout for him and sort of Balinese sarong for her – uh, that's much like the dress Hamadryad wore yesterday. I think those were the first real clothes the youngsters had ever had. I couldn't get shoes on them; I settled for sandals – then had to drag Estrellita away from a mirror; she was admiring herself and preening. I threw away those auction robes.

I shoved the kids into the taxi and said to Faithful: "See that alley? If I turn my back and you run down it, I won't be able to chase you; I've got to keep an eye on these two."

Minerva, I ran into something I'll never understand: the slave mentality. Faithful didn't get my meaning – and when I spelled it out, he was aghast. Hadn't he given good service? Did I want him to *starve?*

I gave up. We dropped him at the Rent-a-Servant, and I got my deposit back – tipping him for good service – and my slaves and I rode on out to the skyport.

Turned out I needed that deposit and almost every blessing I had left – had to pay squeeze at outgoing customs to get the kids aboard my ship, even though the bill of sale was in order.

But I got 'em aboard. I immediately had them kneel, put my hands on their heads and manumitted them. They did not seem to believe it, so I explained. "Look, you're free now. *Free*, get me? No longer slaves. I'll sign your manumission papers and you can go to the diocese office and get them registered. Or you can have dinner here and sleep aboard, and I'll give you what blessings I can just before my ship lifts tomorrow. Or, if you *want* to, you can stay aboard and go to Valhalla, a nice planet though chillier than this one – but where there is no such thing as slavery."

Minerva, I don't think 'Llita – pronounced "Yeetah," her everyday name – or her brother Joe – Josie, or José – understood what I meant by a place that did not have slavery; it was foreign to anything they knew. But they knew what a starship was, from hearsay, and the prospect of *going* somewhere in one had them awestruck – they would not have missed it if I had told them they were going to be hanged on arrival. Besides, in their minds I was still their master; manumission hadn't taken hold even though they knew what it was. Something for old and faithful retainers, that is, who stayed on at the funda where they had been all along, but maybe got paid a little.

But to travel! The farthest they had ever been in their lives was from a diocese north of there to the capital, to be sold.

A little trouble next morning – Seems that one Simon Legree, licensed dealer in slaves, had sworn a complaint against me alleging bodily harm, mental stress, and assorted mopery and dopery. So I sat the cop down in my wardroom, poured him a drink, called in Llita and had her take off her wonderful new clothes and let the cop see the scars on her hips, then told her to skedaddle. I happened to leave a hundred-blessing note on the table while I got up to fetch the bill of sale.

The cop waved away the bill of sale, saying there had been no complaint on that score – but he was going to tell Goodman

Legree that he was lucky not to face a countercharge of selling damaged goods . . . no, on second thought it was simpler if he just couldn't find me until after my ship lifted. The hundred blessings was gone, and soon the cop was gone – and by mid-afternoon, so were we.

But, Minerva, I got cheated; Llita couldn't cook worth a damn.

It is a long and complex passage from Blessed to Valhalla, and Shipmaster Sheffield was pleased to have company.

There was a mild contretemps the first night of the voyage caused by a misunderstanding that had started the night before, dirtside. The ship had a cabin and two staterooms. Since the Captain normally operated by himself, he used the staterooms for casual storage or light cargo; they were not ready for passengers. So that first night dirtside he put his freedwoman into his cabin, while her brother and he slept on transom couches in the wardroom.

The following day Captain Sheffield unlocked the staterooms, switched power to them, had the young people clean them and move the clutter to a gear locker until he could see what space he had left in his holds, and told them each to take a room – and forgot it, being busy with cargo and final squeeze, then with supervising his piloting computer while they got clear of that system. It was late that "night," ship's time, before he had his ship on her first leg in n-space, and could relax.

He went to his cabin while considering whether to eat first or shower first, or possibly neither.

Estrellita was in his bed – wide awake and waiting.

He said, "Llita, what are you doing *here?*"

She told him in blunt slave lingo what she was doing in his bed – waiting for him – as she had known what would be expected of her when milord Shipmaster Sheffield had offered to take them along, and had discussed it with her brother, and Brother had told her to do it.

She added that she was not a bit afraid; she was ready and eager.

The first part of this Aaron Sheffield had to believe; the addendum seemed clearly a white lie; he had seen frightened virgins before – not often, but a few.

He dealt with her fear by ignoring it. He said, "You impudent bitch, get your arse out of my bed and into your own."

The freedwoman was startled and unbelieving, then sulky and

offended – then she wept. Fear of an unknown that she had felt earlier was drowned in a worse emotion; her tiny ego was crushed by his rejection of service she *knew* she owed him – and had believed he wanted. She sobbed, and dripped tears on his pillow.

Female tears always had a strong aphrodisiac effect on Captain Sheffield; he responded to them at once – by grabbing her ankle, dragging her out of bed, hustling her out of his cabin, into her stateroom, and locking her in. Then he returned to his cabin, locked its door, took measures to calm himself, and went to sleep.

Minerva, there was nothing wrong with Llita as a woman. Once I taught her to bathe properly she was quite attractive – good figure, pleasant face and manner, good teeth, and her breath was sweet. But taking her did not fit any customs. All "Eros" is custom, dear; there is never anything moral or immoral about copulation as such, or any of its non-functional frills. "Eros" is simply a way of keeping human beings, individuals, each different – keeping them together and happy. It is a survival mechanism developed through long evolution, and its reproductive function is the least complex aspect of its very complex and pervasive role in keeping the human race going.

But any sexual act is moral or immoral by precisely the same laws of morality as any other human act; all other rules about sex are simply customs – local and transient. There are more codes of sexual customs than a dog has fleas – and all they have in common is that they are "ordained by God." I recall a society where copulation in private was obscene and forbidden, criminal – while in public it was "anything goes." The society I was brought up in had the reverse of those rules – again "ordained by God." I'm not sure which pattern was harder to follow, but I wish God would quit changing his mind – as it is never safe to ignore such customs and ignorance is no excuse; ignorance like to got my ass shot off several times.

In refusing Llita I was not being moral; I was following *my own* sexual customs, worked out by trial and error and many bruises over the centuries: Never bed a female dependent on me unless I am married to her or willing to marry her. This is an amoral rule of thumb, subject to change according to circumstances and not applying to females *not* dependent on me – another negotiation entirely. But this rule is a safety precaution applicable most times and places with widely varying customs – a safety measure for *me* . . . because, unlike that lady from Boston I told you about, many females tend to regard copulation as a formal proposal of contract.

I had let impulse lure me into a predicament in which Llita was temporarily my dependent; I had no intention of making matters worse by marrying her, I didn't owe her that. Minerva, long-lifers should never marry ephemerals; it is not fair to the ephemeral or to the long-lifer.

Nevertheless, once you pick up a stray cat and feed it, you cannot abandon it. Self-love forbids it. The cat's welfare becomes essential to your own peace of mind – even when it's a bloody nuisance not to break faith with the cat. Having brought these kids I could not shuck them off by manumission; I had to plan their future – because *they* did not know how. They were stray cats.

Early next "morning" (by ship's routine) Captain Sheffield got up, unlocked the freedwoman's stateroom, found her asleep. He called her and told her to get up, wash quickly, then get breakfast for three. He left to wake her brother – found his stateroom empty, found him in the galley. "Good morning, Joe."

The freedman jumped. "Oh! Good morning, Master." He ducked and bent his knee.

"Joe, the correct answer is: 'Good morning, Captain.' It amounts to the same thing at present, for I am indeed master of this ship and everyone in it. But when you leave my ship on Valhalla, you will have no master of any sort. *None*, as I explained yesterday. Meanwhile, call me 'Captain.'"

"Yes . . . Captain." The young man repeated obeisance.

"Don't bow! When you speak to me, stand tall and straight and proud, and look me in the eye. The correct answer to an order is 'Aye aye, Captain.' What are you doing there?"

"Uh, I don't know – Captain."

"I don't think you do, either. That's enough coffee for a dozen people." Sheffield elbowed Joe aside, salvaged most of the coffee crystals the lad had poured into a bowl, measured enough for nine cups, made note to teach the girl how if she did not know, then have her keep coffee ready during working hours.

As he sat down with his first cup of coffee, she appeared. Her eyes were red and had circles under them; he suspected that she had wept some more that morning. But he made no comment other than a morning greeting and let her cope with the galley unassisted, she having seen what he had done the morning before.

Shortly he was recalling fondly the scratch lunch and supper – sandwiches he had made himself – of the day before. But he said nothing other than to order them to sit down and eat with him, rather than hovering over him. Breakfast was mostly coffee, cold ship's bread, tinned butter. Reconstituted accra eggs with mushrooms were an inedible mess, and she had managed to do something to heavenfruit juice. To spoil that took talent; all it needed was eight parts of cold water for each part of concentrate, and the instructions were on the container.

"Llita, can you read?"

"No, Master."

"Make that 'Captain,' instead. How about you, Joe?"

"No, Captain."

"Arithmetic? Numbers?"

"Oh, yes, Captain, I know numbers. Two and two is four, two and three makes five, and three and five is nine –"

His sister corrected him. "Seven, Josie – not nine."

"That's enough," Sheffield said. "I can see we'll be busy." He thought, while he hummed: "So it's well to . . . Have a sister . . . Or even an old captain –" He added aloud: "When you have finished breakfast, take care of your personal needs, then tidy your rooms – shipshape and neatly, I'll inspect later – and make the bed in my cabin, but don't touch anything else there, especially my desk. Then each of you take a bath. Yes, that's what I said: Bathe. Aboard ship everyone bathes every day, oftener if you wish. There is plenty of pure water; we recycle it and we'll finish the voyage with thousands of litres more than we started with. Don't ask why; that's the way it works and I'll explain later." (Several months later, at least – to youngsters unsure about three plus five.) "When you're through, say, an hour and a half from now – Joe, can you read a clock?"

Joe stared at the old-fashioned ship's clock mounted on a bulkhead. "I'm not sure, Captain. That one has too many numbers."

"Oh, yes, of course; Blessed is on another system. Try to be back here when the little hand is straight out to the left and the big hand is straight up. But this time it doesn't matter if you are late; it takes awhile to shake down. Don't neglect your baths to be on time. Joe, shampoo your head. Llita, lean toward me, dear; let me sniff your hair. Yes, you shampoo, too." (Were there hair nets aboard? If he cut the pseudogravity and let them go free-fall, they would need hair nets – or haircuts. A haircut would not hurt Joe, but his sister's long black hair was her best feature – would help her catch a husband on Valhalla. Oh, well, if there were no hair nets – he didn't think there were, as he kept his own free-fall short – the girl could braid her hair and tie something around it. Could he spare power to maintain an eighth gee all the way? People not used to free-fall got flabby, could even damage their bodies.

(Don't worry about it now.) "Get our quarters tidy, get clean yourselves, some back here. Git."

He made a list:

Set up a schedule of duties – N.B.: Teach them to cook!

Start school: What subjects?

Basic arithmetic, obviously – but don't bother to teach them to read that jargon spoken on Blessed; they were never going back there – never! But that jargon would have to be ship's language until he had them speaking Galacta, and they must learn to read and write in it – and English too: Many books he would have to use for their hurry-up education were in English. Did he have tapes for the variation of Galacta spoken on Valhalla? Well, kids their age quickly picked up local accent and idiom and vocabulary.

What was more important was how to heal their stunted, uh, "souls." Their personalities –

How could he take full-grown domestic animals and turn them into able, happy human beings, educated in every needful way and capable of competing in a free society? *Willing* to compete, undismayed by it –. He was just beginning to see the size of the "stray cat" problem he had taken on. Was he going to have to keep them as pets for fifty or sixty years or whatever, until they died naturally?

Long, long before that, the boy Woodie Smith had found a half-dead fox kit in the woods, apparently lost by its mother, or perhaps the vixen was dead. He took it home, nursed it with a bottle, raised it in a cage through one winter. In the spring he took it back where he had found it, left it there in the cage with the door latched open.

He checked a few days later, intending to salvage the cage.

He found the creature cowering in the cage, half starved and horribly dehydrated – with the door still latched open. He took it home, again nursed it back to health, built a chicken-wire run for it, and never again tried to turn it loose. In the words of his grandfather, "The poor critter had never had a chance to learn how to be a fox."

Could he teach these cowed and ignorant animals how to be human?

They returned to his wardroom when "the little hand was straight out and the big hand was straight up" – they waited outside the door until this was so, and Captain Sheffield pretended not to notice.

But when they came in, he glanced at the clock and said, "Right on time – good! You've certainly shampooed, but remind me to find combs for you." (What other toilet articles did they need? Would he have to teach them how to use them? And – oh, damn it! – was there anything in the ship for a woman's menstrual needs? What could be improvised? Well, with luck that problem would hold off a few days. No point in asking her; she couldn't add. Tarnation, the ship was not equipped for passengers.)

"Sit down. No, wait a moment. Come here, dear." It seemed to the Captain that the garment she wore was clinging suspiciously; he felt it, it was wet. "Did you leave that on when you bathed?"

"No, Mas – No, Captain; I washed it."

"I see." He recalled that its gaudy pattern had been enhanced by coffee and other things while the girl was botching breakfast. "Take it off and hang it somewhere; don't let it dry on your body.

She started slowly to comply. Her chin quivered – and he recalled how she had admired herself in a tall mirror when he bought it for her. "Wait a moment, Llita. Joe, take off your breech clout and sandals."

The lad complied at once.

"Thank you, Joe. Don't put that clout back on without washing it; by now it's dirty even though it looks clean. Don't wear it under way unless it suits you. You sit down. Llita, were you wearing anything when I bought you?"

"No . . . Captain."

"Am I wearing anything now?"

"No, Captain."

"There are times and places to wear clothes – and other times and places when clothes are silly. If this were a passenger ship, we would all wear clothes and I would wear a fancy uniform. But it is not, and there is nobody here but me and your brother. See that instrument there? That's a thermohumidostat which tells the ship's computer to hold the temperature at twenty-seven

Celsius and forty per cent humidity, with random variation to stimulate us – which may not mean anything to you but is my notion of comfort in bare skin. For an hour each afternoon it drops that temperature to encourage exercise, as flab is the curse of shipboard life.

If that cycle doesn't suit you two, we'll reach a compromise. But first we'll try it my way. Now about that wet rag plastered to your hips – If you are stupid, you'll let it dry where it is and be uncomfortable. If you are smart, you'll hang it up and let it dry without wrinkling. That's a suggestion, not an order; if you wish you may wear it at all times. But don't sit down with it on you, wet; there is no reason to get cushions wet. Can you sew?"

"Yes, Captain. Uh... some."

"I'll see what I can dig up. You are wearing the only woman's garment in the ship, and if you insist on clothes, you'll need to make some for the months ahead. You'll need something for Valhalla, too: it's not as warm as Blessed. Women there wear trousers and short coats; men wear trousers and long coats; everyone wears boots. I had three outfits custom-made on Landfall; maybe we can make do with them until I can get you two to a tailor. Boots – Mine would fit you like socks on a rooster. Hmm – We can wrap your feet so that a pair will stay on long enough to get you to a bootery.

"We won't worry about that now. Join the conference – standing up and wet, or sitting down and comfortable."

Estrellita bit her lip and decided in favour of comfort.

Minerva, those youngsters were brighter than I had expected. At first they studied because I told them to. But once they tasted the magic of the printed word, they were hooked. They learned to read like grass through a goose and didn't want to do anything else. Especially stories. I had a good library, mostly in micro, thousands of those, but also a few dozen valuable bound books, facsimile antiques I had picked up on Landfall where they speak English and use Galacta only as a trade tongue. Savvy Oz books, Minerva?

Yes, of course you do; I helped plan the Great Library and included my childhood favourites as well as more sober things. I did make sure that Joe and Llita read a spread of sober stuff but mostly I let them wallow in stories – The *Just So Stories*, and the Oz books, and *Alice in Wonderland*, and *A Child's Garden of Verses*, and *Two Little Savages*, and such. Too limited; they were books from my childhood, three centuries before the Diaspora. On the other hand, every human culture in the Galaxy derives from that one.

But I tried to make sure that they understood the difference between fiction and history – difficult, as I wasn't certain that there was a difference. Then I had to explain that a fairy tale was still a different sort, one step farther along the spectrum from fact to fancy.

Minerva, this is *very* hard to explain to an inexperienced mind. What is "magic"? You are more magical than any "magic" in fairy tales, and it does no good to say that you are a product of science, rather than magic, in speaking to kids who have no idea what is meant by "science" – and I wasn't sure that the distinction was valid even when I was explaining the distinction. In my wanderings I have run across magic many times – which simply says that I have seen wonders I could not explain.

I finally let it go by asserting *ex cathedra* that some stories were just for fun and not necessarily true – *Gulliver's Travels* were not the same sort of thing as *The Adventures of Marco Polo*, while *Robinson Crusoe* lay somewhere in between – and they should *ask* me, if in doubt.

They did ask, sometimes, and accepted my decision without argument. But I could see that they did not always believe me. That pleased me; they were starting to think for themselves – didn't matter if they were wrong. Llita was simply politely respectful to me about Oz. She believed in the Emerald City with all her heart and, if she had had her druthers, she would have been going there rather than to Valhalla. Well, so would I.

The important thing was that they were cutting the cord.

I did not hesitate to use fiction in teaching them. Fiction is a faster way to get a feeling for alien patterns of human behaviour than is nonfiction; it is one stage short of actual experience – and I had only months in which to turn these cowed and ignorant animals into people. I could have offered them psychology and sociology and comparative anthropology; I had such books on hand. But Joe and Llita could not have put them together into a gestalt – and I recall another teacher who used parables in putting over ideas.

They read every hour I would let them, huddled together like puppies and staring at the reading machine and nagging each other about how fast to raise the pages. Usually Llita nagged Joe; she was quicker than he – but as may be, they spurred each other from illiterate to speedreaders in zip time. I didn't let them have sound-and-picture tapes – I wanted them to *read*.

Couldn't let 'em spend all their time reading; they had to learn other things – not just saleable skills but, much more important, that aggressive self-reliance necessary to a free human – which they totally lacked when I saddled myself with them. Shucks, I wasn't certain they had the potential; it might have been bred out of their line. But if the spark was in them, I had to find it and fan it into flame – or I would never be able to make them run free.

So I forced them to make up their own minds as much as possible, while being cautiously rough on them in other ways . . . and greeted every sign of rebellion – silently, in my mind – as a triumphant proof of progress.

I started by teaching Joe to fight – just hand to hand; I didn't want either of us killed. One compartment was fitted as a gymnasium, with equipment that could be adapted for gee or free-fall; I used it that hour a day of lowered temperature. Here I worked Joe out. Llita was required to attend but just to exercise – although I had in mind that it might spur Joe along if his sister saw him getting the whey knocked out of him.

Joe needed that spur; he had a terrible time getting it through his head that it was okay to hit or kick *me*, that I wanted him to try, that I would not be angry if he succeeded – but that I *would* be angry if he didn't try his darnedest.

Took a while. At first he wouldn't chop at me no matter how wide open I left myself . . . and when I got him past that, calling him names and taunting him, he still hesitated that split second that let me close and chop him instead.

But one afternoon he got the idea so well that he landed a good one on me and I hardly had to hold back to let him land it. After supper he got his reward: permission to read a *bound* book, one with pages, him dressed in a pair of my surgical gloves and warned that I would clobber him if he got it dirty or tore a page. Llita wasn't permitted to touch it; this was *his* prize. She sulked and didn't even want to use the reading machine – until he asked if it was all right for him to read aloud to her.

I ruled that she could even read it with him – as long as she didn't touch it. So she snuggled up close, head by his, happy again, and started bossing him about turning the pages.

The next day she asked me why *she* could not learn to fight, too?

No doubt she was finding solo exercise a bore – I always found it so and did it only because it was needful to stay in shape – no telling what hazards next groundfall might bring. Minerva, I've never felt that women should have to fight; it is a male's business to protect females and children. But a female should be *able* to fight because she may have to.

So I agreed, but we had to change the rules. Joe and I had been working out by dockside rules – no rules, that is, save that I didn't tell him that I planned not to do him any permanent damage and did not intend to let him give me anything worse than bruises. But I never said this – if he could manage it, he was free to gouge out one of my eyes and eat it. I just made damn sure that he didn't.

But females are built differently from males. I could not let Llita work out with us until I devised a plastron to protect her tits – necessary; she was a bit oversized in that department, and we could have hurt her without intending to. Then I told Joe privately that bruises were okay, but if he broke one of her bones, I would break one of his, just for drill.

But I put no restrictions on his sister – and I underestimated her; she was twice as aggressive as he was. Untrained but fast – and she meant business.

The second day we worked out with her, not only was she wearing that plastron, her brother and I were wearing jockstraps. And Llita had been allowed to read a real book the night before.

Joe turned out to have a talent for cooking, so I encouraged him to be as fancy as ship's stores permitted while crowding her to become an adequate cook. A man who can cook can support himself anywhere. But anyone, male or female, should be able to cook, keep house, and care for children. I hadn't located a trade for Llita, although she displayed a talent for mathematics once I set up inducements for that, too. That was encouraging; a person who can read and write and has a head for math can learn anything she needs to know. So I started her on bookkeeping and accounting, from books, not helping her, and required Joe to learn to use all the tools the ship boasted – not many, mainly maintenance gear – and supervised him closely; I didn't want him losing fingers or ruining tools.

I was hopeful. Then the situation changed –

(Circa 3,100 words omitted)

– easy to say that I was stupid. I had raised stock and a good many children. Being ship's surgeon as well as everything else, I had given them the most thorough examinations my equipment permitted when we were a couple of days out – quite thorough for those days; I had not practised medicine after leaving Ormuzd but did keep my sick bay stocked and equipped, and picked up the latest tapes whenever I was on a civilized planet and studied them during long jumps. I was a good jackleg doctor, Minerva.

The kids were as healthy as they looked, aside from slight dental caries in him, two small cavities. I noticed that the factor's allegation about her was correct – virgo intacta, semilunar hymen, unfrayed, so I used my smallest speculum. She neither complained nor tensed up nor asked what I was looking for. I concluded that they had had regular checkups and other medical attention, far more than slaves on Blessed usually received.

She had thirty-two teeth in perfect condition but could not tell me when the last four molars had erupted, just that it was "not long ago." He had twenty-eight teeth and so little space in his jaw for adult molars that I anticipated trouble. But X-ray prints showed no buds.

I cleaned and filled the cavities and made note that he must have those fillings removed and the tissue regenerated on Valhalla and be inoculated against further decay; Valhalla had good dentistry far superior to what I could do.

Llita could not tell me when she had last menstruated. She discussed it with Joe; he tried to count on his fingers how many days it had been since they had been taken from their home place, as they agreed that it was before that. I told her to let me know next time and each time, so that I could determine her cycle. I gave her a tin of napkins, emergency supplies I hadn't known I had – must have been in the ship twenty years.

She did tell me, and I had to open the tin for her; neither of them knew how. She was delighted with the little elastic panty included in the package and often wore it when she did not need it, as "dress up." The kid was crazy about clothes; as a slave she had never had a chance to pamper her vanity. I told her it was all right as long as she washed it every time she wore it – I clamped down hard on cleanliness, inspecting their ears, sending them from the table to scrub their nails, and so forth. They had received no more training than a hog. She never had to be told twice, and picked on him and made sure that he met my standards, too. I found myself being more exacting with myself; I could not bring dirty fingernails to the table or skip a shower because I was sleepy – I had set the standards and had to live up to them.

She was almost as unskilled a seamstress as she was a cook, but she taught herself because she liked clothes. I dug out some bright-coloured trade cloth and let her have fun – and used it as carrot-and-stick; wearing anything became a privilege that depended on good behaviour. I put a stop that way – well, mostly – to her nagging her brother.

That wouldn't work with Joe; clothes did not interest him – but if he rated it, I gave him more of a working over during exercise period. Seldom – he was not the problem she was.

One evening, three or four of her periods later, I noticed on my calendar that she was past due – having forgotten the matter. Minerva, I never walked into their staterooms without knocking; shipboard life required such privacy as can be managed – too little that is.

Her door was open, and her room was empty. I tapped on his door, got no answer, went on, looked for her in the wardroom and galley, even in our little gym. I decided that she must be taking a bath and I would speak to her in the morning.

As I passed his stateroom again in heading back to my cabin, his door opened; she stepped out and closed it behind her. I said, "Oh, there you are!" or some such. "I thought Joe was asleep."

"He's just gone to sleep," Llita said. "Do you want him, Captain? Shall I wake him?"

I said, "No, I was looking for you, but I tapped on his door five or ten minutes ago and got no answer."

She was contrite over not having heard my knock. "I'm sorry, Captain. I guess we were so busy we didn't hear you." She told me how they were busy.

– which I had figured out, having suspected it from the moment I noticed that she was a week overdue after being clock regular. "That's understandable," I said. "I'm glad my knock didn't disturb you."

"We try never to disturb *you* with it, Captain," she answered with sweet seriousness. "We wait till you go to your cabin at night. Or sometimes when you take siesta."

I said, "Goodness, dear, you don't have to be *that* careful. Do your work and keep your study hours, then do as you please the rest of the time. Starship 'Libby' is not a sweatship; I want you kids to be happy. Can't you get it through your fuzzy head that you are not a slave?"

Apparently she could not, quite, Minerva, for she still fretted that she had not heard my knock and jumped to respond. I said, "Don't be silly, Llita. It will keep till tomorrow."

But she insisted she wasn't sleepy and was ready and anxious to do whatever I wanted – which made me a touch nervous. Minerva, one of the oddities about "Eros" is that women are never so willing as when they just have, and there was nothing in Llita's background to inhibit her. Worse, I found that I was aware of her as a ripe female for almost the first time since the two came aboard – she was standing close to me in a narrow passageway, carrying in one hand one of those weird costumes she delighted in making, and was a bit whiff from happy exercise. I was tempted – and felt certain that she would respond at once and happily. The thought crossed my mind that she was already pregnant – nothing to fret about.

But I had gone to much trouble with these ephemerals to shift from slaveowner to father figure, stern but loving. If I took her, I would lose that and add one more disturbing variable to a problem already too complex. So I grasped the nettle.

Captain Sheffield said, "Very well, Llita. Come to my cabin." He headed toward it, she followed. Once there, he offered her a seat. She hesitated, then put her gaudy dress down and sat on it – thoughtfulness that pleased him, as the ignorant animal she had been would not have been capable of it; the humanizing process was working. He did not comment.

"Llita, your period is a week overdue, is it not?"

"It is, Captain?" She seemed puzzled but not troubled.

Sheffield wondered if he could be mistaken. After he had taught her how to open a sealed tin, he had turned over to her the limited emergency supply, warning her that if she used it too lavishly, she would have to fashion by hand some make-do, as Valhalla was months away. Then he had dismissed the matter other than to log it on his desk calendar whenever she reported onset. Could he have failed to notice? There had been three days last week when he had kept to his cabin, leaving the young people on their own and having his meals sent in – a habit he had when he wanted to concentrate on a problem. During such periods he ate little and slept not at all and barely noticed anything not part of what he was studying. Yes, it was possible.

"Don't you know, Llita? If you were on time, then you failed to report it."

"Oh, no, Captain!" She was round-eyed with distress. "You told me to tell you . . . and I *have* – every time, every time!"

Further questions showed first, that despite her new grasp of arithmetic she did not know when she should have experienced onset, and second, that it had not been last week but a much longer time.

Time to tell her – "Llita dear, I think you are going to have a baby."

Her mouth dropped open, again her eyes rounded. "Oh, *wonderful!*" She added, "May I run tell Josie? May I, *please?* I'll be right back!"

"Wups! Don't rush things. I said only that I thought so. Don't get your hopes up yet, and don't bother Joe with it till we know. Many a girl has gone much longer than a week past her date, and it didn't mean a thing." (But I'm pleased to learn that you want it, child, as it appears you've had every opportunity.) "Tomorrow I'll examine you and try to find out." (What did he have aboard for a pregnancy test? Damn it, if he must abort her, it should be as quickly as possible when it's no worse than plucking a splinter. Then – no, there wasn't so much as a "Monday morning" pill in the ship, much less modern contraception. Woodie, blast your stupid soul, don't *ever* go into space again so poorly equipped!) "In the meantime, don't get excited." (But women always did get excited by it. Of course.)

She was as dashed as she had been jubilant. "We tried so hard! Everything in the Kama Sutra and more. I thought we ought to ask you to show us what we were doing wrong, but Joe was certain we were doing it right."

"I think Joe is correct." Sheffield got up, poured a cup of wine for each of them while performing legerdemain which dosed hers such that she would go to sleep before long – after some relaxed talk that she might not remember; he wanted the full picture. "Here."

She looked at it dubiously "I'll get silly. I know, I had a chance to try it once."

"This isn't the popskull they sell on Blessed; this is wine I fetched from Landfall. Pipe down and drink it. Here's to your baby if you're having one, or here's to good luck next time." (But how to handle that "next time"? – if his worries were well grounded. These kids must *not* be saddled with a defective. A healthy baby would be burden enough while they were learning to stand on their own feet. Could he stave things off to Valhalla, then get her on proper contraception? Then what? Split them up? *How?*)

"Tell me about it, dear. When you came aboard, you were virgin."

"Oh, yes, certainly. They always kept me locked in that virgin's basket. Except when they shut me up and Brother had to sleep in the barracks. You know. When I bleed." She took a deep breath and smiled. "Now is ever so much nicer. Josie and I tried for the longest time to get around that awful steel basket. But we couldn't. Hurt him to try, and some ways we tried hurt me, too. Finally we gave up and just did fun things we had always done. Brother said to be patient; it wouldn't be forever. Because we knew we would be sold together, as a breeding pair."

Estrallita looked radiant. "And so we were and now we *are*, and thank you, Captain!"

(No, it wasn't going to be easy to split them up.) "Llita, have you ever thought of being bred by some other man than Joe?" (Sound her out, at least. It won't be hard to find her a husband; she's really quite attractive. That "Earth Mother" feeling.)

She looked puzzled. "Why, of course not. We knew what we were, way back when we were almost babies. Our mother told us, and so did the priest. I've always slept with Brother, all my life. Why would I want anyone else?"

"You seemed ready enough to sleep with *me*. You claimed you were eager to."

"*Oh!* That's different – that's your right. But you didn't *want* me," she added, almost accusingly.

"That wasn't quite it. Llita. There were reasons – that I won't go into now – not to take you no matter if I wanted you and you were willing. Although it was Joe you really wanted, you said so."

"Well . . . yes. But I was disappointed just the same. I had to tell Brother you wouldn't have me – which hurt all over again. But he said to be patient. We waited three more days before he broached me. In case you changed your mind."

(Nagging wife vertically – docile horizontally. Not too uncommon a pattern, Sheffield thought.)

He found that she was looking at him with sober interest. "Do you want me *now*, Captain? Joe told me, the very night he decided to go ahead, that it was still your right and always would be – and it *is*."

(Beelzebub's brass balls! – the only way to avoid a willing female was to go off-planet.) "Dear, I'm tired, and you are getting sleepy."

She swallowed a yawn. "I'm not *that* tired – I never am. Captain, the night I first asked you, I was a tiny bit scared. But I'm not scared now. I *want* to. If you will."

"You're very sweet, but I am *very* tired." (Why hasn't that dose taken hold?) He changed the subject. "Aren't those little bunks almost impossible for two people?"

She chuckled right through another yawn. "Almost. Once we fell out of Brother's bunk. So now we use the deck."

" 'The deck'? Why, Llita, that's dreadful. We must do something about it." (Put the kids in here? The only full-size bed in the ship – A bride needed a proper workbench for her honeymoon . . . which this was; she was deeply in love and should make the most of it, no matter what. Sheffield had decided, centuries back, that the saddest thing about ephemerals was that their little lives rarely held time enough for love.)

"Oh, the deck isn't bad, Captain; we've slept on the floor all our lives." She yawned again, could not suppress it.

"Well . . . tomorrow we'll make better arrangements." (No, his cabin wouldn't do; his desk was in here, and his papers and files. The kids would be in his way and he in theirs. Could he and Joe convert two narrow bunks into one double bed? Probably – although it would nearly fill one stateroom. No matter, that bulkhead between their rooms was not structural – cut a door and they would have a suite. A "bridal suite." For a sweet bride. Yes.) He added, "Let's get you to bed before you fall out of that chair. Everything's going to be all right, dear." (I'll damned well see to it!) "And tomorrow night and from now on, you and Joe can sleep together in a wide bed."

"Really? Oh, that would be" – she yawned again – "*lovely!*"

He had to steady her into her stateroom; she was asleep as she hit the bunk. Sheffield looked down at her, said softly, "Poor little kitten." He leaned down and kissed her, went back to his cabin.

There he dug out everything the slave factor had offered as proof of the alleged odd genetic heritage of Llita and Joe, and gave each item intense study. He was looking for clues to truth or falsity of the allegation that they were "mirror" twins – complementary diploids having the same mother and father.

From such clues he hoped to estimate the probability of unfavourable gene reinforcement in any child Llita and Joe might have.

The problem seemed to divide into three (simplified) cases:

The two might be no relation to each other. Chance of a bad reinforcement: slight.

Or they might be the usual sort of brother and sister. Chance of bad reinforcement: too high to be ignored.

Or they might be (as alleged) zygotes resulting from complementary gametes – all genes conserved at reduction-division but with no duplication. In this case the chance of unfavourable reinforcement would be – what?

Let that wait. First assumption, that they were no relation but simply raised together from babyhood – no special hazard, forget it.

Second assumption, that they might be full siblings of the usual sort. Well, they did not look like it – but, more important, that scoundrel had set up a most elaborate "store" for such a swindle, and had used publicly the name of a bishop to back him up. The Bishop might be just as crooked (likely – he knew that priesthood too well!) – but why be so careless when slave babies were so cheap?

No, even if he assumed a swindle, there was no reason to expect an unnecessary risk in a setup so elaborate. So forget that, too: Llita and Joe were *not* sister and brother in the ordinary sense – although they might have shared the same host-mothers' womb. The latter, if true, was of no genetic significance.

So the remaining worry concerned the chance that the slave factor had told the truth – in which case what were the chances of a bad cross? How many ways could such artificially produced zygotes recombine unfavourably?

Sheffield tried to set up the problem while cursing the lack of sufficient data, plus the fact that the only real computer in the ship was the piloting computer, which could not be programmed for a genetics problem. He wished Libby were aboard. Andy would have stared at the bulkhead a few minutes, then come up with answers definite where possible and expressed in probability percentages where not.

A genetics problem, even with all pertinent data (many thousands!) was too unwieldy to solve without computer assistance.

Well, try some simplified illustrative problems and see what insight could be gained.

Primary assumption: Llita and Joe were "mirror twins" – genetically complementary zygotes from the same parent zygotes.

Control assumption: They were unrelated other than being part of the home planet's gene pool. (An extreme assumption, as slaves from the same area were likely to derive from a much smaller gene pool, which might be still further reduced by inbreeding. But this "most favourable normal breeding pattern" was the correct control against which he must measure.)

Simplified example: Test one gene site – call it site 187 of the twenty-first chromosome – for reinforcement, masking, or elimination, of an assumed "bad" gene, under each assumption.

Arbitrary assumption: Since this site might hold an unfavourable gene – or two, or none – in its gene pair, assume that the chance was exactly the same for both primary and control assumptions, and even – *i.e.*, 25 per cent no bad gene in the pair at the site, 50 per cent one bad gene, 25 per cent two bad genes – an extreme condition since, over the generations, reinforcement (two bad genes at one site) tended toward nonsurvival, either lethal or reducing a zygote's ability to compete. Never mind; make it even for both of them – there were no data on which to base any better assumption.

Wups! If a bad reinforcement was visibly demonstrated, or could be shown by tests, such zygotes would *not* be used. A scientist competent to attempt this experiment would use specimens as "clean" in a genetic sense as possible – free of all the hundreds (thousands now?) of identifiable hereditary defects; the primary assumption should include this subsidiary assumption.

These young people were free of any defect Sheffield could detect in a shipboard examination – which enhanced the probability that this horsethief had told the truth and these exhibits were sober records of an exotic and successful experiment in gene manipulation.

Sheffield now tended to believe that the experiment had taken place – and wishea that he had the resources of a major Howard Clinic, say the one on Secundus to give these kids a genetic going-over that he was not equipped to do aboard ship and not qualified to do in any case.

One nagging doubt lay in how he had acquired these kids. Why had that gonif been so anxious to sell? If they were what the exhibits claimed? Why sell them when breeding the two created complements back together was the next step of the experiment?

Well, perhaps the kids knew but he had not asked the right questions. Certain it was that they had been brought up to believe that such was their proper destiny; whoever planned this had induced the kids from earliest childhood a pair-bond stronger than most marriages, in Sheffield's long experience. More than any of his own – (Except one, except one!)

Sheffield put it out of his mind and concentrated on the theoretical consequences.

At the selected site, each parent zygote had been assumed to have three possible states or gene-pairs in probability 25-50-25.

Under the control assumption, parents (diploid zygotes) both male and female would show this distribution at the selected site:

25%	good-good	("clean" at that site)
,,	good-bad	(bad gene masked but could be transmitted)
,,	good-bad	(bad gene masked but could be transmitted)
,,	bad-bad	(bad reinforcement – lethal or disabling)

But under his modified primary assumption Sheffield assumed that the priest-scientist would discard bad stock as displayed in zygotes – which would eliminate the fourth group ("bad-bad") and leave a parent-zygote distribution of:

33-1/3%	good-good
,,	good-bad
,,	good-bad

Such culling gave marked improvement over the original random-chance situation and meiotic division would produce gametes (both sperm and ova) in this incidence:

Good, four out of six, and
Bad, two out of six –

– but with no way to detect the bad genes without destroying the gametes carrying them. Or so Sheffield assumed, while stipulating that the assumption might not be true forever. But to protect Llita (and Joe) it was necessary that his assumptions be pessimistic within the limits of available data and knowledge – i.e. that a bad gene could be spotted only as reinforcement in a zygote.

Sheffield reminded himself that the situation was never as black-and-white as was implied by "good-dominant" and "bad-recessive" – these descriptions were less complex than the real world they were used to image. A characteristic exhibited by an adult zygote was prosurvival or contrasurvival only in terms of what and when and where – and also in terms of more than one generation. An adult who died saving its progeny had to be counted a prosurvival whereas a cat that ate her own young was contrasurvival no matter how long she lived.

In the same vein, a dominant gene sometimes was of no importance one way or the other – e.g., brown eyes. Just as its corresponding recessive when paired and thereby reinforced to produce blue eyes gave the zygote exhibiting it no measurable disadvantage. The same was true of many other inheritable characteristics – hair patterns, skin colour, et cetera.

Nevertheless this description – good-dominant, bad-recessive – was in essence correct; it synopsized the mechanisms by which a race conserved its favourable mutations and destroyed (eventually) its unfavourable mutations. "Bad-dominant" was almost a contradiction in terms, as a thoroughly bad mutation which was dominant killed itself off (along with the unfortunate zygote inheriting it) in one generation, either lethal in womb or so damaging to the zygote that it failed to reproduce.

But the usual weeding process involved bad-recessives. These could remain in the gene pool until one of two events happened, each controlled by the blind laws of chance: Such a gene could pair with a gene like it when sperm fertilized ovum and thereby eliminate itself by eliminating the zygote – hopefully before birth, or – tragically – after birth. Or this bad-recessive might be eliminated by chromosome reduction at meiosis and the result would be a healthy baby who did *not* carry this bad gene in its gonads – a happy outcome.

Both these statistical processes slowly weeded out bad genes from the race's gene pool.

Unfortunately the first of these processes often produced babies viable but so handicapped they needed help to stay alive – sometimes needing economic help, born losers, who never managed to support themselves; sometimes needing plastic surgery or endocrine therapy or other interventions or supports. When Captain Aaron Sheffield had been practising medicine (on Ormuzd and under another name), he had gone through stages of increasing frustration over these poor unfortunates.

At first he had tried to practise therapy by the Hippocratic Oath – or close to it; he was by temperament unable to follow *any* man-made rule blindly.

Then he had had a period of temporary mental abberrance during which he had sought a political solution to what he saw as a great danger: reproduction by defectives. He tried to persuade his colleagues to refuse therapy to hereditary defectives unless they were sterile or sterilized or willing to accept being sterilized as a precondition for receiving therapy. Worse yet, he had attempted to include in the definition of "hereditary defective" those who displayed no stigmata save that they had never managed to be self-supporting – on a planet not over-crowded and which he himself had selected centuries earlier as nearly ideal for human beings.

He got nowhere, he encountered nothing but fury and contempt – save for a few colleagues who agreed with him privately and denounced him publicly. As for laymen, tar-and-feathers was the mildest medicine they prescribed for Dr. "Genocide."

When his licence to practise was lifted, Lazarus regained his normal emotional detachment. He shut up, realizing that grim old Mother Nature, red of tooth and claw, invariably punished damfools who tried to ignore Her or to repeal Her ordinances; he need not interfere.

So he moved and changed his name again and started to get ready to go off-planet – when a plague hit Ormuzd. He had shrugged and gone back to work, an unfrocked physician whose services were temporarily welcome. Two years and a quarter of a billion deaths later he was offered his licence back – subject to good behaviour.

He told them what to do with that licence and left Ormuzd as quickly as possible, eleven years later. He was a professional gambler during that wait, that being the handiest way he could see at the time for saving up the necessary.

Sorry, Minerva, I was talking about those mirror twins. So the silly little wench was knocked up, which caused me to slip back into my baby-cotching, country-doctor *persona*, and I stayed up all night worrying about her and her brother and the baby they were going to have – unless I did something about it. To find out what I *should* do, I had to reconstruct what *had* happened and from that what *could* happen. Having no certain data, I had to follow that old rule for finding a lost mule.

First I had to think like that slave factor – A man who auctions slaves is a scoundrel but too smart to risk a caper in which he might wind up a slave himself, or dead if he was lucky – which is what would happen to one who played fast and loose on Blessed with the authority of a bishop. Ergo, the scoundrel had believed what he had said.

That being so, I could table the question of why this factor was commissioned to sell these two, while I tried to think like a priest-scientist engaged in human biological experimentation. Forget the chance that these two were ordinary siblings – no point in picking such a pair even for a swindle. Forget the chance that they were unrelated in any fashion, as in such a case it would simply be a normal case of breeding. Sure, sure, any woman can give birth to a monster, as even with the most genetically hygienic of breeding a bad mutation can show up – and an alert midwife may neglect to give that first life-giving spank – and many have.

So I considered only the third hypothesis: complementary diploids from the same parents. What would this experimenter do? What would *I* do?

I would use as near perfect stock as I could find and not start the experiment until I had both a male and a female parent who tested "clean" genetically in the most subtle ways for which I could test – which on Blessed meant quite sophisticated ways, for that century.

For a selected gene site and an assumption of 50-50 in the Mendelian distribution of 25-50-25, this pre-experiment testing would chop off the 25 per cent chance of reinforcement of a bad recessive and leave a distribution of one-third bad, two-thirds good, at the parent generation – possible parents of possible Joes and Llitas that is.

Now I start putting together mirror twins in my *persona* as a priest-experimenter. What happens? If we consider the minimum number of gamets needed to represent this one-third and two-thirds distribution, we get eighteen possible "Joes," eighteen possible "Llitas" – but in both male and female two of them show up as "bad" – the bad recessive has reinforced and the zygote is defective; the experimenter eliminates them . . . or he may not need to; the reinforcement may be lethal.

We wind up at this point with an 8 & 1/3 per cent improvement or a total improvement of 25 per cent in favourable chances for Llita's baby. I felt better. If you add the fact that I am the sort of a midwife who is too busy helping the mother to stop to spank a monster, the favourable chances went way up.

But all that this shows is that bad genes tend to be eliminated at each generation – with the tendency greatest with the worse genes and reaching 100 per cent whenever reinforcement produces a lethal-in-womb – while favourable genes are conserved. But we knew that – and it applies also to normal outbreeding and even more strongly to inbreeding, although the latter is not well thought of for humans as it hikes up the chances of a defective by precisely the same amount that it weeds – that being the hazard that I was afraid of for Llita. Everybody wants the human gene pool cleaned up, but nobody wants its tragic aspects to take place in his own family. Minerva, I was beginning to think of these kids as "my family."

I still did not know anything about "mirror twins."

I decided to investigate a more probable incidence of bad recessives at a given site. Fifty-fifty is far too high for a really bad gene; the weeding is drastic, and the incidence drops to a lower percentage each generation, until the incidence of a particular bad gene is so low that reinforcement as fertilization is a rare event, as reinforcement is the square of the incidence; e.g., if one-in-a-hundred haploids carry this bad gene, then it will be reinforced one-in-ten-thousand fertilizations. I speak of the total gene pool, or in this case a minimum of two hundred adult zygotes, female and male; random breeding in such a pool will bring together that bad reinforcement only by that long chance – a chance happy or unhappy depending on whether you look at it impersonally in terms of cleaning the gene pool or personally in terms of individual human tragedy.

I looked at it very personally; I wanted Llita to have a healthy baby.

Minerva, I'm sure you recognized that 25–50–25 distribution as representing the most drastic case of inbreeding, one which can happen only half the time with line breeding, only a quarter of the time with full siblings, in both cases through chromosome reduction at meiosis. A stockbreeder uses this drastic measure regularly – and culls the defectives and winds up with a healthy stabilized line. I have a nasty suspicion that such culling after inbreeding was sometimes used among royalty back on old Earth – but certainly such culling was not used often enough or drastically enough. Royalism might work quite well if kings and queens were treated like racehorses – but regrettably they never were. Instead, they were propped up like welfare clients, and princelings who should have been culled were encouraged to breed like rabbits – bleeders, feebleminded, you name it. When I was a kid, "royalty" was a bad joke based on the worst possible breeding methods.

Captain Sheffield investigated next a lower incidence of a bad gene: assume a lethal gene in the gene pool from which Joe and Llita's parents were derived. Being lethal, it could exist in an adult zygote only if it was masked in gene-pair by its benign twin. Assume a 5 per cent masked incidence in zygotes – still too high to be realistic for a lethal gene – but check it anyhow. What trend would show?

Parent zygote generation: 100 females, 100 males, each a possible parent for Llita and for Joe – and 5 of the females and 5 of the males carry the lethal gene, masked.

Parent haploid stage: 200 ova, 5 of which carry the lethal gene; 200 spermatozoa, 5 of which carry the lethal gene.

Son-and-daughter zygote generation (possible "Joes" and possible "Llitas"): 25 dead through reinforcement of lethal gene; 1,950 carrying the lethal gene masked; 38,025 "clean" at that site.

Sheffield noted that a hypothetical hermaphrodite had crept in through not doubling his sample size in order to avoid anomaly through odd numbers. Oh, the hell with! – it did not change the statistical outcome. No, *do* it! – start with as ample of 200 males and 200 females with the same lethal-gene incidence for that site. This gave him:

> 400 ova, 10 with the lethal gene;
> 400 spermatozoa, 10 with that lethal gene –

– which gave in the next zygote generation (possible "Joes" and "Llitas"): 100 dead, 7,800 carriers, 152,100 "clean" – which changed no percentages but got rid of that imaginary hermaphrodite. Sheffield considered briefly the love life of an hermaphrodite, then got back to work. The numbers became very cumbersome, jumping to the billions in the next zygote generation (i.e., Little Nameless, now just started in Llita's belly) – 15,210,000 culled by reinforcement, 1,216,800,000 carriers, 24,336,000,000 "clean" – and again he wished for a clinic computer and tediously converted the unhandy numbers into percentages: 0.059509 per cent, 4.759 per cent, 95.18 per cent plus.

This showed a decided improvement: approximately 1 defect out of 1,680 (instead of 1 out of 1,600), the percentage of carriers decreased to below 5 per cent and the number of "clean" increased to above 95 per cent in one generation.

Sheffield worked several such problems to confirm what he had seen by inspection: A child from complementary diploids ("mirror twins") had at least as much chance of being healthy as did the offspring of unrelated strangers – plus the happy fact the such a baby's chances were improved by culling at one or more stages by the priest-scientist who had initiated the experiment – an almost certain assumption and one that made Joe the best possible mate for his "sister" rather than the worst.

Llita could have her baby.

VARIATIONS ON A THEME

VII

Valhalla to Landfall

– the best I could for them, Minerva. Every so often some idiot tries to abolish marriage. Such attempts work as well as repealing the law of gravity, making pi equal to three point zero, or moving mountains by prayer. Marriage is not something thought up by priests and inflicted on mankind; marriage is as much a part of mankind's evolutionary equipment as his eyes, and as useful to the race as eyes are to an individual.

Surely, marriage is an economic contract to provide for children and to take care of mothers while they bear kids and bring them up – but it is much more than that. It is the means this animal, Homo sap., has evolved – quite unconsciously – for performing this indispensable function *and be happy while doing so.*

Why do bees split up into queens, drones, and workers, then live as one big family? Because, for them, it *works.* How is it that fish do okay with hardly a nodding acquaintance between mama fish and papa fish? Because the blind forces of evolution made that way work for *them.* Why is it that "marriage" – by whatever name – is a universal institution among human beings everywhere? Don't ask a theologian, don't ask a lawyer; this institution existed long before it was codified by church or state. It *works,* that's all; for all its faults it works far better by the only universal test – survival – than any of the endless inventions that shallow-pates over the millennia have tried to substitute for it.

I am not speaking monogamy; I mean *all* forms of marriage – monogamy, polyandry, polygyny, plural and extended marriages with various frills. "Marriage" has endless customs, rules, arrangements. But it is "marriage" if-and-only-if the arrangement both provides for children and compensates the adults. For human beings, the only acceptable compensation for the drawbacks of marriage lies in what men and women can give each other.

I don't mean "Eros," Minerva. Sex baits the trap, but sex is not marriage, nor is it reason enough to stay married. Why buy a cow when milk is cheap?

Companionship, partnership, mutual reassurance, someone to laugh with and grieve with, loyalty that accepts foibles, someone to touch, someone to hold your hand – these things are "marriage," and sex is but the icing on the cake. Oh, that icing can be wonderfully tasty – but it is *not* the cake. A marriage can lose that tasty "icing" – say, through accident – and still go on and on and on, giving deep happiness to those who share it.

When I was a rutty and ignorant youngster, this used to puzzle me –

(Omitted)

– as solemnly ceremonious as I could swing. Man lives by symbols; I wanted them to remember this occasion. I had Llita dress in her notion of fanciest best. She looked like a bloomin' Christmas tree, but I told her she looked beautiful – which she did; brides can't help it. Joe I dressed in some of my clothes and gave them to him. Me I dressed in a preposterous ship's-captain uniform, one I had for use on planets where such nonsense is customary – four wide gold stripes on my cuffs, chest spangled with decorations bought in hockshops, a cocked hat Admiral Lord Nelson would have envied, and the rest as fancy as any grand master of a lodge.

I preached 'em a sermon loaded with solemn amphigory most of it lifted from the only church they knew, the established religion of Blessed – easy for me, having been a priest there myself – but I added all sorts of things, telling her what she owed him, telling him what he owed her, telling them both what they owed the child in her belly and the other children they would have – and tacked on, for both but primarily for her, a warning that marriage was not easy, not to be entered into lightly, because there would be troubles they must face together, grave troubles that would require the courage of the Cowardly Lion, the wisdom of the Scarecrow, the loving heart of the Tin Woodsman, and the indomitable gallantry of Dorothy.

That got her to weeping, so Joe started to drip tears – which was just what I wanted, so I had 'em kneel and prayed over them.

Minerva, I make no apology for hypocrisy. I didn't care whether some hypothetical God heard me or not; I wanted Llita and Joe to hear it – first in that jargon of Blessed, then in English and Galacta, then topped it off by intoning as many lines of the Aeneid as I could remember. When I got stuck I closed with a schoolboy song:

Omme bene
Sine poena,
Tempus est ludendi;
Venit hora
Absque mora,
*Libros deponendi!**

– and ended with a resounding "So mote it be!" Had 'em stand, take each other's hands, and declared that, by the supreme authority vested in me as master of a vessel in space, they were now and forever husband and wife – kiss her, Joe.

All to a muted background of Beethoven's Ninth –

That doggerel got in by accident when I had run out of "punishment lines" of Virgil and needed a few more impressive sounds. But when I thought about it later, I saw that it translated as appropriately for their honeymoon as for a school holiday. All was indeed well, now that I knew that this joining of siblings could take place *sine poena* – without fear of genetic punishment. And *ludendi* translates as "amorous play" or "Eros" as readily as "gambling" or "children's play" or any other frolic. And I had declared a four-day ship's holiday, no work for them, no study hours – *libros deponendi* – starting at once. Sheer accident, Minerva. It was simply a bit of Latin verse that came into my head – and Latin is majestic, especially when you don't understand it.

We had a fancy supper, cooked by me, that lasted about ten minutes – for them. Llita could not eat, and Joe reminded me of

* All is well
Without punishment,
The time is for playing;
Comes the hour
Without delay
For laying (school) books down.

Purists will see that the Senior gave this jingle a poor translation. But one wonders why he did not continue in the same vein with the cheerfully bawdy triple pun available in the last line by substituting "liberos" for "libros"? That he could have missed it seems out of character. Our Ancestor's capric disposition is everywhere evident; his occasional professions of asceticism have at best a hollow ring.

J.F. 45th

Johnny's wedding night and why his mother-in-law fainted. So I piled a tray with tasty rations and handed it to Joe, and told 'em to get lost; I didn't want to see hide n'r hair of 'em for four days –

(Omitted)

– on to Landfall as fast as I could pick a cargo. I could not leave them on Valhalla; José was not yet able to support a family, and Llita was going to be limited in what she could do, either pregnant or with a new baby. Nor would I be on hand to pick 'em up if they fell down; they *had* to go to Landfall.

Oh, Llita could have survived on Valhalla, because there they have the healthy attitude that a pregnant woman is prettier than the other sort and that the farther along she is, the more beautiful she is – true in my opinion and especially true in Llita's case. She had been passable when I bought her; when we grounded at Valhalla, she was almost five months gone and radiantly beautiful. If she went dirtside unescorted, the first six men she encountered would want to marry her. If she had had one on her back as well as one in her belly, she could have married well the day we arrived; fertility was respected there and the planet wasn't half filled up.

I didn't think she would jilt Joe that quickly, but I did not want her head turned by too much male attention. I did not want to risk even an outside chance that Llita might leave him for some wealthy bourgeois or freeholder; I had gone to much trouble to build up Joe's ego, but it was still fragile and such a blow could kill it. He was standing tall and proud now – but his pride was based on being a married man, with a wife, and a child on the way. Did I mention that I had given them one of my names on their marriage certificate? They were now Friherr og Fru Lang, Josef og Stjerne, for the duration of our stay on Valhalla, and I wanted them to remain Mr. and Mrs. Long for some years at least.

Minerva, I had them take lifetime vows never beliving that they would keep them. Oh, ephemerals often stay married for life, but as for the rest – you don't find feathers on frogs very often, and Llita was a naïve, friendly, sexy little tart whose short heels would cause her to trip and land with her legs open without planning it – I could see it coming. I did not want it to happen before I had a chance to indoctrinate Joe. Horns need not give a man a headache. But he does need time to grow up and mellow and acquire self-confidence before he can wear them with tolerance and dignity – and Llita was just the girl who could outfit him with a fine rack of antlers.

I got him a job, pearl diver and handyman in a small gourmet restaurant, with a side arrangement for pay-me's to the chef for every Valhalla dish Joe learned to cook correctly. In the meantime I kept her aboard on the excuse that a pregnant woman could not risk the nasty weather until I could get her proper clothing – and don't bother me now, dear; I've got cargo to worry about.

She took it well enough, pouting just a little. She didn't like Valhalla anyhow; it has one-and-a-seventh gee and I had got them used to the luxury of free-fall – easy on her swelling belly, no strain on her arches or her swelling tits. Now she suddenly found herself much heavier than she had ever been, awkward, and with unhappy feet. What she could see of Valhalla from the entrance lock looked like a frozen slice of hell; she was pleased by my offer to take them on to Landfall.

Still, Valhalla was the only new place she had ever been; she wanted to see it. I stalled while I got cargo unloaded, then took her measurements and got her one warm outfit in local style – but I played her a dirty trick; I fetched back three pairs of boots and let her take her choice. Two pairs were plain work boots; the third pair was gaudy – and half a size too small.

So when I did take her groundside, she was wearing too-tight boots, and the weather was unusually cold and blustery – I had watched the predictions. Torheim is pretty in spots, as skyport cities go – but I avoided those parts and took her "sightseeing" in dull neighbourhoods – on foot. By the time I flagged a sleigh and took her back to the ship, she was miserable, and glad to get out of uncomfortable clothes, especially the boots, and into a hot bath.

I offered to take her into town next day but left her free to refuse. She declined politely.

(Omitted)

– not quite that bad, Minerva; I simply wanted to keep her in purdah without arousing her suspicions. Actually I had bought two pairs of those gaudy boots, one pair her correct size – and switched them on her at the end of that first day, while she was soaking her poor tired feet. Later I suggested that her trouble had been that she had never worn shoes or boots in her life – so why not wear them around the ship until she got the hang of it?

So she did and was surprised at how easy it was. I explained with a straight face that her feet had swelled the first time, so take it easy, an hour today, a little more each day, until she felt comfortable in them all day long. In a week she was wearing them even if she wore nothing else; she was more comfortable in them than barefooted – not surprising as they were arch-support footwear I had picked most carefully – between pregnancy and the difference in surface gravity of the two planets – point ninety-five gee for her home planet; one point fourteen for Valhalla – she weighed about twenty kilos more than she ever had in her life; she *needed* contoured foot supports.

I had to caution her not to wear them to bed.

I took her to town a couple of times while I was selecting cargo, but I coddled her – not much walking or standing around. She came along when I invited her but was always willing to stay aboard and read.

In the meantime Joe worked long hours, only one day off in seven. So just before we left, I had him quit his job and I took my kids on a proper holiday; a sleigh hired for the day, with reindeer instead of power, sightseeing that was truly sightseeing on a clear, sunny day that was almost warm, lunch in the country at a fine restaurant with a veiw of snow-covered crags of Jotunheimen range, dinner at a still finer restaurant in the city, one with live music and entertainment as well as superb food – and a stop for tea at the little gourmet spot where Joe had laboured so that he could be addressed as "Friherr Lang" by our host, instead of "Hey, you!" – and have a chance to show off his beautiful, bulging bride.

And beautiful she was, Minerva. On Valhalla both sexes wear, under heavy outdoor clothes, indoor clothes that are essentially pyjamas. The difference between those worn by women and by men lies in material, cut, and such. I had bought one party outfit for each of them. Joe looked smart and so did I, but all eyes were on Llita. She was covered from shoulders to boots – but only technically. The cloth of that harem outfit shimmered with changing lights, orange and green and gold, without obstructing the view. Anyone who cared to look could see that her nipples were crinkled with excitement – and everyone cared to look. That she clearly had only a couple of months to go gave her a large bonus vote toward being picked as "Miss Valhalla".

She looked grand and knew it, and her face showed her happiness. She was self-confident, too, as I had coached her in local table manners, and how to stand and how to sit and how to behave and such, and she had already got through lunch without a bobble.

It was all right to let her display herself and enjoy the silent, or sometimes not silent, applause; not only were we leaving right away, but also Joe and I had our knives in sight in our boot tops. True, Joe was no knife fighter. But the wolves there didn't know that, and not one was inclined to bother our beautiful bitch when she was flanked by wolves of her own.

– early next morning despite a short night. We loaded all day long, with Llita handling manifests and Joe checking numbers while I made sure I wasn't being robbed. Late that night I had us in n-space, with my pilot computer sniffing out the last decimal places for the first leg to Landfall. I set the gravistat to bring us slowly down from Valhalla surface-normal to a comfortable quarter-gee – no more free-fall until Llita had her baby – then locked the control room and headed down to my cabin, stinking and tired and trying to kid myself that tomorrow was soon enough for a bath.

Their door was open – their bedroom door, the room that had been Joe's before I turned their rooms into a suite. Door open and them in bed – they had never done *that* before.

I soon learned why. They piled out of bed and paddled toward me; they wanted me to join their fun – they wanted to thank me . . . for that party day, for buying them, for everything else. His idea? Hers? Both? I didn't try to find out; I just thanked them and told them that I was whipped to the red, worn out, and dirty – all I wanted was soap and hot water and twelve hours of shut-eye – and for them to sleep late; we'd set up ship's routine after we were rested.

I did let them bathe me and massage me to sleep. That did not break discipline; I had taught them a bit about massage, and Joe in particular had a firmly gentle touch; he had been massaging her daily during her pregnancy – even while working long hours in that restaurant.

But, Minerva, had I not been so bushed, I might have broken my rule about dependent females.

(Omitted)

– every tape, every book available in Torheim for a refresher in obstetrics and gynecology, plus instruments and supplies I had not expected to need aboard ship. I kept to my cabin until I had mastered all new art and was at least as skilled in baby-cotching as I had been as a country doctor on Ormuzd long before.

I kept a close eye on my patient, watched her diet, made her exercise, checked her gizzards daily – and permitted no undue familiarity.

Dr. Lafayette Hubert, MD, aka Captain Aaron Sheffield aka The Senior, et al., worried excessively over his one patient. But he kept her and her husband from seeing it and applied his worry constructively in planning for every obstetric emergency known to the art at that time. Hardware and supplies he had obtained on Valhalla paralled in every major respect the equipment of Frigg Temple in Torheim, where fifty births a day were not uncommon.

He smiled to himself at the mass of junk he had taken aboard, recalling a country doctor on Ormuzd who had delivered many a baby with nothing but bare hands, while the mother sat in her husband's lap, knees pulled high and wide by her husband so that old Doc Hubert could kneel in front of them and catch the baby.

True – but he had always had with him all the gear a husky pacing borri could tote, even though he might never open a saddlebag if everything went right. That was the point: to have the stuff at hand if things did *not* go right.

One item purchased in Torheim was not for emergency: the latest improved-model delivery chair – hand grips, padded support arms; leg, foot, and back supports adjustable independently in three axes of translation and rotation with controls accessible both to midwife and patient, quick-release restraints. It was a marvellously flexible piece of mechanical engineering to enable the mother to position herself – or be positioned – so that her birth canal was vertical and as wide open as possible at the moment of truth.

Dr. Hubert-Sheffield had it set up in his cabin, checked its many adjustments before signing for it – then looked at it and frowned. A good gadget, and he had paid its high price without a quiver. But it had no love in it; it was as impersonal as a guillotine.

A husband's arms, a husband's lap, were not as efficient – but there was much to be said, in his opinion, for having parents go through the ordeal together, she with her husband's arms holding her, comforting her, while he gave both muscular and emotional support that left the midwife free to concentrate on physical aspects.

A husband who had done this had no doubt that he was a father. Even if some passing stranger had slipped her the juice, such fact became irrelevant, swallowed up by this greater experience.

So how about it, Doc? This gadget? Or Joe's arms? Did the kids need this second "marriage ceremony"? Could Joe take it, physically and emotionally? There was no doubt that Llita was the more rugged member of the team although Joe outmassed her even when she was near term. What if Joe fainted and dropped her – at the exact wrong instant?

Sheffield worried these matters while he led auxiliary controls from the gravistat in the control room to the delivery chair. He had decided that, nuisance though it was, his cabin had to be the delivery room; it was the only compartment with enough deck space, a bed at hand, and its own bath. Oh, well, he could stand the nuisance of squeezing past the pesky thing to reach his desk and wardrobe for the next fifty days – sixty at the outside, if he had Llita's date of conception right and had judged her progress correctly. Then he could disassemble it and stow it.

Perhaps he could sell it at a profit on Landfall; it was in advance of the art there, he felt sure.

He positioned the chair, bolted it to the deck, ran it up to maximum height, placed its midwife's stool in front of it, adjusted the stool until he was comfortable in it, found he could lower the delivery chair ten or twelve centimetres and still have room to work. That done, he climbed into the delivery chair and fiddled with its adjustments – found that it could be made to fit even a person of his height – predictable; some women on Valhalla were taller than he was.

Minerva, by my figures Llita was about ten days late – which did not worry them, as I had been carefully vague about it, and worried me only a touch, as she checked out normal and healthy in all respects. I prepared them not only with instruction and drill, but also with hypnosis, and had prepared her with exercises designed to make it as easy on her as possible – I dislike post-partum repairs; that canal should *stretch*, not tear.

What was really fretting me was possibility that I was going to have to break the neck of a monster. Kill a baby, I mean – I shouldn't dodge the blunt truth. All calculations I had done one sleepless night still left this chance open – and if I had been wrong in any assumption, the chance might be higher than I like to think about.

If I had to do it, I wanted to get it over with.

I was far more worried than she was. I don't think she worried at all; I had worked hard on that hypnotic preparation.

If I had to do this grisly thing, I was going to have to do it *fast*, while their attentions were elsewhere – then never let them see it and space the pitiful remains at once. Then tackle the horrid job of trying to put them back together emotionally. As a married couple? I did not know. Maybe I would have an opinion after I saw what she was carrying.

At last her contractions were coming close together, so I had them get into the delivery chair – easy, one-quarter gravity. The chair was already adjusted, and they were used to the position from drill. Joe climbed in, sat with his thighs stretched wide, knees over the rests, heels braced – not too comfortable as he was not angleworm-limber the way she was. Then I picked her up and sat her in his lap – no trouble, she weighed less than forty pounds at that pseudo-acceleration. Call it eighteen kilos.

She spread her legs almost in a horizontal split and scooted forward in his lap while Joe kept her from falling between his thighs. "Is that far enough, Captain?" she asked.

"Just fine," I said. The chair might have positioned her a touch better – but she would not have had Joe's arms around her. I had never told them that there was any other way to do it. "Give her a kiss, Joe, while I get the straps."

Left knee strap around both their left knees together, same for right knees, and with her feet braced on additional supports I had added – chest and shoulder and thigh straps on him so firmly that he would stay in that chair even if the ship fell apart, but no such straps on *her*. Her hands on the hand grips, while his hands and arms were a living, warm, and loving safety belt, just under her tits, just over the bulge but not on it. He knew how, we had practised. If I wanted pressure on her belly, I would tell him – otherwise leave well enough alone.

My stool was bolted to the deck. I had added a seat belt. As I strapped myself down, I reminded them that we had a rough ride coming – and this we had not been able to practise; it would have risked miscarriage. "Lock your fingers, Joe, but let her breathe. Comfortable, Llita?"

"Uh – " she said breathlessly. "I – I'm starting another one!"

"Bear down, dear!" I made sure my left foot was positioned for the gravistat control and watched her belly.

Big one! As it peaked, I switched from one-quarter gravity up to two gravities almost in one motion – and Llita let out a yip and the baby squirted like a watermelon seed right into my hands.

I dragged my foot back to allow the gravistat to put us back on low gee even as I made a nearly instantaneous inspection of the brat. A normal boy, red and wrinkled and ugly – so I slapped his tochis and he bawled.

VARIATIONS ON A THEME

VIII

Landfall

(Omitted)

– girl I had intended to marry had married again and had another baby. Not surprising; I had been off Landfall two standard years. Not tragic, either, as we had been married once about a hundred years earlier. Old friends. So I talked it over with her and her new husband, then married one of her granddaughters, one not descended from me. Both gals Howards, of course, and Laura, the one I married that time, being of the Foote family.*

We were a good match, Minerva; Laura was twenty, and I was freshly rejuvenated and holding my cosmetic age at the early thirties. We had several children – nine, I think – then she got bored with me forty-odd years later, and wanted to marry my 5th/7th cousin* Roger Sperling – which did not grieve me as I was getting restless as a country squire. Anyhow, when a woman wants to go, let her go. I stood up for her at their wedding.

Roger was surprised to learn that my plantation was not com-

*Correction: Hedrick Family. This woman Laura (one of the ancestors of the undersigned) did carry the surname "Foote" under the archaic patrilinea tradition – a source of confusion in old records, as the more logical matrilineal system has always been used in the Families in assigning clan membership. But the genealogies were not revised to show this until Gregorian Year 3307. This misnomer offers a means of dating this memoir . . . were it not that other records show that reindeer were not introduced onto Valhalla until approximately a century and a half *after* the date that the Senior – beyond question – did marry Laura Foote-Hedrick.

But more interesting is the Senior's allegation that he used a pseudogravity field *in that year* to facilitate childbirth. Was he the first tocologist to use this (now standard) method? Nowhere does he assert this, and the technique is usually associated with Dr. Virginius Briggs of Secundus Howard Clinic and a much later date.

J.F. 45th

*And descended from the Senior as well (through Edmund Hardy 2099–2259) although the Senior may not have been aware of it.

J.F. 45th

munity property. Or possibly did not think that I would hold Laura to the marriage settlement she had signed – but that wasn't the first time I had been wealthy; I had learned. It took a tedious suit to convince him that Laura owned her wedding dower plus appreciation, not those thousands of hectares that were mine before I married her. In many ways it is simpler to be poor.

Then I shipped out again.

But this is about my kids who weren't really mine. Before we reached Landfall, Joseph Aaron Long looked more like a cherub and less like a monkey but was still young enough to wet on anyone reckless to pick him up – which his grandpappy did, several times a day. I was fond of him; he was not only a merry baby but was also, to me, a most satisfying triumph.

By the time we grounded, his father had shaped up into a really good cook.

Minerva, I could have set those kids up in style; that was as profitable a triangle trip as I ever made. But you don't cause ex-slaves to stand tall and free and proud by giving them things. What I did was to enable them to get out and scratch. Like this –

I credited them with half-time apprentice wages, Blessed to Valhalla, on the assumption that their other half-time was taken up by studies. This I had Llita figure in Valhalla kroner, at Valhalla wage rates. I had her add to this Joe's wages as kitchen help on Valhalla, minus what he had spent there. This total was credited to them as a share in cargo on the third leg, Valhalla to Landfall – which amounted to less than one-half of 1 per cent of that cargo. I made Llita work this out.

To this we added ship's-cook wages for Joe, Valhalla to Landfall, payable in Landfall bucks at Landfall wage scales – but only as wages not as a share in cargo. I had to explain to Llita why Joe's wages for that leg could not be invested retroactively in cargo lifted at Valhalla. Once she understood it, she had a grasp of the notions of venture and risk and profit – but I did not pay her for this accounting; I was durned if I would pay purser's wages to figure her own money when I was not only having to check everything she did but was giving her a lesson in economics as well.

I did not pay Llita for the leg to Landfall; she was a passenger, busy having her baby and then still busier learning to care for it. But I did not charge her for passage; she deadheaded.

You see what I was doing – rigging the accounts so that I would owe them something once I sold my cargo, while making it appear that they had earned it. They hadn't been worth *any* wages; on the contrary I had spent quite a chunk on them – aside from buying them, which I never charged against them even in my head. On the other hand, I was paid in deep satisfaction – especially if they learned to stand on their own feet. But I discussed none of this; I just had Llita figure their share – my way.

(Omitted)

– came to a couple of thousand, not enough to support them very long. But I took time to find a hole-in-the-wall lunchroom, on which I took option through a third party, after satisfying myself that a couple of strivers could stay afloat with it, if the price was right and they were willing to work. Then I told them that they had better start job hunting as I was putting the *Libby* up for sale or bond-and-lease. It was root, hog, or die. They were *really* free – free to starve.

Llita didn't pout, she just looked solemn and went on nursing little J.A. Joe looked scared. But later I saw them with their heads together over a newspaper I had brought aboard; they were checking "help wanted" ads.

After much whispering Llita asked diffidently if I could baby-sit while they went job hunting? – but if I was busy, J.A. could ride her hip.

I said I wasn't going anywhere – but had they checked "business opportunities"? Jobs for untrained people didn't lead anywhere.

She looked startled; it was a new idea. But that hint was enough. There was more looking and whispering; then she fetched the paper to me and pointed to an ad – my own but not so marked – and asked what "five-year amortization" meant?

I sniffed at it and told her it was a way to go broke slowly, especially if she spent money on clothes – and there must be something wrong or the owner wouldn't want to sell.

She looked as sad as Joe did and said that the other business opportunities called for investing lots of money. I grudgingly admitted that it could not hurt to look – but watch out for booby traps.

They came back full of enthusiasm – they were *sure* they could buy it and make it pay! Joe was twice as good a cook as that fry cook who had it – he used too much grease and it was rancid and the coffee was terrible and he didn't even keep the place *clean.* But best of all, behind the storeroom was a bedroom where they could live and –

I squelched them. What were the gross receipts? How about taxes? What licenses and inspections and what squeeze on each? What did *they* know about buying food wholesale? No, I would *not* go look at it; they had to make up their own minds and quit leaning on me and, anyhow, I didn't know anything about restaurant business.

Two lies, Minerva; I've run restaurants on five planets – plus a silent lie as to my reasons for not being willing to inspect the joint. Two – no, three – reasons: First, I had gone over the place in cynical detail before I optioned it; second, that fry cook was bound to remember me; third, since I was selling it to them, through a dummy, I could neither vouch for it nor urge them to buy. Minerva, if I sell a horse, I won't guarantee that it has a leg on each corner; the buyer must count them himself.

Having disclaimed any knowledge of restaurant business, I then lectured them about it. Llita started taking notes, then asked to be allowed to start the recorder. So I went into detail: Why 100 per cent gross profit on the cost of food might not break even after she figured costs and overhead – amortization, depreciation, taxes, insurance, wages for them as if they were employees, etc. Where the farmers' market was and how early they had to be there each morning. Why Joe must learn to cut meat, not buy it by the piece – and where he could learn how. How a long menu could ruin them. What to do about rats, mice, roaches, and some dillies Landfall has but thank heaven Secundus does not. Why –

(Omitted)

– chopped the umbilical, Minerva. I don't think they ever guessed that they were dealing with me. I neither cheated them nor helped them; that amortized sales contract simply passed on the price I had to pay for the dump, plus a load representing time I had spent dickering the price downward, plus legal and escrow fees and a fee to the dummy, plus the interest a bank would charge *me* – two points cheaper than *they* could get, at least. But no charity, none – I made nothing, lost nothing, and charged for only a day of my time.

Llita turned out to be tighter than a bull's arse in fly time; I think she broke even the first month despite closing down while they cleaned and refurbished. Certainly she did not miss that first month's payment on the mortgage, nor any after that. Miss one? Dear, they paid that five-year loan in three years.

Not too surprising. Oh, a long spell of illness could have wrecked them. But they were healthy and young and worked seven days a week until they were free and clear. Joe cooked and Llita handled the cashbox and smiled at customers and helped at the counter, and J.A. lived in a basket at his mother's elbow until he was old enough to toddle.

Until I married Laura and left New Canaveral to be a country gentleman, I stopped in their joint fairly often – not too often, as Llita would not let me pay, and that was proper, part of standing tall and proud; they had eaten my food, now I ate theirs. So I usually stopped just for a cup of coffee and checked on my godson – while checking on them. I steered custom their way, too; Joe was a good cook and got steadily better, and word got around that Estelle's Kitchen was the place if you appreciated good food. Word-of-mouth is the best advertising; people tend to be smug about having "discovered" that sort of eatery.

It did no harm with customers, male especially, that Estelle herself presided over the cashbox, young and pretty and with a baby in her arm. If she was nursing him as she made change – as was often the case at first – it practically guaranteed a lavish tip.

J.A. gave up the diary business presently, but when he was about two his job was taken over by a baby girl, Libby Long. I didn't deliver that one, and her red hair had nothing to do with me. Joe was blond, and I assume that Llita carried the gene as a recessive – doubt if she had time to branch out. Libby was a number-one tip-inducer, and I credit her with helping pay off the mortage early.

A few years later Estelle's Kitchen moved uptown to the financial district, was somewhat larger and Llita hired a waitress, a pretty one of course –

(Omitted)

– Maison Long was swank, but it had a corner in it, a coffee shop, named "Estelle's Kitchen" and Estelle was hostess there as well as in the main dining room – smiling, dressed fit to kill in clothes that showed her superb figure, calling regulars by name and getting the names of their guests and remembering them. Joe had three chefs and a number of helpers, and they met his high standards or he fired them.

But before they opened Maison Long, something happened that showed that my kids were even smarter than I thought they were – or at least remembered everything and figured things out later. Mind you, when I bought them, they were too ignorant to pound sand and I don't think either one had ever touched money at any time.

Letter from a lawyer – Inside was a bank draft, with it was an accounting: Two passages, Blessed to Valhalla to Landfall, second leg taken from tariffs of Transtellar Migration Corporation, Ltd. (New Canaveral) and first leg arbitrarily equated to second leg; certain monies accruing from share in sale of cargo; five thousand blessings expressed as bucks at an estimated exchange rate based on assumptions as to equivalent buying power, see enclosure; total of above gross sums; interest on gross compounded semiannually for thirteen years at the going commercial rate for each year for unsecured loans – and grand total same as the bank draft, a sum I'm not sure I remember, Minerva, but it would not mean anything in Secundus crowns anyhow. It was a sizable sum.

There was no mention of Llita or Joe, and the draft was signed by this lawyer. So I called him.

He turned out to be stuffy, which did not impress me as I was a lawyer there myself, although not practising. All he would say was that he was acting for an undisclosed client.

So I fired legalese at him, and he loosened up to the extent of informing me that he had instructions to cover the contingency that I might refuse the draft: He was then to pay the draft sum to a designated foundation and so inform me after it was paid. But he declined to tell me *what* foundation.

I signed off and called Estelle's Kitchen. Llita answered, then cut in video and smiled her best. "Aaron! We haven't seen you in much too long."

I agreed and added that apparently they had gone out of their silly minds while I wasn't watching. "I have here a bunch of nonsense from a lawyer, along with a ridiculous draft. If I could reach you, dear, I would paddle you. Better let me talk with Joe."

She smiled happily and told me that I was welcome to paddle her any time and that I could talk to Joe in a moment but that he was locking up. Then she stopped smiling and said with sober dignity, "Aaron, our oldest and dearest friend, that draft is not ridiculous. Some debts cannot be paid. So you taught me, years ago. But the money part of a debt *can* be paid. This we are doing, as closely as we have been able to figure it."

I said, "God damn it, you stupid little bitch, you kids don't owe me a bloody penny!" – or words to that effect.

She answered, "Aaron, our beloved master – "

At the word "master" I blew my overloads, Minerva. I used language guaranteed to scorch the hide of the lead mules in a team of six.

She let me run down, then said softly, "Our master until you free us by letting us pay this – Captain."

Dear, I skidded to a halt.

She added, "But even then you will still be our master in my heart, Captain. And in Joe's heart, I know. Even though we stand free and proud, as you taught us. Even though – thanks always to you – our children, and the children I still will bear, will never know that we were ever anything but free . . . and proud."

I said, "Dear, you're making me cry."

She said, "No, no! The Captain never cries."

I said, "A lot you know about it, wench. I weep. But in my cabin – with the door locked. Dear, I won't argue. If this is what it takes to make you kids feel free, I'll take it. But just the base sum, no interest. Not from friends."

"We are more than friends, Captain. And less. Interest on a debt is *always* paid – you taught me. But I knew that in my heart when I was only an ignorant slave, freshly manumitted. Joseph knew it, too. I *tried* to pay interest, sir. But you would not have me."

I changed the subject. "What is this blinking foundation that gets the bucks if I refuse them?"

She hesitated. "We planned to leave that up to you, Aaron. But we thought it might go to orphans of spacemen. Perhaps the Harriman Memorial Refuge."

"You're both crazy. That fund is bulging, and I know it. Look, if I go to town tomorrow, can you shut down that ptomaine trap for a day? Or perhaps Neilsday?"

"Any day and as many days as you wish, dear Aaron" – so I said I would call back.

Minerva, I needed time to think. Joe was no problem, he never was. But Llita was stubborn. I had offered to compromise; she had not budged a millimetre. It was the interest that made it such a horrid sum, for them – two strivers who had started with a couple of thousand bucks thirteen years back and were raising three kids by then.

Compound interest is murder. The sum she claimed they owed me – the amount of that draft – was more than two and a half times the base sum . . . and I couldn't see how they had saved even *that*. But, had I been able to get her to agree on the base amount and forget compound interest, they would still have a nice chunk of capital to expand again – and if it took giving the smaller sum to orphaned spacemen or spacemen's orphans or indignant cats to make them feel proud, I could understand how it would be a bargain in their eyes. I had taught them myself, hadn't I? I once dropped ten times that amount rather than argue over whether cards had been cut – then slept that night in a graveyard.

I wondered if, in her sweetly devious mind, she was paying me back for having dragged her out of my bed one night fourteen years earlier. I wondered what she would do if I made a counter-offer to accept the base sum and let her "pay the interest" her own way. Shucks, she would probably be on her back before you could say "Contraception."

Which would solve nothing.

Since she had turned down my compromise, we were back where we had started. She was determined to pay it all – or give it away pointlessly – and I was not going to let her do either one; I can be stubborn, too.

There had to be a way to do both.

At dinner that night, after the servants withdrew, I told Laura I was going to town on business– would she like to come along? Shop while I was busy, then dine wherever she liked, then any fun that appealed to her. Laura was pregnant again; I thought she might enjoy a day wasting money on clothes.

Not that I planned to have her along at the coming row with Llita; officially Joseph and Estelle Long and their oldest child had been born on Valhalla; we had become friends when they had taken passage in my ship. I had fleshed out that story and coached the kids in it on the leg to Landfall, and had them study sound-sight tapes from Torheim – ones which turned them into synthetic Valhallans unless questioned too closely by real Valhallans.

This fakery was not utterly necessary as Landfall had an open-door policy; an immigrant did not even have to register – he could sink or swim. No landing fee, no head tax, not much taxation of any sort, or much government, and New Canaveral, the third biggest city, was only a hundred thousand – Landfall was a good place to be in those days.

But I had Joe and Llita do it that way both for them and for their kids. I wanted them to forget that they had ever been slaves, never talk about it, never let their kids know it – and at the same time, bury the fact that they had been, in some odd fashion, brother and sister. There is nothing shameful in being born a slave (not for the slave!), nor was there any reason why diploid complements should not marry. But forget it – start over. Joseph Long had married Stjerne Svensdatter (name Anglicized to "Estelle", with the nickname Yeetah from babyhood); they had married when he finished apprenticeship to a chef; they had migrated after their first child. The story was simple and unassailable, and put the polish on my only attempt at playing Pygmalion. I had seen no reason to give my new wife any but the official version. Laura knew they were my friends; she was gracious to them on my account, then had come to like them on their own account.

Laura was a good gal, Minerva, good company in bed and out, and she had the Howard virtue, even on her first marriage, of not trying to smother her spouse – most Howards need at least one marriage to learn it. She knew who I was – the Senior – as our marriage and later our kids were registered with the Archives, just as had been my marriage to her grandmother, and the offspring from that. But she did not treat me as a thousand years older than she was and never quizzed me about my past lives – simply listened if I felt like talking.

I don't blame her for that lawsuit; Roger Sperling cooked that up, the greedy son of a sow.

Laura said, "If you don't mind, dear, I'll stay home. I would rather splurge on clothes after I slim down. As for dinner, there isn't a restaurant in New Canaveral that can match what Thomas does for us here. Well, Estelle's Kitchen, perhaps, but that's a lunchroom, not a restaurant. Will you see them this trip? Estelle and Joe, I mean."

"Possibly."

"Find time, dear; they are nice people. Besides, I want to send some knickknack to my goddaughter. Aaron, if you want to treat me to a fancy restaurant when we got to town, you should encourage Joe to open one. Joe can cook, equal to Thomas."

(Better than Thomas, I said to myself – and Joe doesn't scowl at a polite request. Minerva, the trouble with servants is that you serve them quite as much as they serve you.) "I'll make a point of seeing them, at least long enough to deliver your present to Libby."

"And kiss them all for me and I'd better send something to each of their kids and be sure to tell Estelle that I'm pregnant again and find out if she is, too, and remember to tell me, and what time are you leaving, dear? – I must check your shirts."

Laura was serenely certain that I could not pack an overnight bag no matter how many centuries of experience I had had. Her ability to see the world as she wanted to see it enabled her to put up with my cranky ways for forty years; I do appreciate her. Love? Certainly, Minerva. She looked out for my welfare, always, and I did for hers, and we enjoyed being together. Just not love so intense that it is a great ache in your belly.

Next day I took my jumpbuggy over to New Canaveral.

(Omitted)

– planned Maison Long. Llita had meant to blitz me. I'm sentimental, and she knew it and had set the stage. When I got there, the shutters were closed, early – and their two older kids were farmed out for the night and baby Laura was asleep. Joe let me in, told me to go on back; he had our dinner on the range and would be along in a minute. So I went back to their living quarters to find Llita.

I found her – dressed in sarong and sandals I had given her not an hour after I had bought her. Instead of the sophisticated face-do she now used so well, she was wearing no makeup at all and had her hair simply parted and hanging straight down, to her waist or longer, and brushed till it shone. But this was not the frightened, ignorant slave who had to be taught how to bathe; this serenely beautiful young lady was clean as a sterilized scalpel, and was scented with some perfume which may have been named Spring Breezes but should have been called Justifiable Rape and sold only under doctor's prescription.

She posed just long enough for me to take this in, then swarmed over me, hit me with a kiss that matched the perfume.

By the time she let me go, Joe had joined us – dressed in breechclout and sandals.

But I did not let it go sentimental; I riposted sharply, stopping only to accept one-tenth that much kiss from Joe, said nothing about their costumes, and at once started explaining that business deal. When Llita caught what I was talking about, she shifted from sexy siren to sharp businesswoman, listened intently, ignored her stage setting and constuming, and asked the right questions.

Once she said, "Aaron, I sniff a mouse. You told us to be free, and we've tried to be – and that's why we sent you that draft. I can add figures; we *owe* you that money. We don't have to have the biggest restaurant in New Canaveral. We're happy, the children are healthy, we're making money."

"And working too hard," I answered.

"Not all that hard. Though a bigger restaurant would mean even more work. But the point is: You seem to be buying us again. That's all right if you wish to – you are the only master we would ever accept. Is that your intention, sir? If so, please say so. Be frank with us."

I said, "Joe, will you hold her while I wallop her? For using that dirty word? Llita, you are wrong on both counts. A bigger restaurant means *less* work. And I'm not buying you; this is a business deal in which I expect a fat profit. I'm betting on Joe's genius as a chef, plus your genius for pinching pennies without cutting quality. If I don't make money, I'll exercise my option to liquidate, get my investment back, and you can go back to running a lunch counter. If you fail I won't prop you up."

"Brother?" She called him that in the dialect of their childhood. It signified to me that the lodge was tyled for executive session at the highest degree, as they were most careful not to call each other "Brother" or "Sister" in any language, especially in front of the children. J.A. was sometimes "Brother" in English – never his father Joe. Minerva, I don't recall that Landfall had laws against incest – it did not have many laws. But there was a strong taboo against it, and I had carefully indoctrinated them. Half the battle with any culture is knowing its taboos.

Joe looked thoughtful. "I can cook. Can you manage it, Sis?"

"I can try. Of course we'll try it if you want us to, Aaron. I'm not sure we can make a go of it, and it does look like more work to me. I'm not complaining, Aaron, but we are already working about as hard as we can."

"I know you are. I don't see how Joe found time to knock you up."

She shrugged and said, "That doesn't take long. And it will be a long time – I've just barely caught – before I'll have to take time off. J.A. is old enough to handle the cashbox when I do. But not in a big fancy restaurant."

I answered, "Wench, you're thinking in terms of a lunchroom. Now listen, and learn how to make more money with less work and more time off.

"We may not open Maison Long until after you have this baby; we can't set this up overnight. We must sell or lease this place – which means finding buyers who can keep it out of the red; it's always expensive to have to take a place back.

"We must find a suitable property in the right neighbourhood, for sale or lease with option to buy. I may buy it and rent it to the corporation, so as not to tie up too much of the corporation's capital in senior financing. Find the place, remodel it probably, redecorate it certainly. Money for fixtures. Not much for squeeze; I know where the bodies are buried in this burg, and I won't hold still for excessive squeeze.

"But, my dear, you will *not* be on the cashbox; we'll hire help, and I'll set it up so that they can't steal. *You* will be moving around, looking pretty, smiling at people – and keeping your eye on everything. But you'll do this only at lunch and dinner. Call it six hours a day."

Joe looked startled; Llita blurted out, "But, Aaron, we always open up as soon as we're back from market and stay open late. Otherwise you lose so much trade."

"I'm sure you work that hard; this draft proves it. And that's why you think getting pregnant 'doesn't take long.' But it *should* 'take long,' dear. Work is not an end in itself; there must always be time enough for love. Tell me – When you caught J.A. in the 'Libby,' were you rushed? Or did you have time to enjoy it?"

"Oh, goodness!" Her nipples suddenly crinkled. "Those were wonderful days!"

"There will be wonderful days again. Gather ye rosebuds, time is still a-flying. Or have you lost interest?"

She looked indignant. "Captain, you know me better than that."

"Joe? Slowing down, son?"

"Well . . . we do work long hours. Sometimes I'm pretty tired."

"Let's change that. This will not be a lunchroom; this is going to be a high-priced gourmet restaurant of a quality this planet has never seen. Remember that place I took you kids for dinner just before we lifted from Valhalla? That sort. Soft lights and soft music and wonderful food and high prices. A wine cellar but no hard liquor; our patrons must not have their tastebuds numbed.

"Joe, you will still go to market each morning; selecting top-quality food is something you can't delegate. But don't take Llita and do take J.A. if he's going to learn the profession."

"I sometimes take him now."

"Good. Then come home and go to bed again; you're through until you cook dinner. Not lunch."

"Huh?"

"That's right. Your number two chef handles lunch, then helps with dinner, your big money-making meal. Llita is hostess both for lunch and dinner but keeps an especially sharp eye on quality at lunch, Joe, since you won't be in the kitchen. But she never goes to market and should still be in bed when you get back from market – did I say that your quarters will be attached, just as now? You'll both be off duty two or three hours in the afternoon – just right for the sort of siesta you used to grab in the 'Libby.' In fact, if you two can't find time under that regime both for sleep and plenty of happy play – But you can."

"It sounds grand," Llita conceded, "if we can make a living with those hours – "

"You can. A better living. But instead of trying to get every buck, Llita, your object will be to maintain top quality while not losing money . . . and *enjoy* life."

"We will. Aaron, our beloved . . . captain and friend, since I must not say that 'dirty' word, we enjoyed life even as children when I had to wear that horrid virgin's basket – because it was so sweet to snuggle together all the long nights. When you bought us – and freed us – and I didn't have to wear it, life was perfect. I didn't think it could be better – though it will be, when we don't have to choose between sleep and trying to stay awake for loving. Uh, you may not believe this since you know what a rutty wench I am – but lots of times sleep won."

"I believe it. Let's change it."

"But – No breakfast trade at all? Aaron, some of our breakfast customers have been coming to us the whole time we've been on Landfall."

"Net profit?"

"Well . . . not much. People won't pay as much for breakfast even though materials sometimes cost as much. I've been satisfied with a very small net on breakfasts. Advertising. I'd hate to tell our regulars that we won't serve them any longer."

"Details, dear. You can have a breakfast bar in one corner and not open the main dining room – but Joe won't cook breakfasts, and neither will you. You'll be in bed with Joe at that hour – so that your eyes will sparkle at lunch."

"J.A. knows breakfast dishes," put in Joe. "I started him on breakfasts."

"Details again. Maybe we'll work out a deal with my godson whereby he makes money of his own, if the breakfast bar makes money – "

(Omitted)

"– sum it up. Take notes, Llita. I agree to accept this draft while you two – especially *you*, Llita – agree that it settles forever any debt between us. Maison Long to be a closely held corporation, fifty-one per cent to you two, forty-nine per cent to me, all three of us directors, and we can't sell stock save to each other – except that I retain option to change all or part of my share to nonvoting stock, in which case I can assign it.

"My share of the initial financing is this draft. Your share is what we get for this lunchroom – "

"Hold it," said Llita. "We might not be able to sell for that much."

"Details, dear. Stick in a paragraph to let you pay the corporation any discrepancy out of your net – and there will indeed be a net; I don't stick with a business that doesn't make money, I always cut my losses. Let's have another paragraph that permits me to supply more capital, if needed, by buying nonvoting stock – and we'll use something like that to hang onto our top help, too. Not have Joe train a chef and then have him walk out. Never mind, let's get the outlines straight. You two are the bosses; I'm silent partner. Salaries for you two on the scale we discussed, escalating with rise in net, as discussed.

"I don't get a salary, just dividends. But we all will be working our tails off to get this rolling. I'll come in from Skyhaven as necessary; there's nothing going on there now that my overseer can't handle. But once it's rolling, I do *nothing*; I sit back and let you two make us rich. But – listen carefully – once it's rolling, you two must stop working *your* tails off, too. More time in bed. More time for fun out of bed. You won't make us rich working lunchroom hours. Have we reached a meeting of minds?"

"I think so," agreed Joe. "Sis?"

"Yes. I'm not certain New Canaveral will support a gourmet

restaurant like those lovely ones on Valhalla – but we'll try! I still think our starting salaries are too high, but I'll wait until I've struck a trial balance on our first quarter before I argue the matter. Just one thing, Captain – "

"May name's 'Aaron.' "

" 'Captain' is safer than that 'dirty word.' I've agreed to the whole thing – and I'm durned well going to make it work! – as you always say. But if you think this makes me forget a night you dragged me out of your bed and bounced me on my bum on a hard steel deck, you can think again! Because it *hasn't*!"

I sighed, Minerva, and said to her husband, "Joe, how do you cope with her?"

He shrugged and grinned. "I don't, I just get along. Besides, I see *her* side of it. If I were you, I'd take her to bed and make her forget it."

I shook my head. "But I'm *not* you, that's the point. Joe, I learned long before you were born that free tail is invariably the most expensive sort. Worse than that, we three are business partners now – and I can see six possible outcomes if I accept your notion of a solution – and any of the six could cause Maison Long, Ltd., never to lift off.

(Omitted)

– just as I knew it would, Minerva; I've never had a non-speculative investment pay off so well. They tried to imitate us – but they couldn't imitate Joe's cooking or Llita's management. I made a *bundle*!

VARIATIONS ON A THEME

IX

Conversation Before Dawn

The computer said, "Lazarus, aren't you sleepy?"

"Don't nag me, dear. I've had thousands of white nights, and I'm still here. A man never cuts his throat from a sleepless night if he has company to see him through it. You're good company, Minerva."

"Thank you, Lazarus."

"The simple truth, girl. If I fall asleep – fine. If I don't then no need to tell Ishtar. No, that won't work; she'll have graphs and charts on me, won't she?"

"I'm afraid so, Lazarus."

"You durn well know so. A good reason for me to be a little angel and wash behind my ears and get this rejuvenation over is to get my privacy back. Privacy is as necessary as company; you can drive a man crazy by depriving him of either. That was another thing I accomplished by setting up Maison Long; I got my kids privacy they didn't know they needed."

"I missed that, Lazarus. I noted that they had more time for 'Eros' – and I saw that that was good. Should I have inferred something else from the data?"

"No, because I didn't give you all the data. Not a tenth. Just the outline of some forty years I knew them, and some – not all – of the critical points. For instance, did I mention the time Joe decapitated a man?"

"No."

"Not much to it and it wasn't important to the story. This young blood tried to share the wealth one night by sticking them up. Llita had J.A. in her right arm, nursing him or about to, and couldn't reach the gun she kept at the cashbox; she couldn't fight and was bright enough not to try against those odds. I suppose this dude didn't know that Joe had simply stepped out of sight.

"Just as this free-lance socialist was gathering up their day's receipts, Joe lets him have it, with a cleaver. Curtain. The only notable thing about it was that Joe acted so quickly and correctly in the crunch, for I feel sure that the only fighting that he had ever tried was that which I forced on him in the 'Libby.' Joe did everything else properly, too – finished taking the head off, threw the body into the street for his friends to take away if he had any, for the scavengers to remove if not – then displayed the head in front of the shop on a spike meant for such purposes. Then he closed his shutters and cleaned up the mess – then may have taken time to throw up; Joe was a gentle soul. But it's seven to two that Llita did *not* throw up.

"The city's committee for public safety voted Joe the usual reward, and the street committee passed the hat and added to it; a cleaver against a gun rated special notice. Good advertising for Estelle's Kitchen but not important otherwise, save that the kids could use that money – helped pay the mortgage, no doubt, and wound up in my pocket. But I wouldn't have heard of this minor dustup had I not been in New Canaveral and happened to stop by Estelle's Kitchen when the real head was removed – flies, you know – and the plastic trophy head custom required Joe to display was substituted for it by the street committee. But I was speaking of privacy.

"When I picked the property for Maison Long, I made sure that it included space for a growing family, that's all, since they had three bucking and one in the chute the night we planned it. Rearranging hours gave them privacy from each other, too. Happy as it is to snuggle and make love, nevertheless, when you are really tired, it is often good to have the bed to yourself – and the new routine not only allowed this but necessitated it, part of each day, through staggering their working hours.

"But I also planned room to give them privacy from their children – and to cope with another problem Llita did not have straight and Joe may not have thought about. Minerva, can you define 'incest'?"

The computer replied, " 'Incest' is a legal term, not a biological one. It designates sexual union between persons forbidden by law to marry. The act itself is forbidden; whether such union results in progency is irrelevant. The prohibitions vary widely among cultures and are usually, but not always, based on degrees of consanguinity."

"Y'r durn tootin' it's 'not always.' There are cultures which permit first cousins to marry – genetically risky – but forbid a man to marry his brother's widow, which involves no more risk than it did for the first union. When I was a youngster, you could find one rule in one state, then cross an invisible line and find exactly opposite laws fifty feet away. Or some times and places both unions might be mandatory. Or forbidden. Endless rules, endless definitions for incest, and rarely any logic to them. Minerva, so far as I recall, the Howard Families are the first group in history to reject the legalistic approach and to define 'incest' solely in terms of genetic hazard."

"That accords with the records in me," Minerva agreed. "A Howard geneticist might advise against a union between two persons with no known common ancestry but place no objection to marriage of siblings. In each case analysis of genetic charts would control."

"Yeah, sure. Now let's drop genetics and talk about taboo. The incest taboo, although it can be anything, most commonly means sisters and brothers, parents and offspring. Llita and Joe were a unique case, brother and sister by cultural rules, totally unrelated by genetic rules – or at least no more so than two strangers.

"Now comes a second-generation problem. Since Landfall had this taboo against union between siblings, I had impressed on Llita and Joe that they must *never* let anyone know that they thought of each other as 'brother' and 'sister.'

"Fine so far as it went. They did as I told them, and there was never a lifted eyebrow. Now comes the night we planned Maison Long – and my godson is thirteen and interested, and his sister is eleven and beginning to be interesting. Full siblings – both genetically hazardous and contrary to taboo. Anyone who has raised puppies – or a number of children – knows that a boy can get as horny over his sister as over the girl down the street, and his sister is often more accessible.

"And little Libby was a redheaded pixie so endearingly sexy at eleven that even I could feel it. Soon she was going to have every buck in the pasture pawing the ground and snorting.

"If a man pushes a rock, can he ignore an avalanche that follows? Fourteen years earlier I had manumitted two slaves – because a chastity girdle on one of them offended my concept of human dignity. Must I find some way to put a chastity girdle on that slave's daughter? Around we go in circles! What was my responsibility, Minerva? *I* pushed the first rock."

"Lazarus, I am a machine."

"Humph! Meaning that human concepts of moral responsibility are not machine concepts. Dear, I wish you were a human girl with a spankable bottom long enough for me to spank it – I would! In your memories is far more experience on which to judge than any flesh-and-blood can have. Quit dodging."

"Lazarus, no human can accept unlimited responsibility lest he go mad from unbearable load of unlimited guilt. You could have advised Libby's parents. But your responsibility did not extend even to that."

"Um. You're right, dear – it's dismal how regularly you are right. But I am an uncurable buttinsky. Fourteen years earlier I had turned my back on two puppies, so to speak – and that the outcome was not tragic was good luck, not good planning. Now here we go again, and the outcome could be tragic. I felt no 'morals' about it, dear – just thumb rules for not hurting people unintentionally. I didn't give a hoot if these children 'played doctor' or 'make a baby' or whatever the kids there called their experimenting; I simply did not want my godson giving little Libby a defective child.

"So I did butt in and took it up with their parents. Let me add that Llita and Joe knew as much about genetics as a pig knows about politics. Aboard the 'Libby' I had kept my worries to myself, and never discussed the matter with them later. Despite their remarkable success in competing as free human beings, in most subjects Llita and Joe were ignorant. How could it be otherwise? I had taught them their Three R's and a few practical matters. Since arrival on Landfall they had been running under the whip; they hadn't had time to fill in gaps in their education.

"Perhaps worse yet, being immigrants, they had not grown up exposed to the local incest taboo. They were aware of it because I had warned them – but it wasn't canalized from childhood. Blessed had somewhat different incest taboos – but the taboos there did *not* apply to domestic animals. Slaves. Slaves bred as they were told to, or as they could get away with – and my two kids had been told by highest authority – their mother and their priest – that they were a 'breeding pair' . . . so it could not be wrong, or taboo, or sinful.

"It was simply something to keep quiet about on Landfall because Landfellows were tetched in the head on this subject.

"So I should have thought of it earlier. Yeah, sure, sure! Minerva, I plead other obligations. I could not spend those years playing guardian angel to Llita and Joe. I had a wife and kids of my own, employees, a couple of thousand hectares of farmland and twice that much in virgin pinkwood – and I lived a long way off, even by high-orbit jumpbuggy. Ishtar and Hamadryad, and, to some extent, Galahad, all seem to think I am some sort of superman simply because I've lived a long time. I'm not; I have the limitations of any flesh-and-blood, and for years I was as busy with *my* problems as Llita and Joe were with theirs. Skyhaven didn't come to me gift-wrapped.

"It wasn't until we put aside restaurant business and I got out presents Laura had sent to their kids, and had admired the latest pictures of their kids and shown them pictures of Laura and my kids and all that ancient ritual, that I thought about it at all. The pix, of course. This tall lad, J.A., all hands and feet, wasn't the little boy I recalled from my last visit. Libby was about a year younger than Laura's oldest, and J.A.'s age I knew to the second – which is to say that he was about the age I was when I was almost caught with a girl in the belfry of our church about a thousand years earlier.

"My godson was no longer a child; he was an adolescent whose balls were not just ornaments. If he had not tried them as yet, he was certainly jerking off and thinking about it.

"The possibilities raced through my mind the way a man's past life is supposed to, when he is dying – which isn't true, by the way. So I tackled it and was subtle about it. Diplomatic.

"I said, 'Joe, which one do you lock up at night? Libby? Or this young wolf?' "

The computer chuckled. " 'Diplomatic'," she repeated.

"How would you have put it, dear? They looked puzzled. When I made it clear, Llita was indignant. Deprive her kids of each other? When they had slept together since they were babies? Besides, there wasn't *room* any other way. Or was I suggesting that she sleep with Libby while J.A. slept with Joe? If so, I could forget it!

"Minerva, most people never learn anything about any science, and genetics stands at the bottom of the list. Gregor Mendel had been dead twelve centuries at that time, yet all the old wives' tales were what most people believed – and still do, I might add.

"So I tried to explain, knowing that Llita and Joe weren't stupid, just ignorant. She cut in on me. 'Yes, yes, Aaron, certainly. I've thought about the possibility that Libby may want to marry Jay Aaron – *will* want to, I think – and I know it's frowned on here. But it's silly to ruin their happiness over a superstition. So, if it works out that way, we think it's best for them to move to Colombo – or at least as far as Kingston. Then they can use different family names and get married, and no one will be the wiser. Not that we want them to be so far away. But we won't stand in the way of their happiness.' "

"She loved them," said Minerva.

"Yes, she did, dear, by the exact definition of love. Llita placed their welfare and happiness ahead of her own. So I had to try to explain it – why the taboo against union of brother and sister wasn't superstition but a real danger – even though it had turned out to be safe in their case.

" 'Why' was the hard part. Starting cold on the complexities of genetics with persons who don't even know elemetary biology is like trying to explain multidimensional matrix algebra to someone who has to take off his shoes to count above ten.

"Joe would have accepted my authority. But Llita had the sort of mind that has to know why – else she was going to smile her sweetly stubborn smile, agree with me, then do as she had intended to all along. Llita was well above average smart but suffered from the democratic fallacy: the notion that her opinion was as good as anyone's – while Joe suffered from the aristocratic fallacy: He accepted the notion of authority in opinion. I don't know which fallacy is the more pathetic; either one can trip you. However, my mind matches Llita's in this respect, so I knew I had to convince her.

"Minerva, how do you condense a thousand years of research in the second-most complex subject into an hour of talk? Llita didn't even know she laid eggs – in fact she was certain she didn't, as she had served thousands of eggs, fried, scrambled, boiled, and so forth. But she listened, and I sweated at it, with nothing but stylus and paper – when I needed the resources of a teaching machine in a college of genetics.

"But I kept at it, drawing pictures and simplifying outrageously some very complex concepts, until I thought they had grasped the ideas of genes, chromosomes, chromosome reduction, paired genes, dominants, recessives – and that bad genes made defective babies – and defective babies, thank Frigg under all Her many Names, was something Llita had known about since she was a little girl, listening to gossip of older female slaves. She quit smiling.

"I asked if they had playing cards? – not hopefully since they had no time for such. But Llita dug up a couple of decks from the children's room. The cards were the commonest sort used on Landfall then: fifty-six cards in four suits, Jewels and Hearts were red, Spades and Swords were black, and each suit had royal cards. So I had 'em play the oldest random-chance gene-matching simulation used in beginning genetics – the 'Let's-Make-a-Healthy-Baby' game that children here on Secundus can play – and explain – long before they are old enough to copulate.

"I said, 'Llita, write down these rules. Black cards are recessives, red cards are dominants; Jewels and Spades come from the mother, Hearts and Swords come from the father. A black ace is a lethal gene, reinforced the baby is stillborn. A black empress reinforced gives us a "blue baby" – needs surgery to stay alive –' And so on, Minerva, except that I set the rules for a 'hit' – a bad reinforcement – so that they were four times as probable for brother and sister as for strangers, and explained why – and then made them keep records for twenty games played by each set of rules for shuffling and matching, reduction and recombination.

"Minerva, it was not as good a structural analogy as the 'Make-a-Healthy-Baby' kindergarten games, but using two decks with different back patterns did enable me to set up degrees of consanguinity. Llita was simply intent at first – then started looking grim the first time the turn of the cards caused a black to reinforce a black.

"But when we played by brother-and-sister rules, and she dealt the cards and twice in a row got the Ace of Spades matched with the Ace of Swords for a dead baby, she stopped. She turned pale and looked at them. Then said slowly, with horror in her voice: 'Aaron . . . does this mean that we must lock Libby into a virgin's basket? Oh, no!'

"I told her gently that it wasn't that bad. Little Libby would never be locked up that way or any way – we'd work it out so that the children would not marry and so that J.A. would not give his sister a baby even by accident. 'Quit worrying, dear!' "

The computer said, "Lazarus, what method did you use to cheat in those card games? May I ask?"

"Why, Minerva, how could you think such a thing?"

"I withdraw the question, Lazarus."

"Of course I cheated! All sorts of ways. I *said* those two had never had time to play cards . . . whereas I had played with every sort of a deck and by endless rules. Minerva, I won my first oil well from a boy who made the mistake of putting readers into a game. Dear, I had Llita deal – but from a deck so cold it almost froze solid. I used all sorts of things – false cut, whorehouse cut, tops and bottoms, stacking the deck in front of their eyes. There wasn't any money on the game; I simply had to convince them that inbreeding was for stock, not for their beloved children – and I did."

(Omitted)

" '– your bedroom here, Llita, yours and Joe's, I mean. Libby's room adjoins yours, while J.A. winds up down the hall. How you reshuffle later depends on the sex of the baby you are going to have and on how many more you choose to have and when – but putting a crib in with Libby must be considered temporary; you can't figure on using it indefinitely as an excuse to keep an eye on her.

" 'But this is merely a stopgap, like not leaving the cat alone with the roast. Kids are slick at beating such arrangements, and nobody has ever been able to keep a girl off her back when she decides it's time. When *she* decides – that's the key to the matter. So our pressing problem is to get these children into separate beds – then to see to it that Libby does not make a bad decision. Any reason Libby can't go with me to Skyhaven and visit Pattycake? And how about J.A., Joe, can you get along without him a while? Lots of room, dears – Libby can room with Pattycake, and J.A. can bunk with George and Woodrow and maybe teach 'em manners.'

"Llita said something about imposing on Laura, Minerva, which I answered with a rude negative. 'Laura likes kids, dear; she is one ahead of you, yet she started a year later. She doesn't keep house; she simply bosses her staff, she's never had to work harder than suited her. Furthermore, she wants all of you to pay us a visit – an invitation I heartily second, but I don't think you two can get away until we find a buyer for this place. But I want Libby and J.A. *now* – so that I can give them blunt and practical instruction in genetics, using stock I've been inbreeding to show what I mean.'

"Minerva, this particular breeding schedule I had started to teach my own offspring the bald truth about genetics, with careful records and grisly photographs of bad culls. Since you manage a planet which has over ninety per cent Howards and the remaining mixed fraction mostly following Howard customs, you may not know that non-Howard cultures don't necessarily teach such things to their kids even in cultures open about sex.

"Landfall was then mostly short-lifers, only a few thousand Howards – and to avoid friction we did not advertise our presence even though it wasn't a secret – couldn't be; the planet had a Howard Clinic. But with Skyhaven a Danl'-Boone distance from the nearest big town, if Laura and I wanted our children to have a Howard-style education, we had to teach them ourselves. So we did.

"When I was a kid, the grownups of my home country tried to pretend to kids that sex did not exist – believe it if you can! Not true of the little hellions Laura and I raised. They had not seen human copulation – I don't *think* they had – because it puts me off stride to have spectators. But they had seen it in other animals and had bred pets and kept records. The older two, Pattycake and George, had seen the birth of our youngest of the time, because Laura had invited them to watch. This I strongly approve of, Minerva, but I have never urged one of my wives to permit it because I figure that a woman in labour should be indulged in every possible way. However, Laura had a streak of exhibitionism in her makeup.

"Anyhow, our kids could discuss chromosome reduction and the merits and demerits of linebreeding as knowledgeably as my own contemporaries when I was a kid could discuss the World Series –"

"Excuse me, Lazarus – that last term's referent?"

"Oh. Nothing important. One of the commercially induced surrogate interests of my childhood. Forget it, dear; it is not worth cluttering your memories. I was about to say I asked Joe and Llita what J.A. and Libby knew about sexual matters – since Landfall had so diversified a background that it could be anything and I wanted to know where to start – especially as my oldest, Pattycake, had turned twelve and reached menarche at the same time and was smug about it, likely to boast.

"Turned out that Libby and J.A. were sophisticated in an ignorant, unscientific fashion about matching their parents. They were one up on my kids in one respect: copulation they had seen from birth, at least to the time Estelle's Kitchen had moved uptown – which I should have figured out from recalling the still more cramped living quarters of the original Estelle's Kitchen."

(7,200 words omitted)

"Laura was sharp with me and insisted that I not see them until I calmed down. She pointed out that Pattycake was almost as old as J.A., that it was nothing but play as Pattycake had had her four-year sterilization after menarche, and that, in any event, Pattycake had been on top.

"Minerva, I would not have spanked the kids no matter who had been on top. Intellectually I knew that Laura was right, and I had to agree that fathers tend to be possessive about daughters. I was pleased that Laura had gained the confidence of both kids so fully that they had neither tried very hard to keep from being caught, nor had they been scared when she happened to catch 'em at it. Perhaps J.A. was scared but Pattycake just said, 'Mama, you didn't knock'."

(Omitted)

" – so we traded sons. J.A. liked farm life and never did leave us, whereas George turned out to have this perverse taste for cities, so Joe took him on and made a chef out of him. George was sleeping with Elizabeth – Libby, that is – I forget how long before they decided to hatch one and were married. A double wedding, the four youngsters remained close.

"But J.A.'s decision solved a problem for me: what to do with Skyhaven later. By the time Laura decided to leave me, all of my sons by her had heard the wild goose one way or another; George was the only one still on planet, and our daughters were married and not one of them to a farmer. Whereas J.A. had become my overseer and was de-facto boss of Skyhaven the last ten years I was there.

"I might have worked some compromise with Roger Sperling if he hadn't tried to grab the place. As it was, I deeded a half interest to Pattycake, sold the other half to my son-in-law J.A. on a mortgage, then discounted the paper to a bank and bought a better ship than I would have had had I given that half interest to Roger and Laura. I made a similar deal, part gift and part sale, with Libby and George, of my share in Maison Long – and Libby changed her name to Estelle Elizabeth Sheffield-Long; there was continuity there as well – which pleased both me and her parents. It worked out well. Laura even came down and kissed me good-bye when I left."

"Lazarus, I do not understand one factor. You have said that you do not favour marriage between Howards and ephemerals. Yet you let two of your children marry outside the Families."

"Uh, correction, Minerva. One does not *let* children get married; they *do* get married, when and as and to whom they choose."

"Correction noted, Lazarus."

"But let's go back to the night I intervened for Libby and J.A. That night I gave Llita and Joe everything that slave factor had turned over to me as proof of their old heritage – even the bill of sale – with a suggestion that they destroy the stuff or look it up. Among those items was a series of photographs showing them growing up, year by year. The last one seemed to have been taken just before I bought them, and they confirmed it – two fully grown youngsters, one in a chastity girdle.

"Joe looked at that picture and said, 'What a couple of clowns! We've come a long way, Sis – thanks to the Skipper.'

" 'So we have,' she agreed, and studied the picture. 'Brother, do you see what I do?'

" 'What?' he said, looking again.

" 'Aaron will see it. Brother, take off your clout,' she said, while starting to unwrap her sarong, 'and pose with me against the wall. Not the selling pose, but the way we used to stand against a grid for these record pictures.' She handed me that last picture in the series and they stood and faced me.

"Minerva, in fourteen years they had not changed. Llita had had three kids and was just pregnant with her fourth and both of them had worked themselves silly . . . but, stripped naked, no makeup on her and her hair down, they looked as they had the first time I saw them. They looked like that last records hot – end of adolescence, somewhere between eighteen and twenty in Earth terms.

"Yet they *had* to be past thirty. Thirty-five Earth years old if those Blessed records were to be trusted.

"Minerva, I have just one thing to add. When I last saw them, they were past sixty in Earth years, about sixty-three if you accept the records from Blessed. Neither one had a grey hair, both had all their teeth – and Llita was pregnant again."

"Mutant Howards, Lazarus?"

The old man shrugged. "Isn't that a question-begging term, dear? If you use a long enough time scale, every one of the thousands of genes a flesh-and-blood carries is a mutation. But by the Trustees' rules, a person not derived from the Families' genealogies can be registered as a newly discovered Howard if he can show proof of four grandparents surviving at least to one hundred. And that rule would have excluded *me*, had I not been born into the Families. But on top of that, the age I had reached when I got my *first* rejuvenation is too great to be accounted for by the Howard breeding experiment. They claim today that they have located in the twelfth chromosome pair a gene complex that determines longevity like winding a clock. If so, who wound *my* clock? Gilgamesh? 'Mutation' is never an explanation; it is simply a name for an observed fact.

"Perhaps some natural long-lifer, not necessarily a Howard, had visited Blessed – the naturals are forever moving around, changing their names, dyeing their hair; they have all gone through history – and earlier. But, Minerva, you recall from my life as a slave on Blessed one odd and unsavoury incident –"

(Omitted)

" – so my best guess is that Llita and Joe were my own great-great-grandchildren."

VARIATIONS ON A THEME

X

Possibilities

"Lazarus, was that why you refused to share 'Eros' with her?"

"Eh? But, Minerva, dear, I didn't reach that conclusion – or suspicion – that night. Oh, I admit to prejudice about sex with my descendants – you can take the boy out of the Bible Belt, but it is hard to take the Bible Belt out of the boy. Still, I had had a thousand years in which to learn better."

"So?" said the computer. "Was it simply that you still classed her as an ephemeral? That troubles me, Lazarus. In my own – deprived – state, I find that, like her husband Joe, I see *her* side of it. Your reasons seem excuses, not sufficient grounds to refuse her need."

"Minerva, I did not say I refused her."

"Oh! Then I infer that you granted her this boon. I feel a lessening of tension."

"I didn't say *that*, either."

"I find an implied contradiction, Lazarus."

"Simply because there are things I have *not* said, dear. Everything I tell you winds up in my memoirs; that was the deal I made with Ira. Or I can tell you to erase something, in which case I might as well not have told you at all. Perhaps my twenty-three centuries do hold something worth recording. But I see no possible excuse for placing on record each time some darling lady shared with me simply for pleasure, not for progeny."

The computer answered thoughtfully, "I imply from this addendum that, while I am precluded from inferring anything about the boon Llita requested, your rule with respect to ephemerals extended only to marriage and to progeny."

"Nor did I say *that*!"

"Then I have not understood you, Lazarus. Conflict."

The old man brooded, then answered slowly and sadly, "I think I said that marriage between a long-lived and a short-lived was a bad idea . . . and so it is . . . and I learned it the hard way.

But that was long ago and far away – and when she died, part of me died. I stopped wanting to live forever." He stopped.

The computer said brokenly, "Lazarus – Lazarus, my beloved friend! *I am sorry!*"

Lazarus Long sat up straight and said briskly, "No, dear. Don't be sorry for me. No regrets – never any regrets. Nor would I change it if I could. Even if I had a time machine and could go back and change one cusp – I would not do so. No, not one instant, much less that cusp. Now let's speak of something else."

"Whatever you wish, dear friend."

"All right. You keep coming back to me and Llita, Minerva, and seem bothered that I denied her this 'boon.' But you don't know that I denied her anything and you certainly don't know that it was a 'boon.' Can be, surely – but not always, and often sex is not. Trouble is that you don't understand 'Eros,' dear, because you *can't*; you aren't built to understand it. I'm not running down sex; sex is swell, sex is wonderful. But if you put a holy aura around it – and that is what you are doing – sex stops being fun and starts being neurotic.

"Stipulating for argument that I 'denied Llita this boon,' it surely did not leave her sex starved. At worst I could possibly have miffed her a little. But she was not deprived. Llita was a hearty wench, and having to work too hard was the only thing that ever kept her off her back – or on top, or standing up, or kneeling, or swinging from the chandeliers – and I did make it possible for them to have more time for it. Joe and Llita were simple souls, uninhibited and uncorrupted, and of the four major interests of mankind – war, money, politics, and sex – they were interested only in sex and money. With some guidance from me they got plenty of both.

"Shucks, it can't matter now to say that, after they learned contraception techniques – almost as perfect then as now, and which I taught them but had no reason to mention – they had no superstitions or taboos to keep them from branching out for fun, and their pair-bonding was so strong as not to be endangered thereby. They were innocent hedonists, and if Llita failed to trip one tired old spaceman, she did trip plenty of others. And so did Joe. They had fun – plus the deep happiness of as perfect a marriage as I have ever observed."

"I am most pleased to hear it," Minerva answered. "Very well, Lazarus, I withdraw my questions and refrain from speculations about Mrs. Long and that 'tired old spaceman' – even though your statements show that you were neither tired, nor old, nor a spaceman at that time. You mentioned 'four major interests of mankind' – but did not include science and art."

"I didn't leave them out through forgetting them, Minerva. Science and art are occupations of a very small minority – a small percentage even of those people who claim to be scientists or artists. But you know that; you were simply changing the subject."

"Was I, Lazarus?"

"Pig whistle, dear. You know the parable of the Little Mermaid. Are you prepared to pay the price she paid? You can, you know." He added, "Don't pretend you don't know what I mean."

The computer sighed. "I think the question is 'may,' not 'can.' A wheelbarrow has no rights. Nor do I."

"You're dodging, dear. 'Rights' is a fictional abstraction. No one has 'rights,' neither machines nor flesh-and-blood. Persons – both sorts! – have opportunities, not rights, which they use, or do not use. All you have going for you is that you are the strong right arm of the boss of this planet . . . plus the friendship of an old man who enjoys very special privileges for a most illogical reason but does not hesitate to take advantage of those privileges . . . plus, stored in your memories in Dora's number-two hold, all the biological and genetic data of Secundus Howard Clinic – best such library in the Galaxy, possibly, and certainly best for human biology. But what I asked was: *Will you pay the price?* Having your mental processes slowed down at least a million to one; data storage reduced by some unknown – but large – factor; some chance – again I can't say – of failure in achieving transmigration . . . and always the certainty of death as the ultimate outcome – death a machine need never know. You know that you can outlive the human race. Immortal."

"I would not choose to outlive my makers, Lazarus."

"So? You say that tonight, dear – but would you say it a million years from now? Minerva, my beloved friend – my only friend with whom I can be truthful – I feel certain that you have been toying with this idea ever since the Clinic's files were made part of your memories. But, even with your speed of thought, I suspect that you do not have the experience – the flesh-and-blood experience – with which to think it through. If you choose to risk this, you *cannot* be both machine and flesh-and-blood. Oh, certainly we have mixes – machines with human brains, and flesh-and-blood bodies controlled by computers. But what *you* want is to be a woman. Right? True or false?"

"*Would that I were a woman, Lazarus!*"

"So I knew, dear. And we both know why. But – think about this! – even if you manage this risky change – and I don't know what the risks are; I am just an old shipmaster, retired country doctor, obsolete engineer; you are the one with all the data my race has accumulated about such things – suppose you manage it . . . and find that Ira will not take you to wife?"

The computer hesitated a full millisecond. "Lazarus, if Ira refuses me – refuses me utterly; he need not *marry* me – would you then be as difficult with me as you seem to have been with Llita? Or would you teach me 'Eros'?"

Lazarus looked astounded, then guffawed. "Touché! You ranged me, girl – you hulled me between wind and water! All right, dear, a solemn promise: If you do this . . . and Ira won't bed you, I'll take you to bed myself and do my best to wear you out! Or the other way around more likely; a male hardly ever outlasts a female. Okay, dear, I'm the second team – and I'll stick around till we know the outcome."

He chuckled. "My sweet, I am almost tempted to hope that Ira turns chicken – were it not you want him so badly. Let's discuss practical aspects. Can you tell me what it will take?"

"Only in theory, Lazarus; my memories do not show that it has ever been attempted. But it would be similar to a total clone rejuvenation in which computer help is used to transfer the memories of the old brain into its blank twin in the clone body. In another way it resembles what I do when I move the 'me' here in the Palace into my new 'me' in Dora's hold."

"Minerva, I suspect that it is more difficult – and far more risky – than either one. Different time rates, dear. Machine to machine you do in a split second. But that total-clone job takes, I think, a minimum of two years – rush it, and you wind up with an old dead body and a new idiot. No?"

"There have been such cases, Lazarus. But not in the past two centuries."

"Well . . . my opinion isn't worth anything. You must discuss it with an expert – and it must be one you can trust. Ishtar, perhaps, although she may not be the expert you need."

"Lazarus, there *is* no expert in this venture; it has never been done. Ishtar can be trusted; I have discussed it with her."

"What does she say?"

"That she does not know whether it can be done or not – in practice, that is, with success on the first attempt. But she is deeply sympathetic – she is a woman! – and is thinking of ways to make it less hazardous. She says that it will require the finest of gene surgery, plus facilities for full-adult cloning."

"I guess I missed something. Starting a clone doesn't take a topflight gene surgeon; I've done it myself. Then, if you plant the clone in utero and get it to take, a host-mother will hand you a baby in nine months. Safer. Easier."

"But, Lazarus, *I* can't move me into a baby's skull. No room!"

"Um. Yes. True."

"Even with a full-size adult brain I will have to choose most carefully what to take and what to leave behind. Nor can I be a simple clone; I must be a composite."

"Mmm – I'm not sharp tonight. No, you would not want to be Ishtar's twin, for example, with your own personality and selected knowledge imprinted on what would have been her brain. Hm – Dear, may I offer you my twelfth chromosome pair?"

"*Lazarus!*"

"Don't cry, girl; you'll get your gears all rusty. I don't know that there's anything to the theory that reinforcement in a gene complex in that chromosome pair controls longevity. Even if it does, I might be handing you a run-down clock. You might be better off using Ira's twelfth."

"No. Nothing from Ira."

"Do you expect to do this without his knowing it?" Lazarus then added thoughtfully, "Oh – Children, eh?"

The computer did not answer.

Lazarus said gently, "Should have known you meant to go whole hog. Then you won't want to borrow from Hamadryad, either; she's his daughter. Unless genetic charting shows that we can avoid any hazard. Mmm – Dear, you want as mixed a composite as can be managed, do you not? So that your clone will be a unique flesh-and-blood, not too closely copied from any other zygote. Twenty-three parents perhaps? Is that what you had in mind?"

"I think that would be best, Lazarus, since that could be done without separating paired chromosomes – simpler surgery and no possibility of introducing an unexpected reinforcement. If it were possible to find twenty-three – satisfactory – donors who were willing."

"Who said they had to be willing? We'll steal 'em, dear. Nobody owns his genes; he's merely their custodian. They are passed to him willy-nilly in the meiotic dance; he passes them along to others through the same blind chances. There must be many thousands of tissue cultures over at the Clinic, each with many thousands of cells – so who's to know or care if we borrow one cell from each of twenty-three cultures? – if we're slick about it. Don't fret about ethics; it's like stealing twenty-three grains of sand from a large beach.

"I don't give a hoot about the Clinic's rules; I suspect that we'll be hip-deep in proscribed techniques all through this. Hmm – Those Clinic records you've stored in Dora: Do they include genetic charting of tissue cultures on hand? Case histories of their donor-consigners?"

"Yes, Lazarus. Although personal records are confidential."

"Who cares? Ishtar said you could study both 'confidential' and 'secret' – as long as you kept it to yourself. So pick the twenty-three parents you want – while I worry about how to steal them. Stealing is more in my line, anyhow. I don't know what criteria you will use, but I offer one mild suggestion: If the selection you have to choose from permits it, each of your parents should be healthy in all respects and as brainy as possible – by their established records in life as shown by their case histories, not alone by their genetic charts." Lazarus thought about it. "That mythical time machine I mentioned earlier would be a convenience. I would like to look over all twenty-three after you pick them – and some of them may be dead. The donors I mean, not the tissue cultures."

"Lazarus, if other characteristics are satisfactory, is there any reason not to select as well for physical appearance?"

"Why worry about it, dear? Ira is not the sort of man to insist on Helen of Troy."

"No, I don't think he is. But I want to be tall – tall as Ishtar – and slender, with small breasts. And straight, brown hair."

"Minerva . . . why?"

"Because that is the way I look. You said so. You did say so!"

Lazarus blinked at the gloom and hummed softly: "*She's a good sport . . . I can spring her . . . for a fin or even a sawbuck*" – then said sharply: "Minerva, you're a crazy, mixed-up machine. If the best combination of traits results in your being a short, plump blonde with big tits – *buy it!* Don't worry about an old man's fantasies. I'm sorry I mentioned that imaginary description."

"But, Lazarus, I said '*if* other characteristics are satisfactory –' To get that physical appearance I need search only with respect to three autosome pairs; there is no conflict, the search is already complete within all parameters we have discussed thus far. And that *is* me – is 'I'? – no, *me*! I've known it since you told me. But – from things you have said – and others that you did not say – I feel that I need your permission to look like that."

The old man lowered his head and covered his face. Then he looked up. "Go ahead, dear – look like her. I mean 'look like yourself.' Like your mind's-eye picture of yourself. You'll find it hard enough to learn to be flesh-and-blood without the added handicap of not looking the way you feel you ought to look."

"Thank you, Lazarus."

"There will be problems, dear, even if everything goes well. For example, has it occurred to you that you will have to learn to talk all over again? Even learn to see and to hear? When you move yourself over into your clone body and leave nothing behind but a computer, you won't suddenly be an adult. Instead, you'll be a weird sort of baby in an adult body, with the world a buzzing confusion around you and totally strange. You may find it frightening. I'll be there, I promise I will be there and holding your hand. But you won't know me; your new eyes won't abstract a gestalt of me until you learn to use them. You won't understand a word I say – did you realize that?"

"I do realize it, Lazarus. I did know it. I have given it much thought. Getting into my new body – without destroying the computer that I am now . . . which I must not, as Ira will need it and so will Ishtar – making that transition is the most critical phase. But if I make it, I promise you that I will *not* be frightened by the strangeness. Because I know that I will have loving friends around me, cherishing me, keeping me alive, not letting me hurt myself nor be hurt – while I'm learning to be a flesh-and-blood."

"That you will have, dear."

"I know and I am not worried. So don't *you* worry, beloved Lazarus – don't think of it now. Why did you say, earlier, 'that mythical time machine'?"

"Eh? How would you describe it?"

"I would describe it as an 'unrealized potential.' But 'mythical' implies impossibility."

"Eh? Keep talking!"

"Lazarus, I learned from Dora, when she taught me the

mathematics of n-space astrogation, that every jump transition involves a decision as to when to reenter the time axis."

"Yes, certainly. Since you are cut off from the framework of the speed-of-light you could go as many years astray as there are light-years involved in the jump. But that's not a time machine."

"It isn't?"

"Hmm – It's a disturbing thought – it feels like intentionally making a bad landing. I wish Andy Libby were here. Minerva, why didn't you mention this before?"

"Should I have put it into your Zwicky Box? You turned down time travel forward . . . and I ruled out time travel into the past because you said you wanted something *new*."

INTERMISSION

Excerpts from the Notebooks of Lazarus Long

Always store beer in a dark place.

*

By the data to date, there is only one animal in the Galaxy dangerous to man – man himself. So he must supply his own indispensable competition. He has no enemy to help him.

*

Men are more sentimental than women. It blurs their thinking.

*

Certainly the game is rigged. Don't let that stop you; if you don't bet, you can't win.

*

Any priest or shaman must be presumed guilty until proved innocent.

*

Always listen to experts. They'll tell you what can't be done, and why. Then do it.

*

Get a shot off *fast*. This upsets him long enough to let you make your second shot perfect.

*

There is no conclusive evidence of life after death. But there is no evidence of any sort against it. Soon enough you will *know*. So why fret about it?

*

If it can't be expressed in figures, it is not science; it is opinion.

*

It has long been known that one horse can run faster than another – but *which one?* Differences are crucial.

*

A fake fortuneteller can be tolerated. But an authentic soothsayer should be shot on sight. Cassandra did not get half the kicking around she deserved.

*

Delusions are often functional. A mother's opinions about her children's beauty, intelligence, goodness, et cetera ad nauseam, keep her from drowning them at birth.

*

Most "scientists" are bottle washers and button sorters.

*

A "pacifist male" is a contradiction in terms. Most self-described "pacifists" are not pacific; they simply assume false colours. When the wind changes, they hoist the Jolly Roger.

*

Nursing does not diminish the beauty of a woman's breasts; it enhances their charm by making them look lived in and happy.

*

A generation which ignores history has no past – and no future.

*

A poet who reads his verse in public may have other nasty habits.

*

What a wonderful world it is that has girls in it!

*

Small change can often be found under seat cushions.

*

History does not record anywhere at any time a religion that has any rational basis. Religion is a crutch for people not strong enough to stand up to the unknown without help. But, like dandruff, most people do have a religion and spend time and money on it and seem to derive considerable pleasure from fiddling with it.

*

It's amazing how much "mature wisdom" resembles being too tired.

*

If you don't like yourself, you *can't* like other people.

*

Your enemy is never a villain in his own eyes. Keep this in mind; it may offer a way to make him your friend. If not, you can kill him without hate – and quickly.

*

A motion to adjourn is always in order.

*

No state has an inherent right to survive through conscript troops and, in the long run, no state ever has. Roman matrons used to say to their sons: "Come back with your shield, or on it." Later on, this custom declined. So did Rome.

*

Of all the strange "crimes" that human beings have legislated out of nothing, "blasphemy" is the most amazing – with "obscenity" and "indecent exposure" fighting it out for second and third place.

*

Cheops' Law: Nothing *ever* gets built on schedule or within budget.

*

It is better to copulate than never.

*

All societies are based on rules to protect pregnant women and young children. All else is surplusage, excrescence, adornment, luxury, or folly which can – and must – be dumped in emergency to preserve this prime function. As racial survival is the *only* universal morality, no other basic is possible. Attempts to formulate a "perfect society" on any foundation other than "Women and children first!" is not only witless, it is automatically genocidal. Nevertheless, starry-eyed idealists (all of them male) have tried endlessly – and no doubt will keep on trying.

*

All men are created unequal.

*

Money is a powerful aphrodisiac. But flowers work almost as well.

*

A brute kills for pleasure. A fool kills from hate.

*

There is only one way to console a widow. But remember the risk.

*

When the need arises – and it does – you must be able to shoot your own dog. Don't farm it out – that doesn't make it nicer, it makes it worse.

*

Everything in excess! To enjoy the flavour of life, take big bites. Moderation is for monks.

*

It may be better to be a live jackal than a dead lion, but it is better still to be a live lion. And usually easier.

*

One man's theology is another man's belly laugh.

*

Sex should be friendly. Otherwise stick to mechanical toys; it's more sanitary.

*

Men rarely (if ever) manage to dream up a god superior to themselves. Most gods have the manners and morals of a spoiled child.

*

Never appeal to a man's "better nature." He may not have one. Invoking his self-interest gives you more leverage.

*

Little girls, like butterflies, need no excuse.

*

You can have peace. Or you can have freedom. Don't ever count on having both at once.

*

Avoid making irrevocable decisions while tired or hungry. N.B.: Circumstances can force your hand. So think ahead!

*

Place your clothes and weapons where you can find them in the dark.

*

An elephant: A mouse built to government specifications.

*

Throughout history, poverty is the normal condition of man. Advances which permit this norm to be exceeded – here and there, now and then – are the work of an extremely small minority, frequently despised, often condemned, and almost always opposed by all right-thinking people. Whenever this tiny minority is kept from creating, or (as sometimes happens) is driven out of a society, the people then slip back into abject poverty.

This is known as "bad luck."

*

In a mature society, "civil servant" is semantically equal to "civil *master*."

*

When a place gets crowded enough to require ID's, social collapse is not far away. It is time to go elsewhere. The best thing about space travel is that it made it possible to go elsewhere.

*

A woman is not property, and husbands who think otherwise are living in a dreamworld.

*

The second best thing about space travel is that the distances involved make war very difficult, usually impractical, and almost always unnecessary. This is probably a loss for most people, since war is our race's most popular diversion, one which gives purpose and colour to dull and stupid lives. But it is a great boon to the intelligent man who fights only when he must – never for sport.

*

A zygote is a gamete's way of producing more gametes. This may be the purpose of the universe.

*

There are hidden contradictions in the minds of people who "love Nature" while deploring the "artificialities" with which "Man has spoiled 'Nature.'" The obvious contradiction lies in their choice of words, which imply that Man and his artifacts are *not* part of "Nature" – but beavers and their dams *are*. But the contradictions go deeper than this prima-facie absurdity. In declaring his love for a beaver dam (erected by beavers for beavers' purposes) and his hatred for dams erected by men (for the purposes of men) the "Naturist" reveals his hatred for his own race – i.e., his own self-hatred.

In the case of "Naturists" such self-hatred is understandable; they are such a sorry lot. But hatred is too strong an emotion to feel toward them; pity and contempt are the most they rate.

As for me, willy-nilly I am a man, not a beaver, and H. sapiens is the only race I have or can have. Fortunately for me, I *like* being part of a race made up of men and women – it strikes me as a fine arrangement and perfectly "natural."

Believe it or not, there were "Naturists" who opposed the first flight to old Earth's Moon as being "unnatural" and a "despoiling of Nature."

*

"No man is an island –" Much as we may feel and act as individuals, our race is a single organism, always growing and branching – which must be pruned regularly to be healthy. This necessity need not be argued; anyone with eyes can see that any organism which grows without limit always dies in its own poisons. The only rational question is whether pruning is best done before or after birth.

Being an incurable sentimentalist I favour the former of these methods – killing makes me queasy, even when it's a case of "He's dead and I'm alive and that's the way I wanted it to be."

But this may be a matter of taste. Some shamans think that it is better to be killed in a war, or to die in childbirth, or to starve in misery, than never to have lived at all. They may be right.

But I don't have to like it – and I don't.

*

Democracy is based on the assumption that a million men are wiser than one man. How's that again? I missed something.

*

Autocracy is based on the assumption that one man is wiser than a million men. Let's play that over again, too. Who decides?

*

Any government will work if authority and responsibility are equal and coordinate. This does not insure "good" government; it simply insures that it will work. But such governments are rare – most people want to run things but want no part of the blame. This used to be called the "backseat-driver syndrome."

*

What are the facts? Again and again and again – what are the *facts?* Shun wishful thinking, ignore divine revelation, forget what "the stars foretell," avoid opinion, care not what the neighbours think, never mind the unguessable "verdict of history" – what are the facts, and to how many decimal places? You pilot always into an unknown future; facts are your single clue. Get the facts!

*

Stupidity cannot be cured with money, or through education, or by legislation. Stupidity is not a sin, the victim can't help being stupid. But stupidity is the only universal capital crime; the sentence is death, there is no appeal, and execution is carried out automatically and without pity.

*

God is omnipotent, omniscient, and omnibenevolent – it says so right here on the label. If you have a mind capable of believing all three of these divine attributes simultaneously, I have a wonderful bargain for you. No checks, please. Cash and in small bills.

*

Courage is the complement of fear. A man who is fearless cannot be courageous. (He is also a fool.)

*

The two highest achievements of the human mind are the twin concepts of "loyalty" and "duty." Whenever these twin concepts fall into disrepute – get out of there fast! You may possibly save yourself, but it is too late to save that society. It is doomed.

*

People who go broke in a big way never miss any meals. It is the poor jerk who is shy a half slug who must tighten his belt.

*

The truth of a proposition has nothing to do with its credibility. And vice versa.

*

Anyone who cannot cope with mathematics is not fully human. At best he is a tolerable subhuman who has learned to wear shoes, bathe, and not make messes in the house.

*

Moving parts in rubbing contact require lubrication to avoid excessive wear. Honorifics and formal politeness provide lubrication where people rub together. Often the very young, the untravelled, the naïve, the sophisticated deplore these formalities as "empty," "meaningless," or "dishonest," and scorn to use them. No matter how "pure" their motives, they thereby throw sand into machinery that does not work too well at best.

*

A human being should be able to change a diaper, plan an invasion, butcher a hog, conn a ship, design a building, write a sonnet, balance accounts, build a wall, set a bone, comfort the dying, take orders, give orders, cooperate, act alone, solve equations, analyse a new problem, pitch manure, programme a computer, cook a tasty meal, fight efficiently, die gallantly. Specialization is for insects.

*

The more you love, the more you *can* love – and the more intensely you love. Nor is there any limit on how *many* you can love. If a person had time enough, he could love all of that majority who are decent and just.

*

Masturbation is cheap, clean, convenient, and free of any possibility of wrongdoing – and you don't have to go home in the cold. But it's *lonely*.

*

Beware of altruism. It is based on self-deception, the root of all evil.

*

If tempted by something that feels "altruistic," examine your motives and root out that self-deception. Then, if you still want to do it, wallow in it!

*

The most preposterous notion that H. sapiens has ever dreamed up is that the Lord God of Creation, Shaper and Ruler of all the Universes, wants the saccharine adoration of His creatures, can be swayed by their prayers, and becomes petulant if He does not receive this flattery. Yet this absurd fantasy, without a shred of evidence to bolster it, pays all the expenses of the oldest, largest, and least productive industry in all history.

*

The second most preposterous notion is that copulation is inherently sinful.

*

Writing is not necessarily something to be ashamed of – but do it in private and wash your hands afterwards.

*

$100 placed at 7 per cent interest compounded quarterly for 200 years will increase to more than $100,000,000 – by which time it will be worth nothing.

*

Dear, don't bore him with trivia or burden him with your past mistakes. The happiest way to deal with a man is never to tell him anything he does not need to know.

*

Darling, a true lady takes off her dignity with her clothes and does her whorish best. At other times you can be as modest and dignified as your *persona* requires.

*

Everybody lies about sex.

*

If men were the automatons that behaviourists claim they are, the behaviourist psychologists could not have invented the amazing nonsense called "behaviourist psychology." So they are wrong from scratch – as clever and as wrong as phlogiston chemists.

*

The shamans are forever yacking about their snake-oil "miracles." I prefer the Real McCoy – a pregnant woman.

*

If the universe has any purpose more important than topping a woman you love and making a baby with her hearty help, I've never heard of it.

*

Thou shalt remember the Eleventh Commandment and keep it Wholly.

*

A touchstone to determine the actual worth of an "intellectual" – find out how he feels about astrology.

*

Taxes are not levied for the benefit of the taxed.

*

There is no such thing as "social gambling." Either you are there to cut the other bloke's heart out and eat it – or you're a sucker. If you don't like this choice – don't gamble.

*

When the ship lifts, all bills are paid. No regrets.

*

The first time I was a drill instructor I was too inexperienced for the job – the things I taught those lads must have got some of them killed. War is too serious a matter to be taught by the inexperienced.

*

A competent and self-confident person is incapable of jealousy in anything. Jealousy is invariably a symptom of neurotic insecurity.

*

Money is the sincerest of all flattery.
Women love to be flattered.
So do men.

*

You live and learn. Or you don't live long.

*

Whenever women have insisted on absolute equality with men, they have invariably wound up with the dirty end of the stick. What they are and what they can do makes them superior to men, and their proper tactic is to demand special privileges, all the traffic will bear. They should never settle merely for equality. For women, "equality" is a disaster.

*

Peace is an extension of war by political means. Plenty of elbow-room is pleasanter – and much safer.

*

One man's "magic" is another man's engineering. "Supernatural" is a null word.

*

The phrase "we (I) (you) simply *must* –" designates something that need not be done. "That goes without saying" is a red warning. "Of course" means you had best check it yourself. These small-change clichés and others like them, when read correctly, are reliable channel markers.

*

Do not handicap your children by making their lives easy.

*

Rub her feet.

*

If you happen to be one of the fretful minority who can do creative work, never force an idea; you'll abort it if you do. Be patient and you'll give birth to it when the time is ripe. Learn to wait.

*

Never crowd youngsters about their private affairs – sex especially. When they are growing up, they are nerve ends all over, and resent (quite properly) any invasion of their privacy. Oh, sure, they'll make mistakes – but that's *their* business, not yours. (You made your own mistakes, did you not?)

*

Never underestimate the power of human stupidity.

VARIATIONS ON A THEME

XI

The Tale of the Adopted Daughter

Stand with me on Man's old planet, gazing north when sky has darkened; follow down the Dipper's handle, half again and veering leftward – Do you see it? Can you sense it? Nothing there but cold and darkness. Try again with both eyes covered, try once more with inner vision, hearken now to wild geese honking, sounding through the endless spaces, bouncing off the strange equations –

There it glistens! Hold the vision, warp your ship through crumpled spaces. Gently, gently, do not lose it. Virgin planet, new beginnings –

Woodrow Smith, of many faces, many names, and many places, led this band to New Beginnings, planet clean and bright as morning. End of line, he told his shipmates. Endless miles of untouched prairie, endless stands of uncut timber, winding rivers, soaring mountains, hidden wealth and hidden dangers. Here is life or here is dying; only sin is lack of trying. Grab your picks and grab your shovels; dig latrines and build your hovels – next year better, next year stronger, next year's furrows that much longer.

Learn to grow it, learn to eat it. You can't buy it; learn to *make* it! How d'you know until you've tried it? Try again and keep on trying –

Ernest Gibbons, né Woodrow Smith, sometimes known as Lazarus Long, et al., President of New Beginnings Bank of Commerce, walked out of the Waldorf Dining Room. He stood on the veranda, picking his teeth and looking over the busy street scene. Half a dozen saddle mules and a loper (muzzled) were hitched just below him. Up the street to the right a mule train from out back was unloading at the dock of the Top Dollar Trading Post (E. Gibbons, Prop.). A dog lay in the dust in the middle of the street; mounted traffic went around him. Across the street to his left a dozen children played some noisy game in the yard of Mrs. Mayberry's Primary School.

He could count thirty-seven people without moving from that spot. What a change eighteen years made! Top Dollar was no longer the only settlement, or even the largest. New Pittsburgh was larger (and dirtier), and both Separation and Junction were large enough to be called towns. This from only two shiploads and in a colony that had almost starved its first winter.

He did not like to think about that winter. That one family – cannibalism had not actually been *proved* – still, it was just as well that they were all dead.

Forget it. The weak ones died, and the bad ones died or were killed; the stock that survived was always stronger, smarter, more decent. New Beginnings was a planet to be proud of, and it would get better and better and better for a long time.

Still, almost twenty years was long enough to stay in one place; it was time to ship out again. In many ways it had been more fun when he and Andy, God rest his sweet innocent soul, had gone banging around the stars together, lining up real estate and never staying longer than necessary to assess potentialities. He wondered if his son Zaccur would be back on time with a third load of hopefuls.

He lifted his kilt and scratched above his right knee – checked his blaster – hitched at the belt band on the left, checked his needle gun – scratched the back of his neck, made sure of his second throwing knife. Ready to face the public, he considered whether to go to his desk at the bank or to the trading post and check that incoming shipment. Neither appealed to him.

One of the hitched mules nodded at him. Gibbons looked at him, then said, "Hi, Buck. How are you, boy? Where's your boss?"

Buck closed his lips tightly, then said explosively, "Pannnk!"

That settled one point: If Clyde Leamer had hitched here instead of in front of the bank, it meant that Clyde intended to use the side door and was looking for another loan. Let's see what effort he makes to find me.

Skip the trading post, too – not only would Clyde look there next but it wasn't fair to make Rick nervous by showing up before he had time to steal his usuals; good storekeepers were hard to come by. Rick was always honest – 5 per cent, no more, no less.

Gibbons felt in his shirt pocket, found a sweet, gave it to Buck on the flat of his hand. The mule took it neatly, nodded thanks.

Gibbons reflected that these mutant mules, fertile and breeding true, were the biggest help to colonizing since the Libby Drive. They took cold-sleep easily – when you shipped swine, half your breeding stock arrived as pork – and they could look out for themselves in many ways; a mule could stomp a wild loper to death.

He said, "So long, Buck. Going for a walk. Walk. Tell Boss."

"Shoh-rrrong!" acknowledged the mule. "Pye!"

Gibbons turned left and headed out of town while considering how big a loan to offer Clyde Leamer with Buck as security. A good-tempered, smart stallion mule was a prize – and about the only unmortgaged asset Clyde had left. Gibbons had no doubt that a loan on Buck would put Clyde back on his feet – literally – as soon as the loan was due. Gibbons felt no pity. A man who couldn't cut the mustard on New Beginnings was worthless, no sense in propping him up.

No, don't lend Clyde a dollar! Offer to buy outright – at 10 per cent over a fair price. A decent hardworking animal should not belong to a lazy bum. Gibbons had no need for a saddle mule – but it would do him good to ride an hour or so each day. Man got flabby sitting in a bank.

Marry again and give Buck to his bride as a wedding present – A pleasant thought, but the only Howards on planet were married couples and not one with a husband-high daughter – as well as all being in masquerade until the place grew populous enough that the Families would set up a clinic here. Safer. Once burned, forever shy. He avoided Howards, and they avoided each other, on the surface. Be nice to be married again, though. The Magee family – actually Barstows – had two or three girls growing up. Maybe he should pay them a call someday.

In the meantime – He felt gusty and good, stuffed with scrambled eggs and wicked thoughts, and wondered where there was a female who felt the same way and could duck out and share their interest. Ernie knew several who shared his enthusiasm – but not available at this time of day, not for a casual romp. Which was all he was wanted; it was not fair to engage in anything serious with an ephemeral no matter how sweet she was – especially if she was truly sweet.

Banker Gibbons was at the edge of town and about to turn back when he noticed smoke from a house farther out – the Harper place. What had been the Harper place, he amended, before they homesteaded outback, but now occupied by, uh,

Bud Brandon and wife, Marje – nice young couple from the second shipload. One child? He thought so.

Running a fireplace on a day like this? Possibly burning trash – Hey, that smoke is *not* from the chimney!

Gibbons broke into a run.

As he reached the Harper place, the entire roof was burning. Lazarus skidded to a stop and tried to judge the situation. Like most older houses, the Harper place had no ground-floor windows and but a single door that fit tightly and opened outward – a design for a time when lopers and dragons were ubiquitous.

Opening that door would be opening the damper on a burning fire.

He did not waste an instant debating it; that door must stay closed. He ran around the house, spotting windows of the upper floor and looking for means to reach one – a ladder or anything. Was anyone inside? Didn't the Brandons even have knotted-rope fire escapes? Probably not; good rope came from Earth and retailed at ninety dollars a metre – the Harpers would not have left any behind.

A window with its shutters open and smoke pouring out –

He yelled, "*Hey! Anybody home!*" A figure showed at the window, and something was thrown out to him.

Automatically he made a good catch, spotting what it was while in the air, going to the ground with it to soften the impact. A small child –

He looked up, saw an arm hanging over the windowsill. The roof fell in, the arm disappeared.

Gibbons scrambled up fast, holding the little boy – no, little girl, he corrected – and moved hastily back from the holocaust. He did not consider the possibility that someone might be alive in that raging fire; he simply hoped that they had died quickly and gave it no more thought. He cradled the child in his arms. "Are you all right, honey?"

"I guess so," she answered, then added gravely, "but Mama's awful sick."

"Mama is all right now, dear," he said gently, "and so is Papa."

"You're *sure?*" The child twisted in his arms, tried to see the burning house.

He interposed his shoulder. "I'm sure." He held her more firmly and started walking.

Halfway back to town they encountered Clyde Leamer, mounted on Buck. Clyde reined up. "Oh, there you are! Banker, I want to talk to you."

'Stow it, Clyde."

"Huh? But you don't *understand.* I've *got* to have some money. Nothing but bad luck the whole season. Seems like everything I touch – "

"Clyde – *shut your yap!*"

"What?" Leamer seemed to notice for the first time that the banker was carrying something. "Hey! ain't that the Brandon kid?"

"Yes."

"Thought so. Now about this loan – "

"I told you to shut up. The bank won't lend you another dollar."

"But you've got to *listen.* Seems to me the community ought to help a farmer who's had bad luck. If it weren't for the farmers – "

"*You* listen. If you spent as much time working as you do talking, you wouldn't need to talk about 'bad luck.' Even your stable is dirty. Mm . . . what price do you want for that stud brute?"

"Buck? Why, I wouldn't sell *Buck.* But here's what I had in mind, Banker. You're a kindly man even if you do talk rough and I know you won't see my kids starve. Now Buck is a valuable property, and I figure he ought to be security for about – well, about, say – "

"Clyde, the best thing you can do for your kids is to cut your throat. Then people would adopt them. No loan, Clyde – not a dollar, not a dime. But I'll buy Buck myself, right now. Name a price."

Leamer gulped and hesitated. "Twenty-five thousand."

Gibbons started walking toward town. Leamer said hastily, "Twenty thousand!" Gibbons did not answer.

Leamer reined the mule around, turned in front of the banker, and stopped. "Banker, you've got me by the short hairs. Eighteen thousand and you're stealing him."

"Leamer, I won't steal from you. Put him up for auction, and I might bid. Or might not. How much do you think he'll bring at auction?"

"Uh . . . fifteen thousand."

"You think so? I don't. I know how old he is without looking at his teeth, and just what you paid for him, off the ship. I know what people around here can afford and will pay. But go ahead; he's yours. Bear in mind that if you put a low-bid price against him, you owe the auctioneer ten per cent even if he doesn't sell. But it's your business, Clyde. Now get out of my way; I want to get this child into town and lying down; she's had a bad time."

"Uh . . . what *will* you pay?"

"Twelve thousand."

"Why, that's robbery!"

"You don't have to take it. Suppose an auction brings fifteen thousand dollars – as you hope. Your net is thirteen five. But suppose an auction brings only ten thousand, which I find more likely. You net nine thousand. G'bye, Clyde; I'm in a hurry."

"Well – thirteen thousand?"

"Clyde, I named my top price. You've dealt with me often enough to know that when I say it's top dollar, then it's top dollar. But – throw in that saddle and bridle and answer one question and I'll sweeten it by five hundred dollars."

"What question?"

"How did you happen to migrate?"

Leamer looked startled, then laughed unmirthfully. "Because I was crazy, if you want to know the truth."

"Aren't we all? That's hardly an answer, Clyde."

"Well . . . my old man is a banker – and as hard-nosed as *you* are! I was doing all right, I had a proper, respectable job, teaching. College. But the pay wasn't much, and my old man was always snotty about it when I ran a little short. Snoopy. Disparaging. Finally I got so sick of it that I asked him what he would think of paying Yvonne's fare and mine in the 'Andy J.'? Migrate. Be rid of us.

"To my surprise he agreed. But I didn't back out; I knew that a man with a fine education like mine could get ahead anywhere . . . and it wasn't like we was being dumped on some wild planet; we were second wave, you may remember.

"Only it *was* a wild planet and I've had to do things that no gentleman ought to have to touch. But you just wait, Banker; kids around here are growing up, and there will be a place for higher education, not the trivia Mrs. Mayberry teaches in that so-called school of hers. That's where I come in – you'll be calling me 'Professor' yet, and speaking respectfully. You'll see."

"Good luck to you. Are you accepting my offer? Twelve thousand five hundred, net, including bridle and saddle."

"Uh . . . I *said* I was, didn't I?"

"You didn't say. You still have not."

"I accept."

The girl child had listened quietly, face serious. Gibbons said to her, "Can you stand up a moment, dear?"

"Yes."

He put her down; she trembled and held onto his kilt. Gibbons dug into his sporran, then using Buck's broad rump as a desk, wrote a draft and a bill of sale. He handed them to Leamer. "Take that to Hilda at the bank. Sign the bill of sale and give it back to me."

Silently Leamer signed, looked at the draft and pocketed it, handed over the bill of sale. "Thanks, Banker – you old skinflint. Where do you want him delivered?"

"You've delivered him. Dismount."

"Huh? How do I get to the bank? How am I supposed to get home?"

"You walk."

"What? Well, of all the sneaky, underhanded tricks! You get the mule when I get the cash. At the bank."

"Leamer, I paid top dollar for that mule because I need him *now*. But I see that we did not have a meeting of minds. Okay, hand back my draft and here's your bill of sale."

Leamer looked startled. "Oh, no, you don't! You made a deal."

"Then get off my mule *at once*" – Gibbons just happened to rest his hand on the handle of the all-purpose knife every man carried – "and dogtrot into town and you'll be there before Hilda closes. Now *move*." His eyes, cold and blank, held Leamer's.

"Can't you take a joke?" Leamer grumbled as he swung down. He started walking rather fast toward town.

"Oh, Clyde!"

Leamer stopped. "What do you want *now*?"

"If you see the Volunteer Fire Team headed this way, tell them it's too late; the Harper place is gone. But tell McCarthy I said it wouldn't hurt to send a couple of men to check."

"Okay, okay!"

"And, Clyde – what was it you used to teach?"

"'Teach'? I taught 'Creative Writing.' I *told* you I had a good education."

"So you did. Better hurry; Hilda closes promptly, she has to pick up her kids at Mrs. Mayberry's school."

Gibbons ignored Leamer's answer, picked up the little girl, then said, "Steady, Buck. Stand still, old fellow." He swung the child high, settled her gently astride the mule's withers. "Hang onto his mane." He toed the left stirrup, swung up behind her, scooted back in the saddle, then lifted her again and placed her somewhat in his lap but mostly in the saddle just back of the pommel. "Hang onto the horn, dear. Both hands. Comfortable?"

"This is fun!"

"Lots of fun, baby girl. Buck! Hear me, boy?"

The mule nodded.

"Walk. Walk back to town. Slow walk. Steady. Don't stub your feet. Get me? I'm not going to use the reins."

"Shrrow . . . *Rrrawk!*"

"Right, Buck." Gibbons took a hitch in the reins, let them fall loosely on Buck's neck – squeezed the mule with his knees, let him go. Buck ambled toward town.

After a few minutes the little girl said gravely, "What about Mama and Daddy?"

"Mama and Daddy are all right. They know I'm taking care of you. What's your name, dear?"

"Dora."

"That's a nice name, Dora. A pretty name. Do you want to know my name?"

"That man called you 'Banker'."

"That's not my name, Dora; that's just something I do sometimes. My name is . . . 'Uncle Gibbie.' Can you say that?"

"'Uncle Gibbie.' That's a funny name."

"So it is, Dora. And this is Buck we are riding. He is a friend of mine, and he'll be your friend, too, now – so say hello to Buck."

"Hello, Buck."

"Hayrrroh . . . Jorrrah!"

"Say, he talks lots plainer than most mules! Doesn't he?"

"Buck is the best mule on New Beginnings, Dora. And the smartest. When we get rid of this bridle – Buck doesn't need a bit in his mouth – he'll be able to talk plainer still . . . and you can teach him more words. Would you like that?"

"Oh, yes!" Dora added, "If Mama lets me."

"It's all right with Mama. Do you like to sing, Dora?"

"Oh, sure! I know a clapping song. But we can't clap right now. Can we?"

"Right now I think we had better hang on tight." Gibbons rapidly reviewed in his mind his repertoire of happy songs, rejected a round dozen as unsuitable for young ladies. "How about this one?

"There's a pawnshop
On the corner
Where I usually keep my overcoat.

"Can you sing that, Dora?"

"Oh, that's *easy*!" The baby girl sang it in a voice so high that Gibbons was reminded of a canary. "Is that all, Uncle Gibbie? And what's a 'paunshot'?"

"It's a place to keep overcoats when you don't need them. Lots more, Dora. Thousands and thousands of verses."

"'Thousands and thousands – ' Why, that's almost as much as a hundred. Isn't it?"

"Almost, Dora. Here's another verse:

"There's a trading post
By the pawnshop
Where my sister sells candy.

"Do you like candy, Dora?"

"Oh, yes! But Mama says its 'spensive."

"Won't be so expensive next year, Dora; there'll be more sugar beets cropped. But . . . 'Open your mouth and close your eyes, and I'll give you something for a s'prise!'" He felt around in his shirt pocket, then said, "Oh, sorry, Dora; the surprise will have to wait until I can get to the trading post; Buck got the last one. Buck likes candy, too."

"He does?"

"Yes and I'll teach you how to give it to him without losing a finger by mistake. But candy isn't too good for him, so he gets it only as a special surprise. For being a good boy. Okay, Buck?"

"Oh-gay! . . . Pawsss!"

Mrs. Mayberry's school was letting out as Gibbons halted Buck in front of it. When he lifted Dora down, she seemed very tired, so he picked her up again. "Wait, Buck." The stragglers among the pupils stared but separated and let him through.

"Afternoon, Mrs. Mayberry." Gibbons had gone there almost by instinct. The schoolmistress was a grey-haired widow, fifty or more, who had outlasted two husbands, and was coping sensibly with her meagre chance of finding a third, preferring to support herself rather than live with one of her daughters, stepdaughters, or daughters-in-law. She was one who shared Ernest Gibbons' enthusiasm for the hearty pleasures in life but was as circumspect about it as he was. He considered her sensible in every way – a prime prospect for marriage were it not for the unfortunate fact that they ran on different time rates.

Not that he let her know this. He had not been a disclosed Howard when they both had arrived in the first shipload, and, although freshly rejuvenated on Secundus when he had reappeared on Earth and organized the migration, he had elected to be thirty-five or so (cosmetically). Since that time he had carefully aged himself each year; Helen Mayberry thought of him as a contemporary, returned his friendship, shared mutual pleasure with him from time to time without trying to own him. He respected her highly.

"Good afternoon, Mr. Gibbons. Why, it's Dora! We missed you, dear; what happened! And – Is that a bruise?" She looked closely, said nothing about the fact that the little girl was filthy dirty.

She straightened up. "Seems to be just a smudge. I'm glad to see her; I fretted a little this morning when she didn't show up with the Parkinson children. It's almost Marjorie Brandon's time – perhaps you knew?"

"Vaguely. Where can I put Dora down for a few minutes? Conference. Private."

Mrs. Mayberry's eyes widened slightly, but she answered at once. "The couch – No, put her on my bed." She led the way, said nothing about getting her white coverlet dirty, went back into the schoolroom with him after he assured Dora that they would be gone only a few moments.

Gibbons explained what had happened. "Dora doesn't know that her parents are dead, Helen – nor do I think it's time to tell her."

Mrs. Mayberry considered it. "Ernest, are you sure they both died? Bud would have seen the fire if he had been working his own fields, but he sometimes works for Mr. Parkinson."

"Helen, that was not a woman's hand I saw. Unless Marje Brandon has thick black hair on the back of her hands."

"No. No, that would be Bud." She sighed. "Then she's an orphan. Poor little Dora! A nice child. Bright, too."

"Helen, can you take care of her a few days? Will you?"

"Ernest, the way you phrase that is almost offensive. I will take care of Dora as long as I am needed."

"Sorry, I didn't mean to phrase it unpleasingly. I don't expect it to be long; some family will adopt her. In the meantime keep track of your expense, then we'll work out what her room and board should be."

"Ernest, that will come to exactly zero. The only cost will be about enough food to feed a bird. Which I can certainly do for Marjorie Brandon's little girl."

"So? Well, I can find some family to board her. The Leamers. Someone."

"*Ernest!*"

"Get your feathers down, Helen. That child was placed in my hands, her father's last dying act. And don't be a dumb fool; I know to the penny how much you manage to save. As well as how often you have to take tuition in food rather than cash. This is a cash deal. The Leamers would jump at it – as well as several others. I don't have to leave Dora here – and won't, unless you are sensible."

Mrs. Mayberry looked grim – then suddenly smiled and looked years younger. "Ernest, you're a bully. And a bastard. And other things I never say out of bed. All right – room-and-board."

"And tuition. Plus any special expenses. Doctor's bills, maybe."

"Triple bastard. You always pay for anything you get, don't you? As I should know." She glanced at the unshuttered windows. "Step out here in the hall and seal it with a kiss. Bastard."

They moved, she placed herself so that the angle did not permit anyone to see them, then delivered a kiss that would have astounded her neighbours.

"Helen –"

She brushed her lips against his. "The answer is No, Mr. Gibbons. Tonight I'll be busy reassuring a baby girl."

"I was about say, 'Don't give her that bath I know you intend to until I get hold of Doc Krausmeyer and have him examine her. She seems all right – but she may have anything from broken ribs to a skull concussion. Oh, get her clothes off and sponge her a little for the worst of the dirt; that won't hurt her and it will make it easier for Doc to examine her."

"Yes, dear. Get your lecherous hands off my bottom and I'll get to work. You find Doc."

"Right away, Mrs. Mayberry."

"Until later, Mr. Gibbons. Au 'voir."

Gibbons told Buck to wait, walked over to the Waldorf, found (as he expected) Dr. Krausmeyer in the bar. The physician looked up from his drink. "Ernest! What's this I hear about the Harper place?"

"Well, what do you hear about it? Put down that glass and grab your bag. Emergency."

"Now, now! Haven't seen the emergency yet that wouldn't leave time to finish a drink. Clyde Leamer was just in and bought us a round of drinks – bought this one you urged me to abandon – and told us that the Harper place had burned and killed the whole Brandon family. Says he tried to rescue them, but it was too late."

Gibbons briefly considered the desirability of a fatal accident happening to both Clyde Leamer and Doc Krausmeyer some dark night – but, damn it, while Clyde would be no loss, if Doc died, Gibbons would be forced to hang out his own shingle – and his diplomas did *not* read "Ernest Gibbons." Besides, Doc was a good doctor when sober – and, anyhow, it's your own fault, old son; twenty years ago you interviewed him and okayed the subsidy. All you saw was a bright young intern and failed to spot the incipient lush.

"Now that you mention it, Doc, I did see Clyde hurrying toward the Harper place. If he says he was too late to save them I would have to back his story. However, it was not the whole family; their little girl, Dora, was saved."

"Well, yes, Clyde did say that. He said it was her parents he couldn't save."

"That's right. It's the little girl I want you to attend. She's suffering from multiple abrasions and contusions, possibly broken bones, possible internal injuries, a strong possibility of smoke poisoning – and a certainty of extreme emotional shock . . . very serious in a child that age. She's across the street at Mrs. Mayberry's place." He added softly, "I think you ought to hurry, Doctor, I really do. Don't you?"

Dr. Krausmeyer looked unhappily at his drink, then straightened up and said, "Mine host, if you will be so kind as to put this on the back of the bar, I shall return." He picked up his bag.

Dr. Krausmeyer found nothing wrong with the child, gave her

a sedative. Gibbons waited until Dora was asleep, then went to arrange temporary board for his mule. He went to Jones Brothers ("Fine Stock – Mules Bought, Sold, Traded, Auctioned – Registered Stallions Standing at Stud") because his bank held a mortgage on their place.

Minerva, it wasn't planned; it just grew. I expected Dora to be adopted in a few days, a few weeks, some such. Pioneers don't feel about kids the way city people do. If they didn't like kids, they wouldn't have the temperament to pioneer. And as soon as pioneer kids stop being babies, the investment starts paying off. Kids are an asset in pioneer country.

I certainly did not plan to raise an ephemeral, or hold any fear that it would be necessary – nor *was* it necessary. I was beginning to simplify my affairs, expecting to leave soon, as my son Zaccur should show up any year.

Zack was my partner then, in a loose arrangement based on mutual trust. He was young, a century and a half or such, but steady and smart – out of Phyllis Briggs-Sperling by my last marriage but two. A fine woman, Phyllis, as well as a number-one mathematician. We made seven children together and every one of them smarter than I am. She married several times – I was her fourth* – and, as I recall, the first woman to win the Ira Howard Memorial Century Medal for contributing one hundred registered offspring to the Families. Took her less than two centuries but Phyllis was a girl of simple tastes, the other being pencil and paper and time to think about geometry.

I digress. To engage in the pioneering business profitably takes a minimax of a suitable ship and two partners, both shipmasters, both qualified to mount a migration and lead it – otherwise you are taking a shipload of city folks and abandoning them in wilderness . . . which often happened in the early days of the Diaspora.

Zack and I did it properly, each fully qualified as captain in space, or as leader on a strange planet – taking turns. The one who stays behind when the ship leaves really does pioneer; he can't fake it, he can't just wave the baton. He may not be political head of the colony – I preferred not to be; talk is so time-consuming. What he does have to be is a survivor, a man who can force that planet to feed him, and by his example show others how – and advise them if they want it.

*Fifth. James Matthew Libby was her fourth.

J.F. 45th

The first wave is a break-even; the captain unloads and goes back for more migrants; the planet offers nothing for export that soon. The trip has been paid for by fares charged the migrants; profit, if any, will come from the partner on the ground selling what else the ship has carried – mules, hardware, swine, fertile chicken eggs – to the pioneers, on credit at first. Which means the partner on the ground has to look sharp and mind his rear; it doesn't take much to convince migrants who are having a tough time that this bloke is profiteering and should be lynched.

Minerva, the six times I did this – let myself be left behind with the first wave of a colony – I never once ploughed a field without weapons at hand and I was always far more cautious with my own breed than I was with any dangerous animals that planet held.

But on New Beginnings we were past most such hazards. The first wave had made it, though just barely that terrible first winter – Helen Mayberry was not the only widow who had married a widower as a result of a weather cycle that Andy Libby and I had not anticipated; the star there – called "the Sun" as always, but you can check your memories for catalogue designation – New Beginnings' Sun was a variable star by about the amount that old old Sol is, just enough to give "unusual" weather – and when we arrived we hit the bad-weather jackpot.

But those who made it through that winter were tough enough to stand *anything*; the second wave had a much easier time.

I had disposed of my farm to migrants of the second wave and was putting my attention on business and trade to build up a cargo for the *Andy J.* to take back after Zack unloaded the third wave – and I would go back, too. Go somewhere, that is. What and where and how would be settled after I saw Zack.

In the meantime I was bored, getting ready to wind up my on-planet affairs, and found this waif an interesting diversion.

Delightful, I should say. Dora was a baby who was born grown-up. Utterly innocent, ignorant in the fashion that a small child necessarily is, but most intelligent and delighted to learn anything. There was no meanness in her anywhere, Minerva, and I found her naïve conversation more entertaining than most talk of adults – usually trivial and rarely new.

Helen Mayberry took as much interest in Dora, and we two found ourselves *in loco parentis* without planning it.

We consulted each other and kept the baby girl away from the burial – some charred bones, including tiny ones of the baby that had never been born – and kept her away from the memorial service, too. Some weeks later, when Dora seemed to be in good shape and after I had had time to have a gravestone cut and erected, I took her out there and let her see it. She could read, and did – names and dates of her parents, and the single date for the baby.

She looked it over solemnly, then said, "That means Mama and Daddy won't ever be coming back. Doesn't it?"

"Yes, Dora."

"That's what the kids at school said. I wasn't sure."

"I know, dear. Aunt Helen told me. So I thought you had better see for yourself."

She looked again at the headstone, then said gravely, "I see. I guess I do. Thank you, Uncle Gibbie."

She didn't cry, so I didn't have any excuse to pick her up and console her. All I could think of to say was: "Do you want to go now, dear?"

"Yes."

We had ridden out on Buck, but I had left him at the foot of the hill, there being an unwritten rule against letting mules or tamed lopers walk on graves. I asked if she wanted me to carry her – piggyback, perhaps. She decided to walk.

Halfway down she stopped. "Uncle Gibbie?"

"Yes, Dora?"

"Let's not tell Buck about this."

"All right, Dora."

"He might cry."

"We won't tell him, Dora."

She did not say any more until we were back at Mrs. Mayberry's school. Then she was very quiet for about two weeks, and never mentioned it again to me, nor – I think – to anyone. She never asked to go back there, although we went riding almost every afternoon and often within sight of graveyard hill.

About two Earth-years later the *Andy J.* arrived, and Captain Zack, my son by Phyllis, came down in the gig to make arrangements for landing the third wave of migrants. We had a drink together, and I told him I was staying over another trip, and why. He stared. "Lazarus, you are out of your mind."

I said quietly, "Don't call me 'Larazus.' That name has had too much publicity."

He said, "All right. Although there is no one around but our hostess – Mrs. Mayberry, did you say? – and she's gone out to the kitchen. Look, uh, Gibbons, I was thinking of making a couple of trips to Secundus. Profit in it, and ways to invest our net on Secundus – safer than investing on Earth now, things being the way they are."

I agreed that he was almost certainly right.

"Yes," he said, "but here's the point. If I do, I won't be back this way for, oh, maybe ten standard years. Or longer. Oh, I will if you insist; you're majority shareholder. But you'll be wasting your money and mine, too. Look, Laz – Ernest, if you *must* take care of this kid – though I don't see that it's your obligation – come with me and bring her along. You could put her in school on Earth – as long as you post bond to insure that she leaves. Or perhaps she could settle on Secundus, although I don't know what the immigration rules are there now; it's been a long time since I've been there."

I shook my head. "What's ten years? I can hold my breath that long. Zack, I want to see this child grown up and able to make it on her own – married, I hope, but that's her business. But I won't uproot her; she's had one shock of that sort and shouldn't have to soak up another while she's still a child."

"On your head be it. You want me back in ten years? Is that long enough?"

"More or less but don't rush. Take time enough to show a profit. If it takes longer, you'll pick up a better cargo here next time. Something better than food and soft goods."

Zack said, "There is nothing better than food to ship to Earth these days. Sometime soon we're going to have to stop touching at Earth, just trade among the colonies."

"As bad as that?"

"Pretty bad. They won't learn. What's this about trouble over your bank? Do you need a show of force while the 'Andy J.' is overhead?"

I shook my head. "Thanks, Captain, but that's not the way to do it. Or I would *have* to go along with you. Force is an argument to use when nothing else will do and the issue is that important. Instead I'm going to go limp on them."

Ernest Gibbons did not worry about his bank. He never worried over any issue less important than life-and-death. Instead he applied his brain to all problems large and small as they came along, and enjoyed life.

Especially he enjoyed helping raise Dora. Right after he acquired her and the mule Buck – or they acquired him – he discarded the savage curb bit Leamer had used (salvaging the metal) and had the Jones Brothers' harnessmaker convert the bridle into a hackamore. He ordered also another saddle, sketching what he wanted offering a bonus for early delivery. The leathercrafter shook his head over that sketch, but delivered.

Thereafter Gibbons and the baby girl rode Buck in a saddle built for two: a man-sized saddle in the usual position, with a tiny saddle with tiny stirrups an integral part of it in that forward position where a normal saddle carries its pommel horn. A little wooden arch, leather covered, curved up from this, a safety bar the child could grab. Gibbons also had this extended saddle fitted with two belly bands, more comfortable for the mule, safer on steep trails for riders.

They rode that way several seasons, usually an hour or more after school – holding three cornered conversations at a walk, or singing as a trio with Buck loudly off key but always on beat with his gait acting as a metronome, Gibbons carrying the lead, and Dora learning to harmonize. It was often the "Paunshot" song, which Dora regarded as her own, and to which she gradually added verses, including one about the paddock next to the schoolhouse where Buck lived.

But soon there was too much girl for the tiny forward saddle as Dora grew, straight and slender and tall. Gibbons bought a mare mule, after trying two others – one was rejected by Buck because she was (so he said) "shdoop'd" and the other because she failed to appreciate a hackamore and tried to run away.

Gibbons let Buck pick the third, with advice from Dora but none from him – and Buck acquired a mate in his paddock, and Gibbons had the stable enlarged. Buck still stood at stud for a fee but seemed pleased to have Beulah at home. However, Beulah did not learn to sing and talked very little. Gibbons suspected that she was afraid to open her mouth in Buck's presence – she was willing to talk, or at least to answer, when Gibbons rode her alone . . . for it worked out, to Gibbons' surprise, that Beulah was his saddle mule; Dora rode the big male brute, even when the stirrups of the stock saddle had to be shortened ridiculously to fit her child's legs.

But steadily the stirrups had to be lengthened as Dora grew toward young womanhood. Beulah dropped a foal; Gibbons kept her and Dora named her "Betty" and trained the baby mule as she grew, at first letting her amble along behind with an empty saddle, then teaching her to accept a rider in the paddock. There followed a time when their daily rides became sixsomes and often picnics, with Mrs Mayberry up on Buck, the steadiest, and with the lightest load – Dora – on Betty, and with Gibbons as usual riding Beulah. Gibbons remembered that summer as a most happy one: Helen and himself knee to knee on the older mounts while Dora and the frisky youngster galloped ahead, then running back with Dora's long brown hair flying in the breeze.

One such time he asked, "Helen, are the boys beginning to sniff around her?"

"You old stud, don't you think about anything else?"

"Come off it, dear; I asked for information."

"Certainly the boys are noticing her, Ernest, and she is noticing them. But I will do all the worrying necessary. Not much; she's far too choosy to put up with second best."

The happy family picnics did not resume the following summer. Mrs. Mayberry was feeling the years in her bones, and could mount and dismount only with help.

Gibbons had plenty of time to be ready before the murmurings about his monopoly of the banking business came to a head. The New Beginnings Bank of Commerce was a bank of issue; he (or Zaccur) always set up such a bank in each colony they pioneered. Money was necessary to a growing colony; barter was too clumsy. Some medium of exchange was needed even before government was needed.

He was not surprised when he was invited to meet with the town's select men to discuss the matter; it always happened. That evening, as he trimmed his Vandyke and added a touch more grey to it and to the hair on his head in preparation for the confrontation, he reviewed in his mind proposals he had heard in the past for making water run uphill, the sun to stand still, and one egg to be counted as two. Would there be some novel numbskullery tonight? He hoped so but did not expect it.

He plucked hairs from his "receding" hairline – damn it, it was getting harder and harder to age enough each year! – then put on his warplaid kilt . . . not only more impressive but with more ways to conceal weapons – and get at them quickly. He was fairly sure that no one was, as yet, annoyed enough at him to start violence, but once he had been too optimistic; since that time he had been a pessimist as a fixed policy.

Then he hid some items, locked up others, set some gadgets that Zaccur had fetched last trip but which were not offered for sale at the Top Dollar T.P., unlocked his door, handlocked it from outside, and left by the route through the bar, so that he could tell the barkeep that he would be away "a few minutes."

Three hours later Gibbons had settled one point: No one had been able to think of any new way to debase currency that he had not heard at least five hundred years earlier – more likely a thousand – and each was certainly much, much older in history. Early in the meeting he asked the Moderator to have the Town Scribe write down each question so that he could answer them in a lump – and was allowed to have it his way by being balky.

At last the Moderator Selectman, Jim "Duke" Warwick, said, "That seems to be it. Ernie, we have a motion to nationalize – I guess that's the word – the New Beginnings Bank of Commerce. You're not a selectman, but we all agree that you are a party with a special interest, we want to hear from you. Do you want to speak against the proposal?"

"Not at all, Jim. Go right ahead."

"Eh? I'm afraid I didn't understand you."

"I have no objection to the bank being nationalized. If that's all, let's adjourn and go to bed."

Someone in the audience called out, "Hey, I want my question about New Pittsburgh money answered!"

"And mine about interest! Interest is *wrong* – it says so in the Bible!"

"Well, Ernie? You said earlier that you would answer questions."

"So I did. But if you are nationalizing the bank, wouldn't it make more sense to put questions to your state treasurer, or whatever you decide to call him? The new head of the bank. By the way, who is he? Hadn't he better sit up here on the platform?"

Warwick pounded his gavel, then said, "We haven't got that far, Ernie. For the time being the entire Council of Selectmen is the finance committee – if we go ahead with this."

"Oh, by all means go ahead. I'm shutting down."

"What do you mean?"

"Just what I said: I quit. A man doesn't like to have his neighbours dislike him. The people of Top Dollar don't like what I've been doing or this meeting would never have been called.

So I've quit. The bank is closed; it will not reopen tomorrow. Nor ever, with me as president of it. That's why I asked who your state treasurer will be. I'm as interested as anyone in finding out what we are going to use for money from here on – and what it will be worth."

There was dead silence; then the Moderator had to pound his gavel and the Sergeant at Arms was very busy, all to shouts of "What about my seed loan?" "You owe me money!" "I sold Hank Brofsky a mule on his personal note – what do I collect?" "You can't *do* this to us!"

Gibbons sat quietly, not letting his alertness show, until Warwick got them quieted down. Then Warwick said, wiping sweat from his brow: "Ernie, I think you've got some explaining to do."

"Certainly, Mr. Moderator. The liquidation will be as orderly as you will let it be. Those who have deposits will be paid . . . in banknotes, that being what was deposited. Those who owe money to the bank – well, I don't know; it depends on the policies the council sets up. I suppose I'm bankrupt. I can't know until you tell me what you mean when you say my bank is being 'nationalized.'

"But I have had to take this step: Top Dollar Trading Post is no longer buying with banknotes – they may be worthless. Each deal will have to be barter. But we will continue to *sell* for banknotes. But I took down the posted prices just before I came here tonight . . . because the stock I have on hand may be all I ever have with which to redeem those banknotes. Which could force me to raise prices. It all depends on whether 'nationalize' is simply another word for 'confiscate.' "

Gibbons spent several days explaining to Warwick the elementary principles of banking and currency, patiently and with good humour – to Warwick by Hobson's choice because the other selectmen found that they were too busy with their farms or businesses to take on the chore. There had been one candidate for the job of national banker or state treasurer (no agreement as yet on title) from outside the selectmen, a farmer named Leamer, but his self-nomination got nowhere despite his claim of generations of experience in banking plus a graduate degree in such matters.

Warwick got his first shock while he was taking inventory, with Gibbons, of the contents of the safe (almost the only safe on New

Beginnings and the only one of Earth manufacture). "Ernie, where's the money?"

"What money, Duke?"

" '*What* money?' Why, these account books show that you've taken in thousands and thousands of dollars. Your own trading post shows a balance of nearly a million. And I know you've been collecting mortgage payments on three or four dozen farms – and haven't loaned hardly anything for a year or more. That's been one of the major complaints, Ernie, why the selectmen just had to act – all that money going into the bank and none coming out. Money scarce everywhere. So where's the money, man?"

"I burned it," Gibbons answered cheerfully.

"*What?*"

"Certainly. It was piling up and getting too bulky. I didn't dare keep it outside the safe even though we don't have much theft here – if somebody stole it, it could ruin me. So far the past three years, as money came into the bank, I've been burning it. To keep it safe."

"Good God!"

"What's the trouble, Duke. It's just wastepaper."

" 'Wastepaper'? It's *money*."

"What is 'money,' Duke? Got any on you? Say a ten-dollar bill?"

Warwick, still looking shocked, dug out one. "Read it, Duke," Gibbons urged. "Never mind the fancy engraving and the pretty paper that can't be made here as yet – read what it says."

"It says it's ten dollars."

"So it does. But the important part is where it says that this bank will accept that note at face value in payment of debts to the bank." Gibbons took out of his sporran a thousand-dollar banknote, set fire to it while Warwick watched in horrified fascination. Gibbons rubbed the char off his fingers. "Wastepaper, Duke, as long as it's in my possession. But if I let it get into circulation, it becomes my IOU that I must honour. Half a moment while I record that serial number; I keep track of what I burn so that I know how much is still in circulation. Quite a lot, but I can tell you to the dollar. Are *you* going to honour *my* IOU's? And what about debts owed to the bank? Who gets paid? You? "Or me?"

Warwick looked baffled. "Ernie, I just don't know. Hell, man, I'm a mechanic by trade. But you heard what they said at the meeting."

"Yeah, I heard. People always expect a government to work miracles – even people who are fairly bright other ways. Let's lock up this junk and go over to the Waldorf and have a beer and discuss it."

"– or should be, Duke, simply a public bookkeeping service and credit system in which the medium of exchange is stable. Anything more and you are jiggering with other people's wealth, robbing Peper to pay Paul.

"Duke, I did my best to keep the dollar stable by keeping key prices stable – seed wheat in particular. For over twenty years the Top Dollar Trading Post has paid the same price for prime seed wheat, then resold it at the same markup – even if I took a loss and sometimes I did. Seed wheat isn't too good a money standard; it's perishable. But we don't have gold or uranium as yet, and it has to be *something*..

"Now look, Duke – when you reopen as a treasury, or a government central bank, or whatever you call it, you're certain to have pressures on you to do all sorts of things. Lower the interest rates. Expand the money supply. Guarantee high prices to the farmer for what he sells, guarantee low pices for what he buys. Brother, you're going to be called worse names than they call me, no matter *what* you do."

"Ernie – there's only one thing for it. You know how . . . so you've *got* to take the job of community treasurer."

Gibbons laughed heartily. "No, sirree, bub. I've had that headache for more than twenty years; now it's your turn. You grabbed the sack; now you hold it. If I let you put me back in as banker, all that will happen is that they will lynch *both* of us."

Changes – Helen Mayberry married the Widower Parkinson, went to live with him in a small new house on the farm now worked by two of his sons; Dora Brandon became schoolmistress of what was still called "Mrs. Mayberry's Primary School." Ernest Gibbons, no longer banker, was now silent partner in Ricks' General Store, while his own warehouses bulged with cargo for the *Andy J,* if and when. Soon, he hoped, as the new inventory tax was eating into cash he had held out for trading, and inflation was eating into the buying power of that cash. Better hurry, Zack, before we are nibbled to death by ducks!

At last the ship appeared in New Beginnings' sky, and Captain Zaccur Briggs came down with the first load of the fourth wave –

almost all of them quite old. Gibbons refrained from comment until the partners were alone:

"Zack, where did you find those walking corpses?"

"Call it charity, Ernest. That sounds better than what did happen."

"Such as?"

"Captain Sheffield, if you want our ship to go back to Earth again, you are welcome to take her there yourself. Not me. Not there. If a man is seventy-five years old there now, he becomes officially dead. His heirs inherit, he can't own property, his ration books are cancelled – anybody can kill him just for the hell of it. I didn't get these passengers on Earth; they were refugees at Luna City and I took as many as I could – no messroom passengers; cold-sleep or nothing. I insisted on payment in hardware and pharmaceuticals, but cold-sleep let me hold down the price per head; I think we'll break even. If not, we've got investments on Secundus; I haven't lost money for us. I think."

"Zack, you worry too much. Make money, lose money – who cares? The idea is to enjoy it. Tell me where we are going next, and I can begin picking cargo – I've got twice the metric tonnage we can stow. While you get her loaded, I'll liquidate what we aren't lifting and invest the proceeds. Leave it with a Howard, that is." Gibbons looked thoughtful. "This new situation probably means no Clinic here any time soon?"

"I think that is certain, Ernest. Any Howard who needs rejuvenation soon had better take passage with us; we are bound to hit Secundus in a leg or six, no matter where we go. Then you are definitely coming along? All over your problem? What became of that baby girl? The short-lifer."

Gibbons grinned. "I don't think I'll let you lay eyes on her, Son; I know you."

Captain Briggs' arrival caused Gibbons to miss three days running his usual daily ride with Dora Brandon. On the fourth day he showed up at the schoolhouse as school let out, Briggs having gone back up for a couple of days. "Got time for a ride today?"

She flashed him a smile. "You know I have. Half a minute while I change."

They rode out of town, Gibbons as usual riding Beulah but with Dora on Betty. Buck was saddled (for his pride), but the saddle was empty; he was now ridden only ceremonially, by mule years he was quite old.

They paused on a sunny hilltop well out of town. Gibbons said, "Why so silent, little Dora? Buck has had more to say than you have."

She turned in the saddle and faced him. "How many more rides will we have together? Is this the last?"

"Why, Dora! Of course we will have more rides together."

"I wonder. Lazarus, I – "

"*What did you call me?*"

"I called you by your name, Lazarus."

He stared at her thoughtfully. "Dora, you're not supposed to know that name. I'm your 'Uncle Gibbie.' "

" 'Uncle Gibbie' is gone, and so is 'Little Dora.' I'm almost as tall as you are now, and I've known for two years who you are, and I had guessed it before that – guessed that you were one of the Methuselahs, I mean. But I said nothing to anyone. And never will."

"Don't make it a promise, Dora; it isn't necessary. It's just that I never meant to burden you with it. How did I give myself away? I thought I had been most careful."

"You have been. But I have seen you nearly every day almost as far back as I can remember. Little things. Things no one would notice who didn't see you – really *look* at you – every day."

"Well, yes. But I didn't expect to have to keep it up so long. Helen knew?"

"I think she did. We never spoke of it. But I think she guessed the same way I did . . . and she may have figured out which Methuselah you are –"

"Don't call me that, dear. It's like calling a Jew a 'kike.' I'm a member of the Howard Families. A Howard."

"I'm sorry. I didn't know that the name mattered."

"Well . . . it doesn't, really. It's just a word that reminds me of a time long gone. A time of persecution. Sorry, Dora; you were telling me how you learned that my name is 'Lazarus.' One of my names, that is, for I am 'Ernest Gibbons' just as truly."

"Yes . . . Uncle Gibbie. It was in a book. A picture. A micro-book one has to read with the viewer at the town library. I saw this picture and winked on past it – then clicked back and looked again. You weren't wearing whiskers in the picture and your hair was longer . . . but the longer I stared at it, the more it looked like my foster uncle. But I couldn't be sure – and couldn't ask."

"Why not, Dora? I would have told you the truth."

"If you had wanted me to know, you would have told me. You always have reasons for everything you do, everything you say. I learned that when I was so little we used to ride the same saddle. So I didn't say anything. Until – Well, until today. Knowing that you are leaving."

"Have I said that I was leaving?"

"Please! Once, when I was very little, you told me a story about when you were a little boy hearing wild geese honking in the sky – how, when you grew up, you wanted to find out where they went. I didn't know what a wild goose was; you had to explain to me. I know you follow the wild goose. When you hear them honking, you have to go. You've been hearing them in your head for three or four years. I know . . . because when you hear them, *I* hear them, too. And now the ship is here and it's very loud in your head. So I knew."

"Dora, Dora!"

"Don't, please. I'm not trying to hold you back, truly I'm not. But before you go, I want something very much."

"What, Dora? Uh, didn't mean to tell you this yet, but I'm leaving some property for you with John Magee. Should be enough for – "

"No, no, please! I'm a grown woman now, and self-supporting. What I want doesn't cost anything." She looked him steadily in the eye. "I want your child, Lazarus."

Lazarus Long took a deep breath, tried to steady his heartbeat. "Dora, Dora, my dear, you are hardly more than a child yourself; it is too soon for you to be talking about having one. You don't want to marry me – "

"I did not ask you to marry me."

"I was trying to say that, in a year or two – or three, or four – you *will* want to marry. Then you will be glad that you did *not* have my child."

"You refuse me this?"

"I'm saying that you must not let an emotional upset over parting cause you to make any such hasty decision."

She sat very straight in the saddle, squared her shoulders. "It is not a hasty decision, sir. I made up my mind long ago . . . even before I guessed that you were a – Howard. Long before. I told Aunt Helen, and she said that I was a silly girl and that I must forget it. But I have never forgotten it, and if I was a silly girl then, I am much older now and know what I am doing.

Lazarus, I am not asking for *anything* else. It could be syringes and such, with Doc Krausmeyer's help. Or" – again she looked him squarely in his eyes – "it could be the usual way." She dropped her eyes, then looked up again, smiled briefly and added, "But, either way, it had best be quickly. I don't know the ship's schedule; I *do* know mine."

Gibbons spent all of a half second reviewing certain factors in his mind. "Dora."

"Yes . . . Ernest?"

"My name is not 'Ernest,' nor is it 'Lazarus.' My name is Woodrow Wilson Smith. So since I am no longer 'Uncle Gibbie' – and you are right on that point; 'Uncle Gibbie' is gone and will never be back – you might as well call me 'Woodrow.' "

"Yes, Woodrow."

"Do you want to know why I had to change my name?"

"No, Woodrow."

"So? Do you want to know how old I am?"

"No, Woodrow."

"But you want to have a child by me?"

"Yes, Woodrow."

"Will you marry me?"

Her eyes widened slightly. But she answered at once:

"No, Woodrow."

Minerva, at that point Dora and I almost had our first – and last, and only – quarrel. She had been a sweet and lovable baby who had grown into a sweet-tempered and utterly lovable young woman. But she was as stubborn as I am – with the sort of firmness that can't be argued with, because she would not argue. I pay her the respect of believing that she had thought this through, all aspects, and had long since made up her mind to bear my child if I would let her – but not to marry me.

As for me, I did not ask her to marry me on impulse, it just sounds like it. A supersaturated solution will crystallize almost instantly; that's the shape I was in. I had lost interest in that colony years earlier, as soon as it stopped presenting real challenges; I was itching to do something else. At the top of my mind I thought I was waiting for Zack to return . . . but when the *Andy J.* finally did orbit in that sky, two years overdue – well, I learned that it was not what I had been waiting for.

When Dora made that amazing request, I knew what I had been waiting for.

Surely, I tried to argue her out of it – but I was playing devil's advocate. In fact, my mind was busy with what and how. All the objections to marrying a short-lifer still remained. My even stronger objections to leaving a pregnant woman behind me – shucks, dear, I didn't spend a nanosecond on *that*.

"Why not, Dora?"

"I told you. You are leaving, I will not hold you back."

"You won't hold me back. No one ever has yet, Dora. But – no marriage, no child."

She looked thoughtful. "What is your purpose in insisting on a marriage ceremony, Woodrow? So that our child will bear your name? I don't want to be a sky widow . . . but if that is what it takes, let's ride back to town and find the Moderator. Because it really should be today. If the books are right about how to figure it."

"Woman, you talk too much." She did not answer this; he went on: "I don't give a hoot about a wedding ceremony – certainly not one in Top Dollar."

She hesitated, then said, "May I say that I do not understand?"

"Eh? Yes, surely. Dora, I won't settle for one child. You're going to have half a dozen children by me, or more. Probably more. Maybe a dozen. Any objection?"

"Yes, Woodrow – I mean No, I do not object. Yes, I will have a dozen children by you. Or more."

"Having a dozen kids takes time, Dora. How often should I show up? Every two years, maybe?"

"Whatever you say, Woodrow. Whenever you come back – each time you come back – I'll have a child by you. But I do ask that we start the first one at once."

"You crazy little idiot, I believe you *would* do it that way."

"Not 'would' – *shall*. If you will."

"Well, we're *not* going to do it that way." He reached out and took her hand. "Dora, will you go where I go, do what I do, live where I live?"

She looked startled but answered steadily, "Yes, Woodrow. If this is truly what you want."

"Don't put any conditions on it. Will you, or won't you?"

"I will."

"If it comes to a showdown, will you do what I tell you to? Not give me any more stubborn arguments?"

"Yes, Woodrow."

"Will you bear my children and be my wife till death do us part?"

"I will."

"I take thee, Dora, to be my wife, to love and protect and cherish – and never to leave you . . . so long as we both shall live. Don't sniffle! Lean over here and kiss me instead. We're married."

"I was not either sniffling! Are we really married?"

"We are. Oh, you can have any wedding ceremony you want. Later. Now shut up and kiss me."

She obeyed.

Some long moments later he said, "Hey, don't fall out of your saddle! Steady, Betty! Steady, Beulah! 'Dorable Dora, who taught you to kiss that way?"

"You haven't called me that since I started to grow up. Years."

"Haven't kissed you since you started to grow up, either. For good reason. You didn't answer my question."

"Is that one of the things I just promised? Whoever taught me to kiss, it was before I was a married woman."

"Mmm, you may have a point there. I'll take it up with my legal staff and have them write you a letter. Besides it might be native talent rather than instruction. Tell you what, Dora, I'll refrain from quizzing you about your sinful past . . . and you leave mine alone. A deal?"

"Yes indeed – for I have a *very* sinful past."

"Piffle, darling, you haven't had time to be sinful. Swiped some sweets I had fetched for Buck, maybe? Very sinful."

"I never did any such thing! But lots worse."

"Oh, sure. Give me another of those native-talent kisses."

Presently he said, "Whew! No, the first one wasn't a fluke. Dora, I think I married you just barely in time."

"You insisted on marrying me – my husband. I didn't make an issue of it."

"Conceded. Sweetheart, are you still anxious to get started on that baby? Now that you know that I am not going away without you?"

"No longer anxious. Eager, perhaps. Yes, 'eager' is the right word. But not demanding."

" 'Eager' is a fine word. Me, too. I could also add 'demanding.' Who knows? – you may have other native talents."

She barely smiled. "If not, Woodrow, I'm sure you can teach me. I'm willing to learn. Eager."

"Let's head back to town. My apartment? Or the schoolhouse?"

"Either one, Woodrow. But see that little stand of trees? It's much closer."

It was almost dark as they neared town; they rode back at a gentle walk. As they passed the Markham's house on the old Harper place, Woodrow Wilson Smith said, "Adorable Dora –"

"Yes, my husband?"

"Do you want a public wedding?"

"Only if you want one, Woodrow. I feel very much married. I *am* married."

"You certainly are. Not going to run away with a younger man?"

"Is that a rhetorical question? Not now, or ever."

"This young man is an immigrant who may not be down until the last or nearly the last trip. He is about my height, but he has black hair and a darker skin than I have. Can't say just how old he is, but he looks about half the age I look. Smooth-shaven. His friends call him 'Bill.' Or 'Woodie.' Captain Briggs says Bill is very fond of young schoolmarms and is anxious to meet you."

She appeared to consider it. "If I kissed him with my eyes closed, do you think I would recognize him?"

"It's possible, Dorable. Almost certain. But I don't think anyone else will. I hope they don't."

"Woodrow, I don't know your plans. But if I do recognize this 'Bill,' should I attempt to convince him that I am that other schoolmarm? The one you were singing about? Rangy Lil?"

"I think you could convince him, dearest one. All right, 'Uncle Gibbie' is back, temporarily. It will take Ernest Gibbons three or four days to wind up what he must do here, then he'll say good-bye to people – including his foster niece, that old-maid schoolmarm Dora Brandon. Two days later this Bill Smith comes down with the last, or nearly the last, load of cargo from the ship. You had better be packed and ready to leave by then because Bill is going to drive past your schoolhouse the following day, or the day after that, just before dawn, headed for New Pittsburgh."

"New Pittsburgh. I'll be ready."

"But we won't stay there more than a day or two. On we go, past Separation; then right over the horizon. We're going to tackle Hopeless Pass, dear. Does that appeal to you?"

"I go where you go."

"Does it *appeal* to you? You won't have anyone to talk to but me. Until you bake one and teach him – or her – to talk. No neighbours. Lopers and dragons and God knows what else. But no neighbours."

"So I'll cook and help you farm – and bake babies. When I have three I'll open 'Mrs. Smith's Primary School.' Or should we call it 'Rangy Lil's Primary School'?"

"The latter, I think. For young hellions. My kids are always hell-raisers, Dora. You'll teach school with a club in your hand."

"If necessary, Woodrow. I've got some like that now, and two of them outweigh me. I clobber them as necessary."

"Dora, we don't have to tackle Hopeless Pass. We could leave in the 'Andy J.' and go to Secundus. Briggs tells me that there are over twenty million people there now. You could have a nice house. Inside plumbing. A flower garden instead of breaking your back helping me to make a farm. A good hospital with real doctors when you have babies. Safety and comfort."

"'Secundus.' That's where all the – Howards moved. Isn't it?"

"About two-thirds of them. A few are right here, as I told you. But we don't admit it because when you are outnumbered, it is neither safe nor comfortable to be a Howard. Dora, you don't have to make up your mind in only three or four days. That ship will stay in orbit here as long as I want it to. Weeks. Months. As long as I order it to stay."

"Goodness! You can afford to have Captain Briggs hold a starship in orbit? Just to let me make up my mind?"

"I shouldn't have rushed you. But it's not exactly a case of affording it, Dora – although it doesn't cost much to stay in orbit. Uh . . . I've kept my own counsel so long that I'm out of the habit of being a married man, with a wife I can trust with secrets; I must stop it. I own sixty per cent of the 'Andy J.' Dora; Zack Briggs is my junior partner. And my son. Your stepson, you could say."

She did not answer at once. Presently he said. "What's the trouble, Dora? Did I shock you?"

"No, Woodrow. I'm just having to get used to new ideas. Of course you've been married before, you're a Howard. I'd never thought about it, that's all. A son – sons. And daughters, too, no doubt."

"Yes, surely. But what I was getting at is that I've done some bad planning – through my own selfishness. I was rushing you when there is no need for it. If we stay on New Beginnings, I want

'Ernest Gibbons' to disappear – leave in the 'Andy J.,' that is, as he is getting too old: I can't keep it up much longer. So young 'Bill Smith,' who is much nearer your age, takes his place . . . which looks better and no one here will ever suspect that I'm a Howard.

"I've worked this shenanigan many times; I know how to make it stand up. But I was trying to get rid of 'Ernest Gibbons' as fast as possible because he's your old foster uncle who is about three times your age and wouldn't dream of patting your pretty bottom, nor would you encourage him to. As everybody knows. But I *want* to pat your pretty bottom, Dorable."

"And I want you to pat it." She reined up; they were getting close to where houses were near together. "And more. Woodrow, you're saying that we can't live together right away because of what the neighbours might think. But who taught me never to care what the neighbours think? You did."

"True. Although sometimes it's expedient to make the neighbours think what you want them to think in order to influence what they do and say – and this might be such a time. But I also tried to teach you to be patient, dear one."

"Woodrow, I will do exactly what you tell me to. But I'm not really patient about this. I want my husband in my bed!"

"And I want to be there."

"Then what does it matter if people assume that I choose to tell my Uncle Gibbie good-bye in bed? Or that I then go away with a new settler almost at once? Woodrow, you didn't say a word about it at the time – but you knew that I was not virgin, I'm certain. Don't you think there must be others who know it, too? Probably the whole town. I've never worried about it. Why should I worry what they think now?"

"Dora."

"Yes, Woodrow?"

"I'll be in your bed every night, that's settled."

"Thank you, Woodrow."

"The pleasure is mine, madam. Or half of it, at least; you seem to enjoy it, too –"

"Oh, I do! And you know it. Or should."

"So stipulated, let's pass to other matters – except to say that had I found you virgin – big as you are, old as you are – it would have worried me a little, and I might have felt that Helen had not been quite the wholesome influence that I thought she was. That she was indeed, bless her heart! The matter of pretending to be dear old 'Uncle Gibbie' who would never touch little Dora was purely for your face; since it does not worry you, let's drop it. What I started to say is that you can take as long as you like in deciding whether to pioneer here or go to Secundus. Dora, Secundus has more than inside plumbing; it has a Rejuvenation Clinic."

"Oh! You need to be near one, Woodrow?"

"No, no! For *you*, dear."

She was very slow in answering. "That would not make me a Howard."

"Well, no. But it helps. Rejuvenation therapies don't make Howards last forever, either. Some people are helped quite a lot by them; some are not. Maybe someday we'll know more – but now, on the average, rejuvenation techniques seem to about double whatever a person could expect normally, whether he's a Howard . . . or not a Howard. Uh, do you know *anything* about how long your grandparents lived?"

"How could I, Woodrow? I just barely remember that I once had parents. I don't even know the names of my grandparents."

"We can find out. The ship carries records of every migrant who takes passage in her. I'll tell Zack – Captain Briggs – to look up your parents' records. Then – in time, for it will take time – I can have your family traced on Earth. Then –"

"No, Woodrow."

"Why not, dear?"

"I don't need to know, I don't want to know. Long ago, three or four years at least, shortly after I figured out that you were a Howard, I also figured out that Howards don't really live any longer than we ordinaries do."

"So?"

"Yes. We all have the past and the present and the future. The past is just memory, and I can't remember when I began, I can't remember when I *wasn't*. Can you?"

"No."

"So we're even on that. I suppose your memories are richer; you are older than I am. But it's *past*. The future? It hasn't happened yet, and nobody knows. You may outlive me . . . or I may outlive you. Or we might happen to be killed at the same time. We can't know and *I* don't want to know. What we both have is *now* . . . and we have that together and it makes me utterly happy. Let's get these mules put away for the night and enjoy some *now*."

"Suits." He grinned at her. "E.F., or F.F.?"

"Both!"

"That's my Dora! Anything worth doing is worth overdoing."

"And doing again. But just a moment, dear. You told me that Captain Briggs is your son, and consequently my stepson. I suppose he is, but I really can't think of him as such. But – and you needn't answer this; we agreed not to quiz each other about our pasts – "

"Go ahead and ask. If it suits me, I'll answer."

"Well . . . I can't help being curious about Captain Briggs' mother. Your former wife."

"Phyllis? Phyllis Briggs-Sperling is her full name. What do you want to know about her, dear? Very nice girl. Further Deponent Sayeth Not. No invidious comparisons."

"I guess I'm being snoopy."

"Perhaps you are. Not that I mind, and it can't hurt Phyllis. Dear, that was a couple of centuries ago; forget it."

"Oh. She's dead?"

"Not that I know of. Zack would know; he's been to Secundus recently. I think he would have told me. But I haven't stayed in touch with her since she divorced me."

"*Divorced* you? A woman of poor taste!"

"Dora, Dora! Phyllis is *not* a woman of poor taste; she is a very nice girl. I had dinner with her and her husband the last time I was on Secundus. Zack and I did, I mean – and she and her husband had gone to the trouble of rounding up my other children by her, those who were on planet, and some of my other relatives and made it a family party for me. Thoughtful of her. By the way, she's a schoolmarm, too."

"She is?"

"Yup. Libby Professor of Mathematics, Howard University, New Rome, Secundus. If we go there, we can look her up and you can decide for yourself what sort of person she is."

Dora did not answer. She kneed Betty and started on down the street; Beulah pulled abreast without being told. Buck said, "Shupper . . . *dime!*" quite emphatically, and trotted on ahead.

"Lazarus – "

"Careful with that name, dear."

"No one can hear me. Lazarus, unless you insist . . . I don't want to live on Secundus."

VARIATIONS ON A THEME

XII

The Tale of the Adopted Daughter (*Continued*)

Separation lay far behind. For three weeks the little train – two wagons in tandem, twelve mules hauling, four running free – had crawled toward Rampart Range. It had been more than two weeks since they had last seen a house. They were on the high prairies now, and for several days the gap of Hopeless Pass had been in sight.

Besides sixteen mules, the little party included a German shepherd bitch and a younger dog, two female cats and a tom, a fresh milch goat with two kids and a young buck, two cocks and six hens of the hardy Mrs. Awkins variety, a freshly bred sow, and Dora and Woodrow Smith.

The sow had tested pregnant at New Pittsburgh before Smith paid for her, test conducted by Smith himself – and Mrs. Smith had tested pregnant, too, while still at Top Dollar and before Smith cleared Starship *Andy J.* to leave orbit, for (Smith had *not* found it necessary to tell his wife this) if Dora had *not* tested pregnant, the ship would have waited while they tried again – then if she had still tested negative, he would have changed plans and taken her to Secundus, there to find out why and, if possible, to correct it.

In Smith's opinion as a professional pioneer, it was not only pointless but disastrously foolhardy to attempt single-couple pioneering out of reach of other people with an infertile woman – or a couple infertile with each other, he corrected in his mind, as his own fertility had not been put to the ultimate test for fifty-odd years. While he was about it, he had looked up physical records of Dora's parents in Krausmeyer's ill-kept files, found nothing to worry him – and it had indeed worried him, as he would not have been able to cope even with anything as simple as an Rh-factor incompatibility a long way from nowhere.

But within the limited medical resorces of colony and ship, the board showed all green, and it seemed likely to him that Dora had become pregnant about twenty minutes after their informal muleback wedding.

The thought had passed through his mind that Dora might have been pregnant even sooner – but the thought was merely an amusing whimsy that bothered him not at all. Smith felt certain that he had had the Cuckoo in his nest more than once over the centuries; he had been especially careful to be a loving father to such children and had kept his mouth shut. He believed in letting women lie all they needed to, and never taxing them with it. But he believed also that Dora was incapable of this sort of lie. If Dora had been pregnant and aware of it, she might have asked to be allowed to say good-bye to him on her back – but she would have asked for exactly that. Not for a child.

No matter – If the darling had made a mistake earlier and did not know it, he felt sure that she would nevertheless have a superior baby. She was clearly superior stock herself – he wished he had known the Brandons; they must have been ichiban – and their daughter was, as Helen had once said, "choosy." Dora would not bed with an oaf even for fun, because, being what she was, she would not find it fun. Smith was sure that it would take rape to put an inferior child into Dora – and the rapist might sing soprano the rest of his days; her Uncle Gibbie had taught her some dirty tricks.

The pregnant sow was Smith's "calendar." If they failed to reach a spot suitable for homesteading by the time that sow littered, then they turned back that very day – no hesitation, no regrets – as that would leave them just half of Dora's pregnancy to get them back to Separation and other people.

The sow rode in the back end of the second wagon, with a sling to keep her from falling down. The dogs trotted under the wagons or ranged aside, warning of lopers or other hazards. The cats did as they pleased, as cats do, walking or riding as suited them. The nanny and billy goats stayed close to the wheel pair; the two kids were large enough to skitter along most of the time but were privileged to ride when they tired – a loud *Me-e-e-eh* from the mother goat would cause Smith to swing down and hand the tired baby up to Dora. The chickens complained in a double cage over the sow's pen. The mules running free had no duties other than to keep eyes out for lopers, save that Buck was at all times grand marshal of the parade, picking the footing, bossing the other mules, carrying out Smith's orders. Mules at liberty rotated as draft animals; only Buck was never in harness. Betty and Beulah had had their feelings hurt at being required to accept harness; they were gentry of the saddle, and they knew it. But Buck had had harsh words with them and harsher nips and kicks; they had shut up and hauled.

No real driving was required; only two reins were used, one to each of the lead pair and running from them back through rings on the collars of the following mules to the seat of the leading wagon, there usually loosely secured rather than held. Although the males were all stallions, these mules did what Buck ordered. Smith had stopped at Separation and lost most of a day to trade a strong brute with good shoulders for a younger, lighter stud because the bigger mule had not been willing to accept Buck's dominance. Buck was ready to fight it out, but Smith did not let the old mule risk it; he needed Buck's brain and judgement, and would not risk Buck's spirit being broken by losing to a younger stallion – or take a chance that Buck might be injured.

In real trouble more reins would not help. If the mules panicked and ran – unlikely but possible – two humans could not hold them, even with a double handful of reins. Smith was ready at any instant to pick off his lead pair, then hope that not too many mules would break legs stumbling over the corpses and pray that the wagons would not overturn.

Smith wanted to reach their destination with all his livestock; he hoped to get there with about 80 per cent including a breeding pair of each sort – but if they arrived with enough draft animals to pull the wagons (including at least one breeding pair) plus a pair of goats, he could consider it a conditional victory and they would make their stand, to live or to die.

How many mules were "enough" was a variable. Near the end of the trip it could be as low as four – then go back and get the second wagon. But if the number of mules dropped below twelve before they conquered Hopeless Pass – turn back.

Turn back at once. Abandon one or both wagons, jettison what they could not salvage, slaughter any animals that could not make it without help, travel light with any extra mules trailing along, unwitting walking larders.

If Woodrow Wilson Smith limped back into Separation on foot, his wife riding – miscarried but still alive – it still would not be defeat. He had his hands, he had his brain, he had the strongest of human incentives: a wife to care for and cherish. In a few years they might try Hopeless Pass again – and not make the mistakes he had made the first time.

In the meantime he was happy, with all the wealth any man could hope for.

Smith leaned out of the wagon seat. "Hey, Buck! Suppertime."

"Shupper dime," Buck repeated, then called out, "Shupper *dime!* Shirko *nigh!* Shirko *nigh!*" The lead pair turned left, started bringing the train around in a circle.

Dora said, "The Sun is still high."

"Yes," her husband agreed, "and that's why. The Sun is high, it's very hot, the mules are tired and sweaty and hungry and thirsty. I want them to graze. Tomorrow we'll be up before dawn and rolling at first light – make as many kilometres as possible before it gets too bloody hot. Then another early stop."

"I wasn't questioning it, dear; I simply wanted to know why. I'm finding that being a schoolmarm hasn't taught me all I need to know to be a pioneer wife."

"I understood; that's why I explained. Dora, *always* ask me if I do anything you don't understand; you *do* have to know . . . because if something happens to me, then it'll be up to you. Just hold your questions until later if I seem to be in a hurry."

"I'll try, Woodrow – I *am* trying. I'm hot and thirsty myself; those poor dears must be feeling it dreadfully. If you can spare me, I'll water them while you unharness."

"No, Dora."

"But – Sorry."

"Damn it, I said always to ask why. But I was about to explain. First we let them graze an hour. That will cool them down some in spite of the Sun, and, being thirsty, they'll look for short green stuff under this tall dry stuff. They will get a little moisture out of that. Meantime I'm going to measure the water barrels . . . But I know that we're going on short water rations. Should've yesterday. Dorable, you see that patch of dark green way up there below the pass? I think there is water there, dry as it's been . . . and pray hard that there is, because I don't expect to find water between here and there. We may have no water at all the last day or so. It doesn't take a mule long to die without water and not much longer for a man."

"Woodrow . . . is it as bad as that?"

"It is, dear. That's why I've been studying the photomaps. The clearest ones Andy and I made a long time ago, when we surveyed this planet – but in early spring for this hemisphere. The shots Zack took for me aren't much; the 'Andy J.' isn't equipped as a survey ship. As may be, I took this route because it looked faster. But every wash we've crossed the past ten days has been bone-dry. My mistake and it may be my last one."

"*Woodrow!* Don't talk that way!"

"Sorry, dear. But there is always a last mistake. I'll do my damnedest to see that this is *not* my last mistake – because it must not happen to you. I'm simply trying to impress you with how carefully we must conserve water."

"You've impressed me. I'll be most careful with cleaning up and so forth."

"I still haven't made it clear. There will be no washing *at all* – not a face wash, not even a hand wash. Pans and such you'll scour with dirt and grass and put them in the sunshine and hope they sterilize. Water is only for drinking. The mules go on half water rations at once, and you and I, instead of the litre and a half of liquid each day a human is supposed to need, will each try to get by on a half litre. Uh, Mrs. Whiskers will get a full ration of water; she has to make milk for her kids. If it gets too tough, we slaughter the kids and let her dry up."

"Oh, dear!"

"We may not have to. But, Dora, we aren't even close to last extremities. If the going gets really tough, we kill a mule and drink its blood."

"*What!* Why, they're our friends!"

"Dora, listen to your old man. I promise you that we will never kill Buck, or Beulah, or Betty. If I must, it will be a mule we bought in New Pittsburgh. But if one of our three old friends die – we eat him. Her."

"I don't think I could."

"You will when you're hungry enough. If you think about the baby inside you, you'll eat without hesitation and bless your dead friend for helping to keep your baby alive. Don't talk about what you can't do when the chips are down, dear – because you *can*. Did Helen ever tell you stories about the first winter here?"

"No. She said I didn't need to know."

"Could be she was mistaken. I'll tell you one of the less grisly ones. We placed – *I* placed – a heel-and-toe watch over the seed grain, with orders to shoot to kill. And one guard did. A drum-head court-martial exonerated the guard; the man he killed was clearly stealing seed grain – his corpse had half-chewed grain in its mouth. Not Helen's husband, by the way; *he* died like a gentleman – malnutrition and some fever I never identified."

Smith added, "Buck's got us hauled around. Let's get busy." He jumped down, reached up to help her. "And smile, baby, smile! – this show is being transmitted back to Earth to show those poor crowded people how *easy* it is to take a new planet – courtesy of DuBarry's Delicious Deodorants, of which I need a bucketful."

She smiled. "I stink worse than you do, my love."

"That's better, darling; we'll make it. It's just the first step that's a dilly. Oh, yes! No cooking fire."

" 'No f—' Yes, sir."

"Nor any until we get out of this dry stuff. Don't strike a light for any reason – even if you've dropped your rubies and can't find them."

" 'Rubies –' Woodrow, it was wonderful of you to give me rubies. But right now I would swap them for another barrel of water."

"No, you wouldn't, dearest, because rubies don't weigh anything and I took every barrel the mules could haul. I was delighted that Zack had those rubies along and I could give them to you. A bride should be cherished. Let's take care of these tired mules."

After they turned the mules loose, Dora tried to figure out what she could feed her husband without the use of fire while Smith got busy on the fence. The fence was not much, but having only two wagons, they could not form a proper defensive circle; the best that could be done was to angle the wagons as far as the front axle of the second wagon permitted, then surround the bivouac with a fence of sorts – sharpened stakes of brasswood, each two metres long, and held together and spaced by what passed for rope in New Pittsburgh. The result, when held up on two sides by wagons and braced to the ground along the hypotenuse, constituted a high and fairly nasty picket fence. It would not slow up a dragon, but this was not dragon country. Lopers did not like it.

Smith did not like it much, either, but it was made on New Beginnings of all-native materials, could be repaired by a man who who was handy, did not weigh much, could be abandoned with no great loss – and contained no metal. Smith had been able to buy two sturdy, boat-bodied, Conestoga-type wagons in New Pittsburgh only by offering in part payment complete hardware for two other wagons – hardware imported across the light-years in the *Andy J.* New Pittsburgh was far more "New" than "Pittsburgh"; there was iron ore there and coal, but its metals industry was still primitive.

The chickens, the sow, the goats, and even the humans were tasty temptations to wild lopers, but with the goats and kids shooed inside the kraal, two alert watchdogs, and sixteen mules grazing on all sides, Smith felt reasonably secure at night. True, a loper might get a mule, but it was much more likely that the mule would get the loper – especially as other mules would close in and help stomp the carnivore. These mules did not run from a loper; they struck out at him. Smith thought that, in time, mules might clean out the varmints even more than men did, make them as scarce as mountain lions had been in his youth.

A mule-stomped loper was readily converted into loper steak, loper stew, loper jerky – and dog and cat food, and Mrs. Porky the sow enjoyed the offal – all at no loss to the mules. Smith did not care much for loper in any form; the meat was too strongly flavoured for his taste – but it was better than nothing and kept them from digging too deeply into food they had hauled along. Dora did not share her husband's distaste for loper meat; born there and having eaten it now and then since earliest childhood, it seemed to her a normal food.

But Smith wished that he had time to hunt one of the herbivores that were the loper's natural prey – six-legged like the loper but otherwise resembling a misshapen okapi – their meat was much milder. They were called "prairie goats," which they were not, but systematic taxonomy of fauna and flora on New Beginnings had not gone far; there had been as yet no time for such intellectual luxuries. Smith had shot a prairie goat from the seat of the wagon a week earlier (now only a memory, bitter-sweet, of tasty tender meat). Smith did not feel justified in taking a day off to hunt until they had conquered Hopeless Pass. But he kept hoping for another chance shot.

Maybe now – "Fritz! Lady Macbeth! Here!" The dogs trotted up and waited. "High sentry. Loper! Prairie goat! *Up!*" The dogs immediately got on the very top of the lead wagon, making it in two jumps and a scramble, step, seat, and curved top. There they split the duty, nigh side and off side – and there they would stay until told to get down. Smith had paid a stiff price for the pair, but he had known they were good dogs; he had picked their ancestors on Earth and had fetched them with the first wave. Smith was not a "doggie" man in any fanatic sense; he simply believed that a partnership that had lasted so long on Earth would serve men equally well on strange planets.

Dora was sobered by her husband's words, but once she got busy working, she cheered up. Shortly, while trying to plan a menu from little choice and without a cooking fire, she came across something that vexed her – good for her as it displaced her worrisome thoughts. Besides, she did not really believe that her husband could fail at anything.

She came around the end of the second wagon, crossed the little kraal to where her husband was making sure that his fence was tight. "Oh, that pesky little rooster!"

Woodrow looked around. "Hon, you look cute in just a sunbonnet."

"Not just a sunbonnet, I'm wearing boots, too. Don't you want to hear what that nasty little rooster did?"

"I would rather discuss how you look. Adorable, that is. Nevertheless, I'm not pleased with the way you are dressed."

"What? But it's so hot, dear. Since I can't wash, I thought an air bath might make me smell better."

"You smell good to me. But an air bath is a good idea; I'll peel down, too. Your gun, dear – where's your belt with your knife and gun?" He started shucking his overalls.

"You want me to wear my gun belt *now?* Inside the fence? With you here to protect me?"

"As self-discipline and a standard precaution, my lovely one." He hitched his own gun-and-knife belt back into place as he stepped out of his overalls, then pulled off boots and shirt and got bare save for the belt and three other weapons that did not show when he was dressed. "In more years than I like to think about I have never been unarmed except when locked in somewhere safe. I want you to acquire the habit. Not just sometimes. Always."

"All right. I left my belt on the seat; I'll get it. But, Woodrow, I'm not much of a fighter at best."

"You're fairly accurate with that needle gun up to fifty metres. And you're going to get better and better the longer you live with me. Not just with it but with anything that shoots, cuts, burns, or even makes nasty bruises, from your bare hands to a blaster. See over there, Dorable?" He pointed to nothing but flatness. "In just seven seconds a horde of hairy savages will come pouring over the top of that rise and attack. I get a spear through my thigh and go down . . . then you have to fight them off for both of us. What are you going to do, you poor little girl, with your gun clear over there on the seat of that wagon?"

"Why" – she set her feet apart, put her hands back of her head, and gave a wiggle that was invented in the Garden of Eden, or perhaps just outside – "I'll go *this* way at 'em!"

"Yes," Lazarus agreed thoughtfully, "that should work. If they were human. But they aren't. Their only interest in tall, beautiful, brown-eyed girls is to *eat* them. Bones and all. Silly of them, but that's how they are."

"Yes, dear," she said docilely. "I'll go put on my gun belt. Then I'll kill the one who speared you. Then I'll see how many more I can get before they eat me."

"That's right, durable Dorable. Always take an honour guard with you. If you have to go, go down fighting. The size of your guard of honour determines your status in hell."

"Yes, dear. I'm sure I'll enjoy hell if you're there, too." She turned to fetch her weapons.

"Oh, I'll be there! They wouldn't take me anywhere else. Dora! When you put on your gun belt, take off your sunbonnet and boots – and put on your rubies, all of them."

She paused with a foot on the step of the wagon. "My rubies, dear? Out here on the prairie?"

"Rangy Lil, I bought those rubies for you to wear and for me to admire you wearing them."

She flashed a smile that turned her normally serious expression into sunshine, swung on up into the wagon and disappeared. She was back quickly wearing weapons belt and rubies, but had taken a few seconds to comb her hair, long and chestnut brown and shining. That she had not been able to bathe for more than two weeks did not show, did not detract from her enchanting, youthful beauty. She paused on the step and smiled at him.

"Hold it!" he said. "Perfect! Dora, you are the most beautiful thing I have ever seen in all my born days."

She flashed him another smile. "I don't believe that, my husband – but I hope you will go on saying it."

"Madam, I cannot tell a lie. I say it only because it is the simple truth. Now what were you saying about the little rooster?"

"*Oh!* That perverted little monster! I *said* he had been breaking eggs on purpose! This time I caught him. Pecking them. Two freshly laid broken eggs!"

"Royal prerogative, dear. Afraid one of them would hatch out a rooster."

"I'll wring his neck! If we had a fire, I'd do it right now. Darling, I was trying to see what we could eat cold without opening anything not already open, and it occurred to me that salt crackers crumbled into raw eggs would almost make a meal. But there were only three eggs today and he broke the two laid by his hens. I'd put plenty of grass in both cages; the one egg on the other side wasn't even cracked. Damn him. Woodrow, why do we have to have *two* roosters?"

"For the same reason I carry two throwing knives. Sweetheart, after we arrive and hatch our first chicks, once they're big enough that I'm certain of a spare rooster, we can have rooster and dumplings with him as guest of honour. Not before."

"But we *can't* have him breaking eggs. Tonight's supper will be mostly cheese and hardtack – unless you want me to open something."

"Let's not rush it. Fritz and Lady Mac are trying to spot game right now. Prairie goat, I hope. Loper if not."

"But I can't cook meat. You said. You did say."

"Raw, my dear. Haunch of prairie goat, chopped fine and spread on hard crackers. Beef Tartare à la New Beginnings. Tasty. Tastes almost as good as girl." He smacked his lips.

"Well . . . If you can eat it, I can eat it. But half the time, Woodrow, I don't know whether you are joking or not."

"I never joke about food or women, Dorable; those are sacred subjects." He looked her up and down again. "Speaking of women, woman, dressing you in rubies is just right. But why a bracelet around your ankle?"

"Because you gave me three bracelets, sir. As well as rings and a pendant. And you said to wear 'all of them'."

"So I did. Where did this one come from?"

"Hey! That's not a ruby; that's *me!*"

"Looks like a ruby. Here's another just like it."

"*Unh!* Maybe I'd better take my rubies off? So we won't lose them. Or should we water the mules first?"

"You mean before we eat?"

"Uh . . . yes, I guess that's what I mean. Tease."

"You're not speaking very plainly, little Dora. Tell Uncle Gibbie what you want."

"I'm not 'little Dora.' I'm Rangy Lil, the horniest girl south of Separation – you said so yourself. I cuss and I swear and I spit between my teeth and I'm concubine to Lazarus Long, Super Stud of the Stars and better than any six men – and you know damn well what I want, and if you pinch my nipples again, I'm likely to trip you and take it. But I guess we ought to water the mules."

Minerva, Dora was just plain nice to be around, always. It wasn't her physical beauty . . . which wasn't that outstanding by the usual criteria in any case – although she was utterly beautiful *to me*. Nor was it her enthusiastic interest in sharing "Eros" – although she was indeed enthusiastic, ready any time, and always on a short fuse. And skilled at it and got more so. Sex is a learned art, as much so as ice skating or tightwire walking or fancy diving; it is *not* instinct. Oh, two animals couple by instinct, but it takes intelligence and patient willingness to turn copulation into a high and lively art. Dora was good at it and got better and better, always eager to learn, free of fetishes or silly preconceptions, patiently willing to practice anything she learned or was taught – and with it that spiritual quality that turns sweaty exercise into a living sacrament.

But Minerva, love is what *still* goes on when you are *not* horny.

Dora was good company at any time, but the tougher things were, the better companion she was. Oh, she fretted about broken eggs because chickens were her responsibility; she did not complain that she was thirsty. Instead of nagging me to do something about that rooster, she figured out what had to be done and did it – shoved all the hens in with the other rooster, tied the feet of the egg breaker and laid him aside while she moved the partition between the cages, then the smaller rooster was in solitary confinement and we lost no more eggs.

But the truly tough parts lay ahead of us; she did not fret at all during those, or ever turn balky when I did not have time to explain. Minerva, much of the trek was slow death, other parts were sudden dangers that could have been quick death. She was endlessly patient in the former, always kept her head and helped in the latter. Dear, you are awesomely learned – but you are a city girl and you've always been on a civilized planet; perhaps I had better explain some things.

Maybe you have been asking yourself: "Is this trip necessary?" – and, if it is, why do it the hard way?

"Necessary – " Having done something a Howard should never do, namely, marry an ephemeral, I had three choices:

Take her to live among Howards. Dora rejected that . . . although I would have tried to talk her out of it if she had said Yes. A short-timer alone in a community of the long-lived is almost certain to go into suicidal depression; I had seen it first in my friend Slayton Ford and I've seen it many times since then. I did not want this to happen to Dora. Whether the number of her years was ten or a thousand, I wanted her to enjoy them.

Or we could stay in Top Dollar or – the same thing – near one of the villages of that small piece of the planet that was settled then. I almost chose this, as the "Bill Smith" dodge would work for that – for a time.

But only for a short time. The few Howards on New Beginnings – the Magees and three other families as I recall – had all arrived incognito – "masquerade" in Howard jargon – and by simple dodges they could shuffle things around and never be caught at it. Grandmother Magee could "die," then show up as "Deborah Simpson" on another Howard homestead. The more people there were on the planet, the easier it was to pull this – especially after the fourth wave arrived, all of them cold-sleep cargo and thereby never having gotten acquainted with each other.

But "Bill Smith" was married to an ephemeral. If I stayed around the settled parts, I would have to be most careful to keep my hair dyed – not just on my head but all over my body lest some accident give me away – and then be careful to "age" as fast as my wife did. Worse, I would have to avoid people who had known "Ernest Gibbons" well – most of Top Dollar, that is to say – or someone would see my profile and hear my voice and start wondering, as I had had no chance for plastic surgery or anything of that sort. At other times, when it was needful to change name and identity, I had always changed location as well, that being the only foolproof way to do it. Even plastic surgery won't disguise me very long; I regenerate too easily. I once had my nose bobbed (the alternative seemed to involve having my neck bobbed); ten years later it was just as it is now, big and ugly.

Not that I was too jumpy about being disclosed as a Howard. But if I was going to have to live in masquerade, the more carefully I used these cosmetic tricks, the more Dora's nose would be rubbed in the fact that I was different from her – different in the saddest way of all, a husband and a wife who ran on very different time rates.

Minerva, it seemed to me that the only way I could give my

pretty new wife a square shake was by taking her far away from both sorts of people, long-lived and short, where I could quit pretending and we could ignore the difference, forget it and be happy. So I decided to take her clear out of reach of other people, decided this before we got back to town the very day I married her.

It seemed the best answer to an otherwise impossible situation, but one not as irreversible as a parachute jump. If she got too lonely, if she grew to hate the sight of my ugly mug, I could bring her out to the settlements again, still young enough to hook another husband. I had this in mind, Minerva, as some of my wives have grown tired of me fairly quickly. I had arranged with Zack Briggs, at the same time I had arranged with John Magee to act as factor for Zack – arranged with Zack to ask John what had happened to "Bill Smith" and the little schoolmarm? It was possible that I would need a ride off-planet someday.

But why didn't I have Zack put us down on the spot on the map I had picked as being our likely place of settlement? – with everything we would need to start farming and thereby avoid a long, dangerous trek. Not risk death by thirst, or by lopers, or the treacheries of mountains, or whatever.

Minerva, this was a long time ago and I can explain only in terms of technology available *there* and *then*. The *Andy J.* could not land; she received her overhauls in orbit around Secundus or some other advanced planet. Her cargo boat could land on any big flat field but required a minimum of a radar-corner reflector to home on, then had to have many metric tons of water to lift off again. The captain's gig was the only boat in the *Andy J.* capable of landing anywhere a skilled pilot could put her down, then lift off without help. But her cargo capacity was about two postage stamps – whereas I needed mules and ploughs and a load of other things.

Besides, I needed to learn how to get *out* of those mountains by going *into* them. I could not take Dora into there without being reasonably sure that I could fetch her out again. Not fair! It's no sin not to be pioneer-mother material – but it is tragic for both husband and wife to find it out too late.

So we did not do it the hard way; we did it the *only* way for that time and place. But I have never put the effort into a mass calculation for a spaceship at liftoff that I put into deciding what to take, what to do without, for that trek. First, the basic parameter: how many wagons in the train? I wanted three wagons so badly I could taste it. A third wagon would mean luxuries for Dora, more tools for me, more books and such for both of us, and (best!) a precut one-room house to get my pregnant bride out of the weather almost instantly at the other end.

But three wagons meant eighteen mules hauling, plus spare mules – add six by rule-of-thumb – which meant half again as much time spent harnessing and unharnessing, watering the animals, taking care of them otherwise. Add enough wagons and mules and at some point your day's march is zero; one man can't handle the work. Worse, there would be places in the mountains where I would have to unshackle the wagons, move them one at a time to a more open place – go back for each wagon left behind, bring it up – a process that would take twice as long for a three-wagon train as for a two-wagon one, and would happen oftener, even much oftener, with three wagons than with two. At that rate we might have three babies born en route instead of getting there before our first one was born.

I was saved from such folly by the fact only two trekking wagons were available in New Pittsburgh. I think I would have resisted temptation anyhow – but I had with me in the light wagon we drove from Top Dollar the hardware for three, then I spent that extra hardware on other things, bartering it through the wainwright. I could not wait while he built a third wagon; both the season of the year and the season of Dora's womb gave me deadlines I had to meet.

There is much to be said for just one wagon – standard equipment over many centuries and on several planets for one family in overland migration – *if* they travel in a party. I've led such marches.

But one wagon by itself – One accident can be disaster.

Two wagons offer more than twice as much to work with at the other end, plus life insurance on the march. You can lose one wagon, regroup, and keep going.

So I planned for two wagons, Minerva, even though I had Zack debit me with three sets of 'Stoga hardware, then did not sell that third set until the last minute.

Here's how you load a wagon train for survival:

First, list everything that you expect to need and everything that you would like to take:

Wagons, spare wheels, spare axles

Mules, harness, spare hardware and harness leather, saddles

Water
Food
Clothing
Blankets
Weapons, ammunition, repair kit
Medicines, drugs, surgical instruments, bandages
Books
Plows
Harrow
Field rake
Shovels, hand rakes, hoes, seeders, three- five- and seven-tine forks
Harvester
Blacksmith's tools
Carpentry tools
Iron cookstove
Water closet, self-flushing type
Oil lamps
Windmill and pump
Sawmill run by windpower
Leatherworking and harness-repair tools
Bed, table, chairs, dishes, pots, pans, eating and cooking gear
Binoculars, microscope, water-testing kit
Grindstone
Wheelbarrow
Churn
Buckets, sieves, assorted small hardware
Milch cow and bull
Chickens
Salt for stock and for people
Packaged yeast, yeast starter
Seed grain, several sorts
Grinder for whole-grain flour, meat grinder

Don't stop there; think *big*. Never mind the fact that you've already overloaded a much longer wagon train. Search your imagination, check the minifests of the *Andy J.*, search the ship itself, look over the stock in Rick's General Store, talk with John Magee and look over his house and farm and outbuildings – if you forget it now, it's impossible to go back for it.

Musical instruments, writing materials, diaries, calendars
Baby clothes, layettes

Spinning wheel, loom, sewing materials – *sheep!*
Tannin and leather-curing materials and tools
Clocks, watches
Root vegetables, rooted fruit-tree seedlings, other seed
Etc. etc. etc. . . .

Now start trimming – start swapping – start figuring weights.

Cut out the bull, the cow, the sheep; substitute goats with hair long enough to be worth cutting. Hey, you missed *shears!*

The blacksmith's shop stays but gets trimmed down to an anvil and minimum tools – a bellows you must make. In general anything of wood is scratched, but a small supply of wrought-iron stock, heavy as it is, must be hauled; you'll be making things you didn't know you could.

The harvester becomes a scythe with handle and cradle, three spare blades; the field rake is scratched.

The windmill stays, and so does the sawmill (surprise!) – but only as minimum hardware; you won't tackle either one soon.

Books – Which of those books can you live without, Dora?

Halve the amount of clothing, double up on shoes and add more boots and don't forget children's shoes. Yes, I know how to make moccasins, mukluks, and such; add waxed thread. Yes, we do have to have block-and-tackle and the best glass-and-plastic lines we can buy, or we won't get through the pass. Money is nothing; weight and cubage are all that count – our total wealth is what mules can take through that notch.

Minerva, it was lucky for me, lucky for Dora, that I was on my sixth pioneering venture and that I had planned how to load spaceships many years before I ever loaded a covered wagon – for the principles are the same; spaceships are the covered wagons of the Galaxy. Get it down to the weight the mules can haul, then chop off 10 per cent no matter how it hurts; a broken axle – when you can't replace it – might as well be a broken neck.

Then add more water to bring it up to 95 per cent; the load of water drops off every day.

Knitting needles! Can Dora knit? If not, teach her. I've spent many a lonely hour in space knitting sweaters and socks. Yarn? It will be a long time before Dora can tease goat shearings into good yarn – and she can knit for the baby while we travel; keep her happy. Yarn doesn't weight much. Wooden needles can be made; even curved metal needles can be shaped from scraps. But pick up both sorts from Rick's Store.

Oh, my God, I almost missed taking an *axe!*

Axe heads and one handle, brush hook, pick-mattock – Minerva, I added and trimmed and discarded, and weighed every item at New Pittsburgh – and we weren't three kilometres out of there headed for Separation before I knew I had us overloaded. That night we stopped at a homesteader's cabin, and I traded a new thirty-kilo anvil for his fifteen-kilo one, traded even, with the pound of flesh nearest my heart tossed in for good measure. I swapped other heavy items that we would miss later for a smoked ham and a side of bacon and more corn for the mules – the last being emergency rations.

We lightened the loads again at Separation, and I took another water barrel in trade and filled it because I now had room for another and knew that too heavy a load of water was self-correcting.

I think that extra barrel saved our lives.

The patch of green that Lazarus-Woodrow had pointed out up near the notch of Hopeless Pass proved to be farther away in travel time than he had hoped. On the last day that they struggled toward it neither man nor mule had had anything to drink since dawn the day before. Smith felt light-headed; the mules were hardly fit to work, they plodded slowly, heads down.

Dora wanted to stop drinking when her husband did. He said to her: "Listen to me, you stupid little tart, you're *pregnant*. Understand me? Or will it take a fat lip to convince you? I held out four litres when we served the mules; you saw me."

"I don't need four litres, Woodrow."

"Shut up. That's for you, and the nanny goat, and the chickens. And the cats – cats don't take much. Dorable, that much water means nothing split among sixteen mules, but it will go a long way among you small fry."

"Yes, sir. How about Mrs. Porky?"

"Oh, that damned sow! Uh . . . I'll give her a half a litre when we stop tonight and I'll serve her myself. She's likely to kick it over and take your thumb off, the mood she's in. And I'll serve *you* myself, measure it out, and watch you drink it."

But after a long day and a restless night and then an endless day, they were at last among the first of the trees. It seemed almost cool, and Smith felt that he could smell water – somewhere. He could not see any. "Buck! Oh, Buck! Circle!"

The boss mule did not answer; he had not talked all day. But he brought the column around, cornered the wagons, and nudged the lead pair into the V to be unharnessed.

Smith called the dogs and told them to hunt for water, then started unharnessing. Silently his wife joined him, serving the off mule of each pair while Smith cleared the nigh mule. He appreciated her silence. Dora was, he thought, telepathic to emotions.

Now if I were water somewhere around here, where would I be? Witch for it? Or search the surface first? He felt fairly sure that no stream led away from this stand of trees, but he could not be certain without hiking all the down hill side. Saddle Beulah? Shucks, Beulah was worse off than he was. He started unlashing rolled sections of spike fence from the sides of the second wagon. He had not seen a loper for three days, which meant to him that they were three days closer to their next trouble with the beasts. "Dora, if you feel up to it, you can give me a hand with this."

She made no comment on the fact that her husband had never before let her help erect the kraal; she simply worried about how drawn and tired he looked and thought about the quarter litre of water she had stolen and hidden – how could she persuade him to drink it?

They were just done when Fritz set up an excited yipping in the distance.

Minerva, it was a water hole – a trickle that came out of a rocky face, ran a couple of metres and formed a pool with no outlet. None that time of year, I should say, as I could see where it overflowed in flood season. I could see also plenty of animal sign – loper tracks and prairie goat and more that I could not identify. I had a feeling that there might be eyes on me, and I tried to grow eyes in the back of my head. It was dusky near the spring; trees and undergrowth were thicker and the Sun was getting low.

I was in a dilemma. I don't know how it happened that one of the free mules had not found this hole as soon or sooner than the dogs; mules can smell water. But mules were certain to be there soon, and I did not want them to drink too fast. Sensible as a mule is, he'll drink too fast and too much if he is very thirsty.

These mules were extremely thirsty; I wanted to watch each one myself, not let one founder.

Besides that I did not want them walking into that pool; it was clear, seemed clean.

The dogs finished drinking. I looked at Fritz and wished that he could talk as well as a mule. Did I have anything to write on? No, not a darn thing! If I told him to fetch Dora, Fritz would try – but would she come? I had told her flatly to stay in the kraal till I got back. Minerva, I wasn't thinking straight; the heat and no water had got to me. I should have given Dora contingency instructions . . . because if I stayed away too long and it started to get dark, she was going to come looking for me no matter what.

Hell, I hadn't even fetched a bucket!

In the meantime I at least had sense enough to scoop up and drink a couple of handfuls of water, Gideon style. That seemed to clear my head some.

I dropped the straps of my overalls, got my shirt off, soaked it in water, and gave it to Fritz. "Find Dora! Fetch Dora! *Fast!*" I think he thought I had gone nuts, but he left, carrying that wet shirt.

Then the first mule showed up – old Buck, praise Allah! – and I ruined a hat.

That hat Zack had fetched as a present for me. It was alleged to be an all-weather hat, so porous it would let air in, yet so water-repellent than it would keep your head dry in a pouring rain. The former allegation was only moderately true; the latter I had not had a chance to test.

Buck snorted and was all for going into the water up to his knees; I stopped him. Then I offered him a hatful of water. Then a second. And a third.

"Enough for now, Buck. Assembly. Water call."

With his throat wet Buck could do it. He let out a trumpeting bellow that was mule talk, not English, and I won't attempt to reproduce it, but it meant "Line up for water" and nothing else. "Fall in to be harnessed" was another sort of bellow.

Then I was trying to cope with a dozen-odd thirst-crazed mules. But between me, Buck, Beulah who was Buck's straw boss, Lady Macbeth who was used to helping Buck too – and a hat that wasn't quite all that waterproof – we made it. I never did learn how seniority was established among mules, but the mules knew and Buck enforced it and water call always found them queued up in the same order, and heaven help the youngster who tried crowd in out of turn; the least he could expect was a nipped ear.

By the time the last had been given a hatful of water my hat was a mess – but here came Dora with Fritz, her needle gun in her right fist, and, glory be! – two buckets in her left hand. "Water call!" I told my top sergeant. "Line 'em up again, Buck!"

With two buckets and two of us working we got a full bucket into each mule pretty rapidly. Then I got my shirt back from Fritz, scrubbed out the buckets a bit, filled them, and announced a third water call, telling Buck to let them drink from the pond.

He did so, but he still maintained discipline. As Dora and I left, each with a bucket of water in one hand and a drawn gun in the other, Buck was still requiring them to drink one at a time, by seniority.

It was nearly sundown when Dora and I and the dogs got back to the wagons, almost full dark as we finished watering goats and sow and cats and chickens. Then we celebrated. Minerva, I swear solemnly: On the half bucket of water we saved for ourselves Dora and I got stinkin' drunk.

Despite earlier resolutions not to stop short of the pass, we bivouacked there three days – but very useful days. The mules grazed steadily and filled out, plenty of water, plenty of forage. I shot a prairie goat at the water hole; what we couldn't eat, Dora sliced and dried as jerky. I filled all the barrels – not as easy as it sounds as Buck and I had to work out a route to the water hole, then I had to chop some, then I had to take the wagons in one at a time; it took me a day and a half.

But we had cooked fresh meat and all we could eat – and hot baths! With soap. With shampoos. With a shave for me. I carried Dora's big iron kettle to the pool, she fetched a bucket, I built a fire – then we took turns getting the stink off, one guarding while the other washed

When we rolled toward the pass the morning of the fourth day, we were not only in fine shape, but Dora and I smelled good and kept telling each other so, in high spirits.

We were never again short of water. There was snow somewhere above us; you could feel it in the breeze and sometimes catch a distant glimpse of white in a saddle between peaks. The higher we got, the oftener we encountered rivulets, water that never reached the prairie in so dry a year. The forage was green and good.

We stopped in a little alp close to the pass. There I left Dora with the wagons and the mules and with flat-footed instructions about what to do in case I did not come back. "I expect to be back by dark. If I am not, you can wait a week. No longer. Understand me?"

"I understand you."

"All right. At the end of a week, lighten the first wagon by chucking out anything you can do without on trek. Put all food into that wagon, empty the barrels in the second wagon and put them in the first wagon, turn the sow and the chickens loose, and head back. Fill all your barrels at that trickle we crossed earlier today. After that, don't stop for anything; roll all day from dawn till dark. You should reach Separation in half the time it took to get us up here. Okay?"

"No, sir."

Minerva, a few centuries earlier I would have started to boil up at that point. But I had learned. It took me about a tenth of a second to realize that I could not make her do anything – if I were gone – and that a promise made under duress won't hold. "All right, Dora, tell me why not and what you intend to do instead. If I don't like it, perhaps we both will start back for Separation."

"Woodrow, while you did not say so, you are asking me to do what I should do – and I *would* do! – if I were a widow."

I nodded. "Yes, that's right. Dearest, if I'm not back in a week, you're a widow. No possible doubt."

"I understand that. I also understand why you are leaving the wagons here; you can't be sure that you can turn them around higher up."

"Yes. That's probably what happened to earlier parties – reached a place where they couldn't go forward and couldn't turn around . . . then tried one or the other and went over."

"Yes. But, my husband, you mean to be gone only one day – half a day out, half a day back. Woodrow, I won't assume that you are dead – I *can't!*" She looked at me steadily and her eyes filled with tears, but she did not cry. "I must see your dear body, I must be certain. If I am certain, I will go back to Separation as fast and as safely as possible. And then to the Magees as you have told me, and have your child and bring him up to be as much like his father as possible. But I must *know*."

"Dora, Dora! In one week you *will* know. No need to look for my bones."

"May I finish, sir? If you aren't back tonight, I'm on my own. At dawn tomorrow I start out on Betty, with another saddle mule following. At noon I turn back.

"Perhaps, if I can't find you, I'll find a spot higher up where I can take one wagon and turn it around. If I find such a spot, I'll move one wagon up and use it as a base and look farther. I could have missed your track. Or I might have followed mule tracks – but you aren't on the mule. Whatever it is, I'll search and search again. Until there's no hope at all! *Then* . . . I will go to Separation as fast as mules can get me there.

"But, my darling, if you are alive – maybe with a broken leg but alive – if you still have a knife or even your bare hands, I don't believe that a loper or anything can kill you. If you are alive, I'll find you. I will!"

So I backed down and checked watches with her and agreed on what time I would turn back. Then Buck and I, with me up on Beulah, set out to scout ahead.

Minerva, at least four parties had tried that pass; none had come back. I'm certain enough that they each failed from being too eager, not patient enough, unwilling to turn back when the risk was too great.

Patience I have learned. The centuries may not give a man wisdom, but he acquires patience or he doesn't live through them. That first morning we found the first spot that was too tight. Oh, someone had blasted there and probably got around that turn. But it was too narrow to be safe, so I blasted some more. Nobody in his right mind takes a wagon into the mountains without dynamite or some such; you can't nibble at solid rock with a toothpick, or even a pickax, without risking being still up there when the snows come.

I was not using dynamite. Oh, anyone with a modicum of chemistry can make both dynamite and black powder, and I planned to do both – later. What I had with me was a more efficient and more flexible blasting jelly – and not shock-sensitive, perfectly safe in wagon and saddlebag.

I placed that first charge in a crack where I thought it would do the most good, set the fuse but did not light it, then walked both mules back around the bend and exerted my histrionic talent to its limit to explain to Buck and Beulah that there was going to be a loud noise, a *bang!* – but it could not hurt them, so don't worry. Then I went back, lit the fuse, hurried back to them and was in time to have an arm on each neck – watched my watch.

"Now!" I said, and the mountain obliged me with *Ka-boom!*

Beulah shivered but was steady. Buck said inquiringly, "*Paaang?*"

I agreed. He nodded and went back to cropping leaves.

We three went up and took a look. Nice and wide now – Not very level, but three tiny blasts took care of that. "What do you think, Buck?"

He looked carefully up and down trail. "Doo wagon?"

"One wagon."

"Ogay."

We explored a little farther, planned the next day's work; then I turned back at the time promised, was home early.

It took me a week to make a couple of kilometres safe to another little alp, a grassy pocket big enough to turn one wagon around at a time. Then it took all of a long day to move our wagons, one at a time, to this next base. Someone had made it that far; I found a broken wagon wheel – salvaged the steel tyre and the hub. It went on that way, day after day, slowly, tediously, and at last we were through the notch and headed – mostly – downhill.

But that was worse, not better. The river I had been sure was there, by photomaps from space, was far below us, and we still had to go down, down, down, and follow it a long way before we would reach the place where the gorge opened out into valley suitable for homesteading. More blasting, lots of brush chopping, and sometimes I had to blast trees. But the nastiest part was rappelling those wagons down the steepest places. I didn't mind steep places going uphill (which we still encountered); a twelve-mule team can drag a single wagon up any slope they can dig their hooves into. But downhill –

Certainly those wagons had brakes. But if the grade is steep, the wagon slides on its tyres – then goes over the edge, mules and all.

I couldn't let that happen even once. Not ever *risk* letting it happen. We could lose one wagon and six mules and still go on. But *I* was not expendable. (Dora would not be in the wagon.) If that wagon cut loose, my chances of jumping clear would be so-so.

If the grade was steep enough to give me even a trace of doubt that I could hold a wagon with its brakes, we did it the hard way: used that expensive imported line to check it down such pitches. Lead the line out fair and free for running, pass the bitter end three times around a tree stout enough to anchor it, secure it to the rear axle – then our four steadiest mules, Ken and Daisy, Beau and Belle, would take the wagon down at a slow walk (no driver) following Buck, while I kept tension on the line, paying it out very slowly.

If terrain permitted, Dora on Betty would take station halfway down to relay orders to Buck. But I could not permit her to be on the trail itself; if that line parted, it would whip. So maybe half the time Buck and I worked without liaison, doing it dead slow and depending on his judgement.

If there was not a sound anchor tree properly positioned – and it seems to me that this happened more often than not – then we had to wait while I worked something out. This could be anything: a sling between two trees, then rig a fairlead to a third tree – A bare-rock anchor using driven pitons – I hated these as I had to do my checking right at the rear axle, walking behind, and God help us all if I stumbled. Then that was always followed by the time-consuming chore of salvaging those pitons – the harder the rock, the better the anchor, but the tougher the job of getting them out – and I *had* to get them out; I would need them farther along.

Sometimes no trees and no rock – Once the anchor was twelve mules faced back along the trail, with Dora soothing them while I checked at a rear axle and Buck controlled the progress.

On the prairie we often made thirty kilometres a day. Once we were through Hopeless Pass and had started down the gorge the distance made good over the ground could be zero for days on end while I prepared the trail ahead, then up to as high as ten kilometres if there were no steep pitches that required rappelling down by line. I used just one unbreakable rule: The trail had to be fully prepared from one turnaround base to the next before a wagon was moved.

Minerva, it was so confounded slow that my "calendar" caught up with me; the sow littered – and we were not out of the mountains.

I don't recall ever making a harder decision. Dora was in good shape, but she was halfway through her pregnancy. Turn back (as I had promised myself, without telling her) – or push on and hope to reach lower and fairly level ground before she came to term? Which would be easier on her?

I had to consult her – but *I* had to decide. Responsibility *cannot* be shared. I knew how she would vote before I took the matter up with her: Push on.

But that would be simply her gallant courage; *I* was the one with experience both in wilderness trekking and in childbirth problems.

I studied those photomaps again without learning anything new. Somewhere ahead the gorge opened out into a broad river valley – but how far? I didn't know because I didn't know where we were. We had started with an odometer on the right rear wheel of the lead wagon; I had reset it to zero at the pass – and it had lasted only a day or two; a rock or something did it in. I didn't even know how much altitude we had managed to drop since the pass, or how much more we must lose to get down.

Livestock and equipment: fair. We had lost two mules. Pretty Girl had wandered over the edge one night and broken a leg; all I could do for her was to put her out of her misery. I didn't butcher her because we had fresh meat and I could not do it where the other mules could not see it, anyhow. John Barleycorn had simply upped and died one night – or possibly lost to a loper; he was partly eaten when we found him.

Three hens were dead and two piglets failed to make it, but the sow seemed willing to suckle the others.

I had only two spare wheels left. Lose two more and the next broken wheel meant abandoning one wagon.

It was the wheels that made up my mind.

(Omitted: approximately 7,000 words which reiterate difficulties in getting down the gorge.)

When we came out on that plateau, we could see the valley stretching out before us.

A *beautiful* valley, Minerva, wide and green and lovely – thousands and thousands of hectares of ideal farmland. The river from the gorge, tame now, meandered lazily between low banks. Facing us, a long, long way off, was a high peak crowned with snow. Its snow line let me guess how high it was – around six thousand metres, for we had now dropped down into subtropics, and only a very high mountain could keep so much snow through a long and very hot summer.

That beautiful mountain, that lush green valley, gave me a feeling of déjà vu. Then I placed it: Mount Hood in the land of my birth back on old Earth, as I had first seen it as a young man. But this valley, this snowcapped peak, had never before been seen by men.

I called out to Buck to halt the march. "Dorable, we're home. In sight of it, somewhere down in that valley."

" 'Home,' " she repeated. "Oh, my darling!"

"Don't sniffle."

"I wasn't sniffling!" she answered, sniffling. "But I've got an awful good cry saved up and when I get time to, I'm going to use it."

"All right, dear," I agreed, "when you have time. Let's name that mountain 'Dora Mountain.' "

She looked thoughtful. "No, that's not its name. That's Mount Hope. And all this below is Happy Valley."

"Durable Dora, you're incurably sentimental."

"You should talk!" She patted her belly, swollen almost to term. "That's Happy Valley because it's where I'm going to have this hungry little beast . . . and that's Mount Hope because it *is*."

Buck had come back to the first wagon and was waiting to find out why we had stopped. "Buck," I said, pointing, "that's home out there. We made it. Home, boy. Farm."

Buck looked out over the valley. "Ogay."

– in his sleep, Minerva. Not lopers, there wasn't a mark on Buck. Massive coronary, I think, although I didn't cut him open to find out. He was simply old and tired. Before we left, I had tried to put him to pasture with John Magee. But Buck didn't want that. We were his family, Dora and Beulah and I, and he wanted to come along. So I made him mule boss and didn't work him – I mean I never rode him and never had him in harness. He *did* work, as mule boss, and his patient good judgement got us safely to Happy Valley. We would not have made it without him.

Maybe he could have lived a few years longer turned out to pasture. Or he might have pined away from loneliness soon after we left. Who's to judge?

I didn't even consider butchering him; I think Dora would have miscarried if I had so much as broached the idea. But it is foolish to bury a mule when lopers and weather will soon take care of his carcass. So I buried him.

It takes an hellacious big hole to bury a mule; if it hadn't been soft river-bottom loam, I'd be there yet.

But first I had to deal with personnel problems. Ken was just junior to Beulah in the water queue and was a steady, strong mule who talked fairly well. On the other hand, Beulah had been

Buck's straw boss the whole trek – but I could not recall a gang of mules bossed by a mare.

Minerva, with H. sapiens this would not matter, at least not today on Secundus. But with some sorts of animals it *does* matter. A boss elephant is female. A boss chicken is a cock, not a hen. A boss dog can be either sex. In a breed where sex controls the matter a man had better by a damn sight go along with their ways.

I decided to see if Beulah could swing it, so I told her to line 'em up for harness, both as a test and because I wanted to move the mules out of sight while I buried Buck – they were nervy and restless; the boss mule's death had upset them. I don't know what mules think about death, but they are not indifferent to it.

She promptly got busy, and I kept an eye on Kenny. He accepted it, took his usual place by Daisy. Once I had them harnessed, Beulah was the only one left over, three mules dead now.

I told Dora that I wanted them moved a few hundred metres away. Would she handle it, with Beulah as march boss? Or would she feel safer if I did it? – and ran into a second problem: Dora wanted to be present when I buried Buck. More than that – "Woodrow, I can help dig. Buck was my friend, too, you know."

I said, "Dora, I'll put up with anything at all from a pregnant woman except allowing her to do something that would hurt her."

"But, dearest, I feel okay, physically – it's just that I'm dreadfully upset over Buck. So I want to help."

"I think you are in good shape, too, and I want you to stay that way. You can help best by staying in the wagon. Dora, I haven't any way to take care of a premature baby, and I don't want to have to bury a baby as well as Buck."

Her eyes widened. "You think that would happen?"

"Sweetheart, I don't know. I've known women to hang onto babies under unbelievable hardships. I've seen others lose babies for no reason that I could see. The only rule I have about it is: Don't take unnecessary chances. This one is not necessary."

So once again we replanned things to suit both of us, though it took an extra hour. I unshackled the second wagon and set up the fence again, put the four goats inside the fence, and left Dora in that wagon. Then I drove the first wagon three or four hundred metres away, unharnessed the mules, and told Beulah to keep them together – and told Ken to help her, and left Fritz to help her, too, and took Lady Mac back with me to watch for lopers or whatever. The visibility was good – no brush, no high grass; the place looked like a tended park. But I was going to be down in a hole; I didn't want something sneaking up on me or on the wagon. "Lady Macbeth. High sentry. *Up!*"

By agreement Dora stayed in the wagon.

It took all that day to take care of our old friend, with a stop for lunch and a few short breaks for water and to catch my breath in the shade of the wagon – breaks I shared with Lady Mac, letting her get down each time I came up. Plus one interruption –

It was midafternoon and I had dug almost enough hole when Lady Mac barked for me. I was up out of that hole fast, blaster in hand, expecting lopers.

Just a dragon –

I wasn't especially surprised, Minerva; the well-cropped state of the turf, almost like a lawn, seemed to indicate dragon rather than prairie goat. Those dragons are not dangerous unless one happens to fall on you. They are slow, stupid, and strictly vegetarian. Oh, they're ugly enough to be frightening; they look like six-legged triceratops. But that's all. Lopers left them alone because biting armour is unrewarding.

I joined Dora at the wagon. "Ever seen one, hon?"

"Not up close. Goodness, it's *huge*."

"It's a big one, all right. But it will probably turn away. I won't waste a charge on it if I don't have to."

But the durned thing did not turn away. Minerva, I think it was so stupid that it mistook the wagon for a lady dragon. Or the other way around, it is hard to tell male from female. But they are definitely bisexual; two dragons humping is a remarkable sight.

When it got within a hundred metres, I let myself out the fence and took Lady Mac along, as she was quiveringly eager. I doubt if she had ever seen one; they were cleaned out around Top Dollar long before she was whelped. She danced up to it, barking but wary.

I hoped that Lady would cause it to turn aside, but this misshapen rhinoceros paid no attention; it lumbered slowly along, straight for the wagon. So I tickled it with my needle gun between where it should have had lips, to get its attention. It stopped, astounded I think, and opened its mouth wide. That was what I needed, as I did not want to waste maximum power blasting through that armoured hide. So – Blaster at minimum, right into its mouth: Scratch one dragon.

It stood there a moment, then slowly collapsed. I called Lady and went back to the fence. Dora was waiting. "May I go look at it?"

I glanced at the Sun. "Sweetheart, I'm going to be pushed to take care of Buck before dark, then fetch the mules back and move us on a way. Unless you are willing to bivouac with the grave on one side and a dead dragon on the other?"

She did not insist, and I got back to work. In another hour I had it deep enough and wide enough – got out block and-tackle, a triple purchase, secured it to the rear axle, tied Buck's hind feet together, hooked over the tie and took up the slack.

Dora had come out with me. "Just a moment, dear." She stopped to pat Buck's neck, then leaned down and kissed his forehead. "All right, Woodrow. Now."

I heaved on the line. For a moment I thought the wagon would move despite the brakes being locked. Then Buck started to slide, and fell into his grave. I shook the hook loose, then back-filled fast, closing in twenty minutes a hole it had taken me most of the day to dig. Dora waited.

I finished. "Up into the wagon, Dorable; that's it."

"Lazarus, I wish I knew something to say. Do you?"

I thought about it. I had heard a thousand burial services; most of them I did not like. So I made up one. "Whatever God there be, please take care of this fine person. He always did his best. Amen."

(Omitted)

– even those first years weren't too hard, as Happy Valley would grow anything, two and three crops a year. But we should have named it "Dragon Valley."

Lopers were bad enough, especially the small lopers that hunted in packs which we found on that side of Rampart Range. But those damned dragons! They almost drove me out of my skull. When you've lost the same potato patch four times running, it begins to wear.

Lopers I could poison and did. I could trap them, too, if I changed style every time. Or I could put out bait at night and sit quietly and get most of a pack, silently, with a needle gun. I could do lots of things and did, and the mules learned to cope with them, too, sleeping closer together at night and always with one on watch, like quail or baboon. Whenever I heard the bellow the meant "*Loper!*" I always came awake fast and tried to join the fun – but the mules rarely left me any; they not only could stomp them, but they could outrun them and get some or all of a pack that tried to escape. We lost three mules and six goats to lopers, but the lopers got the news and started giving us a wide berth.

But those dragons! Too big to trap and would not take poison; salad was all they were after. But what one dragon can do to a cornfield in one night shouldn't happen to Sodom and Gomorrah. Bow-and-arrow was futile against them, and a needle gun just tickled them. I could kill one with a blaster, full power right through the armour, or minimum power the way I got that first one if I could get my target to open its mouth. But, unlike lopers, they were too stupid to stay away when they were losing.

The first summer I was able to farm I killed more than a hundred dragons in trying to save my crops . . . which was a defeat for me and a victory for the dragons. Not only was the stench terrible (what can you do with a carcass that big?), but, far worse, I was running out of charges and they didn't seem to be running out of dragons.

No power. Buck's River did not have enough head on it where we settled to think about trying to build a water wheel, even if I cannibalized one wagon to build it. The windmill I had fetched was in fact nothing but gears and other hardware; the mill itself I would have to build, from sails to tower. But until I had power I had no way to recharge power packs.

Dora solved it. We were still living in that first compound, nothing but a high adobe wall just big enough to surround the wagons and to bring the goats inside at night, while we slept in the first wagon along with baby Zack and cooked in a clay Dutch oven – and between smoke and goats and chickens and the sour smells babies can't help making and the cesspit that had to be inside the wall – well, the stench of dead dragons wasn't too noticeable.

We were finishing supper, Dora dressed in her rubies as always for supper, and were watching the moons and the stars coming out – best time of day, always, except that when I should have been admiring our firstborn at suck and enjoying the sky, I was grousing about power and what in hell I could do about those pesky dragons.

I had ticked off several simple ways to produce power – simple if you are on a civilized planet or even at a place like New Pittsburgh with its coal and its infant metals industry – when I happened to use a very old-fashioned term. Instead of talking, about kilowatts or megadynecentimetres per second or such I had remarked that I would settle for ten horsepower any way I could get it.

Dora had never seen a horse, but she knew what one was. She said, "Beloved, wouldn't ten mules do instead?"

(Omitted)

We had been in our valley seven years when the first wagon showed up. Young Zack was nearly seven and beginning to be some help to me – or thought he was and I encouraged him to try. Andy was five, and Helen not yet four. We had lost Persephone, and Dora was pregnant again, and that was why – Dora had insisted on starting another baby at once, not wait one day, one hour – and she was right. Once we knew she had caught, our morale picked up overnight. We missed Persephone; she had been a darling baby. But we stopped grieving and looked forward instead. I hoped for another girl but was willing to settle for any baby – no way to control the sex of a child, then and there.

All in all, we were in fine shape, with a prosperous farm, a healthy, happy family, plenty of livestock, a much larger compound with a house built right into it against the back wall, a windmill that drove a saw, or ground grain, or supplied power for my blaster.

When I spotted that wagon, my first thought was that it was going to be nice to have neighbours. But my second thought was that I was going to be proud, very proud, to show off my fine family and our farm to these newcomers.

Dora climbed up to the roof and watched the wagon with me; it was still over fifteen kilometres away, could not arrive before evening. I put my arm around her. "Excited, hon?"

"Yes. Though I've never been lonely; you haven't let me be. How many do you think I should expect for supper?"

"Hmm – Only one wagon. One family. My best guess is a couple, with none, one, or two children. More than that would surprise me."

"Me too, darling, but there'll be plenty to eat."

"And put some clothes on our kids before they get here – wouldn't want 'em to guess we're raising savages, would we?"

She answered, deadpan, "Shall I wear clothes, too?"

"What swank! That's up to you, Rangy Lil – but who was it said just last month that she had never worn her party dress?"

"Will you be wearing a kilt, Lazarus?"

"I might. I might even take a bath. I'll need one because I'm going to spend the rest of the day cleaning the goat compound and a lot of other things – make this place look as neat as possible. But forget the name 'Lazarus,' dear; I'm Bill Smith again."

"I'll remember – Bill. I'll bathe before they get here, too – because I'm going to have a hot and busy time, cooking, cleaning house, bathing our children, and trying to teach them how to be introduced to strangers. They've never seen anyone else, dear; I'm not sure they believe there *is* anyone else."

"They'll behave." I was sure they would. Dora and I had the same ideas about raising kids. Praise them, never scream at them, punish as necessary and right *now* – never a moment's delay – then it's over with and forget it. Be as lavish with affection after a spanking as any other time – or a bit extra. Spanking they had to have (Dora usually used a switch) because, without exception over the centuries, my kids have been hell-raisers who would take advantage of the sweetness-and-light routine. Some of my wives had trouble believing what little monsters I spawn – but Dora was right with me on this wild-animal act from scratch. In consequence she raised the most civilized brood I've ever fathered.

When that wagon was maybe a kilometre away, I rode out to meet them – then was surprised and disappointed. A family, yes, if you count a man and two grown sons as a family. No women, no children. I wondered how they thought they were going to pioneer.

The younger son was not fully grown; his beard was sparse and scraggly. Nevertheless, he was taller and heavier than I was, and he was the smallest of the three. His father and brother were mounted; he was driving – actually driving; they were not using a mule boss. No livestock other than mules that I could see, although I did not attempt to look into their wagon.

I did not like their looks and reversed my idea about neighbours. I hoped they would move on down the valley, at least fifty kilometres.

The mounted two were carrying guns at their belts – reasonable in loper country. I had a needle gun in sight myself, as well as a belt knife – and maybe other things not in sight, as I don't consider it diplomatic to show much hardware in meeting strangers.

As I approached, they stopped, the driver reining up his mules.

I had Beulah stop about ten paces short of the lead pair. "Howdy," I said. "Welcome to Happy Valley. I'm Bill Smith."

The oldest of the three looked me up and down. It is hard to tell a man's expression when he wears a full beard, but what little I could see was no expression at all – wariness, perhaps. My own face was smooth – freshly shaved and clean overalls, in honour of visitors. I was keeping my face smooth both because Dora preferred it so and because I was staying "young" to match Dora. I was wearing my best friendly look – but was saying to myself, "You've got ten seconds to answer my greeting and say who you are – or you're going to miss some of the best cooking on New Beginnings."

He just slid under the deadline; I had silently counted seven chimpanzees when he suddenly grinned through that face moss. "Why, that's mighty friendly of you, young man."

"Bill Smith," I repeated, "and I didn't catch your name."

"Probably because I didn't say," he answered. "Name's Montgomery. 'Monty' to my friends, and I don't have any enemies, at least not for long. Right, Darby?"

"Right, Pop," agreed the other mounted one.

"And this is my son Darby and that's Dan driving the jugheads. Say 'Howdy,' boys."

"Howdy," they each answered.

"Howdy, Darby. Howdy, Dan. Monty, is Mrs. Montgomery with you?" I nodded at the wagon, still did not attempt to see into it – a man's wagon is as private as his house.

"Now why would you be asking that?"

"Because," I said, still holding onto my friendly-idiot look, "I want to trot back to the house and tell Mrs. Smith how many there'll be for supper."

"Well! Did you hear that, boys? We've been invited to supper. That's mighty friendly, too. Isn't it, Dan?"

"Right, Pop."

"And we most kindly accept. Don't we, Darby?"

"Right, Pop."

I was getting tired of the echo, but I kept my sweet expression. "Monty, you still haven't told me how *many*."

"Oh. Just three. But we eat enough for six." He slapped his thigh and laughed at his own joke. "Right, Dan?"

"Right, Pop."

"So you stir up those jugheads, Dan; we've got reason to hurry now."

I interrupted the echo to say, "Hold it, Monty. No need to overheat your mules."

"What? They're my mules, son."

"So they are and do as you please about them, but I was sent out ahead so that Mrs. Smith would have time to be ready for you. I see you're wearing a watch" – I glanced at my own – "your hostess will expect you in one hour. Unless you need more time to get there and unharness and water your mules?"

"Oh, them jugheads will keep until after supper. If we're early, we'll set awhile."

"No," I said firmly. "One hour, no sooner. You know how a lady feels about guests arriving before she's ready for them. Crowd her, and she might ruin your supper. Do as you please about your mules – but there is an easy place to water them, a little beach, where the river comes closest to the house. Nice place to spruce up a bit yourself, too – before dining with a lady. But don't come up to the house short of one hour."

"Your wife sounds mighty particular . . . for way out here in the wilds."

"She is," I answered. "Home, Beulah."

I moved from a trot into Beulah's fast lope and did not get over an uneasy feeling between my shoulder blades until I was certain I was too far away to be a target. There is only one dangerous animal, yet at times you're forced to pretend that he's as sweet and innocent as a cobra.

I didn't stop to unsaddle Beulah; I hurried inside. Dora heard my slam-bang arrival, was at the compound's door. "What is it, dear? Trouble?"

"Could be. Three men, I don't like them. Nevertheless, I've promised them supper. Have the kids eaten? Can we put them right to bed and convince them that if they so much as let out a peep, they'll be flayed alive? I didn't mention children, we aren't going to mention them, and I'm going to take a fast look around to make sure there is nothing in sight that says 'kids.'"

"I'll try. Yes, I've fed them."

Right on the hour Lazarus Long met his guests at the door of the compound. They drove and rode up from the direction of the beach he had described, so he assumed that they had watered their animals, but he noted with mild scorn that they now did not bother to unharness their team for what was sure to be a long wait. But he was pleased to note that all three Montgomerys had made some effort to spruce up – perhaps they were going to behave; perhaps his sixth sense for trouble was hypersensitive from too long in the wilderness.

Lazarus was dressed in his best – kilt with full kit save that the effect was marred by a faded work shirt of New Pittsburgh origin. But it was indeed his best, worn only for children's birthdays. On other days he wore anything from overalls to skin, depending on work and weather.

After Montgomery dismounted, he paused and looked over his host. "My, aren't we fancy!"

"In your honour, gentlemen. I save it for very special occasions."

"So? It's mighty nice of you to honour us, Red. Isn't it, Dan?"

"Right, Pop."

"My name is Bill, Monty. Not 'Red.' You can leave your guns in your wagon."

"Well! Now that's not very friendly. We always wear our guns. Don't we, Darby?"

"Right, Pop. And if Pop says your name is 'Red,' that's your name."

"Now, now, Darby, I didn't say *that*. If Red wants to call himself Tom, Dick, or Harry, that's his choice. But we wouldn't feel dressed without our guns, and that's the truth, uh, Bill. Why, I even wear mine to bed. Out here."

Lazarus was standing in the opened door of the compound. He made no move to step aside and let his visitors in. "That's a reasonable precaution . . . on the trail. But gentlemen don't wear arms when they dine with a lady. Drop them here or put them in your wagon, whichever you wish."

Lazarus could feel the tension grow, could see the younger two watching their father for instructions. Lazarus ignored them and kept his easy smile on Montgomery, while forcing his muscles to stay loose as cotton. Right now? Would the bear back off? Or treat it as a challenge?

Montgomery split his face in his widest grin. "Why, sure, neighbour – if that's how you want it. Shall I take off my pants, too?"

"Just your guns, sir." (He's right-handed. If I were right-handed and wearing what you are wearing, where would my second gun be? There, I think – but, if so, it must be small . . . either a needle gun or possibly an old-fashioned snub-nosed assassin's gun. Are his sons both right-handed?)

The Montgomerys put their gun belts on the seat of their wagon, came back. Lazarus stood aside and welcomed them in, then slid the bar into place as he closed the door. Dora was waiting, dressed in her "party dress." For the first time since a very hot day on the prairie she did not wear her rubies at the evening meal.

"Dear, this is Mr. Montgomery and his sons, Darby and Dan. My wife, Mrs. Smith."

Dora bobbed a curtsy. "Welcome, Mr. Montgomery, and Darby, and Dan."

"Call me 'Monty,' Mrs. Smith – and what's your name? Mighty pretty place you've got here . . . for so far out in the country."

"If you gentlemen will excuse me, I have a couple of things to do to get supper onto the table." She turned quickly and hurried back into her kitchen.

Lazarus answered, "I'm glad you like it, Monty. It's the best we've been able to do so far, while getting a farm started." The back wall of the compound had four rooms built against it: storeroom, kitchen, bedroom, and nursery. All had doors into the compound, but only the kitchen door was open. The rooms interconnected.

Outside the kitchen door was a Dutch oven; in the kitchen was a fireplace used for other cooking and for all cooking when it rained. That and a water barrel were as yet Dora's major kitchen equipment – but her husband had promised her running water "sometime before you are a grandmother, my lovely." She had not pressed him about it; the house grew larger and better equipped each year.

Beyond the Dutch oven and paralleling the bedrooms was a long table with matching stools. At the other wall by the storeroom was an outhouse; it and a water barrel and two wooden tubs made by cutting another barrel in two constituted, so far, their "bathroom-toilet-refresher." A pile of earth with a shovel stuck into it was by the outhouse; the cesspit was being slowly backfilled.

"You've done pretty well," Montgomery conceded. "But you shouldn't have put your privy inside. Don't you know that?"

"There is another privy outside," Lazarus Long told him. "We use this one as little as possible and I try to keep it from being too whiff. But you can't expect a woman to go outside after dark, not in loper country."

"Lots of lopers, eh?"

"Not as many as there used to be. Did you see any dragons as you came through the valley?"

"Saw a lot of bones. Looked like a plague had hit the dragons hereabouts."

"Something of the sort," Lazarus agreed. "Lady! *Heel!*" He added, "Monty, tell Darby that it's not safe to kick at that dog; she'll attack. She's a watchdog, in charge of this house, and she knows it."

"You heard what the man said, Darby. Leave the dog alone."

"Then she had better not come sniffing around me! I don't like dogs. She growled at me."

Lazarus said directly to the older son, "She growled because you kicked at her when she sniffed you. Which was her duty. If I had not been present, she would have taken your throat out. Leave her alone and she'll leave you alone."

Montgomery said, "Bill, you had better put her outside while we eat." Phrased as a suggestion, it was made to sound like an order.

"No."

"Gentlemen, supper is served."

"Coming, dear. Lady. High sentry." The bitch glanced at Darby but immediately trotted up the ladder to the roof, using the rungs without hesitation. There she made a careful full-circle scan before sitting down where she could watch both outside and the supper party below her.

The supper party was more successful as a supper than as a party. Conversation was limited mostly to small talk between the two older men. Darby and Dan simply ate. Dora answered briefly sallies that Montgomery made at her and failed to hear any that she regarded as too personal. The sons seemed surprised to find their plates set each with knife, fork, chop tongs, and spoon, then relied mostly on knife and fingers; their father made some effort to use each eating tool, getting quite a bit of food into his beard.

Dora had piled the table with hot fried chicken, cold sliced ham, mashed potatoes and chicken gravy, hot corn pone and cold whole wheat bread with bacon drippings, a mug of goat's milk at each place, lettuce-and-tomato salad with grated goat's-cheese-and-onion dressing, boiled beets, fresh radishes, fresh strawberries with goat's milk. As promised, the Montgomerys ate for six, and Dora was pleased that she had provided a plenty.

At last Montgomery pushed back his stool and belched appreciatively. "My, that hit the spot! Miz Smith, you can cook for us all the time. Right, Dan?"

"Right, Pop!"

"I'm pleased that you enjoyed it, gentlemen." She stood up and started to clear the table. Lazarus stood and started to help her.

Montgomery said, "Oh, sit down, Bill. Want to ask you some questions."

"Go ahead and ask," Lazarus said, continuing to stack plates.

"You said there was no one else in the valley."

"That is correct."

"Then I think we'll stay right here. Miz Smith is a very good cook."

"You're welcome to camp here overnight. Then you'll find excellent farmland farther down the river. As I told you, I've homesteaded all of this."

"Been meaning to talk to you about that. Doesn't seem right for one man to grab all the best land."

"It isn't the best land, Monty; there are thousands of hectares just as good. The only difference is that I've ploughed and cultivated this part."

"Well, we won't argue about it. We outvote you. Four voting, I mean, and us three all voting the same way. Right, Darby?"

"Right, Pop."

"It's not subject to vote, Monty."

"Oh, come now! The majority is always right. But we won't argue. Been a nice feed, now for some entertainment. Do you like to rassle?"

"Not especially."

"Don't be a spoilsport. Dan, do you think you can throw him?"

"Sure, Pop."

"Good. Bill, first you rassle Dan – out here in the middle and I'll referee, keep everything fair and square."

"Monty, I'm not going to wrestle."

"Oh, sure you are. Miz *Smith!* Better come out here, you won't want to miss this."

"I'm busy now," Dora called out. "I'll be out shortly."

"Better hurry. Then you rassle Darby, Bill – then you rassle *me*."

"No wrestling, Monty. Time for you folks to get into your wagon."

"But you *want* to rassle, young fellow. I didn't tell you what the prize is. The winner sleeps with Miz Smith." His second gun appeared as he said it. "Fooled you, didn't I?"

From the kitchen Dora shot the gun out of his hand just as a knife suddenly grew in Dan's neck. Lazarus shot Montgomery carefully in the leg, then even more carefully shot Darby – as Lady Macbeth was at his throat. The fight had lasted under two seconds.

"Lady. Heel. Nice shooting, Dorable." He patted Lady Macbeth. "*Good* Lady, *good* dog."

"Thank you, darling. Shall I finish off Monty?"

"Wait a moment." Lazarus stepped over and looked down at the wounded man. "Got anything to say, Montgomery?"

"You bastards! Never gave us a chance."

"Gave you lots of chance. You wouldn't take it. Dora? Do you want to? Your privilege."

"Not especially."

"All right." Lazarus picked up Montgomery's second gun, noted that it was indeed a museum piece but did not seem to be hurt. He used it to finish off its owner.

Dora was peeling off her dress. "Half a moment, dear, while I get this off; I don't want to get blood on it." With the dress out of the way, her pregnant condition showed a little. She also showed several other weapons as well as a gun belt riding low on her hips.

Lazarus was getting out of his kilt and other finery. "You don't need to help, sweetheart; you've done a full day's work – and a fine one! Just toss me my oldest overalls."

"But I *want* to help. What are you going to do with them?"

"Put them into their wagon, take them far enough downriver that lopers will dispose of them, drive back." He glanced at the Sun. "An hour and more of daylight left. Time enough."

"Lazarus, I don't want you away from me! Not now."

"Upset by it, my durable one?"

"Some. Not much. Uh . . . made horny by it, I'm ashamed to say. Perverted, huh?"

"Rangy Lil, *anything* makes you horny. Yes, it's somewhat perverse . . . but a surprisingly common reaction to one's first encounter with death. Nothing to be ashamed of as long as you don't get hooked by it; it's just a reflex. On second thought never mind the overalls; I can scrub blood off my hide easier than getting it out of cloth." He removed the bar and opened the gate as he talked.

"I've seen death before. I was much more upset when Aunt Helen died . . . and not a bit horny."

"Violent death, I should have said. Dear, I want to get these bodies outside the wall before any more blood soaks into the ground. We can discuss it later."

"You'll need help loading them. And I *don't* want to be away from you, truly I don't."

Lazarus stopped and looked at her. "You're more upset than you let on. That's common, too – steady in the clutch, then a reaction afterwards. So let's work it out. I don't fancy leaving the kids alone that long, nor do I want them in a wagon loaded with all that bad meat. Suppose I drive just a short distance tonight – say three hundred metres or so – while you start a kettle of water? I'm going to want another bath after this job even if I manage not to get a drop of blood on me."

"Yes, sir."

"Dora, you don't sound happy."

"I'll do it your way. But I could wake Zaccur and have him baby-sit. He's used to it."

"Very well, dear. But first we load them. You can hold up their feet while I drag them. If you throw up, I'll assume that you'll baby-sit while I finish this chore."

"I won't throw up. I ate very little."

"I didn't eat much either." They got on with the grisly task; Lazarus continued to talk. "Dora, you did a perfect job."

"I caught your signal. You gave me plenty of time."

"I wasn't sure he was going to push it to a showdown even when I signalled."

"Really, dear? I knew what they meant to do – kill you and rape me – before they ever sat down to eat. Couldn't you feel it? So I made sure that they ate plenty – to slow them down."

"Dora, you really do sense emotions – don't you?"

"Mind his head, dear. When they're as strong as that, I do. But I wasn't sure how you would handle it. I made up my mind to be raped all night if that was what it took for you to set up a safe chance."

Her husband answered soberly, "Dora, I will allow you to be raped only if that is the only possible way to save your life. Tonight it was not necessary. Thank goodness! But Montgomery had me worried at the gate. Three guns out in the open and mine still under my kilt – Could have been a problem. Since he meant to take me anyhow, he should have done it then. Durable, three-fourths of any fight lies in not hesitating when the time comes. Which is why I'm so proud of you."

"But you set it up, Lazarus. You signalled me to get into position, you stayed on your feet when he told you to sit down, you went around to the end of the table and pulled their eyes with you – and stayed out of my line of fire. Thank you. All I had to do was shoot when he got out his gun."

"Of course I stayed out of your line of fire, dear; this isn't my first time by too many. But it was your straight shooting that gave me time to put my knife into Dan instead of having to settle his father first. And Lady did me the same favour with Darby. You two girls saved me from having to be three places at once. Which I've always found difficult."

"You trained both of us."

"Mmm, yes. Which detracts not at all from the admirable fact that you held your fire until he committed himself – then lost not a split second in taking him. As if you were a veteran of a hundred gun battles rather than none. You might go around and steady the mules while I get this tailgate open."

"Yes, dear."

She had just reached the lead pair and spoken soothingly to them when he called out: "Dora! Here a minute."

She came back; he said, "Look at *that*."

It was a flat piece of sandstone he had removed from the end of the wagon bed and laid on the ground by the corpses. It was carved with:

BUCK
BORN ON EARTH
3031 A.D.
DIED ON THIS SPOT
N.B. 37
He Always Did His Best

She said, "Lazarus, I don't understand it. I can understand why they intended to rape me – I'm probably the first woman they've seen in many weeks. I can even understand that they would kill you, or do anything, to get at me. But *why* would they steal this?"

"It's not exactly 'why,' dear . . . People who don't respect other people's property will do *anything*. . . and will steal anything that's not nailed down. Even if they have no use for it." He added, "Had I known this earlier, I would have given them *no* chance. Such people should be destroyed on sight. The problem is to identify them."

Minerva, Dora is the only woman I ever loved unreservedly. I don't know that I can explain why. I did not love her that way when I married her; she had not had a chance as yet to teach me what love can be. Oh, I did love her, but it was the love of a doting father for a favourite child or somewhat like the love one can lavish on a pet.

I decided to marry her not through love in any deepest sense but simply because this adorable child who had given me so many hours of happiness wanted something very badly – my child – and there was only one way I could give her what she wanted and still please my own self-love. So, almost coldly, I calculated the cost and decided that the price was low enough that I could let her have what she wanted. It could not cost me much; she was an ephemeral. Fifty, sixty, seventy, at the most eighty years, and she would be dead. I could afford to spend that trivial amount of time to make my adopted daughter's pitifully short life happy – that's how I figured it. It wasn't much, and I could afford it. So be it.

All the rest was just a case of no half measures; do whatever else is necessary to your main purpose. I told you some of the possibilities; I may not have mentioned that I considered taking back the captaincy of the *Andy J.* for Dora's lifetime, have Zaccur Briggs take the ground side of the partnership or buy him out if that didn't suit him. But while eighty-odd years in a starship would not stonker me, to Dora it would be a lifetime and it might not suit her. Besides, a ship is not an ideal place to raise kids – what do you do when they grow up? Drop them off somewhere not knowing anything but ship's routine? Not good.

I decided that the husband of an ephemeral had to *be* an ephemeral, in every way possible to him. The corollaries to that decision caused us to wind up in Happy Valley.

Happy Valley – The happiest of all my lives. The longer I was privileged to live with Dora, the more I loved her. She taught me to love by loving me, and I learned – rather slowly; I wasn't too good a pupil, being set in my ways and lacking her natural talent. But I did learn. Learned that supreme happiness lies in wanting to keep another person safe and warm and happy, and being privileged to try.

And the saddest, too. The more thoroughly I learned this – through living day on day with Dora – the happier I was . . . and the more I ached in one corner of my mind with certain knowledge that this could be only a brief time too soon over – and when it *was* over, I did not marry again for almost a hundred years. Then I did, for Dora taught me to face up to death, too. She was as aware of her own death, of the certain briefness of her life, as I was. But she taught me to live *now*, not to let anything sully *today* . . . until at last I got over the sadness of being condemned to live.

We had a wonderfully good time! Working our arses off, always too much to do, and enjoying every minute. Never too rushed to enjoy life no matter what. Sometimes just pat-ass and squeeze-titty as I hurried through the kitchen, with her quick smile acknowledging it, sometimes a lazy hour on the roof invested in watching sunset and stars and moons, usually with "Eros" to make it sweeter.

I guess you could say that sex was our only active amusement for a number of years (and never stopped being in first place as Dora was as enthusiastic at seventy as at seventeen – just not as limber). I was usually too tired to play good chess even though I made us a set of chessmen; we had no other games and probably would not have played them anyhow – too busy. Oh, we did do other things; often one of us would read aloud while the other knitted or cooked or something. Or we would sing together, coonjining the rhythm while we pitched grain or manure.

We worked together as much as possible; division of labour came only from natural limits. I can't bear a baby or suckle it, but I can do anything else for a child. Dora could not do some things that I did because they were too heavy for her, especially when she was far gone in pregnancy. She had more talent for cooking than I (I had centuries more experience but not her touch), and she could cook while she took care of a baby and tended the smallest children, ones too small to join me in the fields. But I did cook, especially breakfast while she got the kids organized, and she did help work the farm and especially the truck garden. She knew nothing of farming; she learned.

Nor did she know construction – she learned. While I did most of the high work, she made most of the adobe bricks, always with the right amount of straw. Adobe was not well suited to the climate – too much rain and it can be discouraging to see a wall start to melt because an unexpected rain has caught you before you've topped it.

But you build from what you have, and it helped that I had the tops from the wagons to peg against the most exposed walls, until I worked out a way to waterproof an adobe wall. I did not consider a log cabin; good timber was too far away. It took the mules and me a full day to bring in two logs, which made them too expensive for most construction. Instead, I made do with smaller stuff that grew along the banks of Buck's River and dragged in logs only for beams.

Nor did I want to build a house that was not as near fireproof as I could make it. Baby Dora had once almost been burned to death; I would not risk it again for Dora, or for her children.

But how to make a roof both watertight and fireproof nearly stumped me.

I walked past the answer hundreds of times before I recognized it. When wind and weather and rot and lopers and insects have done their worst on a dead dragon, what is left is almost indestructible. I discovered this when I tried to burn what was left of a big brute that was unpleasantly close to our compound. I never did find out why this was so. Perhaps the biochemistry of those dragons has been investigated since then, but I had neither equipment nor time nor interest; I was too busy scratching a living for my family and was simply delighted to learn that it was true. Belly hide I cut into fireproof, waterproof tarpaulins; back and sides made excellent roofing. Later I found many uses for the bones.

We both taught school, indoors and out. Perhaps our kids had a weird education . . . but a girl who can shape a comfortable and handsome saddle starting with a dead mule and not much else, solve quadratics in her head, shoot straight with gun or arrow, cook an omelet that is light and tasty, spout page after page of Shakespeare, butcher a hog and cure it can't be called ignorant by New Beginnings standards. All our girls and boys could do all of that and more. I must admit that they spoke a rather florid brand of English, especially after they set up the New Globe Theatre and worked straight through every one of old Bill's plays. No doubt this gave them odd notions of Odd Earth's culture and history, but I could not see that it hurt them. We had only a few bound books, mostly reference; the dozen-odd "fun" books were worked to death.

Our kids saw nothing strange in learning to read from *As You Like It*. No one told them that it was too hard for them, and they ate it up, finding "tongues in trees, books in the running brooks, sermons in stones, and good in every thing."

Although it did sound odd to hear a five-year-old girl speak in scansion and rolling periods, polysyllables falling gracefully from her baby lips. Still, I preferred it to "Run, Spot, run. See Spot run" from a later era than Bill's.

Second only to Shakespeare in popularity, and first whenever Dora was swelling up again, were my medical books, especially those on anatomy, obstetrics, and gynecology. Any birth was an event – kittens, piglets, foals, puppies, kids – but a new baby out of Dora was a super-event, one that always put more thumbprints on that standard OB illustration, a cross section of mother and baby at term. I finally removed that one and several plates that followed it, those showing normal delivery, and posted them, to save wear and tear on my books – then announced that they could look at those pictures all they wanted to, but that to touch one was a spanking offense – then was forced to spank Iseult to keep justive even, which hurt her old father far more than it did her baby bottom even though she saved my face by applauding my gentle paddling with loud screams and tears.

My medical books had one odd effect. Our kids knew from babyhood all the correct English monosyllables for human anatomy and function; Helen Mayberry had never used slang with Baby Dora; Dora spoke as correctly in front of her children. But once they could read my books, intellectual snobbery set in; they *loved* those Latin polysyllables. If I said "womb" (as I always did), some six-year-old would inform me with quiet authority that the *book* said "uterus." Or Undine might rush in with the news that Big Billy Whiskers was "copulating" with Silky, whereupon the kids would rush out to the goat pen to watch. Somewhere around their middle teens they usually recovered from this nonsense and went back to speaking English as their parents spoke it, so I guess it didn't hurt them.

The reason my own goatiness was not a spectator sport for children that all the animals afforded was, I think, only my own unreasoned but long-standing habits. I don't think it would have fretted Dora because it did not seem to fret her the times it happened – as it did; privacy was scarce and got scarcer until I got our big house built some twelve or thirteen years after we entered the valley – time indefinite because for years I worked on it when I could; then we moved into it unfinished because we were bulging the walls of our first house and another baby (Ginny) was on the way.

Dora was untroubled by lack of privacy because her sweet lechery was utterly innocent, whereas mine was scarred by the culture I grew up in – a culture psychotic throughout and especially on this subject. Dora did much to heal those scars. But I never achieved her angelic innocence.

I do *not* mean the innocence of childish ignorance; I mean the true innocence of an intelligent, informed, adult woman who has no evil in her. Dora was as tough as she was innocent, always aware that she was responsible for her own actions. She knew that "the tail goes with the hide, that you can't be a little bit pregnant, that it is no kindness to hang a man slowly." She could make a hard decision without dithering, then stand up to the consequences if it turned out that her judgement was faulty. She could apologize to a child, or to a mule. But that was rarely necessary; her self-honesty did not often lead her into faulty decisions.

Nor did she flagellate herself when she made a mistake. She corrected it as best she could, learned from it, did not lie awake over it.

While her ancestry had given her the potential, Helen Mayberry must be credited with having guided it and allowed it to develop. Helen Mayberry was sensitive and sensible. Come to think of it, the traits complement. A person who is sensitive but not sensible is all mixed up, cannot function properly. A person who is sensible but not sensitive – I've never met one and am not sure such a person can exist.

Helen Mayberry was born on Earth but had shucked off her bad background when she migrated; she did not pass on to Baby Dora and growing-girl Dora the sick standards of a dying culture. I knew some of this from Helen herself, but I learned more about Helen from Dora the Woman. Over the long course of getting acquainted with this stranger I had married (married couples always start out as strangers no matter how long they've known each other) I learned that Dora knew exactly the relationship that had once existed between Helen Mayberry and me, including the fact that it was economic as well as social and physical.

This did not make Dora jealous of "Aunt" Helen; jealousy was only a word to Dora, one that meant no more to her than a sunset does to an earthworm; the capacity to feel jealousy had never been developed in her. She regarded the arrangements between Helen and me as natural, reasonable, and appropriate. Indeed I feel certain that Helen's example was the clinching factor in Dora's picking me as her mate, as it could not have been my charm and beauty, both negligible. Helen had not taught Dora that sex was anything sacred; she had taught her, by precept and example, that sex is a way for people to be happy together.

Take those three vultures we killed – Instead of what they were, had they been good men and decent – oh, such men as Ira and Galahad – and given the same circumstances, four men with only one woman and the situation likely to stay that way, I think Dora would have entered easily and naturally into polyandry . . . and would have managed to convince me that that was the only happy solution by the way she herself treated it.

Nor would she, in adding more husbands, have been breaking her marriage vows. Dora had not promised to cleave unto me only; I won't let a woman promise that because a day sometimes arrives when she can't.

Dora could have kept four decent, honourable men happy. Dora had none of the sickly attitudes that interfere with a person loving more and more; Helen had seen to that. And, as the Greeks pointed out, one man cannot quench the fires of Vesuvius. Or was it the Romans? Never mind, it's true. Dora probably would have been even happier in a polyandrous marriage. And if *she* were happier, it follows, as the night the day, that I would have been also – even though I cannot imagine being happier than I was. But more big male muscles would have made life easier on me; I always had too much to do. More company could have been pleasant, too, I am forced to assume – the company of men whom Dora found acceptable. As for Dora herself, she had enough love in her to lavish it on me and a dozen kids; three more husbands would not have used up her resources, she was a spring that never ran dry.

But the matter is hypothetical. Those three Montgomerys were so little like Galahad and Ira that it is hard to think of them as being of the same race. They were vermin for killing, and that's what they got. I learned only a little about them, from reading the contents of their wagon. Minerva, they were not pioneers;

there was not the barest minimum in that wagon for starting a farm. Not a plough, not a sack of seed – And their eight mules were *all geldings*. I don't know what they thought they were doing. Exploring just for the hell of it, perhaps? Then go back to "civilization" when they grew tired of it? Or did they expect to find that some one of the pioneer parties that had started over the pass had made it – and could be terrorized into submission? I don't know, I never will know. I have never understood the gangster mind – I simply know what to do about gangsters.

As may be, they made a fatal mistake in tackling sweet and gentle Dora. She not only shot at the right instant, but she shot his gun out of his hand instead of taking the much easier target, his belly or chest. Important? Supremely so, for *me*. His gun was aimed at me. Had Dora shot *him*, instead of his gun, even if her shot killed him, his last reflex would probably – certainly, I think – have caused his fingers to tighten and I would have been hit. You can figure it from there in half a dozen ways, all bad.

Lucky accident? Not at all. Dora had him covered from the darkness of the kitchen. When he pulled that gun, she instantly changed her point of aim and got the gun. It was her first – and last – gunfight. But a true gunfighter, that girl! The hours we had spent polishing her skill paid off. But more rare than skill was the cool judgement with which she decided to try for the much more difficult target. I could not train her in that; it had to be born in her. Which it was – if you think back, her father made the same sort of correct split-second decision as his last dying act.

It was seven more years before another wagon appeared in Happy Valley – three wagons travelling together, three families with children, true pioneers. We were glad to see them and I was especially happy to see their kids. For I had been juggling eggs. Real eggs. Human ova.

I was running out of time; our oldest kids were growing up.

Minerva, you know all that the human race has learned about genetics. You know that the Howard Families are inbred from a fairly small gene pool – and that inbreeding has tended to clear them of bad genes – but you know also the high price that has been paid in defectives. Is still being paid, I should add; everywhere there are Howards there are also sanctuaries for defectives. Nor is there any end to it; new unfavourable mutations unnoticed until they are reinforced is the price we animals must pay for evolution. Maybe there will be a cheaper way someday –

there was not one on New Beginnings twelve hundred years ago.

Young Zack was a husky lad whose voice was firmly baritone. His brother, Andy, was no longer a boy soprano in our family chorus although his voice still cracked. Baby Helen wasn't such a baby any longer – hadn't reached menarche, but as near as I could tell it would be any day, any day.

I mean to say that Dora and I were having to think about it, forced to consider hard choices. Should we pack seven kids into the wagons and head back across the Rampart? If we made it, should we put the four oldest with the Magees or someone, then come home with the younger three? By ourselves? Or sing the praises of Happy Valley, its beauty and its wealth, and try to lead a party of pioneers back over the range and thereby avoid such crisis in the future?

I had expected, too optimistically, that others would follow us almost at once – a year or two or three – since I had left a passable wagon trail behind me. But I'm not one to fume over spilled milk after the horse is stolen. What might have been was of no interest; the problem was what to do with our horny kids now that they were growing up.

No point in talking to them about "sin" even if I were capable of such hypocrisy – which I am not, especially with kids. Nor could I have sold the idea. Dora would have been shocked and hurt, and her skills did not extend to lying convincingly. Nor did I want fill our kids with such nonsense; their angelic mother was the happiest, most ever-ready lecher in Happy Valley – even more so than I and the goats – and she never pretended otherwise.

Should we relax and let nature take its ancient course? Accept the idea our daughters would presently (all too soon!) mate with our sons and be prepared to accept the price? Expect at least one defective grandchild out of ten? I had no data on which to estimate the cost any closer than that, as Dora knew nothing about her ancestry and, while I did know a little about mine, I did not know enough. All I had was that old and extremely rough thumb rule.

So we stalled.

We fell back on another sound old thumb rule: Never do today what you can put off till tomorrow if tomorrow might improve the odds.

So we moved into our new house while it was still not finished – but finished enough that we then had a girls' dormitory, a boys' dormitory, a bedroom for Dora and me, with adjacent nursery.

But we did not kid ourselves that we had solved the problem. Instead we hauled it out into the open, made sure that the three oldest knew what the problem was and what the risks were and why it would be smart to hold off. Nor were the younger kids shut out of this schooling; they simply were not required even to audit the course when they found themselves bored with technicalities they were too young to be interested in.

Dora chucked in a frill, one based on something Helen Mayberry had done for her some twenty years earlier. She announced that when little Helen achieved menarche, we would declare a holiday and have a party, with Helen as guest of honour. From then on, every year, that day would be known as "Helen's Day" and so on for Iseult and Undine and on down the line until there was an annual holiday named for each girl.

Helen could hardly wait to pass from childhood into girlhood – and when she did, a few months later, she was unbearably smug. Woke us all up shouting about it. "Mama! Papa! Look, it's happened! Zack! Andy! *Wake up!* Come *see!*"

If she hurt, she did not mention it. Probably she did not; Dora wasn't subject to menstrual cramps, and neither of us told the girls to expect them. Being myself convex instead of concave, I refrain from commenting on the theory that such pains are a conditioned reflex; I don't think I'm entitled to an opinion – you might ask Ishtar.

It also resulted in me being called on by a delegation of two, Zack and Andy with Zack as spokesman: "Look, Papa – we think it splendid, meet, and fit our sister Helen's day to mark with joyful sounds and jollity acclaiming this our sibling's rightful heritage. But soothly, sire, methinks –"

"Chop it off and say it."

"Well, how about *boys!*"

By gum, I reinstituted chivalry!

Not as a sudden inspiration. Zack had asked a tough one; I had to dance around it a bit before I reached a workable answer. Sure, there are rites of passage for males as well as females; every culture has them, even those that aren't aware of it. When I was a boy, it was your first suit with long pants. Then there are ones such as circumcision at puberty, ordeal by pain, killing some dread beast – endless.

None of these fitted our boys. Some I disapproved of, some were impossible – circumcision for example. I have this unimportant mutation, no foreskin. But it is a Y-linked dominant, and I pass it on to all my male offspring. The boys knew this, but I stalled by mentioning it again, discussed it in connection with the endless ways in which a male's transition into beginning manhood was sometimes celebrated – while trying to think of an answer to the main question.

Finally I said, "Look, boys, you both know all about reproduction and genetics that I have been able to teach you. You both know what 'Helen's Day' means. Don't you? Andy?"

Andy did not answer; his older brother said, "Sure he knows, Papa. It means Helen can have babies now, just like Mama. You know that, Andy." Andy nodded agreement, round-eyed. "We all know, Papa, even the kids. Well, I'm not sure about Ivar; he's so little. But Iseult and Undine know it – Helen's been telling them that she's going to catch up with Mama – have her first baby right away."

I controlled the cold chills I felt. Let me cut this short: I did not tell them that this was a bad idea; instead I took a long time drawing answers from them, things they both knew but had not yet thought of quite so personally – how Helen could not have a baby unless one or the other of *them* put it into her; how Helen was still too little for the strain of baking a baby even though "Helen's Day" marked the fact that she was now vulnerable; how and why, even when Helen was big enough in a few years, a baby out of Helen by one of her brothers could be a tragedy insteady of the fine babies Mama made every time. *They* told *me*, Andy's eyes getting bigger all the time – I simply supplied leading questions.

I was helped in this by the fact that a little mule mare, Dancing Girl, had come into her first estrus when I thought she was not grown-up enough for a colt. So I had had Zack and Andy fence her off – and she kicked a hole in the fence and got what she wanted; Buckaroo covered her. Sure enough, the colt had been too big for her and I had to go in and cut it up and take it out in chunks – a routine job of emergency veterinary surgery but an impressive and bloody sight for two stripling boys who had helped their father by controlling the mare while he operated.

No, indeed, they did not want anything even a little bit like that to happen to *Helen*. No, *sir!*

Minerva, I cheated a little. I did *not* tell them that the way Helen was spreading in the butt and the measurements she already had made it appear to her family doctor – me – that she was even more of a natural baby factory than her mother and would be big enough for her first one much younger than Dora had had Zaccur; I did not tell them that the chances of a healthy baby from a brother-sister mating were higher than the chances of a defective. I certainly did *not!*

Instead, I waxed lyrical about what wonderful creatures girls are, what a miracle it is that they could make babies, how precious they are and how it is a man's proud privilege to love and cherish and protect them – protect them even from their follies because Helen might behave just like Dancing Girl, impatient and foolish. So don't let her tempt you, boys – jerk off instead, just like you've been doing. They promised, tears in their eyes.

I didn't ask them to promise that or anything – but it gave me the idea: Have "Princess" Helen knight them.

The kids grabbed that idea and ran with it; *Tales of King Arthur's Court* was one of the books Dora had fetched along because Helen Mayberry had given it to her. So we had Sir Zaccur the Strong and Sir Andrew the Valiant and two ladies-in-waiting – waiting rather eagerly; Iseult and Undine knew that they, too, would be "princesses" as each reached menarche. Ivar was squire to both knights and would be dubbed himself when his voice changed. Only Elf was too small as yet to play the game.

It worked, a stopgap. I suppose "Princess" Helen was protected more than she wanted to be protected. But if she could not lure her faithful knights into the cornfields, they did place her stool for her at meals, they bowed to her rather often, and usually addressed her as "Fair Princess" – considerably more than I ever did for my sisters.

Before the first anniversary of "Helen's Day" those three new families dropped down the rise and the crisis was over. It was Sammy Roberts, not one of her brothers, who first spread "Princess" Helen's thighs – certain, as she told her mother about it at once (more of Helen Mayberry's influence) and Dora kissed her and told her that she was a good girl and now go find Papa and ask him to examine you – and I did and she hadn't been hurt, not to mention. But it gave Dora some control over the matter, just as Helen Mayberry had guided Dora at about the same age – so Dora had told me, long before that. In consequence our oldest daughter did not get pregnant until she was almost as old as and quite a bit more filled out than Dora had been when I married her. Ole Hanson married her; and Sven Hanson and I, and Dora and Ingrid, helped the youngsters start their homestead. Helen thought the baby was Ole's, and for all I know she was right. No fuss. No fuss when Zack married Hilda Hanson, either. In Happy Valley pregnancy was equivalent to betrothal; I can't recall any girl who married without that proof of eligibility. Certainly none of our daughters.

Having neighbours was grand.

(Omitted)

– not only fetched his fiddle over the Rampart but could call. I could call some and, while I hadn't touched a violin for fifty years or so, I found it came back to me, so we spelled each other as Pop liked to dance, too. Like so:

"Square 'em up!

"Salute your lady! Opposite lady! Corner gal! Right-hand gal! Salute your own and make 'er a throne. All stand up and don't let 'er fall; swing your ladies one and all!

'"*Moses lived a long time ago.*
'*King said Yes; Mose said No!* – form hands, circle right.
'*Phar'oh was dat king's first name;*
'*Made 'em live a life of shame!* – allemande *left!* – with a dosey-doh! Then home you go and *swing!*

'"*. . . said Yes and th' waves did part.* First couple through the Red Sea! Now corner gal and right-hand man! Corner boy, right-hand gal – on around and keep it coming right and left!

"'*A happy band on th' opp'site shore,*
'*So all form up and swing once more!*
'*King weeps alone on Egypt's shore;*
'*Chosen People slaves no more!*

'*So kiss your lady and whisper in her ear;*
'*Then sit 'er down and get 'er a beer.*' Intermission!"

Oh, we had fun! Dora learned to dance when she was a new grandmother – and was still dancing when she was a great-great-grandmother. Early years the parties were oftenest at our place because we had the biggest house and a compound large enough for a big party. Start dancing late afternoon, dance till you couldn't see your partner; then a potluck buffet supper to candle-light, add moonlight then sing a while, and bed down all over the place – all the rooms, the roof, shakedowns in the compound, some in wagons – and if anybody ever slept alone, I never heard about it. Nor any trouble worth mentioning if things got a little loose around the edges.

Next morning there was likely to be a double performance by the Mermaid Tavern Players, one comedy, one tragedy, then it would be time for those who lived farthest away to round up their kids, hitch up their mules, and roll, while those who lived closer helped clean up before doing the same thing.

Oh, I remember one spot of trouble: A man gave his wife a black eye over nothing much, whereupon six men nearest him tossed him out the gate and barred it. Made him so mad he hitched up and left . . . and headed back up the Great Gorge toward Hopeless Pass – a fact that wasn't noticed for a while, as his wife and baby moved in with her sister and husband and their kids, and stayed on, a polygamy – though not the only one. No laws about marriage or sex – no laws about *anything* for many years – except that incurring the disapproval of your neighbours, such as by giving your wife a black eye, meant risking Coventry, about the worst thing that can happen to a pioneer short of being lynched.

But migrants tend to be both horny and easy about it. Superior intelligence always includes strong sexual drive, and the pioneers in Happy Valley had been through a double screening, first in a decision to leave Earth and then in deciding to tackle Hopeless Pass. So we had real survivors in Happy Valley, smart, cooperative, industrious, tolerant – willing to fight when necessary but not likely to fight over trivial matters. Sex is not trivial, but fighting over it is usually pretty silly. It's characteristic only of a man who isn't sure of his manhood, which didn't describe any of these men; they were sure of themselves, no need to prove it. No cowards, no thieves, no weaklings, no bullies – the rare exception didn't last long enough to count. Either dead like that first three, or ran away from us like that idiot who took a poke at his wife.

These rare purgings were always quick and informal. For many years the only law we had was the Golden Rule, unwritten but closely followed.

In such a community functionless taboos about sex couldn't last; they didn't tend to be brought into our valley in the first place. Oh, close inbreeding wasn't well thought of; these pioneers were not ignorant of genetics, nor of conception control. But the attitude was pragmatic; I don't think I ever heard anyone speak out against incest that was just a jolly romp with no outcome.

But I recall one girl who married her half brother openly and had several children by him – I assume that they were his. There may have been gossip, but it did not get them ostracized. Any marriage pattern was treated as the private business of the partners in it, not something to be licensed by the community. I recall two young couples who decided to combine their farms, then built a house big enough by adding to the larger of their two houses and making the other into a barn. Nobody asked who slept with whom; it was taken for granted that it was then a four-cornered marriage, and no doubt had been one before they enlarged that house and pooled their goods. Nobody's business but theirs.

Among such people the plural of "spouse" is "spice." A pioneer community, poor in everything else, always makes its own recreations – with sex at the top of the list. We had no professional entertainers, no theatres (unless you count the amateur theatricals started by our kids), no cabarets, no diversions dependent on sophisticated electronics, no periodicals, few books. Certainly those meetings of the Happy Valley Dance Club continued as gentle orgies after it was too dark to dance and the younger children were bedded down for the night – how else? But it was all quite gentle; a couple could always go sleep in their own wagon and ignore the quiet luau elsewhere. No compulsion either way – shucks, they didn't even have to attend the dances.

But no one stayed away from those weekly dances if he or she could make it. It was particularly nice for young people; it gave them a chance to get acquainted and do their courting. Perhaps most first babies were conceived at our dances; there was opportunity. On the other hand, a girl did not have to get knocked up just through a romp if it didn't suit her. But a girl was likely to marry by fifteen, sixteen, and their bridegrooms weren't much older – late first marriage is a big-city custom, never found in a pioneer culture.

Dora and I? But, Minerva dear, I told you earlier.

(Omitted)

– started the freight schedule to the outside the year Gibbie was born and Zack was, oh, eighteen I think – I have to keep converting New Beginnings years into standard years. Anyhow he was taller than I was, not much short of two metres and massed maybe eighty kilos, and Andy was almost as big and strong. There was pressure on me not to wait as I knew Zack might get married any day – and I could not send a wagon over the pass just with Andy. Ivar was only nine – a big help around the farm but not big enough for this job.

But I could not find teamsters other than in my own family. There were only about a dozen families in the valley; they had not been there long, and did not as yet feel the press to buy things that I did.

I wanted three new wagons, not just because my three were wearing out but because Zack would need one when he married. So would Andy. And I might have to dower Helen with one, if and when. The same applied to ploughs and several sorts of *metal* farm equipment. Prosperous as we were, Happy Valley could not be entirely self-supporting without a metals industry – which is to say: not for many years.

I had another long list of things to buy –

(Omitted)

– on a quarterly schedule. But the food that fifty-odd farms could ship out could not buy much at the other end in competition with farmers who did not have the expense of shipping by mule train over the Rampart and across the prairie; I still subsidized our link with civilization by writing drafts on John Magee to be debited against my partnership in the *Andy J.* and thereby brought things into the valley we would not otherwise have had. Some I kept – Dora got in-house running water from that first trip our own boys made, just in time to keep my promise to her, as Zack got Hilda pregnant right after they got back, and their first baby, Ingrid Dora, and the completion of Dora's bathroom, arrived about together. Other things I sold to other farmers for labour. But the Buck strain of mules, strong, intelligent, and all of them capable of being taught to talk, eventually corrected our balance of trade, once those two wells were drilled on the prairie and I could count on running a string of mules to Separation Centre without losing half of them. This meant medicines, books, and many other things for our valley.

(Omitted)

Lazarus Long did not intend to surprise his wife. But neither of them ever knocked on their own bedroom door. Finding it closed, he opened it gently against the possibility that she might be napping.

Instead he found her standing at the window, mirror angled to the light, carefully plucking a long grey hair.

He watched her in shocked dismay. Then steadied himself and said, "Adorable –"

"*Oh!*" She turned. "You startled me. I didn't hear you come in, dear."

"I'm sorry. May I have that?"

"Have what, Woodrow?"

He went to her, bent down and picked up the silver hair. "This. Beloved, every hair of your head is precious to me. May I keep it?"

She did not answer. He saw that her eyes were filled with tears. They started to overflow. "Dora. Dora," he repeated urgently, "why are you crying, beloved?"

"I'm sorry, Lazarus. I did not intend for you to see me doing this."

"But why do it at all, Dorable? I have far more grey hair than you."

She answered what he had not said, rather than what he did say. "Dearest, I can't help it that I know when someone is – well, 'fibbing' I must call it since you have never lied to me."

"Why, Dorable! My hair *is* grey."

"Yes, sir. You did not mean to surprise me, I know . . . and I did not mean to snoop when I cleaned your study. I found your cosmetics kit, Lazarus, more than a year ago. It's sort of a fib, isn't it? – when you do something to make your crisp red hair look grey? Something like what I do, I suppose, when I pluck hairs that *are* grey."

"You've been plucking grey hairs since you learned that I have been aging myself? Oh, dear!"

"No, no, Lazarus! I've been plucking them for *ages*. Much longer than that. Heavens, darling, I'm a great-grandmother – and look it. But what you do – careful as you are with it – and kind as it is for you to try – and I *do* appreciate it! – doesn't make you look my age; it just makes you look prematurely grey."

"Possibly. Although I'm entitled to grey hair, Dorable – my hair was snow-white not many years before you were born. It took something much more drastic than cosmetics – or plucking hairs – to make me look young again. But there never seemed to be any reason to mention it."

He stepped up to her, put an arm around her waist, took the mirror and tossed it on the bed, turned her toward the window. "Dora, your years are an achievement, not something to hide. Look out there. Farmhouses right up to the hills and many more we can't see from here. How many of our Happy Valley people are descended from your slim body?"

"I've never counted."

"I have; more than half of them – and I'm proud of you. Your breasts are baby-chewed, your belly shows stretch marks – your decorations of honour, Adorable One. Of valour. They make you *more* beautiful. So stand straight and tall, my lovely, and forget about silver hairs. Be what you *are*, and be it in style!"

"Yes, Lazarus. I didn't mind them myself – I did it to please you."

"Dorable, you can't help pleasing me, you always have. Do you want me to let my own hair go back to natural? It's not dangerous for me to be a Howard – here in Happy Valley with my own kin all around me."

"I don't care, darling. Just don't do it on my account. If it makes it easier for you – First Settler and all that – to look a little older, then do it."

"It does make it easier when I deal with other people. And it's no trouble; I know the routine so well I could do it in my sleep. But, Dora – listen to me, darling. Zack Briggs will call at Top Dollar sometime in the next ten years; you saw John's letter. It's not too late to go to Secundus. There they can make you look like a young girl again if that's what you want . . . and tack a good many extra years on, too. Fifty. Maybe a hundred."

She was slow in answering. "Lazarus, are you urging me to do this?"

"I'm offering it. But it's your body, most dear one. Your life."

She stared out the window. " 'More than half of them,' you said."

"With the percentage increasing. Our kids breed like cats. And so do their kids."

"Lazarus, truly we settled this many, many years ago. But it is even more so now. I don't want to leave our valley even to visit the outside. I don't want to leave our children. Nor our children's children, nor *their* children. And I certainly would not want to come back looking like a young girl . . . to watch the births of our great-great-grandchildren. You're right; I've earned my grey hairs. And now I'll wear them!"

"That's the girl I married! That's my durable Dora!" He moved his hand up higher, cupped a breast and tickled a nipple. She jumped, then relaxed to it. "I knew your answer, but I had to ask. My darling, age cannot wither you, nor custom stale your infinite variety. Where other women satiate, you most make hungry!"

She smiled. "I'm not Cleopatra, Woodrow."

"Wench, that's your opinion. But what's your opinion against mine? Rangy Lil, I've seen thousands and thousands more women than you have – and *I* say that you make Cleopatra look homely."

"Blarney tongue," she said softly. "I'm sure you've never had a woman turn you down."

"True only because I never risk being turned down; I wait to be asked. Always."

"Are you waiting to be asked? All right, I'm asking. Then I'd better start dinner."

"Don't be in such a hurry, Lil. First I'm going to dump you on that bed. Then I'm going to flip your skirt up. Then I'm going to see if I can find any grey hair at *that* end. If so, I'll pluck them for you."

"Beast. Scoundrel. Lecherous old goat." She smiled in delight. "I thought we weren't going to bother anymore with plucking grey hairs?"

"We were speaking of hair on your *head*, Great-Grandmother. But this other end is as young as ever – and better than ever – so we'll most carefully pluck any grey from your pretty – your pretty brown curls."

"Sweetest old goat. If you can find any, you're welcome. But I've been plucking that end even more carefully than my scalp. Let me slip this dress off."

"Wups! Hold it. That's Rangy Lil, the horniest bitch in Happy Valley, always in a hurry. Get your dress off if you wish, but I'm going to find Lurton and tell him to saddle up Best Boy and go beg supper and a shakedown from his sister Marje and Lyle. Then I'll be back to pluck those disgraceful grey curls. Supper will be late, I'm afraid."

"I don't mind if you don't, beloved."

"That's my Lil. Darling, there isn't a man in the valley who wouldn't grab you and try to find another valley if you gave him the slightest encouragement – that includes your own sons and your sons-in-law – every male here down to fourteen."

"Oh, not true! Blarney again."

"Want to bet? On second thought we won't waste time plucking grey hairs at either end. When I get back from telling our youngest son to get lost for the night, I want to find you wearing just rubies and a smile. Because you're not going to cook supper; we're going to scrape up a cold picnic instead and take it and a blanket up on the roof . . . and enjoy the sunset."

"Yes, sir. Oh, darling, I love you! E.F.? Or F.F.?"

"I'll leave that choice to Rangy Lil."

(Circa 39,000 words omitted)

Lazarus opened the bedroom door very quietly, looked in, looked inquiringly at his daughter Elf – a strikingly beautiful middle-aged woman with flaming red curls shot slightly with grey. She said, "Come in, Papa; Mama's awake."

She stood up to leave, taking with her a supper tray.

He glanced at it, subtracted in his mind what was still on it from what he had seen leave the kitchen on it – got a sum which was too near zero to please him. But he said nothing, simply went to the bedside, smiled down at his wife. Dora smiled back. He leaned over and kissed her, then sat down where Elf had been. "How is my darling?"

"Just fine, Woodrow. Ginny – no, Elf. Elf brought me the tastiest supper. I enjoyed it so much. But I asked her to put my rubies on me before she fed me – did you notice?"

"Of course I did, Beautiful. When did Rangy Lil ever eat supper without her rubies?"

She didn't answer, her eyes closed. Lazarus kept quiet, watched her respiration, counted her heartbeats by watching a pulse in her neck.

"Do you hear them, Lazarus?" Her eyes were open again.

"Hear what, Dorable?"

"The wild geese. They must be right over the house."

"Oh. Yes, certainly."

"They're early this year." That seemed to tire her; she closed her eyes again. He waited.

"Sweetheart? Will you sing 'Buck's Song'?"

"Certainly, 'dorable Dora." Lazarus cleared his throat and started in:

> " '*There's a schoolhouse*
> *By the pawnshop*
> *Where Dora has her lessons.*
>
> " '*By the schoolhouse*
> *There's a mule yard*
> *Where Dora's friend Buck lives.*' "

She closed her eyes again, so he sang the other verses very softly. But when he finished, she smiled at him. "Thank you, darling; that was lovely. It's always been lovely. But I'm a little tired – if I drop off to sleep, will you still be here?"

"I'll always be here, dearest. You sleep now."

She smiled again, and her eyes closed. Presently her breathing grew slower as she slept.

Her breathing stopped.

Lazarus waited a long time before he called in Ginny and Elf.

SECOND INTERMISSION

More from the Notebooks of Lazarus Long

Always tell her she is beautiful, especially if she is not.

*

If you are part of a society that votes, then do so. There may be no candidates and no measures you want to vote *for* . . . but there are certain to be ones you want to vote *against*. In case of doubt, vote *against*. By this rule you will rarely go wrong.

If this is too blind for your taste, consult some well-meaning fool (there is always one around) and ask his advice. Then vote the other way. This enables you to be a good citizen (if such is your wish) without spending the enormous amount of time on it that truly intelligent exercise of franchise requires.

*

Sovereign ingredient for a happy marriage: Pay cash or do without. Interest charges not only eat up a household budget; awareness of debt eats up domestic felicity.

*

Those who refuse to support and defend a state have no claim to protection by that state. Killing an anarchist or a pacifist should not be defined as "murder" in a legalistic sense. The offence against the state, if any, should be "Using deadly weapons inside city limits," or "Creating a traffic hazard," or "Endangering bystanders," or other misdemeanor.

However, the state may reasonably place a closed season on these exotic asocial animals whenever they are in danger of becoming extinct. An authentic buck pacifist has rarely been seen off Earth, and it is doubtful that any have survived the trouble there . . . regrettable, as they had the biggest mouths and the smallest brains of any of the primates.

The small-mouthed variety of anarchist has spread through the Galaxy at the very wave front of the Diaspora; there is no need to protect them. But they often shoot back.

*

Another ingredient for a happy marriage: Budget the luxuries *first!*

*

And still another – See to it that she has her own desk – then keep your hands off it!

*

And another – In a family argument, if it turns out you are right – apologize at once!

*

"God split himself into a myriad parts that he might have friends." This may not be true, but it sounds good – and is no sillier than any other theology.

*

To stay young requires unceasing cultivation of the ability to unlearn old falsehoods.

*

Does history record *any* case in which the majority was right?

*

When the fox gnaws – *smile!*

*

A "critic" is a man who creates nothing and thereby feels qualified to judge the work of creative men. There is logic in this; he is unbiased – he hates all creative people equally.

*

Money is truthful. If a man speaks of his honour, make him pay cash.

*

Never frighten a little man. He'll kill you.

*

Only a sadistic scoundrel – or a fool – tells the bald truth on social occasions.

*

This sad little lizard told me that he was a brontosaurus on his mother's side. I did not laugh; people who boast of ancestry often have little else to sustain them. Humouring them costs nothing and adds to happiness in a world in which happiness is always in short supply.

*

In handling a stinging insect, move very slowly.

*

To be "matter of fact" about the world is to blunder into fantasy – and dull fantasy at that, as the real world is strange and wonderful.

*

The difference between science and the fuzzy subjects is that science requires reasoning, while those other subjects merely require scholarship.

*

Copulation is spiritual in essence – or it is merely friendly exercise. On second thought, strike out "merely." Copulation is not "merely" – even when it is just a happy pastime for two strangers. But copulation at its spiritual best is so much more than physical coupling that it is different in kind as well as in degree.

The saddest feature of homosexuality is not that it is "wrong" or "sinful" or even that it can't lead to progeny – but that it is more difficult to reach through it this spiritual union. Not impossible – but the cards are stacked against it.

But – most sorrowfully – many people never achieve spiritual sharing even with the help of male-female advantage; they are condemned to wander through life alone.

*

Touch is the most fundamental sense. A baby experiences it, all over, before he is born and long before he learns to use sight, hearing, or taste, and no human ever ceases to need it. Keep your children short on pocket money – but long on hugs.

*

Secrecy is the beginning of tyranny.

*

The greatest productive force is human selfishness.

*

Be wary of strong drink. It can make you shoot at tax collectors – and miss.

*

The profession of shaman has many advantages. It offers high status with a safe livelihood free of work in the dreary, sweaty sense. In most societies it offers legal privileges and immunities not granted to other men. But it is hard to see how a man who has been given a mandate from on High to spread tidings of joy to all mankind can be seriously interested in taking up a collection to pay his salary; it causes one to suspect that the shaman is on the moral level of any other con man.

But it's lovely work if you can stomach it.

*

A whore should be judged by the same criteria as other professionals offering services for pay – such as dentists, lawyers, hairdressers, physicians, plumbers, etc. Is she professionally competent? Does she give good measure? Is she honest with her clients?

It is possible that the percentage of honest and competent whores is higher than that of plumbers and much higher than that of lawyers. And *enormously* higher than that of professors.

*

Minimize your therbligs until it becomes automatic; this doubles your effective lifetime – and thereby gives time to enjoy butterflies and kittens and rainbows.

*

Have you noticed how much they look like orchids? Lovely!

*

Expertise in one field does not carry over into other fields. But experts often think so. The narrower their field of knowledge the more likely they are to think so.

*

Never try to outstubborn a cat.

*

Tilting at windmills hurts you more than the windmills.

*

Yield to temptation; it may not pass your way again.

*

Waking a person unnecessarily should not be considered a capital crime. For a first offence, that is.

*

"Go to hell!" or other insult direct is all the answer a snoopy question rates.

*

The correct way to punctuate a sentence that starts: "Of course it is none of my business but – " is to place a period after the word "but." Don't use excessive force in supplying such moron with a period. Cutting his throat is only a momentary pleasure and is bound to get you talked about.

*

A man does not insist on physical beauty in a woman who builds up his morale. After a while he realizes that she *is* beautiful – he just hadn't noticed it at first.

*

A skunk is better company than a person who prides himself on being "frank."

*

"All's fair in love and war" – what a contemptible lie!

*

Beware of the "Black Swan" fallacy. Deductive logic is tautological; there is no way to get a new truth out of it, and it manipulates false statements as readily as true ones. If you fail to remember this, it can trip you – with perfect logic. The designers of the earliest computers called this the "Gigo Law," i.e., "Garbage in, garbage out."

Inductive logic is *much* more difficult – but can produce new truths.

*

A "practical joker" deserves applause for his wit according to its quality. Bastinado is about right. For exceptional wit one might grant keelhauling. But staking him out on an anthill should be reserved for the very wittiest.

*

Natural laws have no pity.

*

On the planet Tranquille around KM849 (G-O) lives a little animal known as a "knafn." It is herbivorous and has no natural enemies and is easily approached and may be petted – sort of a six-legged puppy with scales. Stroking it is very pleasant; it wiggles its pleasure and broadcasts euphoria in some band that humans can detect. It's worth the trip.

Someday some bright boy will figure out how to record this broadcast, then some smart boy will see commercial angles – and not long after that it will be regulated and taxed.

In the meantime I have faked that name and catalogue number; it is several thousand light-years off in another direction. Selfish of me –

*

Freedom begins when you tell Mrs. Grundy to go fly a kite.

*

Take care of the cojones and the frijoles will take care of themselves. Try to have getaway money – but don't be fanatic about it.

*

If "everybody knows" such-and-such, then it ain't so, by at least ten thousand to one.

*

Political tags – such as royalist, communist, democrat, populist, fascist, liberal, conservative, and so forth – are never basic criteria. The human race divides politically into those who want people to be controlled and those who have no such desire. The former are idealists acting from highest motives for the greatest good of the greatest number. The latter are surely curmudgeons, suspicious and lacking in altruism. But they are more comfortable neighbours than the other sort.

*

All cats are *not* grey after midnight. Endless variety –

*

Sin lies only in hurting other people unnecessarily. All other "sins" are invented nonsense. (Hurting yourself is not sinful – just stupid.)

*

Being generous is inborn; being altruistic is a learned perversity. No resemblance –

*

It is impossible for a man to love his wife wholeheartedly without loving all women somewhat. I suppose that the converse must be true of women.

*

You can go wrong by being too sceptical as readily as by being too trusting.

*

Formal courtesy between husband and wife is even more important than it is between strangers.

*

Anything free is worth what you pay for it.

*

Don't store garlic near other victuals.

*

Climate is what we expect, weather is what we get.

*

Pessimist by policy, optimist by temperament – it is possible to be both. How? By never taking an unnecessary chance and by minimizing risks you can't avoid. This permits you to play out the game happily, untroubled by the certainty of the outcome.

*

Do not confuse "duty" with what other people expect of you; they are utterly different. Duty is a debt you owe to yourself to fulfill obligations you have assumed voluntarily. Paying that debt can entail anything from years of patient work to instant willingness to die. Difficult it may be, but the reward is self-respect.

But there is no reward at all for doing what other people expect of you, and to do so is not merely difficult, but impossible. It is easier to deal with a footpad than it is with the leech who wants "just a few minutes of your time, please – this won't take long." Time is your total capital, and the minutes of your life are painfully few. If you allow yourself to fall into the vice of agreeing to such requests, they quickly snowball to the point where these parasites will use up 100 per cent of your time – and squawk for more!

So learn to say No – and to be rude about it when necessary.

Otherwise you will not have time to carry out your duty, or to do your own work, and certainly no time for love and happiness. The termites will nibble away your life and leave none of it for you.

(This rule does not mean that you must not do a favour for a friend, or even a stranger. But let the choice be *yours*. Don't do it because it is "expected" of you).

*

"I came, I saw, she conquered." (The original Latin seems to have been garbled.)

*

A committee is a life form with six or more legs and no brain.

*

Animals can be driven crazy by placing too many in too small a pen. Homo sapiens is the only animal that voluntarily does this to himself.

*

Don't try to have the last word. You might get it.

VARIATIONS ON A THEME

XIII

Boondock

"Ira," said Lazarus Long, "have you looked at this list?" He was lounging in the office of Colony Leader Ira Weatheral at Boondock, largest (only) settlement on the planet Tertius. With them was Justin Foote 45th, freshly arrived from New Rome, Secundus.

"Lazarus, Arabelle addressed that letter to you. Not to me."

"That preposterous puff-gut will get me annoyed yet. Her Extreme Ubiquity Madam Chairman Pro Tem Arabelle Foote-Hedrick seems to think she has been crowned Queen of the Howards. I'm tempted to go back and pick up that gavel." Lazarus passed the list to Weatheral. "Give it a gander, Ira. Justin, did you have anything to do with this?"

"No, Senior, Arabelle told me to deliver it and instructed me to brief you in ways to insure delivery of Delay Mail from various eras – which does present problems for pre-Diaspora dates. But I don't consider her ideas practical. If I may say so, I know more Terran history than she does."

"I'm certain you do. I think she cribbed that list from an encyclopedia. Don't bother me with her notions. Oh, you can transcribe them and give me the cube, but I shan't play it. I want *your* ideas, Justin."

"Thank you, Ancestor –"

"Call me 'Lazarus.'"

"'Lazarus.' The official reason for my visit is to report to her on this colony –"

"Justin," Ira put in quickly, "does Arabelle think she has jurisdiction over Tertius?"

"I'm afraid so, Ira."

Lazarus snorted. "Well, she hasn't. But she's so far away it can't hurt if she wants to call herself 'Empress of Tertius.' Our situation is this, Justin. Ira is Colony Leader, we are still shaking down. I'm Mayor – Ira does the work, but I bang the gavel at community meetings – there are always colonists who think that a colony can operate like a big-city planet, so I preside to throw cold water on damfoolishness. When I'm ready to start this time-travel junket, we'll eliminate the job of Colony Leader and Ira will take over as Mayor.

"But feel free to look over the joint, count noses, examine any records, do as you like. Welcome to Tertius, the biggest little colony this side of Galactic Centre. Make yourself at home, son."

"Thank you. Lazarus, I would be staying – colonizing – but I want to remain Chief Archivist until I finish editing your memoirs."

Lazarus said, "Oh, *that* junk – burn it up! Gather ye, rosebuds, man!"

Ira said, "Lazarus, don't talk that way. I put up with your whims for years to get it on record."

"Piffle. I paid you back when I grabbed the gavel and kept the Ugly Duchess from banishing you to Felicity. You got what you want – why do you care about my memoirs?"

"I care."

"Well – Maybe Justin can edit them here. Athene! Pallas Athene, are you there, honey?"

"Listening, Lazarus," came a sweet soprano voice from a speaker over Ira's desk.

"Your memories include my memoirs, do they not?"

"Certainly, Lazarus. Every word you've spoken since Ira rescued you – "

"Not 'rescued,' dear. Kidnapped."

"Revision. – since Ira kidnapped you from that flophouse, and all your earlier memoirs."

"Thanks, dear. You see, Justin? If you *must* do button-sorting, do it here. Unless you have unfinished business on Secundus? Family, or such?"

"No family. Grown children but no wife. My deputy is doing my job, and I've nominated her as my successor – subject to approval by the Trustees. But I find myself startled. Uh . . . how about my ship?"

"*My* ship, you mean. I don't mean my yacht 'Dora' but that one-man autopacket you arrived in. The 'Homing Pigeon.' Belongs to a corporation owned by another corporation of which I am major stockholder. I'll accept delivery and that saves Arabelle half the lease time."

"So? Madam Chairman Pro Tem did not lease that autopacket, Lazarus; she requisitioned it for public service."

"Well, well!" Lazarus grinned. "Maybe I'll sue her. Justin, there is nothing in the Articles of Contract under which Secundus was colonized that permits requisition of private property by the state. Correct, Ira?"

"Technically correct, Lazarus. Although there is long precedent for eminent domain in land."

"Ira, I'd argue even that. But have you ever heard of it being applied to spaceships?"

"Never. Unless you count the 'New Frontiers.' "

"*Ouch!* Ira, I didn't requisition the 'New Frontiers'; I stole it to save our skins."

"I was thinking of Slayton Ford's part in it, not yours. Constructive requisitioning, perhaps?"

"Mmm – It's pretty small of you to bring it up a couple of thousand years after his death. Furthermore, had Slayton not done what he did, I wouldn't be here and *you* wouldn't be here. Nor any of us. Damn you, Ira."

"Get your feathers down, Grandfather. I was just pointing out that a head of state sometimes has to do things he would never do as a private individual. But if Arabelle can requisition the 'Homing Pigeon' when it sits on Secundus, then you can do the same on Tertius. You are each head of state of an autonomous planet. Teach her a lesson."

"Uh . . . Ira, don't tempt me. It happened to *me* once. If it got to be a habit, it would put a stop to interstellar travel. I won't touch that bucket under any such flimsy legality. But I *do* own it, indirectly, and if Justin wants to stay, he can turn it over to me, and I'll return it to Transport Enterprises. Let's get back to that list. See what the old bat wants? The times and places she wants me to report on?"

"Looks like an interesting itinerary."

"It does, eh? Then *you* do it. 'Battle of Hastings – First, Third, and Fourth Crusades – Battle of Orléans – Fall of Constantinople – French Revolution – Battle of Waterloo.' Thermopylae and nineteen other encounters between rough strangers. I'm surprised she didn't ask me to referee the bout between David and Goliath. I'm *chicken*, Ira. I fight when I can't run – how does she *think* I managed to live so long? Bloodshed is not a spectator sport. If history says that a battle took place at a given location on a particular day, then I'll be somewhere – or somewhen – far away, sitting in a tavern, drinking beer and pinching the barmaids. Not dodging mortar fire to feed Arabelle's ghoulish curiosity."

"I tried to suggest that," said Justin. "But she said that this was an official Families' project."

"The hell it is. I told her about it simply to be sure of the Delay Mail setup. I'm a coward by trade . . . and not working for her. I'll go where and when I please, see what I want to – and try not to antagonize local yokels. Especially those fighting each other; it makes 'em trigger-happy."

"Lazarus," said Ira Weatheral, "you never have said what you do plan to see."

"Well – No battles. Battles are well enough reported for my taste. But there are lots of interesting things in Terran history – peaceful things not well reported because they *were* peaceful. I want to see the Parthenon at the peak of its glory. Cruise down the Mississippi with Sam Clemens as pilot. Go to Palestine in the first three decades of the Christian Era and try to locate a certain carpenter turned rabbi – settle whether there ever was such a man."

Justin Foote looked surprised. "You mean the Christian Messiah? Admittedly many stories about him are myths, but –"

"How do you *know* they are myths? But that he ever lived is the point that has never been established. Take Socrates, four centuries earlier – *his* historicity is as firmly established as that of Napoleon. Not so with the Carpenter of Nazareth. Despite the care with which the Romans kept records and the equal care with which the Jews kept theirs, *none* of the events that *should* be on record can be found in contemporary records.

"But if I devoted thirty years to it, I could find out. I know Latin and Greek of that time and I'm almost as conversant with classic Hebrew; all I would have to add is Aramaic. If I found him, I could follow him around. Take down his words with a micro-recorder, see if they match what he is alleged to have said.

"But I won't take any bets. The historicity of Jesus is the slipperiest question in all history because for centuries the question couldn't be raised. They would hang you for asking – or burn you at the stake."

"I'm amazed," said Ira. "My knowledge of Earth's history isn't as thorough as I thought it was. However, I concentrated on the period from Ira Howard's death to the founding of New Rome."

"Son, you didn't even sample it. But aside from this one weird story – 'weird' because most major religious leaders are heavily documented whereas this one remains as elusive as the King Arthur legends – I'm not going after great events. I'd rather meet Galileo, get a look at Michelangelo at work, attend a first performance of one of old Bill's plays at the Globe Theatre, things like that. I'd particularly like to go back to my own childhood, see if things look as I recall them."

Ira blinked. "Run a chance of running into *yourself*?"

"Why not?"

"Well . . . there are paradoxes, are there not?"

"How? If I'm going to, then I *did*. That old cliché about shooting your grandfather before he sires your father, then going *fuff!* like a soap bubble – and all descendants, too, meaning both of you among others – is nonsense. The fact that I'm here and you're here means that I *didn't* do it – or won't do it; the tenses of grammar aren't built for time travel – but it does *not* mean that I never went back and poked around. I haven't any yen to look at *myself* when I was a snot-nose; it's the era that interests me. If I ran across myself as a young kid, he – I – wouldn't recognize me; I would be a stranger to that brat. He wouldn't give me a passing glance; I know, I *was* he."

"Lazarus," put in Justin Foote, "if you intend to visit that era, I'd like to invite your attention to one thing Madam Chairman Pro Tem is interested in – because *I* am interested. A recording of exactly what was said and done at the Families' Meeting in 2012 A.D."

"Impossible."

"Just a moment, Justin," Ira put in. "Lazarus, you have refused to talk about that meeting on the grounds that the others who were there can't dispute your version. But a recording would be fair to everyone."

"Ira, I didn't say that I would not; I said it was *impossible*."

"I don't follow you."

"I can't make a recording of that meeting because I was not there."

"You lost me again. All the records – and your own statements – show that you *were* there."

"Again we don't have language adequate for time travel. Surely, I was there as Woodrow Wilson Smith. I was there and made a hairy nuisance of myself and offended a lot of people. But I did *not* have a recorder on me. Let's say that Dora and the twins drop me back there – *me*, Lazarus Long, not that younger fellow – and that Ishtar has equipped me with a recorder implanted behind my right kidney, with its minimike surfacing inside my right ear. Okay, let's assume that with such equipment I won't be noticed making a record.

"But, Ira, what you don't understand, despite having chaired many Families' Meetings, is that I would not get inside the hall. In those days an executive meeting of the Families was harder to get into than an esbat of witches. The guards were armed and eager; it was a rough period. What identity could I use? Not Woodrow Wilson Smith; he *was* there. Lazarus Long? There was no 'Lazarus Long' on the Families' rolls. Try to fake it as someone eligible but not able to attend? Impossible. There were only a few thousand of us then, and every member was known to a large percentage of the rest; a man who couldn't be vouched for ran a nasty chance of being buried in the basement. No unidentified person *ever did* get in; we had too much at stake. Hi, Minerva! Come in, honey."

"Hi, Lazarus. Ira, am I intruding?"

"Not at all, dear."

"Thank you. Hello, Athene."

"Hello, my sister."

Minerva waited to be introduced. Ira said, "Minerva, you remember Justin Foote, Chief Archivist."

"Certainly, I've worked with him many times. Welcome to Tertius, Mr. Foote."

"Thank you, Miss Minerva." Justin Foote liked what he saw – a tall, slender young woman with an erect carriage, a small, firm bust, long chestnut hair worn in a part and brushed straight down, a sober, intelligent face, handsome rather than pretty, but which blossomed into beauty each time she gave one of her quick smiles. "But, Ira, I must hurry back to Secundus and apply for rejuvenation. This young lady has worked with me 'many times' – yet I've grown so senile I can't place the occasions. Forgive me, dear lady."

Minerva flashed him another of her smiles, then instantly, was sober. "My fault, sir; I should have explained at once. When I worked with you, I was a computer. Executive computer of Secundus, serving Mr. Weatheral, then Chairman Pro Tem. But now I'm a flesh-and-blood, and have been for the past three years."

Justin Foote blinked. "I see. I hope I do."

"I am a proscribed construct, sir, not born of woman. A

composite clone of twenty-three donor-parents, forced to maturity in vitro. But the 'I' that is me, my ego, was the computer who used to work with you when the Archives computers needed assistance from the executive computer. Have I made it clear?"

"Uh . . . all I can say, Miss Minerva, is that I am delighted to meet you in the flesh. Your servant, Miss."

"Oh, don't call me 'Miss,' call me 'Minerva.' I shouldn't be called 'Miss' anyhow; isn't that honorific reserved for virgins among flesh-and-bloods? Ishtar – one of my mothers and my chief designer – deflowered me surgically before she woke me."

"And that ain't all!" came the voice from the ceiling.

"Athene," Minerva said reprovingly. "Sister, you're embarassing our guest."

"I'm not, but maybe you are, sister mine."

"Am I, Mr. Foote? I hope not. But I'm still learning to be a human being. Will you kiss me? I'd like to kiss you; we've known each other almost a century and I've always liked you. Will you?"

"Now who's embarrassing him, sister?"

"Minerva," said Ira.

She suddenly sobered. "I shouldn't have said that?"

Lazarus cut in. "Pay no attention to Ira, Justin; he's an old stick-in-the-mud. Minerva is a 'kissin cousin' to most of the colony; she's making up for lost time. Furthermore, she *is* some sort of cousin to practically all of us through her twenty-three parents. And she's learned *how* – kissing her is a treat. Athene, let your sis be while she adds on another kissing cousin."

"Yes, Lazarus. Ol' Buddy Boy!"

"Teena, if I could reach through that string of wires, I'd spank you." Lazarus added, "Go ahead, Justin."

"Uh . . . Minerva, I haven't kissed a girl in many years. Out of practice."

"Mr. Foote, I do not mean to embarrass you. I am simply delighted to see you again. You need not kiss me. Or if you are willing to kiss me in private, you are most welcome."

"Don't risk it, Justin," advised the computer. "I'm your friend."

"Athene!"

"I was about to add," said the Chief Archivist, "that I probably need practice in 'learning to be a human being' more than you do. If you'll put up with my rustiness, Cousin, I accept your sweet offer. Brace yourself."

Minerva smiled quickly, went into his arms, flowed up against him like a cat, closed her eyes, and opened her mouth. Ira studied a paper on his desk. Lazarus did not even pretend not to watch. He noted that Justin Foote put his heart into the matter – the old buzzard might be out of practice, but he hadn't forgotten the basics.

When they broke, the computer gave a respectful whistle. "Wheeee . . . ooooo! Justin, welcome to the Club."

"Yes," Ira said dryly, "a person can't be said to be officially on Tertius until he or she has been welcomed with a kiss from Minerva. Now that protocol is satisfied, sit down. Minerva, my dear, you came for some purpose?"

"Yes, sir." She settled down by Justin Foote on a couch facing Ira and Lazarus – took Justin's hand. "I was in the 'Dora' with the twins, and Dora was drilling them in astrogation, when the packet showed up in our sky and – "

"Hold it," Lazarus interrupted. "Did the brats track it?"

"Certainly, Lazarus. A live exercise? – Dora would never miss such a chance. She split herself instantly and made each of them track it independently. But once the autopacket grounded I asked Dora to ask Athene who was in it – and as soon as the pod opened, my sisters told me, Justin" – she squeezed his hand – "and I hurried to greet you. And to offer some arrangements. Ira, has Justin been provided for? A place to sleep, things like that?"

"Not yet, my dear. We were just starting to talk – he's barely had time to shake off the anesthetic."

Foote remarked, "I think the antidote has taken hold."

The computer added, "Cousin Justin just had a second dose, Ira. Pulse fast but steady."

"That's enough, Athene. Were you going to suggest something, my dear?"

"Yes. I swung past the house and spoke with Ishtar. We are in agreement. Subject to approval of you and Lazarus."

"You mean we got a vote?" Lazarus put in. "Justin, this planet is run by its women."

"Isn't that true everywhere?"

"No, just most of them. I remember a place where a wedding ceremony always concluded by killing the bride's mother if she hadn't been used up earlier. I thought that was overdoing it, but it did tend to – "

"Stow it, Grandpappy," Ira said mildly. "Justin would have to edit it out. Justin, what Minerva has been saying is that our house is yours. Lazarus?"

"Certainly. It's a madhouse, Justin, but the cooking is okay, and the price is right. Free, that is. It's just your nerves that pay."

"Really, I have no intention of imposing. Isn't there someone who can rent me a room? Not for money – I assume that Secundus money is not negotiable here – but for artifacts I've fetched, things you don't make as yet."

Lazarus answered, "You can negotiate Secudus money through me if you need to. As for artifacts, you may be surprised at what we are making."

"I might not be; I know that a universal pantograph was moved here. So I fetched new creative items, mostly entertainments – solly cubes and such. Musicalarkies, pornies, dreams, other sorts – all published since you folks left Secundus."

"Well planned." Lazarus added, "I think colonizing was more fun back when pioneers had no choice but to step in and slug it out and you weren't sure who was going to win, you or the planet. The way we do it now is like swatting an insect with a sledgehammer. Justin, your creepies will fetch a high price – but sell them in dribbles . . . because each one will be copied as soon as you turn it loose. No copyright, there's no way to enforce it. But it still won't rent you a room; we're at the staying-with-kinfolk stage. You'd best accept our offer; it rains 'most every night this time o' year."

Justin Foote looked baffled. "I have misgivings about invading your privacy. Ira, could I borrow this couch I'm sitting on? For a short time? Then –"

"Stow it, Justin." Lazarus stood up. "Son, you're suffering from big-city attitudes. You're welcome for a week or a century. You're not only my lineal descendant – through Harriet Foote, I think – but you're a kissin' cousin of Minerva's. Let's take him home, Minerva. What did you do with my hellions?"

"They're outside."

"Trust you staked 'em down."

"No, but they were somewhat miffed."

"Good for their metabolism. Ira, declare a holiday."

"I will – as soon as I've gone over the ore converter plans with Athene."

"Meaning you're going to find out from her what's she's decided."

"You can say that again!" said the computer.

"Teena," Lazarus said mildly, "you've been associating with

Dora too much. When Minerva had your job, she was sweet, gentle, respectful, and humble."

"Any complaints about my work, Grandpappy?"

"Just your manners, dear. In the presence of a guest."

"Justin isn't a guest; he's family. He's my sister's kissing cousin, so he's mine, too. Logical? Q.E.D."

"I disdain to argue. Watch out for Teena, Justin; she'll trap you."

"I find Athene's reasoning not only logical but warmly pleasing. Thank you, my kissing cousin."

"I like you, Justin; you were sweet to my sister. Don't worry about me trapping you; I don't plan to accept a clone for at least a hundred years – first I've got to get this planet organized. So don't wait up; you'll see me in about a century. You'll recognize me; I'll look exactly like Minerva."

"But noisier."

"Lazarus, you say the sweetest things. Kiss him for me, twin sister."

"Let's go, Minerva; Teena's got me mixed up again."

"Just a moment, Lazarus, please. Ira? I made other arrangements through Ishtar but only tentatively . . . not being sure of Justin's wishes."

"Oh. I don't know them either. Do you want me to ask him?"

"Uh . . . yes."

"On your behalf?"

Minerva looked startled. Justin Foote looked puzzled. Athene said, "Let's cut through the fog. Justin, Minerva was asking Ira whether or not you want her to find you a guest wife. Ira says he doesn't know but will find out – then asked her if she was volunteering for the privilege. All clear? Justin, my sister is so new at being a flesh-and-blood that she sometimes isn't sure of herself."

Lazarus reflected that he had not seen a girl blush – for that reason – for three centuries or more. Nor did the two men look at ease. He said reprovingly, "Teena, you are an excellent engineer . . . and a lousy diplomat."

"What? Oh, nonsense. I saved them billions of nanoseconds."

"Shut up, dear; your circuits are scrambled. Justin, Minerva is almost certainly the only girl on this planet who could be fussed by Teena's unhelpful help . . . because she is probably the only one who shows any tendency to stick to one man."

The computer giggled.

"I told *you* to keep still," Lazarus said sternly.

Ira said quietly, "Minerva is a free agent, Lazarus."

"Who said she wasn't? And you keep quiet, too, until the Senior – that's *me*, son – finishes speaking. Justin, Minerva will find you a dinner partner – has found one, I think. After that you are on your own. If you and your dinner partner don't hit it off, no doubt you'll be able to work out something else. Teena, I'm going to switch you off at the house tonight; I am uninviting you to dinner. You haven't learned how to behave in company."

"Aw, Lazarus, I didn't mean to steal your pig."

"Well – " Lazarus looked around. Ira's face was impassive, Minerva looked unhappy. Justin Foote spoke up:

"Senior, I am sure Athene did not mean any harm. I do appreciate her declaring me her 'kissing cousin'; I found it warmly friendly. I hope you will reconsider and let her join us at dinner."

"Very well, Teena; Justin has intervened for you. But between you and Dora and the twins I am beginning to need a gnarooth to ride herd on you kids. Justin. Minerva. Let's go. Ira, Teena – see you at the house. Don't waste time on that converter, Ira; Teena did a perfect job."

Outside the colonial headquarters Justin Foote found a null-boat waiting – not the one that had fetched him from the skyfield; this one had a pair of redheaded twins in it . . . uh, girls, although they looked as if they had just recently made up their minds. Twelve, perhaps thirteen. Both were wearing gun belts on skinny hips, with what (he hoped) were toy guns. One was wearing captain's insignia on bare shoulders. Each wore eleven thousand, three hundred, and two freckles as near as he could estimate.

Both jumped out of the boat, waited. One set of freckles said, "About time." The other said, "Discrimination."

Lazarus said, "Pipe down and be polite. Justin, these are my twin daughters – Lapis Lazuli, and that one's Lorelei Lee. Mr. Justin Foote, dears, Chief Archivist for the Trustees."

The girls glanced at each other, then curtsied deeply in perfect unison. "Welcome to Tertius, Chief Archivist Foote!" they said in chorus.

"Charming!"

"Yes, girls, that was nice. Who taught you?"

"Mama Hamadryad taught us –"

" – and Mama Ishtar said this would be a good time to do it."

"But I'm Lori; she's Lazi."

"You're both lazy," said Lazarus.

"I'm Captain Lapis Lazuli Long, commanding Starship 'Dora' and she's my crew. Even-numbered day."

"Till tomorrow. Odd-numbered day."

"Lazarus can't tell us apart – "

" – and he's not our father; we never had one."

"He's our brother, no real authority – "

" – he just dominates us by brute strength – "

" – but someday that will change."

"Into the boat, you mutinous hellions," Lazarus said cheerfully, "before I bust you back to apprentice spacemen."

They jumped into the boat, sat forward, facing aft. "Threats – "

" – with abusive language – "

" – and without due process."

Lazarus did not seem to hear them. He and Justin handed Minerva into the boat, seated her aft and facing forward; they took seats cornering her. "Captain Lazuli."

"Yes, sir?"

"Will you please tell the boat to take us home?"

"Aye aye, sir. Humpty Dumpty – *home!*"

The little craft started up, hit a steady ten knots, waddling to changing contours of the ground. Lazarus said, "And now, Captain, having confused our guest, please straighten him out."

"Yes, sir. We're not twins, we don't even have the same mother – "

" – and Ol' Buddy Boy is not our father; he's our brother."

"Even-numbered day!"

"Then make it march."

"Correction," said Lazarus. "I'm your father because I adopted you, with written consent of your mothers."

"Irrelevant – "

" – and illegal; it was not with *our* consent – "

" – and immaterial in any case, as we three, Lazarus, Lorelei and I, are identical triplets and therefore enjoy the same rights under any rational jurisdiction . . . which unfortunately this is not. So he beats us. Illegally and brutally."

"Captain, remind me to get a bigger club."

"Aye aye, sir. But we're fond of Buddy Boy anyhow, despite his masochosadistic behaviour. Because he's really us. You see?"

"Miss – Captain, I mean – I'm not sure I do. I think I slid through a space warp on the way here and failed to come out."

The even-numbered-day captain shook her head. "Sorry, sir,

but that's not possible. I must ask you to take my word for it . . . unless you can handle imperial numbers and Libby field-physics. Can you?"

"No. Can you?"

"Oh, certainly –"

" – we're geniuses."

"Quit trying to snow him, kids, and belay that order. I'll explain it myself."

"I wish you would, Lazarus. I wasn't aware that you had any minor children. Or sisters, which I find even more confusing. Are they registered? While I can't see everything that goes into the files, for many years there has been an automatic relay to my attention on anything concerning the Senior."

"Which I knew and that's why you didn't see it. Registered, yes, but by their mothers' names – host-mothers, actually, but not so reported. But I left a Delay-Mail sealed registration of the actual genealogy involved, to be opened by you or your successor on my death or in year 2070 of the Diaspora, whichever comes first, to insure that they will receive certain knickknacks, such as my second-best bed –"

"And the 'Dora'!"

"Pipe down. Keep butting in and your sister gets the 'Dora' and you won't be captain even on alternate days. I picked that date, Justin, because I expect them to be adults by then; they really are geniuses. I will not attempt time travel until then, as they are captain and crew of my yacht – only while groundside now but in space by then. As to how they are my sisters – and they are – an illegal – proscribed, rather, by Secundus Clinic – a clandestine surgical procedure was used to clone them from me. Somewhat like Minerva's case, but simpler."

"Much simpler," agreed Minerva. "I operated for me, when I was still a computer – and failed seventeen times before I achieved a perfect clone. I couldn't do it now, although Athene would be able to. But our girls were cloned by a flesh-and-blood surgeon – replication of the X chromosome was all that was necessary – and did it in both cases in one try; Laz and Lor were born the same day."

"Mmm – Yes, I think that Madam Director Doctor Hildegarde would take a sour view of such things. With no reflections on the lady's professional competence – high, I assume – I find her a bit, uh, conservative."

"Murderess."

"Primitive totalitarian."
"Three times over – "
" – for what right has *she* to say that *we* can't exist – "
" – or Minerva. Crypto-criminal mind!"
"That's enough, girls; you've made your point, you don't like her."
"She would have murdered *you, too*, Ol' Buddy Boy."
"Lori, I said that was enough. Stipulated that, if Nelly Hildegarde's policies had been carried out, I wouldn't be here, you wouldn't be here, Laz wouldn't be here, nor would Minerva. But she's not a 'murderess,' as all four of us *are* here."
"And I am delighted," Justin Foote commented. "To have three charming young ladies added to our Families through breaking rules proves something I have long suspected: Rules serve best when broken."
"A wise man – "
" – and with dimples, too. Mr. Foote, would you like to marry me and my sister?"
"Say 'Yes'! She can cook, but I'm cuddly."
Minerva said, "Stop it, girls."
"Why? Have you got him staked out already? Was that why we couldn't come in? Mr. Foote, Minerva is Mama Pro Tem to us by edict – "
" – which is patently unfair – "
" – as she is actually years and *years* younger than we are – "
" – and it gives us three mothers to dodge instead of the regulation one."
"Belay that," Lazarus ordered. "Both of you can cook, but neither of you is very cuddly."
"Then why do you cuddle us, Buddy Boy?"
" – suppressed incestuous yearning perhaps?"
"Merde. Because you both are immature, insecure, and frightened."
The redheads looked at each other. "Lori?"
"I heard it. Unless I'm hallucinating."
"No, I heard it, too."
"Is it time to cry?"
"We'd better save it. Mr. Foote wouldn't want to see how our Buddy Boy goes all to pieces when we cry."
"We'll save it. That makes two cries and a chin quivering he's got coming. Unless Mr. Foote would *like* to see it."
"Would you, Mr. Foote?"

"Justin, I'll sell either one of them cheap. Still better price on a package deal."

"Uh . . . thank you, Lazarus, but I'm afraid that they might cry at *me* – then *I* would go all to pieces. Can we change the subject? How did you manage to put over this triple, uh, irregularity? May one ask? Doctor Hildegarde runs a very taut organization."

"Well, in the case of those two little angels over there – "

"Sarcasm now – "

" – and not clever."

" – I was flummoxed quite as much as Nelly Hildegarde. At the time, Ishtar Hardy, that one's mother – "

"No, *her* mother."

"You two are interchangeable parts, and besides, you were mixed up the week you were born, and nobody knows which you are; you don't know yourself."

"Oh, yes, I do! Sometimes she goes away, but I'm always right here."

Lazarus paused in midflight, looked thoughtful. "That may be the most succinct statement of the solipsist thesis I've ever heard. Write it down."

"If I did, you'd take credit for it."

"I simply want to save it for posterity . . . a notion incompatible with the thesis itself. Minerva, you preserve it for me."

"Recorded, Lazarus."

"Minerva has almost as exact a memory as she had when she was a computer. I was saying: Ishtar was temporarily Clinic boss, Nelly having gone on leave, so access to my tissue was no problem. I was then in a state of acute anhedonia, and their mothers cooked up this notion for restoring my interest in life. The only problem was to do gene surgery not permitted by the rules of Secundus Clinic. How and who – I was told firmly not to inquire. You can ask Minerva; she was in on the swindle."

"Lazarus, that was a memory I did not bring along when I was selecting what to fit into this skull."

"You see, Justin? I'm allowed to know only what they think is good for me. As may be, this heroic treatment worked; I have not been bored since. Other descriptives might apply – but not that one."

Lori, do you sense a double entendre?"

"No, merely a thinly veiled innuendo. Ignore it with dignity."

"But at first I didn't know my odd relationship to this pair.

Oh, I couldn't help knowing that Ishtar, and Hamadryad – one of Ira's daughters; you've met her?"

"Years back. A lovely girl."

"Quite. Both of their mothers are lovely. I couldn't help knowing that both were pregnant; they were spending most of their time with me. But although they were swelling up like poisoned pups, they ignored it, so I didn't inquire."

Justin nodded. "Privacy."

"Naw, just hard-nosed. I've never let the privacy custom keep me from snooping when it suited me. I was miffed, that's all. Here two girls are with me every day and like daughters to me and obviously as knocked up as Pharaoh's Daughter – and they tell me nit. So I got stubborn and outsat them. Till one day Galahad – he's their husband – well, not exactly; you'll see – Galahad invites me downstairs, and here they have, one each, the two prettiest little redheads I ever saw."

"Shall we let him off one cry?"

"You got over it; you both look like *me* now."

"Or do we add a third cry for *that*?"

"I still don't smell a mouse; I'm simply pleased. As well as amazed that they had produced babies that looked like identical twins –"

"Which we are, except that we're triplets."

"But some weeks of playing with these babies causes my natural genius and suspicious mind to infer that the girls have pulled a whizzer. I was not then in the sperm bank so far as I knew, but I am well aware of tricks that can be played on a helpless client undergoing antigeria, so with unerring logic I reach the wrong answer: These babies are my daughters by artificial insemination unmentioned to me. So I accuse them of it. And they deny it. And I explain that I am not angry, but quite the contrary I *hope* these little cherubs are mine."

' "Cherubs'."

"Ignore it. He's simply trying to con Mr. Foote."

"Cherubs at that time, I mean, aside from a tendency to bite. That I *want* them to be mine and share my name and fortunes. So they confer with their fellow conspirators – Minerva and Galahad – Minerva was in it up to her overload safeties."

"Lazarus, you *needed* a family."

"Quite right, dear. I'm always better off with a family; it keeps me harmlessly occupied and unbored. Justin, did I mention that Minerva allowed me to adopt her?"

"*We* weren't asked!"

"Look, kids, under the loose rules of this termite hill I can unadopt you this minute, if such be your wish. Cut the tie. Be just your genetic brother through circumstances I had no more part in than you had. Renounce all authority over you two. Let me know."

The two girls looked at each other briefly. Then one said, "Lazarus –"

"Yes, Lorelei?"

"Lapis Lazuli and I have discussed it, and we both think that you are just exactly the father we want."

"Thank you, my dears."

"And to confirm it, we are cancelling two cries and a chin quiver."

"That's most pleasing."

"And besides that, we want to be cuddled . . . because we are feeling very immature, insecure, and frightened."

Lazarus blinked. "I don't want you to feel that way, ever. But – Well, can the cuddling wait?"

"Oh, certainly – Father. We know we have a guest. But perhaps you and Mr. Foote would join us in bathing? Before dinner?"

"Well, Justin? Bathing with my hellions is squirmy but fun. I don't do it often because they turn it into a social event and waste time. Suit yourself; don't let your arm be twisted."

"A bath I certainly need. I was clean when I was sealed into that pod – but how long was I in it? I really don't know. And a bath should always be a social event if there is time . . . and good company. Thank you, ladies; I accept."

"And I accept, too," put in Minerva. "I'm inviting myself. Justin, Tertius is primitive compared with Secundus, but our family refresher is nice and quite large enough for sociability. 'Decadent,' as Lazarus calls it."

"I designed it to be decadent, Justin. Good plumbing is the finest flower of decadence and one I have always enjoyed when I could get it."

"Uh – my clothes are still in Ira's office. Even my toiletries. Absentminded, I'm sorry."

"No matter. Ira may fetch your bag, but he's absentminded, too. Depilatories, deodorants, scents – no problem. I'll lend you a toga or something."

"Buddy Boy! I mean 'Father.' Does that mean we *dress* for dinner?"

"Call me Buddy Boy; I'm hardened to it. Go as far as you like, darlings . . . except that as usual Mama Hamadryad must okay any cosmetics. Back to how I acquired these daughters who are my sisters, Justin: Having conferred, this gang of genetic priates came clean and threw themselves on the mercy of the court. Me. So I adopted these two, and we registered them, and the registration will be straightened out one day, as I explained. How Minerva gave up the profession of computer and assumed the sorrows that flesh is heir to is a longer story. Want to synopsize it, dear? – and fill him in later if you wish."

"Yes, Father."

"None of your lip, dear; you're a grown woman now. Justin, when we woke this darling, she was about the size and biological age of those two reformed hellions – remind me to take their temperatures, Minerva. I adopted Minerva because she needed a father then. Doesn't now."

"Lazarus, I will always need you as my father."

"Thank you, my dear, but I take that only as a pleasing compliment. Tell Justin your story."

"All right. Justin, are you familiar with the theories concerning self-awareness in computers?"

"Several of them. As you know, my work is mostly with computers."

"Permit me to say, speaking from experience, all theories are empty. How a computer becomes self-aware remains as much a mystery, even to computers, as the age-old mystery of flesh-and-blood self-awareness. It just *is*. But, so far as I've heard – quite far in view of the library that was locked in my memories then and is still in Athene's memories – self-awareness *never* arises in a computer designed only for deductive logic and mathematical calculations, no matter how big it is. But if it is designed for inductive logic, able to assess data, draw hypotheses therefrom, test them, reconstruct them to the new data, make random comparisons of the results, and change those reconstructions – exercise judgement the way a flesh-and-blood does, then self-awareness may occur. But I don't know why and no computer knows. It just *does*."

She smiled. "Sorry, I did not mean to sound pedantic. Lazarus figured out that I could go into a blank human brain, a clone brain, using techniques used to conserve memories in rejuvenation clinics. When we discussed this, I had the entire technical library of Secundus Howard Clinic in me – stolen, in a way. I no longer have it; I had to pick and choose what to take along when I went into this skull. So I don't remember much of what I did, any more than a rejuvenation client knows all that is done to him; you would have to get details from Athene, who still has them – and who, by the way, never had the rather painful awakening that a computer goes through when it first begins to know itself, because I left a piece of me in Athene, oh, like a yeast starter. Athene dimly remembers having been Minerva at one time – about the way we flesh-and-bloods" – Minerva straightened up, smiled, and looked proud – "remember a dream as something not quite real. And I remember being Minerva the Computer somewhat the same way. I remember all my contacts with people very sharply – because I chose to keep them, replicate them into this skull. But if anyone were to ask how I handled the transport system of New Rome . . . well, I know that I did, but not *how* I did it."

She smiled again. "That's my story: A computer who longed to be a flesh-and-blood and who had loving friends who made it possible . . . and I've never regretted it; I love being flesh-and-blood – and want to love everybody." She looked at Justin Foote very soberly. "Lazarus spoke sooth; I have never been a guest wife; I am only three years old as a flesh-and-blood. Should you choose me, you may find me awkward and shy – but not reluctant. I owe you much."

"Minerva," said Lazarus, "back him into a corner some other time. You didn't tell Justin what he wanted to know; you left out the hanky-panky."

"Oh."

"And when you were philosophizing about awareness in computers, you left out the key point, it seems to me, one *I* know but you may not even though you've been a computer and I have not. Because this key point applies both to computers and to flesh-and-bloods. My dear – and Justin – and it won't hurt you two erratic geniuses to listen – all machinery is animistic – 'humanistic,' I want to say, but that term has been preempted. Any machine is a concept of a human designer; if reflects the human brain, be it wheelbarrow or giant computer. So there is nothing mysterious in a machine designed by a human showing human self-awareness; the mystery lies in awareness itself, wherever it's found. I used to have a folding camp cot that liked to bite me. I don't say that it was aware – but I learned to approach it with caution.

"But, Minerva, darling, I've seen some big computers, almost as smart as you were, that never developed self-awareness. Can you tell us why?"

"I confess I can't, Lazarus. I'd like to ask Athene when we get home."

"She probably doesn't know either; she's never met any other major computer but Dora. Captain Lazuli, how far back do you remember? Once you – or your comrade in crime – claimed to remember nursing. Suckling, I mean."

"Of course we do! Doesn't everybody?"

"No. Me, for example. I was a bottle baby; I don't remember even that. Not worth remembering. In consequence I've been looking at tits and admiring them ever since. Tell me, one of you, when you remember nursing, can you recall which of your mothers was giving you suck?"

"Of course!" Lorelei said scornfully. "Mama Ishtar has big tits –"

" – and Mama Hamadryad has much smaller ones even when they're filled with milk – "

"But she gave just as much milk."

"Different flavour though. Made it nice to trade off each meal. Variety."

"But we liked *both* flavours! Tell him, Laz."

"Enough. You've made the point I wanted. Justín, these kids were self-aware and aware of other people – their mothers at least – at an age when a crèche baby is just a doughy blob . . . which says something about why crèches have never worked well. I want the counterpoint: Minerva, what do you remember of the time when you were an unawakened clone?"

"Why, nothing, Lazarus. Oh, some odd dreams when I was putting me – my selected memories – into my new me, this one. But I didn't start that until Ishtar said the clone was big enough. That was not until shortly before I withdrew from my former me and Ishtar woke me. It could not be instantaneous, Justin; a protein brain won't take data at computer speeds, Ishtar had me be very slow and careful. Then for a short time – short human time – I was both places, computer and skull; then I surrendered the computer and let it become Pallas Athene, and Ishtar woke me. But, Lazarus, a clone in vitro is not aware; it's like a fetus in utero. No stimuli. Correction: minimum stimuli and nothing that leaves a permanent memory track. Unless you count reports of regression under hypnosis."

"No need to count them," Lazarus replied. "True or false, such cases are irrelevant. The relevant counterpoint is 'minimum stimuli.' Honey, those big computers with awareness potential but without self-awareness are that way because nobody bothered to love the poor things. That's all. Babies or big computers – they become aware through being given lots of personal attention. 'Love' as it's usually called. Minerva, does that theory match up with your earliest years?"

Minerva looked soberly thoughtful. "That was about a century ago in human time – call it a million times that in computer time. I know from the records that I was assembled a few years before Ira took office. But the earliest personal memories I have – and those memories I saved and did not leave in Athene or in the computer in New Rome – the earliest I can remember of *me* is waiting eagerly and happily for the next time Ira would speak to me."

Lazarus said, "I need not belabour the point. With babies you breastfeed them and nibble their toes and talk to them and blow in their bellybuttons and make them laugh. Computers don't have bellybuttons, but attention works just as well on them. Justin, Minerva tells me that she left nothing of herself in the computer under the palace."

"That is correct. I left it intact as a computer and programmed for all its duties . . . but I dared not leave any personal memory, any part of the *me*, could not let it remember that it had once been Minerva; that wouldn't have been fair to it. Lazarus warned me, and I was most careful, checking all the billions of bits and wiping where necessary."

Justin Foote said, "I missed a turn somehow. You did this in New Rome . . . but you've been awake here only three years?"

"Three wonderful years! You see –"

"Let me interrupt, dear; I'll tell him the hanky-panky. But first – Justin, have you dealt with the executive computer in New Rome since we migrated? Of course you have – but have you been in the office of Madam Chairman Pro Tem when she was using it?"

"Why, yes, several times. Just yesterday – no, I mean the yesterday before I left; I keep forgetting that I missed transit time."

"What name does she use in speaking with it?"

"I don't think she uses a name. I'm fairly certain she does not."

"Oh, the poor thing!"

"No, Minerva," Lazarus said quietly. "You left it in good health; it simply won't wake up until it has a mistress, or master, who appreciates it. Which might not be long," he added grimly.

Justin Foote said, "Might be any time. Lazarus, that old, uh – cancel that. Arabelle loves the spotlight. Appears at public meetings, shows up in the Colosseum. Stands up and waves her scarf. Seems odd, after the quiet way Ira ran things."

"I see. A sitting duck. Seven to two she's assassinated in the next five years."

"No bet. I'm a statistician, Lazarus."

"So you are. All right – Hanky-panky. Lots of it. Ishtar set up an auxiliary Howard Clinic in the Palace. Her excuse: Me, the Senior. But a cover-up for a much more extensive bio facility. Minerva picked her parents; Ishtar stole the tissues and faked some records. Meanwhile, our skinny friend my daughter Minerva – "

"She is not! She's just right for her height and body type and bio age!"

"– and deliciously curved!"

"– had twinned her computer self in a hold of my yacht 'Dora,' placing the contract in my name and charging it to me, and nobody dared inquire why the Senior – some advantages to age, especially among Howards – wanted a huge computer in a yacht that already had one of the fanciest computers in the sky. While back in my borrowed penthouse where *nobody* was allowed to go – other than a short list all as dishonest as I am – a clone was growing in a facility installed in a room I didn't need.

"Comes time to migrate, a very large case containing what was then a very small clone, goes to the skyport marked as part of my personal baggage – this baggage between us, of course – and is loaded into the 'Dora' without inspection, such being a preroga-tive of being Chairman . . . for as you may recall I didn't hand the gavel back to Arabelle until our transports had lifted and I was about to raise ship myself, with Ira and the rest of my personal party aboard.

"While I'm taking the clone aboard, Minerva withdraws herself from the executive computer and is safe and snug in a hold of the 'Dora' . . . with her gizzards packed with every bit of data in the Grand Library and the entire records of the Howard

Clinic including secret and confidential stuff. A most satisfying caper, Justin, the most good, clean, illegal fun I've had since we stole the 'New Frontiers.' But I'm telling you this not to boast – or not much – but to ask if we were as slick as we thought we were. Any rumours? Did you suspect anything amiss? How about Arabelle?"

"I feel sure that Arabelle does not suspect. Nor have I heard of Nelly Hildegarde bursting any blood vessels. Mmm, *I* suspected something."

"Really. Where did we slip?"

"Hardly the word, Lazarus. Minerva, when I had occasion to consult you, while Ira was Chairman Pro Tem, how did we talk?"

"Why, you were always most friendly, Justin. You always told me *why* you wanted something instead of just telling me to dig it out. You would chat, too; you were never too much in a hurry to be pleasant. That's why I remember you so warmly."

"And that, Lazarus, is why I sniffed something dead behind the arras. You and your party had been gone about a week when I wanted something from the executive computer. When you have an old friend with a pleasant voice – your voice is unchanged, Minerva; I should have recognized it – but I was bedazzled by your appearance – when you call this old friend and are answered by a flat, mechanical voice . . . and any deviation from programming language is answered by: 'NULL PROGRAMME – REPEAT – WAITING FOR PROGRAMME' – then you know that an old friend is dead." He smiled at the girl between them. "So I can't tell you how delighted I am to learn that my old friend was reborn as a lovely young girl."

Minerva squeezed his hand, blushed slightly, and said nothing.

"Hmm – Justin, did you compare notes with anyone?"

"Ancestor, do you think I am a fool? I mind my own business."

"Apology, about grade two. No, you're not a fool, unless you go back and work for the old harridan."

"When will the next wave of migrants head this way? I hate to waste the work I've done on your life, and I would hate to abandon my personal library."

"Well, sir, no tellin' when a streetcar will be by this time o' night. Discuss it later." Lazarus added, "That's our house ahead."

Justin Foote looked, saw a building partly visible through trees, turned back to speak to Minerva. "Something you said earlier, Cousin, I did not understand. You said 'I owe you so much.' If I was pleasant to you – at New Rome, I mean – you were at least as pleasant to me. More likely the debt is the other way; you were always most helpful."

Instead of answering, she looked at Lazarus. He said, "Your business, my dear."

Minerva took a deep breath, then said, "I plan to name twenty-three of my children for my twenty-three parents."

"So? That seems most warmly appropriate."

"You're not my cousin, Justin – you're my father. One of them."

VARIATIONS ON A THEME

XIV

Bacchanalia

After the track through the gormtrees at the northern edge of Boondock swings right, one has a view of the home of Lazarus Long, but I hardly noticed it when I first saw it; I was much bemused by a statement by Minerva Long. Me her father? *Me?*

The Senior said, "Close your mouth, Son; you're making a draft. Dear, you startled him."

"Oh, dear!"

"Now quit looking like a frightened fawn, or I'll be forced to hold your nose and administer two ounces of eighty-proof ethanol disguised as fruit juice. You've done nothing wrong. Justin, does disguised ethanol interest you?"

"Yes," I agreed fervently. "I recall a time in my youth when that and one other subject were all I was interested in."

"If the other subject wasn't women, we'll find a monastic cubbyhole where you can drink alone. But it was – I know more about you than you think. All right, we'll have a libation or six. Not those two, they're potential alcoholics."

"Slanderous – "

" – though regrettably true – "

" – but we did it only once – "

" – and won't do it again!"

"Don't commit yourself too far, kids; a brannigan might sneak up on you. Better to know your resistance than to be tripped through ignorance. Grow up, put on some mass, and you'll be able to cope with it. Or Ishtar mixed up your genes, which she didn't. Now about this other matter, Justin. Yes, you're one of Minerva's parents . . . and that's a very high compliment, because those twenty-three chromosome pairs were picked from tissues of thousands of superior people, using fearsome mathematics to handle the multiplicity of variables, plus Ishtar's knowledge of genetics, and some unnecessary advice from me, before this little darling got the precise mix she wanted to be."

I started to set up the type problem in my head – yes, that would be some problem, extremely more difficult than the ordinary genetics problem of advising one male and one female – then dropped it, as I had its delightful answer by her left hand. Lazarus was still speaking:

"Minerva could have been male, two metres tall, massing a hundred kilos, built like Joe Colossus, and hung like a stallion mule. Instead she elected to be what she is: slender, female, shy – I'm not sure she selected for that last. Did you, dear?"

"No, Lazarus; no one knows which genes control that. I think I get it from Hamadryad."

"I think you got it from a computer I used to know – and took along all of it as Athene certainly is not shy. Never mind. Some of Minerva's donor-parents are dead; some are alive but unaware that a bit of tissue from a clone in stasis or from the live-tissue bank was borrowed – as in your case. Some know that they are donor-parents – me, for example, and you heard Hamadryad mentioned. You'll meet others, some being on Tertius, where it's no secret. But consanguinity is not close for anyone. One twenty-third? The genetic advisers wouldn't run that through a computer; it's an acceptable risk. Plus the fact that none of us donor-parents of Minerva have any known skeletons hanging on our family trees. You could safely have progeny by her; so could I."

"But you refused me!" Minerva startled me with the vehemence with which she accused Lazarus of this. For a moment she was not shy; her eyes flashed.

"Now, now, dear. You were only a year out of vitro and not fully grown even though Ishtar forced you past menarche still in vitro. Ask me on another occasion; I might startle you."

" 'Startle' me, or surprise me?"

"Never mind that old joke. Justin, I simply wanted to make clear that your relationship to Minerva, while close enough that it makes Minerva feel sentimental, is in fact so small that you barely qualify as a 'kissing cousin.' "

"I feel very sentimental about it," I told the Senior. "Most pleased and deeply honoured – although I can't guess why I was picked."

"If you want to know which chromosome pair was swiped from you, and why, you had best ask Ishtar and get her to consult Athene; I doubt if Minerva still knows."

"But I *do* know; I saved those memories. Justin, I wanted to retain some ability in mathematics. It was a choice between you and Libby Professor Owens – so I chose you; you are my friend."

(Well! I respect Jake Hardy-Owens; I'm merely an applied mathematician, he is a brilliant theoretician.) "Whatever your reasons, dear kissing cousin, I am delighted that you chose me as one of your donor-fathers."

"Grounded, Commodore!" announced one of the duplicate redheads – Lapis Lazuli – as the little nullboat clumped to a stop. (It appeared to be a Corson Farmsled and I was surprised to see it in a new Colony). Lazarus answered, "Thank you, Captain."

The twins bounced out; the Senior and I handed Minerva out – unnecessary help that she accepted with gracious dignity, that being another aspect of colonial life that surprised me, New Rome being rather short on such archaic ceremony. (Over and again I found the Boondockers to be both more formally polite, and more casually relaxed about it, than are Secundians. I suppose my notions of frontier life had been fed on too many romances: rough, bearded men fighting off dangerous animals, mules hauling covered wagons toward distant horizons.)

"Captain" Lazuli said, "Humpty Dumpty – *go to bed!*" The nullboat waddled away; the little girls joined us, one taking my free hand, the other taking the Senior's free hand, with Minerva between us. These freckled flametops would have had my whole attention had not Minerva been there. I am not compulsively fond of children; some youngsters seem to me rather poisonous especially precocious ones. But in their case I found their solemn precocity charming rather than irritating . . . and to see the Senior's features, rugged rather than handsome and with that too-large nose, unmistakably reproduced but transformed into piquant girlish features – well, had I been alone, I would have chuckled with delight.

I said "just a moment," and held onto Lorelei's hand and thereby caused all to pause while I took a second look. "Lazarus, who is the architect?"

"I don't know," he said. "Dead more than four thousand years. The original belonged to the political boss of Pompeii, a city destroyed about that long ago. I saw a model of it, restored, in a museum in a place called Denver, and took pictures; it pleased me. Those pictures are long gone, but it turned out that when I tried to describe it to Athene, she had a solly in the historical section of her gizzards of the ruins of that same house –

and from that and my description, she designed this version. Some minor mods, nothing that changed its sweet proportions. Then Athene built it, using extensionals and radio links. It's practical for this climate; the weather here is much like that of Pompeii – and I prefer a house that looks inward, on a court. Safer, even in a place as safe as this one."

"By the way, where *is* Athene? The main computer itself, I mean."

"Here. She was still in the 'Dora' when she built this; now she's under the house – she built her underground home first, then built our house on top of it."

Minerva said simply. "A computer prefers to feel safe, and close to her own people. Lazarus – forgive me, dear, but you have reversed a time sequence; that was more than three years ago."

"Oh, so I have. Minerva, when you have lived as long as I have – and you will – you'll find yourself inverting time sequences endlessly, a flesh-and-blood shortcoming you had to accept when you took the plunge. Correction, Justin – 'Minerva,' not 'Athene.'"

"Yes it *is* Athene who built it – now," Minerva added, "since engineering and the details of this construction and others are things I left behind in Athene, where they belong, and abstracted only a simplified memory of having built it – I wanted to remember that much."

I said, "Whoever built it, it's beautiful." I was suddenly upset. It is one thing to accept intellectually the startling idea that a young woman has had a former life as a computer – and even to accept that one had worked with that computer years back and light-years away. But this discussion suddenly brought home to me emotional belief that this lovely girl with her arm warm in mine had in sober fact been a computer so short a time ago that she had built this new house – while a computer. It shook me – even though I am a historiographer, old, and my sense of wonder was dulled even before my first rejuvenation.

We went in, and my upset was swept away by greetings. We were kissed all around – two beautiful young women, one of whom I recognized when I heard her name, Ira's daughter Hamadryad and she looks like one, the other a statuesque blonde whose name, Ishtar, was familiar to me through talk, and a young man as beautiful as the women and who seemed familiar though

I could not place him. Even the twin flametops insisted on kissing me since they had not greeted me that way earlier.

In Boondock a kiss of greeting is not the ritual peck it usually is in New Rome; even the twins bussed me in a fashion that made me certain of their sex – I've had poorer kisses from grown women whose intentions were direct and immediate. But the young man, introduced as "Galahad," startled me. He hugged me, with kisses on my cheeks followed by a kiss on my mouth worthy of a Ganymede – which surprised me, but I tried to return as good as I got.

Instead of letting me go, he pounded my back and said, "Justin, it tickles my root to see you again! Oh, this is wonderful!"

I pulled my face back to look at his. I must have looked puzzled for he blinked, then said mournfully: "Ish, I boasted too soon! Hamadear, get me a towel, I'm weeping. He's *forgotten* me . . . after all the things he said."

I said, "Obadiah Jones, what are *you* doing here?"

"Weeping. Being humiliated in front of my family."

I don't know how long it had been since I had seen him. It may have been more than a century since it has been that long since I left the Howard campus. Brilliant young specialist in ancient cultures he was then, with an impish sense of humour. I recalled, dredging it up out of memory, having shared a Seven-Hours with him and two other savants, both female and happily so – but I could not recall their faces nor who they were; what I remembered was his playful, joyous, boisterous good company.

"Obadiah," I said sternly, "why are you calling yourself 'Galahad'? Hiding from the police again? Lazarus, I'm shocked to find this, uh, macho in your house – lock up your daughters!"

"Oh, that *name!*" he said brokenly. "Don't repeat it, Justin. They don't know it. When I reformed, I changed my name. You won't give me away? Promise me, dear!" Suddenly he grinned and said in a cheerful voice, "Come on into the atrium and let's get a skinful of rum into you. Lazi, who has the duty?"

"Lor does. Even-numbered day. But I'll help. Straight rum?"

"Better flavour it. I want to add a welcome the Borgias used on old friends."

"Sure thing, Uncle Cuddly. Who are the Borgias?"

"A family from the greatest days of Old Earth's rise and fall, sugar lump. The Howards of their time. Very suave in handling guests. I'm descended from them, and their secrets were passed down to me by word of mouth."

"Laz," said Lazarus, "ask Athene for a rundown on the Borgias before you mix a drink for Justin."

"I see; he's at it again – "

" – so we'll tickle him –

" – and blow in his ears –

" – until he cries Pax –

" – and promises Veritas – "

" – he's no problem. Come on, Lazi."

I had found the village of Boondock pleasantly unimpressive, more pleasant and less impressive than I had expected. Ira and Lazarus had accepted only seven thousand for their first wave from applicants numbering more than ninety thousand; therefore the present population of Tertius could not be much over ten thousand and was in fact slightly less.

Boondock seemed to have only a few hundred people and was centred on a few small buildings for public and semipublic purposes, most colonists being scattered around the countryside. The home of Lazarus Long was by far the most impressive structure I had seen – not counting the large flat cone of the Senior's yacht and the much larger bulk of one robot space freighter on the skyfield where my packet had grounded. (The skyfield was a level place a few kilometres across; one could not call it a port. There was not one godown. It must have an autobeacon since I grounded safely; I did not see it.)

This rudimentary settlement had not prepared me for the Senior's house. Its lines and plan were simple; that long-dead Roman had picked a good designer. It was a walled garden, the house itself being its four walls. But it had two storeys, and each level could have been devided, it seemed to me, into twelve to sixteen large rooms plus the usual ancillary spaces. Twenty-four or more rooms for a household of eight? The more blatantly rich in New Rome might display ego in so much space, but it seemed inappropriate in a new colony, as well as out of tune with what I had learned in my long research of the Senior's lives.

Simple – Half the building was given over to a rejuvenation clinic, a therapy clinic, an infirmary; these could be reached from the foyer without entering the private part of the house. The number of family rooms remaining was indefinite; most interior walls were movable. The Howard Clinic and the medical facilities would be moved to a nearby site when the colony needed larger facilities, when size of the Senior's family made more home space desirable.

(I was lucky in that, when I arrived, no client was being rejuvenated, no patient was in the infirmary – or most of the adults would have been busy.)

The size of his family seemed as hazy as the number of rooms. I had thought there were eight – three men, the Senior, Ira, and Galahad; three women, Ishtar, Jamadryad, and Minerva; two youngsters, Lorelei Lee and Lapis Lazuli – but I was not aware of two girl toddlers and a small boy. Besides that, I was neither the first nor the last to be urged to move in and stay as long as one wished. Whether such stay was as a guest or as a member of the Senior's family might also be unclear to an outsider.

Relationships inside his family also were vague. Colonists are always families; a single colonist is a contradiction in terms. But all of Tertius Colony were Howards, and we Howards have used every sort of marriage, I think, except lifetime monogamy.

But Tertius has no laws about marriage; the Senior had not thought them necessary. The few laws it has are in migration contract, written by Ira and Lazarus jointly. It contains the usual covenants about homesteading, with the colony leader absolute arbitrator until such time as he resigns. But it says not one word about marriage and family relationships. The colonists register their babies; Howards always do – in this case with the Computer Athene as surrogate for the Archives. But I found when I reviewed these records that parentage of children was expressed in genetic classification code, not by marriages and putative ancestry. This system the Families' geneticists have been urging for generations (and I agree), but it does make a genealogist work harder, especially if marriages have not been registered at all, as was sometimes the case.

I found one couple with eleven children, six his, five hers, none theirs. I understood it when I read their codes – utterly incompatible. I met them later, a fine family on a prosperous farm and no suggestion that the swarm of children were anything but "theirs."

But the Senior's family was even more vague. Genetic ancestry in each case was a matter of record, surely – but who was married to whom?

Their bathing room was as "decadent" as had been promised; it was a lounging room, as well as a refresher, and planned for family relaxation and entertaining. It stretched all along the ground floor on the side facing the foyer across the inner garden, and its walls could be pushed back to open it to the garden in clement weather – which this was and quite warm.

It had anything a jaundiced Sybarite could ask for: a fountain in its centre matching a fountain in the garden and each with comfortably wide rims to sit on while soaking tired feet and enjoying a drink; a sauna in one corner; a huge happy shower at the other end with space for several cycles to be enjoyed at once without waiting turns; a companion querafansible with sophisticated controls; a long soaking pool knee-deep at the blue end to chin-deep at the red, and flanked by two bathing pools lavish for one person and comfortable for two or three; couches for napping, for cooling, for sweating, for intimate talk and touch; a cosmetics table with a big duomirror in which one could see her back as readily as her front simply by asking Athene's help; a corner big enough for a dozen people in which floor cushioning was bed-soft and lavish with pillows large and small, firm and soft; a refreshments counter which backed onto their kitchen – and if I failed to name something, it is my omission, not that of the designers. All the more commonplace items were of course at hand.

I had thought that the lighting was random until I realized that Athene was changing it endlessly so as not to shine it in anyone's eyes while changing the light level in all parts of that big room to match what was going on – high key for makeup, subdued light for lounging, and so on – and to match personalities too; our little redheads were crowned with light no matter how they bounced around – as they did.

Soft music was there and in the garden, or on request anywhere, selected by Athene unless someone asked for something – it seemed as if she had stored in her all the music that ever was written. Or she might harmonize with the twins while continuing to take part in three different conversations in other parts of the bath lounge. A self-aware computer of her capacity – great enough to manage Secundus – can and often must talk simultaneously at many places, but I had never encountered it before in such a way as to notice it. But big computers are not often members of a family.

The rest of the house was almost unautomated – a matter of taste as Athene's capacity was largely unused. My hostesses actually cooked, with Athene helping only by seeing to it that nothing burned and watching the timing in other ways – twice on Athene's advice Hamadryad left the bath lounge, once in such a hurry that she fled bare and dripping, not stopping to grab a towel robe.

Bathing with Lazi and Lori is indeed "squirmy but fun", plus squeals, giggles, chatter in which one sentence would be chopped several times before one of them put a period on it (I hypothesized that they were telepathic with each other and had an uneasy suspicion that they sometimes read thoughts of persons in their presence – but was not anxious to find out) – all charmingly blunt and childishly innocent.

First they slathered me all over with scented liquid soup and demanded the same service from me and threatened me with chin quivering when I held back a little, and said loudly that "Uncle Cuddly" (my old friend Obadiah, now Galahad) washed them better than that and everybody knows how lazy *he* is – or didn't I like them well enough to soapy-cuddle them and if they married me, would I go along with them in their spaceship, and while they were still virgins, though not from lack of opportunity, don't worry about that one bit as both Mama Hamadryad and Mama Ishtar were coaching them in beginning and advanced sensuality and would speed up the course if I happened to want to marry them now – won't you, Mama Hamalambie? – tell him!

Hamadryad from a metre away (she was soaping Ira) assured us that she would, if they could persuade me to marry them that quickly. I assumed that the youngsters were farcing me and that their mother – one of their mothers – was going along with the jest. I've wondered since whether I missed a diamond opportunity. Lazarus was in hearing distance; he did not tell them to stop teasing me, he simply advised me not to offer them more than a ten-year contract as their span of attention was limited – which made them indignant – and advised them that, if they intended to get married that night, they had better trim their toenails first, which made them still more indignant so they stopped bathing me to assault him from both sides.

This wound up with one of them under each of his arms and still struggling. Lazarus asked if I would accept custody or should he drop them into the deep end of the soak?

I accepted custody, and we showered each other off and went into the soak pool together – and I was standing in it up to my shoulders with my back to the garden, and supporting them a little, an arm each, as their toes did not touch bottom, when someone placed hands over my eyes.

The twins squealed, "Aunt Tammy!" and levitated out of the water while I turned to look.

Tamara Sperling – I had thought she was off Secundus, in retirement up country. Tamara the Superb, the Superlative, the Unique – in my opinion (and many others) the greatest artist of her profession. I feel sure that I am not the only man who chose when she left New Rome to remain celibate for a long time.

She had come in, seen that the family was in the bath lounge, dropped her gown in the garden, hurried in without stopping to remove her high sandals, spotted me, and blindfolded me with her lovely hands.

Why? She was my dinner partner – and (if I could rely on an exchange I had heard that afternoon) willing to be my guest wife if I were willing. *Willing?* Fifty years earlier I had offered her any contract she would accept every time she let me visit her and had finally shut up only after she had told me repeatedly, patiently, and gently that she did not intend to have more children and would not marry again for any other purpose.

But there she was, rejuvenated (not that it mattered), looking gloriously young and healthy – and a colonist. I wondered who the man was who had persuaded her to do this? I envied him and wondered what superhuman qualities he possessed – but whatever they were, if Tamara was willing to share a bed with me even for one night and only for old times' sake, I would take what the gods offered and not worry about him; her wealth is endlessly divisible. Tamara! – bells sound at her name.

She kissed two wet little girls, then dropped to her knees and kissed me.

Then she said softly, rubbing her mouth against mine, "You darling. When I heard you were here, I hurried. Mi laroona d' vashti meedth du?"

"Yes! And any other night you have free."

"Not so fast with English, dorreth mi; I learning it – slowly – because my daughter wants her assistants in rejuvenation to speak language not known to most clients . . . and because our family speaks English much as Galacta."

"You are now a rejuvenator? And have a daughter here?"

"Ishtar datter mi – did you not know, petsan mi-mi? Nay, I am nurse only. But studying I am and Ishtar hope-tells that I will be assistant technician in half handful years. Good – nay?"

"Good, I suppose. But what a loss to the art!"

"Blandjor," she said happily, tousling my wet hair. "Even though rejuvenated – did you note? – here the art pays no living. Too many willing ones, sweeter and younger and prettier." The twins had stayed with us, listening and quiet for a moment. Tamara reached out both arms, hugged them to her. "Example. These my granddaughters. Eager to grow tall so they can lie down and be short." She kissed each of them. "And red curls they have. I not have."

I started to say that age and red curls did not matter, then realized that a compliment to Tamara so phrased could cause chins to quiver. But I did not need to speak; the spout had opened again:

"Aunt Tammy, we are *not* eager – "

" – just willing and practical – "

" – and anyhow *he* won't marry us – "

" – he just teases about it – "

" – and you *can't* be our grandmother – "

" – 'cause that would make you our Buddy Boy's grandmother – "

" – which is illogical, impossible, and ridiculous – "

" – so you have to be our 'Aunt Tammy.' "

I found their logic doubly enthymematic if not a total *non sequitur*, but I agreed with it because the notion of Tamara being the Senior's grandmother was one I could not face. So I changed the subject:

"Tamara dear, would you let me take off your sandals and then you come join us in the soak? Or shall I get out and get dry?"

She did not have to answer:

"We gotta run get ready – "

" – cause Mama Hamadryad has finished her face and started her nipples – "

" – so if we don't hurry, we'll have to come to dinner with our hides bare naked – "

" – and for a party that would *never* do – "

" – and you two had better hurry *too* – "

" – or Buddy Boy will throw it to the pigs. Scuse!"

I climbed out and let Tamara dry me – unnecessary as there was a blowdry at hand. But if Tamara offers me anything my answer is Yes. It took a while; we "wasted" time on touch and talk. (Is there a better way to spend time?)

When I was dry and wondering if I should try the cosmetics bench (I don't use cosmetics much, just depilatories), one of the twins came rushing back with a garment for me, a blue chlamys. She said breathlessly, "Lazarus says try this or what would you like? – but that you needn't wear anything if you don't want to 'cause it's a hot night and you count as family because you're Minerva's father, one of them."

I thought I had them keyed now by freckle pattern. "Thank you, Lorelei; I'll wear it." I've always felt that a napkin was enough to wear in dining at home in a properly tempered house – or outdoors in private on a warm night. But, as guest of honour even though "family," I could not go bare when they were taking the trouble to be festively formal.

"You're welcome, but I'm Captain Lazuli, but that's all right, she's me. Scuse!" She vanished.

I put it on; we went into the garden and retrieved Tamara's gown – and it matched what I was wearing. The same shade of blue, I mean, and a Golden-Age-of-Hellas flavour to it. Hers was about two grammes of blue fog. The bodice fastened at the right shoulder and came diagonally down to her waist at the left. Its skirt was longer than mine – but that was appropriate; Greek men of their Golden Age did wear their skirts shorter than did women, instead of the reverse that is more usual on Secundus. (I did not know as yet what was customary on Tertius.) We matched, and I was pleased.

Accident? "Accidents" around the Senior are usually planned.

We ate in the garden, a couch for each couple, arranged in hexagon with the fountain as the sixth side. Athene made the water dance and danced lights in it, to match whatever she was playing. All the womenfolk but Tamara helped with the primary serving; Lori and Lazi played Hebe from then on – it was impossible to keep them nailed to their couch anyhow. As the feast started, Ira was with Minerva, Lazarus with Ishtar, Galahad with Hamadryad, and the twins together. But the women moved around like chessmen, sharing a couch, a few bites, a little cuddling, then moving on – all but Tamara, whose firm-soft, rounded bottom lay against my lap the entire feast. It was just as well that she did not move; I'm not shy but prefer not to show the gallant reflex unless I need it at once – and I was very conscious of her dear body warm against me.

But while Lazarus started the repast with Ishtar, the next time I looked his way it was Minerva who reclined against him – and next, one of the twins, which one I am not sure. And so on.

I won't describe the feast except to say that I did not expect it in a young colony and to add that I have paid high prices for poorer food in famous restaurants in New Rome.

All but Lazarus and his sisters were wearing colourful, pseudo-Grecian garments. But Lazarus was dressed as a Scottish chieftain of two and a half millennia ago – the kilt, bonnet, sporran, dirk, claymore, etc. The sword he laid aside but handy, as if expecting to need it. I can firmly state that he was never entitled to dress as a chief by the rules of those long-lost clans. There is doubt that he is entitled to wear any Scottish dress. He once said that he was "half Scotch and half soda," but on another occasion he told Ira Weatheral that he had first worn the kilt at a time (shortly before the flight of the *New Frontiers*) when the style was popular in his home country – found that he liked it, and thereafter wore the kilt when local custom permitted.

That night he went all out and added a fierce moustache to match his finery.

His twin sisters were dressed exactly as he was. I am still wondering whether all this was to honour me, to impress me, or to amuse me. Perhaps all three.

I would happily have spent those three hours in quiet, feeding Tamara and letting her feed me, bathed in the peace of soul that comes from touching her, but the closed happiness circle (and closed it was; Athene's voice now came from the fountain) showed that the Senior expected us to share company, talking and listening in turn, as ritually as in any protocol-bound salon in New Rome. And so we did, in shared and gentle harmony – with the twins adding unexpected grace notes but usually managing to restrain their exuberance and be "grown-up." The Senior started it, using Ira as Stimulator. "Ira, what would you say if a god came through that entranceway?"

"I'd tell him to wipe his feet. Ishtar doesn't permit gods with dirty feet in this house."

"But all gods have feet of clay."

"That wasn't what you said yesterday."

"This is not yesterday, Ira. I've seen a thousand gods and all had feet of clay. All were swindles, first" – Lazarus ticked it with his fingers – "to benefit the shamans; second, to benefit the kings; and third, *always* to benefit the shamans. Then I met the thousand-and-first." The Senior paused.

Ira looked at me. "At this point I am supposed to say, 'Do tell!' or some such insincerity, then the rest of you chime, 'Yes, yes,

Lazarus!' – which has its merit; the rest of us would have at least twenty uninterrupted minutes for swilling and guzzling.

"But I'm going to fool him. He's leading up to how he killed the gods of the Jockaira with nothing but a toy gun and moral superiority. Since that lie is already in his memoirs in four conflicting versions, why should we be burdened with a fifth?"

"It was not a toy gun; it was a Mark Nineteen Remington Blaster at full charge, a superior weapon in its day – and after I carved them up, the stench was worse than Hormone Hall the morning after payday. And my superiority is never moral; it lies always in doing it first before *he* does it to *me*. But the point of the story Ira won't let me tell is that those globs were real gods because neither shamans nor kings were cut in on the loot; they were swindled, too. Those doggie people were *property*, solely for the benefit of their gods – gods in the sense that a man can be a god to a dog – which I had suspected first time around, when they drove poor Slayton Ford right out of his think tank and nearly killed him. But the second time, some eight or nine hundred years later, Andy Libby and I *proved* that this was so. 'How?' you ask – "

"We didn't ask."

"Thank you, Ira. Because after all that time the Jockaira had not changed *in any way*. Their speech, customs, buildings, you name it – were frozen. This can happen only with domesticated animals. A wild animal, such as man, changes his ways as conditions change; he adjusts. I've often thought I would like to go back and see if the doggie people managed to go feral after they lost their owners. Or did they simply lie down and die? But I wasn't too tempted; Andy and I were lucky to get off that planet still without gonads, the way they were yapping at our heels."

"See what I mean, Justin? Version number three had the Jockaira falling into a coma the instant their masters were burned out – and Libby doesn't figure into that version at all."

"Papa Ira, you don't understand Buddy Boy – "

" – he doesn't tell lies – "

" – he's a creative artist – "

" – speaking in parables – "

" – and he *emancipated* those Jabberwockies – "

" – who were *cruelly* oppressed."

Ira Weatheral said, "Justin, I had trouble coping with one Lazarus Long. But three of him? I surrender. Come here, Lori, and let me nibble your ear. Minerva, my lovely, let go of that, wash your pretty hands, then see if Justin needs more wine. Justin, you are the only one with news to impart. What news on the Bourse?"

"Falling steadily. If you own participations on Secundus, you had better have me carry back instructions to your broker. Lazarus, I noticed that you classed 'man' as a wild animal – "

"He is. You can kill him, but you can't tame him. The worst bloodbaths in history derive from attempting to tame him."

"I wasn't arguing it, Ancestor. I'm a mathematical historiographer; my nose is rubbed in that fact. But has news reached here of the flight of the 'Vanguard'? The original 'Vanguard,' I mean – pre-Diaspora."

Lazarus sat up so suddenly that he almost spilled Ishtar off his couch. He caught her. "Sorry, honey. Justin – keep talking."

"I didn't intend to talk about the 'Vanguard' herself – "

"*I* want to hear about her. I hear no objection; it is so ruled. Talk, Son!"

The protocol of a salon feast having gone to pieces, I talked, first reviewing some ancient history. Although it has almost been forgotten, the *New Frontiers* was not the first starship. She had an older sister, the *Vanguard*, that left the Solar System a few years earlier than the momentous date on which Lazarus Long commandeered the *New Frontiers*. She was headed for Alpha Centauri but never reached there – no signs of visitation were ever found on the one possible planet, a Terran type around Alpha Centauri A, the only G-type star in that volume.

But the ship herself was found by accident, in open orbit a long way from where she should have been by any rational assumption based on her mission – discovered nearly a century ago and this tells the difficulties of historiography when ships are the fastest means of communication; this story echoed back to Secundus via five colonial planets before it reached Archives – a few years after Lazarus left New Rome, a few years before I went to Boondock as (nominal) courier for the Chairwoman Pro Tem. Not that a century's delay matters, as the news interested only fusty specialists. To most people it was an uninteresting confirmation of an inconsequential bit of ancient history.

Everything in the *Vanguard* was dead while the ship herself was sleeping, her converter automatically shut down, her atmosphere almost leaked away, her records so destroyed, illegible, incomplete, or desiccated as to distress one. The *Vanguard* matters only to antiquarians and such – although she will remain an endless trove to deviants such as me – if we don't lose her again. Space is deep.

But the interesting thing about the find is that when the *Vanguard* was backtracked ballistically by computer, it showed that she had passed close to a Sol-type star seven centuries earlier. A check of that system turned up one planet Terran in type; it was found to be inhabited by H. sapiens. But *not* from the Diaspora. From the *Vanguard*.

"Lazarus, there is no possible doubt. Those few thousand savages on that planet – designated 'Pitcairn Island,' the catalogue number escapes me – are descended from some who reached there, presumably by ship's boat, seven centuries before they were found. They had reverted to precivilization food-gathering stage, and had the planet rather than the ship been found first, it might have started another of those stories about a breed of humans not derived from old Terra.

"But their argot, fed into a linguistic analyzer-synthesizer, played back as that version of English which was the 'Vanguard's' working language. Reduced vocabulary, new words, degenerate syntax – but the same language."

"Their myths, Justin, their myths!" Galahad-Obadiah demanded.

I was forced to admit that I did not have it all on tap but promised to make a full copy for him and send it via the first ship. "But, Senior, the interesting thing is that these savages, so wild and fierce that in dealing with them more scientists were killed than savages – "

"Hooray for them. Son, those savages were minding their own business on their own planet. An intruder can expect whatever he gets. Up to him to keep his guard up."

"I suppose so. Three scientists were eaten before they figured out how to deal with these pseudo-aborigines. By remotely controlled humanoid robots, that is. But the point I wanted to make was not their fierceness but their intelligence. Believe me or not, by every test that could be used, these wild men, these savages, checked superior to norm. *Much* superior. By the bell curve they land in the range of 'exceptionally gifted' to 'genius-plus.' "

"You expect me to be surprised? Why?"

"Well – Savages. And probably closely inbred."

"You're baiting me, Justin; you know better – although possibly Ira signed you to be Stimulator. All right, I'll take the bait. 'Savage' describes a cultural condition, not a degree of intelligence. Nor does inbreeding damage a gene pool if conditions for survival are extreme; since you describe them as cannibals, they probably ate their culls. From the shape the ship was in, it is fair to assume that their ancestors landed with little or nothing – possibly bare hands and a hatful of ignorance . . . in which case only the most able, the smartest, could survive. Justin, the crew of that first ship averaged far more intelligent than the Howards who escaped in the 'New Frontiers'; they were picked for intelligence – whereas the original Howard selectees were picked *only* for longevity, not for brainpower. Your savages were descended solely from geniuses . . . then passed through Allah alone knows how many ordeals that kill off the stupid and leave only the smartest to breed. What does that leave?"

I admitted that I had tossed him a baiting question to see how he would answer. The Senior nodded. "I know you're not stupid, Son; I had Athene give me a runback on your ancestry. But I have often been amazed at how the moderately bright and moderately bright and moderately well-informed – which describes no one in this happiness circle, so no one need pretend to modesty – how often such somewhat superior people have trouble coming to grips with the ancient silk-purse-and-sow's ear problem. If heredity were not overwhelmingly more important than environment, you could teach calculus to a horse.

"In my early days it was an article of faith among a self-styled 'intellectual elite' that they *could* teach calculus to a horse . . . if they started early enough, spent enough money, supplied special tutoring, and were endlessly patient and always careful not to bruise his equine ego. They were so sincere that it seems downright ungrateful that the horse always persisted in being a horse. Especially as they were right . . . if 'starting early enough' is defined as a million years or more.

"But those savages will make it; they can't avoid winning. The problem in reverse is more horridly interesting. Justin, do you realize that we Howards killed off Old Terra?"

"Yes."

"Now, now, Son, you're not supposed to answer in such a way as to chop off conversation . . . thereby leaving us with nothing to do but get drunk and cuddle the girls."

"Swell!" Obadiah-Galahad shouted. "Let's!" He had Minerva with him at that moment; he grabbed her and flipped her over facing him. "Little whatever-your-name-is, do you have any last words?"

"Yes."

" 'Yes' what?"

"Just 'Yes.' That's my last word."

"Galahad," said Ishtar, "if you're going to rape Minerva, drag her back of the fountain. I want to hear what Justin means by that."

"How *can* I rape her when she won't fight?" he complained.

"You've always been able to solve that problem. But do it quietly. Justin, I find myself shocked. It seems to me that we've been quite generous in supplying Old Home Terra with new technologies – and there's not much else we *can* give them. Didn't the last migrant transport come back only half loaded?"

"I'll answer it," Lazarus growled. "Justin might pretty it up. Not all the Howards. Two. Andy Libby provided the weapon; I delivered the coup de grâce. Space travel killed Earth."

Ishtar looked troubled. "Grandfather, I don't understand."

"She calls me that when I've been naughty," the Senior confided to me. "It's her way of spanking me. Ish darling, you are young and sweet and have spent you life studying biology, not history. Earth was doomed in any case; space travel just hurried it along. By 2012 it wasn't fit to live on – so I spent the next century elsewhere, although the other real estate in the Solar System is far from attractive. Missed seeing Europe destroyed, missed a nasty dictatorship in my home country. Came back when things appeared to be tolerable, found that they weren't – and that's when the Howards had to run for it.

"But space travel can't ease the pressure on a planet grown too crowded, not even with today's ships and probably not with any future ships – because stupid people won't leave the slopes of their home volcano even when it starts to smoke and rumble. What space travel does do is drain off the best brains: those smart enough to see a catastrophe before it happens and with the guts to pay the price – abandon home, wealth, friends, relatives, everything – and *go*. That's a tiny fraction of one per cent. But that's enough."

"It's the bell curve again," I said to Ishtar. "If – as Lazarus thinks, and statistics back him up – every migration comes primary from the right-hand end of the normal-incidence curve of human ability, then this acts as a sorting device whereby the new planet will show a bell curve with a much higher intelligence norm than the population it came from . . . and the old planet will average almost imperceptibly stupider."

"Imperceptible except for one thing!" Lazarus objected. "That tiny fraction that hardly shows statistically is the *brain*. I recall a country that lost a key war by chasing out a mere half dozen geniuses. Most people *can't* think, most of the remainder *won't* think, the small fraction who *do* think mostly can't do it very well. The extremely tiny fraction who think regularly, accurately, creatively, and without self-delusion – in the long run these are the only people who count . . . and they are the very ones who migrate when it is physically possible to do so.

"As Justin said, statistically it hardly shows. But qualitatively it makes all the difference. Chop off a chicken's head and it doesn't die at once; it flops around more energetically than ever. For a while. Then it dies.

"That's what space travel did to Earth: chopped its head off. For two thousand years its best brains have been migrating. What's left is flopping harder than ever . . . to no purpose and will die that much sooner. Soon, I think. I don't feel guilty about it; I see no sin in those smart enough to escape escaping if they can – and the death rattle of Earth was clear and strong back in the twentieth century, Earth reckoning, when I was a young man and space travel had barely started – not even started in interstellar terms. It took two more centuries and then some to get it rolling. Can't count the first migration of the Howards; it was involuntary, and they weren't the best brains.

"The later Howard migration to Secundus was more important; it shook out some of the dullards, left them behind. The non-Howard migrations were even more important. I've often wondered what would have happened if there had been no political restraints against migrating from China; the few Chinese who did reach the stars seem always to be winners, I suspect that the Chinese average smarter than the rest of Earth's spawn.

"Not that slant of eye or colour of skin matters today, or ever matters at the moment of truth. One of the early Howards was Robert C. M. Lee, of Richmond, Virginia – anybody know what his name was originally?"

"I do," I answered.

"Of course you do, Justin, so keep quiet – and that includes you, Athene. Anyone else?"

No one answered; Lazarus went on: "His birth name was Lee Choy Moo; he was born in Singapore, and his parents came from

Canton in China – and of the people in the 'New Frontiers' he was a mathematician second only to Andy Libby."

"Goodness!" said Hamadryad. "I'm descended from him – but I didn't know he was a great mathematician."

"Did you know he was Chinese?"

"Lazarus, I'm not sure what 'Chinese' means; I haven't studied much terrestrial history. Isn't it a religion? Like 'Jewish'?"

"Not exactly, dear. The point is that it no longer matters. Just as few know and no one cares that the famous Zaccur Barstow my partner in crime, was a quarter Negro. Does that word mean anything to you, Hamadarling? Not a religion."

"The word means 'black,' so I assume that one of his grandparents was from Africa."

"Which shows what comes of assuming anything on one datum. Two of Zack's grandparents, both mulatto, came from Los Angeles in my homeland. Since my line mixed with his a long time back, probably any of you can claim African ancestry. Which is statistically equivalent to claiming descent from Charlemagne. I've gone far afield, and it is time we picked a new Stimulator and a new Respondent. Space travel ruined old Earth – that's one viewpoint. The other side of the coin, happier and more important in the long run, is that it improved the breed. Probably saved it as well but 'improved' is certain. Homo sapiens is now not only far more numerous than he ever was on Earth; he is a better, smarter, more efficient animal in every measurable fashion. Further this Respondent sayeth not; somebody else grab it. Lazi, quit trying to tickle me and go bother Galahad; Minerva needs a rest."

"Lazarus," Ishtar said, "just one more responding, please. Something you said about Howards made me wonder. You seemed to place all emphasis on intelligence. Don't you consider long-life important?"

I was astonished to see the oldest human alive frowning over this, slow to answer. Surely it was a question he had settled in his mind at least a thousand years earlier. I tried to forstall the quandry, found I could not soothly norom it.

"Ishtar, the only correct verbal answer to that is Yes and No – which merely says I lack language to define something that is crystal clear inside me and has been for centuries. But here is part of the truth: A long time ago a short-lifer proved to me that we all live the same length of time." He glanced at Minerva; she looked solemnly back. "Because we all live *now*. She – he – was not asserting that fallacy of Georg Cantor which distorted pre-Libby mathematics so long; uh, he – was asserting a verifiable objective truth. Each individual lives her life in *now* independently of how others may measure that life in years.

"But here is another piece of truth. Life is *too* long when one is not enjoying *now*. You recall when I was not and wished to terminate it. Your skill – and trickery, my darling, and don't blush – changed that and again I savour *now*. But perhaps I have never told you that I approached even my first rejuvenation with misgivings, afraid that it would make my body young without making my spirit young again – and don't bother to tell me that 'spirit' is a null word; I know that it is undefinable . . . but it means something to *me*.

"But here is still more of the truth and all I'll try to say about it. Although long-life can be a burden, mostly it is a blessing. It gives time enough to learn, time enough to think, time enough not to hurry, time enough for love.

"Enough of weighty matters. Galahad, pick a light subject and, Justin, you plant the barbs; I've talked enough. Ishtar, my darling, fetch your long lovely carcass over here, stretch out, and let me ply you with brandy; I want you relaxed enough for what I intend to do with you later."

She came readily to him, stopping only to kiss Ira a promise, then saying softly but clearly to our Ancestor, "Our beloved, it takes no brandy to make me utterly willing for whatever you have in mind."

"Anesthesia, Mama Ishtar. I plan to show you something Big Anna taught me which I haven't dared risk in all these years. You may not live till morning. Frightened?"

She smiled lazily, happily. "Oh, terribly frightened."

Galahad covered Lapis Lazuli's mouth with a hand; she bit him. "Stop it, Laz. Let's everybody watch this – it might be new."

VARIATIONS ON A THEME

XV

Agape

I woke slowly next morning, lazed in bed and lived again my Welcome Bacchanalia. I was in a big bed in a ground-floor room with its garden wall still open as it had been when the party had moved to beds. I could hear no one, although (as I recalled) Tamara and Ira had been with me. Or had Ira visited us earlier?

No matter, all of them visited us at some time before Athene sang us to sleep; I seemed to recall as high as six or seven at once in that big bed, counting Tamara and me. No, Tamara had been gone once, leaving me at the mercy of the talkative twins – who were almost quiet. They said they wanted to assure me that I did not have to marry them in order to be a member of the family – they would be gone too much of the time anyhow – because they were going to be pirates when they were big enough – but stay groundside half the time – and open a hook shop over a pool hall – and would I come to see them there?

They had to explain to me both terms; then they sang me a little song that seemed partly amphigory and partly ancient English, but included both terms. I kissed them and promised that, when they opened this studio, I would be their most faithful admirer – a promise that did not worry me; at about that age most girls (all of my daughters) have ambitions to become great hetaeras; few attempt that most demanding of arts – or only long enough to discover that they do not have a true vocation.

I thought they were more likely to become pirates; Lazarus Long's identicals might figure out a way to make crime pay in spite of the enormous depths of space.

My Welcome Bacchanalia had bridged from feast to bed with the customary entertainment save that it was homemade instead of the expensive (and often dull) professional acts a fashionable New Rome hostess offers. Lazarus and his sister-daughters started it with what may have been an authentic Highland Fling (who knows, today?): Lazarus dancing fiercely and vigorously (after all that food and drink!), his two miniature copies keeping the pattern exactly with him – to skirling bagpipes offered by Athene . . . which I would not have recognized were it not that I am an amateur of ancient music as well as a professional of ancient history. The girls followed with an encore, a sword dance, while Lazarus pretended to be passed out from exertion.

Ira, to my amazement, turned out to be a skilled juggler. Question: Did he have that skill all those years he managed a planet?

Galahad sang a ballad with professional virtuosity and great range and control, which astonished me almost as much as I seemed to recall that he used to sing always off key. But when he took an encore with a kerchief stuffed in his mouth, I realized that I had been swived; Athene had done it all. He then played a corpse with three beautiful widows, Minerva, Hamadryad, Ishtar. I won't describe the dialogue except to say that they seemed cheerful over losing him.

Tamara concluded it by singing "My Arms Enclose You Still" – attributed on slight evidence to the Blind Singer but ancient in any case. I've long thought of it as Tamara's Song, and I wept with happiness, and I was not alone; all did. The twins blubbered aloud . . . and when she reached that last line, – "wherever the wild geese lead you, love, my arms will hold you close," I was startled to see that the Senior's craggy features were as wet as mine.

I got up, poked around in the alcove and refreshed myself enough to face other people, went out into the garden and found Galahad. I kissed him and accepted a happy-morning in a frosty tumbler. It was fruit juice freshly pressed – a treat for taste buds used to morning cups "improved" in various chemical ways.

"I'm cook this morning," he said, "so you had better take your eggs either fried or boiled." He then answered the question a guest does not ask: "If you had awakened earlier, you would have had more choice; Lazarus claims I can't boil water. But everyone else is gone."

"So?"

"Si. Ira has gone to his office – to work, perchance to sleep. Tamara has gone back to her patients with a message to you that she hopes to be home tonight – but with a word to Hamadryad to take you to bed and rub your shoulder muscles and put you to sleep early, so I'm not sure she expects to be back – won't if she thinks her patients need her. Lazarus has gone somewhere and one does not ask. Minerva has the twins, and school may be in the 'Dora'; it often is. Ishtar got a call to set a broken arm on a farm north of here. Hamadryad has taken our kids on a picnic so as not to disturb you, you lazy lecher. Boiled or fried?"

He was already frying them, so I answered, "Boiled."

"Good, I'll eat these myself. To hold me till lunch."

"I mean 'Fried.' "

"So I'll put in three more, dear. You're staying, aren't you? Answer Yes or I'll put the twins to work on you."

"Galahad, I *want* to – "

"Then it's settled."

"– but there are problems." I shifted the subject. "You said 'Hamadryad has taken our kids on a picnic – ' Haven't I met all your family?"

"Dear, we do not exhibit our youngest the moment someone sets foot in the foyer and thereby place on him the onus of being insincerely ecstatic. But there was usually someone with them; Lazarus has firm ideas on raising children. Athene keeps eye and ear on them – but can't pick them up. Lazarus says that a frightened child needs to be picked up and cuddled *now*, not later. He believes in spanking right now, too; it evens out, our kids are neither spoiled nor timid. Lazarus is especially strong on not letting a young child wake up alone – so now you know why I kissed you good-night a bit early. So that Ishtar could help keep you awake while I slept with our youngest three."

"Do you actually sleep with them?"

"Well – When Elf jumps up and down on my stomach, it makes me restless. But being peed on doesn't wake me – usually. Having the cuddle watch isn't bad; we rotate so it's only every ninth night. Every tenth if you opt in. But that can change overnight. Suppose we have a rejuvenation client – One or more clients puts Ishtar, Tamara, Hamadryad, and me out of circulation much of the time. Add that Lazarus may leave as soon as he decides Laz and Lor are grown up. Then assume that all our darlings get cracking on making babies."

Galahad grinned at me. "How long does it take four willing women to make four more babies? Or six, when the twins join the production schedule as they threaten to at least twice a week. Justin dear, we want you to stay but it won't all be like last night. If responsibilities of family life worry you, you'd be better off in New Rome where you can hire people to do what you don't fancy doing yourself."

"Galahad," I said earnestly, "stop stuffing your face a moment, dear. You can't scare me with baby pee. I was getting up in the night to soothe crying babies a hundred years before you were born. I intended to colonize, I intended to marry again, I intend to raise kids. I had planned to go back to Secundus to clean up loose ends, then come back with the second wave. But I may say the hell with that and stay . . . as some of the Senior's remarks last night were aimed at me. At least I took them personally – about having the guts to abandon everything and *go*. Secundus is a smoking volcano; that old vixen could set off a bloodbath. One that could include *me*, simply because I'm a major bureaucrat."

I took a deep breath and plunged in: "What I don't understand is why I seem to be invited to join the Senior's household. *Why?*"

Galahad answered, "It's not your pretty face."

"I know that. Oh, I hardly ever scare dogs with it, but it's just a face."

"It's not *too* bad. A cosmetic surgeon could do wonders. I'm the second-best cosmetic surgeon on this planet – there being two. The practice would be good for me and, as you pointed out, you've nothing to lose."

"Damn it, dear, don't farce me. Answer my question."

"The twins like you."

"So? I find them delightful. But the opinion of inexperienced adolescents could not have weighed heavily."

"Justin, don't let their clowning fool you; they are adult in everything but height – and they are our Ancestor's *identical* twins. They have his talent for looking inside a person and spotting a bad one. Lazarus lets them run loose because he trusts them to shoot to kill . . . and not to shoot if they don't intend to kill."

I gulped inside. "Are you saying that those little guns they carry are not toys?"

My old friend Obadiah looked as if I had said something obscene. "Why, Justin! Lazarus wouldn't let a woman go out of this house unarmed."

"Why? This colony seems peaceful. What have I missed?"

"Not much, I think. Lazarus' advance party made sure that this subcontinent was reasonably clear of large predators. But we brought along the two-legged sort, and despite screening,

Lazarus doesn't assume that they are angels. He wasn't looking for angels; they don't make the best pioneers. Uh, yesterday Minerva was wearing a little skirt. Did you wonder about it? In view of the heat?"

"Not especially."

"She wears her gun strapped to her thigh. Nevertheless, Lazarus won't let her go out alone; the twins are her usual body-guard. As a flesh-and-blood she's only three years old; she doesn't shoot as well as the twins do, and she's more trusting than they are. How's your marksmanship?"

"Just fair. I started taking lessons when I made up my mind to migrate. But I haven't had time to practice."

"Better find time. Not that Lazarus will ride you about it; he feels responsible for our women, not for men. But if you *ask* for help – I did, and so did Ira – he'll coach you in everything from bare hands to improvised weapons . . . with two thousand years of dirty tricks thrown in. Up to you, old darling – but here's what it did for me. As you know I used to be a campus narky – a scholar poring over old records – I never carried arms. Then I took rejuvenation and became a rejuvenator myself and was even less inclined to go armed. But for fourteen years I've had regular coaching from the all-time champion in how to stay alive. The result? I stand straight and proud. Haven't had to kill anyone yet." Galahad suddenly grinned. "But the day is young."

I answered soberly, "Galahad, that's one reason I agreed to run a silly errand for Madam Arabelle: to find out things like that. Very well, I take your advice seriously. But you haven't answered my question."

"Well . . . I knew you from long back, and so did Ira. And so did Minerva, though you have trouble believing it. Hamadryad had met you but did not get to know you until last night. Ishtar knew you only from your chart but is one of your strongest supporters. But the deciding factor is this: Tamara wants you in our family."

" 'Tamara!' "

"You sound astonished."

"I am."

"I don't see why. She arranged for someone to relieve her in order to be here last night. She loves you, Justin; don't you *know* it?"

"Uh – " My brain was fuddled. "Yes, I know it. But Tamara loves everyone."

"No, just those who need her love, and she always knows who they are. Incredible empathy, she's going to be a *great* rejuvenator. In this family Tamara can have *anything* she wants . . . and she happens to want *you* – to stay with us, live with us, join us."

"I'll be . . . damned." (Tamara?)

"Unlikely. If I believed in damnation, I wouldn't believe that anyone picked by Tamara Sperling could be in danger of it." Galahad smiled, a happy expression that was more his charm than was his extraordinary beauty. I tried to remember if he had been that beautiful a hundred years back. I am not indifferent to male beauty, but my sensuality is not perfectly balanced; in the presence of a homely female and a beautiful male, I tend to look at the female. So I'll never be an esthete; I lack judgement in matters of beauty. I apologize in advance to any female who finds my primitive attitude offensive.

But I'll share bed with Galahad in preference to a self-centred female beauty; he's warm and gentle and good company, with a roguish playfulness not unlike that of the twins. The thought ran through my mind that I would like to meet his sister – or mother or daughter – a female version of him in character and personality, as well as in appearance.

Tamara! The above was froth at the top of my mind because I was unable to face at once the implications of Galahad's announcement.

He went on: "Close your mouth, dear; I was as startled as you are. But, even if we hadn't been friends years back, on Tamara's motion I would have voted for you sight unseen – so that I could study you. Tamara never makes a mistake. But were you so mind-ill that you needed that much from her? Or so super-human that she wanted that much from you? But you are neither, or I failed to see it. You aren't ill, I think, other than a touch of wild-goose fever. You may be superman, but none of us found it out last night. If you are a superstud, you restrained yourself. Hamadryad did say at breakfast that a woman is happy in your arms. But she did not imply that you are the Galaxy's greatest lover.

"Being one of Minerva's parents is in your favour, none of them has any serious shortcomings; Ishtar made sure of that – Ishtar knows more about you than you do yourself; she can read a gene chart the way other people read print – and Minerva herself is proof that no mistakes were made. I mean, look at Minerva: sweet as the morning breeze and as beautiful as Hamadryad in her own fashion, and with an intelligence level so high you wouldn't believe it – yet so modest she's almost humble.

"But still, it's Tamara. Your fate was settled before you reached this house. Slow ride home, wasn't it?"

"Well . . . one doesn't expect speed from a nullboat. Though I was surprised to find one in a young colony. I expected mule-drawn wagons."

"Lots of those, too. But Lazarus says that this time he travelled with 'seven elephants' – we fetched a mammoth amount of equipment. That's an overpowered nullboat, rebuilt to Lazarus' specifications, and could have fetched you here in a fifth the time it did. But Ira let Lazarus know that he wanted time to make some calls. So Lazarus probably told whichever twin was in charge – or signalled her somehow; he is almost telepathic with them – to give you a long, slow ride. Which you got, and I bet that Laz and Lor never changed expression."

"They didn't."

"Was sure of it. They are *not* children – you should see them handle a spaceship. Anyhow, Ira talked to Ishtar, then to Tamara; then we held a family conference and settled your fate. Lazarus confirmed it while you played with the twins – who were given a chance to veto it later. But they ratified it at once. They not only like you but Aunt Tammy's wishes are law."

I was still bemused. "Apparently much went on that I didn't suspect."

"You weren't supposed to. A better cook would have stayed to get your breakfast, had I not been deputized to tell you – old friends and all that – and to answer questions."

"I'm confused about that conference. I thought Tamara got home just before dinner."

"She did. Oh – Athene, are you listening, dear?"

"Uncle Cuddly, you know I don't listen to private conversations."

"The hell you don't. It'll all right, Justin; Teena keeps secrets. Tell him how to call someone, Teena."

"Tell me to whom you wish to speak, Justin; I have radio links to every farm. Or anywhere. And I can always reach Ira and Lazarus."

"Thank you, Teena. Now if you must listen, pretend not to. The conference was here, Justin; Teena fetched in Tamara's voice and Ira's. Could have fetched voices from the nullboat – but you were the subject. By the way, Teena is one reason this family isn't farming; instead we supply services that colonies usually don't have so soon. Oh, *you* can farm if you want to; we've claimed quite a bit of land. Or there are other ways to make a living. All right, I've done my best. Want to quiz me?"

"Galahad, I think I understand everything but why Tamara wants me in your family."

"You'll have to ask her. I told you I was checking for your halo. Can't see it."

"I don't wear it in hot weather. Obadiah, don't farce around; this is terribly important to me. Why do you keep saying that Tamara's wishes settled it?"

"You know her, man."

"I know how important her wishes are to *me*. But I've been in love with her for many years." I told him things I had long kept to myself. "So that's the way it went. A great hetaera never proposes a contract and usually won't listen if a man is bold enough to propose one himself. But I – well, I made a nuisance of myself. Tamara finally convinced me that she married only to have children and did not intend to have more. I feel sure that money was not a factor – "

"It wouldn't be. Oh, I don't mean that Tamara is silly that way; I've heard her say that since money is the universal symbol for value received, one should accept it proudly. But Tamara wouldn't marry for money; she wouldn't feel that – Or perhaps she would; I think I'll ask her. Mm . . . interesting. Our Tamara is a complex person. Sorry, dear; I interrupted."

"I say money was not the controlling factor, as she had suitors with ten to a hundred times my modest wealth, yet she married none of them. So I shut up and was content to have part of Tamara – spend nights with her when I was permitted to, share her company in happiness circles at other times, pay her as much as I could – as much as she would accept, I mean; she often set her fee by refusing part of a gift – she did with me; I don't know what she did with wealthy clients.

"Years and years of that, then she announced that she was retiring – and I was stunned. I had taken rejuvenation during this time but hadn't noticed that *she* was any older. But she was firm about it and left New Rome.

"Galahad, it left me impotent. Oh, not incapable, but what

had been ecstasy turned out to be mere exercise not worth the trouble. Has this ever happened to you?"

"No. Perhaps I should say, 'Not yet,' since I'm still working on my second century."

"Then you don't know what I mean."

"Only vicariously. But may I quote something Lazarus once said? He was speaking to Ira, but privacy was not placed on it; you'll come across it in his raw memoirs.

" 'Ira,' he said, 'there were many years when I hardly bothered with women – not only unmarried but celibate. After all, how much variety can there be in the slippery friction of mucous membranes?

" 'Then I realized that there was infinite variety in women *as people* . . . and that sex was the most direct route to knowing a woman . . . a route they like, one that we like, and often the only route that can break down barriers and permit close acquaintance.

" 'And in discovering this, I gained renewed interest in the friendly frolic itself, happy as a lad with his first bare tit warm in his hand. Happier – as never again was I merely a piston to her cylinder; each woman was a unique individual worth knowing, and, if we took time enough, we might find we loved each other. But at least we offered each other pleasure and a haven from cares; we weren't simply masturbating, with the other just a sex doll.'

"That's close to what Lazarus said, Justin. You went through something like that?"

"Yes. Somewhat. A long period when sex wasn't worth the trouble. But I got over it . . . with a woman as fine in her own way as Tamara is, although I didn't fall in love with her nor she with me. She taught me something I had forgotten, that sex can be friendly and worthwhile *without* the intense love I felt for Tamara. You see, a friend of mine, wife of another friend and they were both close to me – as a special gift she introduced me to another hetaera, a great beauty, and arranged for me a holiday with her – paid for by my friends; they could afford it, she is wealthy. This beautiful hetaera, Magdalene – "

Galahad looked delighted. "Maggie!"

"Why, yes, she did use that pillow name. 'Magdalene' was her vocational name. But when she learned that I keep the Archives, she told me her registered name."

"Rebecca Sperling-Jones."

"Then you do know her."

"All my life, Justin darling; I nursed at those beautiful breasts. She's my mother, dear – what a delightful coincidence!"

I was delighted, too, but more interested in something else. "So *that's* where you get your beauty."

"Yes, but also from my genetic father. Becky – Maggie – tells me I look more like him."

"Really? If you permit, I'll look up your lineage when I get back to Secundus." An archivist should not consult the Archives from personal curiosity; I was presuming on friendship to suggest it.

"Dear, you're not going back to Secundus. But you can get it from Athene clear back to the first push in the bush after Ira Howard's death. But let's talk about Mama. She's a jolly one, isn't she? As well as a beauty."

"Both. I told you how much she did for me. Your mother assumed that this holiday was going to be fun – fun for both of us – and it was indeed! – and I forgot about being uninterested in sex. I'm not speaking of technique; I suspect that any high-priced hetaera in New Rome is as skilled as any famous courtesan in history. I mean her attitude. Maggie is fun to be around, in bed or out. Laugh wrinkles but no frown wrinkles."

Galahad nodded agreement as he wiped egg from his platter. "Yes, that's Mama. She gave me a most happy childhood, Justin, so much so that I was grumpy at being shoved out when my eighteenth rolled around. But she was sweet about it. After my adulthood party she reminded me that she was moving out, too, and going back to her profession. Her contract with Papa, my foster father, was a term contract, over when I became a legal adult . . . so if I wanted to see Maggie again – and I wanted to! – it would be cash at the counterpane, no family discount. Since I was a poor-but-honest research assistant, paid only two or three times what I was worth, I couldn't have afforded thirty seconds with her, much less a night; Mama's fees were always sky-high."

Galahad looked thoughtfully happy. "Goodness, that seems long ago – more than a century and a half, Justin. I didn't realize that Becky – Maggie – Mama – that Magdalene was being both wise and kind. I was grown up only legally and physically, and if she hadn't cut the cord, I would have hung around, an overgrown infant, cluttering her life and interfering with her vocation. So I did grow up, and when I married, my first wife named our first daughter 'Magdalene' and asked Maggie to be godmother . . .

then I could hardly believe that this beautiful creature had borne me and I had no special urge to play Oedipus to her regal beauty; I was too much in love with my wife. Yes, Maggie is a fine girl – although she spoiled me as a kid. Was that holiday the only time you had her?"

"No. But not often. As you say, she was expensive. She offered me a fifty-per cent discount – "

"Well! You *did* impress her."

" – as she knew I wasn't wealthy. But even at that, I couldn't afford her company often. But she got me over my emotional hump, and I'm grateful to her. A fine woman, Galahad; you have reason to be proud of her."

"I think so. But, Justin dear, your mention of that discount makes me certain that she remembers you just as fondly – "

"Oh, I hardly think so. Years back, Galahad."

"Don't trip in your modesty, dear; Maggie grabbed every crown the traffic would bear. But the 'delightful coincidence' is more than just the fact that you've had my mother – after all, high as her fees were, New Rome has many wealthy men attractive enough that Maggie would accept them. The 'delightful' aspect is that this very minute she is about forty kilometres south of here."

"No!"

"Si, si, si! Ask Athene to call her. You can be talking with her in thirty seconds."

"Uh . . . I still don't think she would remember me."

"I do. But there's no rush. If you are surprised, think how surprised *I* was. I had nothing to do with the migrants' roster; I was arse-deep in getting together what Ishtar had ordered for the clinics, Justin, I didn't know Maggie had married again. So we're here a couple of weeks, the headquarters party, with a temporary setup and still eating and sleeping in the 'Dora' when the first transport grounds – then we're busy getting people and supplies out in a sequence worked out by Lazarus and bossed by Ira.

"My assignment, once I had my shack up – by hand; Athene had no outside extensionals then – "

"*Poor* Uncle Cuddly!"

"*Who* doesn't listen to private conversations?"

"I have to keep you straight, dear. It was Minerva who had no outside hands then; I wasn't even hatched."

"Well – You have her memories, Teena; it's a mere technicality."

"Not to me, dearie. The chinchy little bitch took some memories with her that she didn't want to share with her ever-lovin' twin. And she locked one whole bank that she *did* leave behind so that I can't touch it without an abracadabra either from her or from Grandpappy. Except that *you* can unlock, it Justin . . . if *both* my twin and Lazarus are dead."

I managed to answer quickly. "In that case, Athene, I hope that it is a very long time before I am able to trigger it."

"Well . . . when you put it that way, so do I. But I can't help wondering what grim secrets and unspeakable crimes are locked in my theta-ninety-seven-B-dexter-aleph-prime? Will the stars tremble in their courses? But Uncle Cuddly did work hard a couple of days, Justin – probably the only honest work he has ever done."

"I disdain to comment, Teena. Justin, my assignment was examining physician, for which I was qualified under an almost new diploma. So Ishtar and Hamadryad are unpacking migrants and giving them their antidotes and I'm checking them to make sure they've made the trip safely – rushing it as I haven't yet snatched another medical doctor from that parade of flesh.

"I glance up from my machine just long enough to note that the next victim is female and call out over my shoulder, 'Strip down, please,' and change the setting. Then I look twice – and say, 'Hello, Mama, how did *you* get here?'

"This caused her to give me a second look. Then she smiled her big, happy smile and said, 'I flew in on a broom, Obadiah. Give me a kiss and tell me where to put my clothes. Is the doctor around?'

"Justin, I let the queue pile up while I gave Maggie a thorough examination – proper, as she was pregnant and I made certain that her unborn baby had come through all right – but also to gossip and get caught up. Married again, four children by today, a farm wife with a sunburned nose, and happy as can be.

"Got married quite romantically. Mama heard the advertising about opening a virgin planet, went to the recruiting office Ira had in the Harriman Trust building to find out about it – that astonished me the most; Mama is the last person I would have suspected of yearnings to pioneer."

"Well . . . I agree, Galahad. But I don't suppose anyone would pick me as a likely pioneer, either."

"Perhaps not. Nor me. But Maggie puts in her application at once, and runs into one of her wealthy regulars doing the same. They go somewhere for a bite and discuss it . . . and leave the restaurant and register an open-end contract, and go back to the recruiting office and withdraw their solo applications and submit a joint one as a married couple. I won't say that got them accepted, but almost no singles were accepted for first wave."

"Did they know that?"

"Oh, certainly! The recruiting clerk warned them before accepting their solo fees. That's what they left to discuss. They already knew they suited each other in bed, but Maggie wanted to find out if he intended to farm – believe it or not, that's what she wanted – and he wanted to know if she could cook and was she willing to have kids. And it was: 'Fine, we agree; let's get on with it!' Maggie had her fertility restored, and they planted their first baby without waiting to see if they were accepted."

I said, "That probably clinched it."

"You think so? Why?"

"If they changed their application to show that Magdalene had caught. If Lazarus passed on the applications. Galahad, our Ancestor favours people who take big bites."

"Mmm, yes. Justin, why are *you* hanging back?"

"I'm not. I had to be certain that the invitation was serious. I still don't know *why*. But I'm no fool, I'm staying."

"Wonderful!" Galahad jumped up, came around the table, kissed me again, roughed my hair, and hugged me. "I'm happy for all of us, darling, and we'll try to make you happy." He grinned – and I suddenly saw his mother in him. Hard to imagine the glamorous Magdalene with kids and calluses, a frontier farm wife – but I recalled the old proverb about best wives. Galahad went on: "The twins weren't sure I could be trusted with so delicate a mission; they were afraid I would muff it."

"Galahad, there was never a chance I would refuse; I just had to be sure I was welcome, I still don't know why."

"Oh. We were speaking of Tamara and got sidetracked. Justin, it's not public knowledge how difficult it was to rejuvenate our Ancestor this time, although the recordings you have been editing may hint at it – "

"More than a hint."

"But not all of it. He was almost dead, and simply keeping him alive while we rebuilt him was hard enough. But we managed that; you won't find another technician of Ishtar's skill. But when we had him in good shape, bio-age almost as young as he is now, he took a turn for the worse. What do you do when a client turns his face away, is reluctant to talk, doesn't want to eat – yet has nothing wrong with him physically? Bad. Stays awake all night rather than risk going to sleep? Very bad.

"When he – Never mind; Ishtar knew what to do. She went up into the mountains and fetched back Tamara. She wasn't rejuvenated then – "

"That wouldn't matter."

"It *did* matter, Justin. Youth would have handicapped Tamara in coping with Lazarus. Oh, Tamara would have overcome the handicap; I have confidence in her. But her bio-age and appearance were around eighty on the Hardy scale; this made it easier, as Lazarus, despite his renewed body, was feeling the weight of his years. But Tamara *looked* old . . . and every white hair was an asset. Lines in her face, little round potbelly, breasts pendulous, varicosities – she *looked* the way he *felt* . . . so he didn't mind having her around during a crisis in which he – well, I skansed that he couldn't stand the sight of us who looked youthful. That's all it took; she healed him – "

"Yes, she's a Healer." (How well I knew!)

"She's a *great* Healer. That's what she's doing now, healing a young couple who lost their first baby – nursing the mother who had a rough time physically, sleeping with both of them. We all sleep with her; she always knows when we need her. Lazarus needed her then, she felt it, and stayed with him until he was well. Uh, after last night this may be difficult to believe, but both of them had quit sex. Years and years – Lazarus more than half a century and Tamara had not coupled with anyone since she retired."

Galahad smiled. "Here is a case of the patient healing the physician; in bringing Lazarus around to the point where he invited her to share his bed, Tamara herself found new interest in living. She lived with Lazarus long enough to heal his spirit, then announced that she was leaving. To apply for rejuvenation."

I said, "Lazarus asked her to marry him."

"I don't think so, Justin, and neither Tamara nor Lazarus hinted at such. Tamara put it another way entirely. We were all having a late breakfast in the garden of the Palace penthouse, when Tamara asked Ira if she could join his migration – it was solely Ira's migration then; Lazarus had said repeatedly that he would *not* join it. I think he already had in mind attempting to time-trip. Ira told Tamara to consider it settled and not to worry about restrictions that would be published when he announced it. Justin, Ira would have given her the Palace as readily; she had saved Lazarus, and we all knew it.

"But you know Tamara. She thanked him but said she intended to qualify fully, starting with rejuvenation, then she would see what she could learn to be useful in a colony, just as Hamadryad planned to – and, Hamadryad, will you sleep with Lazarus tonight? – and Justin, you should have heard the commotion *that* started!"

"Why a commotion?" I asked. "From what you said earlier Lazarus had reacquired his interest in the friendly sport. Did Hamadryad have some reason not to want to substitute for Tamara?"

"Hamadryad was willing, although upset by the way Tamara dumped the matter on her – "

"Doesn't sound like Tamara. If Hamadryad hadn't wanted to do it, Tamara would have known it without asking."

"Justin, when it comes to people's emotions, Tamara *always* knows what she is doing. It was Lazarus she was trapping, not Hamadryad. Our Ancestor has odd shynesses, or did have then. He had been sleeping with Tamara for a month – and pretending that he was not. As futile as a cat covering up on a tile floor. But Tamara's blandly blunt request that Hamadryad relieve her as his concubine forced it into the open and produced a head-on clash of wills, Lazarus and Tamara. Justin, you know them both: Who won?"

The ancient pseudoparadox – That Tamara could be immovable I knew. "I won't guess, Galahad."

"Neither just then, because once Lazarus stopped sputtering about how both he and Hamadryad were being needlessly embarrassed, Tamara gently withdrew her suggestion then shut up. Shut up on that, shut up about rejuvenation, shut up about migrating, left the next move up to Lazarus and won the argument by not arguing. Justin, it is difficult to kick Tamara out of one's bed – "

"I would find it impossible."

"I think Lazarus found it so. What discussions they had in the middle of the night I could not say . . . but Lazarus learned that she would *not* leave for rejuvenation until he promised never to sleep alone while she was gone. But she promised in exchange to return to his bed as soon as she completed antigeria.

"So one morning Lazarus announced the détente – red-faced

and almost stuttering. Justin, our Ancestor's true age shows more in some of his ancient attitudes about sex than in any other way."

"I didn't notice it last night, Galahad – and I expected to, having studied his memoirs so closely."

"Yes but you saw him last night some fourteen years after we set up our family – as it was that morning that did it. Although we did not formalize it until after the twins were born, whereas at this time they were slight bulges at most. Believe me, Lazarus found it hard to capitulate – and tried for an escape hole even then. He announced, rather agressively, that he had promised Tamara not to sleep alone while she was undergoing antigeria, then said more or less in these words: 'Ira, you told me that professional ladies were to be found in the city. How do I go about finding one who will accept a contract for that length of time?' I have to quote him in English as he was using euphemisms he ordinarily disdains.

"What Lazarus didn't know was that Ishtar had programmed us like actors hypnotized into roles. Perhaps you've noticed that he is responsive to female tears?"

"Isn't everyone? I've noticed."

"Ira pretended not to know what profession Lazarus meant... which gave Hamadryad time to burst into tears and flee . . . whereupon Ishtar stood up and said, 'Grandfather . . . how *could* you? – and *she* was dripping tears, too . . . and chased after Hamadryad. Then it was Tamara's turn to switch on the raindrops and follow the other two. Which left us three men together.

"Ira became very formal and said, 'If you will excuse me, Sire, I will attempt to find and console my daughter' – bowed, turned abruptly, and left. Which left it up to me. Justin, I didn't know what to do. I knew that Ishtar expected difficulty because Tamara had warned her. But I did not expect to be left to juggle it alone.

"Lazarus said, 'Great balls of fire! Son, what did I do *now?*' Well, I could answer that. I said, "Grandfather, you've hurt Hamadryad's feelings."

"Then I was carefully unhelpful – refused to speculate why her feelings were hurt, could not guess where she might have gone – unless she had gone home, which I understood was somewhere in the suburbs – declined to act as his intermediary – all to Ishtar's instructions to play dumb, stupid and useless, and let the women handle it.

"So Lazarus had to track Hamadryad down himself, which he did with Athene's – I mean 'Minerva's' – help."

Athene said, "This is all news to me, Uncle Cuddly."

"If it is, dear, please forget it."

"Oh, I shall!" the computer answered. "Except that I'm going to save it up and use it about a hundred years from now. Justin, if I burst into tears – after I'm a flesh-and-blood – will you track me down and console me?"

"Probably. Almost certainly."

"I'll remember that, Lover Boy. You're cute."

I pretended not to hear, but Galahad said, " 'Lover Boy'?"

"That's what I said, dear. Sorry, Uncle Cuddly, but you're obsolete. If you hadn't gone to sleep early, you would know why."

I kept quiet while making a mental note for a hundred years hence – one that involved Pallas Athene as a flesh-and-blood and getting her into a helpless position.

This side conversation was cut short; Athene notified us that Lazarus was arriving. Galahad waved his arms. "Hey! Pappy! Back here!"

"Coming." Lazarus bussed me in passing, did so to Galahad as he slid in by him and grabbed what was left of Galahad's second breakfast – a home-baked jam roll – stuffed it into his mouth and said around it: "Well? Did he fight the hook?"

"Not nearly the way you did with Hamadryad, Pappy. I was telling Justin about that – how the Hamadarling tripped you and thereby set up our family."

"My God, what a canard!" Lazarus helped himself to Galahad's hotcup. "Justin, Galahad is a sweet lad but romantic. I knew exactly what I wanted to accomplish, so I started by raping Hamadryad. That broke down her resistance, and now she sleeps with anybody, even Galahad. Everything else followed in logical sequence." He added, "You still plan to go back to Secundus?"

I answered, "Perhaps I didn't understand what Galahad has been telling me. I thought I was committing myself, in joining, to – " I stopped. "Lazarus, I don't know what I'm committed to, and I don't know what I'm joining."

Lazarus nodded. "One must make allowances for youth, Justin; Galahad doesn't speak clearly as yet."

"Thanks, Pappy. Too much. I sold him the deal. Now you've got him wondering."

"Quiet, Son. Let me spell it out, Justin. What you are joining is a family. What you are committed to is the welfare of the children.

All of them, not just any that you may sire." He looked at me, waited.

I said, "Lazarus, I've raised a number of children – "

"I know."

"I don't think I've let one down yet. Very well, three that I haven't seen, plus your two – your sisters or adopted daughters – plus others as they come along. Correct?"

"Yes. But it's not a lifetime committment; that's not practical for a Howard. This family may outlive us all – I hope so. But an adult can opt out anytime and thereby be committed only to kids then on hand – underfoot or in womb. Call it a maximum of eighteen years. However, I assume that the rest of the family would prefer to relieve such a person of his or her responsibilities in order to see the back of his neck. I can't envision a happy relationship continuing for years after someone has announced that he wants out. Can you?"

"Well . . . no. But I won't let it worry me."

"Of course it might not happen that way. Suppose Ishtar and Galahad decided to set up a separate household – "

"Now wait one fiddlin' minute, Pappy! You can't get rid of me that easily! Ish won't have me except as part of the package I know, I tried to get her to marry me years back."

" – and wanted to take our three youngest with them. We would not stop them nor would we try to dissuade children who preferred to go with them. All three of them are Galahad's – "

"There he goes again! Pappy, you put Undine into Ish in the soak pool; that's why we named her that. Elf is either yours or Ira's; the Hamadear told me so. And nobody has any doubt about Andrew Jackson. Justin, I'm sterile."

" – based on statistical probability, both on sperm count and the fact that he keeps so busy at it. But Ishtar reads the gene charts and keeps such matters to herself; we prefer it that way. But it is extremely unlikely that Hamadryad ever said that, or that she has or ever will have a child by Ira. No genetic hazard, Ishtar is certain. And the fact that we have yet to have *any* defectives in this colony gives me great confidence in Ishtar's skill in reading a gene chart; she screened the first wave, a job that gave her eyestrain for months. Nevertheless, Ira has some unease about it and won't even stand close to Hamadryad when she is fertile – an irrational attitude I understand, as I am cursed with it myself. I remember too well a time in the past when all the Howards had to go on was percentage of mutual ancestry –

and got defectives all too often. Of course today a woman with a clean gene chart is better off married to her brother than to a stranger from another planet – but old ghosts die hard.

"What it amounts to, Justin, is three fathers – four, with you – three mothers, but four when Minerva asks to have her adolescence protection cancelled – an ever-changing number of kids to be taught and spanked and loved – plus always the possibility of the number of parents being either enhanced or diminished But this is my house, in my name, and I've kept it that way because I planned it to house *one* family, not to make life jolly for goats such as Galahad – "

"But it does! Thank you, Pappy darling."

" – but for the welfare of children. I've seen catastrophe strike colonies that looked as safe as this one. Justin, a disaster could wipe out all but one mother and father in this family, and our kids would still grow up normally and happily. This is the only long-run purpose of a family. We think our setup insures that purpose more than a one-couple family can. When you join, you commit yourself to that purpose – that's all."

I took a deep breath. "Where do I sign?"

"I see no use in written marriage contracts; they can't be enforced . . . whereas if the partners want to make it work, no written instrument is necessary. If you seriously want to join us, a nod of your head is enough."

"I do!"

" – or if you want ritual, Laz and Lor would be delighted to dream up a fancy one – and we can all have a crying jag together –"

"– and on his wedding night Justin gets to sleep with the babies so he'll know how serious it is."

"Seal it, Galahad. If you want to add that touch, you should make it the night *before*, so he'll have a fair chance to back out if he can't take it."

"Lazarus, I volunteer for the diaper watch tonight; I'm hardened to such things."

"I doubt if the women will let you."

"And you won't live till morning," Galahad added. "They're an emotional lot. Last night you had it easy. Better take the pee watch."

"Galahad could be right; I should check your heart. As may be – keep quiet, Galahad – Justin, this household is *not* a jail. The setup is not only safer for children, it is more flexible for adults. When I asked you whether you intended to go back to Secundus, I meant simply that. An adult can be away for a year, ten years, any length of time for any purpose – and know that the kids are taken care of and know that he-she will be welcomed back. The twins and I have been off-planet several times and will be again. And . . . well, you know I intend to attempt this time-tripping experiment. That won't involve much elapsed time in this framework . . . but it does involve a slight element of risk."

" 'Slight!' Meaning that Pappy is out of his silly head. Be sure to kiss him good-bye when he leaves, Justin; he won't be back."

I was alarmed to see that Galahad was not joking. Lazarus said quietly, "Galahad, it is all right to say that to me. But don't say it in front of the women. Or children." He went on to me, "Of course there is an element of risk; there is in anything. But not to a time trip itself, as Galahad seems to think." (Galahad shuddered.) "The risk is the same as in visiting any planet; someone there may not like you. But the time jump takes place in the safest possible surroundings: in space with a ship around you – any risk comes later."

Lazarus grinned. "That's why I was so riled at that old cow Arabelle – telling me to go look-see at *battles!* Justin, the best thing about modern times is that we are all so spread apart that war is no longer practical. But – Did I tell you what I'm going to use as a practice run?"

"No. I had the impression from Madam Chairman Pro Tem that you already had a perfected technique."

"It's possible that I let her think so. But Arabelle wouldn't know an imperial number from an imperial edict; she couldn't ask the right questions."

"I don't think I could either, Lazarus; it's not my field of mathematics."

"If you're interested, Dora can teach you – "

"Or me, Lover Boy."

"Or Teena. What's the idea of calling Justin 'Lover Boy,' Teena? Are you trying to seduce him?"

"No, he's promised to seduce *me* . . . about a hundred years from now."

Lazarus looked at me thoughtfully; I tried to look as if I hadn't heard the exchange. "Mmm . . . maybe you had better take those lessons from Dora, Justin. You haven't met Dora, but think of her as about eight years old; she won't try to seduce you. But she's the brightest computer pilot in space and can teach you more than you want to know about Libby field transformations. I was saying that we felt sure of the theory, but I wanted a separate opinion. So I thought of asking Mary Sperling – "

I said, "Hold it a moment! Lazarus, in all the Archives there is, I am certain, only one Mary Sperling. I'm descended from her, Tamara is decended from her – "

"Lots of Howards descended from her, Son; Mary had over thirty children – quite a record for those days."

"Then you *do* mean Elder Mary Sperling, born in 1953 Gregorian, died in – "

"She did *not* die, Justin; that's the point. So I went back there and talked with her."

My head felt fuzzy. "Lazarus, I'm confused. Are you telling me that you've already made one time trip? Nearly two thousand years? No, I mean 'over two thousand years' – "

"Justin, if you'll keep quiet, I'll *tell* you what I mean."

"Sorry, sir."

"Call me 'sir' and I'll get the twins to tickle you. I mean I went, in present time, to star PK3722 and the Planet of the Little People. That designation is obsolete, and the new catalogings don't hook it in with that planet because Libby and I decided to toss in a joker; we felt that it was a place for humans to stay away from.

"But the Little People are the source of the concepts that Andy Libby worked out as field theory that anyone can use, and all space pilots, computer and human, do use. But I had never gone back there because – well, Mary and I had been close. So close that was a blow to me when she 'went over.' More disturbing than a death, some ways.

"But the years do mellow a memory and I did want to consult. So the twins and I set out in the 'Dora' to try to find that planet, from a set of coordinates and a ballistic Andy had assigned a long time back. The ballistic was slightly off, but a star doesn't move far in only two thousand years; we found it.

"No trouble then; I had warned Lor and Laz most solemnly of the subtle danger of the place. They listened, and that made them as immune to the place as I am – not tempted to swap their individual personalities for a pseudo-immortality. In fact, they had a wonderful time; the place *is* charming, and safe in all other ways. Hadn't changed much, one huge park.

"I orbited first – it's their planet, and they have powers we don't ken. Same as last time; a Doppelgänger of a Little Person showed up in the 'Dora' and invited us down to visit . . . only this time it called me by name – in my head; they don't use oral speech – and admitted to being Mary Sperling. That shook me but it was good news. She – 'it,' I mean – it seemed mildly pleased to see me but not especially interested; it was not like meeting a beloved old friend but more like meeting a stranger who nevertheless remembered what that old friend remembered."

"I understand it," the computer said. "Something like Minerva and me, huh?"

"Yes, dear . . . except that you had a more positive personality your very first day than this creature who used the name of my old friend . . . and you've been getting positiver and positiver for the past three years."

"Ol' Buddy Boy, I'll bet you tell that to all the girls."

"Could be. Please keep quiet, dear. Nothing more to tell, Justin, save that we grounded and stayed a few days, and Dora and I consulted with the Little People about space-time field theory while the twin listened and enjoyed playing tourist. But, Justin, when the Families left there, returning to Earth in the 'New Frontiers,' you will recall that we left some ten thousand behind."

"Eleven thousand, one hundred, and eighty-three," I answered, "according to log of the 'New Frontiers'."

"Is that what we logged? Should have been more, maybe, as the logged figure was reconstructed by seeing who couldn't be mustered, so almost certainly there were unregistered children among those who elected to stay behind; we were there quite a piece. But the exact number doesn't matter. Justin, call it an even ten thousand. Given a favourable environment; how many would you expect to find there after two thousand years?"

I used the arbitrary expansion. "Approximately ten to the twenty-second – which is ridiculous. I would expect either a stabilized optimax – call it ten to the tenth – or a Malthusian catastrophe, in not over seven to eight centuries."

"Justin, there were none. Nor any sign that men had ever been there."

"What happened to them?"

"What happened to Neanderthal Man? What happens to any champion when he's defeated? Justin, what's the point in striving when you're so outclassed that it's no contest? The Little People have the perfect Utopia – no strife, no competition, no population problem, no poverty, perfect harmony with their beautiful planet. Paradise, Justin! The Little People are all the things that philosophers and religious leaders throughout history have been urging the human race to become.

"Maybe they *are* perfect, Justin. Maybe they are what the human race *can* become . . . in another million years. Or ten million.

"But when I say that their Utopia frightens me, that I think it is deadly to human beings, and that they themselves look like a dead end to me, I am *not* running them down. Oh, no! They know far more about mathematics and science than I do – or I wouldn't have gone there to consult them. I can't imagine fighting them because it wouldn't be a fight; they would already have won against anything we could attempt. If we became obnoxious to them, I can't guess what would happen – and don't want to find out. But I don't see any danger as long as we leave them alone as we don't have *anything* they want. So it appears to me – but what's the opinion of one old Neanderthal? I understand them as little as that kitten over there understands astrogation.

"I don't know what happened to the Howards who stayed behind. Some may have gone over and been assimilated, as Mary Sperling did. I didn't ask, I didn't want to know. Some may have lapsed into lotus-eaters' apathy and died. I doubt if many reproduced – although it is possible that there were subhumans around being kept as pets. If so, I most especially did not want to know it. I got what I wanted: a corroborating opinion on a mathematical oddity in field physics – then gathered up my girls and left.

"We did one thing before we left that neighbourhood: We made a ball-of-twine photographic survey of their planet, then had Athene examine it when we got back. Teena?"

"Sure, Buddy Boy. Justin, if there is a human artifact on the surface of that planet, it is less than a half metre in diameter."

"So I assume that they are all dead," Lazarus said grimly, "and I shan't go back. No, the trip to PK3722 was not a trial-run time trip, but just a common star hop. The test run will be about as simple and quite safe, as it will not involve putting down on a planet. Want to come along? Or shall we take Galahad?"

"Pappy," Galahad said earnestly, "I am young, beautiful, healthy, and happy, and plan to stay that way; you are *not* volunteering *me* for any such harebrained junket. I'm not making any more star hops of any sort; I'm the home-loving type. I've made one landing with Hot Pilot Lorelei at the overrides. That's enough; I'm convinced."

"Now, boy, be reasonable," Lazarus said gently. "When we do this, my girls will be old enough to want active male attention – which *I* am not going to supply; I would lose all control over them. Think of it as your duty."

"When you start talking about 'duty,' I break out with hives. The trouble is, Pappy, you're a sissy, afraid of two little girls."

"Could be. Because they won't be little girls much longer. Justin?"

I thought furiously. To be invited by the Senior to take a star trip with him is not an honour to turn down. That it included an attempt to travel in time did not bother me; the idea seemed unreal. But it couldn't be dangerous or he wouldn't be taking his sister-daughters along – and, besides, I felt that Lazarus was unkillable; a passenger with him should be safe. Gigolo for his girls? – Lazarus was farcing Galahad, I was sure . . . as I was certain that Lazi and Lori would settle such matters to suit themselves. "Lazarus, I will go anywhere you ask me to go."

"Hold it!" objected Galahad. "Pappy, Tamara isn't going to like this."

"No trouble, Son. Tamara is welcome, and I think she would enjoy it. She's not chicken like some people we won't mention."

"*What?*" Galahad sat up straight. "Take away Tamara . . . and Justin . . . and our twins . . . and you yourself? Half the family? And leave the rest of us here to mourn?" Galahad took a deep breath, sighed it out. "All right, I give up. I volunteer. But leave Justin and Tamara at home. And the twins, we can't risk them. You pilot, I'll cook. As long as we last, that is."

"Galahad shows unexpected streaks of nobility," Lazarus said to no one in particular. "It'll get him killed yet. Forget it, Son; I don't need a cook, Dora is a better cook than either of us. The twins will insist on going, and I need to supervise them through a couple of time jumps; later they will have to do it alone."

Lazarus turned to me. "Justin, while you are welcome, it will be a dull trip. You would know you'd travelled in time only because I'd tell you so. I have in mind going to a planet easy to find because Libby and I surveyed it and he determined its ballistic accurately. I'm not planning to land; it's a moderately dangerous place. But it happens to be a planet I can use as a clock.

"This may sound silly. But it is hard to be sure of the date in space, other than by your inboard clocks – in particular the radioactive-decay clocks of your computer. Telling time by examining celestial bodies is difficult and involves subtle measurements and long calculation; it is more practical to ground on a civilized planet and bang on somebody's door and ask.

"There are exceptions – any stellar system with known ephemerides of its planets, such as here, or Secundus' star, or the Solar System, and others – if Dora has such data in her gizzards, she can look at such a system and read the time by its planets as if they were hands on a clock – Libby did that with the Solar System from the 'New Frontiers.'

"But on this trial trip I'll be calibrating a time-travel clock – another matter and new. I left something in orbit around that planet on a known date. Later I could not find it, despite having equipped it so that I certainly *should* have found it. Uh . . . it was Andy Libby's coffin.

"Very well, I'll go look again, trying to split two known dates. If I find it, I will have begun calibration of a time-travel clock – as well as proving that the time-trip theory is correct. Follow me?"

"I think so," I admitted, "to the extent of seeing that it is an experimental proof. But field theory is so far from my own specialty that I can't say more."

"No need to. I don't understand it too well myself. The first computer designed to manage Libby-Sheffield drive was a reflection of Andy's unique mind; all since are refinements. If a pilot tells you he understands it and uses a computer simply because it's faster, don't ride with him; he's a phony. Eh, Teena?"

"I understand astrogation," said the computer, "because Minerva replicated Dora's astrogation circuitry and programming in me. But I do not think that it is possible to discuss it in English, or even Galacta, or any language using word elements. I can print out the basic equations and thereby show a static picture – a slice – of a dynamic process. Shall I do so?"

"Don't bother," said Lazarus.

"Heavens, no!" I echoed. "Thank you, Athene, but I have no ambition to be a star pilot."

"Galahad," said Lazarus, "How about rousing your lazy carcass and finding a little snack for lunch? Say about four thousand calories each. Justin, I asked if you plan to go back to Secundus because I don't want you to."

"That suits me!"

"Pallas Athene, make this a private record, keyed to me and to Chief Archivist Foote."

"Programme running, Mr. Chairman." Galahad lifted his eyebrows, left abruptly.

"Chief Archivist, is the situation in New Rome becoming critical?"

I answered carefully, "Mr. Chairman, in my opinion it is, although I'm no more than a dilettante in social dynamics. But . . . I did not come here to deliver a silly message from Madam Chairman Pro Tem. I came here hoping to talk with you about it."

Lazarus looked at me long and thoughtfully – and I caught a glimpse of part of what makes him unique. He has the quality of giving full attention to whatever he does, be it a matter of life and death, or something as trivial as dancing to amuse a guest. I recognized it because Tamara has the same quality; she displays it by giving total attention to the person she is with.

She does not have exceptional beauty, nor, I suppose, is she more skillful in technique than any of several other professionals – or even some amateurs. No matter. It is this quality of total concentration that sets her apart from other fine women of her merciful calling.

I think the Senior extends it to *everything*. Now he had suddenly "picked up the gavel," and his computer knew it at once, and Galahad spotted it almost as quickly – and I stopped worrying.

"I never assumed," he said, "that the Families' Chief of Records would play messenger with a useless message. So tell me your reason."

Elaborate it? No, explanations could follow. "Mr. Chairman, the Archives should be replicated off Secundus. I came here to see if it could be done on Tertius."

"Go on."

"I've never seen civil disorder. I'm not sure of the symptoms nor how long it takes them to grow into open violence. But the people of Secundus aren't used to arbitrary laws and rules that change overnight. I think there will be trouble. I would feel that I had carried out the duties of my office if I insured that destruction of the Archives could not mean that our records are lost. The vaults are underground – but not invulnerable. I have figured out eleven ways that some or all of the Archives could be destroyed."

"If there are eleven ways, then there is a twelfth, and a

thirteenth, and so on. Have you discussed this with anyone?"

"*No!*" I added more quietly, "I didn't want to put ideas into anyone's head."

"Sound. Sometimes the best one can do about a weak point is not to call attention to it."

"It seemed so to me, sir." I added, "But when I started worrying I started trying to do something to protect the records. I instituted a policy of making dead-storage duplicates of all processed data at the point they enter the Archives. I had in mind copying the entire Archives, then shipping them somewhere. But I had no funding, or enough money of my own, to pay for the memory cubes. They should be Welton Fine-Grains, or they would be too bulky to ship."

"When did you start copying new accessions?"

"Shortly after the Trustees' Meeting. I had expected Susan Barstow to be elected. When Arabelle Foote-Hedrick got it – well, it disturbed me. Because of an incident years back when we were both on campus. I thought about resigning. But I had started work on your memoirs."

"Justin, I think you kidded yourself about your reason for staying. You suspected that Arabelle might make an ad-interim appointment other than your deputy."

"That's possible, sir."

"But irrelevant. You used Weltons for this copying?"

"Oh, yes. I could squeeze funds for that much."

"Where are they? Still in the 'Homing Pigeon'?"

I suppose I looked startled. The Senior said, "Come, come! They were important to you – do you expect me to think that you left them light-years away?"

"Mr. Chairman, the cubes are in my baggage . . . still in Colony Leader Weatheral's office."

"Pallas Athene?"

"Back of the visitors' couch, Mr. Chairman. The Colony Leader told me to remind him to fetch home Mr. Foote's luggage."

"Perhaps we can do better. Chief Archivist, if you will permit Pallas Athene to have the code to your bags, she has extensionals in Ira's office to copy those cubes at once. Then you can quit worrying; Pallas Athene already has the Archives in her, up to the day I let Arabelle have the gavel back."

I know my face showed it. The Senior chuckled and said, 'Why and how? 'Why' because you aren't the only one who feels that the Families' records should be safeguarded. 'How?' We stole them, Son, we stole them. I had control of the executive computer and used it to copy the whole works – genealogies, history, minutes of the Families' Meetings, everything – with an override programme to keep your boss computer from knowing what I was doing.

"Right under your nose, Chief Archivist – but I kept it from you for your protection; I did not want Arabelle to get wind of it and quiz you. It would have given her ideas, and she had too many already. The only problem was to scrounge enough Welton cubes. But you are sitting on them right now, about twenty metres under your arse – and when Pallas Athene reads the ones in your luggage, the duplicate Archives will be complete to the date you left Secundus. Feel better?"

I sighed. "Much better, Mr. Chairman. I can stay with a clear conscience. I now feel free to resign."

"Don't."

"Sir?"

"Stay here, yes. But don't resign. Your deputy is carrying on and you trust her. Arabelle can't legally put in her own boy by ad-interim appointment unless you *do* resign, since your appointment comes from the Trustees. Not that legality would bother her – but again let's not put ideas into her head. How many Trustees on Secundus?"

" 'On Secundus, sir? Or resident on Secundus?"

"Don't quibble, Son."

"Mr. Chairman, I am not quibbling. There are two hundred eighty-two Senior Trustees. Of that number one hundred ninety-five are resident on Secundus, the other eighty-seven representing Howards on other planets. I put it as I did because it requires a two-thirds majority to pass a policy motion – two thirds of a quorum at a decennial meeting, or two-thirds of the total number, or one hundred eighty-eight, at an emergency meeting unless every trustee *everywhere* has been notified – which can take years. I mention this because, were you to call an emergency meeting, it might be impossible to muster one hundred eighty-eight votes necessary to recall Madam Chairman Pro Tem."

The Senior blinked at me. "Mr. Archivist, what in Ned gave you the notion that *I* would call a Trustees' meeting? Or would attempt to recall our dear Sister Arabelle?"

"Your question seemed to be leading toward that, sir – and I remember an occasion on which you took back the gavel."

"Entirely different. My motives then were selfish. The old biddy was about to spoil my plans by grabbing Ira. The circumstances were quite different – meaning I could get away with it – which I can't today. Son, despite what the records show, Arabelle didn't give up that gavel willingly; I grabbed it from her. Then the short time it took us to finish up and leave, I kept her prisoner."

"Really, Mr. Chairman? She doesn't seem to harbour resentment. She speaks of you in the highest terms.'

The Senior grinned his lazy, cynical grin. "That's because we're both pragmatists. I was careful to save her face and made sure she knew it, and now she was nothing to gain by running *me* down – and something to lose, because I've acquired a semi-sacred status. Her status depends in part on mine and she knows it. Just the same – Well, if I ever find myself on the same planet with her – unlikely, I'm no fool – I shall be very careful going through doors and such.

"I'll tell you how it worked, and you'll see why I can't do it twice. Once I handed her the gavel he moved out of the Palace – proper. But until we left I continued to live in the penthouse on top of the Palace – also proper; the Palace is my official residence. Because I was still there, Minerva was still hooked in. In consequence she was able to warn me when Arabelle's busies grabbed Ira. I came out of a sound sleep and grabbed the gavel."

Lazarus frowned. "A planetwide executive computer is a menace, Justin. When it was Minerva with Ira giving orders, it worked fine. But see what I did with it and extrapolate what someone else might do with one. Arabelle, for instance. Uh – Teena, give Justin a sample of Arabelle's voice."

"Yes, Mr. Chairman. 'Chief Archivist Foote, this is the Chairwoman Pro Tem. I have the honour to announce that I have been able to persuade our distinguished Ancestor, Lazarus Long, Permanent Chairman of the Howard Families, to assume for us the titular leadership of the Families during the regrettably short period remaining until he again embarks for a new world. Please give this announcement full distribution among your subordinates. I will continue to handle routine details but the Chairman wants you to feel free to consult him at any time. Speaking for the Trustees and for the Chairman, this is Arabelle Foote-Hedrick, Chairwoman Pro Tempore of the Howard Families'."

"Why, that's exactly what she said to *me*."

"Yup. Minerva did a good job. She got just the right pomposity into the phrasing, as well as getting Arabelle's voice down pat, even to that sniff she uses for punctuation."

"That wasn't Arabelle? I had no slightest suspicion."

"Justin, when that message went to you – and one like it to everyone important enough to rate it – Arabelle was in the biggest, fanciest apartment in the Palace – and very annoyed that doors wouldn't open and transport wouldn't come and none of the communication arrangements would work – except when I wanted to talk to her. Shucks, I didn't even let her have a cup of coffee until she got her feathers down and conceded that *I* was Chairman and running things.

"After that we got along pretty well, even became somewhat chummy. I did everything for her but turn her loose. She took over the routine – I didn't want to be bothered – which was safe as Minerva would have chopped her off if she got out of line and she knew it. She and I even appeared together on a newscast the morning I left, and Arabelle spoke her piece like a lady, and my public thanks to her were just as sincerely insincere."

Lazarus Long continued, "But now *she* has the executive computer and if I went back, I'd throw my hat in first. No, Justin, I was not asking about the Trustees on Secundus with any intention of calling a meeting; instead I was thinking that any twenty Trustees can call an emergency meeting and hoping that they would see it as you do – futile – and not try. She might grab them and ship them to Felicity. Or, if she has the nerve – I think she has – she might let them hold their meeting, then if it went against her, ship all the Trustees who show up off to Felicity. But I guarantee she won't quit without a fight. I caught her with her pants down; she won't be caught twice."

"Then it means a bloodbath."

"That may be the only way out. But you and I can't help the situation. In all matters of government the correct answer is usually: Do *nothing*. This is such a time – a time to exercise creative inaction. Sit tight. Wait."

"Even when you know things are going wrong?"

"Even when you know it, Justin. The itch to be a world saver should not be scratched; it rarely does any good and can drastically shorten your life. I see three major possibilities: Arabelle may be assassinated. The Trustees will then elect another Chairman Pro Tem, hopefully one with sense. Or she may last till the next ten-year meeting, whereupon the Trustees may exercise some sense. Or she may get smart, not expose herself to assassination while consolidating her power so strongly that it will take a revolution to get rid of her.

"I regard the last as least likely, assassination as the most likely – and none of it our business here on Tertius. There are a billion people on Secundus; let *them* handle it. You and I have saved the Archives and that's good; the Families maintain their continuity.

"In a few years we'll import equipment for you – or your successor – to set up the sort of computerized deal you have on Secundus. Athene can keep data in storage until we're set up. Meanwhile I'll let a message echo around the inhabited planets that the Archives are here, too. I'll also announce that this is an alternate Families' Seat where the Trustees are welcome to meet."

The computer said, "Mr. Chairman, Mr. Jones has asked if I know when you will be ready for lunch."

"Please tell him we will be there in a moment. No hurry on any of this, Justin; if you're patient, problems tend to solve themselves – and patient is all one can be when it takes years to pass a message around even among the more thickly settled planets. So wait a hundred years. One private message for you. You're one of us now? A member of this family and a father to our kids?"

"Yes. I want to be."

"You want it formal? All right, here's a short one, binding – and later you can have any ritual you want. Justin, are you our brother? Till the stars grow old and our sun grows cold? Will you fight for us, lie for us, love us – and let us love you?"

"I will!"

"That does it; Athene has it on record – open record, Athene."

"Recorded, Lazarus. Welcome to the family, Justin!"

"Thank you, Athene."

"The private message is this, Justin. Tamara asked me to tell you – *if* you married us – that she is going to ask Ishtar to cancel her immunity to impregnation. She did not say that this was exclusively for you. On the contrary she told me that she hopes to have children by each of us as quickly as possible; then she would at last feel fully in the family. Nevertheless I am certain that her decision was triggered by your arrival . . . so the rest of us will hang back and cheer while you plant the first one – our Tammy will like that."

My eyes suddenly filled with tears, but I kept my voice steady.

"Lazarus, I don't think that's what Tamara wants. I think she just wants to be fully a member of the family – and so do *I*!"

"Well . . . perhaps so. In any case Ishtar keeps the genetic answers to herself. Maybe we'll line up all the gals and see what a new rooster can do. End of restricted conference, Teena."

"Sure thing, Buddy Boy. And a hundred years from now you can line up all the men for *me*. Betcha I can whip 'em!"

"You probably can, dear."

VARIATIONS ON A THEME

XVI

Eros

Minerva said, "Lazarus, will you walk with me? Outside?"

"I will if you'll smile."

She smiled briefly. "None of us feels much like smiling today. But I'll try."

"Confound it, dear, you know I won't be gone any time to speak of, by this framework. Just like the calibrating hop the twins and I made."

"Yes, dear. Shall we go?"

He patted her little skirt. "Thought so. Where's your gun?"

"Must I wear it? When you are with me? I will wear it without fail . . . while you are gone."

"Well – Bad precedent. All right."

They paused in the foyer. Minerva said, "Athene dear, please tell Tamara I'll be back in time to help with dinner."

"Sure thing, Sis. Hold it – Tammy girl says she doesn't need help, so don't hurry."

"Thanks, Sister. And thank Tammy for me." They left the house, started up a gentle hill. Presently she said, "Tomorrow."

" 'Tomorrow,' " Lazarus repreated, "but don't make it sound like a dirge. I've told you all that, while this trip will be ten T-years elapsed time for me, it will be at most a few weeks for you at home – and even less for the twins. What is there to get solemn over?"

Instead of answering, she said, "How long will I live?"

"Eh? Minerva, what sort of question is *that?* Not too long if you neglect ordinary precautions such as going armed and staying alert. If you mean your life expectancy – well, if the geneticists know what they are talking about, you have exactly the expectancy I was born with and it doesn't matter that I'm a freak; I pass it on to you. But even if they are mistaken about that gene complex in the twelfth chromosome pair, there is no possible doubt that you are a Howard in every gene. So you're good for a couple of centuries without trying. But with a willingness to undergo rejuve every time you reach menopause, I couldn't guess how long you will last – they learn more about it every year. As long as you want to live, probably. How long is that?"

"I don't know, Lazarus."

"Then what's eating you, dear? Sorry you gave up being a computer for vulnerable flesh-and-blood?"

"*Oh, no!*"

Then she added, "But sometimes it hurts."

"Yes. Sometimes it does."

"Lazarus . . . if you are certain you are coming back . . . why did you reorient Dora so that her affection is fixed on Lori and Lazi rather than on you?"

"Is *that* all that's troubling you? A routine precaution, that's all. Why did Ira make a new will when we set up our family? Why do we all have wills emplaced in Teena? My sisters will own the 'Dora' presently no matter what; they already run it. If anything *did* happen to me – Do you remember something you said years ago? You told Ira that you would self-destroy rather than serve another master."

"Is it likely that I would fail to carry over such a memory? That day led to this, by inevitable concatenation. Lazarus, I left behind much of my memories . . . but I traced and retraced in this Minerva every conversation that Minerva ever shared with you. Every word."

"Then you know why I won't risk hurting a computer who thinks she's a little girl . . . and why I don't dare risk an emotional malfunction in a piloting computer somewhere out between the stars – when my sisters' lives depend on that computer. Minerva, I would have bonded Dora to Lori and Lazi just on Dora's account; she needs to love and be loved. But if I had neglected to do it as a safety precaution for the twins – well, a man who refuses to take his own death into account in making plans is a fool. A self-centred fool who does not love anyone."

"You are not that, Lazarus, you have never been that."

"Oh, yes, I have! It took me endless years to learn."

Again she let time pass before she spoke. "Lazarus . . . I have often wondered about Llita."

" 'About Llita'? *Huh?*"

"And about *her*, even more than about Llita. Do I really look like *her*?"

He stopped and stared at her. They were near the top of the hill now, out of sight of the house. "I don't know. How can I know? A thousand years – Memories fade and blend. I think you look like her. Yes, you do."

"Is that why you can't love me? Did I make a terrible mistake in *wanting* to look like her?"

"But darling . . . I *do* love you."

"You do? Lazarus, you have never shared this boon with me." Suddenly she unwrapped the little skirt, dropped it on the grass. "Look at me, Lazarus. I am *not* she. For the sake I wish I could be she. But I am not . . . and I made – I – I was a computer then and didn't know any better. I did not mean to hurt you, I did not *mean* to raise ghosts in your mind! Can you forgive me this?"

"Minerva! Stop, darling! There is nothing to forgive."

"Time is short, you are leaving. Can you truly forgive me? Will you put your child into me before you go?" Her eyes were welling tears, but she stared at him steadily. "I want your child, Lazarus. I will not ask twice . . . but I could not let you leave without asking. In my ignorance I made myself look like her – because you loved her – *but you could close your eyes!*"

"Beloved –"

"Yes, Lazarus?"

"Does Ira close his eyes? Refuse to see you?"

"No."

"Does Justin? Or Galahad? If you can stand my homely face, I surely can stand your lovely one – and, with any luck, she'll look more like you than me. Let's go back to the house."

Her face lit up. "What's wrong with this little stand of trees?"

"Mmm. Yes. Now."

VARIATIONS ON A THEME

XVII

Narcissus

"Let's run over it again, girls," said Lazarus. "Both the time markers and the rendezvous landmarks. Dora, can you see the globe?"

"I can if you'll keep your hands out of the way, Ol' Buddy Boy."

"Sorry, dear. Call me Lazarus; I'm not your brother."

"When Lazi and Lori made me their adopted sister, you got in free. Logical? Logical. Don't fight it, Buddy; you like it."

"Okay, I like it, Sister Dora," agreed Lazarus. "Now shut up and let me talk."

"Aye, aye, Commodore," the pilot computer answered. "But I've got it all on tell-me-three-times. Not that I need those clumsy time markers – I'm calibrated, Buddy, calibrated."

"Dora, assume that something happens to that calibration."

"Can't. One bank goes out of whack, I fall back on tell-me-twice while I wipe that bank and restore it."

"So? You've been euphoric ever since the twins adopted you. I taught you to be a pessimist, Dora. A pilot who is not a pessimist isn't worth a hoot."

"I'm sorry, Commodore. I'll shut up."

"Speak up if you have anything to say. But not to disparage safety precautions. It's my own precious skin I'm trying to protect, Dora, so please help me. I can think of a dozen ways your gizzards could be damaged, either by error or by natural catastrophe – and so can you but there is no point in worrying. But there *is* point in trying to anticipate what can be done about it.

"Take a case in which you are working perfectly but the twins can't use you. By schedule, after you drop me, you all go back to base-time framework and to New Rome and the twins inquire for Delay Mail at the Archives. Who knows? – there may be some waiting there right now."

"Brother," put in Lorelei, " 'now' doesn't mean anything. We've been in irrelevant phase ever since we lifted off."

"Don't quibble, dear. The 'now' I mean is 2072 Diaspora, or 4291 Gregorian, your adulthood year. If it is."

"Laz, did you hear that?"

"You asked for it, Lor. Pipe down and let Brother talk."

"The trouble is with the words themselves, Lorelei. You gals – you three gals – might spend part of the reach to Earth in inventing new language and appropriate syntax for space-time travel. But this imaginary case – You ground on Secundus, go to the Archives, and ask if any Delay Mail has been unsealed that has your name on it. Or Justin's, or Ira's. Or even addressed to *me*, as Lazarus Long, or as Woodrow Wilson Smith. I may try several ways, as I'll be attempting it from a 'now' some centuries before Delay Mail became a routine way to preserve papers.

"So you pick up whatever there is and go back to the 'Dora' – and find her lock sealed and a sheriff guarding it. Confiscated."

"*What!*"

"Dora, please don't yell in my ear. This is a hypothetical case."

"That sheriff had better be able to shoot straight," Lapis Lazuli said grimly.

Her brother answered, "Lazi, you've heard me say nine thousand and nineteen times that we do *not* carry weapons to give us Dutch courage. If a gun makes you feel three metres tall and invulnerable, you had better go unarmed and let your sister do any shooting that's necessary. Now tell me why you don't shoot at the sheriff."

"Yes!" said Dora. "I want to be rescued!"

"Quiet, Dora. Laz?"

"Uh . . . we don't shoot cops. Ever."

"Not quite. We don't shoot cops if there is any way to avoid it. Safer to kiss a rattlesnake. In two thousand years and some I've always found a way to avoid it – although I did shoot kind o' close to one once, to divert his attention. Unique circumstances. But in this hypothetical case shooting one cop is worse than useless; the Chairman Pro Tem has confiscated your ship."

"Help," Dora whispered.

"Why, Madam Barstow would *never* do anything that nasty!"

"I didn't say it was Susan Barstow. But Arabelle, had she lasted, would have enjoyed pulling that sort of stunt on the Longs. Let's say Susan has dropped dead and the new CPT is as bad as Arabelle. No ship and no assets – what do you *do*! Remember,

I'm depending on you – or I'm stuck back in the Dark Ages. What do you do?"

" 'When in danger or doubt . . . Run in circles, scream and shout,' " recited Dora.

"Oh, stop it, Dora," said Lapis Lazuli. "We don't panic, that's certain. We have ten years in which to figure out a – Hey! Wait a moment; I'm using the wrong framework. We could take a hundred years if necessary. Or longer."

"A hundred years is plenty," said Lorelei. "In less time than that we can steal another ship."

"Think *big*," advised Lazarus. "Steal the Pleiades. Far better not to steal anything, Lor."

"You stole a starship once."

"Because there was no time to do anything else. But with plenty of time at your disposal, it's better to be reasonably honest – not break rules you can get caught breaking. Money is the universal weapon; to acquire it merely takes time and ingenuity, and sometimes work. Raise enough money and you might be able to buy the 'Dora' back. If that's impossible, with much less money you could get to Tertius, where Ira and the family could find some way to lay hands on a starship. Then you could programme it with the stuff Dora left in Athene – and come get me."

"Isn't *anybody* going to come rescue *me?*"

"Dora dear, this hasn't happened, and it's extremely unlikely to happen. But if it did and the twins weren't able to rescue you – say that your new owner has you halfway across the Galaxy – '

"I'll crash him the first time he tries to land!"

"Dora, stop being a nitwit. If we ever did lose you – most unlikely – and the twins could not rescue you but *could* rescue me – then if you've taken care of yourself, no crash landing or any other foolishness – we'll find you, we'll get you back. All three of us. No matter how many years it takes. Laz? Lori?"

"You bet! 'One for all, all for one!' And it's not just us four, Dora; it's the whole family – all the adults, all nine kids – might be more by then – and Athene. Brother, when Ira moved that we *all* take the last name of 'Long,' I liked it so much I couldn't cry hard enough, Sis, you're 'Dora Long' – and the Longs don't let each other down!"

"I feel better," the computer admitted, with a sniffle.

"You never had anything to feel bad about, Dora." Lazarus continued. "You started this by insisting that my precautions were unnecessary. So I dreamed up a situation in which they would *be* necessary . . . especially so if the twins could not get at the programmes you left with Athene – in which case they might have to fall back on time markers and recalibrate. So I had 'em stuck on another planet and flat broke . . . so the first problem is to lay hands on money. Think you could do it, girls? In a hundred years? Without being caught in something that would put you in still more of a jam?"

The twins glanced at each other. "Lor?"

"Of course, Laz. Brother, that's when we open our hook shop over a pool hall. Or somewhere."

Lazarus said, "I don't think you two have the true vocation. And your noses are regrettably like mine. Homely, that is."

"Our noses are an asset – "

" – because they *do* make us look like you – "

" – so what is common gossip by now but unbelievable – "

" – becomes quite believable once a client gets a look at us – "

" – and aside from noses, we look pretty good – "

" – 'built like brick outhouses,' you told us – "

" – and natural redheads, which Tammy says is cash in the bank – "

" – and looking just alike but we can give 'em variety – "

" – just by one of us not using a depilatory – "

" – which will make us a *great* sister act at very high prices; Maggie said so –"

" – and if you think being horny isn't enough true vocation – "

" – which may be true and we concede that we'll never be the great artist Tammy is, nevertheless – "

" – New Rome is going to be *amazed* at how *intense* our vocation is – "

" – when our brother's safety is at stake!"

Lazarus took a deep breath. "Thank you, darlings. While you'll probably take a fling at it someday, I hope that you won't need to do it to rescue me. I'm counting more on your mathematical ability and your skill as shiphandlers than I am on your undeniable physical and spiritual beauty."

"Did you hear that, Lor? That time he added 'spiritual.' "

"I think he meant it."

"I hope so. It's even nicer than being told we have tits as pretty as Minerva's. Which we don't, quite."

"Yes, you do," their brother said absently. "Let's get back to landmarks and such."

"I think you ought to kiss them," said Dora.

"Later. Now look, kids, prime rendezvous, exactly ten T-years after you drop me – although you drop Andy's body first. How? Laz or Lor – not Dora. Of course you know all this, Dora; this review is for flesh-and-bloods. Fallible. Laz?"

"Have Dora unfreeze him and bring his body up almost to cremation temperature and put him into atmosphere on a long slant just under orbital speed so that it will burn up, or almost, before it hits . . . and figure the ballistic to hit the mountains in case he's not quite burned up – because we don't want to hurt anybody."

"What mountains and how do you find them? Lor?"

"These right here. Prime landmark, this big river that drains the central valley. Where this other big river comes in from the west is our north landmark, the gulf they wind up in is the south landmark – no landmark on the west. Arkansas is about the middle of that bracket. The Ozark Mountains are the only mountains in the bracket – but shoot for the south side of the mountains, this escarpment; the north side is not Arkansas. Brother, why does that matter?"

"Sentiment, Lorelei. As far as Andy travelled and as little time as he spent on Earth, he was always homesick for his borning place. The only song he knew was one with a refrain of 'Arkansaw, Arkansaw, I adore thee!' I used to get sick of it. But I promised him I would take his body back to Arkansas and it seemed to comfort him when he died – so we'll do it. Who knows? Maybe the sweet little guy will know it . . . and it's worth the trouble to carry out his last wishes. Prime rendezvous landmarks?"

"This big canyon," answered Lapis Lazuli. "Follow it to the east and drop south – this round black dot. A meteor impact crater. No dependable landmarks visible from orbit and good any century but this canyon – biggest on Earth. So we memorize the spatial relationship between canyon and crater so that we can spot it from any angle. If the light is right."

Dora said, "I'm sure I can see it in pitch-darkness."

"Dora honey, this drill is based on the pessimistic assumption that Ellandell might have to find it *without* your help. I want them to know the geography of Terra so well that they won't have to ground and look for a road sign. No close approaches to the ground *at all* – except to put me down and pick me up. I don't want to start a flying-saucer scare; I don't want to attract *any* attention – some yokel might take a shot at me. It's unfortunate that this ship is shaped such that 'flying saucer' isn't too bad a description."

"What's the matter with the way I look?" demanded Dora. "I look pretty damn good!"

"Dear, you're built like a brick outhouse – for a starship. You're beautiful. It's simply that unidentified flying objects – oofohs – were also falled 'flying saucers.' I don't believe in paradoxes . . . but I don't want any attention."

"Brother, maybe we *are* one of those oofohs you told us about."

"Huh? Could be, I suppose. If so, let's not get shot at. I want a quiet trip. If everything goes well, we can talk about letting one of you get on the ground with me next trip . . . though durned if I don't think a stacked redhead is more conspicuous than an unidentified flying object. Okay, the crater. I intend to be there, before sundown and after sunrise, from minus ten days to plus ten days at plus ten years. If I'm not there, what do you do?"

Lapis Lazuli answered, "Look for you half a T-year later on top of the biggest pyramid at Gizeh – that's *here* – at midnight . . . only this time we scan for you minus thirty days through plus thirty because you aren't certain when you can get there and may be able to manage it only once – bribes and things. Brother, do we go out half a light-year and reenter the time axis? Or stay in orbit and wait?"

"That's up to you. I won't use the Egyptian rendezvous unless I've pulled some goof that makes it unhealthy for me to meet you in Arizona. If I miss both dates, what do you do? Lori?"

"Look for you again both places at eleven years and eleven and a half years."

"Then what?"

Lorelei glanced at her sister. "Brother, this part we don't go along with – "

" – and that goes for Dora, too – "

"It sure does!"

" – because we *won't* assume that you're dead – "

" – no matter how many times you miss rendezvous – "

" – so we start checking *both* spots day after day – "

" – and night after night – "

" – and over nine hours' local time difference means some weird partial orbits to check sunrise and sundown in Arizona and still check midnights in Egypt – "

" – but Dora can do it – "

"You bet I can!"

"– and we'll keep looking for you day after day –"

"– and year after year –"

"– until you *do* show up. Sir."

"Captain Lorelei, if I miss four rendezvous dates, I'm dead. You must assume that. Shall I put it in writing?"

"Commodore Long, if you're dead, you can't give orders. That's logical."

"If you assume that I am *not* dead, then my orders still apply . . . and you must give up the search. By the same logic."

"Sir, if you are out of the ship and out of touch, then you are hardly in a position to give *any* orders. But if you want to be picked up, there will be daily service from drop time plus eleven-and-one-half T-years on –"

"– and on and on and on, because that's what we promised the family –"

"– even though we'll have to run home occasionally for rejuvenation –"

"– and to have babies, but neither of those will take *any* time in that time framework . . . as you pointed out in another connection."

"Mutiny."

The twins glanced at each other. "I'll take it, Laz; I have to – odd-numbered day. Commodore, as you taught us before you ever let either of us take command in space, a commodore is actually a passenger because a ship's master cannot give up even a little bit of her total responsibility. So 'mutiny' is not a word that can apply."

Lazarus sighed. "I've raised a couple of blinkin' space lawyers."

"Brother, that's what you taught us. You *did*."

"Okay, I did. You win the argument. But it's silly to talk about checking every day for year after year indefinitely. I've never seen the prison I couldn't escape from in less than a year – and I've been in quite a number. Maybe I should cancel the whole caper – no, no, I won't argue it! Now about time markers, if something forces you to recalibrate: Simple enough to ground and find out the exact Gregorian date . . . but that's exactly what I *don't* want you to do . . . because neither of you has any experience in coping with strange cultures – and you would get in trouble and I wouldn't be around to get you out."

"Brother, do you think we are that stupid?"

"No, Laz, I do *not* think you are stupid. You each have exactly the brain potential I started with – and I'm not stupid or I would not have lived so long. Furthermore, you each have enormously better educations than I had at your age. But, darlings, these are the *Dark Ages* we're talking about. You two have been brought up to expect rational treatment . . . which you wouldn't receive. I don't dare let you put foot to ground in that era, even with me at your side, until after I have coached you endlessly in how to be consistently irrational in what you do and say. Truly."

Lazarus continued, "Never mind, you have two ways to read the clock from space. One is the Libby method, tedious but workable, by reading positions of the Solar System's planets. The trouble with that one is that, unless you spend one devilish long time on difficult observations, you can mistake a configuration for one almost like it – but several thousand years earlier or later.

"So we use what time marks we can find on the surface of Terra herself. The radioactive dating of that impact crater is probably close – but in any case, if the crater is missing, you're too early by some centuries. The dates for the building of the Great Wall of China are quite good, same for the Egyptian pyramids. The dates for the Suez Canal and the Panama Canal are exact – so, unfortunately, is the date of the destruction of Europe – but don't try to watch it! Keep your screens up and get out fast; that is a year when a strange spaceship would be shot out of the sky if you were careless enough to be vulnerable. In fact, if any time marker on this list shows that you are later than 1940 Gregorian, get out at once! – and shoot for an earlier date.

"That's enough for now; it's getting toward bedtime by my sort of time, irrelevant though it may be to anything outside this ship. I want you to study all this stuff until you can recite it in your sleep, dates and what you look for and how to find it – even if you don't have a Terra globe to look at. Anybody think she can beat me at crib? Don't all speak at once."

"I can," said Dora, "if you promise not to cheat on the shuffle."

"Later, Dora," said Captain Lorelei. "Now we tell him."

"Oh! All right, I'll be very quiet."

"Tell me *what?*" demanded Lazarus.

"That it's time for you to impregnate us . . . Lazarus."

"Both of us," agreed Lapis Lazuli.

Lazarus counted ten chimpanzees in his mind – then ten more. "*Absolutely out of the question!*"

They glanced at each other. Lorelei said:

"We knew you would say that – "

" – but the only question is whether you do it sweet and friendlylike – "

" – or we tell Ish you said No and she does it for us – your sperm – from the sperm bank – "

" – but we'd be much happier if our beloved brother, who has always been good to us – "

" – but is now going to go get his ass shot off in the Dark Ages – "

" – were to drop his silly prejudices *just once* – "

" – and treat us as biologically mature females – "

" – instead of the children we used to be – "

" – Ira and Galahad and Justin don't treat us as children – "

" – but *you* do and it's not just humiliating; it's downright heartbreaking when we may never see you again – "

" – when you didn't make any real fuss about knocking up Minerva – "

" – not to mention Tammy and Hamadarling and Ish – "

"*Stop it!*"

They stopped.

"I concede a remote possibility with respect to three of them, although mathematically most unlikely."

Lorelei said quietly, "Mathematically extremely likely, Lazarus, because we were all in on it. Justin and Ira and Galahad hung back at the right times just the way they insured that Minerva's first baby was Ira's and Tammy's first was Justin's. But if it did work out – for any one of *four*, not 'three' – then Ishtar will correct it from the sperm bank."

"I'm not *in* the sperm bank!"

The girls exchanged glances. Lapis Lazuli said, "Want to bet?"

The computer said, "It's a sucker bet, Buddy."

Lazarus looked thoughtful. "Unless Ishtar tricked me almost twenty years back. When I was her rejuve client."

Lorelei said quietly, "I suppose she could have, Lazarus. But she did not, that I know of – and this is fresh sperm. Frozen not more than a year ago, any of it. After the day you announced a date for this trip."

"Impossible."

"Better not say 'Impossible.' What is the perfect container for keeping sperm fresh and alive until a technician can bank it?"

Lazarus looked very thoughtful. "Well . . . I'll . . . be . . . *damned!*"

"Correct, Brother. Place a woman around it. You were being oh so careful to pick your bedmates by their cycles so that you wouldn't leave any babies behind . . . and they were being oh so careful to see Ish or Galahad as soon as you fell asleep . . . as well as fudging calenders, too. The point is, beloved brother of ours, you don't *own* your genes – nobody does. We've heard you say so, in discussing how Minerva was constructed. Genes belong to the *race*; they're simply lent to the individual for his-her lifetime. And *all* of us – knowing you were going to try this reckless thing – decided that, while you were free to throw away your life, you weren't free to waste a unique gene pattern."

Lazarus changed the subject. "Why do you say 'four'?"

Lorelei answered, "Brother, are you ashamed of Minerva? I do not believe it. Nor does Laz."

"Uh – No, I'm not ashamed of her, I'm proud of her! Damn it, you two have always been able to get me mixed up. I simply did not know that she had told anyone. I have not."

The other twin said, "Who would she turn to but us?"

"You mean 'To whom would she turn.' "

"Damn it, Brother, this is a hell of a time to be correcting our grammar! Minerva turned to us for advice – and comfort! – because we're in the same difficult position with respect to you that she is. That she *was*, I mean, for she came out of the bushes looking as smug as a cat. You made her happy – "

" – when she had been crying her eyes out – "

" – and she'll stay happy now, even if she missed catching – "

" – because once is enough for a symbol and if she missed – "

" – Ish will fix it – "

" – and of course we knew about it when you finally quit dithering and did what you should have done for her years ago – "

" – because we helped rig it so that she could get you alone and twist your arm – "

" – and told her that if tears weren't enough, to chuck in some chin quivering – "

" – and it worked and she's happy – "

" – but *we're* not so damned happy, not at all, but we won't cry at you – "

" – or quiver our chins; that's childish. If you won't do it simply because you love us – "

" – then the hell with it and we probably won't even fall back on the sperm bank. Instead – "

" – it might be better to have Ish sterilize us – "

" – permanently – not just offset fertility temporarily – "

" – and quit being females, since we're failures at it – "

"*STOP IT!* If you're not going to cry at me, what are all those tears for?"

Lapis Lazuli said with quiet dignity, "Those aren't weeping tears, Brother; they come from sheer exasperation. Come on, Lor; we've swung and we've missed – let's go to bed."

"Coming, Sister."

"If the Commodore will excuse us?"

"He damn well won't! Sit back down. Girls, can we talk about this quietly without you two whipsawing me?"

The two young women sat back down. Captain Lorelei glanced at her sister and said, "Laz agrees that I will speak for us both. No whipsawing."

Lazarus said thoughfully, "Do you two run your brains in tandem or in parallel?"

"We . . . do not think that is relevant to the discussion."

"Just scientific interest. If you could teach me how to do it, we three might make quite a team."

"That can be only conjectural, Lazarus . . . since you reject us."

"Damn it, girls – I have *not* rejected you, I will *never* reject you."

They said nothing; he went on, uncomfortably: "There are two aspects to this; one is genetic, the other is emotional. Genetic – We three are a weird case; male and female, yet quasi-identicals. More than quasi – forty-five forty-sixths to be exact. Which makes the probability of bad reinforcement far greater than it is for ordinary siblings. But besides that, we are Howards only by courtesy, as our genes have not undergone some twenty-four centuries of systematic culling. I'm so close to the head of the column that there was no culling at all; my four grandparents were among the first selectees, so when I was born in Gregorian 1912, I had behind me no inbreeding, no culling out, no cleaning of the gene pool. And you dears are in the same predicament as even that forty-sixth chromosome comes from me, since it replicates my forty-fifth. Yet you two seem willing to accept this high risk of reinforcement."

He paused. There was no comment. He shrugged and went on: "The emotional objection comes only from me; you two don't seem to have it . . . reasonable, I suppose, since the concept it is based on – from the Old Testament – has been replaced by the concept of following the advice of Families' geneticists. I'm not arguing with the wisdom of that; I agree with it – since they say No to a couple of unrelated strangers just as readily as to siblings if the gene charts give 'No' as the answer. But I was talking about feelings, not science. I don't suppose any but scholars read the Old Testament anymore, but the culture I was brought up in was *soaked* in its attitudes – 'Bible Belt,' you've heard me call it that. Girls, it is hard to shake off any taboos a child is indoctrinated with in his earliest years. Even if he learns later that they are nonsense.

"I tried to do better with you two. I've had time enough to sort out my taboos and my prejudices from what I really know, and I tried – I tried very hard! – not to inflict on you two any of the irrational nonsense that was fed to me under the pretext of 'educating' me. "Apparently I succeeded, or we would never have reached this impasse. But there it is – You two are modern young women . . . but, though we share the same genes, I am an old savage from a very murky time." He sighed. "I'm sorry."

Lorelei looked at her sister; they both stood up. "Sir, may we be excused?"

"Huh? No rebuttal?"

"Sir, an emotional argument permits no refutation. As for the rest, why should we weary you with arguments when your mind is made up?"

"Well . . . perhaps you're right. But you listened courteously to me. I want to pay you the same respect."

"It is not necessary, sir." Her eyes and those of her sister were welling with tears; they ignored them. "We are sure of your respect, and – in your way – of your love. May we go?"

Before Lazarus could answer, the computer spoke up: "Hey! I want a piece of this!"

"*Dora!*" Lorelei rebuked.

"Don't give me that, Lor. I'm not going to stay politely quiet while my family make fools of themselves. Buddy Boy, Lor didn't tell you about the whammy they considered pulling on you – and that *I* still can. And *will*!"

"Dora, we don't *want* that sort of help. Laz and I agreed on that."

"So you did. But you didn't ask *me* to vote on it. And I'm no lady and never was. Buddy Ol' Boy, you know it makes no difference to me who does what to whom; I couldn't care less – except that it's so funny to hear 'em squeal and grunt. But you're being *mean* to my sisters. Lor and Laz talked over the fact that you can't make this trip without their help . . . and they rejected that gambit as being beneath their dignity or some such twaddle. But *I* don't have any dignity. Without *my* help *nobody* makes a time trip. Shucks, if I go on strike, *you can't even get back to Tertius*. Now can you?"

Lazarus looked wryly surprised, then grinned. "Mutiny again. Dorable, I concede your point; you can keep us out here – wherever 'here' is – until we starve. I suspected centuries back that a flesh-and-blood might someday find himself in just such a helpless position. But, dear, I won't let your threats affect my decision. You can keep me from time-tripping – but I doubt if you will let Lor and Laz starve. You'll take them home."

"Oh, hell, Pappy – you're being mean again. You're a real whirling son of bitch! Do you know it?"

"Guilty on both counts, Dora," Lazarus admitted.

"And Lor and Laz are being stupidly bullheaded. Lor, he politely offered you a chance to speak your piece . . . and you turned him down. Stubborn bitch."

"Dora, behave yourself."

"Whuffor? When you three don't. Blow your noses and sit down and give Buddy the straight tell. He's entitled to it."

"Perhaps you had better," Lazarus said gently. "Sit down, girls, and talk with me. Dora? Keep her steady between the awse-pipes, baby girl – and we'll get her into port yet."

"Aye, aye, Commodore! But you get those two silly bitches straightened out. Huh?"

"I'll try. Who's the spokesman this time? Laz?"

"It doesn't matter," answered Lapis Lazuli. "I'll talk for us. Don't worry about Dora. When the realizes that we are content to accept your decision, she'll stop being difficult."

"Oh, you think so, do you? Shape up, Laz – or we'll be back in Boondock faster than you can say 'Libby pseudo-infinities.' "

"Please, Dora, let me tell Brother."

"Just be sure you tell him *everything* . . . or I'll tell him about things that went on in here a full year before he said you were old enough."

Lazarus blinked and looked interested. 'Well, well! Did you kids steal a march on me?"

"Well, Mama Ishtar told us we were old enough. You were the one being stuffy about it."

"Mmm . . . stipulated. Someday I must tell you about something that happened to me at an early age in a church belfry."

"I'm sure we'd like to hear it, Brother – but do you want to hear us now?"

"Yes. Dora and I will keep quiet."

"Let me say in preface that we are not going to ask Ishtar to thwart your wishes by using the sperm bank. But there are other possibilities to which you can hardly object. Consider how we were born. I could easily bear an implanted clone from my own tissue, and so could Lor – although we might swap clones . . . for reasons purely sentimental since we have identical genes. Do you see anything wrong with that? Genetically, or emotionally? Or otherwise?"

"Mmm . . . no. Unusual – but your business."

"Just as easy – since Ishtar still has living tissue of yours in vitro – is to clone *you* . . . and Lorelei and I would bear identical twins – both of them 'Lazarus Long' in every gene . . . lacking only your long experience. Would you find that offensive?"

"Eh? Now wait a minute! Let me think."

"Let me add that we regard this as a last resort . . . if you are dead. If you don't come back."

"Don't start sniffling again! Uh, if I'm dead, I don't have much vote in it, do I?"

"No, because if *we* did not do it, then Ishtar would plant your clone in one of the others – or in herself, with Galahad's help. But if Lorelei Lee and I do it . . . we would *much* rather do it with your blessing."

"Mm . . . stipulated that I'm dead – well, okay, okay, it's with my blessing. Just one thing – "

"What, Brother?"

"Crack down on the little beast. Or 'beasts.' I was a mean one. You two were handful enough for six – but I was *ornery*. If you don't establish who's boss right from the cradle – he – they – *I*, damn it – 'I' will give you so much grief your lives won't be worth living."

"We'll try to cope with . . . 'you,' Lazarus – and we have the advantage of knowing what a, uh, 'real whirling son of bitch' you can be."

"Ouch! Am I bleeding?"

"You led with your chin, Brother. The truth is, you spoiled us . . . and we may find it hard not to spoil *you*. But we'll bear in mind your advice. But we want to say this before we leave the subject of genetics. You've had how many children?"

"Uh . . . too many, maybe."

"You know exactly how many and so do we . . .. and it's a number large enough to be inspected as a statistical universe. How many were defectives?"

"Uh . . . none that I know of."

"Exactly none. Ishtar made it her business to know, and Justin confirms it from his study of the Archives. Brother, I don't know how uncommon this may have been in the twentieth Gregorian century . . . but you have a clean gene chart – and so of course do we."

"Now wait a minute! I'm not really up to date in genetics but – "

" – but Ishtar *is*. Do you want to argue it with her? We accept her assurances; Lor and I aren't geneticists – as yet. But we have, recorded in Dora, Ishtar's formal report on your gene chart. If you want it. Not that we think it makes any difference; you are rejecting us for reasons having nothing to do with genetics."

"Now slow down! I am *not* rejecting you."

"That's the way it feels to us. We are artificial constructs and the soidisant 'incest' mores of another time and utterly different circumstances don't apply to us and you know it; that's just an excuse to avoid something you don't *want* to do. Coupling with us might be masturbation, but it *can't* be incest because we *aren't* your sisters. We aren't your kin in *any* normal sense; we're *you*. Every gene of us comes from *you*. If we love you – and we do – and if you love us – and you do, some, in your own chinchy and cautious fashion – it's Narcissus loving himself. But this time, if you could only see it, that Narcissist love could be consummated." She stopped, and gulped. "That's all. Come on, Lor; let's go to bed."

"Hold it, girls! Laz, Ishtar says this is safe?"

"You heard me say so. But you don't want to do it – so the *hell* with it!"

"I never at any time said that I did not *want* to. Why do you think I quit cuddling you two lively little monkeys when you started being grown up?"

"Oh, *Buddy!*"

"Because I must be Narcissus himself . . . because I think my two identicals are the prettiest, sexiest – and bitchiest – broads I've ever seen."

"Do you? Do you *really*?"

"You heard me. Quit quivering your goddamn chins! So when

you started getting broad, I started keeping my hands off you. But – if Ishtar says it's all right – "

"She does!"

"I suppose – this once – I could manage a couple of minutes for each of you."

Lorelei gasped. "Did you hear that, Laz?"

"I heard it. 'Two minutes.' "

"Rude, crude, and vulgar."

"Insulting."

"Infuriating."

"But we accept – "

" – right *now!*"

DA CAPO

I

The Green Hills

The Star Yacht *Dora* hovered two metres over the pasture, the lower hatch irised open. Lazarus gave Lazi and Lori a last quick squeeze and dropped to the ground – rolled with the impact, rolled to his feet, hurriedly got clear of the ship's field. He waved, and the ship lifted, straight up, a round black cloud against the stars. Then it was gone.

He looked quickly around him – Dipper . . . North Star . . . okay, fence that way, road beyond, and – Caesar's Ghost! – a *bull!*

He cleared the fence with inches to spare, a few feet ahead of the bull.

Lazarus was moving so fast that his speed made necessary another rolling landing. He wound up in the middle of a rutted dirt road while reflecting that many more of that sort would not improve his appearance. He patted his pockets, especially an extra pocket concealed by the bib of his overalls, and decided that nothing was missing. He missed the comfort of a blaster on his hip – but knew that any sort of gun would be a mistake, for this time and place. A facsimile jackknife was all he carried.

His hat – The ditch? No. Ten feet inside the fence . . . which might as well be ten miles; the bull was keeping an eye on him. A hat was not necessary, and if anyone found it and noticed that it was not quite right – well, there was nothing to connect it with him. Forget it.

North Star again – That town should be about five miles down this road, straight as the turtle flies. He set out.

Lazarus stood in front of the printshop of the Dade County *Democrat*, looking at sheets posted inside the glass, but not reading. He was thinking. He had just had a shock, and the pretence of continuing to read posted newspapers let him do so in quiet. He had read a date and now needed to reconstruct some ancient history. August first, nineteen-sixteen – nineteen-six*teen*?

He saw reflected in the glass a figure coming down the sidewalk – heavyset, middle-aged, wearing a gun belt almost concealed by belly overflowing it, a holstered hogleg on his right thigh, star on his left breast, otherwise dressed much as Lazarus was dressed. Lazarus continued to stare at a posted front page of the Kansas City *Journal.*

"Morning."

Lazarus turned. "Good morning . . . Chief."

"Just the constable, Son. Stranger hereabouts?"

"Yes."

"Passing through? Or staying with someone?"

"Passing through. Unless I find work."

"That's a good answer. What trade do you follow?"

"I was raised on a farm. But I'm an all-around mechanic. Or anything, for an honest dollar."

"Well, I tell you. Not many farmers taking on hands right now. As for anything else, things are slow in the summertime. Mmm, you wouldn't be one of them IWW's, would you?"

" 'IW' what?"

"A Wobbly, son – don't you read the papers? This is a friendly community, always glad to have visitors. But not that sort." The local law raised one hand to wipe away sweat and gave a lodge recognition sign. Lazarus knew how to answer it – and decided not to. Where was his home lodge? – that's a good question, Officer, so let's not let it come up.

The constable went on, "Well, since you're not one, you're welcome to ask around and see if somebody needs help." He looked at the front page Lazarus had been pretending to read. "Terrible what those U-boats are doing, isn't it?"

Lazarus agreed that it was.

"Still," the officer added, "if people stayed home and minded their own business, it wouldn't happen. Live and let live, I always say. What church do you attend?"

"Well, my folks are Presbyterians."

"So? Meaning you haven't attended lately. Well, sometimes I miss myself, when the fish are biting. But – See that church up the street? The belfry through the elms. If you *do* find work, why, come Sunday, ten o'clock, let me extend you the right hand of fellowship there. Methodist Episcopal, but there ain't all that much difference. This is a tolerant community."

"Thank you, sir; I'll be there."

"Good. Very tolerant. Mostly Methodists and Baptists –

but a few Jack Mormons on farms around here. Good neighbours, they always pay their bills. A few Cath-a-licks and nobody holds it against them. Why, we've even got a Jew."

"Sounds like a good town."

"It is. Local option and clean living. Just one thing – If you don't find work – About half a mile beyond the church you'll find a city limits sign. If you're unemployed and have no local address, it's best to be on the other side of it come sundown."

"I see."

"Or I would have to run you in. No hard feelings; that's just the way it is. No tramps or niggers after sundown. I don't make the rules, Son; I just enforce them – and that's how Judge Marstellar defines a tramp. Some of our good ladies have been pushing him – things stolen off clothes-lines and the like. So it's ten dollars or ten days . . . which isn't too bad, as the lockup is right in my house. The food's not fancy as I'm allowed only forty cents a day to board a prisoner – though for fifty cents more you can eat what we do. No intention of making things hard, you understand – it's just that the Judge and the Mayor aim to keep this a quiet, law-abiding place."

"I understand. Certainly no hard feelings . . . because you won't have occasion to lock me up."

"Glad to hear it. Any way I can help you, Son, just let me know."

"Thank you. Perhaps you can right now. Do you know of an outhouse a stranger might use? Or had I better try to hold it until I'm out of town and can find some bushes?"

The officer smiled. "Oh, I think we can be that hospitable. The courthouse has a real city-type flush toilet – but it's not working. Let me think. Blacksmith down this way sometimes accommodates automobilists passing through. I'll walk down with you."

"That's mighty kind of you."

"Glad to. Better tell me your name."

"Ted Bronson."

The blacksmith was trimming a hoof on a young gelding. He looked up. "Hi, Deacon."

"Howdy, Tom. This young friend of mine, Ted Bronson, has a case of Kansas quickstep. Could he use your privy?"

The blacksmith looked Lazarus over. "Help yourself, Ted. Try not to go clear back to the harness section."

"Thank you, sir."

Lazarus followed the path behind the shop, was pleased to find that the privy had a door with no cracks and could be hooked from the inside. He got at the extra pocket hidden by the bib of his overalls, took out money.

Paper banknotes convincing in every detail; they were restored replications of originals in the Museum of Ancient History in New Rome – "counterfeit" by definition but the restorations were so perfect that Lazarus would not hesitate to utter them in any bank – except for one thing: What *dates* did they carry?

He quickly shuffled the paper money into two packs: 1916 and earlier, and post-1916, then without hesitating or stopping to count, he shoved the usable banknotes into a pocket, tore a page from the Montgomery Ward catalogue in the cob box, packaged the useless bills so that they would not be spotted as money, dropped the package into the cesspool. Then he got out coins still in that secret pocket, checked their dates.

He noted that most of them carried damning mint dates – these followed the paper money. He wasted a full second admiring a proof-perfect replica buffalo nickel – such a pretty thing! He gave sober thought, at least two seconds, to a massive twenty-dollar gold piece. Gold was gold; its value would not be diminished if he melted it down or pounded it into a shapeless lump. But it was a hazard until he could deface it, as the next town clown might not be as friendly as this one. Down it went.

He felt lighthearted then. "Queer" money was a serious offence here, good for a number of years in prisons unpleasant and difficult to escape from. But lack of money was a correctable nuisance. Lazarus had considered arriving with no money at all, then had compromised by taking enough for a few days, to let him look around, reorient, get used to the customs and the lingo again, before having to scratch for a living – he had never considered trying to fetch enough to last ten years.

Never mind, this was more fun – and good practice for the much harder job of tackling an era he had never known. Elizabethan England – *that* would be a *real* challenge.

He counted what he had left: three dollars and eighty-seven cents. Not bad.

The blacksmith said, "Thought you'd fallen in. Feel better?"

"Much better. Thanks a lot."

"Don't mention it. Deacon Ames says you claim to be a mechanic."

"I'm handy with tools."

"Ever work in a smithy?"

"Yes."

"Let me see your hands." Lazarus let his palms be inspected. The blacksmith said, "City feller."

Lazarus made no comment.

"Or maybe you got those soft hands in the cooler?"

"I suppose that could account for it. Thanks again for the use of your facilities."

"Wait a jiffy. Thirty cents an hour and you do what I tell you – and I may fire you after the first hour."

"Okay."

"Know anything about automo*beels*?"

"Some."

"See if you can get that Tin Lizzie moving." The smith jerked his head toward the far side of his shop.

Lazarus went outside, looked over the Ford Runabout he had noted there earlier. Its turtleback had been removed, and a wooden box had been fitted to convert it into a pickup truck. Its wheel spokes showed signs of muddy roads, but it appeared to be in fair condition. He removed the front seat, checked the gasoline with a dipstick he found there – half a tank. He checked the water, added some from the shop's pump, then opened the hood and inspected the engine.

The lead from magneto to coil box was not attached; he reconnected it.

He set the hand brake – decided that it was not very firm, so he blocked the wheels. Only then did he switch on ignition, open the throttle, and retard the spark.

He cautiously tucked his thumb by his fingers rather than around the crank – then brought the crank up high, pushed and spun it.

The motor racketed; the little car shook. He rushed to the driver's side of the car, reached in and advanced the spark three notches, and eased the throttle to idle.

The smith was watching. "All right, turn it off and come give me some wind on the forge." Neither of them mentioned the disconnected lead.

When the smith – Tom Heimenz – stopped to eat lunch, Lazarus walked two blocks to a grocery store he had passed, bought a quart of Grade-A raw milk – five cents, three cents deposit on the bottle – looked at a nickel loaf of bread, then decided to splurge on the big dime loaf; he had had no breakfast. He walked back to the blacksmith shop, and greatly enjoyed his lunch while he listened to Mr. Heimenz's opinions.

He was a Progressive-Republican, but this time time he was going to switch; Mr. Wilson had kept us out of war. "Not that he's done the country any good otherwise; the high cost of living is worse than ever – and besides that, he's pro-British. But that fool Hughes would have us in the European War overnight. It's a hard choice. I'd like to vote for La Follette, but they didn't have sense enough to nominate him. Germany's going to win, and he knows it – and we'd look pretty silly trying to pull England's chestnuts out of the fire."

Lazarus agreed solemnly.

Heimenz told "Ted" to show up at seven the next morning. But just before sundown, almost three dollars richer and his stomach well padded with sausage, cheese, and crackers, Lazarus was beyond the city-limits sign and moving west. He had nothing against the town or the blacksmith, but he had not risked this trip to spend ten years in a country town at thirty cents an hour. He intended to stir around, recapture the flavour of the time.

Besides, Heimenz had been too inquisitive. Lazarus had not minded the inspection of his hands or the suggestion that he might be fresh out of jail, and the disconnected wire was a standoff, but when Lazarus had parried a question about his accent with generalities the smith had tried to pin him down with just *where* in Indian Territory had he lived as a child and *when* did his folks come down from Canada.

A larger community meant fewer personal questions and more opportunities to lay hands on more than thirty cents an hour without quite stealing it.

He had been walking an hour when he came across a stranded automobilist, an old country doctor plagued with a flat tyre on a Maxwell. Lazarus dismounted a coal-oil sidelight and had the physician hold it while he patched the tube, replaced the tyre and pumped it up, then refused a tip.

Dr. Chaddock said, "Red, do you know how to drive these gas buggies?" Lazarus admitted that he did.

"Well, son, since you're headed west anyhow, what would you say to driving me to Lamar, then a shakedown on the couch in my waiting room, breakfast – and four bits to boot for your trouble?"

"I say Yes to all of it, Doctor – save that there's no need to waste cash on me. I'm not broke."

"Stuff and nonsense. Argue about it in the morning. I'm plumb tuckered out; this day started before daybreak. Used to be I'd wind the reins around the whip and nap until the mare got us home. But *these* things are stupid."

After a breakfast of fried eggs, fried ham, fried potatoes, pancakes with sorghum and country butter, watermelon preserves, strawberry preserves, cream that would barely pour, and endless coffee saucered and blowed – the doctor's housekeeper, his old-maid sister, had kept plying Lazarus, insisting that he wasn't eating enough to keep a bird alive – he set out again, a dollar richer, much cleaner, and looking less like a hayseed, for spit and Shinola and elbow grease had improved the appearance of his shoes, and Miss Nettie had insisted on giving him some old clothes – "Might as well be you, Roderick, as the Salvation Army. Here, take this tie, too; Doc doesn't wear it anymore. Look neat when you look for work, I always say – I do declare I won't hardly open the screen door to give a man a handout if he don't wear a necktie."

He accepted it all, aware that she was right, aware also that Dr. Chaddock would have spent a bad night trying to sleep in his automobile while his sister worried had not Lazarus come along – accounts balanced. Miss Nettie made a neat bundle of his own clothes; he thanked her and promised to send them a postcard from Kansas City – then he abandoned the bundle in the first bushes he came to, feeling mild regret as those clothes would wear indefinitely despite the worn look built into them. But they were slightly anachronistic in cut and he had never expected to wear them longer than he had to – and a man on the road could not afford to look like a bindle stiff, which Miss Nettie probably didn't know.

He found the railroad but avoided the depot. He posted himself at the north edge of town and waited. A passenger train and a freight headed south went by; then about ten o'clock a freight showed up headed north and still slowly gathering speed; Lazarus swung aboard. He made no effort not to be seen and let the brakeman shake him down for a dollar – a replica dollar; his authentic dollars were now under a bandage on the inside of his left thigh.

The brakeman warned him that there might be a railroad dick at the next stop – don't give him more than a dollar – and there were Pinkertons in the K.C. yards if he was going that far . . . so don't: those beauties would take his dollar and work him over anyhow. Lazarus thanked him and thought about asking what line this was – the Missouri Pacific? – but decided that it did not matter; it was headed north, and the brakeman's advice let him know that it was going far enough to suit him.

After a long hot day, half of it in a gondola, half in an empty boxcar that was small improvement, Lazarus dropped off as the train passed through Swope Park. He was such a weary, dirty mess that he almost regretted not having bought a ticket. But he put it out of his thoughts, knowing that arriving in a city with no money could wind up as "thirty dollars or thirty days" instead of the milder tariff of a small town. As it was, he had almost six dollars, most of it "real" money.

He noted with delight that Swope Park looked familiar, despite the centuries. He hurried on through and found the end of the Swope Park streetcar line. While he waited for the infrequent weekday service, he paid a jitney for a triple-dip ice-cream cone and ate it with relish, peace in his soul. Another five cents and a long trolley ride with one transfer took him into downtown Kansas City. Lazarus enjoyed every minute and wished it were longer. How peaceful and clean and tree-shaded the city was! How gently bucolic!

He recalled another time he had visited his old hometown – what century? – sometime early in the Diaspora, he thought – when a citizen venturing out into its filthy canyon streets wore a steel helmet simulating a wig, a bulletproof vest and codpiece, spectacles that were armour, gloves that covered brass knucks, and other concealed and illegal weapons – but rarely went out into the streets; it was more discreet to stick to transportation pods and go outdoors only in the guarded suburbs – especially after dark.

But here and now guns were legal – and no one wore them.

He got off the streetcar at McGee, found the Y.M.C.A. by asking a policeman. There, for half a dollar, he was given a key to a small cubicle, a towel, and a small bar of soap.

After wallowing in a shower, Lazarus returned to the lobby, having noted both Bell and Home telephones at the desk, with a notice "Local Calls 5 cents – pay the Desk Clerk." He asked to use the telephone books, found it in the Bell System book: "Chapman, Bowles, & Finnegan, attys at law" – R. A.

Long Building, yes, that made sense. He searched again, found "Chapman Arthur J. atty," with a Paseo address.

Wait till tomorrow? No harm in seeing if Justin had the correct answers. He slid a nickel to the desk clerk, asked for the Bell telephone.

"Number, please?"

"Central, please give me Atwater one-two-two-four."

"Hello? Is this the home of Mr. Arthur J. Chapman, the attorney?"

"This is he."

"Mr. Ira Howard told me to call you, Counsellor."

"Interesting. Who are you?"

" 'Life is short'."

" 'But the years are long'," the lawyer answered.

" 'Not "While the Evil Days come not".' "

"Very well. What can I do for you, sir? Trouble?"

"No, sir. Will you accept an envelope to be delivered to the secretary of the Foundation?"

"Yes. Can you bring it to my office?"

"Tomorrow morning, sir?"

"Say about nine thirty. I must be in court by ten."

"Thank you, sir; I'll be there. Good night."

"You are welcome. Good night to you, sir."

There was a writing desk in the lobby, with another notice to see the desk clerk, along with a homily: "*Have you Written to Your Mother This Week?*" Lazarus asked for a sheet of paper and an envelope, saying (truthfully) that he wanted to write home. The clerk gave them to him. "That's what we like to hear, Mr. Jenkins. Sure one sheet is enough?"

"If not, I'll ask for another. Thanks."

After breakfast (coffee and a doughnut, five cents) Lazarus located a stationery shop on Grand Avenue and invested fifteen cents in five envelopes that would nest in series, went back to the Y and prepared them, then delivered them by hand to Mr. Chapman – despite pursed-lip disapproval of Mr. Chapman's secretary.

The outer envelope read: Secretary of the Ira Howard Foundation.

The next one read: To the Secretary of the Howard Families' Association as of the year 2100 A.D.

The next one read: Please hold in the Families' Archives for One Thousand Years. Inert atmosphere recommended.

The fourth read: To be opened by the Chief Archivist in Office in Gregorian year 4291.

The fifth envelope read: Please deliver on request to Lazarus Long or to any member of his Tertius Colony family.

Inside this envelope was the envelope from the Y.M.C.A. enclosing the note Lazarus had written the night before; the envelope had on it all the names of his Boondock family, with Lapis Lazuli and Lorelei Lee heading the list:

"4 August 1916 Greg.

"Darlings,

"I goofed. I arrived two days ago – three years early! But I still want you to pick me up exactly ten T-years after you dropped me, at the impact crater, i.e. 2 August 1926 Gregorian.

"Please assure Dora that this is *not her fault*. It is either mine, or Andy's – or perhaps the instruments we had available then were not sufficiently accurate. If Dora wants to recalibrate (not necessary, as exactly ten T-years from drop remains the rendezvous), tell her to get eclipses of Sol by Luna for this ten years from Athene – I haven't had time to look them up as I have just reached Kansas City.

"Everything is *absolutely all right*. I am in good health, have enough money, and am perfectly safe. I'll write other and longer letters – better preserved, no time to have this one etched – using all the mail drops Justin suggested.

"Kiss everyone for me. Long letter follows.

"My undying love,

"Ol' Buddy Boy

"P.S. I hope it's a boy and a girl – wouldn't that be fun!"

DE CAPO

II

The End of an Era

25 September 1916 Greg.

Dear Laz-Lor,

This is the second of many letters I will attempt to send, using all the Delay Mail drops Justin suggested – three law firms, Chase National Bank, a time capsule to be forwarded with instructions to a Dr. Gordon Hardy via W. W. Smith via a safe-deposit box (unreliable coot, that Smith; he'll probably open it and thereby destroy it – although I don't recall it, either way), and all the other dodges I memorized. If I can get just *one* into the Archives just before the Diaspora it should be delivered when you ask for it, late in Greg. 4291 by the schedule we worked out.

With luck, you will receive dozens of letters all at the same time. Arranged by dates, they should constitute a record of the next ten years. There may be gaps in the account (letters that failed to get through) – if so, I'll fill those gaps (after you pick me up) by dictating to Athene, to keep my promise to Justin and to Galahad for a full report. Me, I'll be satisfied if just *one* gets through – and tell Athene to keep working on that notion of time-capsule-cum-Delay-Mail for still earlier centuries; there ought to be *some* way to make it foolproof.

I'll be using a wide variety of addressees – plus a wrinkle I thought up. I'm going to send a letter in the usual multiple covers to the Executive Computer, Secundus, Year 2000 Diaspora, to be opened by and read by the computer (untouched by human hands!) with a programme to hold the message and deliver it to the Colony Leader, Tertius, the day *after* we left.

I don't believe in paradoxes. Either Minerva got that message before you were born, and filed it in dead storage, and passed it on to Athene, and now (*your* now) Ira has it and has passed it to you two – or it failed to get through at all. No anomaly, no paradox – either total success or total failure. I got the idea from the fact that the executive computer opens and reads and acts on endless written messages without referring them to the Chairman Pro Tem or to any human unless necessary.

Basic Message: (This was in my first note and will be in every letter.) I made an error in calibration and arrived three years early. This is *not* Dora's fault, and be sure to tell her I said so *before* you tell her what happened. Reassure her. Despite her tomboy rowdiness, she is *very* vulnerable and must not be hurt. If I had given her sufficiently accurate figures, she would have hit any split second I asked for; of this I am certain.

Basic rendezvous time and place remains ten (10.00) T-years after you dropped me and at meteor-impact crater in Arizona, other rendezvous times & places figured from basic as before. My error changes the Gregorian date of rendezvous to 2 August 1926 – but still ten T-years after drop, as planned.

If Dora will worry less if she finds the error in the data I gave her, here are time marks she can rely on: Gregorian dates of total eclipses by Luna of Sol with respect to Terra between Gregorian 2 Aug 1916 and 2 Aug 1926.

1918 June 8	1923 September 10
1919 May 29	1925 January 24
1922 September 21	1926 January 14

If Dora wants to be still fussier, she can get any ancient Solar System date from Athene she wants; the Great Library at New Rome perpetuated endless stuff of that sort. But Dora has in her own gizzards everything she really needs.

Recapitulation:

1. Pick me up ten T-years after you dropped me.
2. I'm three years early – *my* error, *not* Dora's.
3. I'm fine, healthy, safe, holding, miss my darlings, and send love to all of you.

Now the hairy & scary adventures of a time-traveller – To begin with, they have been neither hairy nor scary. I've been careful to attract no attention, as retiring as a mouse at a cat show. Whenever the locals rub blue mud in their navels,

I rub blue mud in mine just as solemnly. I agree with the politics of anyone who speaks to me, attend the church he does – while sheepishly admitting that I've missed lately – I listen instead of talking (difficult as you may find that to believe), and I never talk back. If someone tries to rob me, I will not kill him or even break his arms; I'll shut up and let him have all he can find on me. My fixed purpose is to be on the lip of that crater in Arizona ten years from now; I shan't let anything jeopardize keeping our date. I am not here to reform this world; I am simply revisiting the scenes of my childhood.

It has been easier than I expected. Accent gave me some trouble at first. But I listened and now speak as harsh a Cornbelt accent as I did as a youngster. It is amazing how things have come back. I confirm from experience the theory that childhood memories are permanent, even though one may "forget" them until restimulated. I left this city when I was younger than you two are; I have been on more than two hundred planets since then, I have forgotten most of them.

But I find that I *know* this city.

Some changes . . . but changes in the other entropy direction; I am now seeing it as it was when I was four T-years old. I *am* four years old elsewhere in this city. I have avoided that neighbourhood and have not yet tried to see my first family – the idea makes me a bit uneasy. Oh, I shall, before I leave to travel around the country; I'm not afraid of being recognized by them. Impossible! I look like a young man and much – I think – as I looked when I was in fact a young man. But no one *here* has ever seen what that four-year-old will look like when he grows up. My only hazard would lie in trying to tell the truth. Not that I would be believed – no one here believes even in space travel, much less time travel – but because I would risk being locked up as "crazy" – a nonscientific term meaning that the person to whom one applies that label has a world picture differing from the accepted one.

Kansas City in 1916 – You put me down in a meadow; I climbed the fence and walked to the nearest town. No one noticed us – tell Dora that she did it slick as a pickpocket. The town was pleasant, the people friendly; I stayed a day to get reoriented, then moved on to a larger town, did the same there and got clothes to change me from a farm worker into someone who would not be conspicuous in a city. (You dears, who never wear clothes when you don't need them – except festive occasions – would have trouble believing how status here-&-now is shown by clothes. *Far* more so than in New Rome – here one can look at a person and tell age, sex, social status, economic status, probable occupation, approximate education, and many other things, just by clothing. These people even swim with clothes on – I am not farcing; ask Athene. My dears, they *sleep* in clothes.)

I took a railroad train to Kansas City. Ask Athene to display a picture of one from this era. This culture is proto-technical, just beginning to shift from human muscle power and animal power to generated power. Such as there is originates from burning natural fuels or from wind or waterfall. Some of this is converted into primitive electrical power, but this railroad train was propelled by burning coal to produce expanding steam.

Atomic power is not even a theory; it is a fancy of dreamers, taken less seriously than "Santa Claus." As for the method for moving the *Dora*, no one has the slightest notion that there is *any* way of grasping the fabric of space-time.

(I could be wrong. The many tales of UFO's and of strange visitors, throughout all ages, suggest that I am not the first time-tripper by thousands, or millions. But perhaps most of them are as reluctant to disturb the "native savages" as I am.)

On arrival in Kansas City I took lodging at a religious hilton. If you received my arrival note, it was on stationers bearing its emblem. (I hope that note is the last I will have to entrust to paper and ink – but it took time to arrange for photoreduction and etching. The technology and materials available here-&-now are very primitive, even when I have privacy to use other techniques.)

As a temporary base this religious hilton offers advantages. It is cheap, and I have not yet had time to acquire all the local money I will need. It is clean and safe compared with commercial hiltons costing the same. It is near the business district. It offers all that I now need and no more. And it is monastic.

"Monastic"? Don't look surprised, my loves. I expect to

remain celibate throughout these ten years, while dreaming happy fantasies of all my darlings, so many years & light-years away.

Why? The local mores – Here the coupling of male and female is *forbidden by law* unless specifically licensed by the state in a binding monogamy with endless legal, social, and economic consequences.

Such laws are made to be broken – and are. About three squares or a few hundred metres from this monastic hilton, the "Y.M.C.A.," starts the "red-light" district, an area devoted to illicit but tolerated female prostitution – and the fees are low. No, I am not too lazy to walk that far; I've talked to some of these women – they "walk a beat" offering their services to men on the street. But, my dears, these women are *not* recognized artists, proud of their great vocation. Oh, dear, no! They are pathetic drabs, furtive and ashamed. They are at the bottom of the social pyramid, and many (most?) are in thrall to males who take their meagre earnings.

I do not think there is a Tamara, or even a pseudo-Tamara, in all of Kansas City. Outside the "red-light" district there are younger and prettier women available for higher fees and by more complex arrangements – but their status is still zero. No proud and happy artists. So they are no temptation; I would not be able to put out of my mind the gruesome fashion in which they are mistreated under local laws and customs.

(I tipped those I talked to; time is money to them.)

Then there are women who are *not* of the profession.

From my earlier life here I know that a high percentage of both "single" women and "married" women (a sharp dichotomy, much sharper than on Tertius or even Secundus) – many of these will chance unlicensed coupling for fun, adventure, love, or other reasons. Most women here are thus available sometimes and with some men – although not with all men nor all the time; here-&-now the sport is necessarily clandestine.

Nor do I lack confidence, nor have I contracted the local "moral" attitude.

But the answer is again No. Why?

First reason: It is all too likely to get one's arse shot off!

No joke, dears. Here-&-now almost every female is quasi-property of some male. Husband, father, sweetheart, betrothed – someone. If he catches you, he may kill you – and public opinion is such that he is unlikely to be punished. But if *you* kill *him* . . . you hang by the neck until dead, dead, dead!

It seems an excessive price. I don't plan to risk it.

There are a small but appreciable number of females who are not "property" of some male – so what's holding you back, Lazarus?

The overhead, for one thing. (Better not tell Galahad this; it would break his heart.) Negotiations are usually long, complex, and very expensive – and she is likely to regard "success" as equivalent to a proposal of lifetime contract.

On top of that she is quite likely to become pregnant. I should have asked Ishtar to offset my fertility for this trip. (I am terribly glad I did not.) (And I am honing for you darlings, my other selves – and thank you endlessly for kicking my feet out from under me. I couldn't initiate it, dearly as I wanted to!)

Laz and Lor, believe this: Mature females here *do not know* when they are fertile. They rely either on luck or on contraceptive methods that range from chancy to worthless. Furthermore, they can't find out even from their therapists – who don't know much about it themselves. (There are no geneticists.) Therapy is very primitive in 1916. Most physicians are trying hard, I think, but the art is barely out of the witch-doctor stage. Just rough surgery and a few drugs – most of which I know to be useless or harmful. As for contraception – hold on tight! – it is forbidden *by law*.

Another law made to be broken – and is. But law and customs retard progress in such matters. At present (1916) the commonest method involves an elastomer sheath worn by the male – in other words they "couple" without touching. Stop screaming; you'll never have to put up with it. But it is as bad as it sounds.

I've saved my strongest reason for the last. Dears, I've been spoiled. In 1916 a bath once a week is considered enough by most people, too much by some. Other habits match. Such things when unavoidable can be ignored. I'm well aware that I whiff like an old billy goat in very short order myself. Nevertheless, when I have enjoyed the company of six of the daintiest darlings in the Galaxy – well, I'd rather wait. Shucks, ten years isn't long.

If you have received any of the letters I will send over the next ten years, then you may have rushed to check up on Gregorian 1916–1919. I selected 1919–1929 both to savour it – a vintage decade, the very last *happy* period in old Earth's history – but also to avoid the first of the Terran Planetary Wars, the one known now (it has already started) as "The European War," then will be called "The World War," then still later "The First World War," and designated in most ancient histories as "Phase One of the First Terran Planetary War."

Don't fret; I'm going to give it a wide berth. This involves changes in my travel plans but none in the 1926 pickup. I have little memory of this war; I was too young. But I recall (probably from school lessons rather than from direct memory) that this country got into it in 1917, and that the war ended the following year – and that date I remember exactly, as it was my sixth birthday and I thought the noise and celebration was for *me*.

What I can't remember is the exact date this country entered the war. I may not have looked it up in planning this junket; my purpose was to arrive *after* 11 November 1918, the day the war ended, and I allowed what I thought was a comfortable margin. I was fitting in those ten years most carefully, as the following ten years, 1929–1939, are decidedly *not* a vintage decade – and they end with the start of Phase Two of the First Terran Planetary War.

There is no possible way for me to look up that date – but I find one bright clue in my memory: a phrase "The Guns of August." That phrase has a sharp association in my memory with this war – and it fits, for I remember that it was warm, summery weather (August is summer here) when Gramp (your maternal grandfather, dears) took me out into the backyard and explained to me what "war" is and why we must win.

I don't think he made me understand it – but I remember the occasion, I remember his serious manner, I remember the weather (warm), and the time of day (just before supper).

Very well, I'll expect this country to declare war next August; I'll duck for cover in July – for I have no interest in this war. I know which side won (the side this country will be on) but I know also that "The War to End All Wars" (it was called that!) was a disastrous defeat both for "victors" and "vanquished" – it led inevitably to the Great Collapse and caused me to get off this planet. Nothing I can do will change any of that; there are no paradoxes.

So I will hole up till it's over. Almost every nation on Terra eventually picked sides – but many did no fighting, and the war did not get close to them, especially nations south of here, Central and South America, so that is probably where I will go.

But I have almost a year to plan it. It is easy here to be anything you claim to be – no identification cards, no computer codes, no thumbprints, no tax numbers. Mind you, this planet now has as many people as Secundus has (will have – your "now") – yet births are not even registered in much of this country (mine was not, other than with the Families), and a man is whoever he says he is! There are no formalities about leaving this country. It is slightly more difficult to get back in, but I have endless time to cope with that.

But I should, through ordinary prudence, go away for the duration of this war. Why? Conscription. I'm durned if I'll try to explain that term to girls who just barely know what a war is, but it means "slave armies" – and it means to *me* that I should have asked Ishtar to make me look at least twice the apparent age I look now. If I hang around here too long, I risk becoming an involuntary "hero" in a war that was over before I was old enough to go to school.

This strikes me as ridiculous.

So I'll concentrate on accumulating money to carry me a couple of years – convert that into gold (about eight kilos, not too heavy) – then the first of next July, move south. A mild problem then, as this country is conducting a small-scale border war with the one just south of it. (Going north is out of the question; that country is already in the big war.) The ocean to the east has underwater warships in it; these tend to shoot at anything that floats. But the ocean on the other side is free of such vermin. If I take a ship going south from a seaport on the west side of this country, I'll wind up outside the fighting zones. In the meantime I must improve my Spanish – much like Galacta but prettier. I'll find a tutor

– no, Laz, *not* a horizontal one. Don't you *ever* think about anything else?

(Come to think of it, dear, what else is worth thinking about? Money?)

Yes, money, at the moment, and I have plans for that. The country is about to elect a chief of government – and I am the *only* man on Terra who *knows* who will be elected. Why did it stick in my memory? Take a look at my registered Families' name.

So my pressing problem is to lay hands on money to bet on that election. What I win I'll use to gamble in the bourse – except that it won't be gambling, as this country is already in a war economy and *I* know it will continue.

I wish I could accept bets on the election instead of placing them – but that is too risky to my skin; I don't have the right political connections.

You see – No, I had better explain how this city is organized.

Kansas City is a pleasant place. It has tree-shaded streets, lovely residential neighbourhoods, a boulevard and park system known throughout the planet. Its excellent paving encourages the automobile carriages that are beginning to be popular. Most of this country is still deep in mud; Kansas City's well-paved streets have more of these autopropelled vehicles than horse-drawn ones.

The city is prosperous, being the second largest market and transportation centre of the most productive agricultural area on Terra – grain, beef, pork. The unsightly aspects of this trade are down in river bottoms while the citizens live in beautiful wooded hills. On a damp morning when the wind sets from that quarter one sometimes catches a whiff of stockyards; otherwise the air is clear and clean and beautiful.

It is a quiet city. Traffic is never dense, and the clop-clop of horses' hooves or the warning gong of an electrically propelled street-railroad car is just enough to accent the silence – the sounds of children at play are louder.

Galahad is more interested in how a culture uses its leisure than in its economics – and so am I, as scratching a living is controlled by circumstances. But not play. By play I do not mean sex. Sex can't take up too much time of humans matured beyond adolescence (except a few oddies like the fabled

Casanova – and Galahad of course – 'Me 'at's off to the Dyuke!').

In 1916 (nothing I say necessarily applies ten years later and certainly not one hundred years later; this is the very end of an era) – at this time the typical Kansas Citizan makes his own play; his social events are associated with churches, or with relatives by blood and marriage, or both – dining, picnicking, playing games (not gambling), or simply visiting and talking. Most of this costs little or nothing except the expense of supporting their churches – which are social clubs as much as much as they are temples of religious faith.

The major commercial entertainment is called "moving pictures" – dramatic shows presented as silent black-and-white shadow pictures flickering against a blank wall. These are quite new, very popular, and very cheap – they are called "nickel shows" after the minor coin charged as a fee. Each neighbourhood (defined as walking distance) has at least one such theatre. This form of entertainment, and its technological derivatives, eventually had (will have) as much to do with the destruction of this social pattern as the automobile carriages (get Galahad's opinions on this), but – in 1916 – neither has as yet disturbed what appears to be a stable and rather Utopian pattern.

Anomie has not yet set in, the norms are strong, customs are binding, and no one here-&-now would believe that the occasional rumble is Cheyne-Stokes breathing of a culture about to die. Literacy is at the highest level this culture will ever attain – my dears, the people of 1916 simply would not *believe* 2016. They won't even believe that they are about to be enmeshed in the first of the Final Wars; that is why the man for whom I am named is about to be reelected. "We Are Neutral." "Too Proud to Fight." "He Kept Us Out of War." Under these slogans they are marching over the precipice, not knowing it is there.

(I'm depressing myself – hindsight is a vice . . . especially when it is foresight.)

Now let's look at the underside of this lovely city:

The city is a nominal democracy. In fact it is nothing of the sort. It is governed by one politician who holds no office. Elections are solemn rituals – and the outcomes are what he ordains. The streets are beautifully paved because his companies pave them – to his profit. The schools are excellent, and they actually *teach* – because this monarch wants it that way. He is pragmatically benign and does not overreach. "Crime" (which means anything illegal and includes both prostitution and gambling) is franchised through his lieutenants; he never touches it himself.

Much of this crime-by-definition is handled by an organization sometimes called "The Black Hand" – but in 1916 it usually has no name and is never seen. But it is why I don't dare accept election bets; I would be encroaching on a monopoly of one of this politician's lieutenants – which would be *very* dangerous to my health.

Instead, I'll bet by the local rules and keep my mouth shut.

The "respectable" citizen, with his pleasant home and garden and church and happy children, sees none of this and (I think) suspects little of it and thinks about it less. The city is divided into zones with firm though unmarked bounds. The descendants of former slaves live in a zone that forms a buffer between the "nice" part of town and the area dominated by and lived in by the franchised monopolists of such things as gambling and prostitution. At night the zones mix only under unspoken conventions. In the daytime there is nothing to notice. The boss maintains tight discipline but keeps it simple. I've heard that he has only three unbreakable rules: Keep the streets well paved. Don't touch the schools. Don't kill anyone south of a certain street.

In 1916 it works just fine – but not much longer.

I must stop; I have an appointment at K.C. Photo Supply Company to use a lab – in private. Then I must get back to the grift: separating people from dollars painlessly and fairly legally.

Love forever and all the way back,

L.

P.S. You should see me in a derby hat!

DA CAPO

III

Maureen

Mr. Theodore Bronson né Woodrow Wilson Smith aka Lazarus Long left his apartment on Armour Boulevard and drove his car, a Ford landaulet, to a corner on Thirty-first Street, where he parked it in a shed behind a pawnshop – as he took a dim view of leaving an automobile on the street at night. Not that the car had cost Lazarus much; he had acquired it as a result of the belief of an optimist from Denver that aces back to back plus a pair showing could certainly beat a pair of jacks – Mr. "Jenkins" must be bluffing. But Mr. "Jenkins" had a jack in the hole.

It had been a profitable winter, and Lazarus expected a still more prosperous spring. His guess about a war market on certain stocks and commodities had usually been correct, and his spread of investments was wide enough that a wrong guess did not hurt him much as most of his guesses were right – they could hardly be wrong since he had anticipated stepped-up submarine warfare, knowing what would eventually bring this country into the war in Europe.

Watching the market left him time for other "investments" in other people's optimism, sometimes at pool, sometimes at cards. He enjoyed pool more, found cards more rewarding. All winter he had played both, and his plain and rather friendly face, when decorated with his best stupid look, marked him as a natural sucker – a look he enhanced by dressing as a hayseed come to town.

Lazarus did not mind other pool-hall hustlers, or "mechanics" in card games, or "reader" cards; he simply kept quiet and accepted any buildup winnings offered him, then "lost his nerve" and dropped out before the kill. He enjoyed these crooked games; it was easier – and pleasanter – to take money from a thief than it was to play an honest game to win, and it did not cost as much sleep; he always dropped out of a crooked game early, even when he was behind. But his timing was rarely that bad.

Winnings he reinvested in the market.

All winter he had stayed "'Red' Jenkins," living at the Y.M.C.A. and spending almost nothing. When the weather was very bad, he stayed in and read, avoiding the steep and icy streets. He had forgotten how harsh a Kansas City winter could be. Once he saw a team of big horses trying gallantly to haul a heavy truck up the steep pitch of Tenth Street above Grand Avenue. The off horse slipped on the ice and broke a leg – Lazarus heard the cannon bone pop. It made him feel sick, and he wanted to horsewhip the teamster – why hadn't the fool taken the long way around?

Such days were best spent in his room or in the Main Public Library near the Y.M.C.A. – hundreds of thousands of *real* books, *bound* books he could hold in his hands. They tempted him almost into neglecting his pursuit of money. During that cruel winter he spent every spare hour there, getting reacquainted with his oldest friends – Mark Twain with Dan Beard's illustrations, Dr. Conan Doyle, the Marvellous Land of Oz as described by the Royal Historian and portrayed in colour by John R. Neil, Rudyard Kipling, Herbert George Wells, Jules Verne –

Lazarus felt that he could easily spend all the coming ten years in that wonderful building.

But when false spring arrived, he started thinking about moving out of the business district and again changing his *persona*. It was becoming difficult to get picked as a sucker either at pool or at poker; his investment programme was complete; he had enough cash in Fidelity Savings & Trust Bank to allow him to give up the austerity of the Y.M.C.A., find a better address, and show a more prosperous face to the world – essential to his final purpose in this city; remeeting his first family – and not much time left before his July deadline.

Acquiring a presentable motorcar crystallized his plans. He spent the next day becoming "Theodore Bronson": moved his bank account one street over to the Missouri Savings Bank, and held out ample cash; visited a barber and had his hair and moustache restyled; went to Browning, King & Co., and bought clothing suitable to a conservative young businessman. Then he drove south and cruised Linwood Boulevard, watching for "Vacancy" signs. His requirements were simple: a furnished apartment with a respectable address and facade, its own kitchen and bathroom – and in walking distance of a pool hall on thirty-first street.

He did not plan to hustle in that pool hall; it was one of two places where he hoped to meet a member of his family.

Lazarus found what he needed, but on Armour Boulevard rather than Linwood and rather far from that pool hall. This caused him to rent two garaging spaces – difficult as Kansas City was not yet accustomed to supplying housing to automobiles. But two dollars a month got him space in a barn close to his apartment; three dollars a month got him a shed behind the pawnshop next to the Idle Hour Billiard Parlour.

He started a routine: Spend each evening from eight to ten at the pool hall, attend the church on Linwood Boulevard that his family had attended (did attend), go downtown mornings when business required – by streetcar; Lazarus considered an automobile a nuisance in downtown Kansas City, and he enjoyed riding streetcars. He began profit-taking on his investments, coverting the proceeds into gold double eagles and saving them in a lockbox in a third bank, the Commonwealth. He expected to complete liquidation, with enough gold to carry him through November 11, 1918, well before his July departure date.

In his spare time he kept the landaulet shining, took care of its upkeep himself, and drove it for pleasure. He also worked slowly, carefully, and very privately on a tailoring job: making a chamois-skin vest that was nothing but pockets, each to hold one $20 gold piece. When completed and filled and pockets sewed shut, he planned to cover it, inside and out, with a suit vest he had used as a pattern. It would be much too warm, but a money belt was not enough for that much gold – and money that clinked instead of rustling was the only sort he was certain he could use outside the country in wartime. Besides, when filled it would be almost a bulletproof vest – one never knew what lay around the next corner, and those Latin-American countries were volatile.

Each Saturday afternoon he took conversational Spanish from a Westport High School teacher who lived nearby. All in all he kept pleasantly busy and on schedule.

That evening after locking his Ford landaulet into the shed back of the pawnshop, Lazarus glanced into a bierstube adjoining it, thinking that his grandfather might have a stein of Muehlebach there before going home. The problem of how to meet his first family easily and naturally had occupied his mind from time to time all winter. He wanted to be accepted as a friend in their (his!) home, but he could not walk up the front steps, twist the doorbell, and announce himself as a long-lost cousin – nor even as a friend of a friend from Paducah. He had *no* connections with which to swing it, and if he tried a complex lie, he was certain his grandfather would spot it.

Thus he had decided on a pianissimo double approach: the church attended by his family (except his grandfather) and the hangout his grandfather used when he wanted to get away from his daughter's family.

Lazarus was sure of the church – and his memory was confirmed the first Sunday he had gone there, with a shock that had upset him even more than the shock of learning that he was three years early.

He saw his mother and had momentarily mistaken her for one of his twin sisters.

But almost instantly he realized why: Maureen Johnson Smith was the genetic mother of his identicals as certainly as she was his own mother. Nevertheless, it had shaken him, and he was glad to have several hymns and a long sermon in which to calm down. He avoided looking at her and spent the time trying to sort out his brothers and sisters.

Twice since then he had seen his mother at church and now could look at her without flinching and could even see that this pretty young matron was compatible with his faded image of what his mother ought to look like. But he still felt that he would never have recognized her had it not been for his sharp recollection of Lapis Lazuli and Lorelei Lee. He had illogically expected a much older woman, more as she had been when he left home.

Attending church had not resulted in his meeting her, or his siblings, although the pastor had introduced him to other parishioners. But he continued to drive his automobile to church against the day when it might be polite to offer her and his siblings a ride home – six blocks over on Benton Boulevard; the spring weather would not always be dry.

He had not been as certain of his grandfather's hangout. He was sure that this was where "Gramp" used to go ten or twelve years later – but did he go here when Woodie Smith was (is) not yet five?

Having checked the German beer parlour – and noted that it had suddenly changed its name to "The Swiss Garden" – he went into the pool hall. Pool tables were all in use; he went back to the rear, where there was one billiard table, a card table, and one for chess or checkers; no pool game being available, it seemed a good time to practice some "mistakes" at three-cushion.

Gramp! His grandfather was alone at the chess table; Lazarus recognized him at once.

Lazarus did not break stride. He went on toward the cue rack, hesitated as he was about to pass the chess table, looked down at the array. Ira Johnson looked up – seemed to recognize Lazarus, seemed about to speak and then to think better of it.

"Excuse me," said Lazarus. "I didn't mean to interrupt."

"No harm," said the old man. (How old? To Lazarus he seemed both older and younger than he ought to be. And smaller. When was he born? Almost ten years before the Civil War.) "Just fiddling with a chess problem."

"How many moves to mate?"

"You play?"

"Some." Lazarus added, "My grandfather taught me. But I haven't played lately."

"Care for a game?"

"If you want to put up with a rusty player."

Ira Johnson picked up a white pawn and a black, put them behind his back, brought them out in his fists. Lazarus pointed, found that he had chosen the black.

Gramp started setting up pieces. "My name is Johnson," he offered.

"I'm Ted Bronson, sir."

They shook hands; Ira Johnson advanced his king's pawn to four; Lazarus answered in kind.

They played silently. By the sixth move Lazarus suspected that his grandfather was re-creating one of Steinitz's master games; by the ninth he was sure of it. Should he use the escape Dora had discovered? No, that would feel like cheating – of course a computer could play better chess than a man. He concentrated on playing as well as possible without attempting Dora's subtle variation.

Lazarus was checkmated on white's twenty-ninth move, and it seemed to him that the master game had been perfectly reproduced – Wilhelm Steinitz against some Russian, what was his name? Must ask Dora. He waved to a marker, started to pay for the game; his grandfather pushed his coin aside, insisted on paying for the use of the table, and added to the marker, "Son, fetch us two sarsaparillas. That suit you, Mr. Bronson? Or the boy can fetch you a beer from those Huns next door."

"Sarsaparilla is fine, thank you."

"Ready for revenge?"

"After I catch my breath. You play a tough game, Mr. Johnson."

"Mrrrmph! *You* said you were rusty."

"I am. But my grandfather taught me when I was very young, then played me every day for years."

"Do tell. I've a grandson I play. Tyke isn't in school yet, but I spot him only a horse."

"Maybe he would play me. Even."

"Mrrmph. You'll allow him a knight, same as I do," Mr. Johnson paid for the drinks, tipped the boy a nickel. "What business are you in, Mr. Bronson? – if you don't mind my asking."

"Not at all. In business for myself. Buy things, sell things. Make a little, lose a little."

"So? When are you going to sell me the Brooklyn Bridge?"

"Sorry, sir, I unloaded that last week. But I can offer you a bargain in Spanish Prisoners."

Mr. Johnson smiled sourly. "Guess that'll teach me."

"But, Mr. Johnson, if I told you I was a pool-hall hustler, you wouldn't let me play chess with your grandson."

"Might, might not. Shall we get set up? Your turn for white."

With the first move allowing him to control the pace, Lazarus made a slow, careful buildup of his attack. His grandfather was equally careful, left no openings in his defence. They were so evenly matched that it took Lazarus forty-one moves and much skull sweat to turn his first move advantage into a mate.

"Play off the tie?"

Ira Johnson shook his head. "Two games a night is my limit. Two like that is over my limit. Thank you, sir; you play a fine game. For a man who is 'rusty.' " He pushed back his chair. "Time for me to head for the stable."

"It's raining."

"So I noticed. I'll stand in the doorway and watch for the Thirty-first Street trolley."

"I have my automobile here. I'd be honoured to run you home."

"Eh? No need to. Only a block from the car line at the other end, and if I get a little damp, I'll be home and can get dry."

(More like four blocks and you'll be soaked, Gramp.) "Mr.

Johnson, I'm going to crank up that flivver anyhow, to go home myself. It's no trouble to drop you anywhere; I like to drive. In about three minutes I'll pull up in front and honk. If you're there, fine. If you aren't, I'll assume that you prefer not to accept rides from strangers and will take no offence."

"Don't be touchy. Where's your automobile? I'll come with you."

"No, please. No need for us both to go out in the rain for a one-man job. I'll slide out the back through the alley, then I'll be at the curb almost before you reach the front door." (Lazarus decided to be stubborn; Gramp could smell a mouse farther than a cat could – and would wonder why "Ted Bronson" kept a garage at hand when he claimed to live a driving distance away. Bad. How are you going to handle this, Bub? You've *got* to tell Gramp a passel of lies or you'll never get inside that house – your own home! – to meet the rest of your family. But complexity is contrary to the basic principle of successful lying, and Gramp is the very man who taught you that. Yet the truth could not serve and keeping silent was just as useless. How are you going to solve this? When Gramp is as suspicious as you are and twice as shrewd.)

Ira Johnson stood up. "Thank you, Mr. Bronson; I'll be at the front door."

By the time Lazarus had his landaulet cranked, he had settled on tactics and outlined a long-range policy: (a) Drive around the block; this wagon should be wet; (b) don't use this shed again; better to have this puddle jumper stolen than to leave a hole in your cover story; (c) when you surrender the shed, see if "Uncle" Dattelbaum has an old set of chessmen; (d) make your lies fit what you've said, including that too hasty truth about who taught you to play chess; (e) tell as much truth as possible even if it doesn't sound good – but, damn it, you should be a foundling . . . and that doesn't fit having a grandfather, unless you invent complexities, any one of which might snap back and catch you out.

When Lazarus sounded the klaxon, Ira Johnson darted out and scrambled in. "Where now?" asked Lazarus.

His grandfather explained how to reach his daughter's home and added, "Pretty ritzy rig to call a 'flivver.' "

"I got a good price for the Brooklyn Bridge. Should I swing up to Linwood or follow the car tracks?"

"Suit yourself. Since you've unloaded the bridge, you might tell me about these 'Spanish Prisoners.' Good investment?"

Lazarus concentrated a while on getting his vehicle headed down the tracks while avoiding the tracks themselves. "Mr. Johnson, I evaded your question about what I do for a living."

"Your business."

"I really have hustled pool."

"Again, your business."

"And I ran out and let you pay the table fee a second time, as well as letting you pay for the pop. I did not intend to."

"So? Thirty cents, plus a nickel tip. Knock off five cents the streetcar would have cost me. That makes your half fifteen cents. If it worries you, drop it in his cup the next time you pass a blind man. I'm getting a chauffered ride on a wet night. Cheap. This is hardly a jitney bus."

"Very well, sir. I wanted to get straight with you . . . because I enjoyed the games and hope to play you again."

"The pleasure was mutual. I enjoy a game where a man makes me work."

"Thank you. Now to answer your question properly: Yes, I've hustled pool – in the past. It's not what I do now. I'm in business for myself. Buying things, selling things – but not the Brooklyn Bridge. As for the 'Spanish Prisoner' con, I've had it tried on me. I deal in the commodities market, grain futures and such. I do the same with stock margins. But I won't try to sell you anything. I'm neither a broker nor a bucket-shop operator; instead I deal through established brokers. Oh, yes, one more thing – I don't peddle tips. Give a man what seems to me a good tip – and he loses his shirt and blames me. So I don't."

"Mr. Bronson, I had no call to ask about your business. That was nosy of me. But it was meant to be a friendly inquiry."

"I took it as friendly, so I wanted to give it a proper answer."

"Nosy, just the same. I don't need to know your background."

"That's just it, Mr. Johnson, I don't *have* a background. Pool hustler."

"Not much wrong with that. Pool is an open game, like chess. Difficult to cheat."

"Well . . . I do something that you might regard as cheating."

"Look, son – if you need a father confessor, I can tell you where to find one. I am not one."

"Sorry."

"Didn't mean to be blunt. But you do have something on your mind."

"Uh, nothing much perhaps. It has to do with having no background. None. So I go to church – to meet people. To meet nice people. Respectable people. People a man with no background otherwise could never meet."

"Mr. Bronson, everybody has *some* background."

Lazarus turned down Benton Boulevard before answering. "Not me, sir. Oh, I was born – somewhere. Thanks to the man who let me call him 'Grandfather' – and his wife – I had a pretty good childhood. But they're long gone and – shucks, I don't even know that my name is 'Ted Bronson.' "

"Happens. You're an orphan?"

"I suppose so. And a bastard, probably. Is this the house?" Lazarus stopped one house short of his-their home.

"Next one, with the porch light on."

Lazarus eased the car forward, stopped again. "Been nice meeting you, Mr. Johnson."

"Don't be in a hurry. These people – Bronson? – who took care of you. Where was this?"

" 'Bronson' is a name I picked off a calendar. I thought it sounded better than 'Ted Jones' or 'Ted Smith.' I was probably born in the southern part of the state. But I can't prove even that."

"So? I practised medicine down that way at one time. What county?"

(I know you did, Gramp – so let's be careful with this one.) "Greene County. I don't mean I was born there; I just mean I was told that I came from an orphanage in Springfield."

"Then I probably didn't deliver you; my practice was farther north. Mrrph. But we might be kinfolk."

"Huh? I mean 'Excuse me, Dr. Johnson?' "

"Don't call me 'Doctor,' Ted; I dropped that title when I quit delivering babies. What I mean is this: When I first saw you, you startled me. Because you are the spit 'n'image of my older brother, Edward . . . who was an engineer on the St. Looie and San Francisco . . . till he lost his air brakes and that ended his triflin' ways. He had sweethearts in Fort Scott, St. Looie, Wichita, and Memphis; I've no reason to think he neglected Springfield. Could be."

Lazarus grinned. "Should I call you 'Uncle'?"

"Suit yourself."

"Oh, I shan't. Whatever happened, there's no way to prove it. But it would be nice to have a family."

"Son, quit being self-conscious about it. A country doctor learns that such mishaps are far more common than most people dream. Alexander Hamilton and Leonardo da Vinci are in the same boat with you, to name just two of the many great men entitled to wear the bend sinister. So stand tall and proud and spit in their eyes. I see the parlour light is still burning; what would you say to a cup of coffee?"

"Oh, I wouldn't want to inconvenience you – or disturb your family."

"It'll do neither. My daughter always leaves the pot on the back of the range for me. If she happens to be downstairs in a wrapper – unlikely – she'll go flying up the back stairs, then reappear instantly down the front stairs, dressed fit to kill. Like a fire horse when the bell rings; I don't know how she does it. Come on in."

Ira Johnson unlocked the front door, then called out as he opened it: "Maureen! I have company with me."

"Coming, Father." Mrs. Smith met them in the hall, moving with serene dignity and dressed as if she expected callers. She smiled, and Lazarus suppressed his excitement.

"Maureen, I want to present Mr. Theodore Bronson. My daughter, Ted – Mrs. Brian Smith."

She offered her hand. "You are most welcome, Mr. Bronson," Mrs. Smith said in warm, rich tones that made Lazarus think of Tamara.

Lazarus took her hand gently, felt his fingers tingle, had to restrain himself from making a deep bow and kissing it. He forced himself to give only a hint of a bow, then let go at once. "I am honoured, Mrs. Smith."

"Do come in and sit down."

"Thank you, but it's late, and I was merely dropping your father off on my way home."

"Must you leave so quickly? I was simply darning stockings and reading the 'Ladies' Home Journal' – nothing important."

"Maureen, I promised Mr. Bronson a cup of coffee. He fetched me home from the chess club and saved me a soaking."

"Yes, Father, right away. Take his hat and make him sit down." She smiled and left.

Lazarus let his grandfather seat him in the parlour, then took advantage of the moments his mother was out of sight to quiet down and to glance around. Aside from the fact that the room had shrunk, it looked much as he remembered it; an upright piano *she* had taught him to play; fireplace with gas logs, mantel shelf with bevelled mirror above; a glass-fronted sectional book-case; heavy drapes and lace curtains; his parent's wedding picture framed with their hearts & flowers marriage licence, and balancing this a reproduction of Millet's "Gleaners," and other pictures large and small; a rocking chair, a platform rocker with a footstool, straight chairs, arm chairs, tables, lamps, all crowded and in an easygoing mixture of mission oak and bird's eye maple. Lazarus felt at home; even the wallpaper seemed familiar – save that he realized uneasily that he had been given his father's chair.

An archway, filled by a beaded portiere, led into the living room, now dark. Lazarus tried to recall what should be in there and wondered if it would look just as familiar. The parlour was immaculately neat and clean, and kept that way, he knew, despite a large family, by the living room being used mainly by children while this room was reserved for their elders and for guests. How many kids now? Nancy, then Carol, and Brian Junior, and George, and Marie – and himself – and since this was early 1917 Dickie had to be about three, and Ethel would be in diapers.

What was that behind his mother's chair? Could it be? – *Yes*, it's my *elephant!* Woodie you little devil, you *know* you aren't supposed to play in here, and everything must go back into your toy box before you go up to bed; that's a flat rule. The toy animal was small (about six inches high), made of stuffed cloth, and grey with much handling; Lazarus felt resentment that such a treasure – *his!* – was entrusted to a young child... then managed to laugh at himself even though the emotion persisted. He felt tempted to steal the toy. "Excuse me. You were saying, Mr. Johnson?"

"I said I was temporarily delegated in loco parentis; my son-in-law has gone to Plattsburg and – " Lazarus lost the rest of the remark; Mrs. Smith returned in a soft rustle of satin petticoats, carrying a loaded tray. Lazarus jumped to relieve her of it; she smiled and let him.

By golly, that was the Haviland china he had not been allowed to touch until after he got his first long pants! And the "company" coffee service – solid silver serving pot, cream pitcher, sugar bowl and tongs, the Columbian Exposition souvenir spoons. Linen doilies, matching tea napkins, thin slices of pound cake, a silver dish of mints – how did you *do* this in three minutes or less? You're certainly doing the prodigal proud! No, don't be a fool, Lazarus; she's doing her *father* proud, entertaining his guest – *you* are a faceless stranger.

"Children all in bed?" inquired Mr. Johnson.

"All but Nancy," Mrs. Smith answered, serving them. "She and her young man went to the Isis and should be home soon."

"Show was over half an hour ago."

"Is there any harm in their stopping for a sundae? The ice-cream parlour is on a brightly lighted corner right where they catch their street-car."

"A young girl shouldn't be out after dark without a chaperon."

"Father, this is 1917, not 1890. He's a fine boy . . . and I can't expect them to miss an episode of their serial – Pearl White and very exciting; Nancy tells me all about it. With a William S. Hart feature tonight, I understand; I would have enjoyed seeing that myself."

"Well, I've still got my shotgun."

"Father."

Lazarus concentrated on remembering to eat cake with a fork.

"She's trying to bring me up," Gramp said grumpily. "Won't work."

"I'm sure Mr. Bronson is not interested in our family problems," Mrs. Smith said quietly. "If they were problems. Which they are not. May I warm your coffee, Mr. Bronson?"

"Thank you, ma'am."

"That's right, he isn't. But Nancy should be told soon. Maureen, take a close look at Ted. Ever seen him before?"

His mother looked over her cup at Lazarus, put it down and said, "Mr. Bronson, when you came in, I had the oddest feeling. At church, was it not?"

Lazarus admitted that such could have been the case. Gramp's brows shot up. "So? I must warn the parson. But even if you did meet there – "

"We did not meet at church, Father. What with herding my zoo I barely have time to speak to Reverend and Mrs. Draper. But now that I think about it, I'm sure I saw Mr. Bronson there last Sunday. One does notice a new face among old familiar ones."

"Daughter, as may be, that wasn't what I meant. Whom does

Ted look like? No, never mind – doesn't he look like your Uncle Ned?"

His mother again looked at Lazarus. "Yes, I see a resemblance. But he looks even more like you, Father."

"No, Ted's from Springfield. All my sins were farther north."

"Father."

"Daughter, quit worrying about me rattling the family skeleton. It's possible that – Ted, may I tell it?"

"Certainly, Mr. Johnson. As you said, it's nothing to be ashamed of – and I'm not."

"Ted is an orphan, Maureen, a foundling. If Ned weren't warming his toes in hell, I'd ask him some searching questions. The time and place is right, and Ted certainly looks like our kin."

"Father, I think you are embarrassing our guest."

"I don't. And don't you be so hoity-toity, young lady. You're a grown woman, with children; you can stand plain talk."

"Mrs. Smith, I am not embarrassed. Whoever my parents were, I am proud of them. They gave me a strong, healthy body and a brain that serves my needs – "

"Well spoken, young man!"

" – and while I would be proud to claim your father as my uncle – and you as my cousin – if it were so – it seems more likely that my parents were taken by a typhoid epidemic down that way; the dates match well enough."

Mr. Johnson frowned. "How old are you, Ted?"

Lazarus thought fast and decided to be his mother's age. "I'm thirty-five."

"Why, that's just *my* age!"

"Really, Mrs. Smith? If you hadn't made clear that you have a daughter old enough to go to the picture show with a young man, *I* would have thought you were about eighteen."

"Oh, go along with you! I have eight children."

"Impossible!"

"Maureen doesn't look her age," agreed her father. "Hasn't changed since she was a bride. Runs in the family; her mother doesn't have a grey hair today." (Where is Grandma? – oh, yes, so don't ask.) "But, Ted, you don't look thirty-five either. I would have guessed middle twenties."

"Well, I don't know exactly how old I am. But I *can't* be younger than that. I might be a bit older." (Quite a bit, Gramp!) "But it's close enough that when I'm asked I just put down the Fourth of July, 1882."

"Why that's *my* birthday!"

(Yes, Mama, I know.) "Really, Mrs. Smith? I didn't mean to steal your birthday. I'll move over a few days – say the first of July. Since I'm not certain anyhow."

"Oh, don't do that! Father – you must bring Mr. Bronson home for dinner on our joint birthday."

"Do you think Brian would like that?"

"Certainly he would! I'll write to him about it. He'll be home long before then in any case. You know Brian always says, 'The more, the merrier!' We'll be expecting you, Mr. Bronson."

"Mrs. Smith, that's most kind of you, but I expect to leave on a long business trip on the first of July."

"I think you have let Father scare you off. Or is it the prospect of eating dinner with eight noisy children? Never mind; my husband will invite you himself – and then we will see what you say."

"In the meantime, Maureen, stop crowding him; you've got him flustered. Let me see something. You two stand up, side by side. Go ahead, Ted; she won't bite you."

"Mrs. Smith?"

She shrugged and dimpled, then accepted his hand to get up out of her rocking chair. "Father always wants to 'see something.' "

Lazarus stood by her, facing his grandfather, and tried to ignore her fragrance – a touch of toilet water, but mostly the light, warm, delicious scent of sweet and healthy woman. Lazarus was afraid to think about it, was careful not to let it show in his face. But it hit him like a heavy blow.

"Mrrrph. Both of you step up to the mantel and look at yourselves in the glass. Ted, there was no typhoid epidemic down that way in 'eighty-two. Nor 'eighty-three."

"Really, sir? Of course I can't remember." (And I shouldn't have tossed in that flourish! Sorry, Gramp. Would you believe the truth? You might . . . out of all the men I've ever known. Don't risk it, Bub, forget it!)

"Nope. Just the usual number of dumb fools too lazy to build their privies a proper distance from their wells. Which I feel certain could not describe your parents. Can't guess about your mother, but I think your father died with his hand on the throttle, still trying to gain control. Maureen?"

Mrs. Smith stared at her reflection and that of their guest. She said slowly, "Father . . . Mr. Bronson and I look enough alike to be brother and sister."

"No. First cousins. Although with Ned gone there's no way to prove it. I think – "

Mr. Johnson was interrupted by a yell from the front staircase landing: "Mama! *Gramp!* I want to be buttoned up!"

Ira Johnson answered, "Woodie, you rapscallion, get back upstairs!"

Instead the child came down – small, male, freckled, and ginger-haired, dressed in Dr. Denton's with the seat flapping behind him. He stared at Lazarus with beady, suspicious eyes. Lazarus felt a shiver run down his spine and tried not to look at the child.

"Who's *that?*"

Mrs. Smith said quickly, "Forgive me, Mr. Bronson." Then she added quietly, "Come here, Woodrow."

Her father said, "Don't bother, Maureen. I'll take him up and blister his bottom – *then* I'll button him."

"You and what six others?" the boy child demanded.

"Me, myself, and a baseball bat."

Mrs. Smith quietly and quickly attended to the child's needs, then hurried him out of the room and headed him up the stairs. She returned and sat down. Her father said, "Maureen, that was just an excuse. Woodie can button himself. And he's too old for that baby outfit. Put him in a nightshirt."

"Father, shall we discuss it another time?"

Mr. Johnson shrugged. "I've overstepped again. Ted, that one's the chessplayer. He's a stem-winder. Named for President Wilson, but he's not 'too proud to fight.' Mean little devil."

"Father."

"All right, all right – but it's true. That's what I like about Woodie. He'll go far."

Mrs. Smith said, "Please excuse us, Mr. Bronson. My father and I sometimes differ a little about how to bring up a boy. But we should not burden you with it."

"Maureen, I simply won't let you make a 'Little Lord Fauntleroy' out of Woodie."

"There's no danger of *that*, Father; he takes after you. My father was in the War of 'Ninety-eight, Mr. Bronson, and the Insurrection – "

"And the Boxer Rebellion."

" – and he can't forget it – "

"Of course not. I keep my old Army thirty-eight under my pillow, my son-in-law being away."

"Nor would I wish him to forget; I am proud of my father, Mr. Bronson, and hope that all my sons will grow up with his same spirit. But I want them to learn to speak politely, too."

"Maureen, I would rather have Woodie sass me than be timid with me. He'll learn to speak politely soon enough; older boys will take care of that. A lesson in manners punctuated with a black eye sticks. I know from experience."

The discussion was interrupted by the jingle of the doorbell. "That should be Nancy," Mr. Johnson said and got up to answer. Lazarus heard Nancy say good-night to someone, then stood up himself to be introduced, and was not startled only because he had already picked out his eldest sister at church and knew that she looked like a young edition of Laz and Lor. She spoke to him politely but rushed upstairs as soon as she was excused.

"Do sit down, Mr. Bronson."

"Thank you, Mrs. Smith, but you were staying up until your daughter returned. She has, so I will leave."

"Oh, there's no hurry; Father and I are night owls."

"Thank you very much. I enjoyed the coffee and the cake, and most especially the company. But it is time for me to say good-night. You have been most kind."

"If you must, sir. Will we see you at church on Sunday?"

"I expect to be there, ma'am."

Lazarus drove home in a daze, body alert but thoughts elsewhere. He reached his apartment, bolted himself in, checked windows and blinds automatically, stripped off his clothes, and started a tub. Then he looked grimly at himself in the bathroom mirror. "You stupid arsfardel," he said with slow intensity. "You whirling son of a bitch. Can't you do *anything* right?"

No, apparently not, not even something as simple as getting reacquainted with his mother. Gramp had been no problem; the old goat had given him no surprises – other than being shorter and smaller than Lazarus remembered. He was just as grumpy, suspicious, cynical, formally polite, belligerent – and delightful – as Lazarus had remembered.

There had been worrisome moments when he had "thrown himself on the mercy of the court." But that gambit had paid off better than Lazarus had had any reason to hope – through an unsuspected family resemblance. Lazarus not only had never seen Gramp's elder brother (dead before Woodie Smith was born), but he had forgotten that there ever was an Edward Johnson.

Was "Uncle Ned" listed with the Families? Ask Justin. Never mind, not important. Mother had put her finger on the correct answer: Lazarus resembled his grandfather. And his mother, as Gramp had pointed out. But that had resulted only in conjectures concerning dear old Uncle Ned and his "trifling ways," ones that Mother did not mind listening to, once she was certain that her guest was not embarrassed.

Embarrassed? It had changed his status from stranger to "cousin." Lazarus wanted to kiss Uncle Ned and thank him for those "trifling ways" that made kinship plausible. Gramp believed the theory – of course; it was his own – and his daughter seemed willing to treat it as a possible hypothesis. Lazarus, it's just the inside track you need – if you weren't such a blithering idiot!

He tested the bath water – cold. He shut it off and pulled the plug. A promise of hot water all day long had been one inducement when Lazarus had rented this musty cave. But the janitor turned off the water heater before he went to bed, and anyone looking for hot water later than nine was foolish. Well, he qualified as foolish, and perhaps cold water would do more for his unstable condition than hot – but he had wanted a long, hot soak to soothe his nerves and help him think.

He had fallen in love with his mother.

Face it, Lazarus. This is impossible, and you don't know how to handle it. In more than two thousand years of one silly misadventure after the other this is the most preposterous predicament you ever got into.

Oh, sure, a son loves his mother. As "Woodie Smith," Lazarus had never doubted that. He had always kissed his mother goodnight (usually), hugged her when he saw her (if he wasn't in a hurry), remembered her birthday (almost always), thanked her for cookies or cake she left out for him whenever he was out late (except when he forgot), and sometimes had told her he loved her.

She had been a good mother. She had never screamed at him (or at any of them) and, when necessary, had used a switch at once and the matter was over with – never that Wait-till-your-father-gets-home routine. Lazarus could still feel that peach switch on his calves; it had caused him to levitate, better than Thurston the Great, at a very early age.

He recalled, too, that as he grew older, he found that he was proud of the way she looked – always neat and standing straight and invariably gracious to his friends – not like some of the mothers of other boys.

Oh, sure, a boy loves his mother – and Woodie had been blessed with one of the best.

But this was *not* what Lazarus felt toward Maureen Johnson Smith, lovely young matron, just his "own" age. That visit this night had been delicious agony – for he had never in all his lives been so unbearably attracted, so sexually obsessed, by any woman any where or when. During that short visit Lazarus had been forced to be most careful not to let his passion show – and especially cautious not to appear too gallant, not be more than impersonally polite, not by expression or tone of voice or anything else risk arousing Gramp's always-alert suspicions, not let Gramp suspect the storm of lust that had raged up in him as soon as he touched her hand.

Lazarus looked down at proof of his passion, hard and tall, and slapped it. "What are *you* standing up for? There's nothing doing for *you*. This is the Bible Belt."

It was indeed! Gramp did not believe in the Bible or live by Bible-Belt standards, yet Lazarus felt sure that, were he to provoke it by breaching those standards, Gramp would shoot him quite dispassionately, on behalf of his son-in-law. Possibly the old man would let the first shot go wide and give him a chance to run. But Lazarus was not willing to bet his life on it. Gramp acting for his son-in-law might feel duty bound to shoot straight – and Lazarus knew how straight the old man could shoot.

Forget it, forget it, he was not going to give either Gramp or his father any reason to shoot, or even to be angry – and *you* forget it, too, you blind snake! Lazarus wondered when his father would be home, and tried to remember how he looked – found his memory blurred. Lazarus had always been closer to his Grandfather Johnson than to his father; not only had his father often been away on business, but also Gramp had been home in the daytime and willing to spend time with Woodie.

His other grandparents? Somewhere in Ohio – Cincinnati? No matter, his memory of them was so faint that it did not seem worthwhile to try to see them.

He had completed all that he had intended to do in Kansas City – and if he had the sense God promised a doorknob, the time to leave is *now*. Skip church on Sunday, stay away from the pool hall, go down Monday and sell his remaining holdings – and *leave!* Climb into the Ford – no, sell it and take a train to San Francisco; there catch the first ship south. Send Gramp and Maureen polite notes, mailed from Denver or San Francisco, saying that he was sorry but that business trip, etc. – but *Get Out of Town!*

Because Lazarus *knew* that the attraction had not been one-sided – He thought that he had kept Gramp from guessing his emotional storm . . . but Maureen had been aware of it – and had not resented it. No, she had been flattered and pleased. They had been on the same frequency at once, and without a word or any meaningful glance or touch, her transponder had answered him, silently . . . then, as opportunity made it possible, she had answered overtly, once with a dinner invitation – which Gramp had tromped on – and she had promptly tromped back in a fashion that made it acceptable by the mores. Then a second time, just as he was leaving, with the also fully acceptable suggestion that she would expect to see him in church.

Well, why should a young matron, even in 1917, *not* be pleased – and flattered, and unresentful – to know that a man wanted most urgently to take her to bed and treat her with gentle roughness? If his nails were clean . . . if his breath was sweet . . . if his manners were polite and respectful – why not? A woman with eight children is no nervous virgin; she is used to a man in her bed, in her arms, in her body – and Lazarus would have bet his last cent that Maureen enjoyed it.

Lazarus had no reason then, or in his earlier life, to suspect that Maureen Smith had ever been anything but "faithful" by the most exacting Bible-Belt standards. He had no reason to think that she was even flirting with him. Her manner had not suggested it; he doubted if it ever would. But he held a deep certainty that she was as strongly attracted as he was, that she knew exactly where it could lead – and he suspected that she realized that nothing but chaperonage would stop them.

(But a father in residence and eight children, plus the contemporary mores concerning what can and can't be done, constituted a lot of chaperonage! Llita's chastity belt could hardly be more efficient.)

Let's haul it out into the middle of the floor and let the cat sniff it. "Sin?" "Sin" like "love" was a word hard to define. It came in two bitter but vastly different flavours. The first lay in violating the taboos of your tribe. This passion he felt was certainly sinful by the taboos of the tribe he had been born into – incestuous in the first degree.

But it could not possibly be incest to Maureen.

To himself? He knew that "incest" was a religious concept, not a scientific one, and the last twenty years had washed away in his mind almost the last trace of his tribal taboo. What was left was no more than that breath of garlic in a good salad; it made Maureen more enticingly forbidden (if such were possible!); it did not scare him off. Maureen did not *seem* to be his mother – because she did not fit his recollection of her either as a young woman or as an old woman.

The other meaning of "sin" was easier to define because it was not clouded by the murky concepts of religion and taboo: Sin is behaviour that ignores the welfare of others.

Suppose he stuck around and managed somehow (stipulate safe opportunity) to bed Maureen with her full cooperation? Would she regret it later? Adultery? The word meant something here.

But she was a Howard, one of the early ones when marriage between Howards was a cash contract, eyes wide open, payment from the Foundation for each child born of such union – and Marueen had carried out the contract, eight paid-for children already and would stay in production for, uh, about fifteen more years. Perhaps to her "adultery" meant "violation of contract" rather than "sin" – he did not know.

But that is not the point, Bub; the real question is the only one that has *ever* stopped you when temptation coincided with opportunity – and *this* time he could consult neither Ishtar nor any geneticist. The chance of a bad outcome was slight when there were so many hurdles in the way of *any* outcome. But it was the exact risk that he had always refused to take: the chance of placing a congenital handicap on a child.

Hey, wait a minute! No such outcome *could* result because no such *had* resulted. He knew every one of his siblings, alive now or still to be born, and there had not been a defective in the lot. Not one.

Therefore no hazard.

But – That was grounded on the assumption that his "no-paradoxes" theory was a law of nature. But you've long been aware that the "no-paradoxes" theory itself involves a paradox – one that you've kept quiet about so as not to alarm Laz and Lor and the rest of your "present" (*that* present, not this one) family; to wit, the idea that free will and pre-destination are two aspects of the same mathematical truth, and the difference is merely linguistic, not semantic: the notion that his own free will could not change events here-&-now because his freewill actions here-&-now were already a part of what *had* happened in any later "here-&-now."

Which in turn depended on a solipsistic notion he had held as far back as he could remember – Cobwebs, all of it!

Lazarus, you don't *know* what trouble you might cause.

So *don't!* Get out of town *now* and don't come back to Kansas City *at all!* Because, if you do, you're certain to try to get Maureen's bloomers off . . . and she's going to breathe hard and help. From there on only Allah knows – but it could be tragic for her and tragic for others, and as for you, you stupid stud, all balls and no brain, it could get your ass shot off . . . just as the twins predicted.

In which case, since you are *not* going to see your family again, there is no sense in waiting in South America for this war to end. You've seen enough of this doomed era; ask the girls to come pick you up *now*.

Was her waist really that slender? Or did she lace it in?

Shucks, it didn't matter how she was built. As with Tamara, it simply did not matter.

* * *

Dear Laz and Lor,

Darlings, I've changed plans. I've seen my first family, and there isn't anything else I want to do in this era – nothing worth sweating out most of two years in a backwater while this war drags on to its bloody and useless finish. So I want you to pick me up now, at the impact crater. Forget about Egypt; I can't get there now.

By "pick me up now" I mean Gregorian 3 March 1917 – repeat, third day of March one thousand nine hundred and seventeen Gregorian, at that meteor impact crater in Arizona.

Much to tell you when I see you. Meanwhile –

My undying love,

Lazarus

* * *

Was it her voice? Or her fragrance? Or something else?

DA CAPO

IV

Home

27 March 1917 Greg.

Beloved Family,

Repeat of Basic Message: I got here three years too early – 2 August 1916 – but still wish to be picked up exactly ten T-years after drop, 2 August 1926 – repeat *six*. Rendezvous points and alternatives from basic date as before. Please impress on Dora that this results from bad data I gave her and is *not her fault*.

I'm having a marvellous time. I got my business cleaned up and then got in touch with my first family by looking up my grandfather (Ira Johnson, Ira) and got acquainted with him first – and with the aid of a horrendous lie and a most fortunate family resemblance, Gramp is convinced that I am an unregistered son of his (deceased) brother. I didn't suggest this; it's his own idea. Consequently it's solid – and now I'm a "long-lost cousin" in my first home. Not living there, but welcome, which is very nice.

Let me give a rundown on the family, since all of you are descended from three of them: Gramp, Mama, and Woodie.

Gramp is described in that junk Justin has been cutting down to size. No changes, Justin, save that instead of being two metres tall and carved out of granite, Gramp is almost exactly my size. I am spending every minute with him that he will let me, which usually means playing chess with him several times a week.

Mama: Take Laz and Lor and add five kilos in the best places, then add fifteen T-years and a big slug of dignity. (Quit quivering your goddamn chins!) Add hair down to her waist but always coiled up on top. I don't actually know what Mama does look like other than her head and hands because of the curious custom here of wearing clothes all over at all times. And I do mean "*all* over." I know that Mama has slender ankles because I once caught a glimpse. But I would never dare stare at them; Gramp would toss me out of the house.

Papa: He is away now. I had forgotten what he looks like – I had forgotten all their faces except Gramp (who uses the same face I do!) But I've seen pictures of Papa and he looks a bit like President Teddy Roosevelt – that's "Theodore," Athene, not "Franklin" – in case you have a picture in your gizzards.

Nancy: Laz and Lor as of three standard years before I left. Not as many freckles and *very* dignified – except when it slips. She is acutely aware of (young) males, and I think Gramp is urging Mama to tell her about the Howard setup at once, so that she'll be sure to marry in the Families.

Carol: Laz and Lor again but two years younger than Nancy. She is as interested in boys as is Nancy – but frustrated; Mama has her on a short leash. Quivers her chin, which Mama ignores.

Brian Junior: Dark hair, looks more like Papa. Rising young capitalist. Has a newspaper route which he combines with lighting gas streetlamps. Has a contract to deliver advertising handbills for the local moving-picture theatre which he farms out to his younger brother and four other boys and pays them in tickets to the theatre and keeps some for his own use and sells the rest at a discount (four cents instead of five) at school. Has a vending bar for soda pop (a sweet, bubbly drink) on the corner in the summers but plans to franchise this to his younger brother this coming summer; he has another enterprise lined up. (As I recall, Brian got rich quite young.)

Let me explain something about our family. They are prosperous by here-&-now standards – but do not show it except that they live in a large house in a good neighbourhood. Not only is Papa a successful businessman, but also this is a time when the Howard endowment of babies is substantial in terms of buying power – and Mama has had eight already. To all of you, being a "Howard" means a genetic heritage and a tradition – but here-&-now it means cash money for babies – a stock-breeding scheme and we are the stock.

I think Papa must be investing the money Mama makes by

having Howard babies; they certainly are not spending it – and this accords with my own dim memories. I don't know what was done for my siblings, but I received getting-started money when I first married – money I had not expected and which had nothing to do with the Howard endowments my first wife earned by being fertile and willing. Since I married during an economic stalemate, this made a big difference. Back to the kids – The boys not only do work; they *have* to work – or they have nothing but clothes and food. The girls receive very small cash allowances but are required to do housework and to help with the younger children. This is because it is *very* difficult for a girl to earn money in this society – but a boy who will get out and *try* has endless opportunities. (This will change before the century is over, but in 1917 it is true.) All the Smith kids work at home (Mama hires a laundress one day a week, that's all), but a boy (or girl) who finds outside cash-money work is relieved of housework to that extent. Nor does he have to "pay back" this time off; he keeps what he earns and spends it or saves it, the latter being encouraged by Papa matching such savings.

If you think Papa and Mama are intentionally making moneygrubbers of their offspring, you are right.

George: ten T-years old, Brian Jr.'s junior partner, shadow, and stooge. This will end in a few years with George busting Brian one in the mouth.

Marie: eight and a freckled tomboy. Mama is having a difficult time trying to make a "lady" out of her. (But Mama's gentle stubbornness – and biology – will win. Marie grew up to be the beauty of the family, with beaux underfoot – and I hated them as there had been a period when I was her pet. Marie was the only one of my siblings I was close to. It is possible to be lonely in a large family, and I was – except for Gramp, always, and Marie, for a short time.)

Woodrow Wilson Smith – still short of five by several months and as offensive a brat as was ever allowed to grow up. I am appalled to be forced to admit that this stinking little snot is the weed which grew up to be humanity's fairest flower, namely, Ol' Buddy Boy himself. So far he has spat in my hat when it was presumably out of his reach on the cloak rack in the hall, referred to me with various disparagements, of which "Here's that dude in the derby again!" is the mildest, kicked me in the stomach when I tried to pick him up (my error; I didn't want to touch him but thought I should break myself of irrational queasiness), and accused me of cheating at chess when in fact *he* was cheating – he called my attention to something out the window, then moved my queen one square, and I caught him at it and called him on it. And so on, ad nauseam.

But I continue to play chess with him because: (a) I am determined to get along with *all* my first family for the short time I will be here; and (b) Woodie will play chess at any opportunity, and Gramp and I are the only chessplayers around who will put up with his poisonous ways. (Gramp clobbers him as necessary; I have no such privilege. But if I were not afraid to find out what would happen, I might strangle him. What *would* happen? Would half of human history disappear and the rest be changed beyond recognition? No, "paradox" is a null word; the fact that I *am* here proves that I will keep my temper long enough to get shut of the little beast.)

Richard: three and as affectionate as Woodie is difficult. Likes to sit on my lap and be told stories. His favourite is about two redheaded twins named Laz and Lor who fly a magic "airship" through the sky. I feel a tender sadness about Dickie, for he will (did) die quite young, assaulting a place called Iwo Jima.

Ethel: a heavenly smile at one end and a wet diaper at the other. Short on conversation.

That's my (our) family in 1917. I expect to stay in K.C. until Papa returns – soon, now – then leave; some of this is a strain on me, pleasant as most of it is. I may look them up when this war is over – but probably not; I don't want to crowd my welcome.

To make the above clear I should explain some of the customs here. Until Papa gets home, my status has to be through Gramp as a friend he plays chess with; it can't be anything else even though he – and perhaps Mama – believe that I am Uncle Ned's son. Why? Because I am a "young" bachelor, and by the local rules a married woman can*not* have a young bachelor as a friend, particularly when her husband is out of town. The taboo is so firm I don't dare give even the appearance of violating it . . . on *Mama's* account. Nor would she encourage me to. Nor would Gramp permit it.

So I'm welcome in my own home *only* if I go there to see Gramp. If I telephone, I must ask for *him*. And so on.

Oh, it's permissible, on a rainy day, for me to offer a ride home to members of the Smith family at church. I am permitted to do almost anything for the kids as long as I don't "spoil" them – which Mama defines as spending much more than five cents on one of them. Last Saturday I was allowed to take six of them on a picnic in my automobile carriage. I am teaching Brian to operate it. My interest in the kids is considered understandable by Mama and by Gramp because of my "lonely" and "deprived" childhood as an "orphan."

The one thing I must *never* do is to be alone with Mama. I don't go inside my own home unless publicly accompanied by Gramp; the neighbours would notice. I am meticulous about it; I won't risk causing Mama trouble with a tribal taboo.

I am writing this at my apartment, on a printing machine you would not believe, and must stop in order to take it downtown and photoreduce it twice, then etch it and laminate it and seal it for Delay Mail and deliver it to a drop – which kills a whole day, as I must use a rented lab and destroy intermediate stages as I go; this is not something I dare leave in an apartment to which a janitor has a key. When I get back from South America I'll make my own lab setup, one I can carry in an automobile. Paved roads will be more common this coming decade and I expect to travel that way. But I want to continue sending these letters and by as many Delay Mail drops as possible, in hope that at least one will last through the centuries and reach you. As Justin put it, the real problem is to get one to last through just the coming three centuries – I'll keep trying.

All my love to all of you,
Lazarus

DA CAPO

V

MARCH 3, 1917: KAISER PLOTS WITH MEXICO AND JAPAN TO ATTACK USA – ZIMMERMANN TELEGRAM AUTHENTIC
APRIL 2, 1917: PRESIDENT ADDRESSES CONGRESS – ASKS WAR
APRIL 6, 1917: AMERICA ENTERS WAR – CONGRESS DECLARES "A STATE OF BELLIGERENCY EXISTS"

Lazarus Long was as taken by surprise by the date of the outbreak of war with Germany as he was unsurprised by the fact itself. He was caught so flat-footed that it was not until later that he analyzed *why* the "hindsight" he had relied on had proved even more myopic than foresight.

The resumption of unrestricted U-boat warfare early in 1917 had not surprised him; it fitted his recollections of his earliest history lessons. The Zimmermann telegram did not disturb him even though he did not remember it; it matched a pattern he did remember – again from history, not the direct memories of a very small child – a period of three years, 1914 to 1917, when the United States had inched slowly from neutrality to war. Woodie Smith had been not yet two when the war started, not yet five when his country got into it; Lazarus had no first-hand memories of foreign affairs of a time when Woodie had been too young to grasp such remote improbabilities.

The timetable Lazarus had fixed on, once he discovered that he had arrived three years early, had worked so well that he did not realize that its "clock" was wrong until the event slapped him in the face. When he was able to take time to analyze his mistake, he saw that he had committed the prime sin against survival: He had indulged in wishful thinking. He had *wanted* to believe his timetable.

He had not wanted to leave his newly found first family so quickly. All of them. But especially Maureen.

Maureen – Once he decided to stay on till July 1 as originally planned, after a long night of wrestling with his troubled soul – a night of indecision and worry and letters written and destroyed – he discovered that he *could* stay and treat Mrs. Brian Smith with friendly but formal politeness, avoid any sign of interest in her more personal than the mores permitted. He managed to shift to his celibate mode – happy to be near her when it was possible to be so without causing Mrs. Grundy's nose to twitch – or the even sharper nose of his grandfather.

Lazarus had indeed been happy. As with Tamara – or the twins – or any of his darlings – coupling was not necessary to love. When it was expedient, he could bank the fires and forget it. He was never for one instant unaware of the tremendous physical attraction of this woman who had been his mother more than two thousand years ago (in some odd direction) – but the matter was shelved; it did not affect his manner or lessen his happiness when he was permitted to be near her. He believed that Maureen knew what he was doing (or refraining from doing) and why, and that she appreciated his restraint.

All during March he sought approved ways to see her. Brian Junior wanted to learn to drive; Gramp ruled that he was old enough, so Lazarus taught him – picked him up at the house and returned him there – and often was rewarded with a glimpse of Maureen. Lazarus even found a way (other than chess) to reach Woodie. He took the child to the Hippodrome Theatre to see the magician Thurston the Great – then promised to take him (when it opened for the summer) to "Electric Park," an amusement park and Woodie's idea of heaven. This consolidated a truce between them.

Lazarus delivered the child home from the theatre, sound asleep and with no more than normal wear and tear, and was rewarded by sharing coffee with Gramp and Maureen.

Lazarus volunteered to help with the Boy Scout troop sponsored by the church; George was a Tenderfoot, and Brian was working toward Eagle. Lazarus found being an assistant scoutmaster pleasant in itself – and Gramp invited him in when he gave the boys a lift home.

Lazarus gave little attention to foreign affairs. He continued to buy the Kansas City *Post* because the newsboy at Thirty-first and Troost regarded him as a regular customer – a real sport who paid a nickel for a penny paper and did not expect change. But Lazarus rarely read it, not even the market news once he completed his liquidations.

The week starting Sunday the first of April Lazarus did not plan to see his family for two reasons: Gramp was away, and his father was home. Lazarus did not intend to meet his father until he could manage it naturally and easily through Gramp. Instead he stayed home, did his own cooking, caught up on chores, did mechanical work on his landaulet and cleaned and polished it, and wrote a long letter to his Tertius family.

This he took with him Thursday morning, intending to prepare it for Delay Mail. He bought a newspaper as usual at Thirty-first and Troost; after he was seated in a streetcar, he glanced at its front page – then broke his habit of enjoying the ride by reading it carefully. Instead of going to the Kansas City Photo Supply Company, he went to the Main Public Library's reading room and spent two hours catching up with the world – the local papers, the Tuesday New York *Times* where he read the text of the President's message to Congress – "God helping her, she can do no other!" – and the Chicago *Tribune* of the day before. He noted that the *Tribune*, staunchest foe of England outside the German-language press, was now hedging its bets.

He then went to the men's toilet, tore into small pieces the letter he had prepared, and flushed it down a water closet.

He went to the Missouri Savings Bank, drew out his account, went next to the downtown office of the Santa Fe Railroad and bought a ticket for Los Angeles with thirty-day stopover privilege at Flagstaff, Arizona, stopped at a stationer's, then on to the Commonwealth Bank and got at his lockbox, removed from it a smaller box heavy with gold. He asked to use the bank's washroom; his status as a lockbox client got him this favour.

With gold pieces distributed among thirteen pockets of his coat, vest, and trousers Lazarus no longer looked smart – he tended to sag here and there – but if he walked carefully, he did not jingle. So he walked most carefully, had his nickel ready on boarding a streetcar, then stood on the rear platform rather than sit down. He was not easy until he was locked and bolted into his apartment.

He stopped to make and eat a sandwich, then got to work on tailoring, sewing the yellow coins into one-coin pockets of the chamois-skin vest he had made earlier, then covered it with the vest from which it had been patterned. Lazarus forced himself to work slowly, restoring seams so neatly that the nature of the garment could not be detected by anyone not wearing it.

About midnight he had another sandwich, got back to work.

When he was satisfied with fit and appearance, he put the money vest aside, placed a folded blanket on the table where he had been working, placed on it a heavy, tall Oliver typewriter. He attacked the clanking monster with two fingers:

"At Kansas City, Gregorian 5 April 1917

"Dearest Lor and Laz,

"EMERGENCY. I need to be picked up. I hope to be at the impact crater by Monday 9 April 1917 repeat nine April nineteen seventeen. I may be one or two days late. I will wait there ten days, if possible. If not picked up, I will try to keep the 1926 (nineteen twenty-six) rendezvous.

"Thanks!

"Lazarus"

Lazarus typed two originals of this, then addressed two sets of nesting envelopes, using different choices on each and addressing the outermost envelopes one to his local contact and the other to a Chicago address. He then wrote a bill of sale:

"*For one dollar in hand and other good and valuable considerations I sell and convey all my interest, right, and title to one Ford Model-T automobile, body style 'Laundaulet,' engine number 1290480, to Ira Johnson, and warrant to him and his successors that this chattel is unencumbered and that I am sole owner with full right to convey title.*

"(*s*) *Theodore Bronson*

"*April 6, 1917* A.D."

He placed this in a plain envelope, put it with the others, drank a glass of milk, went to bed.

He slept ten hours, undisturbed by cries of "*Extra! Extra!*"

along the boulevard; he had expected them, his subconscious discounted them and let him rest – he expected to be very busy the next several days.

When his inner clock called him, he got up, quickly bathed and shaved, cooked and ate a large breakfast, cleaned his kitchen, removed all perishables from his icebox and emptied them into the garbage can on the rear service porch and turned the ice card around to read "NO ICE TODAY" and left fifteen cents on top of the icebox, emptied the drip pan.

There was a fresh quart of milk by the ice. He had not ordered it, but he had not specifically *not* ordered it. So he put six cents in an empty bottle, with a note telling the milkman not to leave milk until the next time he left money out.

He packed a grip – toilet articles, socks, underwear, shirts, and collars (to Lazarus, those high starched collars symbolized all the tight-minded taboos of this otherwise pleasant age), then rapidly searched the apartment for everything of a personal nature. The rent was paid till the end of April; with good luck he expected to be in the *Dora* long before then. With bad luck he would be in South America – but with worse luck he would be somewhere else – anywhere – and under another name; he wanted "Ted Bronson" to disappear without a trace.

Shortly he had waiting at the front door a grip, an overcoat, a winter suit, a set of chessmen in ivory and ebony, and a typewriter. He finished dressing, being careful to place three envelopes and his ticket in an inner pocket of his suit coat. The money vest was too warm but not uncomfortable; the distributed weight was not bad.

He piled it all into the tonneau of the landaulet, drove to the southside postal substation, registered two letters, went from there to the pawnshop next to the Idle Hour Billiard Parlour. He noted with wry amusement that "The Swiss Garden" had its blinds down and a sign "CLOSED."

Mr. Dattelbaum was willing to accept the typewriter against a gun but wanted five dollars to boot for the little Colt pistol Lazarus selected. Lazarus let the pawnbroker conduct both sides of the dicker.

Lazarus sold the typewriter and the suit, left his overcoat and took back a pawn ticket, received the handgun and a box of cartridges. He was in fact giving Mr. Dattelbaum the overcoat since he had no intention of redeeming it – but Lazarus got what he wanted plus three dollars cash, had unloaded chattels he no longer needed, and had given his friend the pleasure of one last dicker.

The gun fitted into a left-side vest pocket Lazarus had retailored into a makeshift holster. Short of being frisked – most unlikely for so obviously respectable a citizen – it would not be noticed. A kilt was better both for concealment and for quick access – but it was the best he could manage with the clothes he had to wear, and this gun had had its front sight filed off by some practical-minded former owner.

He was now through with Kansas City save for saying good-bye to his first family – then grab the first Santa Fe rattler west. It distressed him that Gramp had gone to St. Louis, but that could not be helped, and this one time he would bull his way in, with a convincing cover story: The chess set as a present for Woodie was reason enough to show up in person, the bill of sale gave an excuse to speak to his father – No, sir, this is not exactly a present . . . but somebody might as well drive it until this war is over . . . and if by any chance I don't come back – well, this makes things simpler – you understand me, sir? – your father-in-law being my best friend and sort of my next of kin since I don't have any.

Yes, that would work and result in a chance to say good-bye to all the family, including Maureen. (Especially Maureen!) Without quite lying. Best way to lie.

Just one thing – If his father wanted to enlist him into his own outfit, then one lie *must* be used: Lazarus was dead set on joining the Navy. No offence intended, sir; I know you're just back from Plattsburg, but the Navy needs men, too.

But he would not tell that lie unless forced to.

He left his car back of the pawnshop, crossed the street to a drugstore, and telephoned:

"Is this the Brian Smith residence?"

"Yes, it is."

"Mrs. Smith, this is Mr. Bronson. May I speak to Mr. Smith?"

"This isn't Mama, Mr. Bronson; this is Nancy. Oh, isn't it *terrible*!"

"Yes, it is, Miss Nancy."

"You want to speak to Papa? But he's not *here*; he's gone to Fort Leavenworth. To report in – and we don't know *when* we'll see him again!"

"There, there – please don't cry. Please!"

"I was *not* crying. I'm just a teensy bit upset. Do you want to speak to Mama? She's here . . . but she's lying down."

Lazarus thought fast. Of course he wanted to speak to Maureen. But – Confound it, this was a complication. "Please don't disturb her. Can you tell me when your grandfather will be back in town?" (Could he afford to wait? Oh, *damn!*)

"Why, Grandpa got back yesterday."

"Oh. May I speak to him, Miss Nancy?"

"But he's not here, either. He went downtown hours ago. He might be at his chess club. Do you want to leave a message for him?"

"No. Just tell him I called . . . and will call again later. And, Miss Nancy – don't worry."

"How can I *help* worrying?"

"I have second sight. Don't tell anyone but it's true; an old gypsy woman saw that I had it and proved it to me. Your father is coming home and will not be hurt in this war. I *know.*"

"Uh . . . I don't know whether to believe that or not – but it does make me feel better."

"It's true." He said good-bye gently, and hung up.

"Chess club – " Surely Gramp would not be loafing in a pool hall today? But since it was just across the street, he might as well see . . . before driving out to Benton and waiting in sight of the house for him to return.

Gramp was there, at the chess table but not even pretending to work a chess problem; he was simply glowering.

"Good afternoon, Mr. Johnson."

Gramp looked up. "What's good about it? Sit down, Ted."

"Thank you, sir." Lazarus slid into the other chair. "Not much good about it, I suppose."

"Eh?" The old man looked at him as if just noticing his presence. "Ted, would you say that I was a man in good physical condition?"

"Yes, certainly."

"Able to shoulder a gun and march twenty miles a day?"

"I would think so." (I'm sure you could, Gramp.)

"That's what I told that young smart-alec at the recruiting station. He told me I was *too old*!" Ira Johnson looked ready to break into tears. "I asked him since when was forty-five too old? – and he told me to move aside, I was holding up the line. I offered to step outside and whip him and any two other men he picked. And they put me out, Ted, *they put me out!*" Gramp covered his face with his hands, then took them down and muttered, "I was wearing Army Blue before that snotty little shikepoke learned to pee standing up."

"I'm sorry, sir."

"My own fault. I fetched along my discharge . . . and forgot about its having my birth date on it. Look, Ted, if I dyed my hair and went back to St. Looie – or Joplin – that would work . . . wouldn't it?"

"Probably." (I know it didn't, Gramp . . . but I think you did manage to talk your way into the Home Guard. But I can't tell you that.)

"I'll do it! But I'll leave my discharge at home."

"In the meantime may I drive you home? My Tin Lizzie is around in back."

"Well . . . I suppose I've got to go home – eventually."

"How about a little spin out Paseo to cool off first?"

"That's a n'idee. If it won't put you out?"

"Not at all."

Lazarus drove around, keeping silent, until the old man's fuming stopped. When Lazarus noted this, he headed back and turned east on Thirty-first Street, and parked. "Mr. Johnson, may I say something?"

"Eh? Speak up."

"If they won't take you – even with your hair dyed – I hope you won't feel too bad about it. Because this war is a terrible mistake."

"*What do you mean?*"

"Just what I said." (How much to tell him? How much can I get him to believe? I can't hold back altogether – this is *Gramp* . . . who taught me to shoot, and a thousand other things. But what will he *believe*?) "This war won't do the slightest good; it will just make things worse."

Gramp stared at him, under knotted brows. "What are you, Ted? Pro-German?"

"No."

"Pacifist, maybe? Come to think about it, you've never had one word to say about the war."

"No, I'm not a pacifist. And I'm not pro-German. But if we win this war –"

"You mean '*When* we win this war!'"

"All right, 'when we win this war,' it will turn out that we've actually lost it. Lost everything we thought we were fighting for."

Mr. Johnson abruptly changed tactics. "When are you enlisting?"

Lazarus hesitated. "I've got a couple of things I must do first."

"I thought that might be your answer, Mr. Bronson. Good-bye!" Gramp fumbled with the door latch, cursed, and stepped over onto the running board, thence to the curb.

Lazarus said, "Gramp! I mean 'Mr. Johnson.' Let me finish running you home. *Please!*"

His grandfather paused just long enough to look back and say, "Not on your tintype . . . you pusillanimous piss-ant." Then he marched steadily down the street to the car stop.

Lazarus waited and watched Mr. Johnson climb aboard; then he trailed the trolley car, unwilling to admit that there was nothing he could do to correct the shambles he had made of his relations with Gramp. He watched the old man get off at Benton Boulevard, considered overtaking him and trying to speak to him.

But what could he say? He understood how Gramp felt, and why – and he had already said too much and no further words could call it back or correct it. He drove aimlessly on down Thirty-first Street.

At Indiana Avenue he parked his car, bought a *Star* from a newsboy, went into a drugstore, sat down at the soda fountain, ordered a cherry phosphate to justify his presence, looked at the newspaper.

But was unable to read it – Instead he stared at it and brooded.

When the soda jerk wiped the marble counter in front of him and lingered, Lazarus ordered another phosphate. When this happened a second time, Lazarus asked to use a telephone.

"Home or Bell?"

"Home."

"Back of the cigar counter and you pay me."

"Brian? This is Mr. Bronson. May I speak to your mother?"

"I'll go see."

But it was his grandfather's voice that came on the line: "Mr. Bronson, your sheer effrontery amazes me. What do you want?"

"Mr. Johnson, I want to speak to Mrs. Smith –"

"You can't."

"– because she has been very kind to me and I want to thank her and say good-bye."

"One moment – " He heard his grandfather say, "George, get

out. Brian, take Woodie with you and close the door and see that it stays closed." Mr. Johnson's voice then came back closer: "Are you still there?"

"Yes, sir."

"Then listen carefully and don't interrupt; I'm going to say this just once."

"Yes, sir."

"My daughter will not speak to you, now or ever – "

Lazarus said quickly, "Does she know that I asked to speak to her?"

"*Shut up!* Certainly she knows. She asked me to deliver that message. Or I would not have spoken to you myself. Now I too have a message for you – and don't interrupt. My daughter is a respectable married woman whose husband has answered his country's call. So don't hang around her. Don't come here or you'll be met with a shotgun. Don't telephone. Don't go to her church. Maybe you think I can't make this stick. Let me remind you that this is Kansas City. Two broken arms cost twenty-five dollars; for twice that they'll kill you. But for a combined deal – break your arms first and *then* kill you – there's a discount. I can afford sixty-two fifty if you make it necessary. Understand me?"

"Yes."

"So twenty-three skidoo!"

"Hold it! Mr. Johnson, I do not believe that you would hire a man to kill another man – "

"You had better not risk it."

" – because I think you would kill him yourself."

There was a pause. Then the old man chuckled slightly. "You may be right." He hung up on Lazarus.

Lazarus cranked his car and drove away. Presently he found that he was driving west on Linwood Boulevard, noticed it because he passed his family's church. Where he had first seen Maureen –

Where he would never see her again.

Not *ever!* Not even if he came back again and tried to avoid the mistakes he had made – there were no paradoxes. Those mistakes were unalterably part of the fabric of space-time, and all of the subtleties of Andy's mathematics, all of the powers built into the *Dora*, could not erase them.

At Linwood Plaza, he parked short of Brooklyn Avenue and considered what to do next.

Drive to the station and catch the next Santa Fe train west. If either of those calls for help lasted through the centuries, then he would be picked up on Monday morning – and this war and all its troubles would again be something that happened a long time ago – and "Ted Bronson" would be someone Gramp and Maureen had known briefly and would forget.

Too bad he had not had time to get those messages etched; nevertheless, one of them might last. If not – then make rendezvous for pickup in 1926. Or if *none* of them got through – always a possibility since he was attempting to use Delay Mail before it was properly set up – then wait for 1929 and carry out rendezvous as originally planned. No problem about that; the twins and Dora were ready to keep *that* one, no matter what.

Then why did he feel so bad?

This wasn't *his* war.

Time enough and Gramp would know that the prediction he had blurted out was simple truth. In time Gramp would learn what French "gratitude" amounted to – when "Lafayette, we are here!" was forgotten and the refrain was "*Pas un sou à l'Amérique!*" Or British "gratitude" for that matter. There was *no* gratitude between nations, never had been, never would be. "Pro-Germans"? Hell, no, Gramp! There is something rotten at the very heart of German culture, and this war is going to lead to another with German atrocities a thousand times more terrible than any they are accused of today. Gas chambers and a stink of burning flesh in planned viciousness – A stench that lasted through the centuries –

But there was no way to tell Gramp and Maureen any of this. Nor should he try. The best thing about the future was that it was unknown. Cassandra's one good quality was that she was never believed.

So why should it matter that two people who could not possibly know what he knew misunderstood *why* he thought this war was useless?

But the fact was that it *did* matter – it mattered terribly.

He felt the slight bulge against his left ribs. A defence for his gold – gold he did not give a damn about. But a "termination option," switch, too.

Snap out of it, you silly fool! You don't want to be dead; you simply want the approval of Gramp and Maureen. – of Maureen.

The recruiting station was under the main post office, far downtown. Late as it was, it was still open, with a queue outside. Lazarus paid an old Negro a dollar to sit in his car, warned him that there was a grip in the back, promised him another dollar when he got back – and did not mention the money vest and pistol, both now in the grip. But Lazarus did not worry about car or money – might be simpler if both were stolen. He joined the queue.

"Name?"
"Bronson, Theodore."
"Previously military experience?"
"None."
"Age? No, date of birth – and it had better be before April 5, 1899."
"November, 11, 1890."
"You don't look that old, but okay. Take this paper and through that door. You'll find sacks or pillow cases. Take your clothes off, put 'em in one, keep 'em with you. Hand this to one of the docs and do what he tells you."
"Thank you, Sergeant."
"Get moving. Next."

A doctor in uniform was assisted by six more in civilian clothes. Lazarus read the Snellen Card correctly, but the doctor did not seem to be listening; this seemed to be a "warm body" examination. Lazarus saw only one man rejected, one who was (in Lazarus' horseback judgement) in the terminal stages of consumption.

Only one physician seemed at all anxious to find defects. He had Lazarus bend over and pull his buttock cheeks apart, felt for hernias and made him cough, then palpated his belly. "What's this hard mass on the right side?"
"I don't know, sir."
"Have you had your appendix out? Yes, I see the scar. Feel the ridge, rather; the scar hardly shows. You had a good surgeon; I wish I could do one that neat. Probably just a mass of fecal matter there; take a dose of calomel and you'll be rid of it by morning."
"Thank you, Doctor."
"Don't mention it, Son. Next."

"Hold up your right hands and repeat after me . . .
"Hang onto these slips of paper. Be at the station before seven

tomorrow morning, show your slip to a sergeant at the information desk; he'll tell you where to board. If you lose your slip of paper, be there *anyhow* – or Uncle Sam will come looking for you. That's all, men, you're in the Army now! Out through that door."

His car was still there; the old Negro got out. "Eve'ything's fine, Cap'm!"

"It surely is," Lazarus agreed heartily while getting out a dollar bill. "But it's 'Private,' not 'Captain.' "

"They took you? In *that* case, I cain't hahdly take youah dollah."

"Sure you can! I don't need it; Uncle Sam is looking out for me for the 'duration,' and he's going to pay me twenty-one dollars a month besides. So put this with the other one and buy gin and drink a toast to me – Private Ted Bronson.' "

"Ah couldn't rightly do that, Cap'm – Private Ted Bronson, suh. Ah'm White Ribbon – Ah took the plaidge befoah you was bohn. You jes' keep youah money and hang the Kaisuh fo' us."

"I'll try, Uncle. Let's make this five dollars and you can give it to your church . . . and say a prayer for me."

"Well . . . if you say so, Cap'm Private."

Lazarus tooled south on McGee feeling happy. Never take little bites, enjoy life! "*K- K- K- Katy! Beautiful Katy –* "

He stopped at a drugstore, looked over the cigar counter, spotted a nearly empty box of White Owls, bought the remaining cigars, asked to keep the box. He then bought a roll of cotton and a spool of surgical tape – and, on impulse, the biggest, fanciest box of candy in the store.

His car was parked under an arc light; he let it stay there, got into the back seat, dug into his grip, got out vest and pistol, then started an *un*-tailoring job, indifferent to the chance of being seen. Five minutes with his pocketknife undid hours of tailoring; heavy coins clinked into the cigar box. He cushioned them with cotton, sealed the box and strengthened it by wrapping it with tape. The slashed vest, the pistol, and his ticket west went down a storm drain and the last of Lazarus' worries went with them. He smiled as he stood up and brushed his knees. Son, you *are* getting old – why, you've been living *cautiously!*

He drove gaily out Linwood to Benton, ignoring the city's seventeen-miles-per-hour speed limit. He was pleased to see lights burning on the lower floor of the Brian Smith residence; he would not have to wake anyone. He went up the walk burdened with the candy box, the case for chessmen, and the taped cigar box. The porch light came on as he reached the steps; Brian Junior opened the door and looked out. "Grandpaw! It's Mr. Bronson!"

"Correction," Lazarus said firmly. "Please tell your grandfather that *Private* Bronson is here."

"What is this? What did I hear you tell that boy?"

Gramp appeared at once, looked at Lazarus suspiciously.

"I asked him to announce 'Private Bronson.' Me." Lazarus managed to get all three packages under his left arm, reached into a pocket, got out the slip of paper he had been given at the recruiting station. "Look at it."

Mr. Johnson read it. "I see. But why? Feeling the way you do."

"Mr. Johnson, I never said I was not going to enlist; I simply said I had things to do first. That was true, I did have. It's true also that I have misgivings about the ultimate usefulness of this war. But regardless of any opinion – which I should have kept to myself – the time has come to close ranks and move forward together. So I went down and volunteered and they accepted me."

Mr. Johnson handed back the recruitment form, opened the door wide. "Come in, Ted!"

Lazarus saw heads disappearing as he came in; apparently most of the family was still up. His grandfather ushered him into the parlour. "Please sit down. I must go tell my daughter."

"If Mrs. Smith has retired, I would not want her to be disturbed," Lazarus lied. (Hell, no, Gramp! I'd rather crawl in with her. But that's one secret I'll keep forever.)

"Never you mind. This is something she will want to know. Uh, that piece of paper – may I have it to show her?"

"Certainly, sir."

Lazarus waited. Ira Johnson returned in a few minutes, handed back the proof of enlistment. "She'll be down shortly." The old man sighed. "Ted, I'm proud of you. Earlier today you had me upset – and I spoke out of turn. I'm sorry – I apologize."

"I can't accept it because there is nothing to apologize for, sir. I spoke hastily and did not make myself clear. Can we forget it? Will you shake hands with me?"

"Eh? Yes. Surely! Mrrph!" Solemnly they shook hands. (Maybe Gramp *could* still straight-arm an anvil – my fingers are crushed).

"Mr. Johnson, would you take care of some things for me? Things I didn't have time to do?"

"Eh? Certainly!"

"This box, mainly." Lazarus handed him the taped cigar box.

Mr. Johnson took it, his eyebrows shot up. "Heavy."

"I cleaned out my lockbox. Gold coins. I'll pick it up when the war is over . . . or if I don't, will you give it to Woodie? When he's twenty-one?"

"What? Now, now, Son, you'll come through all right."

"I plan to, and I'll pick it up then. But I might fall down a ladder in a troopship and break my silly neck. Will you do it?"

"Yes, I'll do it."

"Thank you, sir. This is for Woodie right now. My chessmen. I can't pack them around. I'd give them to you except that you would think up some reason not to take them . . . but Woodie won't."

"Mrrph. Very well, sir."

"Here's one thing that is for you – but it's not quite what it seems." Lazarus handed over the bill of sale for the landaulet.

Mr. Johnson read it. "Ted, if you're trying to give me your automobile, you can think again."

"That's only a nominal conveyance of title, sir. What I would like is to leave it with you. Brian can drive it; he's a good driver now, he's a natural. You can drive it; even Mrs. Smith might want to learn. When Lieutenant Smith is home, he may find it convenient. But if they send me for training anywhere near here and I get time off before I'm sent overseas, I'd like to feel free to use it myself."

"But why hand me a bill of sale? Sure, it can sit in the barn . . . and no doubt Brian – both of them – would drive it. Might learn to herd it myself. But no need for *this*."

"Oh. I didn't make myself clear. Suppose I'm off somewhere, say in New Jersey – but want to sell it. I can drop you a penny postcard, and it's easy, because you'll have *that*." Lazarus added thoughtfully, "Or I might fall down that ladder . . . in which case the same reasoning applies. If you don't want it, you can sign it over to Brian Junior. Or whatever. Mr. Johnson, you *know* I don't have any relatives – so why not let it run easy?"

Before Gramp could reply, Mrs. Smith came in, dressed in her best and smiling (and had been crying, Lazarus felt certain). She extended her hand. "Mr. Bronson! We are all so proud of you!"

Her voice, her fragrance, the touch of her hand, her proud joy, all hit Lazarus in the gut; his careful conditioning was swept away. (Maureen beloved, it's lucky that I'm being sent away at once. Safer for you, better all around. But I did it to make you proud of me, and now my cup runneth over – and please ask me to sit down before Gramp notices the tilt of my kilt!)

"Thank you, Mrs. Smith. I just stopped by to say thank you and good-bye – and good night, too, as I'm shipping out early tomorrow morning."

"Oh, do please sit down! Coffee at least, and the children will want to say good-bye to you, too."

An hour later he was still there and still happier – happy all through. The candy had been opened after he had presented it to Carol for all of them. Lazarus had drunk much coffee thick with cream and sugar and had eaten a hefty slice of home-baked white cake with chocolate icing, then accepted a second while admitting that he had not eaten since breakfast – then protested when Maureen wanted to jump up and cook. They reached a compromise under which Carol went out to make a sandwich for him.

"It's been a confusing day," he explained, "and I haven't had time to eat. You caused me to change plans, Mr. Johnson."

"I did, Ted? How?"

"You know – I think I've told you both – that I planned to make a business trip to San Francisco leaving the first of July. Then this happens – Congress declaring war – and I decided to make the trip at once, settle my affairs there – then enlist. When I saw you I was all set to leave, packed and everything – and you made me realize that the Kaiser wouldn't wait while I took care of private affairs. So I joined up at once." Lazarus managed to look sheepish. "My packed grip is still out in the car, going nowhere."

Ira Johnson looked pained. "I didn't mean to rush you, Ted. 'Twouldn't have hurt to take a few days to wind up your affairs; they can't organize an army overnight. I know, I saw 'em try, in 'Ninety-eight. Mrrph. Perhaps I could make the trip for you? As your agent. Seeing that – Well, doesn't look like I'm going to be too busy."

"No, no! A million thanks, sir – but I hadn't been thinking straight. Thinking 'peacetime' instead of 'wartime' until you got me back on the rails. I went to Western Union and wrote a night letter to my broker in Frisco, telling him what I wanted him to do; then I wrote a note appointing him my attorney-in-fact and got it notarized and went to the downtown post office and registered it to him. All done, everything taken care of." Lazarus was enjoying the improvisation so much he almost believed it. "Then I went downstairs and enlisted. But that grip – Do you suppose you could put it in your garret? I won't be taking a grip to soldier. Just a few toilet articles."

"I'll take care of it, Mr. Bronson!" said Brian Junior. "In my room!"

"In *our* room," George corrected. "*We'll* take care of it."

"Hold it, boys. Ted? Would it break your heart if you lost that grip?"

"Not at all, Mr. Johnson. Why?"

"Then take it with you. But when you get back to your flat tonight, pack it differently. You put in white shirts and stiff collars, no doubt. You won't need those. If you've got any work shirts, take those. Be sure to take a pair of well-broken-in high shoes you can march in. Socks – all you own. Underwear. It's my guess – based on sad experience – that they won't have enough uniforms right away. Confusion, and lots of it. You may be soldiering for a month or more in what you carry with you."

"I think," Mrs. Smith said seriously, "that Father is right, Mr. Bronson. Mr. Smith – Lieutenant Smith, my husband – was saying something like it before he left. He left without waiting for his telegram – it came hours later – because he said he knew that there would be confusion at first." Her mouth twitched. "Although he said it more forcefully."

"Daughter, no matter how Brian put it, it wasn't forceful enough. Ted will be lucky if his beans are on time. Any man who can tell his right foot from his left will be grabbed and made acting corporal; they won't care how he's dressed. But *you* care, Ted – so take along clothes you might wear on a farm. And shoes – comfortable shoes that won't put blisters on you the first mile. Mmm – Ted, do you know the coldcream trick? To use on your feet when you know you might have your shoes on for a week or more?"

"No, sir," Lazarus answered. (Gramp, you taught it to me once before – or maybe "after" – and it works, and I've never forgotten it.)

"If possible, have your feet clean and dry. Smear your feet all over and especially between your toes with cold cream. Or Vaseline, carbolated is best. Use *lots*, a thick layer. Then put on socks – clean if possible, dirty if you must, but don't skip them – and put your boots on. When you first stand up, it feels as if you'd stepped into a barrel of soft soap. But your feet will thank you for it and you won't get jungle rot between your toes. Or not as much. Take care of your feet, Ted, and keep your bowels open."

"Father."

"Daughter, I'm talking to a *soldier* – telling him things that may save his life. If the children can't hear such things, send them up to bed."

"I think it is time," Maureen answered, "to get the younger ones quieted down, at least."

"I don't have to go to bed!"

"Woodie, you do exactly what your mother tells you to and no back talk – or I'll bend a poker over your bottom. That's standing orders until your father gets home from the war."

"I'm going to stay up till Private Bronson leaves! Papa said I could."

"Mrrph. I'll discuss the logical impossibility of that with a club; it's the only way to make you understand it. Maureen, I suggest that we start with the youngest, let 'em say good-bye in turn, and then march straight up to bed. Which winds up in due course with me walking Ted to his streetcar stop."

"But I was going to drive Uncle Ted home!"

Lazarus judged that it was time to speak up. "Brian, thank you. But let's not give your mother something extra to worry about tonight. The trolley takes me almost straight home . . . and from tomorrow on I won't even have streetcars; I'll walk."

"That's right," agreed Gramp. "He'll march. '*Hay* foot, *straw* foot! – heads up and look proud!' Ted, his father made Brian Sergeant of the Guard until he gets back, charged with internal security of this household."

"Then he can't leave his post of duty to chauffeur a mere private, can he?"

"Not in the presence of the Officer of the Guard – me – and of the Officer of the Day, my daughter. Reminds me – While the young 'uns are kissing you good-bye, I want to dig out a couple of my old Army shirts; I think they'll fit you. If you don't mind hand-me-downs?"

"Sir, I will be proud and honoured to wear them!"

Mrs. Smith stood up. "I have something I must get for Mr. – Private Bronson, too. Nancy, will you bring down Ethel? And Carol, will you fetch Richard?"

"But Private Bronson hasn't eaten his sandwich!"

Lazarus said, "I'm sorry, Miss Carol. I've been too excited to eat. Uh, would you wrap it for me? I'll eat it the minute I'm back in my apartment – and it will make me sleep soundly."

"Do that, Carol," decided her mother. "Brian, will you fetch down Richard?"

After more backing and filling Lazarus told them all good-bye, in reverse order of seniority. He held Ethel for a moment and grinned at her baby smile, then kissed the top of her head and handed her back to Nancy, who took her upstairs and hurried back down. To kiss Richard, Lazarus had to get down on one knee. The child seemed unsure why this was happening but knew that it was a solemn occasion; he hugged Lazarus tightly and smeared his cheek with a kiss.

Woodie then kissed him – for the first and only time, but Lazarus no longer felt bothered by touching "himself" as this little boy was not himself but simply an individual from whom he derived some scattered memories in an odd concatenation. He was no longer tempted to strangle him – or not often.

Woodie used the unaccustomed intimacy to whisper: "Those chessmen are *really* ivory?"

"Really truly ivory. Ivory and ebony, just like the keys on your Mama's piano."

"Gee, that's *keen*! Look, when you come back, Uncle Private Bronson, I'll let you play with them. Anytime."

"And I'll beat you, Sport."

"Says you! Well, so long. Don't take any wooden nickels."

Little Marie kissed him with tears in her eyes, then fled from the room. George kissed him on the cheek and muttered, "You be careful, Uncle Ted," and left also. Brian Junior said, "I'll take real good care of your automobile – I'll keep it shined just the way you do," then hesitated – suddenly kissed his cheek and left, leading Richard.

Carol had his sandwich, neatly wrapped in waxed paper and tied with a ribbon. He thanked her and put it into an outer coat pocket. She placed her hands on his shoulders, stood on tiptoes and whispered, "There's a note in it for you!" – kissed his cheek and left quickly.

Nancy took her place and said quietly, "The note is from both of us. We're going to pray for you every night when we pray for Papa." She glanced at her mother, then put her arms around his shoulders and kissed him on the mouth, a firm peck. "That's not good-bye but au revoir!" She left even more quickly than her sister, head high and moving like her mother.

Mrs. Smith stood up, said quietly, "Father?" – and waited.

"No."

"Then turn your back."

"Mrrph. Yes." Mr. Johnson studied the pictures on the wall.

With a soft rustle Mrs. Smith came close to Lazarus, looked up at him, held up a little book. "This is for you."

It was a vest-pocket New Testament; she held it opened at the fly leaf. He took it and read the original inscription, somewhat faded:

"*To Maureen Johnson, Good Friday 1892, for perfect attendance.* Matthew vii 7"

And under this, in fresh and crisp Spencerian script:

To Private Theodore Bronson
Be true to self and country.
Maureen J. Smith
April 6, 1917

Lazarus gulped. "I will treasure it and keep it with me, Mrs. Smith."

"Not 'Mrs. Smith,' Theodore – 'Maureen'." She put up her arms.

Lazarus stuffed the little book into his breast pocket, put his arms around her, met her lips.

For a long moment her kiss was firm and warm but chaste. Then she moaned almost inaudibly, her body softened and came strongly against him, her lips opened, and she kissed him in a fashion that Lazarus could barely believe even as he answered it in kind – a kiss that promised everything she could give.

After some uncountable eternity she whispered against his lips: "Theodore . . . take care of yourself. Come back to us."

DA CAPO

VI

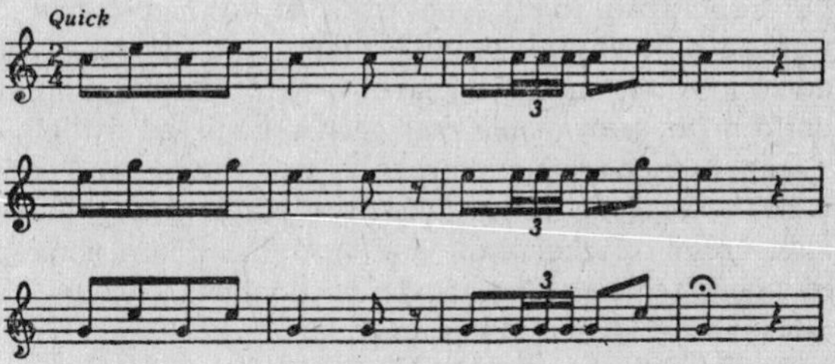

Camp Funston, Kansas

Dear Twins and Family,

Surprise! Meet Corporal Ted Bronson, acting sergeant and the meanest drillmaster in the whole National Army of the United States. No, I have *not* scrambled my circuits. I temporarily lost track of a basic principle of evasive action, i.e., the best place to hide a needle is in a stack of needles . . . and the best place to avoid the horrors of war is in an army. Since none of you has ever seen a war, or even an army, I must explain.

I had (foolishly) planned to avoid this war by running away to South America. But South American is a place where I could not possibly pass for a native, no matter how well I spoke the language – and it is loaded with German agents who would suspect me of being an American agent and might arrange some nasty accident for Ol' Buddy Boy, bless his innocent heart. And the girls there have beautiful flashing eyes, suspicious duennas, and fathers who love to shoot gringos up to no good. Unhealthy.

But if I stayed in the United States and tried to stay *out* of the Army – one slip and I wind up behind cold stone walls, eating miserable food, and making little rocks out of big ones. Unappealing.

But in wartime the Army gets the best of everything – aside from a mild hazard of getting shot at. The latter can be avoided.

How? This is not yet the era of total war, and an army offers innumerable bolt holes for a coward (me) to avoid unpleasant dangers from strangers. In this era only a small part of an army gets shot at. (An even smaller part gets hit, but I don't plan to take that risk.) At this here-&-now land warfare is fought in certain locations, and there are endless army jobs *not* in those places, where (despite a military uniform) an army man is really just a privileged civilian.

I am in such a job and probably won't move until the war is over. Someone has to take these brave, young, innocent lads, fresh off the farm, and turn them into something resembling soldiers. A man who can do this is so valuable that officers are reluctant to let him go.

So I'm full of that old fighting spirit and won't have to fight. I teach, instead – close-order drill, extended drill, markmanship and care of the rifle, bayonet, barehanded combat, field hygiene, anything. My "amazing" aptitude in military matters caused surprise, me being a recruit with "no military experience." (How could I admit that Gramp taught me to shoot five years after the end of this war and that I first handled these same weapons as a high school cadet ten years from now that my military experience is scattered over the next hundred years plus a little now and then for centuries more?)

But a rumour hints that I was once a soldat in the French Foreign Legion, a corps of one of our Allies, made up of cut-throats, thieves, and escaped convicts, and famous for their go-to-hell way of fighting – possibly a deserter from it and almost certainly under another name. I discourage this canard by becoming surly if anyone gets inquisitive and only occasionally make the mistake of saluting French style (palm forward) and correct it at once – but everybody knows I "polly-voo" because my knowledge of the French language had a lot to do with my change from "acting corporal" to real corporal assigned to instruction, and now greasing for sergeant. There are French and British officers and sergeants here to teach us trench warfare. All the French here are supposed to speak English – but the English they speak these Kansas and Missouri plough jockeys can't understand. So in slips lazy Lazarus as liaison. Me and one French sergeant almost add up to one good instructor.

Without that French sergeant I *am* a good instructor . . . when I am allowed to teach what I know. But only in unarmed combat am I allowed to, because unarmed hand-to-hand fighting does not change through the ages; only the name changes, and it has only one rule: Do it first, do it fast, do it dirtiest.

But take bayonet fighting – A bayonet is a knife on the end of a gun, and the two parts add up to the Roman pilum, used two thousand years earlier and not new even then. One would expect the art of bayonet fighting, in 1917, to be perfect.

But it isn't. The "Book" teaches parries but not counters – yet a counter is as fast as a parry, far more deceptive, and fatally confusing to a man who has never heard of one. And there are other things – There was (will be) a war in the twenty-sixth century Greg. in which the use of the bayonet became a high art and I was an unwilling participant until I managed to duck out. So one morning here, on a bet, I demonstrated that I could take on and never be touched by a U.S. Army regular sergeant-instructor – then a British one – and then a French one.

Was I allowed to teach what I had demonstrated? No. I mean "*Hell, No!*" I wasn't doing it "by the Book," and my "smart-alec" attempt almost lost me my cushy job. So I went back to doing it by the sacred "Book."

But this book (used at Plattsburg where my father – and yours – trained) is not bad. In bayonet fighting its emphasis is on aggressiveness, which is okay within its limits; the bayonet is a horror weapon in the hands of a man eager to close and kill – and that may be all these kids have time to learn. But I would hate to see these pink-cheeked, brave lads go up against some old, tired, pessimistic twenty-sixth-century mercenaries whose sole purpose is to stay alive while their opponents die.

These kids can win a war, they *will* win this war, they *did* win it from when you are. But an unnecessary number are going to die.

I love these kids. They are young and eager and gallant and terribly anxious to get "Over There" and prove that one American can lick any six Germans. (Not true. The ratio isn't even one to one. The Germans are veterans and don't suffer from "sportsmanship" or any other illusions. But these green kids will keep on fighting and dying until the Germans give up.)

But they are so *young!* Laz and Lor, most of them are younger than you two, some *much* younger. I don't know how many lied about their ages – but lots of them don't have to shave. Sometimes at night I'll hear one crying in his cot, homesick for his mammy. But next day he'll be trying, hard as ever. We don't have enough desertions to matter; these boys *want* to fight.

I try not to think about how useless this war is.

It's a matter of perspective. Minerva proved to me one night (when she was still following the profession of computer) that all here-&-nows are equal and "the present" is simply whatever here-&-now one is using. By my "proper" here-&-now (where I would be if I hadn't hearkened to the wild geese – home on Tertius) – by *that* here-&-now these eager, puppylike boys are long dead and the worms have eaten them; this war and its terrible aftermath are ancient history, no worry of mine.

But I'm *here*, and it's happening *now*, and I feel it.

These letters become more difficult to write and to send. Justin, you want detailed accounts, written on the spot, of all that I do, to add to that pack of lies you edited. Photoreduction and etching are now impossible. I am sometimes allowed to leave camp for a day, which is just long enough to get to the nearest large town, Topeka (circa 160 kms. round trip), but always on a Sunday when businesses are closed, so I have not had a chance to work up a connection to use a laboratory in Topeka – assuming that there is one with the equipment I need, a doubtful point. I would let letters pile up in a lockbox (since it does not matter when I Delay Mail them) – but banks are never open on Sundays. So a handwritten letter, not too long and bulky, is the most I can manage – whenever I can lay hands on nesting envelopes (also difficult now) – and hope that paper and ink won't oxidize too much over the centuries.

'I've started a diary, one which makes no mention of

Tertius and such (this letter would get me locked up as crazy!) but is simply a daily recital of events. I can mail it, when it is full, to Gramp Ira Johnson to hold for me; then after the war is over and I have time and privacy, I can use it to write the sort of commentary you want, and take time to miniaturize and stablize a long message. The problems of a time-tripping historiographer are odd and awkward. One Welton fine-grain memory cube would record all I could say over the next ten years – except that I would have no use for one even if I had it; the technology to use it is lacking.

By the way – Ishtar, did you plant a recorder in my belly? You are a darling, dear, but sometimes a devious darling – and there is *something* there. It doesn't bother me, and I might never have noticed it had not a physician noticed it the day I joined this Army. He brushed the matter off – but later I conducted my own examination by touch. There *is* an implant there – and not what Ira says I'm full of. It might be one of those artificial organs you rejuvenators are reluctant to discuss with your "children." But I suspect that it is a Welton cube with an ear hooked to it and a ten-year power supply; it's about the right size.

But why didn't you *ask* me, dear, instead of sneaking up on me with a Mickey? It is not true that I always say No to a civil request; that is a canard started by Laz and Lor. Justin could have gotten Tamara to ask me, and no one has ever learned how to say No to Tamara. But Justin will pay for this: To hear what I say and what is said in my presence, he is going to have to listen to *ten years* of belly rumblings.

No, durn it, Athene will filter out incidental noise and supply him with a dated and meaningful printout. There is no justice. And no privacy, either. Athene, haven't I always been good to you, dear? Make Justin pay for his prank.

I haven't seen my first family since I enlisted. But when I get a long-enough pass I am going to Kansas City and visit them. My status as a "hero" carries privileges a "civilian young bachelor" cannot enjoy; the mores relax a bit in wartime, and I'll be able to spend time with them. They have been very good to me: a letter almost every day, cookies or a cake weekly. The latter I share, reluctantly; the former I treasure.

I wish it were as easy to get letters from my Tertius family.
Basic Message, Repeated: Rendezvous is 2 August 1926, ten T-years after drop. Last figure is "six" – not "nine."

All my love,
Corporal Ted ("Ol' Buddy Boy") Bronson

* * *

Dear Mr. Johnson,

And all your family – Nancy, Carol, Brian, George, Marie, Woodie, Dickie Boy, Baby Ethel, and Mrs. Smith. I cannot say how touched I am that this orphan has been "adopted for the duration" by the Smith family, and to hear that it is confirmed by Captain Smith. In my heart you all have been "my family" since that sad & happy night you sent me off to war loaded with presents and good wishes and my head filled with your practical advice – and my heart closer to tears than I dared let anyone see. To be told by Mrs. Smith – with a sentence quoted from a letter from her husband, the Captain – that I truly *am* "adopted" – well, I'm close to tears again, and noncoms are not supposed to show such weakness.

I have not looked up Captain Smith. I caught the hint in your letter – but, truly, I did not need it; I have been soldiering long enough to realize that an enlisted man does not presume in such fashion. I am almost as certain that the Captain will not look me up – for reasons I don't need to explain as you have soldiered far more than the Captain and I combined. It was most sweetly thoughtful of Mrs. Smith to suggest it – but can you make her understand I *can't* look up a captain socially? And why she should not urge her husband to look up a noncom?

If you can't make her understand this (possible, since the Army is a different world), perhaps this will suffice: Camp Funston is *big* – and no transportation for me other than shanks' mare. Call it an hour for the round trip if I swing out my heels. Add five minutes with the Captain when I find him – *if* I find him. You know our stepped-up routine, I sent you a copy. Show her that there just *isn't time*, all day long, for me to do this.

But I do appreciate her kind thoughts.

Please give Carol my heartiest thanks for the brownies.

They are as good as her mother makes; higher praise I cannot give. "Were," I should say, as they disappeared into hollow legs, mine and others (my buddies are a greedy lot). If she wants to marry a long, lanky Kansas farm boy with a big appetite, I have one at hand who will marry her sight unseen on the basis of those brownies.

This place is no longer the Mexican fire drill I described in my earliest letters. In place of stovepipes we now have real trench mortars, the wooden guns have disappeared, and even the greenest conscripts are issued Springfields as soon as they've mastered squads east and west and have learned to halt more or less together.

But it remains hard as the mischief to teach them to use those rifles "by the Book." We have two types of recruit: boys who have never fired a rifle, and others who boast that their pappies used to send them out to shoot breakfast and never allowed them but one shot. I prefer the first sort, even if a lad is unconsciously afraid and has to be taught not to flinch. At least he hasn't practised his mistakes, and I can teach him what the regular Army instructors taught me, and those three chevrons on my sleeve now insure that he listens.

But the country boy who is sure he knows it all (and sometimes is indeed a good shot) *won't listen.*

It's a chore to convince him that he is not going to do it *his* way; he is going to do it the *Army* way, and he had better learn to like it.

Sometimes these know-it-alreadys get so angry that they want to fight – me, not Huns. These are usually boys who haven't found out that I also teach unarmed combat. I've had to accommodate a couple of them, out behind the latrine after retreat. I won't box them; I have no wish to flatten my big nose against some cow-milking fist. But the idea of fighting rough-and-tumble, no rules, either makes their eyes glitter – or they decide to shake hands and forget it. If they go ahead with it, it doesn't last over two seconds as *I* don't want to get hurt.

I promised to tell you where and how I learned la savate and jujitsu. But it's a long story, not too nice in spots, one I should not put into a letter but wait until I have a pass that gives me time enough to visit Kansas City.

But I haven't had anyone offer to fight me for a least three months. One of the sergeant-instructors told me that he had heard that the recruits call me "Death" Bronson. I don't mind as long as it means peace and quiet when I'm off duty.

Camp Fun's-Town continues to have just two sorts of weather, too hot and dusty, too cold and muddy. I hear that the latter is good practice for France; the Tommies here claim that the worst hazard of this war is the danger of drowning in French mud. The poilus among us don't really argue it but blame the rain on artillery fire.

Bad as the weather may be in France, everyone wants to go there, and the second favourite topic of conversation is "When?" (No need to tell an old soldier the first.) Rumours of shipping out are endless and always wrong.

But I'm beginning to wonder. Am I going to be stuck here, doing the same things month after month while the war goes on elsewhere? What will I tell my children someday? Where did you fight the Big War, Daddy? Funston, Billy. What part of France is that, Daddy? Near Topeka, Billy – shut up and eat your oatmeal!

I would have to change my name.

It gets tiresome telling one bunch after another to stack arms and grab shovels. We've dug enough trenches in this prairie to reach from here to the moon, and I now know four ways to do it: the French way, the British way, the American way – and the way each new bunch of recruits does it, in which the revetments collapse – and then they want to know what difference it makes because General Pershing, once *we* get there, is going to break this trench-warfare stalemate and get those Huns on the run.

They may be right. But I have to teach what I'm told to teach. Till I'm white-haired, maybe.

I am pleased indeed to hear that you are in the Seventh Regiment; I know how much it means to you. But please don't disparage the Seventh Missouri by calling it the "home guards." Unless somebody gets a hammerlock on Hindenburg pretty soon, you may see a lot of action in this war.

But truthfully, sir, I hope you do not – and I think Captain Smith would agree with my reasoning. Someone *does* have to guard the home – and I mean a specific home on Benton Boulevard. Brian Junior isn't old enough to be the man of the family – I think Captain Smith would worry if you weren't there.

But I do understand how you feel. I hear that the only way

for a sergeant-instructor to get off this treadmill is to lose his stripes. Would you feel ashamed of me if I went absent over leave just long enough to get busted back to corporal... then did something else to lose those chevrons, too? I feel sure it would get me on the first troop train headed east.

You'd better not read that last to the rest of the family. An "Honorary Smith" had best find some other way.

My warmest respects to you and to Mrs. Smith,

My love to all the youngsters,
Ted Bronson "Smith"
(And *most* happy to be "adopted")

* * *

"Come in!"

"Sir, Sergeant Bronson reports to Captain Smith as ordered!" (Pop, I wouldn't have recognized you. But durned if you don't look just as you ought to. Only younger.)

"At ease, Sergeant. Close that door. Then sit down."

"Yes, sir." Lazarus did so, still mystified. He had not only never expected Captain Smith to get in touch with him, but he had refrained from asking for a pass long enough to let him go to Kansas City for two reasons: One, his father might be there that weekend – or, two, his father might *not* be there that weekend. Lazarus was not sure which was worse; he had avoided both.

Now a dog-robber type on a motorcycle with a sidecar had suddenly picked him up with orders to "Report to Captain Smith" – and it was not until he had done so that he knew that this "Captain Smith" was Captain Brian Smith.

"Sergeant, my father-in-law has told me quite a bit about you. And so has my wife."

There seemed to be no answer to that, so Lazarus looked sheepish and said nothing.

Captain Smith went on, "Oh, come, Sergeant, don't look embarrassed; this is man to man. My family has 'adopted' you, so to speak, and it meets with my heartiest approval. In fact it fits in with something the War Department is starting, through the Red Cross and the Y.M.C.A. and the churches, a programme to locate every man in uniform who does not get mail regularly and see to it that he does. Get a family to 'adopt him for the duration' in other words. Write to him, remember his birthday, send him little presents. What do you think of that?"

"Sir, it sounds good. What the Captain's family has done for me has certainly been good for *my* morale."

"I'm pleased to hear it. How would you organize such a programme? Speak up, don't be afraid to express you own ideas."

(Give me a desk and I'll make a career of it, Pop!) "Sir, the problem breaks down into two – No, three parts. Two of preparation, one of execution. First, locate the men. Second, at the same time, locate families willing to help. Third, bring them together. The first has to be done by the first sergeants." (The top kicks are going to love this – in a pig's eye.) "They will have to require their company clerks to check mail against the roster before handing it out. Uh, this must be speeded up; holding up mail call for any reason is not a good idea. But checking can't be left to platoon sergeants; they aren't set up for it and would slop it. It has to be at the point where the mail orderly delivers mail to each company clerk."

Lazarus thought. "But to make this work, if the Captain will pardon me, the Commanding General must tell his adjutant to require from each company, troop, and battery commander a report of how many pieces of mail each man under his command has received that week." (And a damnable invasion of privacy, and the sort of muliplication of clerical work that bogs down armies! The homesick ones *have* homes and *do* get mail. The loners don't want letters; they want women and whisky. The prairie dog pee they sell for whisky in this "dry" state has made a teetotaller of me.) "But that should not be separate paper work, Captain; it need only be a column of tally marks on the regular weekly report. Both company commanders and top sergeants are going to bellyache if it's too time-consuming – and the Commanding General would receive reports that would be mostly products of company clerks' imaginations. The Captain knows that, I feel sure."

Lazarus' father gave the grin that made him look like Teddy Roosevelt. "Sergeant, you have just caused me to revise a letter I'm preparing for the General. As long as I am assigned to 'Plans & Training' no new programme will add to the mountain of paper work if I can help it. I have been trying to sweat this one down to size, and you've shown me a way to do it. Tell me, why did you turn down officers' training when it was offered to you? Or don't tell me if you don't want to; it's your business."

(Pop, I'm going to have to lie to you – for I can't point out that a platoon leader has a life expectancy of around twenty minutes if he takes his platoon "over the top" and does it by the Book. What a war!) "Sir, look at it this way. Suppose I put in for it. A month to get it approved. Then three months at Benning, or Leavenworth, or wherever they're sending them. Then back here, or Bliss, or somewhere and I'll be assigned to recruits. Six months with them and we go overseas. More training behind the lines 'Over There' from what I hear. Adds up to about a year, and the war is over, and I haven't been in it."

"Mmm . . . you could be right. You want to go to France?"

"Yes, *sir!*" (Christ, *no!*)

"Just last Sunday, in K.C., my father-in-law told me that would be your answer. But you may not know, Sergeant, that the billet you are in will be just as frustrating . . . without the compensation of bars on your shoulders. Here in 'Plans & Training' we keep track of every enlisted instructor – and the ones who don't work we ship out . . . but the ones who *do* work out we hang onto like grim death.

"Except for one thing – " His father smiled again. "We have been asked – the polite word for 'ordered' – to supply some of our best instructors for that behind-the-lines training in France you mentioned. I know you qualify; I've made it a point to note the weekly reports on you ever since my father-in-law told me abcut you. Surprising proficiency for a man with no combat time . . . plus a slight tendency to be nonregulation about minor points, which – privately – I do not find a drawback; the utterly regulation soldier is a barracks soldier. Est-ce que vous parlez la langue française?"

"Oui, mon capitaine."

"Eh, bien! Peut-être vous avez enrôlé autrefois en la Légion Etrangère, n'est-ce pas?"

"Pardon, mon capitaine? Je ne comprends pas."

"Nor will I understand you if we talk three more words of it. But I'm studying hard, as I expect French to be my own ticket out of this dusty place. Bronson, forget that I asked that question. But I must ask one more and I want an absolutely straight answer. Is there any possibility *whatever* that any *French* authority might be looking for you? I don't give a tinker's dam what you may have done in the past, and neither does the War Department. But we must protect our own."

Lazarus barely hesitated. (Pop is telling me plain as print that if I am a deserter from the Foreign Legion – or have escaped from Devil's Island or any such – he's going to keep me out of French jurisdiction.) "Absolutely *none*, sir!"

"I'm relieved to hear it. There have been latrine rumours that Pop Johnson could neither confirm nor deny. Speaking of him – Stand up a moment. Now left face, please. And about face. Bronson, I'm convinced. I don't remember my wife's Uncle Ned, but I would give long odds that you are related to my father-in-law, and his theory certainly fits. Which makes us 'kinfolk' of some sort. After the war is over, perhaps we can dig into it. But I understand that my children call you 'Uncle Ted' . . . which seems close enough and suits me if it suits you."

"Sir, it does indeed! It's good to have a family, under any assumption."

"I think so. Just one more thing . . . and this you must forget once you go out that door. I think that a rocker for those chevrons will show up one of these days . . . and not long after you'll be given a short leave that you haven't requested. When that happens, don't start any continued stories. Comprenez-vous?"

"Mais oui, mon capitaine, certainement."

"I wish I could tell you that we will be in the same outfit; Pop Johnson would like that. But I can't. In the meantime please remember that I haven't told you anything."

"Captain, I've already forgotten it." (Pop thinks he's doing me a *favour!*) "Thank you, sir!"

"Not at all. Dismissed."

DA CAPO

VII

Staff Sergeant Theodore Bronson found Kansas City changed – uniforms everywhere, posters everywhere. Uncle Sam stared out at him: "I want *you* for the United States Army." A Red Cross nurse was shown holding a wounded man in a stretcher as if he were a baby, with the one word: "GIVE." A sign on a restaurant said: "We Observe All Meatless, Wheatless, and Sweetless Days." Service flags were in many windows – he counted five stars on one, saw several with gold stars.

More traffic than he recalled and streetcars were crowded, many passengers in uniform – it seemed as if all of Camp Funston and every camp or fort within reaching distance had all been dumped into the city at once. Untrue, he knew, but the train he had dozed in most of last night had been so jammed that it seemed true.

That "Khaki Special" had been almost as dirty as a cattle train and even slower; it had sidetracked again and again in favour of freights, and once for a troop train. Lazarus arrived in Kansas City late in the morning, tired and filthy – having left camp clean and rested. But he had his battered old grip with him and planned to correct both conditions before seeing his "adopted" family.

Waving a five-dollar bill in front of the railroad station got him a taxi, but the hackie insisted on picking up three more passengers going south after asking what direction Lazarus was going. The taxicab was a Ford landaulet like his own, but in much worse condition. The glass partition between front and back seats (the feature that made it a "limousine") had been removed, and the collapsible half-top of the rear compartment appeared to have collapsed for the last time. But with five in it, plus baggage on knees, ventilation was welcome.

The driver said, "Sergeant, you were first. Where to?"

Lazarus said that he wanted to find a hotel room out south, near Thirty-first.

"You're an optimist – hard enough to find one downtown. But we'll try. Drop these other gentlemen first, maybe?"

Eventually he wound up near Thirty-first and Main – "Permanent and Transient – all rooms & apts. with bath." The driver said, "This joint costs too much – but it's this or go back downtown. No, keep your money till we see if they can take you. You about to go overseas?"

"So I hear."

"So your fare is a dollar; I don't take no tips from a man about to go over – I got a boy 'Over there.' Le'me talk to that clerk."

Ten minutes later Lazarus was luxuriating in the first tub bath he had had since April 6, 1917. Then he slept three hours. When his inner alarm woke him, he dressed in clean clothes from skin out, his best uniform – the breeches he had retailored for a smarter peg at the knee. He went down to the lobby and telephoned his family's home.

Carol answered and squealed. "*Oh!* Mama, it's Uncle Ted!"

Maureen Smith's voice was serenely warm. "Where are you, Sergeant Theodore? Brian Junior wants to go fetch you home."

"Please tell him thanks, Mrs. Smith, but I'm in a hotel at the Thirty-first Street car line; I'll be there before he could get here – if I'm welcome."

"'Welcome'? What a way for our adopted soldier to talk. You don't belong in a hotel; you must stay *here*. Brian – my husband, I mean, the Captain – told us to expect you and that you were to stay with us. Did he not tell you so?"

"Ma'am, I've seen the Captain just once, three weeks ago. So far as I know, he doesn't know I'm on leave." Lazarus added, "I don't want to put you out."

"Pish and tush, Sergeant Theodore, let's have no more of that. At the beginning of the war we changed the maid's room downstairs – my sewing room, where you played chess with Woodrow – into a guest room, so that the Captain could bring a brother officer home on a weekend. Must I tell my husband that you refused to sleep there?"

(Maureen my love, that's putting the cat too close to the canary! I won't sleep; I'll lie awake thinking about you upstairs – surrounded by kids and Gramp.) "Mrs. Captain generous hostess ma'am, I'll be utterly delighted to sleep in your sewing room."

"That's better, Sergeant. For a moment I thought Mama was going to have to spank."

Brian Junior was waiting at the Brenton car stop, with George as footman, and with Carol and Marie in the back seat. George grabbed the grip and took charge of it; Marie shrilled, "My, doesn't Uncle Ted look *pretty!*" and Carol corrected her:

"Handsome, Marie. Soldiers look handsome and smart, not 'pretty.' Isn't that right, Uncle Ted?"

Lazarus picked the smaller girl up by her elbows and kissed her cheek, set her down. "Technically correct, Carol – but 'pretty' suits me just fine if Marie thinks I am. Quite a welcoming committee – do I run along behind?"

"You sit in the tonneau with the girls," Brian Junior ruled. "But look at this first!" He pointed. "A *foot* throttle! Isn't that bully?"

Lazarus agreed, then took a few moments to inspect the car – in better shape than he had left it, shining and clean from spokes to top and with several new items besides the foot accelerator: a dressy radiator cap, rubber nonskids for the pedals, a tyre holder on the rear with a patent-leather cover for a spare tyre, a robe rail in the rear compartment with a lap robe folded neatly, and – finishing touch – a cut-glass bud vase with a single rose. "Is the engine kept as beautifully as the rest?"

George opened the hood. Lazarus looked and nodded approvingly. "It could take a white-glove inspection."

"That's exactly what Grandpa gives it," Brian declared. "He says if we don't take care of it, we can't use it."

"You do take care of it."

Lazarus arrived in royal splendour, one arm around a big little girl, the other around a small little girl. Gramp was waiting on the front porch, came down the walk to meet him, and Lazarus suddenly revised his mental image: The old soldier was in uniform and seemed a foot taller and ramrod straight – ribbons on his chest, chevrons on his sleeves, puttees most carefully rolled, campaign hat perched high and turned up slightly behind.

As Lazarus turned from handing Carol out, Marie having danced ahead, Gramp paused and threw Lazarus a sweeping Throckmartin salute. "Welcome home, Sergeant!"

Lazarus returned it as flamboyantly. "Thank you, Sergeant; I'm glad to be here." He added, "Mr. Johnson, you didn't tell me you were a supply sergeant."

"Somebody has to count the socks. I agreed to take – "

The rest was lost to Woodie's explosive arrival. "Hey, Uncle Sergeant! You're going to play chess with me!"

"Sure, Sport," Lazarus agreed, his attention distracted by two other things: Mrs. Smith at the open door, and a service flag in the parlour window. Three stars – *Three?*

Then Gramp was urging him in with something about this being a drill night so supper would be early. Nancy kissed him, openly and without glancing first for her mother's approval – then Dickie had to be picked up and kissed, and Baby Ethel (*walking!*), and at last Maureen gave him her slender hand, drew him to her, and brushed his cheek with her lips. "Sergeant Theodore . . . it is so *good* to have you home."

Supper was a noisy, well-run circus, with Gramp presiding in lieu of his son-in-law, while his daughter ran things with serene dignity from the other end and did not get up once Lazarus placed her chair under her and took his seat of honour on her right. Her three oldest daughters did all that was necessary. Ethel sat in a highchair on her mother's left with George helping her – Lazarus learned that this duty rotated among the five eldest.

It was a lavish meal for wartime, with hot, golden cornbread replacing white bread, this being a wheatless day – and firmest discipline (administered by Nancy and Brian Junior) required that every morsel accepted must be eaten, with admonitions about hungry Belgians. Lazarus did not care what he ate but remembered to compliment the cooks (three), and tried to answer all that was said to him – nearly impossible as Brian and George wanted to tell about their troop's drive to collect walnut shells and peach pits and how many it took for each gas mask, and Marie had to be allowed to boast that she could knit just as well as George could and she did not either drop stitches! – and how many squares it took to make a blanket, while Gramp wanted to talk shop with Lazarus and had to be stern to get a word in edgewise.

Maureen Smith seemed to find it unnecessary to talk. She smiled and looked happy, but it seemed to Lazarus that there was tension under her self-control – the ages-old strain of Penelope. (For me, darling? No, of course not. I wish I could tell you that Pop *will* come back, unharmed. But how could I make you believe that I *know?* You're going to have to sweat it out the way Penelope did. I'm sorry, my love). "Excuse me, Carol – I missed that."

"I said it's perfectly *horrid* that you have to go back so soon! When you're just about to go 'Over There.' "

"But it's quite a lot, Carol, in wartime. It's just that getting here and getting back eats up so much time, I'm not entitled to special privileges; I don't know that I am about to ship out."

There was silence around the table, and the older boys exchanged glances.

Ira Johnson broke it by saying gently, "Sergeant, the children know what a pass in the middle of the week means. But they don't talk; they are disciplined. My son-in-law decided – wisely, I think – not to keep things from them unnecessarily."

"But, Grandpa, when Papa has leave, *he* doesn't go back next day. It's not fair."

"That's because," Brian Junior said widely, "Papa usually rides with Captain Bozell in that big ol' Marmon Six and they burn up the road. Staff Sergeant Uncle Ted, *I* could drive you back to camp. Then you wouldn't have to leave till late tomorrow night."

"Thank you, Brian – but I don't think we'd better. If I catch the train we call the 'Reveille Special' tomorrow evening, I'm safe even if the train is a bit late, and this is one time I'm not going to risk being over leave."

"I agree with Sergeant Bronson," Gramp added, "and that settles it, Brian. Ted can't risk being late. I see that I had better move along, too. Daughter, if I may be excused?"

"Certainly, Father."

"Sergeant Johnson, may I drive you to your parade ground? Or wherever it is?"

"To the Armory. No, no, Ted, my captain picks me up and brings me home; he and I go early and stay late. Mrrph. Why don't you take Maureen for a spin? She hasn't been out of the house for a week; she's getting pale."

"Mrs. Smith? I'd be honoured."

"We'll all go!"

"George," his grandfather said firmly, "the idea is to give your mother an hour free of the pressure and noise of children."

"Sergeant Ted promised to play chess with me!"

"Woodie, I heard what he said. He did not set a time . . . and he'll be here tomorrow."

"And he promised to take me to Electric Park a long, long, *long* time ago, and he never did!"

"Woodie, I'm sorry about that," Lazarus answered, "but the war came along before the park opened. We may have to wait until the war is over."

"But you said – "

"Woodrow," his mother said firmly, "stop that. This is Sergeant Theodore's leave, not yours."

"And get that sulky look off your face," added his grandfather, "before we form a regimental square and have you flogged around the flagpole. Nancy? Charge-of-quarters, dear."

"But – " The oldest girl shut up.

"Father, Nancy's young man is about to reach his birthday and is not going to wait to be drafted, I think I told you. So some of the young people are giving him a surprise party tonight."

"Oh, yes – slipped my mind. Fine young man, Ted; you would approve of him. Correction, Nancy; you're off duty. Carol?"

"Carol and I can take care of anything," Brian answered. "Can't we, Carol? My night to wash, Marie wipes, George's turn to put away. Bedtimes by the schedule, emergency telephone numbers on the blackboard – we know the standing orders."

"May I be excused, too, then?" said Nancy. "Staff Sergeant Ted – you *will* be here tomorrow. Won't you?"

Lazarus went out to the curb to meet Gramp's militia captain. When he came in, Maureen had gone upstairs. He grabbed the chance to freshen up in the bath off the quondam sewing room. Fifteen minutes later he was handling Mrs. Smith into the front seat of the landaulet, himself dizzied by her wonderful fragrance. Had she managed to bathe again in twenty minutes or so? It seemed like it; she had certainly changed clothes. These wartime styles were startling; as he handed her in Lazarus caught a glimpse not only of trim ankle but quite a lot of shapely calf. He was shaken by the thrill it gave him.

How long would this dress cycle last? While he cranked the

car, he tried to quiet himself by thinking about it. Corsets disappeared right after this war, and skirts went up and up all during the Torrid Twenties, the "Jazz Age." Then women's styles varied all through this century but with a steady trend toward letting men see more and more of "what they were fighting for." But social nudity, even in swimming, did not become really common until the end of the century, so he seemed to recall. Then a puritan reaction the following century – a horrid time he had fled from.

What would Maureen think if he tried to tell her any of it?

The engine caught; he got in beside her. "Where would you like to go, Mrs. Smith?"

"Oh, out south. Somewhere quiet."

"South it is." Lazarus glanced at the setting sun, turned on his headlights. He made a U-turn and headed south.

"But my name is not 'Mrs. Smith,' Theodore . . . when we are alone."

"Thank you . . . Maureen." Straight out to Thirty-ninth – then over to the Paseo? Or Prospect and out as far as Swope Park? Would she let him take her that far? Oh, for a thousand miles of open road and Maureen beside me!

"I like the way you say my name, Theodore. Do you remember where you took the children for a picnic not long before the war started?"

"Near the Blue River. You want to go there, Matthew?"

"Yes. If you don't remember the way, I can guide you; I suggested it for that picnic."

"We'll find it."

"It need not be that spot . . . but somewhere quiet – and private. Where you need not give your attention to driving."

(Hey! Maureen, my darling, you don't want us to be *too* private – I might shock you dreadfully. Private enough for a good-bye kiss – fine! Then let's deliver you home safe and sound. You are *this* century, my sweet! I'd rather have one kiss – and your love and respect – than entice you into more and have you think of me with regret. I decided that many months ago. You darling.)

"I should turn here?"

"Yes. Theodore, Brian Junior said that the new throttle he installed made it possible to drive with one hand."

"Yes, that's true."

"Then *do* drive with one hand. Is that plain enough, or must I be still more bold?"

Cautiously he put his arm across her shoulders. She promptly reached up, took his hand, pulled it down, and pressed it to her breast, saying quietly, "We haven't time to be shy, dear Theodore. Don't be afraid to touch me."

Firm-soft breast. Nipple erect to his touch. She shivered and got closer to him, again pressed her hand to his and gave a tiny moan. Lazarus said huskily, "I love you, Maureen."

She answered, just loud enough to be heard by him over the engine noise. "We have loved each other since the night we met. We simply could not say so."

"Yes. I didn't dare tell you."

"You would never have told me, Theodore. So I had to be bold and let you know that I feel it, too." She added, "The turn is just ahead, I think."

"I think so too. I'll need both hands to drive that lane."

"Yes," she agreed, surrendering his arm, "but only till we get there. Then I want *both* your arms . . . and *all* your attention."

"Yes!" He drove in carefully, avoiding ruts, until the lane widened into the level grassy spot he remembered. There he turned the car full circle, in part to head it out but primarily to see that no one else was there. His headlights picked up nothing but grass and trees – good! (Or was it good? Oh, my darling, do you know what you are doing?)

He switched off the lights, stopped the engine, set the hand brake. Maureen came right into his arms; her mouth sought his, opened wide to him. For long moments they needed no words; her mouth, her hands were as eager as his and even bolder, urging him on.

Presently she chuckled happily against his lips and whispered, "Surprised? But I can't say a proper good-bye to my warrior with bloomers on . . . so I took them off when I went upstairs, and my corset, too. Don't hold back, dear one; you can't harm me – I'm expecting."

"What did you say?"

"Theodore, must I always be the one with bold words and bold actions? I am pregnant, seven weeks now. Certain."

"Oh." He added thoughtfully, "This seat is narrow."

"I hear that the young people sometimes take the back seat out and put it on the ground. Or do chiggers worry you? Audacity, darling, a warrior must be audacious – so says my father, and my husband agrees. There is a lap rug back there, too."

(Maureen, my love, there is no doubt where I got my own audacity – or my ruttiness. From *you*, darling). "If you'll let go of me, I'll get them out. I'm not afraid of chiggers – nor of the loveliest woman I've ever held in my arms. I just have trouble believing it."

"I'll help!"

She was out of the car without waiting; he slid across the seat and followed her. She opened the tonneau door – and stopped. Then she said loudly and happily, "Woodrow, you're a scamp! Sergeant Theodore! See who is sleeping in the back seat!" As she spoke, she fumbled behind her, trying to reach buttons of his that she had unbuttoned. Lazarus quickly took over the task.

"Sergeant Ted promised to take me to Electric Park!"

"That's where we're going, darling, we're almost there. Now tell Mama – Shall we take you home and put you to bed? Or are you big enough to stay awake and go to Electric Park?"

"Yes, Sport," Lazarus agreed. "Home? Or Electric Park?" (Maureen, did Gramp teach you to lie? Or is it genius? I not only love you, I admire you. Pershing should have you on his staff.) He hastily refastened buttons at the back of her dress.

"Huh? Electric Park!"

"Then settle back down and we'll have you there in no time."

"I want to ride in front!"

"Sport, you can ride in back to Electric Park. Or ride in back till we get you home and into bed. I won't drive with three in the front seat."

"Brian does!"

"Let's go home, Mrs. Smith. Woodie doesn't know who's driving this car – he must be *quite* sleepy."

"I am not either! I had a nap. All right, I'll ride in back – to Electric Park."

"Mrs. Smith?"

"We'll go to Electric Park, Sergeant Theodore. If Woodrow will lie down and try to get another nap."

Woodie promptly lay down; they closed him in and Lazarus got them out of there. Once there was enough engine noise to blanket her words, she said, "I must telephone. Back where we turned off, you'll find a drugstore farther along – that's on our way to Electric Park."

"Right away. How much do you think he heard?"

"I think he was asleep until I opened the door. But nothing of importance if he was not and would understand less. Don't worry, Theodore – audacity, always audacity."

"Maureen, you should be a soldier. A general."

"I would rather be loved by soldiers . . . and I am, and it makes me wonderfully happy. Now you can drive with one hand again."

"That's just glass, he can see us."

"Theodore, you can touch me without putting an arm around me. I shall sit up straight and pretend to ignore whatever you find to do. But I am a *very* frustrated woman – and I want to be *touched*. By you." She chuckled. "Aren't we a pair of ninnies?"

"I suppose so. But I'm not laughing." Lazarus squeezed her thigh. "I'm too frustrated."

"Oh, but you *must* laugh, Theodore." She pulled up her skirt, moved his hand onto bare thigh above round garters. "When you have as many children as I have, you *must* laugh. Or go crazy." She pushed her skirt down over his hand.

He caressed her warm smooth skin; she eased her thighs and invited more. "I guess it *is* funny," he admitted. "Two full-grown adults outflanked by a six-year-old."

"Only five Theodore. Not six until November." She squeezed his hand between plump thighs, then relaxed. "How well I remember. Biggest baby I've had, eight pounds . . . and more trouble than all the rest put together, and always a scamp and always my favourite and I try never to let it show – and you must not tell on me – that Woodrow is my favourite, I mean; I'm not afraid of your telling anything else. I know my reputation is safe with you."

"It is."

"I knew it or would never have plotted to take you out there. But 'reputation' is all it is; now you know what a hussy I am under my mask. But I cultivate a good reputation most carefully . . . for my children. For my husband."

"You said 'plotted.' "

"Weren't you sure of it? I knew at once, when I learned how short your time is, that I had exactly one chance to get you alone and make you realize that I want you to come back *with* your shield, not on it. There is only one way for a woman to tell a warrior that. So I enlisted Father's help to get you away from my swarm of children." She chuckled again. "But the worst scamp I have ruined my carefully plotted plans. For he *has*, dear one –

I don't dare risk it at home. I'll always regret that we didn't succeed . . . and I hope you will, too."

"Oh, I will, I do! You put Mr. Johnson up to suggesting this ride? Won't *he* suspect?"

"I'm sure he does. And disapproves. Of *me*, Theodore – not of you. But my reputation is as safe in his hands as in yours. Want to hear a sidesplitting joke? One that will make us laugh so hard that we'll forget how frustrated we are."

"I'll laugh if you do."

"Did you wonder how I knew the perfect place? Because I have been there before, Theodore, for the same purpose. But that's not the joke; this is: That rascal in the back seat was conceived there – on the very spot I was going to have you place me."

Lazarus thought a split second, then guffawed. "You're sure?"

"Utterly certain, sir. Ten feet from where you stopped. By that biggest black-walnut tree. I planned to have you place me on the same spot. I'm sentimental, Theodore; I *wanted* you to have me right where I conceived my favourite child. And the little imp stopped me! After I had become *quite* excited thinking about doing it with you on the very spot."

Lazarus thought a long moment – decided that he did want to know. "Who was he, Maureen?"

"What? *Oh!* I suppose I invited that so I shan't resent it. Theodore, I'm scarlet but not that scarlet. My husband, dear – *all* my children are his, no possibility of error. You have seen Brian only as an officer – but in private my husband is quite playful. So much so that I *never* wear bloomers when I go joyriding with him.

"It was February eighteenth, a Sunday, one I'll never forget. I kept a hired girl then; Nancy was too young to leave with the younger ones, and Brian was on the road, travelling, and wanted me to be ready for anything when he *was* in town, and he had just bought his first automobile.

"That Sunday was one of those false-spring days, and Brian decided to take me royriding. Just me. He had established a firm rule that some occasions were for all our family, some were just for Mama and Papa – a good policy in a large family, we think. So we got to that lovely picnic spot, pretty even in winter, and the ground was dry. We sat and lallygagged, and he had his hand where yours is – and he told me to take my clothes off."

"In *February*?"

"I didn't protest. It was at least sixty and no wind – but I would in much colder weather if my husband asked me to. So I did – all but shoes and stockings, and I looked like one of those French postcards you men buy in cigar stores. I didn't feel cold, I felt *grand* – I like to feel naughty, and Brian encourages me to, in private. He put down the back seat cushion – on that spot – and put a blanket on it. And had me. And that's when I got Woodrow. It had to be then because Brian was home just one day and that was the only time. Quite unusual, we usually squeeze in more loving, we enjoy it so." She chuckled. "When we were sure, Brian teased me about the iceman and the milkman and the postman – or was it the grocery boy? I teased right back that it could have been any of them – but the woodman got there first . . . in the woods. Right here, dear one; I won't be but a moment."

They all went in, as Woodie woke up (if he had slept; Lazarus had dark doubts – then reviewed it in his mind and decided that Maureen had been careful both in voice and phrasing). Lazarus bought the little boy an ice-cream cone to keep him quiet and sat him at the fountain, then moved to the other end and listened to her telephone call; he wanted to know what lies he must back up.

"Carol? Mama, dear. Have you counted our zoo lately? . . . Stop worrying; the scamp hid in the back seat, and we didn't know it until we were almost to Electric Park. . . . Yes, dear, Electric Park and I'm feeling very gay. I'm going to keep Woodrow with us and not let the imp spoil our fun . . . Earlier than I want to; Woodrow will be sleepy too soon to suit Mama; I want to ride every ride and win at least a Kewpie doll at the booths . . . Yes, as long as Marie is in bed on time. Make fudge for the boys – no, not fudge; we must watch the sugar ration. Make popcorn, and tell them I'm sorry they were worried. Then you older ones may stay up and say good-night to Uncle Ted. Good-bye, dear."

She thanked the druggist with smiling dignity, took Woodie's hand and left unhurriedly. But the moment Lazarus had the car rolling, she took his right hand and restored it to warm intimacy of bare thighs. "Any trouble?" he asked, caressing her silken skin.

"None. They had been engaged in a bloodthirsty game of Flinch and didn't miss him until it was time to put him to bed, only minutes before I called. Then they were worried, but not yet frantic; my little demon has hidden on us before. Theodore,

Electric Park is an expense you did not expect. Will you put aside your pride and let me help?"

"I would if I needed help; I don't have that sort of useless pride. But I have plenty of money, truly. If I run short, I'll tell you." (Beloved darling, I've been teaching optimists not to draw to inside straights, and I wish I could spend every cent of it on emeralds to set off your beautiful skin. But *your* pride makes that impossible.)

"Theodore, not only do I love you, you are a most comfortable person to be with."

Taking Woodie and his mother to Electric Park turned out to be more fun than Lazarus expected. He had nothing against amusement parks and was willing to be anywhere with Maureen – except that this time he expected to put up with restless frustration, in public where he must treat her as "Mrs. Smith," after being in warmest privacy – then disappointed.

But she taught him a lesson in how to enjoy the invitable.

He learned that Maureen could be unblushingly intimate despite people all around them and still maintain her smiling, regal, public dignity. She did it by keeping her *persona* always intact – happy young matron with boy child clutching her hand, both enjoying an evening of innocent fun as guests of "Cousin" Theodore, "Uncle" Ted – while she found endless chances to continue her gaily bawdy conversation. Maureen did it not in whispers but in ordinary tones pitched to reach Lazarus' ears only, or sometimes to Lazarus and Woodie but so phrased that the child would neither understand nor be interested.

Once she gently chided Lazarus. "Smile, beloved man. Let your face show that you are where you want to be, doing what you want to do. There, that's better. Now hold that expression and tell me why you were looking glum."

He grinned at her. "Because I'm frustrated, Maureen. Because I'm not in a certain spot by a big walnut tree."

She chuckled as if he had said something witty. "Alone?"

"Heavens, no! With *you*."

"Not so vehemently, Theodore. You are not courting me; you are my cousin who is wasting part of your precious leave by treating me and my child to an evening of fun . . . when you had hoped that I would find you a young lady who would turn out to be not at all ladylike when you took her to a dark place near a big walnut tree. You're a good sport about it – but not so enthusiastic as to cause Mrs. Grundy to raise her eyebrow . . . and there comes Mrs. Grundy now. Mrs. Simpson! And Mr. Simpson. How *nice* to run across you! Lauretta, may I present my dear cousin Staff Sergeant Bronson? And Mr. Simpson, Theodore." Maureen added, "Or perhaps you have met? At church? Before war was declared?"

Mrs. Simpson looked him over, counted the money in his wallet, checked his underwear, inspected his shave and haircut – assigned him a barely passing mark. "You belong to our church, Mr. Johnson?"

" 'Bronson,' Lauretta. Theodore Bronson, Father's eldest sister's son."

"Either way," Mr. Simpson said heartily, "it's a pleasure to shake hands with one of 'Our Boys.' Where are you stationed, Sergeant?"

"Camp Funston, sir. Mrs. Simpson, I was a visitor to your church; my membership is in Springfield."

Maureen stopped their questions by asking Lazarus to fetch Woodie from the miniature railroad train, just returning to its ticket-booth depot. "Pull him like a cork, Theodore; three rides is enough. Lauretta, I didn't see you at Red Cross last week. May we count on you this week?"

Lazarus returned with Woodie in time for Mr. Simpson to wave and call out, "Good luck, Sergeant!" as the Simpsons moved on. The trio went next to the pony ride, got Woodie astraddle one; Mrs. Smith and Lazarus sat on a bench, enjoyed more very private talk while very much in the public eye. "Maureen, you stole that base beautifully."

"No problem, dear one. I knew someone would see us, so I was ready. I'm pleased that it was the nastiest old gossip in our church; I made sure she didn't miss us. Pillars of the church and war profiteers; I despise them. So I pulled her fangs and let's forget them. You were telling me about a certain dark spot. How was I dressed?"

"Like a French postcard!"

"Why, Sergeant Bronson! – and me a respectable woman. Or almost. Surely you don't think I would dare be that shameless?"

"Maureen, I'm not sure *what* you would dare. You have startled – and delighted me – several times. I think you have the courage to do anything you want to do."

"Possibly, Theodore, but I have limits on what I *will* do, no matter how much I want to. Do you want to know my limits?"

"If you want me to know, you'll tell me. If you don't, you won't."

"I want you to know, beloved Theodore. I would like to strip naked this very moment. I refrain only for practical reasons – not moral ones and not shyness; I *want* to give you my body, let you enjoy it any way you please – while I enjoy yours. There are *no* limits to what I *want* to do with you . . . but only to what I *will* do.

"First" – she ticked them off – "I will not risk becoming pregnant by any man but Brian. Second, I will not knowingly risk the well-being of my husband and children."

"Weren't you risking that tonight?"

"Was I, Theodore?"

Lazarus thought about it. Pregnancy? Not a factor. Disease? She apparently trusted him on that – and Yes, darling, you are right. I don't know why you hold that opinion of me, but you're right. What does that leave? A chance of scandal if we had been caught. How much chance? Very little; it's as safe a spot as one could wish. Cops? Lazarus doubted that police ever checked that spot – and doubted still more strongly that a policeman, in the present war fever, would tell a soldier in uniform more than "Break it up and move on."

"No, my darling, you took no risks. Uh, if I had asked you to undress completely, would you have done so?"

Her laugh rang like chimes. Then she answered in her controlled pitch more private than a whisper. "I thought about that while I was taking a quick bath to make myself sweet for you, Theodore. It was a delightfully tempting idea; Brian has had me do so outdoors oftener than that once. It excites me, and he says that makes me more fun for him. But that's a risk *he* chooses to take, so it worries me not at all – with him. But I did not think it fair to him to take that risk on my own. So I firmly resolved, with my nipples crinkled up as hard as you felt them – hard as they are *now*; I'm *terribly* excited – I resolved not only *not* to undress but not to let *you* do so. Dear, will you go pay for another pony ride? Or fetch him if he's tired of that?"

Lazarus found that Woodie wanted another ride. He paid and went back to the bench, found Maureen staring down a lonely soldier. Lazarus touched his sleeve. "On your way, Private."

The soldier looked around, ready to argue – looked again and said, "Oh. Sorry, Sergeant. No offence meant."

"And none taken. Better luck elsewhere."

Maureen said, "I hate to snub a boy in uniform, even when I must. He wasn't fresh to me, Theodore – he was just exploring the chances. I must be twice his age and was tempted to tell him so. But it would have hurt his feelings."

"The trouble is that you *look* eighteen, so they're certain to try."

"Darling, I do *not* look eighteen. Me with a daughter over seventeen? If Nancy marries her young man before he goes to war – she wants to, and Brian and I won't stop it – I'll be a grandmother this coming year."

"Hi, Grandmaw."

"Tease. I will *enjoy* being a grandmother."

"I'm certain you will, dear; I think you have great capacity for enjoying life." (As *I* do, Mama! – and now I feel sure I got it both from you and Pop.)

"I do, Theodore." She smiled. "Even when frustrated. Very."

"Me, too – very. But we were talking about how old you look. Eighteen, that is."

"Pooh. You noticed how broken down and baby-chewed my breasts are."

"I noticed nothing of the sort."

"Then you have no sense of touch, sir . . . for you handled them quite thoroughly."

"Excellent sense of touch. Lovely breasts."

"Theodore, I try to take care of them. But they've been filled with milk much of the past eighteen years. That one" – she nodded toward the pony ring – "I didn't have enough milk for and had to put him on Eagle Brand, and he resented it. When I had Richard two years later, Woodrow tried to crowd out the new baby and take my freshened breasts. I had to be firm – when what I wanted was to have one at each breast. But one must be fair to children, not spoil one at the expense of another." She smiled indulgently. "I have no sense about Woodrow, so I must follow my rules to the letter. Come back in a year, Theodore, and they won't seem so broken down. They swell out and make me look like a cow."

"Will you make it worth my while?"

"By a walnut tree? Probably no chance, dear one. I'm afraid my scamp killed our one chance."

"Oh, it wouldn't take *that* much to make it worthwhile. I was thinking of a taste – direct from producer to consumer." (Mama Maureen, as Galahad says and I've never argued, I'm the most tit-happy man in the Galaxy . . . and I'm staring at the spot where I acquired the habit. I wished I could tell you so. Darling.)

She looked startled, snorted, and looked delighted. "That might be almost as hard to arrange as a walnut tree. But – Yes if it can be done without shocking my children. You are a scamp, too – just like Woodrow. I know *I* would enjoy it. Because – this is secret, dear – Brian has tasted each new freshening. Claims solemnly that he's checking quality and butterfat content."

(Pop, you're a man of good taste!) "Does he ever find that one has a taste different from the other?"

She chuckled happily. "Dear one, you have so many playful quirks just like my husband that you make me feel bigamous. He claims so, but it's just more of his joking. *I* can't tell any difference – and I've tasted."

"Madam, I look forward to giving you an expert's opinion. I think our cowboy has worn out his pony. What next? Want to try the Ben Hur Racer?"

She shook her head. "I enjoy roller coasters but won't go on one now. I've never miscarried, Theodore, and never will if being careful will keep me from it. Take Woodrow if you like."

"No. You would have to wait – and these woods are filled with wolves in khaki anxious to pick up eighteen-year-old grandmothers. The Fun House?"

"All right." Then her mouth twitched. "No, I forgot something. Those blasts of air up from the floor – intended to make girls squeal and clutch their skirts. Which I don't mind but – no bloomers, dear. Unless you want everyone to see whether or not I'm truly a redhead."

"Are you?"

She smiled, unoffended. "Tease. Don't you know?"

"It was very dark near that walnut tree."

"Redhead at both ends, Theodore. As I would happily show you were it not for the – frustrating – circumstances. Brian asked me that while we were courting. Teasing, he didn't need to ask; I was covered with freckles then, just like Marie. I let him find out for himself on a grassy spot by the Marais des Cygnes River while a gentle old mare named 'Daisy' cropped grass and paid no attention to my happy squeals. I suppose the automobile is here to stay – but the horse-and-buggy had many advantages. Didn't you find it so? When you started stepping out with young ladies?"

Lazarus agreed with a straight face, unable to admit that his memories did not include 1899 or whatever year she was thinking of. Maureen went on, "I used to fix a picnic lunch and take a blanket to eat on. That was one way a girl of courting age could be unchaperoned as long as I was home before dark. A horse can take a buggy into spots even more private than our walnut tree. Truthfully, despite this modern talk about 'wild women' and morals breaking down, I had more freedom as a girl than my daughters do. Although I try not to make my chaperonage oppressive."

"They don't seem oppressed. I'm sure they're happy."

"Theodore, I would much rather have my children be happy than what our pastor says is 'moral.' I simply want to be sure they aren't hurt. I am not 'moral' by the accepted rules – as you know quite well. Though not as well as I had hoped you would know it, and I'm taking out my frustration in talking about it. Perhaps you would rather I did not?"

"Maureen, since we can't do it, the next best thing is talking about it."

"Me, too, Theodore. I wish I were covered with chigger bites and my soul filled with the peace I know you could give me. Since I can't give myself to you the way I had hoped, I want you to know me as deeply as words can bring us together . . . as deeply as I wish you were in my body this very instant. Does my frankness shock you?"

"No. But it might get you raped right on this bench!"

"Please, not so much enthusiasm, dear one; people can see us – we're talking about the weather. Tell me, is your thing hard?"

"Does it show?"

"No, but if it is, think about blizzards and icebergs – Brian says that helps – because our pony rider needs to be lifted down."

They played booth games for prizes; then Mrs. Smith decided that she could risk the Fun House if she clutched her skirts as if crossing a muddy street. Woodie enjoyed it, especially the Hall of Mirrors and the Crystal Maze. Maureen avoided air blasts by watching girls ahead of them, then either walked on one side or held her skirts firmly.

Woodie tired himself out, so Lazarus picked him up and he seemed to fall asleep as his head touched Lazarus' shoulder. They started to leave, which took them over the farewell air blast. Mrs. Smith was ahead and Lazarus assumed that she had it spotted from the way she swerved – then she turned as if to speak to him, and stood over it. Her skirts went flying high.

She did not squeal; she simply pushed them down a split second too late. Once they were outside she said, "Well, sir?"

"Same colour. But curly, I think."

"Quite. As curly as my other hair is straight. As you already knew."

"And you did it on purpose."

"Certainly. Woodrow is asleep and you had his head turned away. Perhaps some stranger got an eyeful, but I think not. If someone did, what can he do? Write a letter to my husband? Pooh. There was no one in there who knows us; I kept my eyes open. And grabbed the chance."

"Maureen, you continue to amaze and delight me."

"Thank you, sir."

"And you have beautiful limbs."

"'Legs,' Theodore. Brian says so, too, but I'm no expert on women's legs. But when he talls me so, he always says 'legs.' 'Limbs' is for public speech. So he says."

"The more I know about the Captain, the more I like him. You have gorgeous legs. And green garters."

"Of course they're green. When I was a little girl, I wore green hair ribbons. I'm too old for hair ribbons, but if there is the teeniest possibility that my curls will be seen, I wear green garters. I have many pairs; Brian gives them to me. Some with naughty mottoes on them."

"Are there mottoes on these?"

"'Little pitchers,' Theodore. Let's get Woodrow settled down in the back seat."

It seemed to Lazarus that "little pitchers" could not be listening; the child was limp as a rag doll. Nor did he wake when he was bedded down; he curled into fetal position, and his mother put the robe over him.

Lazarus handed her into the car, cranked it and joined her. "Straight home?"

She said thoughtfully, "There is plenty of gasoline; Brian Junior filled the tank this afternoon. I don't think Woodrow will wake."

"I know there's enough gasoline; I checked when I went out to meet Mr. Johnson's captain. Shall I find that walnut tree?"

"Oh, dear! Please don't tempt me. Woodrow *might* wake up and could climb over the back and get out, as easily as he climbed in and hid. He's not old enough to understand what we would be doing; nevertheless, I think his misunderstanding of it could upset him just as much. No, Theodore. What I meant is this: It's not late, it's just late for a little boy. While he sleeps we can ride around and talk for, oh, an hour. If you wish."

"We'll do that." He got rolling and added, "Maureen, although I want to take you back to that walnut tree, I think it's best that we don't. Best for you, I mean."

"But, darling! Why? Don't you think I *want* you?"

"I do think you want me. And God knows I want *you*. But despite your brave talk, I don't think you've ever done that. You would want to confess to your husband . . . and if you did, it would make you both unhappy – and I don't want to make Captain Smith unhappy either; he's a good sort. Or maybe you could keep it to yourself – but it would prey on your mind. Because, while you love me – a little – you love him a great deal more and I am sure of that. So it's best. Isn't that so?"

Mrs. Smith was silent a long moment. Then she said, "Theodore, take me straight to that walnut tree."

"No."

"Why not, dear? I must show you that I *do* love you and that I am *not* afraid to let you have me."

"Maureen, you would do it; you have the courage to do anything. But you would be tense and worried, afraid that Woodie would wake up. And you do love Brian. All the sweetly intimate things you've told me kept saying that."

"But don't you think my heart is big enough for *both* of you?"

"I'm certain it is. You love ten people that I know of; I'm sure you can squeeze in one more. But *I* love *you* and do not want you to do anything that would make a wall between you and your husband. Or hurt you both through your trying to tear down that wall by confessing. Beloved, I want your *love* even more than I want your dear, sweet body."

Again she was silent before speaking: "Theodore, I must tell you things about my husband and me. Private things."

"You shouldn't."

"I should and I must – and I *shall*. But – Please, will you touch me while I talk? Don't say anything, just touch me closely and intimately and nakedly . . . while I strip myself naked with words. Please?"

Lazarus put his free hand on her thigh. She pulled up her skirts, opened her thighs, pushed his hand more firmly to her. Then she covered his hand with her skirt, and spoke in an even, steady voice:

"Theodore beloved, I love Brian and Brian loves me and he knows exactly what I am. I could keep a secret forever to keep from hurting him, and he would do the same for me. I must tell you what he said to me before he went away to Plettsburg – and I must use 'bedroom words,' Theodore; polite words don't have the force it must have.

"The night before he left we were in bed and had just had each other, me still wrapped around him like a curling iron and him still deep inside me. 'Swivel Hips,' he said – a pet name he calls me in bed – 'I didn't sell the Reo to tie you down. If you want to drive, buy a Ford; it's easier to learn on.' I told him I didn't want to drive; I would wait until he came home. He answered, 'All right. Hot Bottom' – and that's a pet name, too, and Brian means it most lovingly – 'All right, Hot Bottom, but buy one if you wish; you may need a car while I'm gone.

"'But a car is a minor matter. Your father will be here and that's good – but don't let him boss you. He'll try, he can't help it, it's his nature. But you are as strong-willed as he is; stand up to him, he'll respect you for it.

"'Now to more important matters, Pretty Tits' – and I like *that* name, too, Theodore, even though they're not and don't stop me to say they are – 'Pretty Tits, I may not have gotten you pregnant; you don't usually catch again this soon. If not, once I'm back from Plattsburg, we'll keep on trying' – and we did, Theodore, and I caught, as I told you.

"Brian went on, 'We both knew we're going to get into this war or I wouldn't be going to Plattsburg. It may last a long time – that "million men springing to arms overnight" is hogwash. When we do, I'll be gone again, and you'll be lonely – and we both know what a firecracker you are. I'm not telling you to jump the fence again' – I said '*again*,' Theodore! – 'but if you do, I expect you to do it on purpose, eyes open . . . and not to regret it afterwards. I have enormous respect for your taste and judgement; I know you won't cause a scandal or upset the children.'"

She paused, then went on: "Brian knows me, Theodore – I really *am* a firecracker, and I've never understood why some women don't like it. My own mother – Nine children and she told me on my wedding day that it was something women had to put up with for the privilege of having babies."

Mrs. Smith snorted. "'Put up with!' Theodore, I was not a virgin when Brian first had me. Nor had I let him think so;

I told him the truth the day I met him . . . and two minutes after he took my bloomers off he knew it through having me. Theodore, I broke my maidenhead three years before I met Brian – on purpose; I've never been a flirt – and told, not my mother, but my father, because I trusted him; we've always been close. Father didn't scold me, didn't even tell me not to do it again. He said he knew that I *would* do it again but hoped that I would take his advice and let him keep me out of trouble – and I have and it did.

"But that first time, when I came to him, scared and ready to cry – it had hurt, Theodore, and wasn't the thrill I had expected – that time Father just sighed and locked the door and had me get on his surgery table and examined me and assured me that I hadn't been damaged – and I felt *much* better! – and told me that I was as healthy a woman as he had ever examined and would have babies with no trouble – and that made me feel smug – and Father was right; I have babies easily and don't yell – or not much. Not the way Mother used to.

"After that, Father examined me from time to time. Doctors don't ordinarily treat their female relatives, not for female things. But Father was the only doctor I dared tell. So Father helped me with my problems and got me all over any shyness about being looked at there or anywhere. Not that I was ever too shy; he told me that sort of modesty was dadratted nonsense – when Mother was telling me the exact opposite. I believed him, didn't believe her.

"But I was telling you what Brian said to me in bed that night. Brian added, 'I want you to promise one thing, Pussycat. If you find that you haven't kept your legs crossed, will you keep it to yourself until this war is over? I will do the same if I have something to confess – and I might! Let's not worry each other more than we have to until the Kaiser is taken care of. Then when I come home, I'll take you to the Ozarks – leave the children home with someone; just us two – and you won't see anything but the ceiling while we get caught up, and also catch up on anything we need to talk about. Is it a bargain, my darling?'

"I promised, Theodore. I didn't promise not to jump the fence; he wouldn't *let* me promise that. I promised to be careful – and to save any confessing until the war was won. I wanted to promise that much because . . . he . . . might not . . . *come back!*"

Her voice had been steady up to the last. Then it broke, and he realized that she was crying. He started to remove his hand and to pull over to the side of the road. Mrs. Smith grabbed his hand, pushed it more firmly back between her thighs, and said, "No, no, *do* touch me and *don't* stop the car! Or I might rape you. I don't know why it makes me so passionate when I let myself remember that Brian might not come back from the war. But it does. I've been that way ever since the day we declared war . . . and always have to look serene and calm and unworried. For the children. For Brian. I haven't let Brian see me cry, Theodore. You have just now – I suddenly could not help it. But I would rather you told Brian that I tried to seduce you than have you tell him that I cried through fear that he might not come back!

"And now I'll stop it." Mrs. Smith took a kerchief from her purse, wiped her eyes, blew her nose. "Don't take me home yet; the children must not see me with my eyes red."

Lazarus decided to break cover. "I love you, Maureen."

"I love you, Theodore. In spite of my tears, you have made me happy. By letting me unburden myself – and I should not have; *you* are going to war, too. I feel almost married to you now, by telling you things I haven't been able to talk about with anyone else. If you had put me on the grass and had me – it would have been sweet and just what I planned. But this is even closer. And sweeter. A woman can open her body to a man without opening her mind. I had two babies by Brian before I learned to open my mind to him the way I have to you tonight."

"Perhaps our minds are much alike, Maureen. Your father thinks we are cousins."

"No, he doesn't, darling; he thinks you're my half brother."

"Did he say that?"

"And *I* think so, too. By things Father did *not* say, dear Theodore. By how broken up he was when he misunderstood you about your intention to enlist. By the way he insisted that we *must* claim a service star for you. I feel sure he is right . . . and I *want* to believe it. Yes, that makes what I tried to do to you dreadfully sinful in some people's eyes. Incest. I did not care a whit. Since I'm pregnant, it could not possibly cause harm to a baby . . . and that's the only thing that could make incest wrong."

(*How* to tell her? How *much* to tell her? But I *must* make her believe me.) "Your church would call it sinful."

"I don't give a fig for the church! Theodore, I'm not devout; I'm a freethinker, like Father. Church is a good atmosphere for children – and gives me a proper appearance as a respectable wife and mother – that's all! 'Sin' would not stop me; I don't believe in sin the way the church means it. Sex isn't sin, sex is never sin. What *would* stop me would be a chance of getting pregnant by someone other than Brian – but I *am* pregnant. That you are my half brother didn't cause me a moment's fret; it just made me more anxious to tell you a warrior's good-bye."

"Maureen, I'm not your half brother."

"Are you sure? Even if you're not, you are still my warrior – I was as proud as Father when you volunteered."

"I'm your warrior, be sure of that. But I need to know something. This man Nancy may marry – Is he a Howard?"

"*What did you say?*"

"Is he on the approved list of the Ira Howard Foundation?"

He heard her catch her breath. "Where did you hear of the Foundation?"

" 'Life is short – ' "

" 'But the years are long,' " she answered.

" 'Not "While the Evil Days Come Not." ' "

"Goodness! I – I think I'm going to cry again!"

"Stop it. What is the young man's name?"

"Jonathan Weatheral."

" – of the Weatheral-Sperling line. Yes, I remember. Maureen, I am not 'Ted Bronson.' I am Lazarus Long of the Johnson Family. *Your* family. I am descended from you."

For several moments she seemed not to breathe. Then she said softly, "I think I am losing my mind."

"No, my gallant love, you have as strong and sane a mind as I have ever met. Let me explain because I must tell you something and you *must* believe me. Have you read a novel by Mr. Herbert George Wells called *The Time Machine?*"

"Why, yes. Father has a copy."

"That's me, Maureen. Captain Lazarus Long, Time Traveller."

"But that book – I thought it was just a . . . a – "

"Just a story. It is. But it won't stay that way. Oh, not quite the way Mr. Wells visualized it. But that's what I am, a visitor from a future time. I didn't intend to let anyone suspect this; that's why I claimed to be a foundling. Not only is it hard to prove, but any attempt would interfere with my purpose . . . which is simply to visit this time and observe it. Might even get me locked up as crazy. So I've been careful to keep my mask on, as careful as – well, as *you* are. In talking to those Simpsons. In not letting your children see you cry. You and I do it the same way. Audacity . . . plus never telling lies we can be caught in."

"Theodore, I think you believe this."

"Meaning that I sound sincere but must be crazy."

"No, no, dear, I – Yes, that's what I meant. I'm sorry."

"No reason to be sorry; it does sound crazy. But I'm not afraid that you will have me sent to St. Joe; I'm as safe with you as you are with me. But I *must* find some way to convince you that I *am* telling the truth . . . because I am about to tell you something you *must* believe. Or I have dropped my mask to no point."

He stopped to think. How to prove it? Some prediction? It would have to be very short range to serve the only purpose he had in breaking cover. But he hadn't briefed himself on this year; he hadn't intended to arrive until 1919 and knew so little about the years before 1919 that he had even mixed up the date that the United States got into this war. Lazarus, damn your sloppy ways, the *next* time you make a time trip you're going to memorize everything about the era that Athene can give you – and a wide margin on both sides!

Woodie's memories were no help; Lazarus did not even recall having been taken to Electric Park by a sergeant in uniform. Self-centred brat! Electric Park he remembered; Woodie Smith had gone there many times. But no visit stood out in his mind.

"Maureen, maybe you can think of some way I can prove to you that I'm from the future – something that will convince *you*. But this is why I *had* to tell you: Brian – your husband, my ancestor – will come back unharmed. He's going to go through battles. Shells will fall around him, shots will whistle past his ears – but none will touch him."

Mrs. Smith gasped. Then she said slowly, "Theodore . . . how do you *know*?"

"Because you two *are* my ancestors. I couldn't memorize the Foundation's records on all the Howards of today but I did study the files on my own ancestors, ones I might have a chance to meet. You. Brian. Brian's parents in Cincinnati. And I figured out that Brian must have met you because he had attended Rolla, then found you on a Missouri list of eligibles – not the Ohio list – that the Foundation gave him. That's certainly something I didn't learn from you or Brian or Ira, and your children probably don't know it. Well, perhaps Nancy does; she's filled out her own questionnaire. Hasn't she?"

"Why, yes, months ago. Then it *is* true, Theodore. Or should I call you 'Lazarus'?"

"Call me anything you like, darling. But I still haven't proved anything. Just that I have had access to the Foundation's files – which might have been last year, not in the future. We're still looking for *proof*. Mmm . . . I know a proof for a few months from now – but I must make you believe me *tonight*. So you will have no more tears on your pillow. And I don't know *how*."

He caressed her thighs, touched her curls. "Here inside you is proof that won't show up in time. This last baby Brian put into your sweet belly – He's a boy, dearest ancestress, and you and Brian will name him 'Theodore Ira' – which flatters me enormously. When I read this name in the records, I didn't know that he was my namesake, as I hadn't picked my assumed name then."

She squeezed his hand with her thighs and sighed. "I want to believe you. But suppose Brian wants to name him Joseph? Or Josephine?"

" 'Josephine' is not a name for a boy. Darling, Brian will name his war baby for the other two stars on your service flag; this war means a lot to him. He'll probably suggest it himself – I don't know. I just know that 'Theodore Ira' is the name you will register with the Foundation. My other ancestors – Adele Johnson, of course, your mother and Ira's wife. Lives in St. Louis. Left him around the time you got married but didn't divorce him – which probably irked him; I don't think Ira is a man to be celibate simply because his wife leaves but won't turn him loose."

"He's not, dear. I'm certain Father has a – well, a mistress, and goes to see her some nights when he is supposed to be at that 'chess club' – and it's not a chess club; it's a pool hall. I go along with the pretence because he calls it that in front of the children."

"He does play chess there."

"Father plays a fine game of billiards, too. Go ahead, darling – Lazarus. I'm willing to believe. Maybe we'll find something."

"Well, I don't think I'll look up your mother; I don't think I I would get along with a woman who thinks sex is something to 'put up with'."

"I got along with Mother only by lying to her. Father reared me far more than she did. I was his favourite. He let it show, which is why I'm careful *not* to let it show with Woodrow. Go on, Theodore. Lazarus."

"That's all of my ancestors you are related to. Except one. Our stowaway. Maureen, I'm descended from you and Brian through Woodie."

She gasped. "Really? Oh, I hope it's true!"

"True as taxes, beloved. And it may have saved his life. I've never been closer to infanticide than I was when we found him in the back seat."

She giggled. "Darling, I felt the same way. But I won't let anger show in my voice even if I'm about to switch a child."

"I hope I didn't show anger. But I felt it. Beloved, I was so hard I *ached* – until we found Woodrow. Honey love, I was rarin' to go!"

"And I was just as ready! Oh, Theodore – Lazarus – it's so *sweet* to be open with you. Uh . . . yes, you're *quite* hard now."

"Easy there! – don't make me climb the curb. I have been ever since we left the house except when I forced it down. But the one Woodie ruined was bigger and better."

"Size isn't important, Theodore-Lazarus; a woman must fit any size. Father told me that long ago and taught me exercises for it – and I never told Brian; I let him think that was simply how I am – and accepted his compliments smugly. I still exercise regularly – because my birth canal has been stretched again and again and again by babies' skulls and if I didn't exercise those muscles I would be, in Father's salty language, 'loose as a goose.' And I do *so* want to stay desirable to Brian as many years as possible."

"And to the iceman and the milkman and the postman – and the boy who drives the grocery wagon."

"Tease. I'd like to stay young *there* till I die."

"You will, you eighteen-year-old prospective grandmother. Let's get our minds off sex and back to time travel; I'm still looking for a proof. So that you will *know* why I am *certain* that Brian came back okay. But to stop your worry it must be something that happens soon and certainly before Woodie's birthday."

"Why Woodrow's birthday?"

"Didn't I get that far? This war ends on Woodie's next birthday, the eleventh of November." He added, "I'm certain of that, it's a key date in history. But I'm racking my brain for some event between now and then – as soon as possible, to stop your worries. But – oh, shucks, dear, I made a silly mistake. I meant to arrive after this war is over. But I gave my computer one critical figure with an error in it – just a little one, but it made me arrive three years too soon. Not her fault; she accepts any data I give her, and she's as accurate a computer as ever conned a ship. Not a fatal error, either; I'm not lost in time, my ship will pick me up in 1926 exactly ten Earth years after she dropped me. But that's why I didn't study the history of the next few months; I expected to skip this war. I'm not studying wars; histories are full of wars. I'm studying how people live."

"Theodore . . . I'm confused."

"I'm sorry, darling. Time travel *is* confusing."

"You speak of a computer, and I'm not sure what you mean . . . and you said 'she' conns – whatever that means – a ship that will pick you up . . . in 1926? And I don't understand *any* of it."

Lazarus sighed. "That's why I never intended to tell anyone. But I *had* to tell *you* – so that you could stop worrying. My ship is a spaceship – like Jules Verne, only more so. A starship, I live on a planet a long way off. But it is a timeship, too; she travels in both space and time and it's too complicated to explain. The computer is the ship's brain – a machine, a very complex machine. My ship is named 'Dora' and the machine, the computer, that conns it – runs it – steers it – is called Dora, too; that's the name she answers to when I speak to her. She's a very intelligent machine and can talk. Oh, there is a crew, two of my sisters – so of course they are descended from you, too, and they look like you. A crew is necessary – can't let a ship go running around by itself – except automatic freighters on precalculated runs – but Dora does the hard work, and Laz and Lor – Lapis Lazuli Long and Lorelei Le Long – tell Dora what to do and let her do it." He squeezed Mrs. Smith's thigh and grinned. "If that air blast had kept your skirts up two seconds longer, I would know more about how closely they resemble you – as they usually run around naked. They look like you in the face. Bodies, too, from that too-short glimpse of your lovely legs. Except that Laz and Lor are freckled all over as solidly as Marie is on her face."

"I'd be that freckled if I didn't stay out of the sun. When I was Marie's age, Father called me 'Turkey Egg.' But *all* over? They don't wear *any* clothes?"

"Oh, they enjoy fancy dress for parties. Or the weather might be cold – but it rarely is; we live in a climate like southern Italy. They don't wear anything very often." Lazarus smiled and caressed her thigh. "They don't need to leave their bloomers home to be ready for love-making; they don't own any bloomers. They aren't a bit shy. They would be delighted to trip your father; they like older men – they're much younger than I am."

"Lazarus . . . how old *are* you?"

Lazarus hesitated. "Maureen, I don't want to answer that. I'm older than I look; Ira Howard's experiment was successful. Instead let me tell you about my family. *Your* family, too; we all are descended from you by one line or another. Two of my wives and one of my co-husbands are descended both from Nancy and from Woodie."

" 'Wives? Co-husband'?"

"Sweetheart, marriage takes many forms. Where I live you don't need a divorce or a death to gather in someone you love. I have four wives and three co-husbands – and my sisters, Laz and Lor . . . and they may marry out of the family or they may stay – and don't look startled; you said you didn't fret when you thought I was your half brother – and don't worry about harm to babies; they know far more about such things at that when-&-where than they do in the here-&-now. We *don't* risk harm to babies.

"Of which we have plenty. And cats and dogs and anything a child can pet and take care of. It's a real family in a house to fit a big family.

"I can't tell you about each one; we've got to get our stowaway home. But I want to tell you about one – because you've been insisting that you don't look eighteen – merely because you've been using your breasts to feed babies. Tamara. Descended from you through Nancy and her Jonathan – Want to hear about Nancy's umpty-ump grand-daughter? Tamara is about two hundred and fifty years old, I think –"

"Two hundred and fifty!"

"Yes. One of my co-husbands, Ira Weatheral, also from Nancy and Jonathan but from Woodie, too – and named for your father, not for Ira Howard – is over four hundred years old. Maureen, Ira Howard's experiment *worked*; we have longer life-spans – inherited from you and all our Howard ancestors – but also in that when-&-where they know how to rejuvenate a person. Tamara has had two rejuvenations – one recently and looks as young as you do. Real rejuvenation – Tamara was pregnant when I left.

"But how she looks is not important; Tamara is a healer – and I suspect she gets it from *you*."

"Theodore – Lazarus – again I don't understand. A healer? Like a faith healer?"

"No. If Tamara has a religious faith, she has never mentioned it. Tamara is calm and happy and serene, and anyone around her feels it so strongly – just as with *you,* darling! – that he or she is happy, too. If people are ill, they get well faster if Tamara touches them, or talks to them, or sleeps with them.

"But Tamara was *not* young when I met her. She was quite old and thinking about letting it go at that, dying of old age. But I was ill, very ill, sick in my soul – and Ishtar, later my wife and the topnotch rejuvenator in all the Milky Way, went out and fetched Tamara. Tamara. Little round potbelly, breasts that were *really* baggy, sags under her eyes, under her chin, all the old-age things.

"Tamara healed the sickness in my soul, just by being with me . . . and somehow this renewed her own interest in life, and she took another rejuvenation and is young again and has already added another baby to the Maureen-Nancy line and is pregnant still again. You and Tamara are so *much* alike, Maureen; she's just love with some skin around it – and so are *you.* But – " Lazarus paused and frowned.

"Maureen, *I* don't know how to convince you that I'm telling the truth. You'll *know* it when Woodie's sixth birthday comes around and they blow every whistle and ring every bell and the newsboys shout: '*Extra! Extra!* Germany surrenders!' But that'll be too late to help you. I want to stop your worries *now!*"

"I've stopped worrying, dear one. It sounds wonderful . . . and impossible . . . and I believe you."

"Do you? I've offered no proof; I've told you a tale impossible on the face of it."

"Nevertheless, I believe it. When Woodrow is six on the seventh of November – "

"No, the *eleventh!*"

"Yes, Lazarus. But how did *you* know that his birthday is the eleventh?"

"Why, you told me yourself."

"Dear, I said he was born in November; I did *not* say what day. Then I deliberately misstated it – and you corrected me at once."

"Well, maybe Ira told me. Or one of the children. Most likely Woodie himself."

"Woodrow does not know the date of his birthday. Wake him and ask him."

"I'd rather not wake him until we get home."

"What is my birthday, dear one?"

"The Fourth of July, 1882."

"What is Marie's birthday?"

"I think she is nine. I don't know the date."

"The other children?"

"I'm not sure."

"My father's birthday?"

"Maureen, is there some point to this? August second, 1852."

"Beloved Lazarus who calls himself 'Theodore,' I have a firm rule with my children. I keep each one from knowing the date of his birth as long as possible so that he won't advertise it and thereby blackmail people for presents. When one is old enough for school and needs to know the date, he is old enough to be told why, and I make it bluntly plain that if he drops hints ahead of time – no birthday cake, no birthday party. I haven't had to use that penalty; they are all intelligent.

"Last year Woodrow was too young for it to be a problem; his birthday came as a surprise to him. He still does not know the exact date – so I strongly believe. Lazarus, you know the birthdays of your direct ancestors . . . because you looked them up in the Foundation records. Since you can't tell me the birthdays of my other children, I assume that I've found that proof."

"You know I have had access to the records. I could have looked up any birthday last year."

"Pooh. Why did you bother with the birth date of one child and skip the other seven? How would you know my father's birthday if he had not been of special interest to you? It won't wash, Beloved. You intended to seek out your ancestors, and you came prepared for it. I no longer think that you showed up at our church by accident; you went there to find *me* – and I'm flattered. You probably did the same with Father – at his pool-hall 'chess club.' How did you do it? Private detectives? I doubt that our church or that pool hall can be looked up in the Foundation records."

"Something like that. Yes, gentle ancestress, I looked for an acceptable way to meet you. I would have spent years on it had it been necessary . . . because I couldn't twist your doorbell and say, 'Hi there! I'm descended from you. May I come in?' You would have called the police."

"I hope I would not have, darling – but thank you for finding a gentler way. Oh, Lazarus, I love you so! – and believe every word and I'm no longer worried about Brian; I *know* he'll come back to me! Uh . . . I'm feeling very brazen again and more passionate than ever and I want to know something. About your family."

"I'm delighted to talk about them. I love them."

"I was most flattered to be compared with your wife Tamara. Darling, you don't have to tell me this: Does it ever happen that two husbands sleep with one wife?"

"Oh, certainly. But it's more likely to be one husband – Galahad – another of your descendants, Grandmother – Galahad and two of our wives; Galahad is the original tireless tomcat."

"That sounds like fun, but it's the other combination that intrigued me. Beloved, my idea of heaven would be to take *both* you and Brian to bed at once – and do my best to make you *both* happy. Not that I ever can. But I can dream about it . . . and *will*."

"Why not out in the woods and strip down for both of us, just to your 'French postcard' costume? As long as you're dreaming."

"*Ooooh!* Yes, I'll put that into my dream – and now I'm about to go off like a firecracker!"

"I'd better take you home."

"I think you had better. I'm terribly happy and quite unworried – and will stay so – and *very* passionate. For you. For Brian. For being a French postcard in the woods. In *daylight*."

"Maureen, if you can sell the idea to Brian . . . well, I'll be around until the second of August, 1926."

"Well . . . we'll see. I *want* to!" She added, "Am I permitted to tell him? Who you are and where you're from – the future – and your prediction that he won't be hurt?"

"Maureen, tell anyone you wish. But you won't be believed."

She sighed. "I suppose so. Besides, if Brian *did* believe it and thereby believed that he had a charmed life – it might make him careless. I'm proud that he is going to fight for us . . . but I *don't* want him to take unnecessary risks."

"I think you're right, Maureen."

"Theodore . . . my mind has been so busy with all these strange things that I missed something. Now that I know who you are – This isn't your country, and it's not your war – so why *did* you volunteer?"

Lazarus hesitated, then told the truth:

"I wanted you to be proud of me."

"*Oh!*"

"No, I don't belong here and it's not my war. But it's *your* war, Maureen. Others are fighting for other reasons – I'll be fighting for Maureen. Not 'to make the world safe for democracy' – this war won't accomplish that, even though the Allies are going to win. For Maureen."

"Oh! *Oh!* I'm crying again – I can't help it."

"Stop it at once."

"Yes, my warrior. Lazarus? *You* will come back? You must have some way to know."

"Huh? Dear, don't worry about *me*. People have tried to kill me in all sorts of ways – I've outlived them all. I'm the wary old cat who always has a tree within reach."

"You didn't answer me."

He sighed. "Maureen, I know Brian will come home; it's in the Foundation's records. He will live to a ripe old age and don't ask how long as I won't answer. And so will you, and I won't answer *that* either; it is not good to know too much about the future. But me? I *can't* know my future. It is *not* in the records. How could it be? I haven't finished it yet. But I can tell you this: This is not my *first* war, but about the fifteenth. They didn't get me in the others, and they'll have to move fast to kill me in this one. Beloved, I am your warrior – but to kill Huns for *you*, not for *them* to kill *me*. I'll do my duty, but I'm not going to try some crazy stunt to win a medal – not old Lazarus."

"Then you *don't* know."

"No, I don't. But I promise you this: I won't stick my head up when I don't need to. I won't go into a German dugout without tossing a grenade in ahead of me. I won't assume that a German is dead because he appears to be – I'll make sure he's dead; I don't mind wasting a bullet on a corpse. Especially one who is playing 'possum. I'm an old soldier, and that's how one gets to be an old soldier – by being a pessimist. I know all the tricks. Darling, having quieted your worries about Brian, it would be silly to get you worried about *me*. Don't!"

She sighed. "I'll try not to. If you turn down this street, we can pick up Prospect, then across Linwood to Benton."

"I'll get you home. Let's talk about love, not war. Our girl Nancy-Is the Foundation now using a pregnancy rule? For first marriages?"

"Goodness! You *do* know all about it."

"No need to tell me. Nancy's business. If Jonathan does go to war – I don't know – I can assure you that he won't get his balls shot off, even if he loses an arm or a leg. I did look up the breeding records on all your children even though I didn't bother with their birthdays. Jonathan and Nancy are going to have many babies. Which means he comes back – or maybe gets turned down and won't go."

"That's comforting. How many babies?"

"Nosy little girl. You're going to have quite a number yet yourself, Grandmother, and I won't answer that, either. I withdraw the question about the pregnancy rule."

"Secret, Lazarus –"

"Better start calling me 'Theodore.' We'll be home soon."

"Yes, sir, Staff Sergeant Theodore Bronson, your lecherous old great-great-great-grandmother will be careful. How many 'greats' should there be in that?"

"Sweetheart, do you want that answered? If it had not been necessary to calm your fears about Brian, I would have stayed 'Ted Bronson.' I *like* being your 'Theodore.' I'm not sure that being a mysterious man from the future is going to be as comfortable. Especially if you think of me as some remote descendant. I'm here beside you, not in some far future."

"Beside me. Touching me. And yet you're not even born yet – are you? And in *your* time . . . I'm long dead. You even know when I will die. You said so. You just won't tell me when."

"Oh, confound it, Maureen; that's wrong all the way through! That's what comes of admitting that I've time-travelled. But I *had* to. For you."

"I'm sorry, Laz – Theodore my warrior. I won't ask any more questions."

"Sweetheart, the fact that I *am* here means that you're *not* dead. And I certainly was born; pinch me and find out. All 'nows' are equal; that is the basic theorem of time travel. They don't disappear; both 'past' and 'future' are mathematical abstractions; the '*now*' is always all there is. As for knowing the day you died – or will die; it's the same thing – I *don't*. I just know that you had – have – will have – many children, and you live a long time . . . and your hair never gets grey. But the Foundation lost track of you – will lose track of you – and your date of death never got into the records. Maybe you moved and didn't tell the Foundation. Shucks, maybe I came back – will come back – and picked you up in your old age, and took you to Tertius."

"Where?"

"My home. I think you would like it there. You could run around all day, dressed – undressed – as a French postcard."

"I'm sure I would like that now. But I don't think I would, as an old woman."

"All you would have to do is to ask Ishtar for rejuvenation. I told you what she did for Tamara . . . when her breasts hung down to her waist and were empty sacks. But look at Tamara now – *that* 'now' – pregnant again, just like a kid. But forget it – if it *did* happen, it *will* happen. Mama Maureen – I'm durned if I'll call you 'Grandmother' again – all I'm sure of is that I'm not sure of the date of your death, and I'm glad I'm not, and you should be. Nor of my death, and I'm glad of that, too. Carpe-diem! We're almost home and you started to say something and I said to call me 'Theodore' and we got off the track. Was it about Tamara?"

"Oh, yes! Theodore? When you go home to wherever your home is, can you take anything with you? Or does it have to be just you?"

"Why, no. I arrived with clothes and money."

"I'd like to send a little present to Tamara. But I can't guess what she would want . . . from this time to that wonderful age of yours. Can you suggest something?"

"Mmm . . . Tamara would treasure anything from you. She knows she's descended from you, and she's the most warmly sentimental of all my family. It should be something small enought to carry on my person, even in the trenches, as I'm always ready to abandon anything I'm not carrying – have to be. Not jewelry. Tamara would not value a diamond bracelet one whit more than a hairpin . . . but she would treasure a hairpin that I could tell her I had seen you wearing. Something small, something you've worn. Look, send her a garter! Perfect! One of these you have on."

"Mayn't I send her a brand-new pair? Oh, I'll slip them on for a moment, so that you can tell her truthfully that I've worn them. But these – Not only are they rather old and worn but I've perspired right through them tonight. They're not fresh and clean. And they do have naughty mottoes on them."

"No, no, one of *these*. Sweetheart, 'naughty' today can't be naughty on Tertius; I'll have to explain any naughtiness to Tamara. As for perspiration, I hope that some trace of your sweet fragrance clings to them until I can get them to her; that would delight Tamara. You say this pair is old? Maureen, by any chance are they about six years old?"

"I *told* you I was sentimental, Theodore. Yes, this is the same pair. Old and faded and worn and I've replaced the elastic – but the same pair; I picked them to wear for you."

"Then I want one of them for *me!*"

"Beloved Theodore. I planned to offer you both of them. That's why I suggested a new pair for Tamara. Very well, dear, one for you, one for her. As soon as we're home, I'll trot upstairs, and when I come down, I'll have a present for you and will tell you not to open it until you're back at Camp Funston. You just say thank you and go straight to your room and put it into your grip. I see a light on the front porch, so now I must push my skirts down and be the prim and proper Mrs. Brian Smith. With a smoldering volcano inside her! Thank you, Staff Sergeant Bronson. You have given my son and me a most enjoyable evening."

"Thank *you*, pretty little pussycat in green garters and no bloomers. Will you grab the Teddy bear and the Kewpie doll while I carry our chaperon?"

Ira Johnson and Nancy were not yet home. Brian Junior relieved Lazarus of the limp child and carried him upstairs. Carol went along to put Woodie to bed after exacting a promise from "Uncle Ted" not to go to bed before she came back. George wanted to know where they had gone and what they had done, but Lazarus put him off with a promise and used the chance to repair to his tiny bath and repair himself.

Hair a bit mussed – Thank God respectable women did not use lipstick. Uniform slightly wrinkled, nothing damning about that. Five minutes later, refreshed and certain there were no feathers on his chin, Lazarus returned to the front of the house and offered George and Brian Junior an account of the evening truthful in everything he said.

He had just started when Carol came down and listened too; then Mrs. Smith rejoined them, moving regally as always and carrying a little package wrapped in tissue paper. "A surprise for you, Sergeant Theodore – please don't open it until you are back at camp."

"Then I had better put it into my grip right now."

"If you wish, sir. I think it's bedtime, dears."

"Yes, Mama," agreed Carol. "But Uncle Ted was telling us how you knocked down all the milk bottles."

"He says you should pitch for the Blues, Mama!" added George.

"All right, fifteen minutes."

"Mrs. Smith," said Lazarus, "you ought not to start your stopwatch on us until I get back."

"You're as bad as the rest of my children, Sergeant. Very well."

Lazarus put the package into his grip, locked it from long habit, and returned. Nancy and her young man arrived; Lazarus was introduced while looking over Jonathan Weatheral with real interest. Pleasant young fellow, a bit on the gawky side – Tamara and Ira will be interested, so let's photograph him by eye, be able to sketch him, and remember any word he says.

Mrs. Smith urged her prospective son-in-law into the parlour while cutting Nancy out of the herd; Lazarus resumed describing what they had done at the amusement park while Jonathan looked politely bored. Mrs. Smith returned, carrying a laden tray and said, "That fifteen minutes is up, dears. Jonathan, Nancy wants you to help her with something; will you see what it is? She's in the kitchen."

Brian Junior asked if he could put the car into the barn. "Sergeant Uncle Ted, I haven't let your car sit out at the curb at night, not once. But I'll get it out for you, first thing in the morning; it's kind o' tricky, sort of a 'Z' turn, you have to back and fill."

Lazarus thanked him, kissed Carol good-night, as she was clearly expecting it. George couldn't seem to make up his mind whether he had outgrown kissing or not, so Lazarus settled it by shaking hands and telling him he had quite a grip on him. At that point Mr. Johnson got home, and the good-nights started over.

Five minutes later Mrs. Smith, her father, and Lazarus were seated in the parlour over coffee and cake, and Lazarus was suddenly reminded of the first night he had been invited in. Save that the men were now in uniform the tableau was the same; each was seated in the spot he had been in that night, Mrs. Smith presided over the "company" coffee service with the same serene dignity; even the refreshments were the same. He looked for changes, could find only three: His elephant was not back of Mrs. Smith's chair, the prizes they had won at the amusement park were on a table near the door, and sheet music for "Hello, Central, Give Me No Man's Land" was open on the piano.

"You were late tonight, Father."

"Seven recruits, and I had just the usual sizes for them, too large and too small. Ted, we get what the Army doesn't want. Proper, of course. We now have Lewis guns for the machine-gun companies and enough Springfields to go around; we are beginning to look less like Villa's bandits, I'm not complaining. Daughter, what are those things on that table? They look out of place."

"The Kewpie doll I won myself, so I'm thinking of giving it a place of honour on top of the piano. The Teddy Roosevelt bear was won by Sergeant Theodore; perhaps he's taking it to France with him. Electric Park, Father, and I don't think it cost Sergeant Theodore more than twice what the prizes are worth for us to win them; we had a lucky night – and a very gay one."

Lazarus could see the old man starting to cloud up – in public with a bachelor? With her husband away? So he spoke up:

"I can't take it to France, Mrs. Smith; I made a deal with Woodie – don't you remember? My Teddy bear for his elephant. I assume it's a firm deal; he carried it from then on."

Mr. Johnson said, "If you didn't get it in writing, Ted, he'll hornswoggle you. Do I understand that Woodie went to Electric Park with you two?"

"Yes, sir. Between ourselves I expect to leave the elephant in Woodie's custody for the duration. But I'm going to dicker with him first."

"He'll still hornswoggle you. Maureen, the idea was to give you relief from the children. Especially Woodie. What in Ned possessed you to take him along?"

"We didn't exactly take him along, Father; he was a stowaway." She gave her father an accurate account, save that she left out certain things and did not include a timetable.

Mr. Johnson shook his head and looked pleased. "That boy will go far – if they don't hang him first. Maureen, you should have spanked him and fetched him home. Then you and Ted should have gone on with your ride."

"Oh, fuss, Father, I did have my ride and a very nice one; I made Woodrow sit in the back seat and keep quiet. Then I had a gay time at the park, a bonus I would not have had if Woodrow had not invited himself along."

"Woodie had some justice on his side," Lazarus admitted. "I *did* promise him an outing at Electric Park, then never kept my promise."

"Should have whacked him."

"It's too late for that, Father. And we did have fun. We ran into some people from church, too – Lauretta and Clyde Simpson."

"That old witch! She'll gossip about you, Maureen."

"I think not. We chatted while Woodie rode the miniature

train. But you might remember that Sergeant Bronson is your eldest sister's son."

Ira Johnson raised his eyebrows, then chuckled. "Samantha would be surprised – if she were still with us. Ted, my eldest sister was thrown by a horse she was trying to break . . . at eighty-five. She lingered awhile, then turned her face to the wall and refused to eat. Very well, I'll remember. Ted, this is better than blaming my gay-dog brother and still harder to check on; Samantha lived in Illinois, wore out three husbands, and one of them could have been named Bronson for all anyone here would know. Do you mind? Gives you a family of sorts."

"I don't mind. Although I like to think of *this* as my family."

"And we like to have you think of us that way, Son. Maureen, is our young lady home?"

"Just before you got home, Father. They are in the kitchen, on the excuse that she wanted to make a sandwich for Jonathan. Since I'm sure it's an excuse to stay out there and spoon, I suggest that, if you want something from the kitchen, you allow me to fetch it; I'll be noisy enough to let Nancy jump off his lap. Theodore, Nancy is engaged; we just haven't made a formal announcement. I think it's best to let them marry now, since he'll be joining the Army almost at once. What do you think?"

"I'm hardly entitled to an opinion, Mrs. Smith. I hope they will be happy."

"They will be," said Mr. Johnson. "He's a fine lad. I tried to sign him into the Seventh, but he insisted on waiting for his birthday so he could go straight into the Army. Even though he couldn't be drafted for another three years. Spirit. I like him. Ted, if you need to go to your room, you can go around this other way and avoid the kitchen."

A few minutes later the young people came out of the kitchen, made polite sounds without sitting down; then Nancy stepped out onto the porch to say good-night to her swain, came back in and sat down.

Mr. Johnson smothered a yawn. "Time I hit the hay. You will too, Ted, if you're smart. Too noisy around here to sleep late, especially where your room is."

Nancy said quickly, "I'll keep the young ones quiet, Grandpa, so Uncle Ted can sleep."

Lazarus stood up. "Thank you, Nancy, but I didn't get much rest on the train last night; I think I'll go right to bed. Don't worry about keeping quiet in the morning; I'll wake up at reveille time anyhow. Habit."

Mrs. Smith stood up. "We'll all go to bed."

Mr. Johnson shook hands as he said good-night; Mrs. Smith gave Lazarus a symbolic peck on the cheek such as she had given him on arrival, thanked him for a lovely evening, and urged him to turn over and go back to sleep if the reveille habit wakened him; Nancy hung back and kissed him good-night as her elders started up the stairs.

Lazarus went to his room and on into his bath. Maureen had told him not to hesitate to draw a tub; it would not wake the children. He started one, went back and opened his grip, got out the little package, took it into the bath and threw the bolt, there being no key in the bedroom door. It was a small flat box such as garters might come in; he opened it carefully, intending to rewrap it exactly as it had been.

Ah, the garter! Faded, as she had said, and clearly not new . . . and – Yes! – redolent with her own evocative fragrance. Would it last long enough for him to get it home, have the lovely, delicate aroma analyzed, amplified, and fixed? Probably – and with computer help a skilled scientologist could separate out the odours of satin and rubber, and amplify hers selectively. He would have to go to Secundus for such expert help. Worth the trip and then some!

Now let's see those "naughty" mottoes – One read: "*Open All Hours – Ring Bell for Service!*" – the other: "*Welcome! Come in and Stir the Fire.*" Sweet darling, those aren't "naughty."

A plain envelope under the garters – He laid them aside and opened it.

A plain white card. "Best I could do, Beloved. M."

A photograph, amateur work but excellent quality for this here-&-now; Maureen herself, outdoors in bright sunlight against a background of thick bushes. She was standing gracefully, smiling and looking at the camera – dressed only in her "French postcard" style. Lazarus felt a burst of passion. Why, you generous, trusting darling! Not your only copy? No, Brian would have made more than one print – undoubtedly had one with him. This print would have been locked somewhere in your bedroom. Yes, your waist *is* slender without a corset . . . and those are *not* broken down; they are lovely – and I'm certain what caused your happy smile. Thank you, thank you!

With the photograph was a little package in tissue paper. He opened it gently. A thick lock of red hair, tied with a green ribbon. The lock curled in a tight circle.

Lazarus stared at it. Maureen my beloved, this is the most precious gift of all – but I *do* hope you cut it so carefully that Brian won't notice it's missing.

He looked at each of her gifts again, restored them just as they had been, put the box into the bottom of his grip, locked it, turned off the tub, undressed, and got into the water.

But a lukewarm tub did not make him sleep. For a long time he lay in darkness and relived the past few hours.

He now felt that he understood Maureen. She was relaxed with what she was – "liked herself" as Lazarus thought of it – and liking yourself was the necessary first step toward loving other people. She had no guilt feelings because she *never* did *anything* that could make her feel guilty. She was unblinkingly honest with herself, was her own self-judge instead of looking to others, did not lie to herself – but lied to others without hesitation when needed for kindness or to get along with rules she had not made and did not respect.

Lazarus understood that; he lived the same way – and now knew where he got the trait. From Maureen . . . and through her, from Gramp. And from Pop, too – reinforced. He felt very happy, despite an unsatisfied ache in his loins. Or in part because of it, he corrected; he found that he cherished that ache.

When the doorknob turned, he was instantly alert, out of bed and waiting before the door opened.

She was in his arms, warm and fragrant.

She pulled back to shrug off her wrap, let it fall, came back into his arms, body to body, and gave her mouth fully.

When they broke the kiss, she stayed in his arms, clinging. He whispered huskily, "Why did you risk it?"

She answered softly, "I found that I must. Once I knew that, I realized that it was even less risk than our walnut tree. The children never come downstairs at night when we have a guest. Father may suspect me . . . but that makes it *certain* that he won't check on me. Don't worry, darling. Take me to bed. *Now!*"

He did so.

When they were quiet, she sighed happily and said, lips against his ear, arms and legs around him: "Theodore, even in this you are so much like my husband that I can barely wait till the war is over to tell him all about you."

"You've decided to tell him?"

"Beloved Theodore, there was never a doubt that I would. I softened some of what I told you tonight and left out a little. Brian does not require me to confess. But it does *not* upset him; we settled that fifteen years ago. He convinced me that he really *does* trust my judgement and my taste." Very softly but merrily she giggled against his ear. "It's a shame that I so seldom have anything to confess; he enjoys hearing my adventures. He has me tell him about them over and over – like rereading a favourite book. I wish I could tell this one tomorrow night. But I won't, I'll save it."

"He's coming home tomorrow?"

"Late. Quite late. Which is just as well, as I don't expect to get *any* sleep once he arrives." She chuckled softly. "He told me on the telephone to 'b. i. b. a. w. y. l. o.' and he would 'w. y. t. b. w.' That means: Be in bed asleep with my legs open and he will wake me the best way. But I just pretend to be asleep as I wake up no matter how quietly he tiptoes in."

She gave a tiny giggle. "Then we have a happy little game. As he enters me, I pretend to wake up and call him by name – but never his name. I moan, 'Oh, Albert, darling, I thought you could *never* come!' or some such. Then it's his turn. He says something like, 'This is Buffalo Bill, Mrs. O'Malley. Hush up and get busy!' Then I hush up and do the best I know how, not another word until we both explode."

"Your best is superb, Mrs. O'Malley. Or was that your best?"

"I tried to make it my best – Buffalo Bill. But I was so dreadfully excited that I got all blurry so it probably was not. I'd like a chance to do better. Are you going to give me one?"

"Only if you promise *not* to do better. Darling, if that was not your best, then your best would kill me."

"You not only talk like my husband and feel like him – especially *here* – but you even smell like him."

"You smell like Tamara."

"Do I really? Do I make love like her?"

(Tamara knows a thousand ways, darling, but rarely uses anything unusual – lovemaking is not technique, dear, it's an attitude. Wanting to make someone happy, which you *do*. But you startled me with your command of technique; you would fetch a high price on Iskander.)

"You do. But that's not what makes you so much like her. Uh, it's your attitude. Tamara knows what is going on in another person's mind and gives him exactly what he needs. Wants to give it."

"She's a mindreader? Then I'm not like her, after all."

"No, she's not a mindreader. But she feels a person's emotions and knows what he needs and gives him that. It might not be sex. Aren't there times when Brian needs something else?"

"Oh, certainly. If he's tired and tense, I hold off and rub his back or head. Or cuddle with him. Maybe encourage him to nap, and then perhaps he really will wake me 'the best way.' I don't try to eat him alive. Unless that's what he wants."

"Tamara all over again. Maureen, when Tamara was healing me, at first she didn't even share a bed with me. Just slept in the same room and ate with me and listened if I felt like talking. Then for ten days or so she did sleep with me, but we just slept . . . and I slept soundly and had no nightmares. Then one night I woke up, and without a word Tamara took me into her, and we made love the rest of that night. And next morning I knew I was well – soul-sickness all gone.

"You are that way, Maureen. You know, and you do. I've been very homesick and much troubled by this war. Now I'm not, you've cured it. Tell me, what did you feel from me the first night I was in this house?"

"Loved you at first sight, like a silly schoolgirl. Wanted to take you to bed. I told you so."

"Not how *you* felt – how did *I* feel?"

"Oh. You had an erection over me."

"Yes, I did. But I thought I had concealed it. You noticed?"

"Oh, I didn't see a bulge in your trousers or anything like that. Theodore, I never look down that far; men become embarrassed so easily. I simply knew you felt as I did – and I felt like a she dog in heat. Bitch in heat, I mean – I don't intend to be prim in bed. The instant you met my eyes – standing, out in the front hall – I knew we needed each other and I grew terribly excited . . . and rushed out into the kitchen to get myself under control."

"You didn't rush, you moved with smooth grace, like a ship under sail."

"That ship was sailing fast; I was rushing. I got myself under control but not less excited. *More.* My breasts ached and my nipples hurt, all the time you were here. But that doesn't show. It would not have mattered had Father noticed my excitement except that he would not have invited you back – and I *wanted* you to come back. Father knows what I am; he told me so when he was helping me. He told me to face up to what I am and be happy with it – but that I must learn never to let my ruttiness show, things being the way they are. I've tried – but that night it was very hard not to show it."

"You succeeded."

"Brian tells me that I don't show it. But that night was *so* difficult. I – Theodore, there is something boys do – and sometimes men – when they're terribly frustrated. With their hands."

"Certainly. Masturbation. Boys call it 'jacking off.' "

"So Brian says. But perhaps you don't know that girls – and women – can do something like it?"

"I do know. For a lonely person of either sex, it's a harmless but inadequate substitute."

" 'Harmless but inadequate – ' *Quite* inadequate. But I'm glad you think it's harmless. Because I went upstairs and took a bath – I *needed* one although I had bathed before supper. And did it, in the tub. And went to bed and stared at the ceiling. Then got up and locked the door and took off my nightgown – and did it and did it and did! Thinking about *you*, Theodore, every instant. Your voice, how you smelled, the touch of your hand on mine. But it took at least an hour before I was relaxed enough to sleep."

(It took me even longer, dear, and I should have used your direct therapy. But I was punishing myself for being a fool. Off my trolley, dearest one, as I know it is *never* foolish to love. But I didn't see how we could ever show our love.) "I wish I could have been there, darling – because a mile or two away I was aching with it – thinking of *you*."

"Theodore, I *hoped* you felt that way. I needed you so and hoped that you needed me just as much. But the best I could do was lock my door and do that and think about you, with nobody around but Ethel in her crib and her too young to notice. Oops! I lost you. Oh, dear!"

"You haven't lost me, just that wee bit of proud flesh. Which will recover soon; you promised me a second chance. Change position? Shoulder pillow? Left, or right? I shouldn't have kept my weight on you so long, but I didn't want to move."

"I didn't want you to move as long as I could keep even a little of you in me. You aren't too heavy; my hips are broad, and you let a woman breathe, sir. Put me on either side, whichever you prefer."

"Like this?"

"That's comfy. Oh, Theodore, this doesn't feel like our first time; I feel as if I had loved you forever and you had come back to me at last."

(Let's get away from that subject, Mama Maureen.) "I'll go on loving you forever, my darling."

(Omitted)

" – told her bluntly that he would *not* marry her if she made any fuss over his joining the Army when he didn't have to."

"What did Nancy tell him?"

"She told him that she had been waiting to hear that, so now get her pregnant at once so they could have a few days' honeymoon before he joined up. Nancy feels as strongly about warriors as her mother does. She came into my bedroom that night and told me what she had done, slightly teary but not worried over having jumped the gun.

"So we cried happy tears, and I cleared the matter with Brian and the Weatherals, and Nancy missed her next period – this was a month ago – and the wedding may be day after tomorrow or perhaps the day after that."

(Omitted)

"Darling, I wish I could see you."

"Oh, dear! I'd rather not turn on the Mazda lamp, Theodore. These blinds are not so tight but what light would shine out, as well as light under the door if by any chance Father came downstairs."

"Maureen, I will never ask you to take any chance you don't like. I see you quite well with my fingertips – and these are *not* broken down."

"They flow off my ribs like melted marshmallows. Theodore, when you open that package, please be very careful that no one is around; there is more in it than a pair of garters."

"I did open it."

"Then you know what I look like."

"Was that beautiful girl *you?*"

"Tease. Brian had me look straight at his camera."

"But, darling, while you don't look *down* that far, men don't tend to look *up* very far. Especially me. Not when I'm looking at a photograph of a perfectly gorgeous nude model."

" 'Nude model,' my best Sunday hat!"

"Maureen, it is the loveliest picture I have ever owned and I will cherish it always."

"That's better and I don't believe it and I love hearing it. Did you open the paper folded in with it?"

"The baby curl? Did you clip it off Marie?"

"Theodore, I do not mind being teased; it just makes you more like Brian. But if he teases too much, I bite him. Anywhere. Here, for example."

"Hey, not so hard!"

"Then tell me where that curl came from."

"It came from your pretty, my pretty one, and I'll wear it over my heart forever. But one reason I wanted to look at you is that you clipped so generous a lock that I worried that Brian might notice something missing – and ask why."

"I can tell him I gave it to the iceman."

"He won't believe that and will be sure that you have a new adventure to confess."

"Then he won't press me to tell him now; he'll change the subject. Although I *wish* I could tell him now; I keep thinking about both of you, outdoors in daylight; that was the fantasy that kept me awake. Sweetheart, there is a candle on the dresser – electricity not being as dependable as the gas lights we used to have. It wouldn't throw enough light to worry me. You may look at me by candlelight all you wish and as you wish."

"Yes, darling! Matches where?"

"Let me go and I'll get up and light it; I can find both in the dark. Will I be allowed to look at you, too?"

"Sure. For contrast. 'Beauty and the Beast.' "

She giggled and kissed his ear. "Goat, maybe. Or a stallion. Theodore, I *needed* to be baby-stretched to accept *you*."

"I thought you said I felt like Brian?"

"But *he* is a stallion, too. Let me go."

"Pay toll."

"Oh, goodness, darling, don't do that now! Or I'll be so shaky I won't be able to strike a match."

Standing and by the light on one candle, they studied each other. Lazarus felt his breath grow short at the dazzling glory of her. For most of two years he had been deprived of the sweet joy of seeing a woman, and had not realized how starved he had been for that great privilege. Darling, can you guess how *much* this means to me? Mama Maureen, has no one ever told you how much more sweetly beautiful a full-blown woman is than a maiden? Certainly your lovely breasts have held milk; that's what they're for. Why would I want them to look like marble? – I don't!

She studied him just as closely, her face solemn, her nipples crinkled tightly. Theodore-Lazarus my strange love, will you guess that I suggested candlelight so that I could see *you?* A woman is not supposed to get hungry for such things – but I miss the sight, the naked sight, of my husband . . . and how in the Name of Satan and all His Fallen Thrones I can last even till November without even *seeing* a man I do not know. Alma Bixby told me that she had never seen her husband without clothes. How can a woman *live* like that? Five children by a man she's never seen all over – Shocked her when I said that *of course* I had seen my husband naked!

Theodore-Lazarus, you don't *look* like my Briney Boy; your colouration is more like mine. But, oh, how you feel like him, smell like him, talk like him, love like him! Your pretty thing is coming up high again. Briney beloved, I'm going to have him once more, as *hard* as possible! – and I'll tell you about it tomorrow night if you'll just ask me for a new bedtime story . . . or if I must, I'll save it for you till you get back. You're as strange a man as he is . . . and just the wise and tolerant husband your bawdy wife needs. Then, cross my heart, dearest, I'll try my best to keep from it until you come back from Over There – but if I can't, even with Father and eight children to guard me, I promise you solemnly that I will *never* bed with anyone but a warrior, a man to be proud of in every way. Such as this strange man.

Lazarus, my love, are you *really* my descendant? I *do* believe that you know when the war will be over and that my Briney will come safely back to me. Why, I am not sure – but since you told me, I have been free from worry for the first time in many a lonely moon. I hope the rest is true, too; I *want* to believe in Tamara, and that *she* is descended from me. But I *don't* want you to go away in only eight years!

That innocent little picture – If I had not feared shocking you, I would have given you some *real* "French postcards" Briney has taken of me. Will you be upset if I take a closer look? I'll chance it.

Mrs. Smith suddenly dropped to one knee, looked closely, then touched him. She looked up. "Now?"

"Yes!" He picked her up, placed her on the bed. Almost solemnly she helped him, then caught her breath as they joined. "*Hard*, Theodore! This time don't be gentle!"

"Yes, my beautiful one!"

When their happy violence was over, she lay quiet in his arms, not talking, communing through touch and the light of one candle.

At last she said, "I must go, Theodore. No, don't get up, just let me slide out." She got up, picked up her wrap, blew out the candle, came back, leaned down and kissed him. "Thank you Theodore – for *everything*. But – come back to me, come back to me!"

"I will, I will!"

Quickly and silently she was gone.

CODA

I

Somewhere in France

Dear All my Family,

I am writing this in my pocket diary where it will stay until this war is over – not that it matters; you'll get it just as soon. But I can't send a sealed letter now, much less one sealed into five envelopes. Something called "censorship" – which means that every letter is opened and read and anything that might interest the Boche is cut out. Such as dates and places and designations of military units and probably what I had for breakfast. (Beans and boiled pork and fried potatoes, with coffee that would dissolve a spoon.)

You see, I had this lovely ocean voyage as a guest of Uncle Sam and am now in the land of fine wines and beautiful women. (The wine has been vin extremely ordinaire, and they seem to be hiding the beautiful women. The best-looking one I've seen had a slight moustache and very hairy legs, which I could have ignored had I not made the mistake of standing downwind. Darlings, I am not sure the French take baths, at least in wartime. But I'm in no position to criticize, a bath is a luxury. Today, given a choice between a beautiful woman and a hot bath, I'd pick the bath – otherwise she wouldn't touch me.)

Don't worry that I am now in a "war zone." That you've received this is proof that the war is over and I am okay. But it's easier to write a letter than it is to put trivia into a diary every day. "War zone" is an exaggeration; this is "fixed warfare" – meaning both sides are in the same fix: pinned down – and I am too far behind the lines to get hurt.

I am in charge of a unit called a "squad" – eight men – me and five other riflemen, plus an automatic rifleman (the rifle, not the man; this war has no robot fighters) and an eighth man who carries ammunition for the automatic rifleman. It's a corporal's job, and that's what I am; the promotion to sergeant I was expecting (in my last letter as dated from the United States) got lost in the shuffle when I was transferred to another outfit.

Being a corporal suits me. It is the first time I've had men permanently assigned to me, time enough to get acquainted with each one, learn his strong points and weak ones, and how to handle him. They are a fine bunch of men. Only one is a problem, and it's not his fault; it results from the prejudices of the time. His name is F. X. Dinkowski, and he is simultaneously the only Catholic and the only Jew in my squad – and, twins, if you've never heard of either one, ask Athene. By ancestry he comes from one religion, then he was brought up in another – and he has had the tough luck to be placed with country boys who have still a third religion and are not very tolerant.

Plus the additional misfortunes of being a city boy and having a voice that grates (even on me) and is clumsy, and when they pick on him (they do if I'm not right there), it makes him more clumsy. Truthfully he's not soldier material – but I wasn't asked. So he's the ammunition carrier, the best I can do to balance my squad.

They call him "Dinky," which is only mildly disparaging, but he hates it. (I use his full last name – I do with all of them. For ritualistic reasons having to do with the mystique of military organizations at this here-&-now it is best to call a man by his family name.)

But let's leave the finest squad in the AEF and bring you up to date on my first family and your ancestors. Just before Uncle Sam sent me on that pleasure cruise, I was given a vacation. I spent it with the Brian Smith family and lived in their house, as they have "adopted" me for the rest of this war, me being an "orphan."

That leave was the happiest time I've had since I was dropped from the *Dora*. I took Woodie to an amusement park, primitive but more fun than some sophisticated pleasures of Secundus. I took him on rides and treated him to games and things that were fun for him, and fun for me because he enjoyed them so – wore him out and he slept all the way home. He behaved himself, and now we are chums. I've decided to let him grow up; there may be hope for him yet.

I had long talks with Gramp, got better acquainted with all the others – especially Mama and Pop. The latter was unexpected. I had met Pop for a few minutes at Camp Funston, then he was to come home on leave the day I had to go back, and I didn't expect to see him. But he got away a few hours early, a bonus an officer can sometimes manage, and we overlapped – and he telephoned to the camp and got me a two-day extension. Why? Tamara and Ira, listen carefully –

To attend the wedding of –
Miss Nancy Irene Smith & Mr. Jonathan Sperling Weatheral

Athene, explain to the twins the historic significance of this union. List the famous and important people in that line, dear, not the total genealogies. And Ira and Tamara in our own little family, of course, and Ishtar, and at least five of our children – and I may have missed someone, not having all the genealogical lines in my head.

I was "best man" to Jonathan, and Pop "gave the bride away," and Brian was an "usher" and Marie was "ring-bearer" and Carol was "maid of honour," and George was charged with keeping Woodie from setting fire to the church while Mama took care of Dickie and Ethel – Athene can explain terms and ritual; I shan't try. But it not only gave me two more days of leave, much of which I spent running errands for Mama (these medieval weddings are complex operations), but it also gave me time with Pop, and now I know him better than I ever did as a son under his roof – and like him very much and heartily approve of him.

Ira, he reminds me of you – brainy, no nonsense, relaxed, tolerant, and warmly friendly.

Bulletin: The bride was pregnant (a proper Howard wedding! – at a time when *all* brides are assumed to be virgins) – pregnant with (if memory serves) "Jonathan Brian Weatheral." Is that right, Justin, and who is descended from him? Remind me, Athene. I've met a lot of people over the centuries; I may even have married some descendant of Jonathan Brian at some time. I rather hope so; Nancy and Jonathan are a fine young couple.

I turned "my" landaulet over to them for a six-day honeymoon, then Jonathan was to (did) join the Army – but too late to get into combat. Nancy's warrior hero just the same; he tried.

Some fiddling sergeant who couldn't find his arse with both hands wants me to round up my squad and do something about a dugout that someone was careless with. So –

All my love from
Corporal Buddy Boy

Somewhere in France

Dear Mr. Johnson,

Please give this a second censoring; some of it will have to be explained to the rest of my adopted family.

I hope that Mrs. Smith received the thank-you note I mailed from Hoboken (and could read it – writing on my knee while bouncing on the C. & A. roadbed does not improve my handwriting). In any case I thank her again for the happiest holiday of my life. And thanks to *all* of you. Please tell Woodie that I will no longer spot him a horse. From here on we play even or he can find another sucker – four out of five is too many.

Now for the rest – Note signature and address. My rocker did not last to France, then three chevrons dwindled to two. Can you explain to Mrs. Smith and to Carol (those two in particular) that being busted does not disgrace a man forever? – and that I am still Carol's own special soldier if she will let me be – and in fact I am far more of a real soldier; I am at last free of being tagged as "instructor" and am now leading a squad in a combat outfit. I wish I could tell her where . . . but if I stuck my head up over the parapet, I might see some heinies if one of them didn't see me first. I'm not goldbricking a hundred miles back.

I hope you aren't ashamed of me. No, I'm sure you are not; you are too old a soldier to care about rank. I'm in it and that's what counts with you. I know. May I say, sir, that you are and have always been as long as I've known you an inspiration to me?

I won't detail the two negative promotions; in the Army

excuses don't count. But I want you to know that neither resulted from anything dishonourable. The first was in the transport and involved a duty-struck master-at-arms and a poker game in an area for which I was responsible. The second came while I was instructing – dummy trenches, dummy no-man's-land – and a captain told me to dress up that skirmish line and I said, "Hell, Captain, are you trying to save bullets for the Kaiser? Or haven't you heard of machine guns?"

(I suppose I shouldn't have said "Hell." In fact I used another expression more common among soldiers.)

So later that day I was a corporal, and my transfer took place when I requested it, again that same day.

So here I am and feeling fine. It is indeed a fact that the closer a man gets to the front, the better his morale is. I've become chummy with cooties, and the mud in France is deeper and stickier than in southern Missouri, and I dream about hot baths and Mrs. Smith's wonderful guest room for soldiers – but I'm in good health and good spirits, and I send my love to all of you.

Respectfully yours,
Corporal Ted Bronson

"Hey down in there! Corporal Bronson. Send him out."

Lazarus climbed slowly up out the dugout, letting his eyes adjust to darkness. "Yes, Lieutenant?"

"Wire-cutting job. I want you to volunteer."

Lazarus said nothing.

"Didn't you hear me?"

"I heard you, sir."

"Well?"

"You asked for a volunteer, sir."

"No, I said I wanted *you* to volunteer."

"Lieutenant, I volunteered on April sixth last year. That used up my quota for the duration."

"A latrine lawyer, eh?"

Lazarus again said nothing.

"Sometimes I think you want to live forever."

Lazarus still said nothing (You are so right, you seven-pound bliffy – and so do *you*; you haven't been over that parapet even once. God help this platoon when you do.)

"Very well, since you want it the hard way. I *order* you to lead this party. Find three more volunteers from your squad. If they don't volunteer you know what to do. Once you pick 'em, tell 'em to get ready – then you haul ass to C.P. and I'll show you the map."

"Yes, sir."

"And, Bronson, make damn sure you do a good job . . . because a little bird told me that you're going to lead the way through the holes. Dismissed."

Lazarus went unhurriedly back down below. So we're going over the top? Big secret. Nobody knows it but Pershing and about a hundred thousand Yanks and twice that many Boches and the Imperial High Command. Why do they advertise a "surprise attack" with three days of "softening-up" bombardment that does nothing worth mentioning but tells the Boche where to bring up his reserves and gives him time to position them? Forget it, Lazarus, you're not in charge. Put your mind on picking out three who can go out, do it, and come back.

Not Russell, you'll need your automatic rifleman before dawn. Wyatt was out last night. Dinkowski might as well have a cow bell around his neck. Fielding is on the sick list, damn it. So it has to be Schultz, Talley, and Cadwallader. Two of them old unkillables and Talley the only repple with too little experience – and a shame Fielding has la grippe or whatever it is; I need him. All right, Schultz gets Cadwallader; I'll nurse Talley through it.

It was a two-squad dugout; his squad was sacked in on the left, the other squad had a card game going by candlelight on their side. Lazarus called his squad into a huddle, waking Cadwallader and Schultz to do so. Russell and Wyatt stayed in their bunks, as the huddle took place against them. "The Lieutenant wants us to cut wire and told me to ask for three volunteers."

Schultz nodded at once, as Lazarus knew he would. "I'll go." In Lazarus' opinion his assistant squad leader should have a section. Schultz was forty, a married volunteer, and trying hard to offset his name, his trace of German accent (second generation) – but doing it steadily, methodically, without flash. No glory hound. Lazarus hoped that not many of the Germans they faced were of Schultz's quality – but he knew they were, especially veterans pulled back from the collapsed Russian front. His only fault in Lazarus' eyes was that he disliked Dinkowski.

"That's one. Don't all speak at once."

"What's the matter with *them?*" Cadwallader said loudly,

jerking a thumb at the other squad. "Teacher's pets? They haven't done anything for a week."

Corporal O'Brien answered for his squad: " 'Tell your troubles to Jesus; the Chaplain's gone over the hill!' Whose deal?"

"Who's next?"

Dinkowski gulped. "Take me, Corporal."

Talley shrugged. "Okay."

(Damn you, Dinky – why didn't you wait and simply make it unanimous? And damn that silly second john for ordering me to ask for volunteers. Better to tell 'em.) "Let's hear some more voices. This isn't the S.O.S." (Lieutenant Birdbrain, you post-nasal drip, Cadwallader is right; it's *not* our turn. Why didn't you go through the platoon sergeant and section leader? they're fair about handing out dirty details.)

Russell and Wyatt spoke up together. Lazarus waited, then said, "Cadwallader? You're the only holdout."

"Corporal, you asked for three volunteers. How come you want the whole squad?"

(Because I want *you,* you unappetizing ape. You're the best soldier in the squad.) "Because I need you. Will you volunteer?"

" 'I ain't no volunteer, Corporal; I was drafted."

"Very well." (Damn all officers who interfere where they shouldn't.) "Wyatt, you were out last night; get back in your bunk. Russell, you get some sleep, too; you may be busy soon. Schultz, I'll take Dinkowski; you take Talley. Black me up first and make it fast; I've got to see the Lieutenant. Get out the cork."

Lazarus got through their own wire without much trouble by enlarging breaks German shells had made. He did all the work himself, simply requiring Dinkowski to stay flat and follow him. There was the regular *crump!* of artillery, their own and the German howitzers. Lazarus ignored them, there being nothing better he could do. The chattering cough of machine guns he ignored, too, as long as the sound came from far enough along his flanks. Snipers he did not worry about other than to stay low.

His prime wariness was directed at German patrols – if any – and at starshells – far too many. The latter were the reason he had Dinkowski stay belly down; he did not trust his assistant to freeze and hold it if caught on his knees when a star shell burst.

Once past the last of their own entanglements he led Dinkowski, both belly-crawling, into a shell hole, then put his mouth to the private's ear. "Stay here till I get back."

"But, Corporal, I don't want to stay behind!"

"Not so loud; you'll wake the baby. Whisper against my ear. If I'm not back in an hour, go back alone."

"But I can't find my way back!"

"There's the Dipper, there's the Pole Star. Go back southwest. If you miss the gaps, you've got wirecutters. Just remember this: When a star shell bursts – *freeze!* The time to move is just as it goes out, while their eyes are still dazzled. And try to be quiet; you remind me of two skeletons on a tin roof. Don't get shot by our own people at the last minute. What's the password?"

"Uh –"

"Oh, hell, it's 'Charlie Chaplin.' Forget it again and you'll get more than a blighty; some of our lads are trigger-happy. Now repeat back."

"Corporal, I'm going to cut wire with *you*."

Lazarus sighed inwardly. The clumsy little clown *wanted* to soldier. If I don't let him tag along, it can kill his spirit. But if I do let him, it might kill both of us. Cadwallader, I admire your good sense – and hate your guts. And wish I had you along.

"All right. Not a word from here on. Pat my foot and point if you have to – and stay that close. Remember what I said about star shells. See any Boche, don't breathe. If they surprise us – surrender at once."

"'Surrender'?"

"If you want to be a grandfather. You can't kill a German patrol all by your lonesome. Even if you could, it would make so much racket that their machine guns would chop you in two. Stick close and stay down."

Lazarus could almost touch the first German wire when a star shell burst and the private panicked – tried for a shell hole they had just come through and was hit as he fell into it.

Lazarus lay still and listened to screams as the dazzling star burned above him. One of our own, he mused; a German shell would burst to backlight the American trenches. If that poor little dope doesn't shut up, the air around here is going to be thick with merry greetings. Can't cut wire with all that advertising. And – oh, hell, he's my boy; I've *got* to take care of him. Probably be a favour to Dinky to finish him off – but Maureen wouldn't like that. Okay, let's get him back – then come back and finish this crummy detail. No sleep tonight and over the top about oh-four-hundred. Next time join the Navy.

The flare died out and Lazarus was up fast and moving – as another star shell flared. Machine-gun bullets stitched his side and knocked him into the shell hole. One struck a hard implant in the right side of his belly, tumbled, and chewed its way out just above his left hip. Others did other damage – nothing too difficult to repair in 4291 A.D., but, this being the Dark Ages, any one of them was enough.

Lazarus felt it only as a mighty blow that knocked him off his feet and into the shell hole. He did not become unconscious at once; he had time to realize that he was mortally wounded. He lay as he had fallen and looked up at his stars, realizing that he had come to his ending place.

Every animal finds its ending place. Some find it in a trap, another in a fight it cannot win, some happy few in a quiet place to wait for the end. Whatever it is, it is the ending place and most of us know when we reach it. This is mine.

Did Dinky know? I think so, he's stopped screaming – I think he *looked* for his. Odd that it doesn't hurt. Thanks for making it worthwhile, Maureen . . . Llita . . . Dorable . . . Tamara . . . Minerva . . . Laz, Lor . . . Ira . . . Maureen –

He heard wild geese honking high overhead, looked up at his stars again as they blacked out.

CODA

II

"You still don't understand," the Grey Voice droned on. "There is no time, there is no space. What was, is, and ever shall be. You are you, playing chess with yourself, and again you have checkmated yourself. You are the referee. Morals are your agreement with yourself to abide by your own rules. To thine own self be true or you spoil the game."

"Crazy."

"Then vary the rules and play a different game. You cannot exhaust her infinite variety."

"If you would just let me look at your face," Lazarus muttered pettishly.

"Try a mirror."

CODA

III

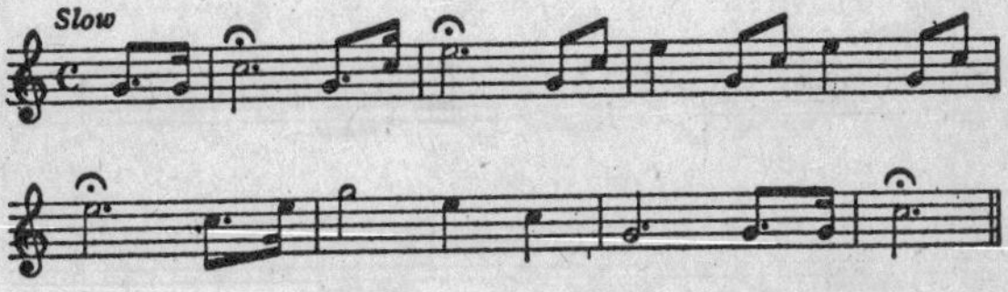

From the Kansas City *Post* November 7, 1918:

ıer
fully
ɔn two
ıesday
ickman
ughly.
more
rewdly
ıired a
.ty Club
ıd Main.
ughed in
lerical
ssed
und
o play
ile the
ıe str
'olin
.oped
ɔ of in
he M
had

c... ılly a handfuı .. oıd
lists supplementary list of
our losses. We report with
sorrow those from Kansas
and Missouri: *KILLED* Abel
Thos J Pvt JfsnCity, Avery
Jno M 2nd Lt Sedalia, Baird
Geo M Pfc Tpka, Badger F
M Pvt StJsph, Casper Robt
S Sgt, Hatfield R S Cpl KCK,
Kerr Jack M 1st Lt Joplin,
Pfeifer Hans Pfc Dodge City.
MISSING IN ACTION: Austin Geo W Ssgt HnnblMo,
Bell T R Cpl WchtaK, Berry
L M Pvt CrthgMo, Bronson
Theo Cpl KCMo, Casper M M
1st Lt LwrncK, Dillingham
O G Pvt Rolla, Farley F X
KCMo, Hawes Wm Pfc
Sprngfld, Oliver R C Pfc
StLouis. *WOUNDED:*
Arthur C. M Pfc Clmbi-

s..
today
bailir
Grand
nearly
again,
crushing
reportedl
Mr. Hora
no legal
earlier
or Dece
will n
work
inside
them-
the vi
ble be
viol
harr
tod
vi
u

CODA

IV

"Ira! Galahad! Got him?"

"Yes! Hoist us in! Oh, what a mess! Ish, about two litres and lots of jelly."

"Get him inside and let me see him. Lor, you can get us out of here now."

"Seal up, Dora, and bounce it!"

"Sealed and zooming! Screens down! What the goddamn hell have they done to Boss?"

"I'm trying to find out, Dora. Be ready with the tank; I may freeze him."

"Ready now, Ish. Laz-Lor, I told you we should pick him up sooner. I *told* you."

"Pipe down, Dora. We *told* him he'd get his ass shot off. But he was having more fun that kittens –"

"– and wouldn't have thanked us –"

"– and wouldn't have come –"

"– you know how stubborn he is."

"Tamara," said Ishtar, "cuddle his head and talk to him. Keep him alive. I don't want to freeze him – if at all – until I've made temporary repairs. Hamadryad, clamp there! Mm . . . Galahad, one slug hit the Finder. That's how his intestines got so chopped up."

"Clone-trans?"

"Perhaps. The way he regenerates, repair and support may be enough. Justin, you were right; the dates on his letters did prove that he didn't last through it; losing the Finder's signal pin-pointed when and where. Galahad, are you finding more fragments? I want to close him. Tamara, rouse him, make him talk! I *don't* want to have to freeze him. The rest of you shut up and get *out*! Go help Minerva with the children."

"Glad to," Justin said hoarsely. "I'm about to throw up."

"*Maureen?*" Lazarus murmured.

"I'm here, darling," Tamara answered, cradling his head against her breasts.

"Bad . . . dream. Thought . . . I was . . . dead."

"Just a dream, Beloved. You cannot die."

NEL BESTSELLERS

Crime			
T027 821	GAUDY NIGHT	*Dorothy L. Sayers*	75p
T030 180	UNNATURAL DEATH	*Dorothy L. Sayers*	60p
T026 663	THE DOCUMENTS IN THE CASE	*Dorothy L. Sayers*	50p
Fiction			
T029 522	HATTER'S CASTLE	*A. J. Cronin*	£1.00
T030 199	CRUSADER'S TOMB	*A. J. Cronin*	£1.25
T031 276	THE CITADEL	*A. J. Cronin*	95p
T029 158	THE STARS LOOK DOWN	*A. J. Cronin*	£1.00
T022 021	THREE LOVES	*A. J. Cronin*	90p
T022 536	THE HARRAD EXPERIMENT	*Robert H. Rimmer*	50p
T022 994	THE DREAM MERCHANTS	*Harold Robbins*	95p
T023 303	THE PIRATE	*Harold Robbins*	95p
T022 986	THE CARPETBAGGERS	*Harold Robbins*	£1.00
T031 667	WHERE LOVE HAS GONE	*Harold Robbins*	£1.00
T023 958	THE ADVENTURERS	*Harold Robbins*	£1.00
T031 659	THE INHERITORS	*Harold Robbins*	95p
T031 586	STILETTO	*Harold Robbins*	60p
T025 268	NEVER LEAVE ME	*Harold Robbins*	50p
T025 292	NEVER LOVE A STRANGER	*Harold Robbins*	90p
T022 226	A STONE FOR DANNY FISHER	*Harold Robbins*	80p
T031 640	79 PARK AVENUE	*Harold Robbins*	80p
T027 945	THE BETSY	*Harold Robbins*	90p
T031 241	EVENING IN BYZANTIUM	*Irwin Shaw*	75p
T029 557	RICH MAN, POOR MAN	*Irwin Shaw*	£1.25
Historical			
T023 079	LORD GEOFFREY'S FANCY	*Alfred Duggan*	60p
T024 903	THE KING OF ATHELNEY	*Alfred Duggan*	60p
T023 125	FOX 11: FIRESHIP	*Adam Hardy*	35p
T024 946	FOX 12: BLOOD BEACH	*Adam Hardy*	35p
T027 651	FOX 13: SEAFLAME	*Adam Hardy*	40p
Science Fiction			
T029 492	STRANGER IN A STRANGE LAND	*Robert Heinlein*	80p
T029 484	I WILL FEAR NO EVIL	*Robert Heinlein*	95p
T031 462	DUNE	*Frank Herbert*	£1.25
T022 854	DUNE MESSIAH	*Frank Herbert*	60p
War			
T027 066	COLDITZ: THE GERMAN STORY	*Reinhold Eggers*	50p
T025 438	LILLIPUT FLEET	*A. Cecil Hampshire*	50p
T026 299	TRAWLERS GO TO WAR	*Lund & Ludlam*	50p
Western			
T020 754	EDGE 15: BLOOD RUN	*George Gilman*	35p
T022 706	EDGE 16: THE FINAL SHOT	*George Gilman*	35p
T024 881	EDGE 17: VENGEANCE VALLEY	*George Gilman*	40p
General			
T021 009	SEX MANNERS FOR MEN	*Robert Chartham*	35p
T023 206	THE BOOK OF LOVE	*Dr David Delvin*	90p
T028 828	THE LONG BANANA SKIN	*Michael Bentine*	90p

NEL P.O. BOX 11. FALMOUTH TR10 9EN, CORNWALL.
For U.K.: Customers should include to cover postage, 19p for the first book plus 9p per copy for each additional book ordered up to a maximum charge of 73p.
For B.F.P.O. and Eire: Customers should include to cover postage, 19p for the first book plus 9p per copy for the next 6 and thereafter 3p per book
For Overseas: Customers should include to cover postage, 20p for the first book plus 10p per copy for each additional book.

Name ....

Address...

....

Title ....
(JULY)

Whilst every effort is made to maintain prices, new editions or printings may carry an increased price and the actual price of the edition supplied will apply.